THE GIRL WITH THE LIGHTNING BRAIN

THE GIRL WITH THE LIGHTNING BRAIN

A NOVEL
BY CLIFF RATZA

The Girl with the Lightning Brain

THIS ACTION-ADVENTURE THRILLER, LACED with terrorism and political intrigue, constructs from the latest technological and sociopolitical trends one plausible scenario resulting from a viral pandemic occurring early in the 22nd century, all seen through the microcosm of an extraordinary female—eighteen-year-old Electra Kittner. As it traces her growth, the book explores some of the timeless questions that are part of the human condition.

The novel's theme reveals that no matter how extraordinary the person, anyone can be a victim in a primitive world that can't handle the truth, and must deal with the complexities of being "merely human, "best handled with an optimistic and pragmatic philosophy.

The book contains three storyline threads:

1. From the start of the novel (August 2115) going forward.
2. From Electra's birth (February 2097) to the novel's start.
3. From the start of the Worldstars' career (September 2092) to Electra's birth. Worldstars refers to Indira Ramanujan, Su-Lin Chou, Jason Kittner, and Adom Ola. They are biotech PhDs who met in grad school and work together for the National Institute of Health. Indira and Jason are Electra's parents.

Readers should enjoy the book on whatever level they wish:

- Gripping action-packed thriller
- Glimpse into a plausible near-term future

- Insight into dealing with the "human condition"
- Illustrative optimistic and pragmatic worldview philosophy
- Fast-paced emotive narrative and imagery

There are glossary and appendix at the back of the book for readers who wish to know more about terms or topics referenced.

An entire "Lightning Brain series" follows. Two subsequent novels have already been written; three more have been outlined.

Main Characters

Electra "Kit" Kittner
Jason Kittner
Indira "Indy" Jaswinder Ramanujan
Justin "Doc" Kittner
Su-Lin Song Chou
Adom Ola
Chris Conklin
Jennifer Conklin
Russell Conklin
Moses "Mo" Solstein
Robin Setdarova
Jared Gardner
Hudson "Hud" Haller
Hollis "Holy" Haller
Zoe Vargas

Book Series Dedication

I wish to thank my parents, Clyde and Betty Ratza, for their loving patience and generosity, giving me the freedom to explore the limits of my world. And I wish to thank my sister Claudia for introducing me while still a pup to the lyrical magic of poetry and literature. Thanks also to our book manager L.P. Brown and Martin Caylor for their careful reading and suggestions. And thanks to John Kane and his people at Prime Solutions support teams for turning a manuscript into a market reality. Finally, I want to thank the bold explorers from the past, present, or future. Whether found in science, commerce, or the arts, they are the ones pushing the envelope of what is possible, always asking why not, rather than why.

I wish to dedicate this series to the readers, who have given me the greatest gift any author could hope for: their desire to reach out to the world and characters that emerge when reading the series. A poem from Indira touches each of us.

Beyond The Pale

We're story-tellers in our soul,
Heralding what the World should be.
Laced with fear and ecstasy,
Perfect paradigms to extol.

But Life is not a scripted play,
Cherished wishes go unfilled.
Castles are so hard to build,
Plans revised by end of day.

Still be inspired by the tale,
Audacious hope for what we thirst.
Reach for the dream you may be first,
You may end up beyond the pale.

Contents

CHAPTER 1	"In the Dark"	13
CHAPTER 2	"The Lightning Explosion"	15
CHAPTER 3	"In the Beginning"	23
CHAPTER 4	"Ominous Conversations"	33
CHAPTER 5	"The Secret Within"	41
CHAPTER 6	"The Little Girl with a Curl"	50
CHAPTER 7	"School Bells Ringing"	59
CHAPTER 8	"Bonds of Friendship"	66
CHAPTER 9	"The Prize"	75
CHAPTER 10	"Moses and the Promised Land"	91
CHAPTER 11	"Boy's Night In"	102
CHAPTER 12	"A Distant Storm Brewing"	116
CHAPTER 13	"The Buddhist Monk"	127
CHAPTER 14	"Summer-Autumn Interlude"	145
CHAPTER 15	"Washington Outbreak"	152
CHAPTER 16	"A Pregnant Pause"	167
CHAPTER 17	"Great Expectations"	175
CHAPTER 18	"Into the Void"	189
CHAPTER 19	"On the Town"	196
CHAPTER 20	"Game Face Lessons"	203
CHAPTER 21	"In the Moment"	215
CHAPTER 22	"The Cause of Effects"	223
CHAPTER 23	"Rites of Passage"	246

CHAPTER 24   "The Chosen Path" 260
CHAPTER 25   "Changing of the Guard" 279
CHAPTER 26   "Run for Nurse" 290
CHAPTER 27   "The Competitive Landscape" 303
CHAPTER 28   "Blow-Up" 325
CHAPTER 29   "The Next in Line" 346
CHAPTER 30   "The Monster from the Id" 360
CHAPTER 31   "Dodging Bullets" 392
CHAPTER 32   "Drilling into Danger" 413
CHAPTER 33   "What Bloody Messes" 437
CHAPTER 34   "The Love You Make" 453
CHAPTER 35   "Godspeed Farewell" 464
CHAPTER 36   "The Eyes of Texas" 477
CHAPTER 37   "Run for Nurse Redux" 492
CHAPTER 38   "Three Queens—Redux" 502
CHAPTER 39   "Murder in the House" 517
CHAPTER 40   "Blown Away" 532
CHAPTER 41   "The Deadly Mole" 540
CHAPTER 42   "Second Strike" 552

Glossary 570
Appendix 575

CHAPTER 1
August 2115

"In the Dark"
(Thread 1 Chapter 1)

ELECTRA IS EXCEPTIONAL. SHE knows that. And she also knows her extraordinary abilities—the paranormal aftermath of a near-fatal experience at birth—are secrets that must never be revealed. Her life depends on it.

Taller than most eighteen-year-olds, stiletto-thin Electra Kittner—no one is allowed to use her childhood nickname Kit—combines striking features and an emergent musculature that imply superior strength and catlike agility. All this concealed beneath careless attire and indifferent grooming. She rarely wears makeup or fusses with her raven-black longish hair. The boys would notice if she did. But she prefers never to be noticed by anyone. Ever.

Now she's stuck in a National Institute of Health underground lab near Washington, DC. Power failures occur much too frequently, even in self-contained environments maintained by the nation's "best and brightest." Biosafety Level 5,the highest possible, should be able to deal with the nation's number one crisis that mysteriously emerged twenty years ago, the Techno-Plague, now raging globally. But not even America can cope. It too has joined the "Great Dimming" Era. The world is degenerating: populations becoming dumber and paranoid, governments becoming autocratic and suspicious. The Dark Ages is on the horizon. Advancing. Electra has the right words to describe the mess: the world is devolving intellectually, culturally, politically.

Effective vaccines are unavailable. This plague—caused by an incredibly resilient, mutant manmade virus—rarely kills. It's much worse than that, for it's a living death, causing cognitive impairment similar to Alzheimer's but progressing much faster and affecting all types, all age groups.

Even the United States is approaching a pandemic tipping point. Though it's the first country to develop a vaccine, these "smart pills" are only a temporary solution, and Washington is losing control because neither the people nor the Administration trusts one another. Add to this the spreading terrorism fomented by Isilabad—the rogue Middle East state—and you have a sociopolitical train wreck.

The government's chosen few are given advanced smart pills that put the plague temporarily into remission, allowing them to function better and giving the illusion of a healthy infrastructure. But the smart people still left know better, and they are terrified.

Is Electra worried about contracting the plague? No. She has built-in immunity, but has much bigger problems that she keeps hidden from everyone.

Is she worried about being stuck in the dark? Hardly. Experience has equipped her to deal with situations like this, so she pulls out a flashlight-equipped keyring and pans the room, seeing nothing alarming.

Today is her first inter-lab assignment. She's the newest data retrieval clerk assigned to a project team, sent to retrieve a recently discovered "Project Zero" file. She has two objectives, one obvious and one covert: get the file, pick it apart. She needs only a minute to scan for clues before the Security Center seals it. Even if she finds no clues, she will come away knowing about Alpha Lab's layout and security procedures, which might come in handy if she ever needs to make an unannounced visit.

A glimmer catches her attention. Smiling inwardly, Electra says to herself *It must be from a security guard's flashlight.* The glimmer becomes brighter. *I'm ready to practice my low-vocation disguise. Let the acting begin.*

CHAPTER 2
February 11, 2097

"The Lightning Explosion"
(Thread 2 Chapter 1)

JASON ADJUSTED ALL BURNERS on the stove to high so there would be plenty of hot water. He knew that what he was doing was unnecessary, but he followed his mother's orders anyway because she wanted to keep him busy and out of the way. Perhaps doing so had swept his throbbing headache away, or maybe he should thank the two smart pills taken earlier. Whatever the reason, Jason was sure it added to his euphoric certainty that his first child would be exceptional.

And he had every reason to be confident, for here was, safely ensconced in his childhood home, a wooden Colonial in a middle-distance suburb of DC, where his wife-to-be Indy was upstairs, about to give birth. His mother Dora—a practical nurse—was assisting; his father—Doctor Justin Kittner—would be arriving shortly. "Doc" Kittner, an old school general practitioner, had instilled in his impatient son a love for biology. Indy and his parents were the only people other than two grad school friends he could tolerate for more than an hour, but Indy predicted their first child would enchant a sometimes-dour Jason to the max.

They had met in graduate school where both pursued PhDs in biotechnology, and over time her playful spirit softened his blunt manner. She did her best to brighten his life, nicknaming him

Sunny, but it didn't stick because he didn't appreciate its carefree irony, nor did anyone associate that adjective with him because his mood usually sat near the opposite end of the brightness scale. Still, she coaxed him to expand his interests, introducing him to the fine arts, hoping he would eventually share her special love of poetry. Her lighthearted prodding began to work its magic; at least now he could tolerate some of the liberal arts.

Jason opened the kitchen door to check the weather—a swirling, intensifying wind with thunder rumbling and tumbling in the distance. He thought how extraordinary it is for thunder to accompany an approaching snow squall. A fragment from a folklore rhyme came to mind:

> "Happy is the corpse the rain falls on,
> Happy is the bride the sun shines upon."

And he wondered what lines might be added shortly for mother and child.

As he turned to re-enter, a flash brighter than a thousand suns burst in the kitchen, and the concussion from a thunderous crash propelled him over the porch railing, stunning him for a minute. As he regained his footing and staggered through the doorway, greedy flames and hissing gas blocked his path to the stairway. In spite of his shock-filled fog, Jason lurched out the kitchen door, running mechanically to the front door, where flames dancing madly blocked him again. He screamed out to his mother and Indy, but heard nothing except the whooshing of the spreading fire.

GET THE LADDER FROM THE GARAGE! screamed through all his senses. He did so with all the speed his muddled brain could muster. NOW CLIMB TO THE BEDROOM WINDOW! Jason snapped out of the fog and climbed like a SWAT commando. Once there he saw the disaster; room engulfed in flames, his mother collapsed on the floor, and Indy—horribly burned below the waist— at the open window clutching their newborn. Jason was dumbstruck.

"LIGHTNING GOT US ALL! "rasped Indy as she thrust the infant into his arms. She choked out "ELECTR—"just as the floor gave way with a crunching groan and the bedroom collapsed inward and downward, sucking her into the inferno now raging below.

The survival instinct thrust Jason down the ladder. He reached the ground a second before the living room exploded, catapulting him across the front lawn, unconscious but still clutching the infant.

JEEZUS JEEZUS JEEZUS! shouted Doc Kittner into the windshield. He was driving madly from his personal holocaust: his home a blazing torch in swirling darkness of the late afternoon storm, his wife and his soon to be daughter-in-law missing in action, his severely lacerated son unconscious in the back seat, and his lobster-red grandchild squirming in the passenger seat. His adrenaline-charged strength had been just enough to drag Jason into the van and then dash back for the infant. Now it was a race for their lives to the county hospital on a route he knew instinctively from years of practice. He prayed his staff would be up to the challenge.

Doc nearly skidded off the road as he careened around the sleet-slick turn into the entrance drive. He was in luck; the backup power generator had kicked in and the lights were on. JEEZUS THANK YOU! he bellowed, brakes screeching the van to a sliding halt as an EMT ran to assist.

Doc yelled, "Get a stretcher and someone to help you. Jason's unconscious in the back seat. He's got head injuries and bad cuts." Then he charged into the hospital, clutching his grandchild. Anna, the on-duty nurse, scurried towards him gasping, "Mother of God," freezing for an instant before snapping into action.

"Go to Neonatal!"

"It's my grandchild. Clarence is wheeling in Jason. I'll be in E.R. My house burned down! "Anna swooped the infant into her arms, then disappeared down the corridor.

Doc's adrenaline rush was wearing off after three hours helping patch Jason. The deep cuts had been stitched and though badly bruised, he had no broken bones or internal injuries, so he was out of danger and though groggy, was able to talk. In a stuttering voice, he described as best he could the disaster. A lightning bolt had struck through the bedroom while he was in the kitchen. Mother, child, and grandmother had been electrocuted. Somehow, a mother's love had given Indy the strength to rise almost from the dead to thrust her newborn into his waiting arms just before she plunged to her fiery death. "Jeezus, Jeezus, Jeezus," Doc mumbled as he slumped in a chair, tears rolling down his cheeks as he drifted into a grief-stricken stupor.

Anna had never seen anything like this. Doc's grandchild—granddaughter actually—had been lobster red a couple of hours ago. With her little hands grasping the air and her dark hazel eyes scanning about, she looked like a lobster struggling to avoid a pot of boiling water. But now her skin was the pinkish-white expected in a typical newborn. And she was not crying or screaming. Instead, her alert eyes peered intensely at Anna as her tiny mouth uttered indistinct syllables. Anna bustled away to talk with Doc.

"Doc, wake up." Anna's words seeped into his brain and he began to stir.

"All gone, all gone. Just me and Jason left," he mumbled. Anna shook him by the shoulders.

"Justin! Doctor Kittner! Snap out of it. Your granddaughter survived. Come with me. You need to see this."

"What? Jeezus!" Doc suddenly grasped the situation as Anna's words galvanized him to action.

"Let's freshen you up so you can see her. Then we'll talk with your son."

"Here's your granddaughter." Anna carefully placed a blanket-wrapped baby into Doc's strong but gentle arms.

"Jeezus, she looks dandy as can be. And all her responses are normal?"

"Yes. This is one alert young lady. Her eye and head movements are as if she can follow the conversation." Doc was mesmerized. Bright smiling eyes, exploring hands reaching towards his face, and a smile forming on that tiny mouth. Anna took his arm as she led the way to Jason's room.

Jason's memory was a blank slate. What fire? What explosion? What baby? And then in a flash it all came rushing back.

"And that's it. I hope to God Mom and Indy died instantly, but I couldn't tell." Jason sobbed silently. Doc wore his brave face.

"Don't you worry, son. We'll get through this. Now just get some rest. We'll start fresh in the morning. "They started to leave, but the infant started squirming in Anna's arms, pointing towards the bed.

"If it's OK, can I hold her for a while. I can't sleep, and I need something to do or I'll go off the deep end."

"That's a good idea. I'll check later to see how you and your daughter are doing."

Indy's prophesy came true. Jason was mesmerized too, suspended in the moment, wanting to hold his daughter forever. How light, yet how strong. Her sparkling eyes made frequent contact with his after gazing purposefully around the room, while her hands touched and brushed his face. "My little girl is no crybaby. I think she wants to tell me something, but what could possibly be flowing through her brain? Could she remember what she just went through?"

As he rocked her gently, Jason said aloud, "I'm so sorry, little kitten that I have to take your Momma's place. Momma holding you would have looked so lovely. And I'm so sorry I was not at Momma's side. Only you and Grandma and Momma were there." He mused that someday she would share what happened but then changed his mind. How agonizing that would be. "Momma and I didn't pick a name for you. We wanted to meet you first. And when we did, Momma had to leave right away."

A crash thundered in Jason's head. Indy's last word—ELECTR. Jason instantly knew what to name his daughter. Tears welled in his eyes as he kissed Electra and spoke again.

"Before Momma left, she named you Electra, after the Greek goddess. You are Electra, our little princess, our little kitten. And I shall give you the nickname Kit, for our last name Kittner."

Electra seemed to return his kiss, nodding in agreement. "Impossible, but what the hell. Why not pretend she understands?

It'll be like talking to Indy." A wan smile lit his face as he held Electra close.

"I think you know what I'm saying, little kitten. Momma wants me to keep talking so you'll know all about Momma and me. And you can talk to us when you're ready." Fatigue finally settled in;

Jason slept as his daughter snuggled in his arms. They would be safe for tonight.

Anna came by to check her special patients. Jason was asleep, daughter wrapped in his arms, gazing intently at his face while her hands brushed lightly over every feature within reach. She carefully retrieved the infant.

"Time for you to rest, Little Lady. You can come back tomorrow and play with your Daddy."

Jason was too busy the next week arranging funerals to spend much time with his daughter, so Doc filled in. He needed something to do while moving temporarily into Jason's house, bringing what few belongings remained, and Jason needed him to talk with their minister to arrange an ecumenical service. Indy had been Christian and Hindu.

Doc's patient, empathetic persona bonded instantly with his granddaughter, who did likewise. He chuckled as he held the sparkling and inquisitive infant, then spoke as if she understood. "I like talking to you, and I hope you'll be talking back to me soon. And I think I'll use your nickname Kit, or maybe call you Kit-Kat, until you get to be an adolescent. By then, you'll probably want to be called by a more adult, ladylike name. You can tell us what you like."

Keeping busy helped father and son get through the week, keeping darker thoughts away. Both appreciated the consoling words offered by friends, but even during the service nothing that was said helped much.

After the service, Jason insisted he carry both urns on that cold misty morning. As he shuffled towards the burial vault, he did not know how long it would take to work through his grief but realized he had to keep busy, to keep occupied or risk sinking into a deeper depression. The folklore rhyme again came to mind:

"Happy is the corpse the rain falls on."

How can I make them happy? What can I do for them now? The answer came in a flash, freezing him in his tracks. They'd want me to do to everything possible to keep Electra safe. But how can

I protect her from the uncertainties facing us? How can I keep the T-Plague away?

Jason suddenly felt lighter, as if a dreaded darkness that had filled him to the core were lifting. He completed the march, then left with straightened shoulders and quickened pace. He knew what to do.

Late that night, Jason sat in the safety of the house he and Indy had planned to turn into their home. His father and daughter were asleep, so he wouldn't be interrupted as he carried out Indy's last command. Indy had given him a sealed envelope containing instructions if some catastrophe befell her. He was to open the envelope and read the letter as soon as possible. Jason knew it was time to obey.

"My dearest Jason. You are reading this because an unforeseen tragedy will forever separate us in the physical world. I know you loved me dearly, as did I you. You are now working through the grief you feel. I would be doing the same if you had been taken from me. Grieving is but one of the steps for coming to terms. You must get past it right now. You have yourself, your parents, and our daughter to live for. Move forward right now into your future. Pretend I am sitting across from you, encouraging you to do what is right. Start by listening to a poem I learned in high school."

> "Do not stand at my grave and weep.
> I am not there, I do not sleep.
> I am a thousand winds that blow.
> I am the diamond glints upon the snow."

Streaming tears forced him to stop. After the wave of emotion had washed away, Jason continued.

> "I am the sunlight on the ripened grain and
> I am the gentle autumn rain.
> When you awaken in the morning hush,
> I am the swift uplifting rush, of
> Quiet birds in circled flight.

—

I am the soft star that shines at night.
Do not stand at my grave and cry,
I am not there, I did not die."

"Dearest, I am with you always in the recesses of your memory. I command you now to pack all my belongings and put them away. Hold one last remembrance, then follow the sentiments in this poem, which I appropriately named *Dead Reckoning*."

"I've grieved too long about the past,
Once joys of life have passed away.
Happier times a distant day,
So sad that even love won't last.

But silly me for now I know,
Can't clone emotions that I feel.
Nor conjure the day to make it real,
The world moves on all life is flow.

And love transforms what's deep inside,
Reckon the past no more concerned.
Move forward with the lessons learned,
And bury the past with all that's died."

Jason worked into the early hours of next morning.

CHAPTER 3
September 2092

"In the Beginning"
(Thread 3 Chapter 1)

JASON'S DREAM WAS BLOSSOMING like a flower kissed by the sun. He and his closest grad school friends—Indy, Su, and Adom—all held promising positions at NIH labs near Washington, and his outlook had brightened even further because Indy had just reviewed his co-friend marriage contract, making only a couple of revisions.

Indira Jaswinder Ramanujan, whose name means beautiful possessor of an Indian God's thunderbolt, occupied the center of Jason's life. She had that rare combination of academic and social intelligence that made everyone like her immediately rather than envy all her talents. They had met in Boston, he studying genetic engineering at MIT and she virology at Harvard. He had a fatal attraction for smart, trim, and fit women, traits Indy possessed in spades. When adding to that her long and leggy look, Jason was a goner, head over her shapely heels and other killer anatomical parts. Realizing she had unwittingly hooked him, she playfully reeled him in, reminding that anything worth having is worth working for. She told him he was her favorite for all his S-words: smart, serious, solid, stocky, slightly shorter than she, and so on. What great sport it was! She had grown up in India, the daughter of a wealthy Indian family that encouraged her to be a professional woman of Modernity. She attended the best schools and selected Harvard for graduate virology.

Indy's roommate, Su-Lin Song Chou, grew up in China, the only daughter of a middle class Chinese couple that had recently emigrated from Beijing to London. Su's name says it all—a cute gem of a young lady. Unlike Indy's effervescent personality, Su was cerebral rather than athletic, reserved and delicate, possessing subtle charm only Asian women possess. She was the smartest on a team comprised of Mensa-only members, placing near the top in most classes, especially in her neuroscience and biostatistics specialties.

Jason's roommate Adom Ola came at the age of six from Kenya when his parents immigrated to Atlanta. He had academic and athletic talents—high school valedictorian and state cross country champion were among his achievements. He and Jason were cast from the engineering-type mold, but he distinguished himself from typical bio-tech drones (including Jason) because he was a "cool guy"—tall, affable, and handsome—who enjoyed socializing to break the grind. Women found his name fitting—a gift from the Gods—worth his weight in gold.

The four bonded immediately. Given the cultural mix and how well their skills and personalities blended, Indy nicknamed them the Worldstars Team. Each had an NIH grant that fast-tracked them through respective degree programs. Indy predicted the world will be their "genetically modified oyster "because the 21st century is indeed the "Biotechnical Age," even though technological progress is still hampered by swaths of society fearing what they don't understand. But the Worldstars were undaunted; the arrow of change points relentlessly forward, driven by science and pragmatic reason. An NIH recruiter, recognizing their collective breadth and depth, offered a deal no one could refuse. The four were on their way.

Today they would have lunch after the Home Base Monthly Update Meeting attended by newer researchers. Jason needed to hurry; he had to be there by nine-thirty, and Indy had a head start.

The moderator concluded every meeting by showcasing a topic meant to capture the imagination of his aggressively talented junior researchers, and today's choice was among the best. The audience liked how he blended respect for senior researchers with encouragement for the younger generation. NIH must retain the best and brightest of both junior and senior researchers to ensure America's health and safety against whatever comes, and the mysterious disease he was about to describe might be on the horizon.

"Listen up, young turks and tigresses. Here is a problem that appeared on our Bio-Risk Environmental Scanner three weeks ago. Our Far East Monitor detected a Beijing outbreak of an unidentified infectious disease. The Chinese have not reached out for assistance. They're tight-lipped so our facts are minimal. This slide shows there's much we don't know..."

- Case Fatality Rate (CFR) unknown.

- Symptoms—Severe headache, nausea and fever. Cognitive impairment.

- Symptoms clear without intervention in 48 hours.

- Headache and cognitive impairment follow a two-month cycle. Intensity grows.

- Cause unknown. Contagion duration unknown.

- Transmission mode unknown. Treatment unknown.

After summarizing the points, he challenged the juniors with a career-accelerating opportunity.

"Quite a cool conundrum, wouldn't you agree? We've tasked Atlanta CDC to set up an intervention team to monitor its trajectory, assigning it code X status until more data comes in. There's a high probability it will transition into a Go status project, part of which will be open to a junior researcher team proposal contest. And if the winning proposal gets greenlighted by our senior researcher committee, all members on the winning team will be promoted two grades to Senior Researcher. That's a significant step up in career and compensation, so consider forming into four-person teams to enter the contest. Additional details to follow when appropriate. And on that exciting note, we conclude today's meeting." As the lights came up, the audience, buzzing with excitement, filed to the cafeteria.

Jason spotted Indy's table. She was quicker than he in just about everything, and Su was about to join her. The Worldstars made a game of arrival sequence: last person sitting had to clean the clutter when they left. Jason hurried through the shortest line and seated himself next to Indy, who kidded Adom as he glided in.

"You gave Jason too big a head start. He hasn't been going to the fitness class often enough to make him quicker than you."

"Right you are, Indy. I couldn't make up my mind which dessert I wanted, so I took two." The four bantered while eating, making plans for a weekend hike and trading ideas about how they could prepare for a proposal contest. Su wanted to hear Adom's ideas first, so she asked him to speak up.

"You're a pretty cool guy. What do you think of that pretty cool problem?"

"I don't know, but let's use it to play our Proposal Generation Game. Remember how we would pick a research topic and practice writing up a grant proposal? We were going to write up a whole batch for real once we launched our biotech company. Indy, what's the name you gave it?"

"Worldstar Biologicals, and you thought it was a pretty cool name. Hey Jason, chime in please."

"Adom has a good idea. I guess those two desserts delayed his after-lunch siesta. Why don't we discuss it after Sunday's hike? Hey Su, since you planned it, don't forget to tell everyone what to bring. And speaking of taking a hike, we better start hiking for the shuttle vans so we don't miss our ride back to the labs. Glad I don't have to clean up the table."

Adom could never wear a fake scowl for more than a second or two, so when Indy offered to clean her side he smiled and kidded with her.

"If you go through with this co-friend thing, better add more clauses to your contract or he'll have you cleaning up more than dirty dishes."

"You're right, and since he's my work in progress, I'll clean him up so we can stand him." Su added to the teasing.

"He's standing in our way. We'll have to work our way around him." Jason decided to put up a light-hearted defense.

"I'll be the last man standing when push comes to shove. My fitness class might not add speed, but it's converting flab to muscle." Adom couldn't resist adding the final barb.

"Why don't the ladies shove off for the vans with me? Jason will then be in his usual place when trying to keep up, standing in our wake." Indy gave Jason a playful push as she moved next to Su.

The Sunday hike through Rock Creek Park pleased everyone because Su could plan as well as Jason. Since she knew the park's history, she acted as tour guide. Indy kidded that even the gorgeous weather had been orchestrated by Su's wizardry, to which she replied climate change would be next on her "to-solve" list. Even Jason cracked a smile, admitting he didn't have a project planning template big enough to handle the weather.

The hike ended mid-afternoon at a shade-dappled, gently rolling picnic grove. Indy and Su had packed cheese and veggie snacks, Jason the beverages, and Adom the desserts, all contributing to a balanced blend of healthy and hedonic. The girls staked out a table while the guys retrieved coolers and hampers from Adom's van. Indy started the discussion after Adom's appetite had been appeased.

"It's proposal game time. Jason and I have a head start because we've already considered several ideas. Let him be our proposal leader because he's always so thorough filling in his planning templates. Jason, you're up."

"If we're going to win, we'll need a big idea that draws from all areas of our expertise. Let's identify possible causes and then select the biggest payoff scenario. A virus might be the root of the problem. Indy's our virology expert. Indy, please go on."

"A virus is just one of the possible causes. We don't know if we're dealing with bacterial or viral infection, or maybe environmental exposure. I looked for a big idea and chose a synthetic virus that periodically switches between remissive and aggressive states, even though it's a long shot because recurring viral infections in cranial neurons are virtually unknown." Adom liked what he heard.

"Indy, I'm with you. For a potentiation pathway, I'll go big or go home. Research journals are reporting the existence of short-lived but highly active biomolecules in deep brain tissue, like the conjectured nano-proteins or enzymes. That's my choice for scenario number one." Su was next to offer an opinion.

"But what keeps generating these molecules? Our immune system kills off rogue organisms if they don't kill us first. I won't know until I get more data, but let's assume conventional disease transmission modes and revisit Indy and Adom's choices." As the discussion rolled on, Jason offered several ideas that Su liked. Jason's idea that DNA alteration could play a big role seemed the best choice, and she wanted Indy to explain how that fit with her virus ideas, but Jason was losing patience.

"Let's cut to the chase. What we have is a genetic mutation of a synthetic virus. Like gene slicing and dicing, but at warp speed. Let me explain my bullet point summary of what we've come up with." Jason recited from his notes.

- A previously undetected state-changing virus infects unspecified bacteria.
- Bacteria spread virus to unspecified brain control centers.
- Nano-biochemicals cause genetic mutation.
- Mutation leads to neural pathway entanglement causing cognitive impairment.

"We've wasted enough time. What we've got should be enough to build into a proposal if there's actually a contest. Su can handle that, and the rest of us will fill in where needed."

"Slow down, Jason. I can't handle it without Indy's help. And we should consider other scenarios, because the ones we have use too many low probability choices that are all independent. When we multiply the probabilities of each one occurring, the odds are better for all of us being struck by lightning. But we have time to evaluate further, because the contest hasn't started. And I've been thinking about transmission modes. Until I get some timeline data, I can suggest only my educated guesses. I don't believe in far-fetched entanglement theory or a spontaneous generation analogy, so I'll consider the standard modes, narrowing my selection once I get data on how fast and how far the disease spreads." As Su talked on, Indy noticed Jason fidgeting with his pen, so she said, "I think we've done enough for a Sunday, so let's adjourn. But before we go, let's think about how we'll handle the diplomatic piece if there's a call for proposals. Other teams might think we have an unfair advantage because we've been working together for a couple of years. Most of the researchers know we're a package deal, so let's keep our proposal generation game to ourselves." Only Jason disagreed.

"Come on, Indy, this is career advancement stuff. All the researchers are adults, and if we happen to be better, which I know we are, too bad for the competition."

Su said, "Jason's making a valid point, but we must keep in mind the human side of the equation. Research, just like business, is a contact sport and we're dealing with smart people with big egos. Indy's right. Let's be diplomatic." As usual, easygoing Adom waited until everyone's position was on the table so he could smooth out any wrinkles; today he offered advice to Jason.

"I'm glad you're a bull dog and push hard for what you want. That's what makes you a talented project manager. But you need to dial down your assertiveness so we can get along with the other researchers. You have a reputation for being good at managing details, but sometimes you're too blunt."

"OK, OK. I get it. I'll make more of an effort to be kind and gentle and not ruffle other teams, and I'm counting on the three of you to let me know how I'm doing. Are we done now? Can we go home?" Indy spoke for everyone.

"Yes, but let's remember the seniors are watching. Many of them have bigger egos than the juniors, and deservedly so in some cases. They'll think we're too inexperienced to build an industrial strength project, so they might not support our proposal. We haven't been here long enough for them to know how good we are. Let's make an effort to get along. Are we copacetic?" Everyone nodded, and the Worldstars packed up and into Adom's van for the drive home.

Adom drove and Su rode alongside, gossiping about his social life and her volunteer work. Both cool in different ways: Adom the fun-loving extrovert, Su the refined intellectual. While Indy dozed against his shoulder, Jason considered all the good things going on. He wondered if Su and Adom would transition into co-friendship. The term originated years ago in the LBGT Community to describe an intimate pairing regardless of Y chromosome count or sexual orientation. Jason wouldn't hazard a guess, but regardless what they decide, what marvelous serendipity for the Worldstars to meet in America, where outstanding careers await those with talent, where people seem more youthful and healthier than ever before. Advanced cosmetic surgery could peel years off appearances; new weight loss procedures or appetite-suppressing drugs could eliminate obesity.

Medical advances, however, had limits; proper nutrition, exercise, and genes remain the major determinants for feeling and looking good well past today's extended middle age decades. Too bad magic medical bullets to counteract too much or too many sensual pleasures remain a pipe dream, for human nature knows what it likes and will not be denied.

Jason's physical condition illustrated that the same applies to fitness. He needed to firm up and slim down, difficult to achieve because contemporary lifestyles burn fewer calories than a couple of generations ago. Too bad drugs or shortcuts to fitness work only when used in marketing infomercials. Jason was not one of those people willing to endure sweat-producing levels of exercise often enough to reach his goal.

I hope Indy doesn't point this out in her revisions to my Vow-Cer marriage contract.

As Jason thought more about the current socioeconomic climate, he concluded that the time's right for living in America. Although gender discrimination still festered, racial or sexual orientation confrontations were mostly in the past, as were thoughtless microaggression behaviors, because society had become more tolerant; political parties had made good progress shoring up their moral shortcomings while relearning the art of civilized negotiation and compromise towards the middle. Though government regulation and meddling, along with a frayed welfare system, were still issues, the middle class grew once again towards prosperity. The country was a work in progress, advancing gradually towards ever better times.

Though the Washington Establishment often underperformed— it fought a losing battle to keep in touch with Main Street— the public usually tolerated its missteps. Congress and the courts too often cooperated implicitly with imperial presidents pushing agendas favoring cronyism rather than the greater good, but the public looked the other way as long as conditions were improving. People had become more self-reliant, reaching out through collaborative consumption to share with others while balancing unnecessary wants against actual needs, and thanks to an omnipresent and increasingly powerful Worldwide Web, volunteerism and crowdsourcing empowered people to help one another in areas the government neglected.

Far-sighted pundits warned that too much public indifference towards government could lead to a government not working for the people but instead working for itself and controlling the people. They pointed to the number of people who, instead of participating in the democratic process, withdrew into binge watching, video games, or other virtual reality worlds. Blunders like these could be avoided by having an educated population demanding more accountability and reducing the size of a bloated government. But the country's mood continued to downplay long-term concerns in favor of short-term optimism.

The rest of the world continued advancing by fits and starts. After a stormy beginning to the 21st century, many countries moved to a kinder and gentler place, even though technology delivered less than promised and some governments were impediments to progress. Dire global warming, energy, environmental, or population predictions turned out to be largely figments of special interest group imaginations. South America began to stabilize its political and economic systems, and Europe dealt with declining population by assimilating Middle East immigrants who craved modernity. Census numbers ticking upwards registered the impact for all countries but Russia, whose population imploded, further marginalizing it on the world stage. Meanwhile, China's burgeoning middle class wrested a share of power from its Communist Party, while India's enormous population finally endorsed both democracy and human rights. And Africa's commitment to democracy boosted economic output to yield hard-won fruits of labor.

That left only the Middle East. Too bad the rogue Islamic State—officially named Isilabad, same as its capital—refused to accept modernity, continuing the centuries-long war pitting Islam against Christianity. It still had one economic weapon, oil reserves seized when it carved out its geography from the underbelly of neighboring countries, but fortunately for the civilized world, oil's declining economic importance counterbalanced Isilabad's belligerent stance. None of the Middle East countries had yet mastered weapons of mass destruction, though according to rumors, WMD is Isilabad's top priority. And to make the Middle East even more of a muddle, none of the Arab states had made much progress moving beyond an oil-based economy.

As his thoughts meandered, Jason recalled a Biblical warning: tomorrow is promised to no one. Though true, Jason had confidence that his promised tomorrow was attainable. Determination, Indy, his loving parents, and the Worldstars would make it so. *Indy nicknamed me Sunny. It didn't stick, but I feel that way today. It fits my mood to a T. I'm going to work to be more cheerful. Perhaps that will help my career blossom even faster. I need to show Indy I've got what she's looking for.*

CHAPTER 4
August 2115

"Ominous Conversations"
(Thread 1 Chapter 2)

ALTHOUGH ALPHA LAB'S POWER hadn't been restored, Electra could tell from a flashlight's glare that help was nearly at the window she was peering through, so she stopped banging on the door, then reminded herself to underact the role of a lost data collection clerk. I'll thank the guard and be apologetic so I can ask him more questions.

The guard stepped haltingly down the corridor, certain he would find a lost soul even though the pounding sound he'd been tracking had stopped abruptly. He had been a capable employee, scoring close to the new normal for his job grade when hired, and he used to be less paranoid, less anxious when blackouts occur, but smart pills no longer kept symptoms in remission, and his latest test score was barely above cutoff. Like so many other T-Plague victims, he worried constantly about losing his job.

The guard lurched backwards when he beamed his flashlight through the next window, for it illuminated the terror-stricken head of a young woman, making it look like a disembodied orb floating eerily in a black void. Though his heart was pounding, he steeled his nerves and opened the door just before the lights blinked back to life with a click and then a soft buzzing sound that stopped when the current stabilized. All seemed back to normal.

"Come on missy, let's get you back to level 1." He had never seen this girl before, but she was obviously upset, tripping when reaching for his outstretched hand, falling awkwardly and scattering some papers clutched in one hand. He helped her up before speaking again.

"Missy, are you OK?"

"Ye-yes. "Oh my gosh, my papers! I gotta get them back in order or my boss will be so mad at me, and this is my first assignment. Please wait while I get organized."

"Sure, sure. You just take your time. Sit at the workstation and settle down. How'd you get so lost anyway? Few clerks wander into this part of the lab."

"I didn't get off the elevator at the right level and then I must have gone the wrong way down the wrong corridor, and I got all turned around so I couldn't backtrack, and I ducked in here to calm down, and then the lights went out and I got scared."

"OK, OK. I understand. No harm done. We'll get you on your way soon." She was now sitting, carefully counting the pages, dividing them into appropriate piles, her lips silently mouthing page numbers.

Poor thing, he said to himself. *I hope they keep her. She seems like a right nice young lady.*

After the papers were sorted, the guard escorted her to the Security Center so she could depart on the next inter-lab shuttle van. The guard commented afterwards to his associates how polite she was. "She sure did her best to apologize for getting lost, and tried to make me feel important by asking a lot of questions. I don't know how much sunk in because she still looked pretty confused. Nice young lady, though."

Electra had accomplished her mission. The contents of the file were stored in her lightning brain, while on her lap she held the sealed file. She reviewed while gazing out the window what she had memorized. By the time the van parked, she concluded the file contained no clues. She had known in advance it was a long shot, so she would now pursue other options for ferreting out additional vaccine data, but at least she had learned more about Alpha Lab.

"I'm pleased she found what I sent her for. This is her first trip, and with more coaching, she'll get to know the procedures better. I'll talk with her in about fifteen minutes." As Jalen Kamare disconnected the call, a headache twitched and then subsided. Alpha Lab had just reported that his data retrieval clerk, despite getting lost during a power failure, had completed her assignment. He was happy about that but worried about an intermittent headache because it might be a warning his smart pills no longer work. He felt all right otherwise so he calmed down, joking to himself that some of his associates panic if they burp the wrong way, but nevertheless he was concerned. Jalen, the Training Department Manager for DC labs, supervised Electra's initial training she was completing today, and she would start work Monday for a project team. Jalen didn't know which one because Security guard uses a double-blind assignment protocol to stymie mole infiltration. And he didn't know if the protocol worked because no one knows who or where the moles might be. Jalen had given up trying to keep track of all the political intrigue swirling about, but at last count there were rumored to be at least three covert operations infiltrating labs, hunting for reasons why

T-Plague projects are standing still.

Jalen was certain Electra isn't a mole, which made her even more likeable. She seemed smart enough for her low-skill position, pleasant, and non-threatening. Her background was a bit of a mystery. Something about traumatic accidents dulling her cognitive abilities. Because NIH might have been partly to blame, a senior administrator gave her a job. *Perhaps she's recovering from the T-Plague, and if so, maybe smart pills are working better for her than for me. But I'll never know her medical history, for only high-level administrators can see it, and then only on a need to know basis.*

When Electra returns, Jalen would explain to her and another employee what to expect next Monday because both would begin working on the same project. As he saw her approaching, he called Nick Rossi to join them in his office, then motioned for Electra to sit in a chair on the other side of his desk. As soon as she was sitting, Jalen asked about her day.

"How was your first trip?"

"I think it went OK, although I got lost. But other workers did too. The blackout confused me." Jalen's smile offered encouragement.

"I had a call from the Security Center and they said you did fine. We'll make sure you get more assignments like this one so you learn your way around."

"That will help, and I'll do better next time."

"Well, we're almost done for today, and all that's left is briefing you for next week. I'm going to introduce you to another person wrapping up training. His name is Nick Rossi, and as luck would have it, both of you are assigned to the same project team. I wish I could tell you what team it is, but our security protocols keep that info off limits. I hear him now."

Nick entered the office, exuding youthful confidence expected from an intelligent and well-groomed young man built like a soccer player. He had graduated with honors last spring from the University of Pennsylvania, majoring in political science and minoring in biology. The NIH Intern Program would be his first job in his chosen career, government healthcare services.

"Hello Nick. I would like you to meet Electra Kittner. You're both assigned to the same team in our Zeta Lab Complex and will report there Monday at nine a.m. Your intern position reports to the Bus-Admin Project Leader, and you will handle whatever tasks he assigns. Electra, you report to the Tech Project Leader. You still report to me, but only on a dotted line basis, so if I ever need temporary resources, I can call on you. I know it's been a full week for each of you, but before you go, do you have any questions?" None came up, so Jalen ended the meeting.

"Why don't you get to know each other better? Here's a cafeteria voucher, so dinner is on me. And don't worry. Both of you will do well in your new assignments."

Neither Electra nor Nick had ever eaten at the Home Base cafeteria and were surprised by selection and quality. Nick told her the labs run 24/7 and was sure the cafeteria served up improved employee morale along with tasty entrees. Electra smiled at his attempt to break the ice as he led her to a table suitable for holding a get-acquainted conversation.

"Jalen told me your friends called you Kit when you were a kid, but that's no longer allowed. I'll remember that when we become friends."

"I outgrew it long ago, so please call me Electra. It's too soon to know if we'll be friends, but I like your preppy look. You must have graduated from a top school to land an intern position here. Tell me more about yourself."

As he talked, Electra listened to herself too. *Nick's skills are way beyond those of a basic trainee. He's got great social intelligence, and he must have rehearsed the elevator speech that he's putting on me. In less than five minutes he's said enough for a company to make him a job offer. He must have used it on interviews. This guy's going places.*

"That's my background. I'm solid all the way around, and ready to work for the government's healthcare system. And what about you? How'd you get the Data Clerk position?" Electra launched into a well-rehearsed story.

"I've had a couple of health issues affecting my thinking skills. Don't worry, it's not the T-Plague. NIH has been nice enough to keep me on so I could qualify for a clerk position."

"I'm sorry to hear you've had medical problems, but cog-impair symptoms often clear. I hope that's the case. What kind of project would you like to work on?"

"It doesn't matter to me as long as I can keep practicing my skills. What would you like?"

"I hope it's a T-Plague project. That's where the excitement and conspiracy theories are. We'll know Monday if we got lucky. "The conversation switched to the social scene because Nick had recently relocated and wanted to join an appropriate social network. Electra offered what little advice she had.

"I'm not active socially, but I have a couple of friends who are. I'll give you their numbers next week after I clear the way." Nick glanced at his cell phone, then replied.

"I'm good with that, and I better get going. I need to sort through a bunch of messages when I get home. Come on, I'll walk you to your car."

"Thanks for the offer, but I'm going to get a hot fudge sundae. I'll talk to you Monday."

That evening, Electra sat in her darkened living room, expecting a call from Hector who had texted her earlier, asking for an invite to play his favorite game: strip poker a la Electra. Her return text told him to call back at nine.

Electra's game replaced poker with a popular question and answer game. First person reaching "Emperor's New Clothes" status was declared the loser, and the winner could claim a mutually acceptable prize. Electra never lost except when she needed to boost her opponent's morale. If they lost too often, they might lose interest and move on to "easier" girls.

Electra set eligibility standards high enough for her own protection. *I'm not expecting a perfect ten, but too many young guys are emotionally insensitive, grabbing for sex before I'm ready. And facial hair styles on some of them rub my skin the wrong way. So, I flush guys who can't pass these standards. But if they do, I go easy on them after that.*

Though the T-Plague had reduced the eligibility pool even further, Electra did have three current players: Hector, Joe, and Chris. Hector, a mechanic she knew from high school, met her standards. He was sensible, good looking, and helped fix her car, but whenever he did, Electra knew his ulterior motive: he offered to trade a tune-up for a head start. Electra would wear only a bikini thong and blouse. Hector's emphatic hormones made games exciting, but of all the players, he earned the most penalty points for playing too rough. If he ripped clothing, he was immediately declared the loser.

Joe, a handsome healthcare professional several years older, liked to dance and like all healthy males enjoyed the physical more than the cerebral aspects Electra had to offer, but he was captivated by the different personalities she could reveal whenever she granted him an evening out.

Chris was Electra's secret lover, more considerate and always taking the time to please. They knew each other from early school days, from which their best friend relationship morphed into physical attraction as they grew into adolescence and beyond. Electra struggled for years to keep her emotions reined in by her rational self, but physical demands must be met. Modern parenting acknowledges that sex is a survival instinct which must be obeyed, so adolescents are given adequate freedom to learn by experimenting. ("Show don't tell" was Electra's description).

Electra's vaunted self-control helped, but sometimes primal instincts would break through, bringing fantasies of shredding her clothes, running naked on deserted streets at midnight, howling at the Moon. These feelings were addictive, simultaneously exciting and terrifying in their power over her cognitive self.

She had always been afraid Chris would reject the passion and intensity of her feelings, so she kept them hidden. But a year ago Electra summoned the courage to show them and was rewarded. Now she must protect Chris as well as herself from all the uncertainties swirling everywhere, so they decided to keep their intimacy a secret, dating others to mask their love affair.

Finally, her cell phone chimed. *What shall I do? Shall I toy with Hector, or let him win? Tonight, I'll flip a coin.*

Two deadly adversaries who had never met were also waiting for calls that evening, calls from their field agents who controlled the moles. One used the code name Invisible Man, the other Mrs. T. Washington's political intrigue had become a deadly game affecting covert operations players and their unsuspecting targets alike.

The Invisible Man sat stone-faced in a vacant office buried deep inside a Guardian Party building. The Guardian Party, having ascended to prominence by opposing the Washington Establishment, had built a covert operations team that had planted moles where they would learn the most. The Invisible Man, known only by that code name to the Guardian inner circle, is the direct link through his anonymous agent (code-named the Invisible Hand) to their moles. When his cell phone rang, the Invisible Man came to life.

"This is the Invisible Man. Identify yourself." "This is the Invisible Hand awaiting instructions."

"Your moles report T-Plague approaching a political tipping point. When reached, you must be ready to roll up what you have. How long will that take?"

"What priority do I have?"

"Conclude with extreme prejudice. Ignore collateral damage. Do you copy? "The Invisible Hand smiled. *Screw them all and save the last six for pall bearers.*

"Copy that. It will take forty-eight hours."

"Good. Report again at your scheduled time and let us know if you need additional assets."

Mrs. T, the mirror image of the Invisible Man, coordinated covert operations for another organization that opposed the current Administration and its Washington Establishment cronies. It's known to the media as the Opposition Group, but because it's a relative new-comer, it struggles to gain traction, despite how badly the Administration bungles with terrorism and the T-Plague. Mrs. T's mole handler (code-named the Bad Boy) was doing his best to close the infiltration gap between the Opposition and the Guardians. When her cell chimed, she answered promptly.

"This is Mrs. T. Please identify."

"This is your Bad Boy, ready for instructions."

"Your moles are telling us T-Plague may go politically viral soon. Please make plans for extraction and delivery. Let us know what resources you'll need and how long that will take."

"Copy that. I will have an answer for you shortly." "Very well. Call again as previously arranged."

No one could predict when the tipping point would come, but as America's downward spiral accelerated, the question became a matter of when, not if. Both covert operations teams would be ready to roll at a moment's notice. No one could predict which would prevail, but each followed prudent advice: hope for the best but plan for the worst. No matter what comes, each made plans to survive.

CHAPTER 5
November 2097

"The Secret Within"
(Thread 2 Chapter 2)

Electra loved her father and grandfather, but she was dissatisfied with the way they were handling her. She wanted to be treated like a mini-adult because her brain was developing at lightning speed. Though she would tolerate her grandfather's using a kidlike nickname Kit, from now on the preferred name is Electra. Luckily for Jason, that's what he liked to use, so Electra was confident he would have no trouble dealing with their very first father-daughter talk that she had rehearsed. *After all, isn't a little princess supposed to wrap Daddy around her little finger? That's what the tele-kids I see on TV do.* She giggled in anticipation, expecting her father to toe the lines she would draw now and in the future.

It was an early Sunday morning, and Electra had just hopped back into her crib. She had been watching her mega-media monitor, which she referred to as the tele or TV. Jason wanted her to have a constant stream of sensory input, so he let broadcasts run nonstop when she was awake, no matter which room she was in. She had learned to operate the remote control by trial and error, and two months ago had begun thinking in complete sentences, picking up different accents and favorite phrases from assorted TV characters. She was pleased she could do this, even though her speed of speaking was nowhere near her speed of thinking. Her brain was a fast-growing spongy, organic dynamo, sprouting neural connections and absorbing information at the speed of neural circuitry. TV fascinated her, especially the Learning Network, where she had already mastered all the pre-school reading and arithmetic lessons. News, history channels and comedy series retro-runs were favorites too. Now her very first dialogue was about to begin, for she could hear her father approaching.

Jason always had concerns, for he was a natural-born worrier. *Is there something wrong with Electra's growth pattern, or am I misinterpreting what I see? Her arms and legs seem longer and stronger than normal for her age. I hope she doesn't have some freakish growth malady. Dad hasn't said anything, and she seems normal and remarkably happy otherwise. And best of all, she has none of those T-Plague early warning symptoms so many infants get. I'll keep giving her my advanced smart pills.*

Jason's home front concerns extended to himself, his father, and Electra, and this morning included worrying why he never recalled setting the station Electra was watching, as well as hoping Doc would continue in the role of Electra's omni-parent. *Dad has the right touch. I think Electra loves him more than she loves me, and I can't blame her. I don't have the time or patience to make up for Indy.* All this was weighing on Jason's mind as he walked into Electra's bedroom, wishing for something to happen that would chase his dull headache away.

"Good morning, Electra. Let's open the curtains and let the sun shine in. That always make us feel good." Jason noticed the TV's shutting down indicator blinking and its remote control wand on the floor, but before he could convert the observation into another worry, he heard a British-accented chipper little voice talking to him.

"Daddy, talk like tele-people." When Jason turned abruptly to face the crib, he gaped in awe, gobsmacked to the max. There she stood, strong fingers grasping the bars, and a perky little grin on her face, as if expecting an immediate reply. Electra had spoken.

"Daddy, Daddy," she chirped. "Talk please. "He couldn't. He was dumbstruck. And since he didn't obey, she did what she had learned from telekids when not getting their way: she started crying. That worked. Jason rushed to the crib, picked her out and smothered her with light kisses, then sat her on his lap and stared at this amazing creature.

Electra loved fatherly attention and said pertly, "Daddy, I good. Help me learn. Please talk." Holding her at arm's length, Jason searched for what to say.

"Electra, how can you talk like this?"

"I watch tele. Please talk more." Jason's thoughts finally caught up with the flow of words from his daughter.

"Let's go see your grandfather right now."

Doc was in the kitchen preparing breakfast. After the catastrophic fire, Jason insisted his father move in permanently. At first, Doc was reluctant because he didn't want to meddle in a father infant daughter relationship. But when Jason struggled handling basic baby care, Doc stepped in, becoming Electra's omni-parent, giving her what Jason couldn't, while making Jason's life easier. It was convenient too; the drive to his clinic was shorter. And now that his son and granddaughter were the center of his life, this house was the only place he wanted to be. He turned off the burners just before the duo came in.

"Dad, let's sit down. We have something to tell you." Doc didn't know what Jason's grin preceded, but figured it concerned Electra because he had just placed her in the chair.

"Hi Grampa. I Electra. I Kit to you. Love you. Daddy too. Please talk." Doc's coffee mug nearly slipped from his grip. He was speechless, so Jason supplied the words.

"It stunned me too. Electra's gone overnight from making nary a peep to talking in complete sentences. What do you think?"

"Jeezus, I don't know. How old is she now? Nine months? Infants start babbling and forming syllables about then, but I never heard of them talking in sentences. She sure fooled us."

"I have an idea. As soon as we finish breakfast, let's drive to your clinic and take a couple of brain scans." Doc nodded mutely, so Electra piped up.

"Grampa, who is Jeezus?" Doc was still fumbling for words, so Jason answered.

—

"Grampa will tell you all about him later. Right now, let's have breakfast and then go for a drive." Doc dished up breakfast, doing his best to digest bacon and eggs along with the words he had just heard.

By mid-afternoon, Doc had Electra's brain scan and DNA map displayed on a wide-screen color monitor in his clinic's network center. Doc served as her pediatrician, so the staff didn't think it unusual for him to examine his granddaughter on a Sunday. Neural testing was commonplace because the Healthguard agency mandated scans and DNA screening for infants at least twice a year to look for plague-related neural entanglement. An array of Internet cloud-based testing software provided immediate analysis of scanning or mapping data, giving a diagnostic report Doc had just finished reading. Electra sat nearby, playing with her father's multi-media wristband.

Jason asked "What's your assessment?" Doc muttered back after rubbing his chin for a second or two.

"Jeezus, I've never in all my life seen such a saturated pattern. The bright color-coded spots are centers of neural activity. It looks like a forest of lighted Christmas trees. And the 3-D scan confirms activity from the outer surface all the way down to the brain stem. We're gazing at world's most active brain. "After a few more minutes studying other cross section images, Jason tapped the keyboard to activate DNA deconstruction software. He spoke ten minutes later after studying the new images.

"This is incredible. I see a normal female chromosomal pattern, but genetic cross-linking patterns on several DNA segments are unrecognizable. And when I try reading DNA coding on the oddballs, seminal sequences are different. I'm unsure how much of Electra's DNA would match mine or Indy's. I don't know what to compare it with. Let me think."

"I'll get us something to drink while you keep thinking. You want a Coke?"

"Thanks Dad." Electra understood many of the words and decided to chime in.

"Coke fizzy. "That stopped Doc in his tracks. When he turned towards her, he saw eyes beaming with delight. Electra was having a great time playing with the two men in her life, and the gadgets and wires she was wearing tickled.

"Kit, how do you know about Coca Cola?"

"I Electra too. Call me Electra. I watch tele. Things go with Coke. I thirsty," came the sprightly reply. Doc scratched his head, then spoke to Jason.

"Jeezus, where'd she learn to talk like a Brit? I'll bring her some fruit juice. Do you suppose she knows about caffeine? We won't mention it unless she brings it up."

Doc returned with the drinks; father and son sat at the conference table, sipping and thinking in silence. Finally, Jason spoke.

"Near as I can tell, what we have here is a mega-mutation. Right now, the pattern is localized to the brain. Maybe you can do a DNA scan on other organ tissues."

"Sure thing. I'll bring her with me tomorrow. "They sat quietly for several more minutes finishing their drinks, occasionally glancing at the screen. Then Jason spoke again.

"Do you remember the science-thriller classic, Jurassic Playground or Park or something like that?"

"Dinos big! I like dinos." That was another momentary conversation stopper, courtesy of Electra. It was dawning on the menfolk that they better include her in future conversations.

"In that movie, the scientists brought the past into the present through gene slicing and dicing. When I look at the patterns here, it's like bringing the future into to the present. In the movie it's dinosaurs, but on this screen, it's the human species. The electrical surge from the lightning bolt must have caused all this. Let me sketch what I'm thinking." Jason continued a minute later.

"Here's the evolutionary tree for homo sapiens. Time is the vertical axis and genetic diversity is the horizontal." Doc followed Jason's finger-pointing. "Here's where man is today, and here's my guess for Electra. I've placed her to the right and above man's current location, which means she's genetically more diverse and temporally ahead of us, as if she comes from the future. How many millennia into the future is she? We don't have any data to tell us. How different is she or how different will she become due to this mega-mutation? We don't know that either. The lightning bolt jolted her into one possible future location. Will mankind evolve to where she is? We don't know. All we do know is she's much different. And let's think about this. Evolution caused by natural selection always leads to an improved, better-adapted species if they survive the mutation. Organisms get stronger, smarter, and fitter, or they go extinct. What about Electra? Is she physically and mentally superior? I hope so, and the little we've seen indicates her brain is much more active. So, I'm assuming she is mentally superior to us mere mortals. But physically, emotionally, or ethically? We don't know. We'll have to see how they develop. My guess is, once they start, they'll develop rapidly because neural connections and signals force multiply, reinforcing one another. We may be witnessing a recent neuroscience conjecture, self-directed design replacing intelligent design. Cognitive processes within an organism can self-direct its growth or mutation."

"Jeezus, should we maybe get a second opinion? Who do you think we could talk with?"

"Nobody! Even in the best of times, bad things could happen to her: burned at the stake or dissected. And with the trouble now brewing because of T-Plague, terrorism, and government policy? It'll get worse and she'll be lucky to survive. Look at all the pushback against high-tech development. If the government got wind of Electra, they'd label her a genetic freak and consider her a Frankenstein monster. And they wouldn't be kind or gentle either."

He rose abruptly, returning to the table with Electra in his arms. He began to speak, looking directly into her accepting eyes.

"You are the most exceptional creature in the whole wide world. I think you can understand me, and all three of us must pay close attention to what I'm saying. No one but the three of us, and only the three of us, can ever know what we're talking about today. We must keep it a secret forever. Electra, do you understand what I'm saying?" Electra blinked and giggled.

"Secret game. I like games. Just for Daddy, Grampa, me." Jason hugged her, then gently handed her to his father.

"Kit, you and your Daddy are all I have. I'll never tell anyone." As he hugged his extraordinary granddaughter, Electra spoke. "Love you, Grampa. Love you, Daddy. Help me learn. Don't tell Jeezus secret." Doc placed Electra back in her chair while Jason added final instructions.

"I have an idea. When you start doing her organ DNA scans, why don't you do a DNA hybridization comparison test to measure percent difference between hers and a homo sapiens reference standard? Each percent difference is equivalent to five million evolutionary years. That will give us an estimate of how advanced her brain is."

"I can do it, but what is it going to tell us? Suppose the test shows she's a million years ahead. Does that mean she's a million years better or a million years different?" Jason shook his head.

"We won't know, because most of DNA sequencing has no known function. Only the 50 thousand segments we call genes are important for controlling protein synthesis and related processes. I would have to determine where her gene sequences differ and what characteristics they control. Someday I'll do that, but the best way to see what it all means is just let her grow up. You and I can watch how she develops. She'll be like most kids in some ways, but different in others. Some of the differences we'll observe, but others might go undetected. But we know right now Electra is extraordinary, and we must keep that secret to ourselves."

"OK, I'll do the tests and we can look at the results later this week."

In bed that night with Electra asleep beside him, Jason sorted through today's revelations. He wept silently, uncertain if the tears were caused by sorrow or joy. He didn't know whether his daughter was cursed or blessed. He recalled part of a verse spoken at the first atomic blast, an event that forever changed the world:

"Now I become Death, the destroyer of worlds."

In the flash that changed his daughter, perhaps the same could be said. He couldn't even speculate at the unimagined power, either creative or destructive, that might be hidden in her brain. He was simultaneously fearful and hopeful.

Jason's epiphany at the burial site had abruptly ended his grieving. As if by some conjuring of the gods, Electra magically filled the void left when Indy departed. He needed to keep her close, to protect this fragile and gentle creature until she was ready. Ready for what he did not know. Not even the gods knew what might unfold, but Jason did know that he and his father must explain to her how remarkable she is. They should wait until she's old enough to understand, maybe wait until she's an adolescent. Until then, they should help her enjoy as best as possible being just a normal little girl. As he drifted into sleep, another verse from an Indy poem echoed:

> "The secret is unknown for now,
> Locked in a vault of mind.
> To which I say on rare Spring day,
> Winter stay far behind!"

Jason descended into his deepest sleep since the Big Bang of Electra's creation.

Later that week, Jason and Doc interpreted DNA tests and scans done on organ tissue. DNA hybridization comparisons between Electra's DNA and a reference standard measured a 0.3 percent difference, which would take evolution over a million years to account for that much difference. The lightning brain was indeed a visitor, a stranger from a distant future. Organ scans also detected trace mutations. They didn't know how extensive or fast changes might continue. To answer, they would need to track Electra's growth and behavior. But one thing was certain; Jason's life would be much different than he ever could have imagined. What would Indy say? He smiled when recalling one of her aphorisms:

"Life is what happens when you're making plans for something else."

I'll have to make sure Indy would approve how Dad and I raise Electra. And I wonder what name she would have picked for a daughter. I'll never know, but I'm sure she'd like Electra, no matter her first choice. I can't think of it, but if Indy were here, she'd quote that famous poem that says the same. I wish Indy were here, but as she told me, I must keep moving forward and keep busy. Electra will help me do both, and Dad and I will help her learn as much as she can as fast as possible. Someday her lightning brain will electrify the world.

"The Little Girl with a Curl"
(Thread 2 Chapter 3)

"Grampa, please tell me the story about Jeezus, and start all the way at the beginning."

"This is a good time for me to do just that. Your Aunt Su and Uncle Adom won't be here for a couple of hours, and your Dad's cooking dinner. So here we go..."

The Kittner household was about to celebrate Easter, a holiday that fascinated Electra because her grandfather often spoke the name Jeezus. Because she knew about the parts of speech, she understood that Doc used the "J" word to enliven his speaking. She liked his rendition of religion's greatest story, from which he recited from twice a year—Easter and Christmas. Each year he added more details, making the stories more realistic. Electra always asked probing questions, which she "dummied down" to her chronological age. She already knew the Bible better than adults, but she asked questions to learn what others believe or how they interpret Bible stories.

Electra knew many things better than most adults because the lightning brain's neural connections had mushroomed far beyond that of mere mortals, bestowing extraordinary mental powers. As soon as her two-man support team recognized her inquisitive nature, they provided all the books or Internet access they could. Electra absorbed it all.

She also knew it would be easier to hide her secret if she pretended to have the mental ability of a smart—but not exceptional—little girl, so she acted the part of a well-behaved child unless someone called her Kit, and that would trigger a nasty outburst. Only Doc could call her Kit, but not too often.

Doc had become her special person, an amalgamation of parent, grandparent, and mentor. He spent more time with her than with anyone else because she had become his focal point, giving him joy and purpose. His empathy force multiplied their relationship as well as her development, and Electra basked in the glow of his protective nurturing. Jason doted on her too, but in a distracted way. Though trying to be close, he worried too much and shut out the past, opening gaps between them. She sensed his flaws but loved him anyway, adjusting her expectations accordingly.

Electra's cognitive persona emerged first and its growth accelerated, but two other personas—the physical and the emotional—would become extraordinary as well, although developing more slowly because their neural development circuits ticked to slower clocks. Electra would come to realize that her cognitive self could influence physical and emotional development. Neuroscience had recently replaced intelligent design with self-directed design where a person's thoughts can—within limits— control growth, and since the number of interconnections and control centers in Electra's brain exceed man's evolutionary limit, what she wills herself to become might be startling.

Brains need sensory input to stimulate interconnections, and though Jason prohibited "dangerous" contact with strangers, Electra's active imagination compensated for the lack of playmates by inventing friends. She also studied subjects or learned skills found on the Internet, such as history or martial arts. Retro-flick movies featuring car chases and fight scenes were among her favorites, as were sci-fi classics.

But Electra's exceptional abilities came with drawbacks. Children have a grace period—between the emergence of awareness and the emergence of self—where they live in a world of unconditional happiness and worry-free security. Not so for Electra. She had already sensed life's contingent nature. Not even her precious father or grandfather could protect her forever, or vice-versa, but the men in Electra's world had kept her safe for the first three years, resulting in a happy and healthy early childhood.

Doc was wrapping up his story. "And so, we celebrate Easter because Jeezus died to save us from our sins. We must believe in him to gain everlasting life."

"Grampa, I love to hear you tell the story."

"And I love to tell it to you. You often ask questions, but today you just listened. Would you like to ask me something?" Electra asked a question appropriate for this year.

"Do you think there is more than one way to believe in Jeezus?"

"That's a great question. Yes, there are several ways, and everyone must pick a way that makes the most sense. You might believe Jeezus is the son of God and can work all sorts of miracles. Or you might believe Jeezus gives us everlasting life if we practice his teachings and his kind of love. We'll talk more about this when you get a little older. But for right now, just enjoy being here talking with me." Electra hugged Doc, then ran off to play on her computer while he headed to the kitchen to check in with the chef.

"The aroma's tantalizing. I'm impressed with how quickly you've mastered the art of cooking." Jason kept stirring as he replied.

"Cooking is chemistry. My lab work has made me an expert for handling any biochemical reaction, and that's what cooking is. I overheard your Jeezus story. Thanks for entertaining Electra. And thanks for being so good with her. You mean more to her than I do. She frowns at me when I call her Kit, but she lets you get away with it. You've got the right touch."

"She loves you as much as she loves me. Just in a different way. We are blessed to have such an exceptional little lady."

"So far so good, I guess. I try not to fret about what she'll become, but I'm a worrier by nature."

"I know the drill. It took me over sixty years to learn how to enjoy today and let tomorrow take care of itself. So, don't kick yourself for worrying. It comes with being a parent." Just then the doorbell rang.

"That must be Su and Adom. I'll get the front door, and you keep cooking."

Doc was right. He hugged Su, shook Adom's hand, and ushered them into the living room after putting coats in the hallway closet. Electra bolted into the living room, singing out a greeting.

"Aunt Su. Uncle Adom. Happy Easter, Happy Easter!" Jason, attired in his chef's apron, soon joined the group.

"Happy Easter everyone." Adom seized the greeting to tease Jason.

"Hey buddy, nice wardrobe. Isn't that Su's Christmas present?" "Sure is, and now that my chef skills are improving, I have to dress the part." Su handed Jason a plump shopping bag.

"I baked some of Electra's favorites. I hope they match the quality of your cooking."

"I could cook for a thousand years and never match your kitchen wizardry, so thank you for the goodies. Why don't all of you chit-chat while I get back to the kitchen? I'll have dinner on the table in about twenty minutes. Would anyone like an appetizer or a drink?" Everyone declined the offer and let appetites build. Electra sat on the sofa between her godparents, who were long-time friends of her parents, and the only adults allowed into her life. They always came to family celebrations and were considered part of the family.

Doc asked, "Jason tells me all about you two and what's going on at the lab, but what's been going on outside of work? Adom, how is life treating you?"

"I'd say it's a mixed bag. I didn't renew my sports club membership. Some of the members contracted the T-Plague, and that scared some people away, including me. You remember my girlfriend Whitney Cantrell? She contracted the T-Plague late last year and is still recovering. I talk to her occasionally, but we're no longer dating. Su said I should join a volunteer group to fill the gap, and I'm still looking for one. But I've spent more time in the lab's fitness center, so I feel pretty good. And at Su's prodding, I joined an online book club. It's a nice change from the stuff I have to read at work." Doc nodded and added more.

"Yes, the T-Plague has impacted lots of people, directly or indirectly. But you look darn fit. Su, what about you? You always look good."

"I'm fine, thank you. I see my friend Kayed occasionally when I attend my Middle East lecture series. Between that and piano practice, I have a nice balance with work. Now, how about you?"

"I still keep my medical practice going, but I cut my schedule back so I have more time to take care of Kit. She and I are best buddies, and thanks to her I keep physically and mentally fit. Isn't that right, Kit?"

"Yes. Grampa is my best friend, and I made him promise to stay healthy and wise. And I like when Grampa takes me with him when he goes out. I always learn so much, and we have lots of fun. And today, he told me again his Jeezus story. Aunt Su, would you tell me your Jeezus story?"

"Of course. You and I will talk after dinner." Electra smiled and clapped her hands. Just then Jason announced that dinner was ready, and the party headed to the table.

Electra waited patiently for dinner to end so she could have Su all to herself. She planned for them to curl up in her bedroom, sitting on the floor while she peppered Su with questions. Each felt a mutually strong emotional bond, different and more dimensional than with other people, always coming to the surface when talking about Indira. Though Electra had no recollection of her mother, Su provided missing links that helped piece together a multidimensional picture. Unlike Jason, who usually ignored his feelings, Su allowed them to come out when talking with Electra, even though Electra sensed they were sometimes painful. Her brain stored everything Su mentioned, continuing to paint a picture of her practically perfect mother.

"Aunt Su, how do you believe in Jeezus? Grampa told me there are a couple of ways." After three years—and even though Electra acted her age—Su suspected her godchild was exceptional. When they were together, it seemed that she was in the presence of a mini-Indy reincarnation, making the moments special.

"That is a very good question. It can be answered on many levels, some easy and some more difficult to understand. Do you think you are ready for a more difficult answer?" Electra needed to be careful, never to expose too much of her secret, even to Su.

"Oh, yes. Please give me an answer that's just right, sort of like what Goldilocks chose."

"Very well. Some people believe Jesus is exactly what the Bible says, and everything told in the Bible happened exactly as it's stated. Then there are other people like me who think it's allegorical. Now that's an adult word. Do you know what allegory means?" Electra played along. "In Sunday School, the teacher says Jeezus used parables. Is an allegory like a parable?"

"Very good. Yes, an allegory is an adult version of a parable. So, I like to consider Jesus a great teacher who gave the world the best rules for living and helping one another. Would you agree with this?" Electra wanted Su to answer more questions, so she let fly another zinger.

"I like that, but why don't you believe in miracles, like the ones in the Bible?" From her expression, Electra knew Su was scrambling for a suitable answer.

"Well, ah, your father, Uncle Adom, and I are scientists, and you know what scientists do. We study the real world using our brains, knowledge, and facts to figure things out. When we apply all this to the Bible and the miracles it talks about, it sometimes seems unreasonable that things happened just that way. So, we come up with different explanations that make more sense. I think you and I should talk more about Bible miracles when you get a little older. For now, why don't you just enjoy what great stories the Bible has?"

Su's words provided a segue for Electra to ask about Indira's religion. As she folded her hands in her lap, sparkling eyes and a charming smile accompanied the next question.

"I like talking with you about Momma. You were Momma's best friend. Did Momma believe in Jeezus like you do?" Su reflexively glanced away, pausing to gather what to say.

"Yes, she did. Your mother and I were best friends, and we talked about many things. She believed in Jesus the same way. Your mother knew a lot about religion. As a little girl, she learned about the Hindu religion. And when she was older, her parents converted to Christianity. When you get a little older we'll talk about other religions. Learning about them makes you smarter. But for now, I think you should learn all you can about Jesus and the Bible. After that, I'll teach you about other religions."

"Would you teach me next year?"

"Yes, and we'll let your Uncle Adom join us."

"Do you think Uncle Adom brought chocolate Easter Eggs? I like them almost as much as I like him."

"Let's go ask him." Electra led a relieved Su to the living room.

Doc listened stoically as Adom described Cognicom's sad state of affairs. Even the Worldstars team was making little progress since Indy's death, and the news Jason quoted on the political front wasn't encouraging either, confirming what he said all too often: the Worldstars were no longer kissed by the sun, but cursed by a devil instead. All teams felt pressured to get results. Doc welcomed a change of topics when Electra bounded into the room, curtsying to Adom before asking a question.

"Grampa said if I was good today that maybe you would give me a chocolate Easter Egg. Grampa, have I been good today?" Doc winked at Su.

"We'll have to ask your Aunt Su." Everyone's attention focused on Su, who thought for only a moment before replying.

"Electra has been very good today. Her behavior reminds me of a Longfellow poem Indy told me long ago. It's about a little girl."

> "There was a little girl,
> Who had a little curl,
> Right in the middle of her forehead.
> When she was good,
> She was very good indeed,
> But when she was bad she was horrid."

"Electra is always very good, and sometimes I think she's the most extraordinary little girl in the whole wide world." Adom picked her up, then swung her back and forth.

"You're getting bigger and stronger. Pretty soon I'll need help from your Dad swinging you like this." He set her down and then gave her two fudge-filled chocolate Easter Eggs. "Be sure to save one for later."

"Thank you! I'll share them with Daddy and Grampa too." Electra hugged everyone before scampering off to play on the computer while the adults finished talking.

On the drive home, Adom asked Su for her view on Electra.

"I think she's thriving. When I'm with her, I get this feeling that Indy's spirit is present. I cannot imagine what she will become, but I think it will surprise all of us. How do you think the fellows are doing with her?"

"I think they're doing a great job. Jason's lucky his Dad's so good with kids. And I'm impressed with Jason's cooking. He has a lot more to worry about than I do. Between his professional and personal lives, he's booked solid. No wonder he hasn't taken me up on the double-dating offer."

"Speaking of dating, are you seeing anyone now?" Su didn't pry into why he dropped Whitney; perhaps he'd explain.

"I feel bad she contracted the T-Plague, but I was ready to break things off before then. She wanted more of a commitment, and I'm not ready for that big of a step."

"Our private supply of stronger smart pills puts us at a lower risk for contracting T-Plague. You could see her without worrying you'll get sick. Don't let Jason's hypochondriac tendencies infect you. But, no sense prolonging a relationship that's one-way." Adom changed to a safer subject.

"Doc knows he's lucky his clinic isn't a T-Plague testing center. I bet Jason gives everyone at home our better smart pills. Jason worries that if the T-Plague spreads much further, our medical system won't be able to handle the load and there'll be a smart pills black market."

They drove on in silence to Su's condominium. As he walked her to the front door, Su's comment regarding a mini-Indy reincarnation came to mind. "Too bad Indy's gone. The two of you were the brains driving our project. No wonder we made progress when she was alive. I wish Jason and I could pick up the slack, but you work at a higher level. But you by yourself are moving us ahead. And like Indy used to tell me, I'm responsible for moving myself forward. So, I'll follow Indy's advice and find a Whitney replacement."

Su repressed an urge to tell Adom that he was too self-centered, that he needed to look beyond himself for a commitment to someone or something, or else he would never become the responsible adult that was inside. Tonight she would not criticize, knowing the time for a tongue lashing would come if Adom didn't change, so she smiled instead and said goodnight.

CHAPTER 7
August 2102

"School Bells Ringing"
(Thread 2 Chapter 4)

Jason couldn't recall why the school district had sent a reminder to enroll Electra in first grade until he remembered she had turned five last February. The letter instructed him to provide a copy of her medical records when bringing her next week for cognitive and behavioral testing that would determine slotting into the proper education track.

Could Electra be that old? So much has happened since her birth, and it's gone by like a streak of lightning. There, I used the word again. Ever since her birth and Indy's death, words like flash or lightning strike me. The bolt that changed our lives is always near.

Electra exhibited all outward signs of a normal child. Her abnormal growth spurt ended after the first year. She was long-limbed, making her appear even taller, and according to Doc she was in the 90th percentile for height and 50 for weight. These measurements, when decked out on her thin-boned frame, added to a lithe yet resilient look. She had surprising strength and agility as well as paranormal immunity to the T-Plague. Doc believed it was a side effect of the lightning bolt, but just to be safe he gave her Jason's stronger smart pills.

Electra's menfolk were relieved when precocious emergence of her cognitive skills dissipated, for she no longer asked them

—
59

embarrassing questions. They concluded she must have above-average intelligence because she had mastered computers, playing with them for hours on end. Everyone agreed she had a lovely little personality: bright, cheerful, and loving with a clever sense of humor. She rarely cried, and was "difficult" only if Jason tried to pull her away from the computer. Then she would throw a nasty temper tantrum that ended immediately when she got her way. All told, she seemed like a healthy, well-balanced little girl who loved to laugh and play games. But Jason didn't trust leaving her with anyone other than Doc. He worried incessantly that someone might discover her secret, so he limited her social contact, especially with other children.

Like most fathers, Jason thought his daughter was cute and might become pretty as she grew into adolescence and beyond. She inherited all of Indy's striking Indian features: high cheekbone profile, dark hazel-green oval eyes, raven-black hair, a complexion considered darker for Caucasian and lighter for Asian.

But just beneath the surface everything was different. According to brain scans run periodically, Electra's neural and genetic patterns were becoming more and more extraordinary. Jason obsessed that if Healthguard ever finds out she's a genetic freak immune to the T-Plague, it would experiment with her in ways that made him cringe. *Secrecy is paramount so her cover isn't blown. First grade's about to begin and adjustments must be made to keep her secret. I need to talk with Doc.* Jason hustled to the kitchen where his father was setting the breakfast table. He explained the predicament, after which the two went to the living room so Electra couldn't eavesdrop. The tone of Jason's voice matched his concern.

"So, what do you think we can do?"

"I can fudge the medical records you'll bring so Kit looks normal, and if we get her in the home-school track, we're home free because I'll be responsible for periodic medical testing. But she has to score either real low or real high on all the exams. Otherwise, they'll put her on a track we don't control, and that means Healthguard will handle medical testing. If she doesn't qualify for the home-school track, we'll have to file an exemption that'll be handled by a Healthguard inspector.

They could get suspicious and do their own brain scan, and then we're in big trouble." Jason became increasingly agitated.

"Damn the T-Plague! And damn that upstart Guardian Party for their damn fear-mongering. They're to blame for creating Healthguard and Security guard agencies. Mo's network warned us that the political situation could get bad because people are getting too dumb or scared to take care of themselves, and he thinks the government will get even more intrusive. You remember Mo, don't you?"

"Jeezus Jason, calm down. We can work this out. Sure, I remember Mo. He's your bus-admin leader, and he's plugged in politically. He says the Administration is scared that T-Plague outbreaks will grow, and if that happens everyone better watch out for Healthguard and Securityguard poking into private lives."

"You got it right. What do you think we should do?"

"I figure it like this. We'll tell Kit enough so we can make a game of getting really high-or-low test scores. If she gets on the home track we're safe. If she doesn't, we'll ask for an exemption. We can tell the Healthguard administrator about her bad accident at birth, Indy's death, anything to get sympathy. Maybe he'll feel sorry and use my scan data. If not, we'll protest further. We're running out of time, and I think this is our best shot." Jason thought for a minute, his look of concern changing to resolution.

"Thanks for being such a brick. I couldn't handle the situation without you. Let's go with your plan. We might as well tell her now." Off they went to find Electra.

Doc always had Electra by his side when watching or reading local news, so she knew school would be starting soon, and she had another reason for wanting home schooling. It would give her more freedom to study whatever she wanted. But no matter the track, she would have more opportunities to play a new game only she knows about.

Electra had invented game-inside-a-game to shield her father and grandfather from the whole truth. Her thinking skills already exceeded those of mere mortals, but it was risky for her to show others how smart she is. She knew her father worried excessively that outsiders—especially Healthguard administrators—would wonder why, possibly putting her through tests that might reveal her secret, so she decided to dummy down by acting her chronological age.

Electra knew much about people's behavior from watching TV or surfing the Internet. The more sensory input she gets, the more neural circuits the lightning brain creates, becoming a virtuous cycle further increasing lightning brain capabilities. Electra is indeed human but had been jolted at birth to a distant branch of the family tree. She didn't know where, but did know this: she was much, much different, perhaps better in some ways or worse in others. Only time would reveal.

Game-inside-a-game started when the three of them decided to play a game containing only two rules. Rule number one: whatever any of them said or did, they could never reveal that Electra is a genetic freak. Rule number two: no one else could play the game. It's a dangerous game because one false move might be lethal, so that's why the new game was created. She would pretend, even to father and grandfather, that her capabilities were only a little above average. Only she would ever know about game-inside-a-game. Besides, she already knew that even well-intentioned parents meddle too much. The players were approaching. Electra knew what they were up to and what moves to make, so she yelled silently, *Let the games begin.*

"Hello, Electra. Would you like to hear the good news Grampa and I have for you?" Electra clicked off the computer before talking back. "Hi Daddy. Hi Grampa. Will it let us play a game?" Doc jumped right in.

"Yes, it will and it's a brand new one. You'll like it a lot." She sat quietly, listening attentively, and when the menfolk were finished, she compared what they had said to what she thought. The match was spot-on. She needed to get on the home-schooling track so her grandfather could submit bogus brain scans and supporting medical tests.The home-schooling track was good because her "Schooling Team"—father, grandfather and a school district counselor—would control a customized program. The only drawback would be less social contact with classmates, but home-schooled children attend bi-weekly play sessions for more interaction with other children, and besides, parents often preferred less social contact to lower the risk of contracting the T-plague.

To qualify, she needed exceptionally high or low scores on a complete battery of tests. Because she was well adjusted socially, Doc figured on high scores for those parts of the exam, so they told her to think real hard on psycho-social adjustment questions and pick the right answer. They also told her to pick the wrong answer "just for fun" on most of the intelligence test questions. She saw through their deception: she was supposedly not as smart cognitively as socially, so it would be easier for her to find wrong answers on I.Q. tests because not only are they easier spot, but there are more of them. Electra told them she could handle what they wanted. She liked this game.

Jason brought Electra to the testing center the following Thursday. Two hundred children in groups of fifty took a battery of four tests, two for cognitive and two for psycho-social traits, each lasting twenty minutes. Parents waited in the lobby adjacent to the testing rooms, and because Jason knew several of them, he chatted to get the scoop on parental concerns. All worried about T-Plague because a serious case would devastate academic performance, effectively shutting the door to college or professional careers. Parents were first in line for monthly smart pill allocations which they force-fed their children, even though everyone knew these pills were at best marginally effective. Most parents didn't worry about track assignment because there were enough college or vocational training slots available for every child able to complete primary and secondary education, as long as their cumulative twelve-year performance met minimum standards. Not so for Jason. Only home-schooling gave Doc the cover to submit fake medical tests. Jason's calm expression covered his agitated state where he worried enough for both father and daughter.

Jason and Electra met briefly with a Healthguard counselor afterward to schedule a debriefing session for discussing performance and track placement, as well as for answering any additional questions. Online testing allowed for rapid scoring and evaluation, reducing Jason's worry-about-results limbo. Electra's session would be held Friday afternoon.

Jason asked on the drive home if today had been fun.

"It was fun playing our game while taking all the tests. I bet I did just like you and Grampa said."

"I'm sure you did." He didn't want his concern to show further so he stopped talking and turned on the radio, but his stomach churned on. Jason wouldn't stop worrying until the results came in.

He took Electra to the lab on Friday so they could go directly to the testing center after work, leaving early in case traffic was heavier than usual. An assigned counselor called Electra's name at the scheduled time, ushering them into her office.

"Hello Mr. Kittner, and hello Electra. My name is Stenice Maze. Thank you for being so punctual. My job is to provide you with test results, track assignment and first day instructions. This will take about twenty minutes. We'll retrieve this information online as soon as I logon with Electra's Healthguard I.D. May I please see her card."

Jason smiled, saying nothing when handing her the card, but complaining to himself how intrusive the Healthguard Agency had become. *Kids with Healthguard cards and I.D.'s my ass! They damn well better not be in charge of my daughter's medical testing.*

"Let's take a look at her account. I see that the medical test data you gave us yesterday has been stored. According to Healthguard analytic software, your daughter's medical history is complete and indicates no abnormalities. We won't need additional medical tests until next January. Healthguard will do periodic testing at school unless Electra is placed on the home-schooling track, for which her pediatrician submits test results. Were you aware of that?" Jason nodded yes and yelled silently *Let's get on with it!*

"Let's look at scores and track assignment…"

Electra jumped out of the car before Jason toggled off the ignition; she wanted to be the first to tell Grampa. Jason sat in relieved silence for a moment, wondering how could he have been so wrong. According to Mrs. Maze, Electra's intelligence scores placed her in the top percentile; her psycho-social scores placed her in the bottom five percentile. A most unusual combination, which meant home-tracking would work best. Jason was finally able to put worry away for the day. *It doesn't matter what scores she got as long as she got into the hometrack program. I guess it's hard for any parent ever to know what's going on inside their kid's brain. And now I know how and why parents agonize during the wait for results even more than kids. I wonder if it'll be the same if Electra plays sports. At least in sports, we get instant feedback. But she could get injured. Come on, stop worrying. It's silly to look too far ahead. I have to ease up and be a patient dad. I have a lot to learn, and I learned a lot today. And we got what we needed, so today's a victory.* Jason's sunnier outlook reappeared as he hurried in to join the celebration.

Electra played on the computer after dinner while her menfolk considered the day's excitement.

"We lucked out. Kit's on the Home Track, and I can fake the medical tests, so our secret is safe. And don't be concerned about the psycho-social test scores. She's got no adjustment problems. Those scores are flukes."

"You're right. I'll stop worrying so much." Doc nodded but said nothing, for he knew his son would worry until gravity stops working. But for Electra's grade school years, Jason could worry less. All medical testing would be in safe hands.

CHAPTER 8
October 2102

"Bonds of Friendship"
Thread 2 Chapter 5

THE KITTNER HOUSEHOLD BUSTLED the next month adjusting to school. Jason installed a better computer for Electra to use whenever she came to the lab, and Doc reduced his clinic hours even further. He took Electra shopping for school clothes she would wear to the lab or playmate sessions, and she surprised him by knowing the latest grade school clothing fads. *She must have inherited an eye for fashion from her mother. Jason's socks don't always match. I'm glad she knows about kid's clothes because I can let her pick and choose. I'm sure she'll pick nice playmates too.* So far so good, or so he thought.

Home-schooling fit Electra to a T. She reveled in her expanding world, modifying a line from Star Trek—her favorite retro sci-fi series—to describe her newfound freedom: she boldly goes to Websites where no kids her age had gone before. Electra did even more online whenever at Jason's lab because she could play on a computer that had access to more channels than the one at home. The lab also put her in contact with scientists; several even told stories about Indira. Electra's spongy brain absorbed everything she heard or viewed, including NIH seminars and certification courses. Though she didn't understand the details, she picked up terms and basic concepts, building foundation knowledge. Everyone thought

—

66

she was just playing, so now she had additional game-inside-a-game players.

Play sessions at her assigned school furnished a new crop of playmates who gave her up close and in person opportunities to develop social skills and form relationships with children her own age. Electra's cohort would be granted cellphone privileges in a couple of years, but until then she needed in-person contact that helped her social intelligence grow like Jack's beanstalk. Though her brain was already beyond the age of fairy tales, Electra played along with her new friends just for fun.

She liked all the kids, but hadn't found a best friend yet. Perhaps her menfolk could help; she was ready to play a new game just as soon as an opportunity presented itself: Pin the Matchmaker label on the Father.

Jason provided the perfect segue during dinner a week before Halloween when he asked Electra a timeless conversation starter.

"So, how was your day?"

"It was lots of fun. I always like playing at school. And today, Miss Bahnta let me pick the story she read to us. I picked Cinderella." Jason's follow-up questions followed Electra's script perfectly. When he asked, "Why did you choose that one?" Electra made her move. Her smile faded when she answered in a quavering voice.

"Sometimes I'm sad having no friends to play with when I'm home. When Miss Bahnta asks us to tell about our home friends, I have to make them up. And I like to play Cinderella with one of my make-believe playmates." That brought Doc into the game.

"Why didn't you tell us before? If we'd known, we could have started looking for some that live close by."

"Because I have you and Daddy. But I'd like to have kid-size playmates too." That was a conversation stopper, the pause allowing Electra to finish another dessert cookie.

"I have an idea for getting some. Your daddy and I will talk first, and then we'll surprise you. Will you like that?" Electra's smile reappeared. She said yes, then skipped off to watch a retro-flick. The men cleared the table, then discussed the situation further.

"You and Indy had a nice circle of friends. Why don't you call some of them to find out if they have any playmate-age kids?"

"I don't know. That was so long ago. I doubt they'll remember her." Doc could see that Jason might need a suggestion or two.

"A lot of Indy's friends reached out to you after the fire, and you said you'd get back to them. Why don't you try reconnecting? Everyone likes to talk about kids."

"I don't even remember their names. How do I start?"

"Didn't Indira have a home-birth class members' list? I thought you told me she joined a support group. You even went to a couple of sessions. Start there." Doc's hints began to take hold.

"You're right. Now I remember. She kept stuff like that in the night stand I put in your bedroom. If I didn't clean out the drawer, it'll be there."

"I hope you didn't, but if you did, we'll think of something else. You could search online for hover-parent groups."

"A what? Never heard of it."

"Don't you read some of the parenting magazines I subscribe to? I read an article that described what young mothers can do to guard against the T-Plague. It said the term originated in the 1960's.I imagine some of the Baby Boomer parents hovered like helicopters over their kids. But today, some parents over-hover and smother instead."

"I get it. If I can't find her address book, I'll search online for parent support groups. I'm gonna look right now. If I find it, I'll start making calls tomorrow evening."

Jason found what he was looking for, so next evening he began calling, starting with check-marked names. He jotted down notes after each chat, and his words came easier by the time he made the fourth call.

"Hello, may I please speak with Jennifer Conklin?" "This is she. May I help you?"

"Good evening, Jennifer. My name is Jason Kittner. Do you remember my significant other, Indira Ramanujan? She met you at the home birth classes."

"Why, yes. I called you when I heard about your tragedy. I imagine your life has been filled with first-child excitement. I know mine is."

"Yes, and that's the reason for my call. My daughter Electra started first grade this year and has playmates at school, but I haven't found any for her she can play with at home. I'm calling Indy's friends, looking for kids she could play with. Do you have any kids close to Electra's age?"

"Why, yes. I gave birth the same week. And I'm hosting a Halloween party next Sunday for a group of friends and their children. Why don't join us?"

"I apologize for my spotty memory. Everything was a blur back then. And I didn't connect the dots between what you said regarding first-child excitement. Indy was teaching me to be more socially aware, but I was a slow student. I'm happy to say that Electra takes after her mother, not me."

"Don't be so hard on yourself. Raising a daughter by yourself is daunting. I'm fortunate to have my husband Russell, who enjoys sharing the responsibility."

"I'm fortunate too. My father, Justin Kittner, lives with us and is Electra's omni-parent. He's a doctor, but he cut back his practice to be with Electra. He's great with kids, and I think she likes him better than me."

"Please invite him. And tell him adults don't need to wear costumes. But if they did, he could come as is. Doctors' costumes are always fitting."

"Everyone calls him Doc, and the name fits his personality. Do you still live at the same address? The list I'm calling from has addresses too."

"We haven't moved. The party starts at four. Please join us. I'm sure Electra will find playmates."

Jason gratefully accepted, then hunted for Doc to share the good news.

"Bingo, I connected on the fourth call. And we're going to a kid's Halloween party next Sunday."

"Good for you. I'll take Kit shopping for a costume. Where're we going?"

"To Jennifer Conklin's. I don't remember meeting her, but she and Indy must have hit it off. They had lunch at her place a couple of times. By the way, Jennifer invited you too, but not to worry. Parents can come as they are. Or maybe, you could dress up as a doctor." Doc chuckled before replying.

"It's so good when you lighten up. I wish you'd practice more often." "Indy always said I was her work in progress. I wish she were here to finish the job."

"Why don't you let Adom set you up with a friend of his latest lady friend? He's offered before."

"I'm just not in the mood. I'll wait until Electra's older. Then I can double date with her to keep her boyfriend's hormones under control." Jason's sense of humor made a cameo appearance as he recalled a long-forgotten story.

"Did I ever tell you about my friend Gene Timberlane? He married right after high school and had three daughters. His brother did too, achieving the same results. I guess females were in guys' genes, and Gene and his brother were in the wives' jeans too. Anyway, they decided their daughters could date all they wanted, but only after they turned thirty-five. But don't worry about me. I won't stick around that long."

"Nice pun. Indy's word games stuck with you after all. Did any of her poems do the same?"

"I haven't thought about her poetry in a long time. I'll have to sit with Su sometime so we can write them down. If anyone could remember, she'd be the one. They'd be a nice keepsake for Electra. But let's talk about tomorrow. Do you think you can find a costume?"

"That'll be easy. She can shop online for it, and then we'll pick it up at whichever mall it's at. She likes going to malls, and every time I take her shopping for clothes she knows about the latest kid styles."

"She gets that from her mother, not from me. Indy was a snappy dresser. She always looked good in tight-fitting jeans. I guess a sense of style is in Electra's genes too, along with other surprises."

"I think I'll surprise her while we're out by treating her to lunch at McDonalds. It'll be a reward for being such a good little girl."

"Whatever you do, don't buy her a McDonalds Kids Meal. Remember what happened the time I said, 'Kit, let's get you a Kids Meal.' You don't want a repeat of that performance."

"You're right. Electra can be hard to handle when she's angry. Good thing hardly anything makes her angry. We're fortunate she's what she is."

Jason tried to be nonchalant when Jennifer greeted them, but afterwards joked with Doc that he almost dropped his eyeballs— Jennifer was drop-dead gorgeous, at the top end of modeling agency quality. She introduced her little Chris, who was wearing a prince's costume that complemented Electra's princess attire. One look was all it took for the kids to latch on to one another with an enthusiasm found only in children when suddenly finding something they want to hold. Electra and Chris skipped off to play, and Jennifer introduced her husband, Dr. Russell Conklin, a senior NIH executive, perhaps forty-five and quite distinguished looking.

While ten costumed kids played, twenty adults mingled. The fathers were professionals close to Jason's age except for Russell. Most of the mothers stayed home to manage the household and their children's activities, T-Plague protection being top priority. To help reduce the risk, mothers screened playmates' medical histories and were constantly looking for possible replacements, because no matter how careful parents were, the T-Plague could strike. One couple that lived nearby extended an invitation for Electra's mother to bring her during weekday afternoons. Jason pointed to Doc, who was busy chatting with the children clustered around Electra, explaining that he was Electra's omni-parent who would call next week to arrange for playtime.

When it was time to leave, both Electra and Chris begged to have regular playtime, so the adults said they would look into it. Electra chattered happily on the drive home, explaining why she liked Jennifer's little prince best of all the kids. When she asked for more friends, Jason promised to find some, happy that he and Doc had made Electra's day special.

"I had such a good time. And Chris is so much fun to be with. And she has two names. Christi is her real name, but she likes Chris better because she likes boys better than girls. But she says she likes me best of all. I told her my real name is Electra, but I don't like my nickname Kit because it makes me sound like a silly little girl." Doc patted her head.

"We're pleased you like Chris, and I'm sure we can arrange more playtime for the two of you."

"We like to play the Cinderella game, because when we grow up we'll get married and live happy ever after and play games in bed." Jason wasn't sure where this was leading, but gamely played along.

"In fairy tales you can do that, but not when you and Chris grow up. The real world is different."

"Sure, we can. I see pictures of pretty ladies in bed playing lots of games. But it must be a summertime game because they aren't wearing clothes. And when Chris grows up, she'll be as pretty as her Mommy, and she'll make me call her Mr. Christi or she won't play with me."

Jason decided on the spot that Doc should chat about "the birds and the bees" with the household's leading lady, but then it dawned. *She already knows a whole lot more because of the Internet. Better not make a big deal out of it. She'll learn about boys soon enough.*

After Jennifer called the next evening, Jason hurried to the kitchen, where Doc was measuring out oatmeal for tomorrow's breakfast. "We're in luck. Jennifer says Chris wants to play again with Electra. We picked next Saturday morning. Can you take her? Jennifer will bring her home after dinner."

"Will do. I'll tell her the news right now." Electra insisted she wear her princess costume once again to play Cinderella.

Jennifer brought Christi on the return trip because Electra wanted to show her Internet surfing skills. She was an expert navigator, and when the adults heard giggles coming from the bedroom, Jason didn't explain his ulterior motive for looking in on girls.

"Let me make sure Electra has the computer working properly." He hustled away, leaving Doc to carry on.

"It was nice of you to invite us to your Halloween party. I enjoyed chatting with Russell. Please tell me more about your family."

"I met Russell while working as a convention hostess. He offered to help me continue working towards nursing certification while I was still working at the talent agency, and nature took its course after that."

"Sounds like you have the perfect family. And thanks for being so nice to Electra. I know Indy would be so happy."

"Indy and I would have become close friends, so having our children play together is only natural."

"I've been a family practitioner for fifty years, and I know how selective NIH is. Russell must have an outstanding background."

"Russell has medical and hospital administration degrees from prestige schools. I liked him right away for his professional bearing and the way he looked out for my best interests. He's very social-minded, and NIH likes his medical and administrative expertise." Jason heard NIH mentioned as he reentered the room.

"Did I mention that I work at an NIH lab? I'm on the tech side and try to avoid all the political intrigue, but my project's business leader tells us how demanding the political situation is. Russell must be under a lot of pressure."

"Come on, Jason. It's the weekend. Leave the shop talk until Monday. Why don't you two chit-chat about family affairs while I get us something to drink?"

"Thanks, Dad. Sorry to be so boring. I sure hope Electra inherits Indy's social skills instead of mine."

"Indy told me about you during home-birthing classes. One thing she shared was your healthy appetite. I imagine taking care of Electra and working at the lab burn up a lot of calories because you're thinner than I expected. I'll check with Russell, but I'm sure he would be happy if we invite your family for Thanksgiving. The kids can play and the adults can talk."

"On behalf of the Kittners, I gratefully accept your invitation. I'll bring wine, and please let me know what else you'd like." When Doc returned with the drinks, Jennifer proposed a toast.

"To our little princesses, who will all too soon become queens. Let's make sure they play together often. I think they're destined to be best friends forever."

CHAPTER 9
March 2093

"The Prize"
(Thread 3 Chapter 2)

THE MODERATOR'S CONCLUDING REMARKS stirred the audience, for seldom did junior researchers get an opportunity to advance so quickly; seldom did a disease of possibly epic proportions emerge so mysteriously. Only one team would triumph, so the competition would be keen.

"Listen up, young turks and tigresses. CDC has upgraded to Code Red one of the Code X events they've been monitoring, and that means we're initiating an official project. Code name is Cognicom. As you can guess, it's for the mysterious, rapidly spreading Chinese outbreak, for which we have more information. It appears to be caused by a virus of unknown origin, perhaps naturally-occurring but more likely synthetic. Rumors attribute the outbreak to a mutant strain that leaked into the environment from an Alzheimer's-focused research lab. The media has named it the Techno-Plague, or T-Plague. We have named our project Cognicom, standing for cognition compromise. The project is comprised of three separate projects. Senior researchers must develop proposals for two of them, one for the immunization vaccine and another for reversal. We're starting a contest, open to NIH junior researchers nationwide, for a third proposal. It will develop a vaccine to suspend the illness and provide symptomatic relief. All members of the winning team will be promoted two levels in job classification and pay grade. Quite a prize, wouldn't you agree?" The moderator continued after the buzz died down.

"But there's a catch to winning the prize. A majority on the Senior Researchers Committee must vote in favor of using the winning proposal. We know you juniors are bright and understand cutting-edge technology, but we need results ASAP, not in ten years. The T-Plague could become a serious threat worldwide, so we need to stop it as quickly as possible. If the winning proposal's solution is considered unattainable within a suitable time frame, it will not be green-lighted and a senior researchers' team will prepare a more realistic proposal." The audience buzz picked up again; the moderator paused briefly, then concluded the session.

"If you wish to enter the contest, form a team of four and submit online your proposal by the end of April. You can login using your normal security code. Then fill out the RFP, which by now you should know stands for Request for Proposal, and download the background information packet. The winning team will be announced at our June session. Before we head to the cafeteria, I'll try to answer your questions…"

Jason hustled to the cafeteria, confident the Worldstars could win if their proposal game paid off. He was first to the table, gulping down lunch before the others arrived. Minutes later his enthusiasm bubbled out once his teammates were seated.

"We are kissed by the Sun. We've already come up with a half-dozen proposals, so all we need is to pick the best one and away we go. When can we do that?" Even normally reserved Su shared his enthusiasm, but toned down his certainty.

"We've made a good start, but we have to develop more details before we can narrow the choices, and then we'll have to scope out solution paths for each before picking the one for our proposal. And we need a timeline the seniors will buy. Indy, what do you think?"

"You're right. Why don't we do this? You and Adom come over next Sunday so all of us can work through what to do."

"Jason, you can be leader, Su and Indy can be the brains, and I'll be the support guy to keep everyone loose. I'll start by loosening up

Jason so he doesn't get wound too tight. Just like in grad school, I'll keep him from being too much of a grind." Even Jason had to grin before replying.

"We'll have even more fun than we did back then. You know, the further from grad school I get, the more I dislike that time in my life. If it weren't for the three of you, I probably would have ground out my thesis while living in my advisor's lab. I promise to avoid making that mistake."

Adom crowed, "And I'll do my best to keep you from making new ones." Indy caught Su's eye, which reflected a shared optimism. The Worldstars were on their way.

Indy cleared the great room table for a place the team could work while watching on the wall monitor the Co-NFL championship game. The Co-NFL, a football league comprised of elite male and female athletes, had become a fan favorite of both sexes. A joint offshoot of the National Football League and the Cross-Fit Training Association, the Co-NFL started ten years ago patterned after football, rules adjusted to accommodate male and female differences, which meant height and weight limits for the males. Its loyal fanbase grew every year because this league's well-matched team competition offered the most exciting blend of sports and entertainment.

During the last fifty years, athletic excellence in many areas of fitness approached parity between males and females, making Co-NFL games lightning fast and competitive. Many of the athletes could have been models or in movies, so it was no surprise that the sport earned top media ratings, paving the way for the Co-NBA, a similar basketball league formed five years later.

Indy adjusted the volume to a low background level. *Jason and Adom like the sight of the females more than the sound of the males. I'll make sure they sit facing the screen so they have something to watch while Su and I do the thinking. I hope she gets here before they bring back the carry outs. We can talk about Vow-Cer issues while setting the table.* Indy wanted private time for just the two of them to discuss Jason's marriage contract. If she approves it, she and Jason can begin planning their Contract Vow Ceremony—a modern version of a wedding ceremony. But first, Jason had some growing to do.

Jason contained all the S-words Indy wanted, such as serious, smart, and sensible, and at least one that she wanted him to remove from all capitals: SEX. She could read him like a children's book, for she was smarter intellectually, emotionally, and socially. She was a better athlete too, but whenever Jason noticed her physical gifts, he automatically re-focused whatever he was thinking about to bedroom activities. Few could match her combined talents. Su was in the neighborhood for some, but Jason and Adom floundered in the ladies' collective wake, so it took continual coaching from Indy and Su to keep the fellows within hailing distance.

The Indy-Jason pairing puzzled everyone, but no one said a word about her choice. Yes, Jason was smart and would do well in his career, but ladies labeled him anything but sexy, unless it meant a stocky, average looking guy with an engineer's personality. He could be insensitive, blunt, and occasionally abrasive. When asked about Jason's personality, Indy would reply with a smile that Jason's best traits take time to appreciate. She would use a true story dramatized in a retro-flick for an analogy: a famous rivalry between two world champion F1 racecar drivers. One of them fit the glamorous image: sexy beyond handsome, charismatic personality, affable, lived each day as if it were his last. He was a media favorite and a darling of the beautiful people. The other was just the opposite: ordinary looking (nicknamed "the Rat" because of his overbite profile), blunt-talking, socially inept, annoying personality, lived a dull lifestyle when not behind the wheel. Yet his marriage to a talented, wealthy, and beautiful woman was a lasting success because she found in him everything she wanted.

Indy had a few minor flaws, and like everyone, tried not to advertise them. She was a genuinely nice person because she was comfortable with herself, never drawing comparisons with others. Too many people with looks and talent have oversized egos that trip them up. Not so with Indy; she made a game poking fun at herself whenever appropriate.

She also made a game of tweaking Jason's tail whenever it needed adjusting. Sitting across from her, he'd blabber about whatever theory he thought was his own, like the time he explained how love works. Then she would re-cross her legs. Game, set, match over. Someday, when his hormone levels subside, Jason would get to know the true Indy better, minor flaws and all. Until then, she would let nature run its course.

A tap at the front door announced Su's arrival. Indy and Su were yin and yang that might have blossomed into even more had not the Jason-Adom tandem crossed their path. Su was surprised that Indy had chosen Jason instead of Adom (or more importantly, herself), but she concealed her disappointment behind an oriental veil of impenetrable reserve. Indy believed Su was genuinely happy for her co-friendship with Jason. He was too insensitive to detect Su's feelings, and Adom was too wrapped up in his social life to notice. Indy's hug matched what Su refused to show.

"How are you? And what desserts have you cooked up for our teammates?"

"My usual assortment of brownies and cheesecake cups for the guys, and for us, some fruit tarts from a new recipe." Indy was about to mention that she wanted to talk about marriage contract revisions when the fellows charged in, Adom leading the way.

"Hello, ladies. Game on yet?"

Su replied, "Which game do you mean? The Co-NFL or the Pro-Po-Sal?"

Adom countered, "Su-shi the Quiet, you are a riot."

"I have qui-et many skills, but I prefer not to reveal them too often. I prefer keeping you off balance." Jason poked Su and then said,

"Touche, or should I say touch-e?" Indy pointed at the wall monitor.

"Why don't you fellows watch the game. Su and I will put stuff on the table." Soon they were watching the game while snacking and chatting. Adom said that Indy could be a player if she did enough weight training and conditioning.

"I'd rather be a player on the Worldstars Team. After all, our proposal's going to win." After helping Indy clear the table, Jason redirected the conversation.

"OK team, let's continue playing our proposal game. Indy, why don't you kick things off?"

"Let the games begin. I'll review our starting point, and then Jason will lead us from there."

For the next two hours, the debate raged regarding which proposal had the best odds for winning. Su cautioned about too much creativity because senior researchers would be skeptical, while Indy warned against being too ordinary. Jason facilitated, hammering out a proposal draft containing the right mix of cutting-edge bioscience and achievable short-term goals, and Su predicted it would have the best chance of winning, even though a riskier choice would have been more exciting. Jason summarized next steps.

"We're good to go with what we've got. Let's assign to-dos for the coming week. Adom and I will rewrite the proposal according to RFP specifications, then Indy and Su will make any final corrections. And then the real fun begins when we win. We'll put in the nitty gritty hard work to make a killer vaccine." Adom added a finishing touch.

"Of course, it's a T-Plague killer and a patient lifesaver. And fame and fortune for us."

Indy said, "We're all tired from the work we've done, but we should be happy because we know what to do to make a winning proposal. Why don't you fellows collect all the notes while Su and I take care of the leftovers?"

As Jason walked Adom to the van, Electra cornered Su. "We need to talk about my Vow-Cer plans. I've tentatively agreed to Jason's marriage contract, but I need a second opinion. Why don't we go shopping next weekend and discuss it over lunch? I'll send you a copy tomorrow. And please, be brutally honest. I want your frank opinion on the modifications I'm proposing."

"Now you're talking sense. Would you pick me up next Saturday at nine?"

"Will do. And please don't say anything to Adom. He and Jason like to blab."

Su was her typically quiet self on the drive home, so Adom broke the silence.

"You and Indy are a two-headed genius for biotech drugs. I can't imagine another proposal beating ours. Just like I can't imagine how Jason's marriage contract could be beat. But he told me Indy's gonna revise it. What do you know about that?"

"Nothing. Indy hasn't shared it with me. But you should remind Jason how particular she can be."

"You're right. I should talk with him so he knows to expect some changes. Well, here we are. I'll walk you to the door."

The team stuck to its plan as the week sailed by. Not even Su could recommend improvements to the RFP, so Jason submitted it on Friday. As he pushed the enter button, he paused for an instant to salute his team's superior brainpower that had just built an unbeatable proposal, then returned to his research bench. Jason was too pragmatic for sentimental daydreams; he'd let Indy handle that.

Su mused how much she enjoyed being with Indy. Grad school days had revealed how compatible they were, for no matter how mundane the day or trivial the task, just being together gave pleasure. Today would be even more-so because a shopping-lunching combination always satisfies. It's a social activity designed for people, even for people as controlled and reserved as Su. *We're all social animals, enjoying in-person contact, especially with friends. That's something online social networking can't do yet.*

Su had come up with several marriage contract recommendations Indy might like. When they were roommates, they had often talked late into the night about male-female relationships, and each took a different approach. Unlike Su, who would consider only males that took her breath away, Indy took a wider view, and had even written a poem that addressed both sides. Su remembered the verse that spoke to her:

"Oh, for godlike creations that take my breath away,
And leave me suspended in the timeless presence of their being!
Search wherever, find them if I can,
And I'll feel forever magic, turning eternity into but a single day."

And the verse for Indy:

"But what about those ordinary people of our days? Don't discard—they're magic too—a slower-acting kind. It likely takes more living for their import to emerge,
For then you'll say quotidian ways have power to amaze."

I know what's right for me. I hope Indy makes the choice that's right for her.
Today's conversation would be enlightening.

Saturday morning mall traffic was lighter than normal, so the ladies cruised through, picking out new slacks appropriate for the lab or for socializing. Indy's body was built to display the best any garment had to offer, for a willowy frame equipped with long, slender arms and legs is a designer's dream. Su's shorter stature required a little more care, but both had an eye for fashion and would look good among any group of well-tailored professional women.

Sipping drinks after lunch, neither was in a hurry to trek for shoes. Indy was usually the lead-off talker, but today Su surprised her. "You and I are, and I hope always will be, best friends. I want you to be happy, so let me give you my recommendations for what to add to your marriage contract. Are you ready?" "I am, and please don't hold back."

"Here's how I view it. The amendments you added tell Jason to move past sex and get to committed love. They also tell him to be less self-centered and to treat you as at least his equal. I would add three more. Stop taking you for granted. Lose the love handles. Be more considerate of other people and points of view."

"Wow, I didn't pick up on being taken for granted, but now it comes to me that he is. He's getting too comfortable living with me. But I've been teasing him about losing weight, and it seems to be working. He's going to the fitness center regularly with me." Indy's voice took on a philosophical tone.

"It's harder than I thought trying to understand what's going on inside Jason's head, or how to deal with his flaws. I better tell him to face the facts. And thanks for pointing out he's taking me for granted. That connects with something he's started doing. He opens my mail. I guess he thinks all the mail that comes is for him. I'm going to call him out on that. So how does this sound? I'll add your three points and the one about opening my mail, and I'll push back the VowCer date. That should put him on notice, but not shove him out the door. And I'll see if he comes around."

"That should work, especially when you're pushing back the date. Make sure Jason's the right work in progress." The conversation paused briefly while Indy finished her drink, allowing Su to glean a thought about her best friend's talents.

"I like how you can write poetry to capture the essence of whatever strikes your fancy. I compare poetry to the elegance of mathematical proofs. They, like your poetry, cut right to the heart of the matter."

Indy replied, "I like to write poetry because it lets the reader expand the message into what works for them. For example, when you told me what you needed from a committed relationship, I used a verse describing romance as taking your breath away."

"Do you have a poem for how to deal with long-term relationships or commitment? Those are things Adom needs to work on."

"Yes. I named it 'The Memory Garden.' Its message is pretty simple; don't overanalyze relationships. Simply act on your feelings."

"Please recite it. I'll summarize the message for Adom.

"It's too bad the guys don't have your ear for poetry, or music for that matter. Anyway, here's the poem:

"Tomorrow's memories are made today,
It's good you are too close to see.
Just go about your merry way,
They are a future mystery.

No crystal ball for where things lead,
What fruit your current efforts bring.
Just tend the present plant the seed,
For the flower to bloom and blossoms take wing.

Tomorrow's harvest depends on you,
Its bounty and whether short or long.
So remember today in the things you do,
Blow a kiss to the future then keep moving on."

"How do you remember all these poems?"

"The same way you remember all the notes you play on the piano. Why don't we change the subject? I'm tired of talking about Jason or Adom. Tell me about your volunteer work."

"I just found another organization. I'm assisting the Middle East Refugee Assistance Program. Volunteering adds another dimension to my life by putting me in social settings and giving me an interlude from my passion, which is biotech research, and complementing my avocation, which is piano. I'm happy with the overall mix, and I don't need to settle for a mediocre male. I'm better without, because I won't be taken for granted or have to put up with a disappointing sex partner. If Jason doesn't make the cut, make sure you have a contingency plan."

"I have something even better than that. I have you as my best friend forever, and it fits us to a T. I've sat long enough. Let's look for your running shoes." And off they trotted.

Indy was sitting on a fitness store bench when she felt a tap on her shoulder. When she turned around, she recognized Monica, one of the junior researchers.

"Indy! I thought it was you. How's shopping? Can I join you for a minute?" Indy flashed her always engaging smile.

"Monica, hi. Please sit next to me. Su's somewhere testing running shoes." Monica sat down, then replied in a half-joking manner.

"I don't want Su getting any faster. Her mind's too quick right now. How's your team doing on the contest proposal? Just between you and me, my team's struggling. We haven't put a proposal together before, and although it's good practice, ours isn't very good."

"We submitted ours last Friday. It's the best we could come up, and we didn't think more time would help, so we'll just have to see. If it would help, Su and I would be happy to talk with you about yours."

"It sure would. I tried reaching out to some people I thought were friends, but they're unwilling to provide suggestions. I didn't realize how competitive junior researchers are. No matter who wins, there'll be hard feelings due to egos. And I'm sure some of the seniors will be skeptical if they're unfamiliar with the winning proposal's concepts. Many of the seniors are pretty smug."

"Some of them are, but some of them are pretty talented too. I try to be diplomatic whenever talking with them. Why don't you pick a time for the three of us to meet?" Monica did, then commented further.

"No wonder the juniors think you and Su are AOK."

"Thanks for the compliment, and just between you and me, what do they say about Adom and Jason? Be honest. You won't hurt their feelings because I won't tell." Monica answered in a more confidential tone.

"In general, Adom is well liked, and why not? He's friendly, clever, and good looking. But Jason, he has a knack for turning people off. I'm sure you know his better qualities, but sometimes the juniors can't find them. Is it true you're planning a Vow-Cer with him?" Indy smiled and gave a well-practiced reply.

"Jason's best traits take time to appreciate…"

Junior researchers' excitement built as the June briefing session drew near. Numerous rumors had spread concerning the committee's scoring, including proposals are unrealistic, the winner wouldn't be greenlighted, proposals are unimaginative, and committee chairperson is prejudiced against the younger generation. Neither

Indy nor Su paid attention, but the guys agonized over what might be, unable to sleep the night before, unable to understand how Indy and Su could be so calm. Jason heard Indy's point—don't worry about what's outside your control—but couldn't wrap his head around it.

Finally, announcement day arrived, bringing with it the Regional Director of NIH labs, who would provide welcoming remarks.

"Good morning, everyone. We're going to begin by announcing the contest's winning team. In my day, everyone would have to wait until the very end of the session to know the results, but we're kinder and gentler now than way back then.

"Let me provide some details. Twenty proposals made it into the semi-final round. Of course, they weren't all equal, but every one of them demonstrated competence and creativity. The committee picked the best three for final evaluation, and we'll post them along with scores on our Interlab Website. The committee chose one that was good enough to greenlight, so it's now part of the overall Cognicom Project. And the winner is the Worldstars team."

Scattered applause, plus disappointed groans, arose from the audience, none of which stopped a wave of euphoria from washing over Jason and his teammates. The Regional Director called Jason to the stage, handing him a commemorative plaque, then announced that the winning team would have lunch with the Director of Human Resources, who would brief the team further. The moderator asked Jason what he thought about that, and Jason surprised the audience with an amiable quip that his team is starving for more information, so lunch couldn't come soon enough.

Lunch was served in a small but elegant dining room used only for special events like the one today, and the Regional Director's remarks matched the occasion.

"All of you are to be congratulated for your winning proposal. Our seniors committee is demanding, and several members thought your approach might be too ambitious to achieve results in the target timeframe. But enough of them thought your approach has merit, so they greenlighted your proposal. Three senior researchers will meet with you once a month to review progress, but after reviewing your H.R. files, I think you have the technical skills to deal with them. But you must also hone your business, project management, and negotiations skills. I'm going to have our H.R. Manager give you all the details on what to expect."

The Human Resources manager was none other than Dominic Herrera, the erstwhile Worldstars recruiter who had recently been promoted to coordinate campus recruiting and junior researchers' career development. He was as pleased as the Worldstars.

"Your new job levels and pay grades show the importance of what you'll be doing, and I know you've got what it takes to deliver. After all, I recruited you, I have utmost confidence you will be successful. Let me first describe Cognicom Project structure. It is divided into three separate projects.

Cognicom-R/Z for the reversal vaccine. R for reversal; working in Zeta Lab

Cognicom-I/Z   for   the   immunization vaccine.I for immunization; also in Zeta Lab

Cognicom-S/Z for the suppression vaccine. This is yours. S for suppression; Zeta Lab."

Dominic paused to let what he said sink in, then continued. "Next week, each of you will wrap up your current assignment,

and the following week you'll coordinate setting up your new lab. Have any of you ever been to the Zeta Lab?" All shook their heads no.

"It's our newest facility, and it's where many top priority projects are assigned. It's about five miles west of where we are now, so your commute should be fine. Who is your Tech-Development Leader? Let me guess, it's Jason." Jason smiled and nodded.

"Good. In addition to Indy, Su, and Adom, we're assigning two lab techs and a data collection clerk. We're also assigning a business administration leader, who will be liaison between the lab and NIH headquarters. Jason, you and the bus-admin person are co-managers, but you should defer to him on business and political issues that are bound to come up. You must have a lot of questions so please ask away."

Indy had already been coaching Jason's people skills, so he knew what to say. "We are honored that our proposal was selected, and we'll do a great job for you. We've heard that T-Plague projects might become politically sensitive. Can you fill us in here?" Indy noticed Dom's slight twitch.

"Of course. We don't know how far or fast the disease might spread, but we need to be prepared for all eventualities. Think back to the Polio or AIDS or Ebola or Zika epidemics of long ago. People had good reason to be afraid, but back then our political climate was more settled than today's. Now we have rogue nations and upstart political parties fostering fear and uncertainty. We don't want all this to stampede the public's T-Plague fright into a panic that might cause political unrest. It's a long way from happening, but we need to be proactive. Your bus-admin leader will be your interface between the lab and the usual government channels. He'll insulate you from any political blowback. We want the four of you to think only about developing the S-vaccine." Jason nodded in agreement and was ready with another question.

"Could you give us some insights into what the seniors think about Cognicom? And what's their opinion of us?"

"Excellent questions. They think R-Vac will be the toughest to crack, followed by I-Vac,and then S-Vac. That's why you have S-Vac, but I'm sure you realize it will be challenging too. Regarding their opinion of the Worldstars, they acknowledge all of you are bright, but you'll need to show them you can get results. They think Indy could be a great team leader, know Su is brainy, and like the way Adom gets along. Jason, you have excellent project management skills, but you'll need to improve your people and diplomacy skills. Don't be insulted if I ask you to get pointers from your bus-admin leader and also take a couple of our online leadership or high-performance team-building courses. It'll help you now and as you move up." Nothing could possibly bother Jason at this moment.

"You are correct, sir. I'll pay attention to constructive criticism. And how about if my team members ask some questions? Indy, why don't you start?"

Indy was proud how Jason was handling himself and pleased with Dom's overall assessment. Yes, Jason's my work in progress, and NIH recognizes his potential. Let's showcase Adom next.

"Adom, we know you've got keen insight, so why don't you go next."
"Thanks, Indy. Dom, I'm concerned about the junior researchers. Do you think they might be resentful? I sure don't want hard feelings."

"Adom, you're one of the nicest guys I've recruited. But in technical careers at NIH, talent matters most. It's better that they respect your ability rather than like you personally. Some might be glad you won even if they didn't, but others might be glad if you fail. I'll leave it at that." Dom knew how quiet Su could be, so he drew her out.

"Su, you are always so quiet, yet always thinking. Do you have any questions for me?"

"Yes, I do. I am concerned about the senior researchers. What are their expectations for us, and how much support should we expect?"
"The senior researchers are even more competitive than the juniors, so don't expect them to give you suggestions. Be alert. They might try picking holes in your approach, but don't let that bother you. They're skeptical because they don't know you very well, but I know you'll show them what you can accomplish."

Adom and Su's concerns were pretty much what Indy thought they would be, and Dom's answers were to her liking, so now it was Indy's turn to talk.

"It's just like Jason said. We're honored to be the winners and will do our best. I think we've asked enough questions for today, and it's time for the four of us to move ahead. We need to map out our plan for the next two weeks. Jason, why don't you take it from here?"

While Jason talked, Dom listened to his own thoughts. *What an exceptional blend of technical and social skills Indy has. Why not appoint her tech leader? But no, she must have other plans. She clearly wants Jason to take charge, and she'll put everything in motion so he succeeds. Good for Jason, good for Cognicom S-Vac, and good for NIH. It's time to adjourn.*

"Why don't you take the rest of the day off. Then get ready for Monday when you'll meet your bus-admin leader. I think you'll be impressed with Moses Solstein. With Mo and Jason leading, S-Vac is primed for success."

Later that night, Indy gave Jason her takeaway from this extraordinary day. "I think your favorite saying is correct: we are kissed by the sun. Can you believe it? All of us on the same high priority project at the same location. You and I can drive together. Adom and Su can too, if they want to." Jason was still aglow from the day's victory.

"Yes, and I'm sure the bus-admin guy will fit in with our style, as will the lab techs and the data clerk. But I do have a concern. Dom talked about defusing political blowback. What do you think he meant? And why do we need a data collection clerk? And what ab–." Indy pressed a finger against Jason's lips so he would stop babbling. "Will you please stop worrying. All things in due time." Then she re-crossed her legs.

"Come sit next to me and tell me what's on your mind." Jason immediately stopped worrying.

CHAPTER 10
May 1093

"Moses and the Promised Land"
(Thread 3 Chapter 3)

MOSES SOLSTEIN ALWAYS FOUND ways to come out on top, always positioning his teams to be winners. He captained a high school baseball team the year it won the city championship. At Harvard, his B-School study groups always cracked the toughest cases. He had been the pilot of a highly decorated Navy helicopter crew, and as a newly appointed Bus-Admin Leader for one of Cognicom's top priority projects, he was confident the winning streak would remain intact. Today Mo would meet the Worldstars.

Mo inherited street smarts and business savvy from his father, a Baltimore merchant serving the Jewish community; from his mother came social skills and a respect for community and country. Looks and personality inspired trust, and he moved with an alert step shared among fighter pilots and quarterbacks. Associates and superiors alike found him friendly and competent. Senior NIH administrators commented that "the Boy Scout" has a great future, and they weren't surprised that, at the age of only thirty-three, he had earned merit badge assignments for his performance, Cognicom considered one of the biggest plums.

Mo reviewed preparations while driving to the Home Base Facility, a fenced one-story complex located in a rural DC setting, unobtrusively but securely guarded. He knew from previous visits conference room locations. He would be in the audience during the kick-off session, after which his work would begin at a team break-out session. Having already skimmed personnel files, he knew the caliber of his people and confirmed it by asking his network about the different personalities. He liked what he had heard, especially comments regarding the one who had it all: Indira Ramanujan. He wondered why she wasn't the team's tech leader but decided she must have good reasons. *I'll bet she wants to promote her designated co-friend. If so, she'll be the power behind Jason's throne. I've got a good reading on my duties and my team. I'm ready to seize the opportunity.*

"Hello Worldstars." My name is Moses Solstein, also known as Mo the gofer, because my job is to go and get whatever we need so we're a big success. I had an opportunity to review backgrounds and your Worldstars nickname says it all. I hope to show that my bus-admin skills complement your biotech smarts. So, please ask any questions about me or Cognicom." Jason spoke for the team.

"Welcome to the Worldstars orbit. We look forward to your administrative and networking savvy. We all have questions, and how about we go around the table, introducing ourselves and asking questions. Indy, would you please start?" Indy liked what intuition told her. Mo comes across like the real deal, prepared and professional. I hope he's competent too.

"I'm certain you and Jason will make an outstanding leader duo. No sense asking too many questions right now, but let me offer one; why the nickname "Techno-Plague" when so little is known about what we're dealing with? It seems so sensational."

"I agree with you, but the media spinners are hyping it. They're saying technology is to blame for bringing this disaster, and we did it to ourselves. Nothing like fear to attract viewers."

Su asked, "What's the current T-Plague status in other countries?" "Tight-lipped China told us an outbreak reoccurred in Shanghai, and Israel notified CDC they have a handful of cases in Tel Aviv. China isn't cooperating, but Israel is working with us. We should get tissue samples and preliminary test results no later than next week. They'll be sent directly to the Zeta Lab, and Jason will sign for our allocation. Once you've looked at them, let me know what additional resources you need." Adom spoke next.

"How much are the teams supposed to share, and why do we have data retrieval clerks?"

"Cognicom has top priority, so we want the teams to cooperate and to share as much data as the tech leaders think necessary. Just be aware that you'll be working with senior researchers who won't consider you their equals. Regarding data retrieval clerks, on dark projects like Cognicom, data is confidential and encrypted. The clerks handle encryption, decryption and document the audit trail. We've gone around the table, so we're back to Jason. Fire away."

"Dom from H.R. talked about political blowback. Could you expand on that?"

"Sure. The world is not as kind and gentle as hoped for. Just look and listen to Isilabad, that rogue Islamic state. And here at home we have the startup Guardian Party making a play for far left and right factions. Some think tanks have developed worst case scenarios containing a worldwide pandemic that destabilizes weaker governments. Sounds like the apocalypse. Is it possible? Sure, but so is all of us being struck by lightning in a snowstorm. It's too soon for alarm. I'll wait until there's a good reason, and you should too. Let me run interference so you can focus on the tech stuff. Jason, since you're the tech lead, can you summarize how our team's going to start?

"Sure, can do. As you said, we'll analyze the samples and data as soon as we get them, then figure out what else we need. We're wrapping up our previous assignments. Our team will hold weekly status meetings every Friday which we'd like you to attend whenever you're available, so we'll set up a workstation in the lab for you. Will that work?"

"Yes, thanks. And I like the division of labor. I handle business and you handle biotech. Well if there are no further questions, I'm off to my boss's weekly staff meeting. I'll be happy to report the Worldstars are up and running Cognicom's S-Vac project. I'll touch bases with you Friday afternoon."

The Worldstars had more to talk about after Mo marched out, so Jason led off.

"He sure talks a good game. I hope he can back it up. What do you think, Indy?"

"I think he's solid. You'll learn a lot about negotiating and diplomacy by watching him in action. And also, how to handle people. Did you notice how he focused on us, not himself? He didn't talk about his accomplishments. Su was going to check him out on social media. What did you find?"

"His resume is impressive. Strong academic and military credentials. Been with NIH for five years and has moved up quickly. Has handled a wide range of assignments, and he's still active in the Air Reserves." As usual, Adom would be the last to offer an opinion.

"I like the guy. Between Jason and Mo, our project team is in good hands. They'll lead us to the promised land. Not the land of milk and honey, but the one that holds golden careers and bucks we take to the bank. I'm ready."

By the end of a hectic transition week, the Worldstars needed a change of pace weekend, so Su suggested they tour the National Gallery of Art, then have a mid-afternoon Sunday lunch at one of her favorite restaurants. Adom chauffeured while everyone chatted on the drive. Even Jason, not known for his fine arts appreciation, found some of the paintings to his liking.

"You ladies are never at a loss for places to go and things to do, and I must say today was better than I expected. Indy knows a lot about literature, so I depend on her for book and poetry tips, and I can count on you for music tips, but how'd you learn so much about art?"

"It's a hobby, and I'm glad you enjoyed my comments. We can do it again sometime. It's better to have several shorter tours than one that's too long. That way, you don't wear out your eyes and legs." Adom's takeaway was about the same as Jason's.

"I never thought much about connections between art, music, and literature until you pointed out how artists create a mood and a setting for whatever they're describing. Isn't that what you do when you play the piano?"

"Yes. Just like what Indy does when she uses words to paint poetic imagery."

"Su's right, but here in the museum we see the great artists. By any standard of comparison, my poems are barely mediocre. But that's OK, because I enjoy writing them." Indy's comment triggered Jason's discouraging observation.

"I feel so one-dimensional compared to the three of you. Look, we're all smart and have great jobs. But Su plays the piano, knows lots about art and does volunteer work. Indy writes poetry and shares lots of activities with a great circle of friends. Adom was a champion runner and is socially engaged. Then there's nerdy me. All I've got going is my career and Indy. And I sometimes wonder what she sees in me."

Indy's empathy stepped right in as she put her arm around him and said, "You have lots going for you. People find them when they get to know you better. I've already teased about all the S-words you've got, but you've got lots more than that. And since you are my work in progress, we'll polish other hidden talents." She let the words sink in and then continued.

"And no matter how good we think we are, only a few of us ever get beyond mediocrity. So, all of us should just be happy with the best we can do." Su nodded in agreement.

"I seem to recall a poem you wrote about this. I'd like to hear it again if you can remember it."

"OK, but don't anyone fall asleep from boredom, especially Adom, because he's driving. There's nothing worse than listening to someone drone on and on when you're not interested. Anyway, since Su asked, here goes. I named it 'Mediocrity's Stepchild,' and I start by making comparisons with numbers, using 1, 2, 3 and so on. Numbers can get big by counting, but they can't go beyond, to infinity, by sticking just to counting. Somewhere in counting, you have to make the leap to infinity if you want to go beyond. So, here's the first verse.

> Numbers always tell the score,
> But they can't reach infinity.
> They can't even get up close,
> By using only 1, 2,3.

"Now I bring myself into the poem. You might think I'm pretty good, but I'm not even close to being in the same league with the great ones. That's the point of the second verse.

> The same applies to you and me,
> Reaching beyond our mundane place.
> I've looked inside for what I need,
> I haven't found a single trace.

"But, suppose I try lots of careers and attempt lots of things. It still won't make me great, because the sum of mediocrity is still mediocrity. Here's the third verse.

> And I have tried a lot of things,
> In each I did not get too far.
> But what if I add up all my scores?
> I'm sorry to say it's barely par.

"But, so what if I'm only mediocre? I won't care or be jealous. Instead, I'm in awe of what the great ones can do.

> Brilliance and genius are rarified gifts,
> Have it and use it and reach for your star.
> And cast your mysterious spell on the world,
> I'm in awe of those gifted wherever they are.

Jason, does this help?"

"Yeah, I get the point, but I need to let it sink in." Adom was pulling into the parking lot, so he added a final comment.

"Diners, we are arriving at our destination restaurant. Please have your appetites ready."

The conversation eventually turned to the upcoming week and who should be doing what. Adom groaned when Jason handed everyone a sheet of paper listing what tasks, including completion dates, were assigned to whom.

"Here's where we start tomorrow. I'll brief our new team members on our SVac project and what their roles are, and then I'll have the new lab techs work with me to sketch the lab's layout and begin arranging equipment. Adom will develop a list of additional items we'll need and get Mo to sign off. As soon as the tissue samples arrive, Adom and I will analyze the virus structure. Indy and Su have the most important task. They'll draft the S-Vac solution path details by extending our proposal. Then they'll explain it to Adom and me so we know what's going on. Won't that be good for starters?" Su wasn't sure.

"I don't think we can hit the solution path completion date. We'll have to see how tough it is to unravel the virus."

"I'll buy that, so we'll keep the timeline flexible. And since this is our kick-off meeting, I'll also buy dinner."

"Will you look at that. Now that my best buddy has expense account privileges he's Mr. Big Bucks. Can I order a dessert to go?" "Only if you let Indy and Su test it." Adom declined the offer so dinner was over and out they went.

Early that evening, Indy could tell from reading Jason's pensive body language that something was amiss, so she led him into living room that was softly aglow from the setting sun and parked him on the sofa before speaking.

"Tomorrow's the start of the next leg up in your career. And everyone always feels overwhelmed on the first day. But you've got what it takes to make our team great, so what's troubling you?"

"I want you to be proud of me. I want to lead a successful team. I want to be a great team leader. And I want to compensate for being so one dimensional. I'm afraid I won't measure up. And it's hard for me to admit all this, even to you." Indy gave him a reassuring hug.

"I'm proud of who you are and the effort you're making. And all of us working together will make our project a big success. And you, the team leader, will earn the lion's share of the credit for making it so."

"You'd make a better tech lead than I be—" Indy put a finger to his lips.

"You deserve to be the leader. You are great at organizing and following up on details. Let me help you when you need it, and let Mo teach you what he can." Indy could feel Jason's tension drain away.

"You are so right, as always." Indy pulled away, then re-crossed her legs, knowing exactly what to say.

"Now, why don't you tell me what's on your mind?"

The first month rolled out according to Jason's plan. The lab techs, under Adom's direction, arranged and calibrated all equipment in only two weeks. Jason coordinated tissue sample analysis and asked the data collection clerk to teach all team members the latest encryption methods.

Meanwhile, Su and Indy devoted full effort to the critical task on the project's critical path: constructing a solution path to an effective S-Vac. Without it, the project would go nowhere.

Su would provide cutting edge concepts and Indy would help piece them into place using her sixth sense to adjust Su's conjectures. And the ladies refused to gossip, sharing nary a hint about progress with the fellows. Adom joked that Su was so focused she wouldn't bat an eye if he came to the lab buck naked, but he and Jason knew it was best not to disturb the quiet genius. Su relied exclusively on Indy. The breakthrough occurred Sunday of the third week.

"You've cracked the T-Plague code. Theoretically, we're able to develop all the vaccines." Su couldn't conceal her delight, sharing her victory with her best friend.

"I couldn't have come up with the solution path without you. I'd better write a white paper explaining it, so the fellows understand why and how it works. It's strictly for our team. Only Jason and Adom get to read it. This breakthrough belongs to us. Here, let me write down a bullet point summary and go over it with you. Let's make sure I have all the steps covered." Indy sat back while Su came up with a bullet point outline, and when finished, Indy began reviewing, taking twenty minutes before announcing her verdict.

"I can't think of anything to add. What you've given us is a path to the holy grail of T-Plague vaccines. If we make it so, it'll make our careers. Let me explain it back to you because that's the best way to confirm I understand your breakthrough." Su simply nodded, so Indy proceeded.

"It starts by describing the four bioengineering disciplines incorporated in the solution path, one for each of us. I'm virology, Jason's genetic engineering, Adom's molecular biology, and you handle neuroscience and stats combined. It then gives a high-level picture of the solution path connecting bacteria to virus to brain control center, and from there to enzyme production causing DNA mutation leading to symptoms and cognitive impairment. Am I on target?"

"Yes, and of course you and I will develop the details for each step along the path. Jason and Adom have primary responsibility for implementation. Go on."

"Now comes your breakthrough. It lists the quantum biology concepts used to weave the entire solution together. I can pronounce them, but I can't explain them. I'll leave that for you. Finally, it outlines how the path leads to three separate vaccines. And our project will develop only the S-Vac, which is for suppression and symptomatic relief. And that concludes my takeaway. What grade do I earn?"

"You earn an A-plus. Knowing you, I would imagine you'll ask the next question, which is how do we proceed? I've prepared a plan that answers it. Let me walk you through it.

"Our project is my raison d'etre, my reason for living. I have to make a biotech breakthrough, and that's what I've done. You've helped me apply it to T-Plague vaccine development. And it can make all of us wealthy. Even though I keep quiet, I like money as much as Adom does. You and I just cracked the code, and our team has what it takes to make the vaccines. And with it comes recognition and money. But only our team should control vaccine development and get credit." Su waited for Indy to ask a question, but it didn't come yet, so she continued.

"Our solution's a biotech development paradigm shift. The senior researchers are good, but they aren't on the cutting edge like we are. They won't understand or support our approach, so let's keep most of our work below the radar. Otherwise, we'll draw too much attention, or they won't approve what we want to do. Or they might steal from us. So, we're going to use our official project as cover for a stealth project. Are you with me?"

"Yes. I'll offer comments when you're through. Go on."

"Our official project is the suppression vaccine. We'll knock that off first according to our official timeline. Meanwhile, we keep working on our stealth project, which is our comprehensive solution path for all vaccines. Whatever solutions the other teams develop won't work. We can give them some help if they ask for it, but we won't give any details about my breakthrough. We'll resign at the earliest opportunity and start Worldstar Biologicals, using what's rightfully mine. The rest is history, our history."

"Su, I'm surprised. I never thought you could be you so assertive. Do you think this is legal or ethical? Aren't we going to be stepping into risky territory?"

"I've worked all that out. We're giving NIH everything they want. We'll help other teams if they ask. And we'll keep everyone else out of the loop. This is my discovery, and I won't let anything or anyone stand in my way. We're smarter than the seniors, and it's time we harness our brainpower, but we'll keep it undercover. Believe me, between the two of us and the guys, we can make it work. Adom and Jason can implement our solution path. Remember our discussion a couple of weeks ago about your marriage contract? It helped me confirm what I want. For you, Jason plays a big part. For me, this is it."

"So, what's next?"

"Monday, we hold a meeting for only the four of us. I'll give everyone a copy of my white paper, and everyone has to buy in and swear to secrecy or we don't proceed. I'll summarize why our solution works, and how we'll roll it out. It's a win-win-win."

"What about Mo?"

"We all like Mo, but he's on the outside. And he'll never discover our project-in-a-project. Jason will give him a list of additional equipment. No one will be suspicious because of all the unknowns at startup. And Mo will look good because we'll be the only team making progress."

"How do you know?"

"At the team briefing, the seniors provided conventional overviews that won't work. They haven't a clue how to combine virology, molecular biology, genetic engineering, and cognitive neuroscience as we do. And my breakthrough comes from integrating some of the quantum biology and intra-cellular macromolecular factory concepts. If I'm wrong, may Zeus strike me with a lightning bolt. I need you to get the guys onboard. Tell Jason, and have him call Adom so they're primed for tomorrow."

Indy took a deep breath then said, "I thought I knew you well, but today you've revealed what I haven't seen before. Makes me wonder how well I know Jason, or maybe I'm just fooling myself. Maybe I should talk with him again about the marriage contract. I think it's time for me to go home and drop some hints. See you tomorrow." Su's hint of a smile went undetected.

Monday's meeting couldn't have gone better even if Su had scripted what the guys were thinking. Her quantum biology primer and white paper explained enough so they understood the supporting theory. Jason would get the recognition he wanted, and Adom liked the money the stealth project approach could deliver. Keeping Mo in the dark didn't bother anyone since he wasn't a biotech contributor to the cause. Jason said it best at meeting's end. "We've just kicked off our race to the future, and defeating the T-Plague will take us to our promised tomorrow. Nothing can stop us now."

Sometime later that week, another kick-off meeting took place in the bowels of a CIA facility. It was the start of Project Death Shield, a covert operation that would make sure no T-Plague project or related political fallout would get out of control. No matter how widespread, no matter what timeframe, the administration and the government would survive.

CHAPTER 11
July 2093

"Boy's Night In"
(Thread 3 Chapter 4)

ADOM'S BRAIN ALWAYS WORKED better on a full stomach. The delivery van had just departed, and since the fridge contained plenty of beer, he'd be able to dish up pizza and advice, the combination meant to ease Jason's appetite and worry. They were holding a guy's only Saturday night, which usually started at Adom's apartment, and tonight would stay there so Jason could unload at his favorite safe space a tale of woe regarding Indy's marriage contract.

Adom lived a modern professional lifestyle, which included good job and career prospects, encouraged kinder and gentler morality, emphasized fitness and health, and embraced open relationships. His success told that he knows what ladies want, and males puzzled by females often asked him for advice, which Adom would advisedly dispense. A knock at the door announced tonight's designated worrier.

"Hi, Jason. Five minutes more and the pizza would have been history. So, how's it going?"

"Thanks for letting me cut into your Saturday social scene. On a scale of one to ten, I'm sitting at two. I need help."

"Hey, you're my best friend. The ladies can wait for one night. Grab a seat by the screen and switch on whatever sports channel you want. I'll grab the pizzas and beer."

The duo enjoyed pizza while swapping a few stories, simply enjoying time together, waiting for Adom to switch to Jason's number one concern.

"Hey guy, marriage contract and Vow-Cer stuff are significant steps for you and your significant other. Even I, Mister No-Commit, realize it takes time to get to know your partner, and you and Indy are still adjusting. Why don't you tell me about the latest revisions she's making and we'll take it from there?"

"Indy thinks I've started taking her for granted. She also wants me to lose my love handles, and she reminded me that I need to move past sex if I want our relationship to grow. And I need to be less self-centered. And listen to this one. She doesn't want me opening her mail."Adom smiled, having heard similar stories from other clueless guys.

"I know Indy pretty well, and I'm sure she didn't mean to hurt you. And I think it's good she's pushing back your Vow-Cer date. You and I look at relationships differently, and the biggest difference is your decision to make a long-term commitment. I'm not there yet, but I understand your predicament, and if I were you I'd do what Indy's pointing out. And the last one, about opening her mail. How would you like it if she started opening yours?"

"I wouldn't mind. I have nothing to hide. I'm just curious, and want to know all about her. Sometimes, she gets letters postmarked from Hollywood. Why's that? I never opened one of those, but I asked her what's the connection. She told me she has college friends working there."

"If I were you, I'd take her word for it. If you can't trust Indy, you can't trust anyone. She's been completely open with you, so stop opening her mail. What else is bothering you?"

"I'm trying, but it's hard to be perfect."

"Get real. Indy's not looking for a perfect ten. She would have picked me instead of you if she were. Indy loves you for all the S-words and more. All she wants is for you to do your part. By the way, Indy isn't perfect either, but damned if I can find any flaws." Adom paused for another sip of beer, then continued.

"You're the prime example of a guy who doesn't understand women. You try to read them like a science book. I've seen you in action hustling them. You get impatient, don't pick up on nuances, and often are emotionally blind. For females, patience and empathy play big roles. Haven't you noticed this in Su or Indy? And when it comes to committing, women handle it much better than men. As Indy points out, you need to get beyond sex and get to know her in other ways. Tell me again your stages of love theory."

"Sure. Everyone goes through the stages of love in this order. First, there's attraction or infatuation. Then you move to physical love, where I'm hung up. Then you move to committed love, which is the place I'm trying to reach. Finally, the highest form is unconditional love, like the love my Mom and Dad have."

"I'll buy into that, but make sure you know what you're looking for. Didn't you divide them into looks, background, personality, intelligence, and character? Maybe you can divide further, but that's putting too fine a point on it. Just go with it and talk with Indy."

"Give me an example."

"Try this. Indy knows you're not a ten, but under the character heading, she loves you because you try to correct your flaws and become the guy she knows is inside. And make sure you put what you're looking for in the right order."

"Uh, I don't follow. What do you mean?"

"What do you think is more important? Looks or character? Talk it out with Indy. You may find the order switches once you get to know someone. I've given you enough to think about. Study it and talk with Indy."

"You're right. I'll try to change, and please let me know if you see me backsliding."

"I'll be happy to, but just don't start throwing punches. I know criticism can be hard to take, especially for you. This talking makes me thirsty. I'll get us both another beer."

Jason shifted topics when Adom returned.

"How do you like where Su's solution is taking us?"

"I've known since grad school how smart she is, but until she walked us through her white paper I never realized how far ahead of me she is.I heard about quantum biology the last year in school. It was way over my head, but I didn't feel bad because no one understood.Now here she is, integrating our four areas of expertise with quantum biology. If this unfolds according to her solution path, our Wordstars team is golden as far into the future as I can see. Not only at NIH, but when we start our own company."

Jason said, "It looks the same to me. Worldstar Biologicals will make us millions, but Su doesn't come up with all this by herself. I think it's the Indy-Su duo. Just step back and watch them in action." "Yes, they're great friends. If you got hit by a bus or struck by lightning, maybe the two of them would go beyond co-friendship." "I don't think so, because Indy likes sex.Maybe you're the good-looking guy she'd go for if she gets rid of me.But let's not go there. I want all of us to stick around. You're the best Vow-Cer counselor I know."

"Now that we've got your current worry taken care of, let's pay attention to the Co-NFL game. The Washington Ambassadors' female jocks sure are looking good…"

Early September weather matched the team's mood; both were glowing in an aura of well-being. Su's white paper empowered collective action, allowing the Worldstars to run like a well-oiled machine needing no adjusting, so this afternoon's status meeting would be brief, after which Jason would take Indy on a dinner date. "We're three months into the project. All of us have made excellent progress on our assignments, and I've asked Su to summarize why it's all working so well. Su, would you please do the honors?"

"Preliminary analysis of the samples and data Mo obtained confirm our white paper approach is viable. And from what I've seen, our solution path is far superior to the senior's M.O. Since each of us has identified a large number of options, all we need to do is multiply our four numbers to come up with the number of scenarios we must evaluate. I've run the numbers, plugging in time estimates for each, and it will take us twenty years to test them all. So, we'll need to streamline our search procedure. That's where my quantum-bio piece fits in. I can eliminate improbable scenarios. I'll work with everyone to identify the best ones. That way, we'll be able to get the best vaccine for our piece of Cognicom in no more than three years. Jason, why don't you explain what three years means?"

"Three years for the ne plus ultra. Adom, did I stump you with that?" Jason was in a terrific mood and wanted to tease, but Adom was a step ahead and shot back the answer.

"The perfect or ultimate."

"OK, wise guy. Indy must have given you the correct answer. Anyway, NIH doesn't need to wait for the ultimate S-vaccine. They'll want to roll out a stopgap formulation ASAP and let us come up with improved formulations later. And that's when we might be able to start assisting the seniors if they're still struggling, but only if they ask. According to Su, we should have our first formulation approved no later than the middle of next year, especially if we get fast-track FDA approval. Su, why don't you explain how this impacts our stealth project?"

"Only we know about stealth. It's our project-in-a-project that covers all my break-through elements. And let me repeat what I've said previously. Our approach is pragmatic and ethical. The seniors won't understand our complete solution, even though it's correct. Our official project delivers what Cognicom needs, so they'll be happy with our stopgap smart pill first and then our more effective S-Vac later. And we'll keep my breakthrough to ourselves. I've figured out how to spread the credit for success among all of us, which means no one person is under the microscope and it'll be impossible for anyone to uncover stealth."

"Sounds like you have this nailed. Does anyone have questions or comments? Does anyone need additional equipment? Now's the time to get all we need." The answer was no, so Jason ended the meeting.

"We'll let Su decide who she'll work with next week. She has the entire weekend to pick the first victim. And whoever it is, their worries are over, unless she picks me. After all, I'm the designated team worrier. I hope you enjoy the weekend as much as Indy and I will. We're about to spend a night on the town." Ten minutes later, they were on their way.

"I'm proud of you. What a wonderful meeting you ran today. Your touch of humor at the end added an exclamation point to how well we're doing. You're handling the project management details like a pro, and I like how you lead by example. Adom's beginning to put in almost as much time as you." High praise indeed from Indy. The ambiance and wine coolers served at a late-night bistro helped Jason relax after Indy had coaxed him onto the dance floor earlier that evening.

"I'm trying to be the best Cognicom tech-lead, just like I'm trying to stick to the marriage contract changes you made. How am I doing?"

"Please stop worrying. You're doing your best, and that's all I can ask."

"Good. I'll stop worrying about that, but here's something else bothering me. Have you ever felt frightened because things are going so well? Lately, I've been feeling that way, and I need your help working through it." Indy reached across the table, taking Jason's hand.

"People feel that way at special times. And I know this is a special time for us. We have great careers, great friends, and most of all we have each other. And I know you've taken to heart my suggestions for making our relationship work. I love you for it."

"So how can I lose my fear?"

"You've made solid plans and are working to make them real, so don't worry about what will be. Enjoy right now and let the future unfold. Try to embrace the advice given in this couplet."

It's not the quarry but the chase,
It's not the laurel but the race.

Indy coyly removed her hand. "I know a better place for us to continue our discussion." Jason started feeling better immediately.

Where have the months gone? I can't believe the Christmas Holidays will start in only two weeks. Musing as he drove to have dinner with his Cognicom busadmin associates, Mo thanked the Worldstars more than his lucky stars for what a great year was now winding down.

It began auspiciously when he was officially promoted to Senior Business Manager, adding two related projects considered plum assignments: Cognicom S-Vac, and Middle East Environmental Scanning. Scanning provided a window into Middle East current events, giving advanced warning how T-Plague might impact that part of the world. His boss Bobbi Tarla gave him top marks during last week's annual performance review, and his unassuming personal life had contributed to a satisfying year. *I'm sure Candy picked a restaurant that'll get top marks too.* Candice Tarnell, lead for the I-Vac Project, had chosen the restaurant, noted for Italian cuisine and quiet elegance, because Spencer Harris, the R-Vac lead, rated its ravioli four stars.

All three were accelerating upwards among the ranks of thirty-something government healthcare professionals. They were smart, socially adept, and politically connected. *You need all three to get ahead in Washington. And you have to know the best places to go for info or for dining. I like the looks of the restaurant.* Mo walked purposefully from his car, ready to lead a conversation mixing business with pleasure. Food and ambiance matched Spencer's rating, making the conversation flow comfortably. When the topic turned to Cognicom projects, Mo summarized why S-Vac's team is a manager's dream: Su the intellectual dynamo, Adom the clever jokester, Jason the designated worrier, and Indy the thread seamlessly stitching all together.

"You're lucky your researchers have such synergy. Mine do too much sniping. What about yours, Spence."

"Mine don't snipe, but some have egos bigger than hat sizes. A couple of them are skeptical about Mo's tech-lead, so you better warn your team to be on its toes when talking with the seniors. But even the seniors say Indy's special."

As they sampled desserts, Mo complimented Candice for her choice of restaurants. It fostered a quiet intimacy perfect for comparing project notes. Mo was considered first among equals, so Candice and Spencer let him continue leading the conversation. "I can't thank you enough for how well our collective Cognicom work has gone this year. I'm lucky to have you as partners. And my team's ahead of schedule. We could have a smart pill ready by the end of next year, and we'll follow up with first generation S-Vac. Candy, how do things look for you?"

"My I-Vac researchers are talented, but sometimes they're a bit too self-satisfied, thinking they know it all when they don't. They haven't made much progress yet. They're surprised your team's done so well, but they tell me Jason's pushy. Spence, what's your take?"

"My seniors haven't come up with a solution path yet. They tell me all three vaccines are tough nuts to crack, but theirs is the hardest. Their best estimate is five years to have an R-Vac that'll work. And we know that's politically unacceptable if outbreaks become widespread. I haven't paid that much attention to inter-team friction, but my people probably would say what Candy did. Too bad we can't clone Su and Indy."

Mo said, "My team has an exceptional background. They met in grad school, came to NIH as a Worldstar package deal, and they're tops in their complementary disciplines. And somehow, Su tied them all together using quantum biology. Do you know what that is?" A silent pause gave Mo the answer, so he continued.

"I tried to read up when Su mentioned it. I'm no dummy, but it's way beyond me. Newtonian physics is my limit. And Su talks about wave-particle duality, tunneling, and instantaneous action-at-a-distance. Somehow, these laws of nature apply to biology and dominate at the molecular level. Su even talks about intra-cellular nano-molecular factories. She applies all this when selecting research paths. But there's more to it. Have you ever talked with Indira Ramanujan?"

Candy said, "I've chatted with her a couple of times. She's very impressive, and I can see why she's the one person on your team everyone likes. Some of my researchers think she should be the tech-lead."

"She's the glue that binds my team together, and I don't think Su could do what she does if Indy weren't there to help."

Spencer added, "I think it shows that Youth will be served. Sooner or later, our senior researchers will have to give way to the young turks and tigresses. And the three of us should be thankful for our career choices. Business and sociopolitical skills have much longer shelf lives than techie skills." Spencer had just served up a conversation segue Mo was waiting for.

"Let's compare notes on sociopolitical issues. Each of us is leading an "EnviroScan" Project, so I'll start with a Middle East recap. Only two countries have reported outbreaks, Israel and China. We're lucky that Israel reached out to NIH for help. They're working with us, and their research teams have shared what little success they've had. Israel's deathly afraid of a widespread outbreak. Remember Ebola about a century ago? We dodged a bullet back then because transmission was by physical contact. We might not be so lucky this time. The Israelis are saying transmission is airborne and active for days. They think it's a virus that goes dormant in soil or water below critical levels of temperature and humidity. All this is bad news. And there's more. No age, sex or ethnic group is immune.

"Now the good news. So far, fatalities are nil. The fever, nausea, and headache clear in forty-eight hours, but the cognitive impairment lasts longer. The Israelis don't know if or when cog impairment clears. If an outbreak spreads regionally, the political consequences would be bad. Most of Israel's neighbors still don't have modern healthcare systems. With population densities and sanitary conditions being what they are, an outbreak could lead to widespread fear and instability. Not a cheery ring out the old ring in the new message. Candy, what do you see?"

"The Chinese have a tight lid on events in Beijing. We do know the second outbreak was bigger than the first but hasn't spread too far geographically. Our contacts are almost certain the virus is a biotech research blunder, not a natural occurring mutation. They think the outbreaks are caused by accidental containment breaches from an unidentified lab. Did the Israelis talk about what caused their outbreak?"

"No, our preliminary briefings were sketchy, but that's on our list of follow-up questions. But the similarities are compelling. Both countries have active biotech R&D, and outbreaks occur in urban areas close to research parks. Maybe Israeli containment and clean-up work better. The Chinese middle class is a growing power, and if they connect the T-Plague with the government's directed growth policy there could be problems. But nothing like that has surfaced. Spencer, what have you learned?"

"My Enviro-Scan covers Western Europe, and those countries are afraid of genetic engineering. They claim its risks outweigh benefits. Do you know who invented the T-Plague moniker? We can thank European media. Perhaps they and their social networking sources know more than our official channels are letting on. It might become a finger-pointing conspiracy theory because a growing number of naysayers believe tinkering with nature has brought a plague on all our houses. If this thing spreads to Europe, watch out. Europeans demand their government safety nets take care of them, especially when it comes to healthcare."

Mo asked, "Do you think the American public feels threatened, or that our government is doing all it can to deal with it?" Candice answered first.

"That's a great question. All of us work in government healthcare and take for granted what a great job the system does. But the Administration is often criticized for being out of touch with Main Street. And the public thinks too much money is wasted on foreign aid, rather than spent at home rebuilding infrastructures, namely transportation, energy, and communications systems. So, the public will demand action if T-Plague outbreaks occur in the U.S. Spence, what does European coverage say about America?"

"Pretty much the conventional wisdom. We feel safe because the oceans are big buffers. And if no cases are reported, we aren't

concerned. Europe doesn't see the Guardian Party gaining traction unless outbreaks become widespread. Mo, you're politically connected more than either of us. What's your reading on the Guardian Party?"

"It isn't for mainstream Democrats or Republicans yet. But the Far Right likes them because they're for American Exceptionalism and the use of military force. They're also against the Big Government's big safety net. And the Far Left likes them because they push for increased surveillance and security-related gun control, as well as using high-tech to improve the quality of life. And listen to this doomsday scenario conjured by a government think tank.

"T-Plague eventually becomes a worldwide pandemic and our government can't come up with vaccines that work. America's economy, infrastructure, and military are degraded. Our government's misguided belief in a "kinder and gentler world" is confounded by the world becoming a dangerous place. America becomes a pushover for terrorists who strike on American soil.

"And the political fallout? People run to the Guardian Party for shelter. Not just the extremes, but mainstreamers as well. This could lead to an orderly transition or maybe an overthrow or a revolution orchestrated by the Guardian Party that represses certain minorities. It gets worse, but let's stop here. Frightening to consider, wouldn't you say?"

Candice was incredulous. "Does anyone in the Administration believe this? It seems so far-fetched."

Mo answered, "Until the 19th century, black swans were considered an impossibility. Then they were found in Australia. This T-Plague could be a gigantic black swan, and think tanks are in business to think outside the box. They're supposed to figure out what damage the T-Plague could cause. Look what happened to Europe in the Middle Ages. The Black Death killed sixty percent and turned the clock back a century. Look, this is the season of comfort and joy. Can't we come up with a happy ending?" Spencer found a cheery spin to end the evening.

"Sure. Our teams develop effective vaccines, and the T-Plague is history. We get big promotions for jobs well done, and NIH sells the vaccines to the rest of the world for big bucks. No more national debt or balance of payments problems."

Mo said, "I like it, and I know three teams to get us there. So, let's call it a night and get going."

The Worldstars were about to put an exclamation point on a banner year. Jason's parents were hosting a New Year's Eve party for them and their dates. Jason was in the living room watching for Su and Adom, his parents bustling in the kitchen, Indy dressing upstairs. Jason idolized his parents, a doctor-nurse team practicing in this rural community for forty years. They had given Jason the best of what old and new lifestyles had to offer, and were proud how promising his future should be.

As he gazed at the front yard's moonlit contours, splendid memories of past New Year's Eves drifted into his thoughts. Tonight promised to be happiest of all. Many good things had come his way this year. Thanks to Indy, he was enjoying the present more and worrying less about unknown risks the future might bring. Though worry was part of his DNA, Jason was learning how to keep in perspective what was outside his control. Headlights swept across the lawn, announcing the guests.

Party preparations showed Dora's attention to details: holiday decorations adorned the room, and appetizers were already placed. Jason did the honors by introducing everyone.

"Su, Happy New Year to you and Kayed. Let me introduce you to Mom and Dad, Dora and Doc Kittner. And Adom, the same to you and Whitney." Jason's mother added her greetings.

"I am so pleased all of you are here. What a handsome collection of youth. I love your boundless energy and enthusiasm." Her smile and sparkling eyes brought everyone into a lively conversation that eventually moved to what the new year might hold.

"Your Mother and I try to keep up with younger generation lifestyles, but sometimes I fall behind. All of you are smart, attractive, have good careers, and all the things that go with it, but all of you are still single. Why is that?" Indy replied before Jason.

"Social norms are much broader than ever, and young people like having the freedom to explore a range of interests or lifestyles. And unlike a generation or so ago, females can have rewarding lives without husbands or children. Those are some of the reasons why the younger generation postpones marriage or having kids. Whitney, what's your view?"

"I agree but also say some people know what they want much earlier than others. And a popular family counselor said if you wait too long before committing, you miss out on many sharing opportunities. You and Jason are thinking about moving ahead. Su, how do you look at the commitment decision."

"I think it's important for a person not to settle. You should wait until you have what you want. "Adom, how about you?"Adom dodged the barb. "How about more appetizers? Mrs. Kittner, your Swedish meatballs are just tangy enough. Best I've ever had." The conversation rolled through dinner and the rest of the evening, finally ending after a New Year's toast.

Guests were gone and Jason's parents had gone to bed, giving Jason an opportunity to quiz Indy about Su's love life.

"Kayed seems nice enough, but do you think he's right for Su? I'm not the most diversified guy, but what else other than the Middle East conundrum does he think about?"

"You do have a point. I think she sees him only when doing volunteer work for a Middle East refugee relocation program. That's where she met him, and according to Su, he keeps in close touch with friends living in that part of Isilabad previously belonging to Syria. She told me that he's convinced the Arab World will ultimately accept Modernity, but not in his lifetime."

"I don't suppose there's a romantic interest on Su's part. Do you?"

"Su is private. I don't ask, and she doesn't tell, but my intuition tells me no. However, Su does like to follow world events. I hope she connects him with Mo. He might be able to help Mo keep ahead of the headlines. Now, what about Whitney and Adom?"

"She's got a lot to offer. Works for a public relations firm. Good career and good looking. And like all the women he dates, she knows he's a great catch. But he's not ready to commit. He says he'll do that when he finds someone like you." Jason paused but Indy didn't comment, so he carried on.

"I apologize if Dad asked too many questions about our marriage plans. Thanks for explaining what co-friend, marriage contract, and Vow-Cer stuff's all about."

"Your Dad has a youthful outlook and understands a lot about the younger generation, even better than your Mom. Family and marriage are different today than twenty years ago, so let's not worry about setting dates. Let the future come to us."

"One of your poems captures what I'm feeling right now. I think you named it 'The Quiet Realm.'"

"I'm proud of you for remembering some of my poems, and here's the first verse.

'A peaceful stillness fills the room,
That bustled once with life.
Like King and Queen and all that's seen,
My peerless man and wife.'

I'm pleased you like it. And I think I know something else you'll like."

Jason hugged Indy, letting joy fill him to the brim. He would be worry-free, at least until sunrise.

CHAPTER 12
March 2094

"A Distant Storm Brewing"
(Thread 3 Chapter 5)

THE T-PLAGUE LASHED OUT with unexpected fury early in the new year, spreading rapidly beyond Shanghai,then leapfrogging to other urban centers. After stonewalling for over a year, the Chinese government yielded to intense pressure from its assertive middle class, forcing it to reach out for help. America's CDC led the international community's efforts to contain a potential pandemic.

Israel's outbreak spread at an alarming rate to adjoining Arab territories, and the rumor mill reported cases in Isilabad and Iran, but Muslim countries were uncooperative so information was sketchy, obtained primarily from Israeli covert contacts. Additional outbreaks subsided, but media pundits and fear-mongers alike hyped they would soon resume. Conjectures and conspiracy theories were rampant; social networking pulsed with late-breaking extras.

Not even Mo's boss Bobbi Tarla could find anything positive in the T-Plague briefing session hastily arranged for senior NIH administrators. Now she was back in her office, working on notes she would distribute to her direct reports. She had just summoned the brightest rising star in her galaxy of mid-level managers to help.

Bobbi could be a poster child for what social support programs can achieve. She was raised in Chicago's inner city by a single father who gave her the attention an orchid breeder would lavish on his prize-winning specimen, using every opportunity to further her education. Bobbi blossomed to become a respected public healthcare administrator dedicated to her career, country, and father. Her professional manner and careful grooming enhanced her unexceptional looks that kept improving when compared with other mid-forties women because of fitness classes. Bobbi's career had plenty of upward momentum that she would apply to Mo's as well.

Mo strode into Bobbi's office. She and her superiors liked his direct, confident manner and had picked him for bigger responsibilities going forward. Bobbi glanced up from her desk, and without smiling, started right in.

"Thanks for getting here so quickly. I just came from a T-Plague meeting, and I want you to give the update at our next staff meeting. I'll go over what I found out and let you finish. And there's more. You've been doing a great job with your piece of the Cognicom Project. Your team's the only one making progress. We want you to get more exposure to the political side, so you're assigned to the Inter-Agency Committee that controls all T-Plague-related actions. You'll be working with congressional and CIA staffers and meeting with high-ranking officials. Consider this an unofficial promotion because it's a real plum. Congratulations. Now let's get to work." Mo reached across the desk to shake Bobbi's hand.

"I'm nearly speechless, which is rare for me. I'll do my best to deliver the results you want."

"Your career has a long way to go if you keep producing. It might take you into the political arena. But today's topic is the T-Plague. Here's what I know." Bobbi gave her notes to Mo after summarizing them. He was surprised he knew more than she did but kept that to himself.

"I'm good with this, and I can add to it. I can see what you said playing out in Europe or Africa. My gut instinct tells me the U.S. isn't as concerned because outbreaks have occurred only offshore. The oceans buffer us, but we'll pay attention big-time when we get our first outbreak. And I would look for outbreaks near biotech development clusters, such as Boston or San Diego. Would you like to hear my take on the political landscape?" Bobbi nodded so Mo pushed on.

"The current Administration has low approval ratings for two main reasons. Too soft on national security and terrorism, and too lax on controlling access to information and protecting us from ourselves. So, the extreme left or right doesn't like us, but that's nothing new. The moderates share some of these views but go along with the Administration, at least for now. The upstart Guardian Party pushes for a tougher stance on national security and terrorism. They also push for more government intervention to obtain personal information and to control biotech research better. All in the name of guarding our country. So, the fringe left or right likes them. I've heard their fund-raising campaign pitches. They use slogans like 'The Guardian Party, growing to protect the best in all of us,' or 'Harsh times demand harsh measures.' Some of their arguments are convincing too, so it's no wonder they've started winning congressional seats. And they criticize Washington for being out of touch with Main Street, and for neglecting infrastructure and job creation. OK so far?"

"Yes. Keep going."

"So, the Guardian Party is a slow-growing threat to the Establishment, but if the T-Plague breaks wide open it's a game-changer. The Guardian Party will use it to get themselves voted into the Oval Office, or if that doesn't work, maybe to lead a populist-supported government take-over. And they already pushed through legislation that converted their two agencies, Healthguard for public health and Securityguard for terrorist-type protection, into government bureaucracies the public clamored for. The public will pay even more attention if T-Plague comes ashore. And it's not a question of if, but when."

Bobbi asked Mo to stop, then said, "You know more than I do. You have a smart network, and when you start working with the Committee, you'll have even more people in it. I have another meeting, so let's be on our way." Mo thanked Bobbi one more time, then set sail.

July's nice weather nationwide added to the public's belief that the T-Plague would never strike America. It only showed up in media reporting, but since no outbreaks had occurred at home, people paid little attention. But not so for the Cognicom project teams that were working feverishly but gaining little ground. Jason's reasons for worry would be the focal point at a mid-July team meeting.

"We can congratulate ourselves for the progress we've made, and the seniors believe Su's explanation that the hunch we played—Adom's nano-enzyme conjecture—paid off. Our stealth project is flying under the radar. But I have two worries. Our S-Vac progress is slowing, and Mo reports Cognicom will become a political football if our current Administration can't handle outbreaks or its socioeconomic fallout. And he says if that occurs, watch out for the Guardian Party. So, my question to the team is this, how should we proceed?" Su spoke first.

"Your concerns are justified, and what we do depends on what unfolds politically. We're fortunate Mo is so well connected."

Jason asked, "Do you think we should bring Mo into our inner circle?"

"No, not yet. First, we don't know him well enough to trust him with our future, or if darker scenarios unfold, with our lives. Second, S-Vac's still ahead of schedule, so we don't need to make a snap decision."

"I get the part about being ahead of schedule," Adom said, "but I don't follow the rest. What are you getting at?"

"Suppose T-Plague outbreaks become widespread. Suppose only we can make effective vaccines. Suppose moles infiltrate NIH and uncover our stealth project. If that scenario gets out of control, we'll be lucky to survive."

Indy replied, "No one knows if we're heading to a pandemic, to a political crisis, or possibly to both. We could be victims, targets, or collateral damage. So, let's be proactive. Su and I will recheck our solution path to figure out why progress has slowed; you guys think through how political scenarios impact Cognicom. And we'll all keep pushing ahead on stealth. If the political situation stabilizes, we stay the course. If it spirals downhill, we bring Mo into the loop.

And let's remember what Benjamin Franklin said. Either we hang together or we hang separately. And Jason, perhaps we are kissed by the sun. But it's possible we're cursed by a devil instead."

"That's a grim thought, but let's be positive because we have a plan of action." Jason planned to say more, but stopped suddenly. "I've lost my train of thought. Who can say something positive so we can end on a cheerier note?" Indy broke the uncomfortable silence. "The future is written on the winds of change, not in stone, and we'll help write it to our liking. And remember, media talk always hypes the worst outcomes that usually don't play out. It's a distant storm they're forecasting. Much can happen to keep it away, so, let's follow our new plan, starting today. Meeting adjourned."

Adom made progress the next week piecing together political scenarios from information found on the Internet. Jason admitted he had nothing to add, so Adom gave his notes to Indy, who agreed to summarize them for the team as soon as she and Su completed their S-Vac review. Indy had what she needed by mid-August, so the team rendezvoused at Indy and Jason's apartment on a Saturday afternoon. Indy rewarded the fellows by giving them tickets to that evening's Co-NBA game, suggesting they leave early. Only Su detected an ulterior motive. Indy wanted only Su to stay because the fellows would only be in the way. After the guys cleared out, Indy cleared the great room table while Su fired up her tablet and systematically arranged stacks of notes.

"I'm glad you bought tickets for the guys. They need a break, and tonight's game should help. Even Adom seems stressed."

"Both of them have been too grim lately. I think watching the Co-NBA females will pick them up. Why don't you start by going over why we've slowed down, and I'll write a summary?" Su did so after finding the notes she needed.

"We shouldn't worry about slow S-Vac progress. We simply haven't picked the right combination of parameter changes. We got lucky on the first combinations and hit a sweet spot that gave us safety and efficacy. But even though I've already eliminated many follow-up combinations, we must keep testing the others, picking from my prioritized candidate list. I'm convinced we've come up with a generalized bio-development solution path that will work for many viral diseases. What we've done so far confirms I'm right."

"I guess that's why we're ahead of the other teams. And you're sure the seniors haven't a clue about what we're doing?"

"They don't, and I'm not being arrogant, just brutally honest. We're smarter and know how to combine current procedures with quantum biology. I read the journals. Nothing out there comes close to what we have. They're jealous, and their egos won't admit we're better."

"What if we gave them suggestions? Do you think it would help?"

"They'd ignore, scratch their heads, or apply them incorrectly. If they ask Mo for help, we can point them in the right direction, but that's all. We'll capitalize on my breakthrough as soon we resign to start Worldstar Biologicals."

"The guys will like that. It gives us lots of options. We can keep working on the commercial side, or return to academia if venture capitalists buy us. And you're sure our solution path is valid?"

"Without a doubt. I never stop thinking about it. We have a major breakthrough."

"I've got enough notes to write all that up. And Adom gave me his notes on possible political scenarios, so let me summarize for you." Indy sorted through a stack of papers before saying more.

"First, the optimistic one. I-Vac and R-Vac teams come up vaccines within five years, needing no help. T-Plague is wiped out, first here and then worldwide. There's no political instability.

"Next, the likely one. The seniors need our help. It takes them ten years to come up with effective vaccines. The plague is controlled, but not before pandemics erupt and political fallout disrupts developing countries. Our government is pushed by the Guardian Party to make reforms, but we don't have a revolution.

"Finally, worst case scenario. The I and R vaccines take too long; they're too little and too late. American infrastructures and military readiness deteriorate. Terrorist groups hijack weak countries, attack us, and bring back the Dark Ages to much of the world. Economies at home and abroad decline. The public's I.Q. and tolerance decline.

The Guardian Party takes control. And if it's ever leaked that we're the only reason for any effective vaccines, we'll be lucky to escape with our lives. We'd be targeted by terrorists or hostile groups because we have the cure for the T-Plague. Our own government might put us under lock and key because we can't be trusted."

"Please stop. If you say another word, I'll be tempted to slit my wrists. But let me add a final observation on the technical side. I can explain why symptoms and outbreaks cycle. The virus switches between infectious and remissive states. You know what this means? A patient we think is cured might become contagious again when the virus changes states. And we won't know if site decontamination works or if the virus has just gone remissive. Aren't these cheery chestnuts?" Indy hoped her reply would help.

"We're getting way ahead of ourselves, so let's bring this back to a shorter time horizon. When the guys get back, we'll tell them the good news first. We do have a generalized solution path, and we'll keep it to ourselves. We'll help other teams only if they ask. When the time is right, we'll leave NIH and start Worldstar Biologicals.

"Now for a good spin on the bad news. Our progress has slowed because we haven't found better parameter combinations, so we keep working through your hit list. On the political front, things could get darker, but we're nowhere near a partial eclipse because all the scenarios are conjecture, nothing confirmed. So, we stick with our plan. If the political situation begins to spiral downhill, we'll change our plan after bringing Mo into the loop."

Su said, "That should keep Jason from worrying too much. He and Adom will like it because we keep doing what we're doing. Nothing changes. And while you finish writing, I'll get us a treat from the kitchen. I made another batch of fruit tarts."

Indy completed the write-up by the time Adom and Jason returned, and she forced everyone to listen to her summary. Though tired, everyone agreed with what she said, and appreciated Adom's attempt to leave on a lighter note.

"I like what I hear because we don't change a thing. And it fits a joke I heard at a drug development seminar. The only person that likes change is a wet baby. Let's keep ourselves away from the storm so we stay nice and dry."

The remainder of summer slipped away uneventfully, but that changed as summer turned to autumn. T-Plague struck without warning in Boston and San Diego, causing an eruption of sensational stories and conspiracy theories that infected news media and social networks. The Administration assured the public they had a firm grip on the situation, but the Guardian Party attacked from both the left and right ends of the political spectrum. China added to the malaise: the plague was fast reaching epidemic proportions in several urban centers. All the commotion swelled Guardian Party town hall meetings to standing room only.

Mo came back from his September inter-agency meeting ready to brief his team so they could help him come up with better insights into the festering T-Plague muddle. If that happened, he could make more network connections that would help him stay ahead of events. Jason had already told his people Mo needed help deciphering the latest ground reports, so they were swapping ideas before he arrived.

Mo walked in with his trademark meeting mood elevators: gourmet cookies and fruit slices. "Hey everyone, the sky isn't falling, so cheer up. Have some snacks and grab a drink before we get started." The short break helped lighten the mood before Mo continued.

"I just attended a special inter-agency briefing that let me in on the latest. I want to include some of their concerns in my assessment update that will include technical and political issues, and you're my best choice for adding to the list." Mo handed out a bullet point chart containing technical concerns.

"I know this is short notice, but what can we add or expand on either the technical or political side?" Jason felt obligated to begin. "Your list is a good starting point, but we've got some items to add. Indy, why don't you fit them in?

"Here's what we came up with. New outbreaks are found in urban industrial or research centers, like the special economic zones in Shanghai, because the virus is synthetic, not naturally occurring.

It's an accidental leak or contamination. China's safety precautions and contamination clean-up are inadequate compared to the Israeli's. Maybe joint projects are spreading contamination among other research centers. Su, please tell us more about the virus."

"The virus cycles between infectious and remissive states, making it difficult knowing if a patient is cured, or if a contamination site has been scrubbed cleaned. No fatalities pose major long-term problems. Treatment centers will be overwhelmed; cognitive impairment will impact healthcare, the economy, and national security. I'll stop here and ask for comments." None were forthcoming, but Mo asked a question.

"Any ideas on what will stop it from spreading?"

Su continued, "It'll stop when the virus mutates to a non-infectious form, or when it runs out of susceptible hosts. I don't see much hope in either. We need vaccines. Our marginally effective S-Vac could be ready for U.S. distribution in six months if we get fast-track approval and production ramps up. The I and RVacs are nowhere near being ready. Mo, what can you tell us about the countries working with us?"

"China is providing more data and claims it knows where the contamination is coming from. Maybe they do, but we aren't betting on it. Israel says their contamination is from a government lab working on Alzheimer's. We have nothing concrete from Iran, other than they deny having anything to do with it."

Jason added, "Boston and San Diego have a number of biotech startups. It's possible they have joint projects we don't know about. Maybe they caused external cross-contamination, or maybe they are working with the same protovirus. Adom, any ideas here?"

"My Boston contacts think the same. And they say to watch out for San Francisco's Bay Area too. From what they're telling me, no one is close to a vaccine, but several unnamed labs might have a stopgap by next year like our smart pill. I wonder when Europe will get drawn in?" Mo turned to the political situation.

"You've come up with excellent technical insights. Now I have something new to take back to Bobbi, and believe me this is going to help. Now, let's look at the political assessment. Here's the latest."

Mo handed out another bullet point list. "What can you add to it?" Jason spoke for the team.

"We would agree with these points, but there are others we can add that hit closer to home. Has your committee thought about consequences if the names of Cognicom researchers are leaked? Might we be in danger? And the public is going to want some type of vaccine or smart pill ASAP. How are we going to deal with that? Our healthcare system could be overloaded and our economy impacted." Mo shook his head before replying.

"We haven't, but you've given me some new issues I can use. And they'll help me watch our backs. We can stick to our game plan. The other teams are being pressured, but we're not in the crosshairs because we've made some progress. Don't worry about any sniping by the seniors. Just be understanding and noncommittal. Indy, please give me the expanded list and we'll call it a day."

Unlike Jason, Mo was a doer, not a worrier. He always faced facts, deciding what steps to take, and then moving on. The Worldstars had given him some troubling facts, and he needed his boss to help keep the situation from deteriorating. Early the next week, Mo dropped in unannounced to chat with Bobbi, giving her his technical and political assessment notes. While she skimmed his report, Mo sat across the desk observing body language that implied she liked his report.

"I'm impressed with what you've done on your own. We knew you were good, and that's why you're on the Inter-Agency Committee. How did you come up with this?"

"After the last meeting, I brainstormed with my Worldstars, then did some Internet searches. And wouldn't it make sense for me to do brainstorming with NIH persons who have higher level access to what's going on?"

"It does, and like you point out, identity leaks could put our researchers at risk. We don't want the press distorting what NIH is doing."

"We'll be better off if we stay ahead of what's trending. Here's another example. The public will demand the government provide effective T-Plague protection by handing out some sort of smart pill, something to keep cognition from deteriorating. If our Cognicom projects get lucky, maybe we'll have some vaccines before we're hit with a major outbreak. But if we don't, we need to have a response ready. And a major outbreak is coming. We just don't know where or when."

"Do you think the Guardian Party poses a threat?"

Mo replied, "A threat to whom? I've paid attention to their recruiting pitches, and they aren't a threat to the man on the street. Mainstreet thinks they're doing a better job guarding public health and security than the guy in the White House. The Administration better wake up, or it'll be swept away by a tidal wave of public resentment when the storm hits."

"What do you think we need to do?"

"NIH and the Administration must already have teams in place working on response scenarios. I think I can contribute. Would you be able to place me, or put me in touch with the right people?"

"I'm sure you realize this could put you at odds with influential people. If and when the Administration changes, the pecking order gets reshuffled and different straw men come to the fore. Are you ready to play a political game?"

"Yes."

"Let me work my channels, and for now, keep doing what you're doing."

"Thank you, Bobbi. I'll do my best."

A call came two weeks later, just as Mo was turning out the lights for the night.

"Hello Mr. Sunstein. We understand you're the real deal, a genuine patriot. And you want to help guard what makes America great. How would you like to join our stealth think tank and help us prepare for the coming storm?" The call lasted for two hours.

CHAPTER 13
December 2094

"The Buddhist Monk"
(Thread 3 Chapter 6)

THE WORLDSTARS WERE LIVING the lifestyles of their dreams: upwardly mobile biotech careers unfolding in Washington's exciting milieu offering numerous social venues. Thanks to Indy, even Jason attended social events. She was an active member of NIH's New Vista Club and often convinced him to join its tours or happy hours. She had joined a fitness center and belonged to its professional women's group that sponsored activities for couples. And she belonged to a literary society that sponsored monthly lectures, so when all this was added to local college concert schedules, every weekend offered plenty to do. Indy never forced Jason to come along. Sometimes he did, and when he did, sometimes he actually enjoyed himself.

The T-plague remained the public's subliminal concern, but people still went out and about taking normal precautions, and since no DC outbreaks had occurred, everyone went on with their daily lives, pointing for the Holidays a week away. Washington's December weather added to a sense of well-being. A dusting of snow sparkled in the Sunday morning sunlight, confirming Christmas is approaching.

Jason had planned to take Indy this Sunday on a tour of neighborhoods meeting his first home criteria: young professional families, reasonable commute to work, newer and affordable construction, progressive schools. He figured there would always be buyers should they need to sell, no matter the state of the union. Indy liked what she saw.

"Our tour reminds me of two more of your S-words: systematic and sequential. Sometimes I think your greatest pleasure is filling up our bucket list and then checking items off. I never have to worry about planning ahead because you do that so well."

"It's my nature to be a planner and a worrier. They go together. My biggest fears are failing to achieve my goals, and losing the things that mean the most. Don't these bother you?"

"I look at them differently. Instead of worrying about not reaching my goals, I focus on reaching out for what I want. Lots of stories tell about people feeling a letdown after achieving success because now they have nothing to reach for. So, I try to enjoy each day by working towards something. Results will follow."

"It's not an S-word, but I wish I had your optimism."

"Su told me about a neuroscientific research paper that concluded humans are predisposed to optimism, which equips us to handle adversity. So, practice being optimistic. It's foolish to worry about losing what means the most. All of us ultimately lose all that's dear, ashes to ashes, dust to dust and so forth. Try to enjoy the present. My fear is losing interest in life and having nothing or no one to care about. But that's a worry for my old age. Right now, I appreciate you and how you're planning for our future. And I certainly don't need to worry about where we'll buy a house. I like all the neighborhoods you've picked. Why don't you prioritize them so we know where to start looking when we're ready?"

"How about we look next year and be ready to buy sometime in 2096?"

"I like that." Jason's next question switched subjects. "What's on your bucket list?"

"It's about time you asked me. My bucket list contains emotional things instead of the material things you like to focus on. There's nothing wrong with putting material items in a bucket list, mind you, and you're taking care of that for us. But mine contains more of the emotional experiences that make for a life well lived."

"So, what're in your first couple of buckets?"

"By now, you should have a good idea what they are. Experiencing the intimacy of a truly committed relationship is number one, followed by the experience of natural childbirth. To me, they are the essentials of being human."

"I wish I had a higher emotional I.Q. No wonder you and Su are best friends. I'm sorry if I come up shallow when it comes to deep thinking. I guess that's another S-word in my collection." Indy chuckled, then replied.

"You're better than most guys, and time is on your side. And don't worry, I'll help you because you're my work in progress."

"I don't think I told you, but Adom's invited us to his sports club New Year's Eve party. It'll be a noisy, fun-filled place, filled with people, food, and dancing you'll like. He asked Su, but she's already made plans. Will you want to go?"

"It's an excellent choice. Did Adom give you any hints on what to wear?"

"Anything from jeans to tuxedo or gown. He showed me pics from last year. The partygoers looked like your kind of people. He's bringing Whitney and I said we'd join them. And I expect you'll have even more fun than I."

"Don't be that way. Be optimistic because a positive outlook always helps. Remember this. Whether you think you can or you can't do something, what you're thinking is likely to happen. And it helps to prepare for what might happen if you picture yourself actually dealing with the situation. I've seen enough neighborhoods on this tour. Let's go home and deal with a situation I know you can handle."

Jason was helping Indy in the kitchen late Sunday afternoon when he received a text message ordering him to call Lab Security. Jason's expression told her something bad had happened; when the call ended, he blurted the news.

"We're in big trouble! T-Plague virus has contaminated I and R-Vac labs. Two I-Vac researchers have tested positive, and I was in that lab last Friday. I bet I've been exposed. What are we gonna do?"

"Jason, stop worrying. You can get tested tomorrow. How do you feel?"

"My stomach feels queasy."

"Stop acting like a hypochondriac. You look fine, and here's what we're going to do. Call Adom and Su. Have them drop everything and come over so we can plan how to handle the situation. They can spend the night with us. Adom will drive all of us to the lab tomorrow. We need to set an example for the other teams."

Su and Adom knew about the emergency and would be right over. Jason prepared coffee and snacks while Indy cleared the table and outlined an agenda. Indy, a natural-born leader, rarely panicked and she started talking as soon as everyone grabbed a seat.

"Thanks for getting here so soon. Look, this situation is not a crisis for us. It's an opportunity we need to use. We'll come up with a plan Mo will like, and he can sell it to his boss. But first, let's have Jason summarize what we know."

Jason repeated what Lab Security had told him. T-Plague virus had escaped into I and R-Vac labs, but not into the Worldstars S-Vac lab. Two I-Vac researchers tested positive. Emergency containment procedures had been implemented, forcing lab evacuation and decontamination; those infected were quarantined and given massive doses of developmental S-Vac smart pills. All I and R-Vac researchers would be tested tomorrow and quarantined if results were positive. There would be an all hands emergency meeting nine a.m. tomorrow at Home Base for everyone working on Cognicom. Mo would run the meeting, assisted by the other leads.

"That's the latest. And to make matters worse, I might have been exposed." Adom didn't think so.

"Come on. Don't be such an alarmist. Indy, what do you think?"

"I think he's fine. And I have an idea what went wrong. I-Vac and R-Vac teams are under so much pressure they took short cuts that caused some sort of containment breach. I don't think it spread, so only they were directly exposed. And it'll be cleaned up fast.

NIH de-tox procedures are top notch. We're in the clear because no intrusion alarms sounded in our lab."

Su added, "We need to be careful with the other teams. They'll resent us even more unless we're part of whatever restrictions follow. And it's possible their tech leads will be fired. If so, we're candidates for promotion. So, let me ask, do you want promotions or do you want us to stay together?"

"Jason and I have been best buddies since grad school, and I want it to stay that way. That's been our plan all along, both short and long-term."

"I think Indy and Jason agree, so if Mo's boss suggests one of us be promoted, we can say that our team's synergy would be destroyed. Let's tell Mo we'll be happy to provide assistance to other teams if they request it, but we make no promises it'll help. And we keep our stealth project under wraps. We need to make doubly sure it's hidden from any and all prying eyes. We'll give lots of credit to Mo for insulating us from the political squabbling, and we need him to defuse any back-biting from the seniors. We want him to be the hero among all the leads. He already is the acknowledged leader, and his position will be even more solid if he can handle this crisis."

Indy said, "Let's prepare a list of what additional resources we need if the other teams ask for help. And we can include whatever will help make faster progress on our stealth project. One more thing. Word of the containment breach should be kept from the media. There's no need inflaming the public's fears." Jason remained a silent observer, but Adom had more to say.

"I like that. Mo can tell the other leads we'll help, but only if they ask for it. And he should say we volunteer for testing and informal quarantine over the Holidays as a gesture of solidarity. We won't go to my club's New Year's Eve party even though the odds are nil that any of us have been infected." Indy decided it was time for Jason to play the team lead role.

"Let's give all our notes to Jason so he can write up a plan of action for Mo. He's probably home alone thinking about what to do, so let's have Jason call him as soon as possible." Jason finally began to emerge from a funk.

"I apologize for being so useless. I've worried myself sick that I might be infected, even though I'm probably not. Adom, maybe you can work with me."

"I'll be happy to do that, but you better wear a surgical mask. I don't want you breathing down my neck." Adom's good-natured humor brought smiles even to Jason.

It didn't take long for Jason to draft a summary that the team approved. Then he called Mo, who liked what he heard and asked for an Emailed copy and an agenda for tomorrow's meeting. "I've been struggling all evening getting nowhere for tomorrow. Now I've got a starting point. I'll see you before I start the meeting." Jason disconnected the call and turned to his team.

"Indy, you were so right. Mo needs what we'll send. We're set for tomorrow, so let's get some sleep. And we can rest easy, knowing the stealth project is our hidden wildcard no matter what the future holds."

Mo pulled the Worldstars aside as soon as they arrived.

"Thanks for what you pulled together. I'll use it in the meeting and when I meet with Bobbi later today. I won't know until early January what she'll get approved, so consider yourselves on holiday break until then. The other teams need to stay after the meeting, but you don't. We'll meet ASAP in January, so you'll be the first to know where Cognicom's heading. Any questions?" There were none, so the Worldstars found a place to sit in the auditorium just before Mo began talking.

"Good morning everyone, and thanks for being here on such short notice. I'm not going to mince words because we have a big problem that's gonna impact Holiday plans. All teams, including bus-admin and tech leads, will work together after this meeting to come up with a game plan we need to get approved. So, let me outline the approach you'll fine-tune afterwards. This afternoon the bus-admin leads will nail down the plan, and I'll take to my boss. Here's the starting point." Mo paused briefly for everyone to focus on him.

"We think the virus was contained and cleanup successful at I and R-Vac labs. Everyone on those teams must be tested immediately;

anyone testing positive will be quarantined. And we want all team members, including the S-Vac team, to limit voluntarily their Holiday social activity just in case. All three labs are closed until early January." Mo paused for the message to register, then continued.

"We need to identify the cause of the leak, so we want all teams to review their safety and handling protocols. Ask me if you want assistance. I need each team to give me a list of additional equipment or people needed so we don't get another breach. Be aware there's heightened urgency for us to get results. Think about what you need to make it so. Finally, there should be no leaks to the media. Nothing got into the environment. The public is safe. Please keep your mouths shut. Otherwise, there could be public or political blowback. Any questions before breaking into teams?" An outspoken senior researcher raised a question that many others wanted answered.

"Do you think any heads are going to roll?" Mo never hid the truth or pulled punches, but always spoke with enough diplomacy so even those taking the hits couldn't complain.

"That's an excellent question. I don't know, but I'm sure the review committee will consider all extenuating factors. Let's focus on the task at hand and not get too far ahead. Any other questions?" None of the grim faces spoke up. Mo hoped that hypochondriacs weren't on any Cognicom team.

The bus-admin leads met early afternoon to finalize a game plan. Nothing was added to what Mo already had; later that afternoon he met with Bobbi.

"My boss already told me we have to find what caused the breach. There's gotta be procedural and maybe personnel changes on the I-Vac and R-Vac teams. Your team's in the clear. You've been doing a great job and if I get my way, you'll be promoted to Senior Manager. Do you think it makes sense to promote some of your people into tech lead positions?"

"Thanks for your confidence in me. I'll keep doing my best. And let's remember that for my team, the whole is greater than the sum of the parts. If we promote anyone to lead another team, we'll lose synergy. Better to have them assist where needed, keeping them together so they stay focused on S-Vac. Let's see how this goes, at least for the first part of next year."

"Sold. Please tell Candice and Spencer their teams are on break until next year. You and your team can take a break too. All of you have earned it. And now, I better hustle to my boss's office." Mo smiled as he shook Bobbi's hand, wishing her the best for the Holidays as well as for the next meeting.

Adom's van had a party-like atmosphere on the drive home. Even Jason stopped worrying and joined the merriment.

"We came out of that looking good. Mo's the hero, and the seniors are on their heels." Adom butted in, half joking.

"Yeah, we've been dodging bullets, thanks to quick-thinking Indy and Su." Su waited for Indy to speak up.

"I guess so. Su, how about you?"

"I'm with Jason. We're looking good, but let's continue downplaying how good we are. And if we help come up with effective I and R-Vacs in the next three years or so, we'll have done our patriotic duty. Then Jason can lead the plan for launching Worldstar Biologicals. By then, Mo can join our inner circle. And everyone, remember to take extra doses of our improved smart pills. All of us must stay healthy." Adom found another opportunity to needle Jason.

"Hey Jason, now don't start acting like a hypochondriac. I swear that every time you pass gas, you think it's colon cancer." Not even Jason could resist smiling. Indy added last words.

"Since we are self-quarantined for New Year's Eve, how about spending it at our place? Last night was good practice." The decision was unanimous.

Another member's only party took place that New Year's Eve: the first meeting of the Guardian Party's inner circle, attended only by "charter members" of this hand-picked group. Congratulations were in order because November elections voted more Guardian members into office.

The inner circle needed to guard the Guardian Party by constructing its version of a CIA. Tonight, someone would be given that assignment, and it didn't take long to reach a unanimous agreement on that person's code name: the Invisible Man.

The Invisible Man already had a plan for the new year. He would recruit moles to collect data or track suspects, placing his snoopers where they would be most useful. The first two locations were obvious: somewhere within the current Administration to track actual intentions, somewhere within NIH to track T-Plague progress. Future events would dictate placement of others. And he already knew his first recruit, his right-hand man, codenamed the Invisible Hand. 2095 would be a very good year.

During the Holidays, Mo spent a couple of days in Baltimore with his parents. They were Jewish and many of his friends where Christian, the combination equipping Mo with an ecumenical approach to religion (celebrated Hanukkah and Christmas) that for him was pragmatic (ignored religion during the week). His mother reminded him again to start a family soon, but his father liked Mo's career-minded attitude, encouraging him to parlay his current position into political or business opportunities, and kidding that father knows best. Mo should build a family after following the money trail.

Mo came back to DC midway between Christmas and New Year's Eve, using the break to prepare for a hectic January. He was pleased with his job because it gave him a sense of patriotic accomplishment. Now his career was beginning to open doors into the political arena where he might walk into business opportunities. With so much going for him, Mo was happily pushing the envelope of his comfort zone.

Mo met with Bobbi early in January, ready to roll out the plan his team had helped build.

"What you gave me has been approved. Now you must make it work. And congratulations on your promotion to Senior Bus-Admin Manager. And here's another plum. You'll be part of an

NIH special committee that will meet with Israel. They're coming to Washington, seeking to license some of our T-Vac patents. Any thoughts on that?"

"Yes, but first I want to thank you for my promotion. You've been my mentor, and I'll keep plugging away. Regarding Israel, I think they want to stockpile smart pills by manufacturing them, rather than buying from us. According to our research people, Israeli R&D is way behind so they're in a weak bargaining position. We aren't going to give anything away, so we can use smart pill stockpiling as leverage to get better Islamic State monitoring. We need to wary of Isilabad, especially if they use a T-Plague crisis to put America on its heels."

"That sounds like solid proactive thinking. You should bring one of your Worldstars to the meetings. Who will you pick?"

"Indy's the best choice. Now let me ask you a question since I have meetings set with Candice and Spencer. Are there any personnel changes on their teams?"

"No changes for the time being, but if I and R-Teams don't show progress, that will change."

"Well, I'm ready to roll. I'm meeting this afternoon with my team and first thing tomorrow with Candice and Spencer. I'll keep you posted."

Jason started the meeting early because Mo had already called him, sharing the good news.

"Do we think the Israeli's have anything to offer us on the development front?" Su shook her head no.

"From what I've read in blogs or research journals, they've made zero progress. They haven't even considered using atomic force microscopy, which is just one of the techniques Adom used to determine virus activation pathways."

Jason said, "Our job will be to tell our negotiators that the Israeli's have a weak bargaining position. Su, who do you think should go with Mo?"

"Indy, without a doubt. She knows the sci-tech, and she reads people well. I'm sure Mo will agree. We should be happy his star is rising. It shields us from a lot of disruptive changes."

"Amen to that," Jason said, then added, "Indy, are you OK with this?"

"Yes. I'll watch the Israeli body language and listen to what they. I can help Mo read between the lines. And speaking of the devil, here he comes."

As he always did, Mo strode in with the team's favorite mood elevators. Since the fridge was stocked with an ample supply of beverages, everyone grabbed food and drink before Mo waded into the meeting.

"The Israeli's want to manufacture smart pills, which means they're coming to license our T-Vac patents, or to trade some of theirs for some of ours. Do you think they have any patents we can use?" Jason spoke first.

"Definitely not. They've made little progress and are not even close to picking the right solution path. And we don't think you want to give our stuff away."

"You are correct, sir. But maybe we can improve our Islamic State monitoring if they let us place some of our covert agents with theirs. So far, we've been relying on what they tell us. We trust them, but only so far. Adom, any thoughts?"

"I've heard additional rumors about an outbreak in Iran. That could be important for tracing possible sources or uncovering links to Isilabad. Let's get Israel to confirm."

"Our think tank agrees with you, so quid pro quo is on tap. I'll need one of you to be with me at our Israeli meetings. Have you decided who?"

Indy smiled as she said, "Yes, we voted and I lost, so you're stuck with me." Mo's smile showed he was pleased.

"I can't think of a better person to be stuck with. Well, that wraps things up. Details to follow."

The delegation leader kept Mo posted on preparations because he and Indy would be key players for technical evaluation. The meeting would be a three-day affair starting on a mid-March Wednesday. The morning session would be an overview attended by both delegations. The afternoon would be devoted to Middle East political issues, followed by a dinner. Thursday morning each delegation would meet separately to assimilate what they had learned, and an afternoon joint session would focus on technical issues. Friday morning each delegation would meet again separately to consider the technical landscape, followed by a luncheon where delegation leaders would conclude the event.

Mo kept Indy in the loop and offered suggestions for how to act. Little did he know how well she had already prepared, but she kept this to herself to conceal her advantage. Mo considered Indy his "stealth weapon" and insisted she attend all sessions, even though some resistance came from those who thought a researcher would be out of place in political style negotiations. How wrong that would prove to be.

March weather turned cold and blustery, adding to the gloom arising from T-Plague rumors. And like many state meetings, it was a low-profile, tight security affair, allowing the press only after the meeting had adjourned.

An unexceptional plenary session launched the affair, and since Mo had briefed Indy thoroughly, she knew what to look and listen for. Mo would be one of the meeting facilitators; Indy's role was listening to words and watching body language, noting any inconsistencies between what was said and what was implied.

Mo presented part of the American position: U.S. needs more soft assets—covert agents—placed in the Middle East for reconnaissance to track T-Plague outbreaks. The Israeli's postured how much they knew and how much they were already sharing. Occasionally they would side-bar, speaking in Hebrew, which frustrated some U.S. delegation members. But when the afternoon session adjourned and one of the Israeli's learned Mo spoke his language, smiles faded from the Israeli delegates.

Mo talked with Indy to compare notes. "What have you picked up?"

"The Israeli's are evasive. Their lead negotiator's body language sent that message loud and clear. Watch for a slight shift in his body position. He twists ever so slightly when dodging uncomfortable questions. By the way, Su and her friend Kayed briefed me last week on Middle East issues Iranians care about. I didn't learn anything new at the morning session."

"I didn't pick up on the lead negotiator's body language. If we play poker, I'll stake you. You'll do some of the presenting at tomorrow morning's session. Just tell everyone what you observed, and compare what you learned with what you already knew. And don't pull any punches. Don't be shy. Can you handle that?"

"Yes. And I'll mingle with the Israeli delegation tonight for some additional signs. We'll have a good time tonight, and an even better time tomorrow."

Mo was uncharacteristically nervous at the start of next morning's session. He summarized how they would build on yesterday's results, then explained why Doctor Indira Ramanujan would speak next. As she stepped to the podium, scrutinized by a skeptical audience, she too had a case of nerves, but it vanished the moment she began to speak.

"Thank you, Mo. And I want to thank all of you for including me. Mo tells me I have a great combination of sociopolitical skills and tech know-how, but you can judge for yourself. I know many people from the Middle East because I talk with people doing refugee volunteer work, and that gives me insight into current events and concerns. I already knew everything the Israelis told us about Iran and possible connections with Isilabad terrorism. And they didn't mention Iran's ongoing drug development with China. We can connect the dots to conclude their outbreak is connected with China's.

"Regarding the Islamic State and terrorism, the Israeli's say they don't know much about possible connections with Iran, and that contradicts what they say about the accuracy of their intelligence. Their body language told me that much is being withheld. My assessment is this. We should push Israel hard for what we want. Any comments on this?" Only silence. The delegation was starting to realize that Indy was more than a mere researcher. Mo picked up where she left off.

"Thank you, Doctor Ramanujan. Let's talk about what we should push for. Then we'll adjourn for lunch, followed by the afternoon tech session..."

Before heading for lunch, several delegates complimented Indy, and she was quick to deflect any praise to Mo. They confessed ignorance about T-Plague, and she said tomorrow's presentation would help. Mo spoke to Indy after the delegates moved on.

"Great job. You spoke like a seasoned negotiator. You earned style points with our delegates. Are you ready for the afternoon session?"

"Yes. I'll ask appropriate questions and mention nothing that's confidential. I'll try to earn more points this afternoon."

Mo let the Israeli negotiator kick off the afternoon tech session. Indy soon realized just how weak the Israeli R&D position is. Nano-techniques or quantum connections, critical for understanding T-Plague, were beyond Israeli capabilities. After asking just one question about the use of atomic force microscopy—Adom had used it to map T-virus topology—she knew the Israeli researchers were clueless; she wouldn't embarrass them further. Mo realized he didn't need to reveal anything about NIH patents. It was abundantly clear the Israelis had struck out. After the meeting, Mo told the American delegation that he and Indira would summarize T-Plague development tomorrow morning.

Friday's morning session was easy for Mo. He simply turned it over to Indy.

"Thank you, Mo, and good morning. Let me say the Israelis are good friends of the United States, but they aren't in our league for drug development. Their procedures aren't as good, and their solution paths are off target. It's not our job to train them, so I would recommend we let them buy more of our smart pills rather than license our patents. And give them a better price if they help us gather intelligence." Indy paused as she shifted to science.

"I believe some of you would like to know more about T-Plague drug development, so my team has put together a slideshow that will help. All this is NIH-confidential, so please treat it accordingly. Here we go."

Although Mo had not yet seen Indy's presentation, he knew he was in for a pleasant surprise. Lights dimmed for the first slide which Indy summarized.

"My team has known each other since grad school days where we coined our nickname, the Worldstars, because of our varied ethnic backgrounds. Our skills and personalities fit together. NIH hired us as a team and Mo knows best how to manage us."

And like all science, drug development is a matter of controlling the matter and energy interaction." Indy showed her next slide.

"As we drill down into the fine-grained details, common sense no longer rules. As we go from the dimensions of our everyday world where classical physics holds, and into the atomic world beyond molecules, even the best minds struggle to grasp the concepts." Indy paused for a moment, then went to the next slide.

"As we summarize here, biotechnology has begun applying the findings of modern physics, and that's a major contributor to why biotech R&D is making headway today in many areas. Nanotechnology allows us to probe deep into matter's structure, and we're learning how life's physical processes originate at the micro level. The next slide highlights some of the major reasons.

"As you can see, we are beginning to deconstruct cellular functioning in ways that, until modern physics came along, were inaccessible. But today, e can model the cell as a factory containing molecular machines. Large molecules, like DNA or RNA, are the machines. Enzymes and proteins function like machines too. And it's not magic, but rather it's governed by subtle laws of nature encapsulated in quantum mechanics. Let me summarize what my S-Vac team is doing.

"This slide shows that we use nanotechnology and quantum biology to integrate four biotechnology disciplines. Each member of my team is an expert in one of the disciplines, and we use advanced techniques to determine how organisms like the T-Plague virus impact humans. We expect our efforts will lead to a route or a pathway we can follow to create an effective drug or vaccine for our piece of the Cognicom Project, which is for symptomatic relief or symptomatic suppression. The next slide summarizes our development steps.

"As you can tell, there are numerous complex steps comprising a T-Plague vaccine development pathway. We must reverse neural entanglement using brain control centers to manufacture appropriate neuro-chemicals. The saying that the devil's in the details holds in R&D. It's hard work, and NIH researchers are among the best biotech workers there are. But take a look at the next slide for some of the reasons why it takes so long to come up with T-Plague vaccines.

"As you can see, drug development is both science and art. We can apply science to identify possible solution paths, and we know how to evaluate each one. But researchers develop the art of knowing when to use intuition gained through experience to leap ahead. I remember an appropriate quote: Serendipity and the prepared mind power us to the future. That is what my team is doing. And as our Cognicom Projects unfold, we need to remember the points I've outlined on the next slide.

"My team knows what it's doing. That's why we have made progress. Perhaps my team can assist the others, but there's no guarantee we can duplicate our success. Lightning rarely strikes twice. And Moses Solstein, our bus-admin leader, has done all he can to harness my team's collective synergy. We need that to continue.

"I know that for most of you, this morning's presentation is a first-time introduction to difficult concepts, and I hope my remarks have given you a better understanding of how my team does its job. In closing, I would like to thank all of you for being such an attentive audience. I'll be happy to answer any questions you might have."

No questions accompanied a smattering of applause. The audience was just beginning to grasp the complexity of this brave new world as Mo returned to the podium to conclude the morning session.

"Thank you, Doctor Ramanujan, for your clear explanation of a most difficult subject. And at this point, I recommend we adjourn for lunch."

While the room emptied, Mo introduced Indy to the delegation leader, Brad Harmon. "Doctor Ramanujan, thank you for your contributions. Our people have learned a lot from you."

"You are most welcome Mr. Harmon, and please call me Indy. Doctor is so formal."

"Indy it is. I've spent my career at NIH, and you are one of the best at combining science and diplomacy. I'm glad you're on our side."

"Thank you, Mr. Harmon. My team wants to reach closure on the T-Plague. The best way is for us to stay together, focused on vaccine formulations."

"Sounds like a plan Mo will implement. But I would like to ask you a question, if I may. Why aren't you the team leader? I can't imagine anyone better qualified than you." Mo spoke for Indy.

"Brad, all four of my R&D scientists are outstanding. And I will go on record stating that Doctor Ramanujan and Doctor Su-Lin Chou combined are the driving force. Current team leader Jason Kittner is an excellent project manager. Having him as official tech leader lets Indy and Su-Lin work better. Indy, am I right?" Indy smiled, nodding in agreement.

"Mo, just keep your team doing their thing. Well, we're set for the afternoon's closing remarks. See you there."

That evening, Mo and the Worldstars would have sandwiches at Jason and Indy's apartment, a perfect way to brief the team while decompressing from a hectic week. When they arrived, Jason hugged Indy and then shook Mo's hand.

"Thanks for covering for all of us. From what Indy phoned in, there won't be any big changes. We want to hear your recap after we have something to eat." Everyone picked a sandwich and drink, and after taking a couple of bites, Mo was ready to unwind by spinning a summary of today's excitement.

"Indy and I were well prepared, thanks to your help. We won't be licensing any patents because Israel has nothing to offer in return. We'll give them a better price on smart pills only if they let us place covert agents. Indy gave our delegation a presentation on biotech drug development that even the skeptics liked. And she pointed out that it's best we keep our team together, assisting the other teams only if they request help. Indy, is there anything you want to add?"

"Just that Mo stays in control as our bus-admin manager."

"Sometimes, I get the feeling you're in control of the entire situation, including me. You're all much brighter, and I know your intentions are good, so I'm happy to be along for the ride. But please, bring me a little closer to your inner circle. And how do you know so much about current events in the Middle East?"

Su said, "I'm the reason because I do volunteer work for Middle East organizations. Let me know if you would like to attend a meeting. You might meet some immigrants that can help you fill in your think tank information gaps."

"I appreciate the offer. Let me check upcoming weekend dates to see what works."

Everyone was ready to call it an evening earlier than usual because the week had been stressful. Many hands made for a quick clean-up, then all departed for well-earned weekends. Afterwards, Indy and Jason sat in the living room, sorting through what had taken place.

Thanks to Mo and you, events broke our way, so wouldn't you say all's well that ends well?" Indy suppressed a yawn before answering.

"Although the optimist in me agrees, I know the future is clouded with uncertainty. Listen to my story of a Buddhist monk. No matter what happened, when people asked if he thought the outcome was good or bad, his answer was always the same: Perhaps. He explained it this way. Sometimes an event leads to a bad outcome, which in turn leads to a good outcome, which in turn leads to a bad outcome. And so, on and on. So, the outcome might be judged good or bad, depending on when the question is asked. So that's why 'perhaps' might be the best answer. Let's leave it there and go to bed. I'm exhausted. Perhaps you can reenergize me." Jason was certain he could make it so.

CHAPTER 14
July 2095

"Summer-Autumn Interlude"
(Thread 3 Chapter 7)

THE WORLDSTARS KEPT SPINNING in all the right directions that summer. Su made everyone recheck their calculations to find mistakes that might be hindering progress, and even though they couldn't find any, Su's confidence satisfied Mo. He told them the other bus-admin leads had encouraged their teams to reach out for help because nothing they had tried got them moving. When Su introduced Mo to several immigrants from the Middle East, they were pleased to explain what Isilabad might be planning, and Mo came away impressed by their solidarity and desire to be part of the modern world, for which they believe America offers the most opportunities. They told him what relatives told them about rumors of Isilabad's terrorist network launching attacks in America, using T-Plague virus obtained from Iran or China. Mo would share at the next think tank meeting all that he was hearing.

Mo did just that, but didn't expect the response. Some of the skeptics thought the Administration's thinking was better, adding that Mo's alarmist predictions were too implausible, too far into the future. There'd be plenty of time to take action once tangible evidence surfaces. Mo listened patiently, then offered a story.

"I understand why you think I'm an alarmist, but I'm trying to be proactive. Are you familiar with the 'Salamander on the Stove' story?" Since they weren't, Mo told his tale. "If you put a salamander in a pot of water and gradually turn up the heat, it ignores the danger and boils alive. I know we don't have much hard evidence, but we must be vigilant. I'm not in charge, only a foot soldier reporting in, but I hope you'll remember what I've said." The meeting chairman added a final comment before switching to another member.

"I want to thank you for your initiative, and please keep doing what you're doing. We'll be as proactive as possible, given the political climate."

The Labor Day weekend marked the unofficial end of summer, bringing with it perfect outdoor activity weather, so the Worldstars planned a Sunday hike ending with a picnic before going to a late afternoon concert. The trail ended near a shady grove; the guys retrieved the food while the ladies picked a table partly in the sun. A pleasant silence accompanied snacking until Jason asked Adom about the music.

"How did you hear about the concert?"

"I never heard of the band, but Whitney follows the music scene and said they're a must see and must hear. Thanks to her public relations connections, she got us free tickets. Su, do you think Kayed will like it?"

"Yes, I think so. He likes new century music even more than I. But that's not the reason I came. I'm here to chaperone you." Indy added to Su's teasing.

"We'll both make sure you stay grounded. No crowd surfing for you." Bantering continued until Jason announced it was time to go, for there remained just enough time to pick up Whitney and Kayed before the show. The guys carried the coolers to Adom's van while the ladies cleaned the table. A minute later the ladies were strolling to the parking lot when Su noticed a commotion.

"Jason looks upset. Why do you think he's arguing with Adom? Once within earshot, Jason's words held the answer.

"I thought I gave you the keys."

"Nope. You had them in your hand when you took the cooler out." Su peered into the van while the squabble continued, and then reported what she saw.

"The keys are sitting on the back seat." Indy added to that.

"Jason, don't look so panic-stricken. It's not the end of the world."

"This is awful! We'll miss the start of the concert. What are we going to do?" Indy handed her cell phone to Jason before answering.

"Why don't you and Adom call his Internet roadside assistance provider to unlock the van?"

"I'm sorry, but I let the service lapse because I never used it. I guess I shouldn't have." Jason tried to cover his mistake by further criticizing Adom.

"I can't believe it. You're always so insistent at the lab that I renew service contracts. I guess when it comes to spending your own money you'd rather risk getting stuck, like we are now." Jason would have said more, but Su intervened.

"Now hold on, Jason. According to Consumer Reports studies, you actually save money in the long run if you don't buy extended warranty or service contracts since the cumulative costs usually exceed the benefits, and that means Adom made the right decision." The three of them kept debating until Indy interrupted.

"I wish Mo were here to give all of you a lesson in crisis management. You're arguing about what caused the problem rather than solving it. And here's the solution. You guys should use my cell phone to search for then call a garage that'll drive here to open the van."

Su was the only one other than Indy to see the humor in the situation. "I think the three of us should enroll in an online contingency planning workshop." Indy's smile said all is forgiven.

"You guys are in charge. Su and I are heading back to the table so I can tell her how Jason's behavior might force me to make additional revisions to his marriage contract." Although she was joking, Jason's expression said otherwise until he caught on.

The gals chatted more while the guys fumed less. Jason calmed down enough to call Whitney and Kayed about the delay, then he rationalized the incident.

"Maybe it's good the keys are locked inside. Perhaps the traffic will be lighter when we get out of here. Who knows, maybe we missed a bad accident."

"Could be, but come on, we'll be outta here as soon as the service truck shows up."

The Worldstars were back on the road an hour later. Although they would miss the start, the best part of the concert awaited. Adom reminded Indy to call again.

"Hi Whitney, it's Indy. We'll pick you up in fifteen minutes." Her tone changed abruptly. "Oh my God, that's awful! Stay put." She disconnected the call, then spoke.

"There's been shooting at the concert. Two gunmen sprayed the crowd with bullets as the concert began. Thank God we weren't there. I'll call Kayed and tell him the news." Plans changed because of the attack. No one had much of an appetite, so Adom dropped everyone off and then drove home.

Su stayed with Indy and Jason that evening. After watching the news, Jason gave his opinion of the day's events.

"The Buddhist monk's answer sure fits us today. Locking the key inside kept us out of harm's way. We didn't have to dodge real bullets. I wonder what the police will say."

"Could be any number of possibilities," Indy replied. "Maybe they're a terrorist sleeper cell. Maybe they're disgruntled morons getting even for something that happened to them. Su, what do you think?"

"All that, and I'll add maybe the shooters are insane. Even the U.S. is not as kind and gentle as everyone had hoped. This will be on national news for the next couple of days."

Indy added, "I hope there's no connection between this and Middle East terrorism. That would put people on edge. We'll have to hear what the police find out. I don't know about you, but I've seen and heard enough for one day. I'm going to bed."

The shooting turned out to be the work of two psychologically disturbed mid-twenties high school dropouts, just one of the high-risk profiling groups Securityguard planned to monitor more closely. The Guardian Party publicized the attack, hoping to convince the public the government had become too soft, but further complaints about the Administration retreated into the background once the shooting faded from the front page.

Autumn that year stayed warm and clear. Indy decided the time was right for an October outing to Baltimore's historically rich Inner Harbor, for it was her duty to keep Jason and Adom from becoming R&D drudges. She recruited Su to help plan a weekend that would be sure to please. The Worldstars would leave early Saturday morning to tour Baltimore's Inner Harbor, including the National Aquarium. Sunday would be their fine arts day, combining a morning tour of Baltimore's Art Museum and an afternoon concert at Symphony Center. Since Indy was teaching Jason to appreciate the fine arts and Su thought Adom should learn about them too, the ladies lectured on the drive why the guys would like the sights and sounds.

Saturday went like clockwork, ticking in step with Indy's itinerary that kept track of all they packed into one day. The foursome toured two of the historic ships, then waded through much of the Aquarium until stopping for a late lunch. Adom was given an assignment he was well qualified for—scouting out a restaurant—and he met everyone's expectations because there were so many to choose from. Afterwards, they took an Inner Harbor boat cruise that ended only a couple of blocks from Old Otterbein Church, Baltimore's oldest, built in 1785. Indy wanted to walk there but she could tell Jason was wearing out, so she suggested he choose a snack bar before the group went to the hotel.

Sunday gave Indy a reading on her work in progress. If she and Jason were to go the Vow-Cer route, she wanted him to like the things she did because she wouldn't force him to go places with her if he weren't interested. Today would be a chance for Jason to show how much progress he had made.

The Worldstars were sitting in a restaurant near Symphony Center when Jason asked Su for help. "Could you explain again why I should like all the music we just heard?"

"Let me guess. I imagine you didn't enjoy the first piece, Verklarte Nacht."

"I sure didn't. Indy, did you?"

"I can understand why you didn't like it. For some composers, a listener needs to prepare for what they'll hear, and that's why Su gave us an intro to Schoenberg and his twelve-tone technique, and I talked about the poem the piece reflects. Did I like it? Intellectually I did because I could hear a connection between the music and the poem it alludes to. But emotionally, I didn't. There's a lot of contemporary and post-contemporary symphonic music that leaves me out in the cold. That's just the way I feel. Some people might feel the same and others might differ. Su, chime in please."

"I tend to agree. Too much of post-modern symphonic music substitutes an orchestra for rock music instruments and it's a mismatch, like a tin whistle on a fire truck. Jason, did you like the second piece better?"

"I did. I could almost feel the rhythm of the sea in the music. Adom, how about you?"

"Me too, and according to Su, Debussy's music matches up with impressionistic paintings, where the mood or subject is implied. Am I right?"

"You get an A for paying attention to our lecture. Most people like impressionistic paintings because their imaginations can picture what's in them. That's why you liked La Mer. And the melody's more traditional than the Schoenberg piece."

"Jason and I are on the same page. And maybe he's with me when I say I liked the third piece best. Indy, what Beethoven symphony is that?"

"It's his seventh, called the Dance Symphony because of its rhythmic dancelike cadence. It's his most popular. Everyone likes its melodies, right Jason?"

"You bet. Adom and I see eye-to-eye on this. I mean ear-to-ear. If I don't correct myself, he will, so I got there first." Adom found a clever way to change the subject.

"I think we fellows should finally get high marks from the ladies for our efforts, and we can talk more about fine arts later. But for now, let's do some fine dining. Here comes the food."

The drive home reminded Jason of a Worldstars outing three years ago. Then as now, Adom driving, Su sitting next to him chatting, Indy sleeping against Jason's shoulder. *Our dream careers started so well back then. We won the prize; Su cracked the T-Plague code. But events since December make me worry, and our progress has slowed.*

It's time for me to practice what Indy's teaching me. I won't worry about what I can't control, and I'll remember the Buddhist monk's answer. But I do know one thing for certain: I'm lucky to have Indy. She keeps me centered. I'll keep her safe.

Jason stopped worrying all the way home.

CHAPTER 15
November 2095

"Washington Outbreak"
(Thread 3 Chapter 8)

Washington's T-Plague outbreak occurred the week before Halloween, as if cued by the Guardian Party's public relations department. Public concern was palpable, especially for parents with young children. Cynical headlines like "White House tricks Public with unwanted Treat" appeared in major news media, expressing the overall sentiment.

The outbreak wasn't as bad as the banners blared. Only twenty-five confirmed cases were reported and immediately quarantined, but a wave of panic swamped emergency rooms. An NIH press release announced that virus escaping from their BSL-5 labs would be virtually impossible because they were equipped with state-of-the-art safety measures, listing its failsafe mix of double airlocks, micro filters, and negative pressure air systems. No mention was made about last December's lab containment breach.

Adom guessed some unwitting traveler brought the virus to Washington. CDC continued backtracking all cases, identifying Boston as the prime source. And with only a handful of new cases reported during the next two weeks, CDC announced the Washington outbreak had been successfully contained. But the damage had been done; the public's fear persisted because non-government health organizations asserted that once a virus escaped into the environment, additional outbreaks are inevitable, and to date, even the experts had little to say about safety precautions, other than staying locked in a germ-free room until vaccines are available.

Adom expected to learn more about T-Plague current events at a Guardian Party town hall meeting that would double as a date with Whitney. He thought Indy would like to see Guardian Party P.R. in action so he extended an invitation and was pleased she and Jason accepted. Adom would drive the foursome Saturday evening.

Indy had concerns not only for the T-Plague but also for Whitney. *I like Whitney and so does Adom. But she might like him more than vice-versa. I hope he's being fair. Women deserve honesty in new-wave relationships. I know Adom's intentions, play now and settle down later. As long as Whitney knows this too, she can deal with Adom on her terms. I'll chit-chat while Adom's driving.*

"So, how's life been treating you? Adom hasn't told us what you've been up to lately."

"It's been good. I went sailing in Chesapeake Bay late September with a fellow I met at a social club. I liked it, and I plan to do more. We're vacationing between Christmas and New Years at a Caribbean sailing school." Indy smiled, thinking *Good for you. Keep your social life afloat.*

"Jason and I have never gone sailing, but I'm sure he'll add that to our bucket list."

"It's already on the list, but it hasn't come to the surface yet. But when it does, it'll be smooth sailing for Indy and me." Adom groaned a reply before Jason could continue.

"There he goes again, playing with words. I swear, Indy's polishing his literary skills even faster than I'm trimming his love handles."

"Please leave Jason to me. I'll take care of reducing his rough edges. But I want to hear more about Whitney. How has work been?"

"It's been busy. Some of our clients are worried about how public T-Plague concerns will impact their businesses. We have a number of service industry clients, and if too many people are afraid of being exposed to the T-Plague, business is going to suffer because people won't go out."

"Does your agency do any work for political parties like the Guardian Party?"

"We handle some public-sector clients, but we haven't done work for the Guardians yet. I've heard they're professional and well organized. And they capitalize on high visibility movers and shakers. Look at who's speaking tonight, the popular Maryland senator David Rushman who defected from traditional parties early on and helped launch the Guardian Party. That's why he's considered its founding father." Jason's ears perked up.

"What do you think of their message? Is it resonating with the public?"

"Well from what I've heard, they do make a convincing case that all recent administrations have let the public down. And as far as we know, Guardians are what they say. Altruistic and for the greater good. No hidden agendas uncovered yet. But let's see what happens as they gain more power. And we'll get a reading tonight on what the public thinks."

"Whoa. Traffic is heavy. If this is any indication of public interest, Rushman's crew will do well in next year's elections. I was going to drop you off and find you inside, but that won't work in this crowd. Let's walk after I park."

The hall was packed but Jason shouldered them to a spot just behind the seating area that would be good for watching and listening. Indy noted right from the start how resonant the welcoming remarks sounded.

"Good evening fellow Patriots, and thank you for your support. The Guardian Party is growing to protect the best values we stand for and the best in all of us. Our Government is failing us across the board! Current Administration is weak on National Security, weak on surveillance, weak on controlling runaway biotechnology, weak on maintaining our nation's infrastructure. They're spending billions on foreign aid rather than investing right here at home. Look at what their bungling has brought us: the T-Plague. Do you believe them when they say it's under control? Well, listen to the facts we present and you'll know it's not. So please join our ranks to win back America.

"Our speaker tonight is one of America's leading statesmen. He knows it's time for a change and has championed our cause right from the get-go. I won't chronicle his stellar resume because his qualifications are obvious. So without further ado, ladies and gentlemen, please welcome Maryland's senior senator, the Honorable David Rushman."

Rushman's remarks summarized what he did to start the Party and what the Guardian Party wants to accomplish, then followed up with convincing evidence showing the current Administration is unable to deal with impending crises.He urged voters to empower Healthguard and Securityguard agencies to coordinate what needs to be done, and then opened the floor to questions.

The breadth and depth of audience concern surprised Jason, as did the panel's convincing answers. Adom lobbied to leave soon to avoid a traffic jam, recommending they stop at a coffee bistro to recap the night's adventure. Whitney gave directions to one of her favorites, and twenty minutes later the group was enjoying biscotti and latte.

Jason remarked, "I never realized how concerned people are. And most of them seem to know more than I do. I guess I spend too much time at the lab, rather than looking at the world around me." Indy said, "Don't be too hard on yourself. I give you high marks for branching out. Whitney, what's your take on what you heard?"

"That meeting was right on point for the Guardians. Well planned and well executed. Clear message. Convincing speakers. Turnout and questions show how worried the public is. I think the Guardians came away with new members, along with donations and signatures. I want to see how local media pick up on tonight's meeting and what happens when other cities have outbreaks. A story like this has legs."

Adom made one comment that put a lighter spin on what they had heard. "Well I'm not ready to donate. I'm still guarding my wallet. Hey, let's beat the feet."

Adom dropped off Indy and Jason first, then Whitney, but declined her invitation to come in. Even the most care-free Worldstar was beginning to worry.

Media furor subsided in the coming weeks, but T-Plague remained a topic people talked about; fear of exposure cut into attendance at social venues or public places, disrupting Holiday travel plans; airport traffic was down fifteen percent.

Indy refused to live her life in fear, for there was no reason if she and Jason kept taking stronger smart pills and were sensible about where they went. That's why she invited the team to an early December literary society holiday party. After appetizers and a light meal, invited speakers from New York and Philadelphia would present recent book or poetry summaries.

Adom drove on that seasonally cold but snow-free Sunday afternoon, and Indy, being the Worldstars' poet laureate, led the discussion.

"Now fellows, please consider the party a pleasant way of learning more about literature. The speakers will give an overview of current trends and then describe how their works fit in."

Su added, "Indy has written enough poetry to fill two books. She occasionally sprinkles them into our conversations. And she's continued studying poetry since our college days."

"She sometimes quotes a couple of lines to me," Jason said. "And she says I'm getting better connecting them to the topic we're talking about. Maybe someday she'll be a speaker at a club meeting." "We're here and parking's good, so let's go in for some good food and drink. And don't worry about me, Jason. I'll save room so

I can digest at least some of what I hear."

Turn-out disappointed the party organizers. One of them was Julisa, a good friend of Indy, who greeted the Worldstars.

"Hi, Indy, and thanks for bringing your friends. I'm sorry so many people didn't show. Maybe they'll be here later. Maybe other plans got in the way, or maybe they're scared of the T-Plague. Even our invited poetry speaker canceled at the last minute."

"A smaller audience simply makes the talk more inviting and personal. I think it'll go just fine." Julisa looked at her fellow organizers and then made an offer.

"We've been friends for a couple of years. You've shared some of your poetry, and we've encouraged you to get it published. Have you done that?"

"No, not yet. I'll do that when I get old."

"Well, how about this. Would you be willing to fill in for the guest poet? It would be a big help, and as you said, a small audience is easy to handle. I'll introduce you and everyone will understand you're helping make the evening enjoyable. Would you?" Su didn't give Indy a chance to decide.

"Indy's been my best friend for years, and I've pushed her to publish but she hasn't. Maybe tonight will push her in the right direction if she reads a couple of her poems. It'll be good for her and the audience." Indy folded her arms, smiling while resting her chin on an uplifted hand.

"How can I possibly refuse an offer like that. But I'm making no promises about my poems or my delivery. And I'll need to write down several of them along with some remarks." Julisa was delighted; one of the other organizers scurried to get paper and pen.

"Thank you so much! And don't be nervous. You'll have a most appreciative audience."

The party-goers didn't mind the reduced attendance. While Adom joked there'd be more appetizers for everyone, the organizers mingled, letting everyone know about the last-minute change. Indy would be the final speaker. Though she tried not to appear nervous, anxiety had taken her appetite away, but as she rose to speak, a calm clarity took over.

"Good evening, everyone. My name is Indy Ramanujan, and like many of you, not only do I like poetry, but I've studied it and have even tried writing some. There's a saying that you should always save the best for last. Well tonight, that probably won't apply, but what we can say is our organizers have saved the surprise speaker for last. And I hope you get something out of my comments or a couple of my poems.

"Let me start by saying an appreciation of poetry, like that of music or art, is intensely personal. Human beings are designed to react to music or painting or writing. You might say it's in our

DNA. And it helps, though it's not always necessary, if you have a little background understanding of the particular fine art you're interacting with. So, let me give you my take on what poetry is all about.

"Poets use words to create a context and a mood in which they convey a message to the reader. Poetry comes in many styles. Some are easier for the listener to relate to than others. As for my style, I would label it modern metaphysical or lyrical poetry. I try to paint with words a picture that gives insight that connects emotionally with some aspect of the human condition, the life we experience. And I use words and meter and rhyming schemes that are pleasing to the ear. My poetry might not be considered modern or post-modern, and might not be currently fashionable. But the style I use is considered timeless. There will always be people who enjoy it, for it was created by the great poets of the past, and it speaks to us today. "I'd like to read several of my poems to illustrate what I mean. The first is called 'The Spiral Stairway,' which is my metaphor for our path through life. I won't insult your intelligence by interpreting it. You'll easily find a meaning that suits you. It's eight verses in length, and I would like to read it to you now.

We each explode into the world,
On trajectory all our own.
Ignited by our parent's love,
A gift for us alone.

Intending you to reach your dream,
With everything it holds.
And so that bold ascent begins,
Star-bound odyssey unfolds.

Onward upward so you go,
Stepping higher and higher.
Surpassing all the boundaries,
An ever-widening gyre.

But then one day an odd event,
You're suddenly startled to find,
The arc's no longer upward bound,
The apex is behind.

But don't despair the downward stair,
There's an opportunity.
To better view what you've come through,
And assess reality.

The mind's eye sees more clearly now,
It's the lens you see life through.
How sharp becomes the focal point?
That answer's left for you.

Dwell only briefly in the past,
Don't rest on laurels won.
Better to inhabit now,
And build on what's been done.

And if you give back more to those,
No matter who they be.
A priceless gift awaits for you,
Glimpse immortality."

Indy paused for her words to take hold. "It takes me several readings to get comfortable with a poem, and maybe you're the same way. There's a famous quote by Francis Bacon:

'Some books should be tasted, some devoured, but only a few should be chewed and digested thoroughly.'

"I think the same applies to poetry. Wouldn't you agree? It's getting late, and I don't want to wear out my welcome. Besides, there's hardly anything worse than listening to someone drone on when you've had enough. So, I'll end with a poem that's a bit of a self-portrait. I call it 'The Simple Scholar.' It's brief but to the point.

I'd say that I'm mediocre,
In all I've aspired to be.
And though I have tried it can't be denied,
What's lacking is profundity.

But still I can study life's drama,
And consider from singular view.
Wise persons may find they've left nothing behind,
My wish simple wisdom shows through.

"So, there you have it, two poems from Indira. Thank you for being such an accommodating audience, and best wishes for the Holidays."

The applause was genuine, as were Julisa's closing remarks thanking Indy for being such a good sport, and as people started leaving, several complimented Indy.

A party atmosphere prevailed on the drive home, during which Indy confessed to being stressed before delivering her poems. "Public speaking is exciting, but tiring. I'm drained."

Su said, "You're a natural, and here's why. You project a command of what you're talking about. You're comfortable with who you are, and you have so much social intelligence and empathy. Not everyone has that blend. It's a gift you've been blessed with." Indy smiled and said, "Perhaps."

All Cognicom teams ended this year better than the last when a containment breach shut down the labs. They used the weeks before Christmas to prepare for Holiday parties and for steps that all researchers wished would finally unleash progress. The Worldstars made up for last year by celebrating at a New Year's Eve party hosted at Adom's sports club. Su surprised everyone. She was a better dancer than anyone expected, but then she explained why: playing the piano requires hand-foot coordination of keys and pedals. Adom kidded back, saying her explanation sounded good, even though she's on the dance floor, not at the keyboard.

Jason needed no explanation why his primal instincts were aroused. The dance floor featured a bevy of attractive ladies prancing in the New Year. He was primed to get in bed with Indy, confident she would let him add an exclamation point to the evening.

Indy awoke at first light having slept fitfully, disturbed by Jason's snoring and a swarm of unsettling thoughts flitting through her head. She had big plans for the new year and was worried Jason might not be ready to share the load. As she got up to make coffee, the Buddhist monk story flickered in her mind.

The New Year roared in like an unchained beast. T-Plague charged into Boston, then leapfrogged over America's midsection to infect San Diego, spreading relentlessly either by accidental containment breaches or unwitting travelers, then spreading locally by air,water,or human contact.Rural areas were last to be impacted. Thanks to aggressive CDC protocols, outbreaks were quickly contained, limiting the number of confirmed cases in each location to at most fifty.But the numbers would balloon if outbreaks spread, and testing centers could become overloaded because people often mistook Flu symptoms for the T-Plague.

The CDC had tracked enough cases to draw frightening conclusions: the virus spontaneously switches from remissive to active states, causing flare-ups in old cases. There is no natural immunity, and the worst side effect is cognitive impairment. Fuzzy thinking improves but not completely, and worsens every time symptoms reoccur.

China, Israel, and the U.S. are slow-moving train wrecks that riveted the media. Governments hadn't come up with effective crisis intervention plans, and Europe braced itself because it's only a matter of time before it too becomes a viral battle zone.

Mo knew more about the political situation than most of his associates, but never revealed how or how much he knew. Nor did he reveal the depth of his concern. He decided to tap into the Worldstars for more assistance but had to proceed carefully for although they liked him, there were limits to their trust. *Now's the time for the Worldstars to bring me into their confidence. I'll make an unannounced visit and plead my case.*

Mo was lucky. The Worldstars were holding an impromptu meeting when he walked in, bringing an air of confidence and favorite mood elevators that helped him redirect the conversation.

"It comes as no surprise there's urgency surrounding Cognicom. There's no breathing room on the tech front, and none on the political front either. I'm plugged into sources that tell me the situation is much more serious than what's officially given to the media. It's not a full-blown crisis yet, and I hope it doesn't come to that, but some of the think tanks are drawing up contingency plans. And that's where I need your help. And look at it this way. By helping me, you're helping yourselves. For this to work, you need to trust me as I trust you. I know how close-knit you are. And I hope by this time you have confidence in me." Mo stopped there, waiting for Jason to break the pregnant pause.

"What are your intentions?"

"I'll level with you. NIH likes me. I'm part of a stealth think tank that's trying to stay ahead of the situation. We've got a good handle politically, but it would help if we had more of a window into R&D possibilities going forward. I would like us to form sort of a companion stealth project inside our official project. Believe me, this could be our life preserver if some of the dire predictions come true." Mo's beeper went off; his boss was assembling her direct reports. "Damn, just when I was getting to the good part. How about we reconvene first thing Monday?" Indy knew instinctively what to say. "Mo, please call Jason at home tonight. You go, and we'll finish up here." Mo agreed, then dashed off.

Jason was the first to speak. "Am I missing something or did Mo just make us an offer we can't refuse? Su, what's your take?"

"I want to hear Adom, then Indy's position before I give you mine. Adom, what do you think?"

"I think Mo's being honest. I don't think it's some sort of loyalty test, and I don't think he's aware of our stealth project. And his political network must be onto something. We already have enough tech tidbits to help him. Indy, how about you?"

"My instincts tell me we can trust him. And he doesn't need to know about our actual stealth project. We'll control the amount and timing of what he gets. And isn't it better to be part of the action than a bystander, especially when it's win-win? Su, how about you?"

"Yes, it's in everyone's best interest. And let me add some tech details. We need to use our pilot runs to stockpile our supply of improved smart pills, because NIH hasn't geared up manufacturing for what's going to be needed. But they'll need to, and soon. There'll be pressure to launch an improved S-Vac, so we need to get something approved ASAP. We do that and we'll be out of the crosshairs. Then Mo can control how much assistance we give to the I and RVac teams. They'll need it if they ever wake up. We need to be useful, but not tip our hand. Otherwise, we'll be back in the crosshairs. And let's start monitoring ourselves for symptoms."

Indy was the first to spot a problem.

"We'll have to adjust our solution path and timeline if we want to get something approved ASAP, but that'll work because we can follow up with another formulation that works better. Look at it this way. We've just engaged the enemy in the first battle, but this is a war. Jason, how about you summarize for us."

"Will do, but let me add a concern Mo didn't mention. I think long-term cognitive impairment will be an enormous drain on the healthcare system and the economy. And now for the summary. We go with Mo but don't tip our hand. We provide enough stuff to help but not so much we draw attention. And we build up a supply of smart pills just in case outbreaks spread faster. That should do it." Indy added what Jason had overlooked.

"And all of us, including Mo, will join us Sunday noon at our place to nail it down."

"Sorry. I didn't think of that. But let me add final requirements. Adom brings drinks, Su brings dessert, Indy and I handle the rest." Indy answered Mo's call that evening. "Please join the Worldstars Sunday noon at our place for an induction ceremony. You've been voted into the Worldstars inner circle. Just bring yourself and your acceptance speech."

Sunday went even better than Mo's greatest expectation. He had earned Worldstars' trust, and they rewarded him with novel ideas he could take to his think tank. In return, he would requisition additional equipment for which he hadn't a clue what it would do but was sure he'd have no trouble getting. Before he left, Mo warned that Healthguard and Securityguard agencies were political wildcards; he and his think tank would need to track their moves.

"Thank you all for your vote of confidence. No matter what happens, our team is moving in the right direction. I'll make sure my boss knows how much you're doing. It'll earn all of us a bunch of atta-boys we can cash in when we need to. And I bet we never need to use them to cancel an aw-shit. The joke goes that no matter how many atta-boys you earn, one awe-shit cancels them all."

Spring came early that year, helping bolster the nation's sagging spirits. No serious outbreaks had occurred since mid-January, so a skittish public was beginning to settle down, but a foreboding always lurked close to the surface.

Mo did an excellent job managing NIH expectations, and the Worldstars were confident their just-approved formulation would be enough to demonstrate tangible progress. Adom kidded that the Worldstars were "in the flow," but when Jason replied he hoped their efforts weren't flowing down the drain, Indy snapped at him.

"Come on, a team leader's words set an example. You can do better than that."

"Sorry. I'll try harder to project a PMA. You know, a positive mental attitude." Su added to the reprimand.

"Sometimes you project PMS instead of PMA. And since you're working to understand women better, I shouldn't have to explain what I mean." Indy winked at Su because Adom had to explain the acronym. *Jason's lucky I don't have it, and for women that do, it lessens with age. Perhaps I won't suffer from postmenopausal symptoms either.*

Even with Indy's assistance, Su struggled to improve S-Vac further but wouldn't quit, often working weekends. She agreed when Indy cautioned her to avoid burning out, replying that her Middle East volunteer group gives her a stress-relieving change of pace, pointing to one such example. Kayed, the Syrian immigrant she dated casually, would take her Sunday to a current events Islamic State lecture for which he'd lead a Q&A session. He could speak authoritatively from experience, having been a humanities professor at an Isilabad university until its government put even more oppressive restrictions on what he could say.

Mo joined them afterwards for dinner at Kayed's favorite Middle East restaurant. He treated Kayed to a dessert favorite—cakelike Nammourah and Turkish coffee. In return, Kayed answered Mo's questions about how Isilabad's leader, the Exalted Ruler, views the West.

"Do you think the Islamic State will soften its criticism of Modernity?"

"It depends on the time frame. Short-term, say five years or so, yes. But only to appear more flexible. Long-term, I think not. The hardliners want to dismantle progress, take us back to Muhammad's world. The liberals in America have this kinder and gentler world view that doesn't work when confronting Middle East terrorism. It ultimately takes boots-on-the-ground to get terrorists' attention. And the longer we dance around the problem, the bigger it becomes."

"Isn't the Islamic State hypocritical by ranting against the West and then using 22nd century technology? They make great use of the Internet and megamedia, not to mention weapons they buy from China and Russia. And their leaders seem to enjoy the trappings of the privileged."

"Yes, it's expedient for them to use whatever works. They use a traditional Middle East quotation, 'The enemy of my enemy is my friend,' to rationalize what they do. They're using modern medical technology because they're concerned T-Plague will cross the border from Israel or Iran. They're supposed to be studying the virus, but my sources hear nothing about what they're up to or what luck they have controlling outbreaks. But I agree with you. Their ranting hides a private agenda for raw power." Su added her comments.

"I study neuroscience and behavioral psychology, and when I consider the situation in this context, I draw two conclusions. First, emotions or faith outweigh logic or reason in the short-run. Second, societies always struggle adapting to progress. But don't you think most of your people want Modernity? How long will it take for the extremists to wither away?"

"You are correct. The majority crave Modernity, but a small band of extremists, once they gain power and weaponry,are hard to dislodge.North Korea's a prime example.As long as we can contain them, I think the West will let the situation ride. But if they get their hands on WMD's, the West will escalate to a shooting war."

Mo said, "It's been a long afternoon for you. You must be tired. Thanks again for letting me pester you with questions.And I hope to Allah or Yahweh or whatever name we choose, that we stay strong enough to keep Isilabad under control."

"That is my wish also, and that of the civilized world. I will be pleased to talk with you anytime you like.I hope my answers help." "They do, and that's why I'll always buy you at least a dessert.

I don't want free advice, because you know the joke. Free advice is worth what it costs.Your answers are worth a lot to me."

CHAPTER 16
June 2096

"A Pregnant Pause"
(Thread 3 Chapter 9)

EUROPE'S T-PLAGUE IMMUNITY EXPIRED in May when outbreaks occurred in Berlin and Paris, following the now predictable pattern: metropolitan area hit first,spreading into the countryside.But panic is always unpredictable; emotions always overwhelm reason in the so-called superior social species—homo sapiens. Media coverage hyped the ensuing hysteria.

Indy and Jason were watching a weekend news special that spotlighted the situation, but seeing public reaction added a deeper dimension. Indy could see Jason's optimism for their promised tomorrow draining away.

"Stop worrying.Our world isn't ending.Don't let external events we can't control dominate our world."

"But think about what you like to say.Let the future come to us. And from the looks of it, I don't like what's coming our way."

"You're not paying attention.Yes, we have to let external events come our way. We have no control over them. But we can't live our own lives contingently. Otherwise, we're victims of the future, not participants."

"You're much bolder than I am. Sorry if I disappoint you. Will you be mad at me if I push back our Vow-Cer date?"

"Of course not, silly. Sooner or later you'll come to terms with your sentiments. Let me match you with a George Bernard Shaw character in his play *The Devil's Disciple*. Setting is our Revolutionary War. The main character is a mild-mannered minister who becomes a leader because those turbulent times are for him a call to action. Something will either call you to action or not. It'll be your choice, so make it for yourself and not for anyone else. Otherwise, you'll always regret it."

"Does this mean you're tearing up our marriage contract?"

"Of course not. I'm not going anywhere, at least not until something better comes along. Look, our personal lives won't be much affected if another local outbreak occurs. We'll simply raise our smart pill dosage and lower our crowd-level socializing. Public concern will grow, especially for families with young children. But for the time being, that doesn't concern us." Jason felt better, but he failed to notice Indy's body language; this time she did not re-cross her legs.

It was after dinner on an early June Friday when Indy announced she was going to a Saturday talk hosted by a local wellness center. She invited Jason, but he begged off, claiming he was in good enough shape and would rather watch an afternoon Co-NFL game. *He didn't even ask why I'm going.* Indy shrugged before getting up to leave the kitchen. "Suit yourself."

"Sorry. I should have asked you why you want me to go."

"The talk is about home childbirth. If I like what I hear, I'm going to enroll because I'm pregnant." Jason froze, as if struck by lightning.

"Damn, this changes everything! How can we possibly handle a kid with the world all topsy-turvy?"

"Look, the world is indifferent to us, whether or not it's in a state of panic. And I'm perfectly capable of handling pregnancy, so join me if you want to. It starts at one-thirty and lasts until three. I'm going shopping before and running errands after. Maybe we can have dinner out later." Jason corrected his blunder, accepting on the spot.

Nearly one hundred persons attended, mostly couples, but also a handful of single women. Jason could tell from questions that many were concerned about the T-Plague. Birth at home seemed to be a lower risk if expectant mothers would follow the speaker's safety precautions. She was thorough and competent, and most of the women—including Indy—registered afterwards for classes. Sessions included bi-weekly lectures followed by exercise on Saturday mornings.

Jason made up at dinner for his morning faux pas, ordering a decadent chocolate dessert for Indy that he paired with Brandy Alexander.

"This is tasty. I like it. I'll have to add the S-phrase 'sometimes surprising' to your description. Where did you learn to match desserts with drinks?"

"I got it from Adom, and he should know because he specializes in desserts. He asked about the occasion, and I told him we're celebrating your pregnancy. I hope you aren't mad I told him."

"No, but he's the first, other than you, to know. I'll have to tell Su, now that he knows."

"I thought he'd be happy for us, but the news seemed to trouble him. He stumbled for what to say. He recovered, but seemed only lukewarm. Maybe he thought as I did when you first told me. What do you think is bothering him?"

"You're his best friend. He's probably worried you won't pal around with him anymore. But tell him not to worry. Having a child won't crimp your lifestyle."

"I know. But as I learned this afternoon, yours will be if I don't share the load. I promise to do my part. The couples I talked with seemed to know what to expect. Nearly half are like we are, co-friend committed, awaiting the right time for the Vow-Cer. And most of the fellows I talked with are professionals.

"And since you've added 'surprise' to my S-list, I have another for you. I've come up with a delivery plan. You can give birth at my parent's home. Mom can be midwife and Dad your physician."

"Why that's a wonderful idea. Do you think they'll agree?"

"I called them last night and they were thrilled. Mom invited us for dinner tomorrow. Is it OK I accepted?"

"Of course. And by the way, I joined an expectant mothers support group. I talked with a bunch of the women this afternoon, and I like them, one in particular. Jennifer Conklin's her name. We have the same early February due date. And her husband Russell attended too. Older and distinguished looking. He's a senior NIH administrator who knows about Cognicom projects. Small world after all."

The weeks trudged by for Mo because Cognicom was barely creeping forward, posing his biggest challenge, but instead of complaining, he transformed the problem into an opportunity by seeking additional networking connections. His superiors, noticing his resilience, opened doors to higher levels. Though he wasn't the self-promoting type, Mo's star kept rising. He continued delivering technical insights, thanks to the Worldstars' efforts, and in return he kept them posted about the political landscape. Mo decided to surprise everyone by canceling a Friday meeting, replacing it with a Saturday afternoon of horse racing at Pimlico, the nation's second oldest race track. But there was one condition: Adom must drive because his van offered a refreshing change of venue from their lab's humdrum conference room. On the drive to Baltimore, Mo would steer a Worldstars-only meeting.

"Jason, you were right. The government wants to stockpile smart pills ahead of an outbreak. That means our S-Vac formulation will be the primary line of defense after victims take our smart pill. Su, how effective will it be?"

"The latest formulation that passed acceptance testing does a fair job on symptomatic relief. It also slows down the onset of dementia. But we don't know how quickly it loses potency. That's what we're working on now."

"My boss can live with that, especially since the other teams have nothing to show. If an outbreak occurs, we might be asked to assist them even more, but we don't need to do anything yet."

Jason added, "Building a stockpile takes time, so here's what I think the government will do. They'll start by rationing smart pills to the people who need them the most, probably including politicians who have the most pull. But I don't think the public will stand for it, especially if the government can't show progress, and that will tighten the screws further on Cognicom. And then Healthguard starts dispensing bogus pills, like placebos, and places the blame on us."

"Now you're thinking like a politician. I think I'll take you too my next think tank meeting. Hey, don't panic! I'm just kidding. But I haven't looked at stockpiling that way, and that's something to consider. Any others ideas?" Indy offered one.

"We might find some variation among different ethnic types if there were cooperation among different countries. Any chance for this?"

"Afraid not. Every country is guarding what they're doing. But our sources tell us we're the only one with anything promising, even though it's minimal."

Adom asked, "When do you think we might be in danger from kidnapping or hacking into our research?"

"I think that's a long way from happening, but it's worth considering. Cognicom researchers won't be the only ones who'd be in danger, and that's the pitch the Guardian Party makes for extending Securityguard and Healthguard meddling. My think tank predicts the Guardian Party will gain seats in the November elections even if there's no major outbreak. We haven't found tangible threats to Cognicom researchers, but a betting man might bet on it in the future. But let's table your worry because we're at the track. It's time to focus on the thoroughbreds, not the Techno-Plague, so our meeting is adjourned."

Outbreaks occurred before summer's end, this time in urban centers of developing countries, hitting Brazil the hardest, followed closely by Argentina, but India and all of Africa remained untouched. Media coverage hyped the human suffering intensified by substandard healthcare systems. The U.S. had no abnormal increase in reported cases, but once again the psychological damage had been done. The public was on high alert; Labor Day gatherings shrunk because people feared exposure. The media pundits predicted major Guardian Party gains while the G-7 bloc of post-industrialized democracies called for a special meeting, inviting the BRICS so all could discuss how best to work together.

Another meeting took place late September, attended by Project Death Shield members only. In operation for two years, its agents had been monitoring any T-Plague related activity in suspect organizations that could destabilize the government. The section chief provided a sobering appraisal.

"So far we haven't detected tangible activity to leverage public paranoia against the Administration. If the Guardian Party gains too much in November, or if outbreaks swell, that might change. We need to stay ahead of the curve, so you need to recruit additional moles or leakers. We need to burrow into NIH, so focus on Cognicom. For now, our role is observation, not interdiction. Stay alert, but stay invisible."

A happier meeting took place on an October Saturday; Indy was having lunch at Jennifer Conklin's, comparing lifestyles and husband-wife relationships. Their backgrounds were much different, and each wanted to know more about the other. When Indy arrived, the first thing she wanted was a tour of the house.

"Your home is lovely. Jason and I will be closing on our first house next month. Perhaps you can give me pointers on interior decorating. How long did it take you to furnish your home?"

"It takes forever. You never finish but simply keep making changes that you hope improve the place. Russell and I were fortunate because his salary let me hire a professional decorator who bought furniture right away. Depending on your budget and the amount of time you want to spend, maybe you and Jason can do it yourself. But with your first child on the way, maybe you'll put in just the basics and grow from there. Come on, I'll show you the kitchen and we'll have lunch."

Jennifer served chicken breasts with rice and stir-fried vegetables, a healthy selection for expectant mothers. Each had gained the normal amount of weight after the first trimester, and because the home birthing class included regular fitness sessions, both felt as good as they looked. They were now in the family room, enjoying each other's company.

"You might say I have what used to be considered the traditional family lifestyle. Married only once and able to quit working because the husband's job brings in lots of money. I worked for a talent agency as a trade show presenter until becoming pregnant, and I won't go back to work until my kids are old enough not to need a hover mother. I came close to completing my nursing degree, and I plan to finish when the kids are older so I can have my own career. And we're not sure if we want more than one child. Now, tell me about yourself. I don't want to pry, but are you planning a Vow-Cer with Jason?"

"I consider myself a professional young woman of Modernity. I grew up in India and moved to the United States for my advanced biotech degree. Jason and I met in Boston. We're committed to each other, but he worries too much about events out of our control, so he's pushing back our Vow-Cer date, and that's fine with me. I'm perfectly capable, because of my career, to raise a child on my own."
"I admire your independence. My background didn't equip me as well as yours. I love Russell, and we both give and get what we need. Russell needs a companion to complete his life, and I need someone I care about who can provide the security I never had. We're well matched. I imagine you plan to go back to work, but aren't you worried about infant T-Plague exposure? I think I can minimize it if I'm a stay-at-home mom."

"I'm fortunate because the lab has onsite daycare. Hardly any risk of exposure there. And I'm sensible when out in public. With all of that, plus the smart pills, I think we'll be safe. But I'm concerned about handling work and all the additional chores at home."

"I never had to worry about that. And even though we had plenty of money so I could hire cleaners or nannies, I wanted to do it myself. And Russell, because he's older, understands why he should pitch in. Russell's a caring and sharing type of man."

"I kid Jason that he's my work in progress. I'm still working to make him more like Russell, and I'm making more progress there than at work. Has Russell told you much about all the challenges posed by the T-Plague? I know he works at NIH."

"He tries to keep work and home separate, but now and then we talk about the headaches it gives him. I hope your projects have happy endings soon. But let's talk about what we know will have happy endings, giving birth at home."

"Jason came up with our plan. I'll deliver at his parent's home because we won't be settled into our new place. His mom's my midwife and his dad's my doctor. I just wish I could make Jason understand how hard pregnancy is on my body and emotions."

"I'm fortunate that Russell is older. I know it takes men a long time to understand women. After we deliver, why not have our men chat regularly? I know you and I will."

And so, the afternoon flitted by. By the time she left, Indy knew that she and Jennifer were destined to become close friends, looking forward to years of family friendship. They made plans to meet next Saturday at the health bar after the home birthing exercise class.

On the drive home, Indy wondered what Jason would be like in fifteen years—mentally, physically, and emotionally. That was the age differential between Russell and Jason. Indy decided her work in progress had a lot of maturing to do. Perhaps time was still on his side.

CHAPTER 17
October 2096

"Great Expectations"
(Thread 3 Chapter 10)

Mo says I should thank him, but I'll wait until I know how I did. His phone call yesterday helped, and at least I get a free lunch. I always think better on a full stomach. Adom left his jitters in the van as he walked from the parking garage to Bobbi's office.

Mo had been called away to douse the flames on another project, so he picked Adom to attend a lunchtime meeting his boss Bobbi had called for Cognicom bus-admin leaders. Mo recognized that Adom had a combination of tech smarts and social skills that could help expand his career by working both sides—technical and business-political—and he knew only one person could convince Adom to "go for it;" motivation comes from within. He hoped Adom would grab the opportunity and score points at Bobbi's meeting; she had connections.

Adom had been forced to grow in another way during the past four months. Indy's pregnancy had unnerved him, forcing a permanent pecking order rearrangement among Indy, Jason, and himself, pushing Adom to move on. Making more of a career commitment was taking him in the right direction.

Bobbi treated Adom with the same regard she would have given Mo. She asked him to summarize the current T-Plague outlook, respecting what he said, and after that asked for an S-Vac project status update,for which Adom glanced only twice at the notes Mo had helped him prepare.

"Well done. Now Candice and Spencer know why all NIH projects have tighter information security requirements than ever before. We can thank Securityguard for that. And your data retrieval clerks have to deal with longer screening and audit trails. Cognicom is under the microscope. And according to our Enviro-Scan sources, the T-Plague prognosis is disheartening here and abroad. It's hit major urban areas on most continents, with every indication it'll spread further.Election results should galvanize the Administration to do more, and that may impact us hard. Got all that?"What Candice got caused concern.

"My researchers are all big brains, but their big egos get in the way. I think it's time for them to admit the problem is bigger than they can handle. I'd like Mo's team to help us even more."Spencer asked for the same.

"When Mo gets back, he and Adom will figure out what they need to make it happen. And unless there's more you'd like to discuss, lunch is over.Adom,make sure you take the extra brownies. You earned them."

Adom hurried back to share the news with his team. When he reported the other teams finally asked for additional help, Su spoke before Jason.

"We'll need two junior researchers to handle some of our routine work, and we've already scoped out what additional equipment is needed. We can't promise success, so all we'll say is we'll do our best." Indy added more.

"And we don't want to step on toes or egos, so we have to be diplomatic.When he gets back, we'll let Mo defuse any ego issues by talking directly with the seniors. Jason, why don't you go with him to watch how he handles people."

"I've jotted down all your suggestions.I can't think of any to add, so let's get back to work."

When Mo returned home Friday evening, he called Adom after first contacting Bobbi.

Adom was pleased that Bobbi had praised his performance and thanked Mo again for supporting his modified career path. When Mo emphasized the need to provide more help to the other teams, Adom already knew what to say.

"Jason and I want to discuss that with you in person. That's why we're treating you to an afternoon at my sports club. We're picking you up Sunday at eleven."

Today's sports clubs put a new twist on the time-honored sports bar tradition. Open dining areas contain an array of widescreen TV monitors flanking the room which is partitioned into box seating, each containing controllable loudspeakers for tuning into any game. Parking or weather never interfere, and tailgate-like buffet stations cater to every palate. Because Adom had reserved a box, he and his partners were seated immediately and began watching the local Co-NFL team—The Washington Ambassadors. The Co-NFL had more sex appeal than any other professional sport, giving fans enticing sights no matter the score. Mo agreed.

"You sure know how to pick your spots and sports. We should hold more of our meetings here. And no one will fall asleep if we tune in to Co-NFL games. The competition's exciting and the athletes are good looking. I'm sure Indy and Su could find players to root for. Who are you rooting for, Adom?"

"The one that looks like Indy before she got pregnant. You might not know it, but Indy has more athletic talent than any of us. If she wants to change careers, we're watching where she might be a star if she trained hard."

"She looks fit to me, and she wears her pregnancy well. Maybe she'll be even stronger afterwards. Several elite women marathoners ran faster times after their first pregnancy. Jason's a lucky fellow to have a partner like Indy."

"I'm lucky Indy is what she is. Have either of you ever fallen head-over-heels for someone? It's one of life's great experiences, but I don't recommend repeating it too often. It's a big emotional drain."
"I don't know about Adom, but I never have. I've been more career-minded than marriage-minded. Wrong term. Co-friend or Vow-

Cer minded. I'm not as with-it as you guys regarding the new-wave stuff, but you know what I mean. Adom, what about you?"

"I'm becoming more career-minded too. But I've never found a partner like Indy. If I did, I might commit. Jason knows all about how that fits in his love theory. Why don't you tell Mo about all the stages?"

"Glad to. Everyone goes through four stages. First is infatuation, which I think each of you has experienced. Then comes physical love, where sex is dominant. If you work at it the sex remains exciting but physical love morphs into committed love, and finally into unconditional love. I'm trying to move to committed love. Indy says I worry too much about events I don't control. Says that's why I keep pushing back our Vow-Cer date."

"When Jason and I were in grad school, I saw him put his love theory into practice. And if you ever want to know how physical attraction works, ask Su. She can add science to the mix. I've listened to her make mind-brain and neuro-scientific connections to falling in love. I don't follow all of it. Su's brain is way beyond mine. But Indy must know you're getting better at making commitments. The two of you just closed on a house, and that says a lot. When do you move in?"

"Week before Thanksgiving. Next year we'll invite all the Worldstars for Thanksgiving. Mo, don't forget. You're now part of our inner circle. You bring a pragmatic business dimension to the mix. Sometime when we're all assembled, we should talk about plans beyond Cognicom and NIH. By the way, when did you join the Air Reserves? Are you still active?"

"After I was discharged from the Navy, and yes, I'm still active. It scratches my itch to fly. And it gives me networking contacts too." Adom was ready to switch from talking to tasting.

"All this talk is making me hungry. Why don't we make another tail-gate pass and settle in for the second half? I'm committed to the cookies and cheese cake."

While the guys were at the sports bar, Su had Indy all to herself. She needed to say things that were for Indy's ears only.

"I'm happy you're pregnant. I know you want a child and you don't need to wait for an official Vow-Cer commitment. As you've said so often, we are professional females of Modernity." Indy smiled whimsically.

"Both of us are way ahead of Jason intellectually and emotionally. He loves me more than I love him, but I care deeply for him. And the lifestyle we'll have makes me happy."

"You and I have talked often about lifestyles. And you have often teased about my Oriental veil of privacy. And you are correct. It's my nature to be reserved, not to reveal myself until fully prepared. Perhaps I've waited too long, but I need you to listen to my proposal. Please hear me out before answering. And you'll need time to consider what I'm offering." Su paused, glancing away to gather what she would say.

"I am in love with you. I have been for years. I love you intellectually, emotionally, physically. It will be that way always. You complete me, you give me something to love other than my biotech research passion. And in return I can give you breadth and depth you'll never get from Jason. Our lifestyle by co-friending at the next level will give you all you want. We can raise a child better than most couples. I'm telling you this because Jason's closing in. I think you can love me more than you love him. Please think carefully about what I've said. I don't expect an answer until you have fully considered what our relationship could be. Let your mind and emotions play with the possibilities."

They sat for a moment looking at one another, Su on the sofa and Indy in her favorite chair. Indy rose quietly, then gently sat next to Su, tears welling softly. Though she appeared calm, troubling thoughts churned inside.

November snuck by, bringing the worst-case election results the Administration had imagined. The Guardian Party gained enough seats to prevent a majority even if old guard partisans from the traditional parties combined forces. Many of the Guardian demands would have to be implemented or the public might take action against Washington.

Mo attended a flurry of post-election meetings, saving the best for last, the final Worldstars briefing before the holidays. Since the lab would be closed for the remainder of the year, even Jason responded to Mo's cheery comments.

"What a year, and the world's still here. Even the cities hardest hit by T-Plague are still standing. And we don't expect serious outbreaks in urban centers because containment works. It's basic blocking and tackling. Quarantine those infected; trace their footsteps to find others; decontaminate infected sites; hope for the best. Next year we'll watch for outbreaks in rural areas or in developing countries, but we'll put that worry away until after the Holidays.

"And thanks to your collective efforts, I've supplied ideas my think tank is using to shape longer-term political scenarios, such as dealing with economic and healthcare issues if T-Plague dementia puts too many victims out of work and onto welfare. Here's some of the collateral damage. Productivity will go down and healthcare costs will skyrocket. Military readiness and the nation's infrastructure will deteriorate if we don't have enough smart people left to fill critical jobs. And if that unfolds, watch out for terrorism." "All you've said could happen," Jason replied, "but it's too soon for even me to worry, and if it does come our way there should be plenty of warning. And maybe some of the Guardian Party reforms will help. What do you see the Guardian Party doing? Do you think they have a hidden agenda?"

"They don't seem to have one, but if they do, I hope we find out before they push us too far the wrong way. I think they'll make Healthguard and Securityguard even more intrusive and restrictive. From where I sit, the Administration is more concerned about themselves than the public, but I keep that to myself, so please do likewise. Su, would you please give us a yearend tech progress summary?"

"From our S-Vac point of view, the year has been barely OK. Since progress on improved formulations has stalled, Indy and I are looking for solution path revisions. The current formulation is marginally successful for suppressing side-effects and keeping some victims in a remissive state, but after three months dementia accelerates. We're counting on our subsequent formulations to be better.And here's a big concern.Demand will exceed manufacturing capability if NIH doesn't ramp up production. And that doesn't include worldwide demand, just domestic. Indy, why don't you tell about the other teams."

"It was good Mo told their leads right up front we make no promises about coming to the rescue, because we're not optimistic. Su and I have our work cut out because I-Vac and R-Vac solution paths are flawed, leading nowhere. The equipment and junior researchers you brought us will help next year if Su and I figure out what changes to make. We hope to have partial breakthroughs by April."

"Sorry, but I can't give that to Bobbi. Starting February, you're on maternity leave. Do you expect Su to handle the load all by herself?"

"I forgot to mention we've been coaching Jason and Adom. While I'm out, they'll fill in. And that leads to a final point. Each of us needs to stay healthy. No one gets the T-Plague. Please watch for symptoms and keep taking our improved smart pills. We all need to stay in the game. I can't think of anything to add. Mo, what's next?"

"It's time for my holiday surprise. I ordered a catered lunch, and it should be arriving in ten minutes. The rest of the day is not for business, but for pleasure."

Lunch rolled in as advertised, bringing a selection of salads, cold cuts, cheeses, and desserts that impressed even Adom. As everyone dished up, Adom kidded about his choice.

"I'm going to act like a Brit and start with dessert. I've heard that's what they do in London."

Su said, "That's incorrect. But I read a London Imperial College research report that suggests eating dessert first can keep appetites in check. If you load up on dessert before the main course, the brain protein glucokinase, which keeps track glucose levels, tells you to stop eating. Why don't you go ahead and eat dessert first, then tell us if the experiment worked?"

"I will. And how about after lunch we each report what we want next year to bring us."

A happy mood lasted beyond lunch. Jason jested about Adom's experiment, pointing to the empty brownie tray to prove his point. Adom told Mo to reward Jason's powers of observation by letting him be the first to tell his hopes for the coming year.

"Indy and I have great expectations, what with just buying our first house and having our first child due in early February. And I plan to worry less. Indy's better with words, so let's hear from her."

"My top priority is early February delivery, and thanks to the seminars we went to, I know what to expect and Jason knows what to do. Thanks also to the lab's childcare center. I plan to return to work in two months. Many expecting moms I've met will stay home to minimize newborn T-Plague exposure. But the risk is minimal at our lab. There'll never be another containment breach." Mo asked, "Is birth at home as safe as at a hospital? How do you control for germs, and what about complications?"

"I'm not worried. Jason's parents are a doctor-nurse team. Besides, giving birth at home feels natural. It's more comfortable. Hospitals can be so barren."

Jason added, "I'll be doing my part, too. As soon as we move in, I'll set up a baby's bedroom. And I'll be at my parent's home when Indy delivers, so that I can help out. It'll be even easier the next time."

"Well, let's take it one baby at a time. Besides, I might revise your marriage contract afterwards. We haven't set the Vow-Cer date."

OK, OK. I'll slow down and enjoy right now. Will that satisfy you?" Indy's smile said yes. Adom's comment spoke for all.

"We want a happy outcome for you and Jason, and we want you back soon working with Su. Jason and I will do our best, but only you can keep up with her."

"You'll do fine in my absence. But enough about me. Let's hear about next year's plans from the rest. Mo, why don't you start."

"I plan to do more of the same next year, including more Air Reserves training. Flying is too expensive a hobby if I weren't in the Air Reserves. It's the best way to stay chopper-certified. Su, how about you?"

"I plan to take additional online courses that integrate quantum physics and nano-science into my research. And I plan to continue my Middle East volunteer work. That and piano practice keep me balanced."

Adom asked, "Are you still seeing Kayed? He seems like a nice guy."

"We sometimes go out for dinner after a volunteer meeting. Nothing serious, so don't worry. I still have my eye on you. Now it's your turn."

"I'm going to work on expanding my career.Mo says I work well with people, so I'll ask him to let me do more on the business and political side next year.His boss liked how I filled in when Mo was out of town. And when I'm prepared, talking with business and political types is easy."Adom had more to say, but Jason interrupted. "Let me cut in here.I forgot to mention my parents have invited all of us for a Worldstars only New Year's Eve party at their place. Please bring a date if you like. And they especially want to meet Mo. Indy and I had planned to host it at our place, but my folks don't want Indy stressing herself out. Next year will be our turn. Mo, do you plan to bring a partner?"

"I recently met a lawyer who's in my politico-network. You'll like Rebecca. Indy, do you still play your S-word game? You would say she's smart and socially attuned. And Adom would say she is soothing to look at." Adom dived back in.

"If she's as good as that, I'd say you've made an excellent choice. I can't wait to see for myself."

Mo wrapped up the post-lunch discussion saying, "That's only two weeks away. And between now and the party, all of us are on break. Go home and get ready for the new year…"

This year's party was even better than the last. It had a comfortable, coming-home feeling, accented by a dash of new friendship because Mo brought Rebecca. Everyone voiced optimism for what next year would bring. The guests departed soon after midnight, all pledging to attend next New Year's Eve party that Jason and Indy would host.

183

A pleasant stillness filled the house. Jason's parents were asleep; Jason and Indy were sitting next to one other, sharing the moment in the living room, softly lighted by candles.

"Everyone said how lovely, how radiant you look in your last month of pregnancy. I hope you keep feeling as good as you look."

"I'm completely engaged in the moment, enjoying right now. Maybe my hormone levels cause heightened awareness because I feel such a connection to everything around me. I hope I can capture these feelings in a poem. And how about you?"

"I'm trying to worry less about the future, but I still have to remind myself that all we have are the people we care about and the moment we're living in. And each moment is not a dress rehearsal. I try to follow the advice in one of your poems. I don't remember which one, but I remember the verse that grabs me."

> "So busy yourself with what is now,
> Focus on what's here.
> Enjoy the most that fate allows,
> Future memories will be dear."

"I have something else for you. I'll be right back." Indy walked away, leaving Jason alone with his thoughts. *I can't imagine what she's getting. And that's one of her charms. She always keeps me guessing. I'll never figure out what's in store. Makes me love her that much more.*

Indy returned a few minutes later carrying a large sealed envelope. She sat in a chair across from him, wearing an elusive smile.

"Let me describe what this contains and what the rules of the game are. Inside are some papers and sealed envelopes. The papers are for you. The sealed envelopes contain letters that are to be given to the person addressed. Under no circumstances are you allowed to open the large envelope without my permission. And you must return it to me as soon as I ask for it. If something terrible happens to me before I ask, you must open the envelope as soon as you are ready, read the papers, and deliver in person the letters. You must instruct each person to read their letter in the privacy of their own thoughts." Indy reached across the coffee table and gave him the envelope.

"I've got the envelope, but I don't get what all this means. Is this like a will? Why are you giving it to me now?"

"You'll just have to wait to find out."

"And what is the envelope supposed to do?"

"Why, it's to keep you from worrying what to do if I disappear. I'll probably ask for it back in a month or so, but maybe not. Let's see what the future brings."

Earlier that evening the Invisible Man was awaiting a phone call from the Invisible Hand, expecting to hear good news. He answered on the first ring.

"This is the Invisible Man."

"This is the Invisible Hand reporting success. We now have moles placed in Cognicom. Both confirmed a T-Plague containment breach late last year."

"Excellent work. NIH kept that hidden from everyone. We will use that against the Administration when the time is right. What do your Admin moles report?"

"The Administration thinks they can limit our party's growth if they pretend to follow our lead."

"Good for us. We will exploit complacency. Remember to tell your moles to observe and not to interdict until the time is right. Report back as arranged. Happy New Year to you and your moles."

Jason awoke on a cold and blustery late January Friday with a pounding headache and upset stomach, just what was needed to trigger the hypochondriac within. He felt his forehead, confirming his worst nightmare. *I'm burning up! I'm infected with the T-Plague and Indy's due date is only two weeks away! Why is this happening to me now?*

Jason's panic attack awakened Indy from a dream about delivering a boy. Though a boy would be fine, she would prefer a daughter. Jason was hoping for a boy, but she wouldn't tell what she already knew.

"Morning, Jason. What's all the commotion?" Jason rushed into the bedroom.

"I've got the T-Plague! I have all the symptoms and feel terrible. What are we going to do?" Indy sat up, then spoke.

"Let's get dressed and go to the lab's screening center to get tested. And don't worry. You've been taking smart pills. If we test positive, we'll nip it in the bud."

Indy had to drive because Jason was an emotional wreck. She told her story to the guard, who in turn called the screening center. "Please drive to the entrance and wait for a technician to come get Jason." Two minutes later an EMT escorted Jason into the building. Indy parked in her assigned space, then trekked to the screening center as fast as her late stage pregnancy would allow. Two hours later the examining physician gave Indy the news.

"Well Mrs. Kittner, I have good news and bad news. First the good news. Neither you nor Jason tested positive. He has a mild case of the Flu, but that's all. Just take him home for bed rest and aspirin."

"Thank you, Doctor. You mentioned bad news. What is it?"

"Mr. Kittner said you were expecting your first child, but you already have one. Jason seems to be a big baby when it comes to getting sick."

"Well at least it's not sympathetic morning sickness. He'd be down for the count if that were the case. Thank you for diagnosing my big baby's condition."

Jason recovered quickly, and Indy worked for one more week before starting maternity leave. On Sunday afternoon before the due date, Jason's mother was hosting a Worldstars only baby shower, welcoming all the guests.

"As you can see, Indy's in perfect health, the picture of what an expectant mother should look like. She put on just the right amount of weight in all the right places. And Doc and I have everything in place for delivery. I'm a registered nurse who knows all about midwife practices, and Doc is her physician. I'll let him tell you more."

"Indy will have the best possible care, as good as what she'd get at a hospital and more comfortable. Many women today are opting for birth at home to reduce the risk of T-Plague exposure. We sanitize Indy's bedroom every day, and all of us have just tested negative for T-Plague. We are ready to welcome Indy's baby into the world."

Adom kidded, "All that is all to the good, but what about Indy's other baby, the big one that we all work with?" Su couldn't resist piling on.

"Adom has a point. What precautions should we take for him?" Now it was Mo's turn.

"Here's what a Jewish grandmother would recommend. Sedate him for six months, then have him wake up in a barber shop."

"OK everyone, I get the point. Indy and I have already talked about this. I am ready to assume the mantle of parenthood." A round of applause congratulated Jason, after which Indy added a compliment.

"Yes, Jason is still a work in progress, but he's making good progress. He's up to the challenge."

Mo added, "I hope he's up to the challenge at the lab too, because he and Adom have to fill in for you while you're out of action."

"Jason wants me to be home for a couple of months, but I plan to be back in about four weeks. The daycare facilities at the lab are excellent, and I'll be right there. And Jason says he's ready to share night duty, but I think our child will be exceptional: bright, beautiful and well behaved. I'm playing the B-word game for our first child."

Adom asked, "Do you want a boy or a girl? Any favorite names?"

"Indy wants a girl, and I want a boy, but I'll be happy with either as long as Indy comes through as she promises. She opted out of the gender tests so we don't know. We'll sort through names when we know what we have."

Su said, "The mild weather is a good sign, and if it stays as good as it's been, I predict a trouble-free delivery. I imagine Jason has already checked the forecast."

"Yep, and it's supposed to be the same this week as last. There's one outlier forecast for bad weather later in the week, but I think it's wrong. I'm betting on good weather, but no matter what, everything's all set right here. No driving to the hospital. Indy, what do you want to add?"

"Please stop worrying about the weather. We can't control it, and you've done all you can to get our new house ready. You and I are as ready as we can be."

The remainder of the afternoon flitted gaily away; Jason promised to call everyone as soon as possible after Indy's delivery. Before leaving, everyone gave Indy final hugs and kisses, along with promises to visit next weekend.

That evening, Indy reviewed the coming week's drill one more time for Jason.

"You'll stay at our house, going to work every day and visiting me at night. At the first sign of labor, we'll call so you don't have to rush to get here. And when you get here, your mother will tell you what to do, just like she did when you were a kid." It pleased Indy to see Jason smile.

"And I already know what your mother will say. She'll tell you to stay out of the way, boil some water in the kitchen, and call your father when the time comes. Jason my love, I'm certain you'll be fine."

"I know, and I won't worry if you won't worry. Do we have a deal?" Indy sealed it with a final kiss.

CHAPTER 18
February 2097

"Into the Void"
(Thread 3 Chapter 11)

Su's CALL CAME WHILE she was hurrying out the door, forcing her to search madly through her shoulder bag. Power had been restored after yesterday's freak snowstorm blew itself out, and she was anxious to drive to the lab, now that main roads were drivable. She was even more anxious to hear good news about Indy, and was happy to see Jason's number flashing on her cell phone.

"I'm so glad to hear from you. How are Indy and the baby?" Her expression changed to one of horror. "Oh my God! No! I'll call Adom and Mo right now. Call me back as soon as you can!"

Su numbly disconnected the call, trying to collect her thoughts which were whirling as fast as her spinning emotions. She punched in the number and spoke as calmly as possible when the call connected.

"Adom, please listen. Jason just called. The unthinkable happened. Indy was killed yesterday in a fire. He'll call me back when he can. Please call Mo."

That tragedy had taken place a week ago but Jason never called back, for too much was swirling about in his life and he needed time to sort through the rubble, as did Su. But he did visit her the day after the funeral, delivering a letter marked for her eyes only. She could not read it immediately because the knifelike pain stabbing her heart was too great. She had to wait until her trembling hands and emotions could handle whatever was inside. Late that night, sitting on the living room sofa with only an end table lamp lighted, Su steeled herself to read Indy's final words.

She and Indy had sat here so many times, sharing whatever came to mind. But never again, for Indy was dead, leaving a gaping void. Su mechanically opened the envelope, and as she began to read, vanished into the sound of Indy's voice.

"My dearest Su, if you are reading this letter something unforeseen happened to me while giving birth. And I have secrets to share only with you. I know you hide behind a veil of reserve, so you are reading in private. Please imagine I am sitting across from you, as I did so many times.

I love you more than anyone else! More than I love Jason. Together we would have made a wonderful life. Jason would eventually understand and be happy for all of us. I am so sorry it took me too long to make my choice; I robbed us of special times and memories. Please forgive me.

I do not want you to grieve long about my passing! Hold one last remembrance with Jason and Adom, and then all of you must move on. And I have one last wish: please help Jason raise my daughter. Yes, a daughter! Help him as soon as he is ready. Please be her godmother and aunt. Jason's heart is in the right place, but he never understood women. My love is with you always."

Su read the letter over and over into the early morning hours, emotions screaming what she already knew. Indira was her kindred spirit, never to be replaced. She would have to make other plans to compensate for this devastating loss. Never again would she share an intimacy only Indy could satisfy. How she wished she had a copy of her poems. Indy had told her that she might publish them when she was old and had nothing better to do. Now that would never happen; Indira would remain thirty-one forever.

Su held a solo vigil until the dawn, locking all of Indira into memory. A verse from Indy came painfully to mind:

> "The problem is Time turned its back,
> On the search for my Kindred One.
> The World and I have gone separate ways,
> It's a harder fit for me.
> Only one match for all of our days,
> Comes and goes and no more will be.
> So I'll have to settle for a lesser God,
> If my search continues on."

Su would never settle for a lesser God.

A month after the funeral, Su was ready to hold Indira's life celebration remembrance that would help bring closure. Everything was in place—snacks and wine awaiting on a coffee table—so she sat back simply waiting, mind completely blank. When the doorbell roused her, she greeted Jason and Adom. Words weren't necessary; she hugged them both then set them in living room, groping for what to say. After two false starts, words barely audible began to flow.

"The three of us are Indy's best friends. We loved her, each in our own special way, and will never replace her. But she would want us to get over the grieving and move on with our lives. One of her last wishes was for me to host for only the three of us a celebration remembrance of her life. So here we are." It was Jason who spoke next.

"Indy was always way ahead of me. She gave me an envelope containing instructions just in case something bad happened during childbirth. And damn if it didn't."

Adom said, "Indy was way ahead of me too, and Jason gave me my last letter from her that I want you to hear." Adom removed it from his vest pocket and began to recite.

"Dear Adom, if you are reading this letter something unexpected happened to me during childbirth. You were a great friend, and I thank you for all we shared. You are Jason's best friend, and he needs your help. You know how much he loved me, but he must leave that in the past and move into the present and future. Please help him do just that. Try to keep him socially engaged. In due time, introduce him to some ladies you think I would approve of. Please be a godfather and uncle to my daughter. And follow Su's lead to your promised futures. My love to you all."

Jason was unable to speak, so Su picked up where Adom left off.

"Indy left a final letter for me as well, and I will share it. She wanted us to hold one last remembrance and then put away our memories. And she knew she'd have a daughter. Her final wish for me is to help you raise her when you need assistance. Only time will tell if you need it, but it's there for the asking." Jason had regained control of his emotions and was able to talk.

"Indy told me some of the same. One last remembrance and then move on. Thank you both for helping me."

"Come on Jason, don't you make me all weepy. It'll just increase my appetite for Su's snacks. All of us are still coming to terms with our loss, but tonight will help us all."

"Well said," replied Su. "Let's sample snacks and share memories."

The three remaining Worldstars talked late into the night, sharing all they could. Adom summarized it best.

"Indy wasn't perfect, but I never found a flaw worth mentioning. I guess I never will. Su, you're the smart one. Did you find any?"

"No, but maybe Jason did. Did she leave the cap off the toothpaste?"

"No, and she never left a bathtub ring either. But wait a minute. Once in a while she'd leave me a list of household chores. At least I was man enough to handle them, and Indy gave me high marks for trying."

"I know you're fully loaded coming to terms with your new lifestyle, but as your best friend, let me know when you're ready for some social R&R. Just like Su, I'm here to help."

"I will when my life settles down. And I imagine I'll be able to sleep better, but so far all I do is toss and turn, even when I'm tired. Maybe tonight will be a turning point for me. I think it's time to go home and try to get a good night's sleep."

As he and Adom departed, Jason thanked Su for helping put away memories. Indira was gone, and though she would always be in his memory, he subconsciously began to construct a mental barrier that would relegate the past to remote corners so that emotional pain would subside. *I'll keep so busy I won't have time to think about her, and if anyone asks me what she was like, I'll just change the subject.*

Indira's death affected Mo more than was apparent. He too kept his feelings to himself, and like Su showed a calm demeanor in public. He had attended the funeral, being careful not to intrude into Jason's private world.

The funeral had been held a month ago, and today he would hold the first team meeting since then. Afterwards, he would talk with Bobbi so she could get whatever the team needed for filling a void that would always remain.

Jason started the meeting long before Mo arrived.

"Let me state the obvious. We lost the person who glued us together. She helped me run the project. She helped Su crack the T-Plague code. She helped Adom understand the politics. She helped Mo understand the science. Did I miss anything?" Silence gave the answer. Jason continued.

"We'll never find a replacement, but we must adjust best we can. Mo will recruit a senior researcher to handle virology. Let's choose someone who fits our style. I'll improve my project leadership skills, and I promise to be positive and proactive. Adom will help Su improve our solution path. And Su, please tell us what you'll need to make that happen."

"I'll be brutally frank. Indy and I were the R&D dynamo because we fitted together so well. I know Adom will do his best, but I'd rather work alone. Let Adom help Mo deal with the sociopolitical piece. You can take Indy's place when I need assistance. And get another lab tech for me."

"It's decided. I know what I'll say to Mo. Let's take a break until he gets here."

Mo arrived a half hour later, bringing muffins and a can-do attitude into the conference room.

"Words can't express my sadness for our loss. All I can do is my best to get what you need so we can move ahead. Jason, please tell me what the team wants."

"Thanks Mo, for all the support you give us. We'll never replace Indy, but we've come up with a plan. Here's what we want to do…" Mo liked everything he heard. After Jason finished, he summarized the details, then ended the meeting.

"I'll chat with Bobbi this afternoon to get her buy-in. I'm certain she'll like what you've outlined, and I'll report back ASAP."

Mo marched into Bobbi's office, projecting man-with-the-plan bravado but hoping she didn't see through to his concern. As he was about to speak, Bobbi signaled that she would talk first.

"I met the Worldstars only twice, but from what I saw and what you say, Indira was special. Please give my condolences to Jason. She'll be hard to replace. You have a big problem figuring out what to do, so tell me, what are your intentions?" She listened impassively as Mo rattled off details. When he finished, she picked up where she left had off.

"I understand what you need and where you want to go. And I'll believe your story if you say it's the best you can do. But I'll have to spin it better. Otherwise, my boss will never buy in. Let me explain why. He doesn't want me to tell him about your problems. All he wants to know about are your team's accomplishments. I can just hear him lecturing me if I say what you just did. Did you ever hear the fist in the bucket principle?" Mo shook his head no, so Bobbi continued.

"Pretend your S-Vac project is a bucket containing water. Now form a fist, pretend it's Indira, and push it into the water. Wait ten seconds, then remove it. Ten seconds later, look at the water. Tell me what you see and what's the lesson." Mo was stumped, so Bobbi told him the answer.

"Now I get it. The water looks the same before and after removing the fist. No one is indispensable. My team should be able to get moving again without Indy. That's what I have to tell my team."

"Whether or not it's true, that's what you'll have to say, and what they'll have to do. And I expect the pressure to build on all of you. Get used to it."

As he paced back to his office, Mo recognized Bobbi's dilemma and, though making headway on vaccines would be difficult, he would do his best to get everything possible to make his team successful. Mo called Jason immediately.

"Bobbi will get our plan approved. I'll have to keep her bosses happy, and you'll have to get results, but it's good you have lots to do. By the way, you haven't told me what you named your daughter." "I named her Electra. And now I have two things to help fill the void, my work and my daughter. You, Su, and Adom help me at work, and Dad helps me at home. And I'll do my best at both places so Indy will be proud of me. Just wait and see."

CHAPTER 19
June 2105

"On the Town"
(Thread 2 Chapter 6)

JASON WAS SO IMMERSED calibrating his DNA nano-sequencer that he was unaware of his cell phone chiming until Adom yelled at him.

"Hello, this is Jason Kittner."A concerned school administrator began telling Jason that Electra had gone missing from a tour group.

"No, my daughter hasn't called me. She doesn't have a cell phone. I'm leaving right now!"

Gorgeous mid-June weather heralded the end of Electra's third year in school. Achievement exams had already been completed, and DC area grade schools were invited to an annual "Kid's Day at the National Zoo," which would be open only to registered tour groups. To qualify, a grade schooler must have scored in the exam's top quartile and tested negative for T-Plague, implying the outing would be a risk-free reward for motivated students and an instructive start to summer vacation. Home-schoolers were invited too, which meant Electra would go with her best friend Christi. She was chirping with delight when Jason dropped her off at the Conklins before driving to the lab.

Electra's third year in the home-schooling track had provided perfect protective cover because her grandfather handled medical testing, making her look like a healthy normal little girl. Meanwhile, she followed a study program that matched her extraordinary brain,

—

196

and as long as her achievement scores were satisfactory she was home free. She played her Goldilocks game with the exams, always obtaining scores that were just right.

Electra's neural connections placed her beyond mere mortals. She had left the enchanted world of childhood far behind and long ago. And her brain was able to synchronize conscious with subconscious to self-direct organic growth—cognitively and physically within the bounds of her DNA—to match her intentions. Her abilities for one so young are extraordinary yet subtle, difficult for others to detect unless she flaunted them, which she promised never to do. Only her emotional development is proceeding at a normal pace. At first, she wanted that to accelerate also, but then she understood why it was better letting it develop more slowly. The lightning brain knew instinctively in its darker recesses that with emotional complexity comes the challenging and sometimes unpleasant realities of the adult world, from which there would be no return.

This explained why Electra loved her first three years in school. They gave constant contact with children her age who glowed with innocence and imagination, focus and enthusiasm, which all too soon adolescence would eclipse. She didn't know how her more nuanced emotions would behave when they emerge, but she hoped for the best.

Jennifer Conklin delivered a lecture to the girls just before dropping them off at school.

"Please stay with your group. I don't want you getting lost. Hold hands and help one another. Do you need any money?"

"No, Mother. Father gave me money last night."

"Mrs. Conklin, Dad said we'd get a box lunch, and he gave me money for candy. And Christi and I will be good, won't we?" Christi poked Kit in the ribs; both were giggling.

Christi was a lovely child; fair hair, blue eyes, and child model features inherited from her mother. She and Electra made a striking pair: smart, vibrant, and usually well-behaved, one fair and one darker. They jumped from the car, ready to seize the day.

Childhood school bus rides are among the happiest journeys, camaraderie of companions and excitement of destinations etched forever in memory. In later years, Electra would follow them to happier times, but today she was already there. She and her classmates bounded from the bus and into assigned groups.

"I want each of you to pick a partner and form a line holding hands. Please keep up with the pair in front of you. Please do this every time we leave an exhibit area. Are we ready?" A boisterous chorus of yeses followed the guide's directions, so they were off.

Electra had prepared for the trip by studying on the Web details of the DC

Zoo and many of its animals, but was more interested in mingling with other children to learn how little humans tick. She already knew Christi's classmates because the school included her in social activities. Today she would add to her understanding of childhood behavior and make new friends along the way, for like mother like daughter; everyone instinctively liked Electra.

It seemed impossible they were already stopping at the picnic area for lunch. The kids buzzed with delight, enjoying the food and fun-filled atmosphere. Christi was aglow when she and Electra locked arms, exclaiming, "This is so much fun, being with you like this!" And then an impish smile swept across her face.

"I have an idea. Why don't we go with some other groups? We can make a game of how long it takes for us to get caught. And we'll meet a lot of kids too. And if we get lost or in trouble or something, I can call Mother on my cell phone."

Electra wanted a cell phone; perhaps she could use today's adventure to get one. She replied surreptitiously.

"We'll stick together and see how far we get. But let's not get into trouble. If we get caught, let me talk first." With so many children milling about, the duo tucked in where they didn't belong, latching on at the end of a procession and acting as if they belonged. If other children asked, they had two ready answers. For the wide-eyed innocent ones, they would say they had transferred in late; for the more kid-wise, they would say they were playing a game and would beg to have it kept it a secret. Both excuses worked. The duo went from group to group unnoticed by supposedly wise and watchful adults.

"What's the next exhibit?" Christi asked the girl ahead.

"The big apes. They're scary!" Electra thought differently.

"They're very smart and usually like people. They'll be fun to see." As they approached, their group was overrun by young and old, screaming and running helter-skelter. And that's when Electra spotted the poor gorilla, frightened by all the commotion and fleeing from the crowd back to the safety of its enclosure. The poor brute knew how dangerous homo sapiens—even little ones—could be and wanted no part. The effect was like yelling "Fire!" in a theater; everyone panicked. The girls hugged one another as the throng surged by. Then Christi spotted an opportunity.

"This is our chance. Let's go exploring! Don't let go my hand! I saw an exit sign." The girls raced away, ducking under an exit turnstile. They had escaped the confines of adult supervision and were on their own venturing into unexplored territory.

The immediate vicinity held popular tourist attractions, so it was not unusual to see pairs of children walking about. The lovely weather and time of the year added to the crowd, allowing the girls to blend in, and they were thrilled to see so much that was new. They stopped to read all the signs, eavesdropping when standing next to adults, then zigged and zagged to take in all the attractions. When Christi saw a sign she recognized, she decided they should hike in a new direction.

"Mother told me all about the Metro. Let's follow the arrows and sneak on."

"If we do that, where should we go?"

"We'll take it to Father's office. I know how to get there. Won't he be surprised!" What great adventure, so off they went.

What a lark Electra was having. Perhaps the adult world was less threatening than her father warned. The child inside dialed down the lightning brain's warning system, but it was still active because both father and grandfather had coached her always to be aware of surroundings. She noticed a well-dressed fellow close to her father's age following them. When he caught up he started talking to Christi, who still trusted all adults.

"Young ladies, a gorilla escaped at the Zoo! That would be very frightening."

"Oh no! It was exciting, and it gave my friend and me a chance to explore on our own." As they approached the Metro entrance, Christi kept chattering while Electra plotted a good-bye.

"Why don't you come with me and we'll explore some more. I'll bet you might like something to drink." The chap took Christi by the arm and started leading her away, unnoticed by the people walking past. Electra sprang into action.

"Don't forget me!" Electra sang out as she ran towards them. The fellow turned around a second before she arrived, just in time to catch her swift knee kick squarely between his legs. As he fell forward diagonally, she executed a perfect mawahi geri—a karate roundhouse kick—to the side of his head, just as she had practiced while watching karate training videos.

Lights out, Mr. Prevert! screamed inside her brain. As his head thudded on the concrete, she grabbed Christi's arm and hissed, "Follow me! Run under the turnstiles!" The girls disappeared into the Metro station before a gathering crowd could figure out what had happened.

Christi was not aware she had been in danger. Instead, she was laughing breathlessly because of the excitement-filled dash. Electra knew it was time to wrap up the adventure before something bad might spoil the end of a marvelous afternoon.

"Call your Dad and tell him where we are. He can pick us up. And by the time he gets here, I'll make up a great story how we got here."

The girls were in luck because Russell Conklin was in his office when the call came in. It took him only twenty minutes to retrieve the girls from a spot just far enough away from the commotion. They bounded into the back seat, ready with a whale of a tale.

"Christi, I already called Mother. And Electra, your father is with her. The school called them when you didn't show up at the bus. They heard about a gorilla getting loose and the stampede it caused. Were you scared?"

"No, but Christi saved us by calling you. We'd be lost without the cell phone."

"I'm proud of how you took care of yourselves. We'll have pizza at our house, and you young ladies can tell us the whole story." The girls clapped hands as Electra whispered, "Let me tell the story first. I have it all figured out."

Jennifer and Jason greeted the girls like mini-heroines, all grownups visibly relieved to see them safe and sound. What with the excitement of their great adventure, topped with pizza—their favorite food—today was becoming more and more magical. And now it was story time. Jason asked a leading question.

"I was worried when the school called me. They couldn't find you, so I called Mrs. Conklin and she said the same thing. Weren't you scared being lost?"

"Daddy, it wasn't at all like that. The two of us make a great team, and we know how to take care of ourselves. You should give us credit for using our brains. And Christi used her cell phone. I wish you'd get me one. We didn't panic like everyone else. We knew the gorilla wouldn't hurt us. We ran out of the Zoo, so we weren't trampled. That's when Christi remembered how to use the Metro. But when we got there we called Christi's Dad to get us." Christi was going to tell about the fellow they met, but Electra kicked her shin before she veered into risky territory.

Christi said, "Let's go see what the Internet says about gorillas." So off they went, letting the adults marvel how mature their children were becoming. The girls chirped about today's lessons once inside Christi's room.

"That man who grabbed you was a prevert—uh, pervert. He wanted to do bad things to you. We have to be careful around adults. Don't trust them unless you know them."

Christi nodded in agreement as Electra lectured more about lessons learned.

"And here's another thing. We can trick our parents if we stick together. We can have lots of adventures as long as we're careful and don't cause big problems."

"This is so good! We should be together forever!"

"Me too you too!" As the girls hugged, the child in Electra was back in control, but the lightning brain's cognitive persona subliminally knew that Electra's unconditional childhood joy was a cherished memory. And it was preparing for whatever would come. Electra completed her marvelous day by holding a father-daughter talk that turned out to be no contest. Jason agreed she could handle more independence, promising to buy her a cell phone. He realized that today was another Electra epiphany; more ah-ha moments would follow as she matures.

"You're very smart and act like a grownup in many ways. I'll tell Gramps you're ready for a bit more independence and a cell phone. But please remember to keep our secret. And please, always trust and talk with us. You have more to learn from the two men in your life." Her hug told him better than words she would always remember.

CHAPTER 20
April 2108

"Game Face Lessons"
(Thread 2 Chapter 7)

ELECTRA'S EARLY CHILDHOOD HAD been remarkably happy, and the start of her preteen years followed suit. Home life and home schooling gave her the protection and freedom necessary for her extraordinary abilities to take shape. The T-Plague touched her life only tangentially; every so often a classmate or playmate would drop out of sight and never reappear, a casualty of the inexorably growing epidemic.

Jason could not say the same because he was in the trenches fighting an incredibly challenging virus. Cognicom progress was at a standstill in spite of best efforts; Indy's death had dealt a devastating blow that crippled the Worldstars. Electra was not yet aware of T-Plague R&D, but that day would come, perhaps sooner than desirable.

Two dimensions of Electra's being—the cognitive and the physical—continued developing rapidly but invisibly to all but her father and grandfather, far exceeding her peers, but when comparing her cognitive and physical abilities, her mental powers far exceeded those of her muscles because she had not yet focused on the physical.

Preteen years trigger a new set of hormone-induced emotions. Many of Electra's friends were further along the sexual awareness spectrum, her best friend Christi being the leader of her pack. Electra listened intently to their chatter but stayed on the sidelines because she was not ready to experiment. Instead, she learned as much as possible about the science and psychology of sex by surfing the Web. She understood why her friends transitioned from childhood innocence and openness to a worldly, more adult sentiment. She too would change when her hormones came calling, but until then simpler pleasures enchanted her world.

Among all of her social activities, co-ed age group soccer topped of the list. She and Christi played on the same team, part of an area-wide league, practicing once a week and competing every Saturday. Girls were as good as boys until adolescence when hormones took control, making boys bigger, stronger, and faster, but until then co-ed soccer teams took center stage.

Hover mother Jennifer Conklin watched over both girls whenever Doc could not chaperone Electra. Jennifer and Indy would have become great friends had not a stroke of lightning short-circuited so much. Jennifer had grown up the only daughter of a working-class family in New York City. Bright and bashful as a child, she wanted to be a nurse but as she matured her stunning looks launched a successful modeling career. Talent agents detected star quality if only she would be more assertive, but that was not Jennifer's strong suit. She was happy to settle for photo ops and trade show presenter or greeter assignments while taking practical nursing courses. She wanted to have a professional career whenever her looks faded, but as Jason had already observed, that was not in the offing.

Jennifer met psychiatrist Russell Conklin at an NIH seminar where she filled a hostess role. His noble intentions rescued her from the clutches of two circling surgeons. He knew they were "swordsmen" and simply wanted to keep her untarnished. When he learned she eventually wanted to be a nurse, he offered to help her focus on healthcare assignments, which brought her to a Washington talent agency. He also used his influence to help transfer credits for enrolling in a DC nursing school. Nature took its course from there. Jennifer was in awe of Russell's mature, distinguished appearance that accentuated his senior NIH executive position. She liked him well enough to settle for his marriage proposal, even though he was fifteen years older. With him came the security and lifestyle she desperately wanted.

Russell's friends warned he was making a terrible mistake. He would never be able to keep a woman that beautiful and that much younger happy. Russell smiled and thanked them for their concern. But his reaction was the same as asking the Sphinx for a cigarette: stone cold silence. He was hopelessly in love and would accept whatever consequences came with the goods. He gave her all the freedom she wanted, and in return she gave him the love and affection he needed.

They had been happily married for five years when Jennifer became pregnant, and it was an easy decision for her to become a stay-at-home mom. Russell couldn't be happier. He had a high-powered career, a gorgeous wife, a lovely daughter, and a privileged social life. He was living his dream.

On a warm late-April afternoon, Electra and Christi were at soccer practice. Even though she was careful not to show off, Electra still had moments when she wanted to cut loose. Coaches had noticed her speed and footwork, and under their tutelage she had become the star of her team: talented, popular, and modest most of the time. She and Christi were walking in a group back to the girls' locker room, laughing and joking the way pre-teen girls do.

Ruby, the smallest player on the team, said, "When we get older we'll play in the girls-only leagues. And that'll be fine with me. Boys play too rough and dirty when they get older." Christi smirked knowingly.

"Yeah, but they become interesting in other ways. You know what I mean." Most of the girls understood, giggling and gesturing provocatively.

"Maybe so," Ruby continued, "but just look at those two bullies playing keep-away from the little guy. Poor kid wants his ball back." Electra glanced where Ruby pointed, quickly sizing up how she could correct the situation. She was feeling a bit too full of herself lately, in spite of her warning system reminders to look before leaping. But she was Electra the exceptional, able to take care of herself and situations, so she loped over, ready to take control.

The boys didn't notice her approaching, and unbeknownst to Electra were merely three brothers enjoying a game of keep-away. Electra tripped the boy about to catch the ball.

"You guys should pick on somebody your own size." She was pleased with herself and threw the ball to the little guy, ready to run back to her teammates when the boy she tripped tackled her from behind, pinning her to the ground.

"Mind your own business, bozo!" he shouted, then punched several times, landing solid blows to Electra's mouth and nose. She was defenseless, blood coming from her nose and split lip. She was stunned, more mentally than physically, because until this moment she had never been challenged in any way by kids her own age. She simply assumed others would defer to her superiority. Big mistake; Electra needed more real-world seasoning. As a small group gathered around the fray, one of the coaches rushed to break up the fight before serious damage could be done, then scolded winner and loser alike.

"Come on, kids! That's not the way to behave. What happened?" Electra was flummoxed but managed to stammer a reply.

"I, uh, I thought they were gonna keep his ball."

"He's my brother, you dummy!" The coach knew how to make the episode a lesson for everyone.

"I want the two of you to shake hands. Young lady, apologize for your mistake. Young man, apologize for hitting her. You belong to the same club, and we do not want any hard feelings. And I have to report this incident to your parents. Both of you, come with me."

Christi and her mother waited patiently outside the coach's office for Electra to be dismissed. The nurse had treated the cuts, but Electra looked worse for the wear. Skinned knees, swollen lip, and a blood-blotched jersey matched her dejected shuffle.

"Electra darling, please don't look so sad. Christi told me what happened. It's only a minor scrape."

Electra sniffed, "Hi Mrs. Conklin; hi Christi. It was my fault."

"It wasn't your fault! It looked like those guys were picking on the little guy, and you were the only one brave enough to do something."

"The coach called Gramps. He and Dad will be mad."

"Come on, girls. Let's stop for something to drink on the way home. You'll soon feel better." As they walked to the car, Christi saw a single tear curve slowly down Electra's cheek, so she put her arm around the shoulder of her crestfallen partner.

"You're my best friend forever. I love you." Then she kissed her on the cheek. Electra started sobbing, hugging Christi in return. "Me too you too."

Christi's backseat twitter on the drive home stopped the flow of tears. The minor wounds no longer hurt, and the lightning brain had already made adjustments for next time. But Electra was still upset, needing guidance from her father and grandfather to settle her emotions. As she moped into the kitchen, Doc called out in his always upbeat manner.

"Hey champ, let me take a look at you." He hugged her, examined the damage, and after determining she needed no further patching, rubbed her head.

"The nurse did a nice job. You'll be good as new in no time. Now go wash up and change your clothes for supper. Your Dad will be home in about a half hour and you can tell us all about what happened. We're having one of your favorites, sloppy joes. And for dessert we have some of your Aunt Su's brownies."

Jason talked briefly with Doc, then went upstairs where Electra was brooding behind a closed door. "Electra, I'm home. Can I come in?" Electra came running out, folding herself into Jason's open arms.

"I'm sorry I goofed." Jason examined her tear-streaked face before replying.

"You didn't goof this afternoon. You just ran into a situation you didn't expect, and it's a lesson for how to handle yourself when dealing with strangers. The real world isn't a kind and gentle place. We'll talk about it at supper. I'm going to change, so I'll see you at the table in a couple of minutes."

Doc had supper on the table when his two partners sat down. He gave a quick blessing, then dished up everyone's plate. He and Jason used evening meals to share what happened that day, picking examples for teaching Electra more about the emotional side of life. Because he was a better storyteller, Doc led the table talk.

"I remember many times when your dad got into fights. Sometimes they were his fault, and sometimes not. But we always learned from them. Let's see what we can learn from today. Tell us about this afternoon."

Electra provided a blow-by-blow description, complete with facial expressions and arm gestures. Doc knew what lessons to draw and launched into the first after Electra finished the last brownie.

"As you get older, you're learning more about how other people behave. And you must be careful when dealing with real life situations. It's good you want to have more independence. All children do as they grow. But with independence comes responsibility for your actions. That's lesson number one. Jason, please add another."

"Here's the most important one. Always keep our secret. Don't let it slip out by jumping into situations where people can see how exceptional you are. You've done a good job keeping it hidden. But as you get older, you'll be tempted to show what you can do. But if you show too much, the consequences will be bad. So, let's renew our pledge to protect our secret."

Doc added, "We know how good you are. You don't have to prove anything to strangers. And, remember from Bible class what's the worst of the seven deadly sins. It's P-R-I-D-E. Never get carried away by how smart or talented you think you are. Be modest. People like you better that way, not when you show off. And pride sometimes gets in the way of clear thinking. Maybe that happened today. What do you think?"

"I guess I thought I knew what was going on and I could handle it. I didn't stop to think it through. I promise I won't let that happen again."

Jason patted Electra's head. "And here's another thing we learned. Whenever you get in a fight, make sure you have your game face on. Do you know what that means?"

"Yes, Dad. It means I have to zone in with my brain as well as brawn. I have to focus on what I'm getting into. Otherwise, I'll get clobbered, like today."

"You forgot about emotions. They force-multiply muscles, so make sure you turn them on when you put your game face on. But make sure your brain keeps your emotions under control. What else, Doc?"

"Let me emphasize the importance of putting your game face on. It's all about shifting your brain into a different cognitive state that matches your muscles. Look at it this way. Your brain's like a dynamo, able to generate loads of power. But you have to learn how to control it, how to shift from one state to another so the power goes where it should. Your brain is always in some cognitive thinking state. You don't give it a second thought because it's always there. You live in it. It's like the air you breathe. It's all around, and you don't pay attention to it. Maybe we can teach you how to shift states. Jason, didn't Indy mention something about Buddhist monks shifting gears?"

"Yes. She said Buddhist monks train so they can control physical and mental actions, like pulse or brainwave patterns, through meditation. They combine conscious, subconscious, and physical states. Hey, I just thought of something. You and Electra can play a new game. Call it the change of state game. Here are the rules for Electra.

"When you start doing something particularly important, stop for a moment and pay attention to how you're feeling. And then try to imagine what you can think about to make yourself feel that way again. Over time, we'll be training your brain to synchronize your thoughts and emotions with your actions. If you can focus like that, you'll be a world beater."

"I got it. My game face is on when I zone in on what I want to do. And now, you've told me how to practice. I see what went wrong today. I picked the wrong fight. I was in the wrong, so my brain and muscles didn't want to work together." Doc saw it too.

"Here's how you and I can practice. I'll take you to the clinic for brain scans so we can see how your neural pattern changes when you try to sync brain and emotions with physical activity. We'll be getting immediate feedback on how well you're learning to shift states." Jason saw even more.

"If it works, you can teach her how to dial down her brain pattern, to make it appear normal. And if Electra can do that, she'll be able to fool all Healthguard brain testing, other than DNA pattern analysis. And DNA pat-match testing isn't required after grade school. That means we'll be in the clear. What do you think about that?"

"We're all set for Electra and me to play a new game. Why don't we celebrate what we've just figured out by going for ice cream. Do you have room after that last brownie?"

"I sure do. There's always room for ice cream…"

Before bed that night, Jason constructed a reading list of online articles describing adolescent psychology and emotional development.

"Why don't you and Electra read a couple of these articles tomorrow. They'll help you explain more about dealing with emotions.

"I will, and I'll add a couple that cover sex and adolescence, but she has probably covered much of this in the social development class she takes at Christi's school. And we can go one better. Let's give them to Su and have the two of them talk. They can start this weekend. Isn't Su taking her shopping this Saturday for summer clothes?"

"I forgot about that. Thanks for reminding me. I don't know what I'd do without you. You know more about Electra than I do. We'll turn it over to Su, and we'll invite her to spend the night. I'll do my part by cooking dinner."

Electra jumped out of bed early Saturday, even more energy-filled than usual because shopping at the mall was a favorite activity. Even in the online age, and in spite of potential T-Plague exposure in public places, people still like being out and about socializing. Evolutionary biologist Richard Dawkins coined over a century ago the term meme:an inherited trait stored in a culture and its people's behaviors, learning, arts, or institutions that are able to transmit people's social behaviors from one generation to the next. Memes are to culture what genes are to living organisms, so consider them socially transmitted inherited traits. Thus humans,being preeminent social animals,must have the shopping instinct embedded in their memes, which means businesses have built-in customers, young and old alike.

Su spent more time with Electra than typical aunts or godmothers, partly because she was fulfilling Indy's wish, partly because she felt an uncanny attraction similar to what she had towards Indy. As she did in all aspects of her life, Su hid the depth of her feelings, deciding not to reveal her deeper affection until Electra was much older.

The two made a gala day of hunting for clothes. The combination of Su's impeccable taste and Electra's list of "with-it" items young girls wanted allowed them to bag Electra's summer wardrobe. Electra glowed from all the fun, and Jason would too because Su purchased a decadent dessert at a favorite gourmet food store.

Enough time remained before dinner for Electra to stage a fashion show, Aunt Su providing commentary. It was touching to see how natural the relationship between them was. Doc made a note to mention it to Jason.

Dinner conversation was high spirited, and Electra informed everyone that after dessert she and Su would have a woman-to-woman talk about some of the latest emotional twitter popping up among her friends. After she cleared the table, Electra spirited Su into her bedroom, where they sat on the floor, surrounded by throw pillows.

"I got in a fight with a couple of boys last week. It was my fault. I made a mistake and picked the wrong fight. But I learned a lot from it, and Gramps and Dad explained a lot of things to me."

"Your father told me. Fights like that are natural, and it's good they happen when you are young, so you learn how to handle different types of people in different social situations."

"Gramps and Dad explain all sorts of things, but sometimes things come up that they don't know much about." Su's smile widened as she continued in the direction Electra's words were leading.

"I know what you're talking about. Your father and grandfather love you dearly, but they aren't equipped to talk with you about female issues. Your mother and I used to joke about your father. How could such a smart fellow be so dumb when it comes to women?" Electra's laughter was infectious. "Please tell me, what girl things are on your to-ask list?"

"My best friend Christi is beginning to like boys, almost as much as she likes me. She says she likes them in a different sort of way, and I'm still her best friend. She says it comes as we grow adult emotions. I guess I'm not growing them as fast as Christi or the other girls. Aunt Su, I'm not a retard, am I?" In Electra's world, being a retard was worse than death.

"Of course, you aren't! You are the smartest child I've ever known. And remember what your Dad has already taught you. Every person has three dimensions. You have Electra the mental, that's your mind and brain which are one and the same. You have Electra the physical, that's your strength and agility. And you have Electra the emotional, which are your moods and feelings. They each grow on their own, somewhat independently from one another. Try as we like, we cannot consciously will the physical or the emotional to obey our brain. When I was a young girl, just like you, I wondered about my slow-growing emotions. But don't worry about them. They'll come out when you're ready. And when you get older, you might look back on slow-growing emotions being a good thing."

Electra knew what Su was implying but liked to hear Su speak so she could compare her understanding with the explanation given. Electra pretended to take the bait and asked with wide eyes, "Aunt Su, what do you mean?"

"Being an adult is much different than being a child. In some ways better, in some ways worse. Do you know where the expression 'letting the genie out of the bottle' comes from? It comes from jinn, an Arabian word. They were an ancient mythical people who had magical powers, like granting wishes to people who rubbed the lamp in which they lived. When you let a genie out of the bottle, you can't put the genie back in. Once your adult emotions come out, you can't bottle them up again. You have to live with them, which most of the time is good. But there will come times when you'll wish you were a child again. Don't think about emotions further. Just enjoy the fun and excitement of being what you are right now."

"I get it. My emotions will come out when the time is right. Until then, I'm going to enjoy being just what I am."

"Good for you. You and I can talk more about emotions whenever you like."

"Let's go tell Gramps and Dad I'm not a retard after all."

"Electra, I'm certain they already know, but let's see what they're up to."

Late that night, Doc was lying awake in bed, reflecting on what a wonderful day it had been. He was pleased with Electra's relationship with Su because she provided a mother's touch in places he couldn't reach. Today he saw how strong the bond and hoped it would hold as Electra grows into adolescence and beyond.

On balance, he was satisfied with the collective results he and Jason were achieving. *Kit's a gem, sparkling with life and balancing her brain in a normal childhood setting. Jason loves her dearly, but like many dads he's career-driven, putting him out of touch. He's lucky I can fill in, but I'm lucky too. It gives me something to do. And when it comes to raising his daughter, I'm better than Jason. He's not naturally sensitive or empathetic, and he buries his emotions. And he never mentions Indira unless Electra asks. Even then, he doesn't say much. I think I'll ask Su to tell her more about her mother.*

Though he recognized Jason could use a touch more patience and empathy, Doc was proud how well his son balanced all the demands confronting him, carrying career and family responsibilities better than most fathers. But Doc worried about Jason's T-Plague predictions. In spite of NIH best efforts, Cognicom still struggled to develop effective vaccines, and Jason hinted that sociopolitical fallout would cause a downhill spiral. Perhaps not immediately, but trouble loomed on a more distant horizon.

I wish Jason weren't a Type A personality. He's a focus-focus push-push worrier type, and he's gonna burn out or blow up. Too bad he won't go on double dates Adom lines up. A change of pace would do him good, but he says he's just not interested. Maybe that will change when Kit's older. I'll tell him to double date so he can check out Adom's pick while checking out the young fellow who's dating his daughter.

Rome wasn't built in a day, nor did it fall apart very fast. Our private world seems to be spinning the right way. And if we need to change direction, we'll have plenty of time to figure out where to go. Tomorrow will be another day for all of us to get better. There's a famous quote from Candide's Doctor Pangloss: All is for the best in the best of all possible worlds. Jason and I are doing our best for Electra, and that counts for a lot. That final thought brought Doc a good night's sleep.

CHAPTER 21
October 2108

"In the Moment"
(Thread 2 Chapter 8)

MARYLAND'S SENATOR DAVID RUSHMAN knew all about the political saying "When the whistle blows you better get on the train." Not only was he on the Guardian Party train, but he was driving the locomotive.

David was one of many politicians who disliked the current string of feckless presidents that mishandled security and healthcare, steering America away from traditional values while a complicit Washington Establishment neglected the nation's infrastructures and stalled technological progress. And he became more outspoken when T-Plague came ashore, using the outbreak to galvanize the upstart Guardian Party, catapulting himself to the forefront and allowing him to recruit movers and shakers into his camp.

As national security and health fears climbed, the Guardian Party became official, growing a constituency that elected Guardians at local and national levels. Even its toughest critics found no duplicity or hidden agendas. In fact, they grudgingly admitted Rushman championed values that had made the nation great, and was committed to guarding the people against terrorism and T-Plague. He installed smart, aggressive lieutenants in key positions, all of them looking almost as good as himself whenever in the public spotlight.

The Guardians were new in name only because its leadership was politically savvy and connected, quickly building a cohesive organization. Several years ago they had even established an internal security group termed the "Guardian Agency," complete with its own covert operations team. Today David led a meeting for his top echelon, describing preparations and predictions for the upcoming elections.

"We wouldn't be where we are without your commitment to the cause. I appreciate your faith in my ability to recognize where our country needs to be, and in my leadership style the public respects, but without a cadre of talented lieutenants like yourselves, we'd be like all the other opposition parties that have come and gone: all words and no results. And I'm now going to turn the meeting over to my second in command, Jared Gardner, who will tell us what he sees coming, both short-term and long-term. Jared, the floor is yours."

"Thank you, David. For the coming elections, the political landscape looks like we'll gain congressional seats in the Midwest and East, and hold our own in the West. The Administration will hold serve nationally. But longer-term we gain, and they lose if the T-Plague continues to grow and national security continues to decline." One of the lieutenants interrupted.

"Do we know what's going on at NIH regarding Cognicom projects?"

"No. We did too good a job building Healthguard and Securityguard agencies. Cognicom is now a dark project and its double-blind security protocols make it difficult for us to develop contacts. We need to get more of our people placed closer; the elections should help us do that. Say the word, and we'll put more covert effort into it. Then we'll have eyes on the inside." David thought for a minute while glancing around the table, then replied. "Do it. Either way, we can turn it to our advantage. Tell us what you see on the terrorist front. Is there any truth to rumors linking T-Plague and terrorism?"

"No sir, not yet. The major terrorist threat comes from Isilabad and its Middle East proxies. They don't have the technology to deal with biotech, so T-Plague is off limits. But that's not to say they couldn't get it elsewhere by swapping oil for virus technology or forging an alliance with China. We don't think they're doing it, but it could happen. And that brings us to a disturbing trend at home. I assigned one of my guys to dig into it. I'll let him tell us what he uncovered." Another sharp looking lieutenant snapped to attention.

"This damned T-Plague is invisibly sapping America in three ways. First, healthcare costs for long-term care are skyrocketing. We have a growing population of mental incompetents. Second, growing shortages of skilled people in critical areas are crippling GNP growth and infrastructure maintenance. Third, our military and defense posture is compromised by the first two. Not a pretty picture if the trends continue. And all of this negatively impacts public spirit and government support."

Slapping the table, Rushman said, "Not only do I damn the T-Plague, but I damn the current Administration for being so weak. But all this plays into our wheelhouse. Let's have our spin doctors hype it. And let's have covert operations tap into Securityguard as well. Short and long-term, we're going to get more control."

Several other lieutenants provided facts and figures, and an hour later David concluded the meeting. "That's a wrap. Nice work all of you, especially Jared. We'll reconvene end of November to finalize next year's plans. If the election breaks the way Jared says, we can enjoy the moment and then plan for a happy new year."

The first Saturday in November preceded election Tuesday, dawning clear and cool, unveiling perfect weather for the area soccer league's championship games. Excitement ran high that morning in the Kittner and Conklin households because Electra's team had earned a spot in its age group final.

There would be a total of five championship games, each consisting of two twenty-minute periods. Electra's team would play in the second contest that morning. Doc had coached her the night before on preparation and sportsmanship, telling her to put her game face on and avoid showing off. He emphasized that victory goes to the team, not to an individual, and Electra assured him she had learned lessons from last spring's fight. She was more mature, more aware, and more adept at synchronizing muscles and emotions with her thinking.

Five rode in Doc's van, all three Kittners, plus Jennifer and Christi. Jennifer's husband Russell had to attend a special joint agency pre-election meeting, but he would know the score because Jennifer planned to text results as they unfolded.

Both girls excelled at soccer, and all team members had bonded during the course of the season. Parents and players alike respected whatever abilities each member contributed, and the kids were still at an age where good sportsmanship and the thrill of competition trumped winning. Each player had earned an appropriate soccer nickname: Electra's was "Legs" because of blazing speed and adroit footwork, while Christi's was "Goldi" because of her honey-blonde hair and ability to make valuable passes. Other clubs knew the team capitalized on the "Goldi-Legs" duo and had nicknamed it "the Sisters," a source of pride for team and parents.

This was the last year the girls would be able to play co-ed soccer, for next year when they turned twelve the "same sex only" policy would apply. All clubs playing co-ed soccer observed an unwritten rule that prohibited stacking a team with oversized or overage players. The league would—but rarely had to—suspend any club that blatantly violated the spirit of this law. It was neither possible nor desirable to enforce complete equality of size or ability. Besides, the league knew that all sports fans have a time-honored tradition of rooting for the underdog. Officials, coaches, and parents simply wanted fair and fun-filled competition for the kids, and all cooperated, resulting in co-ed soccer meeting everyone's expectations.

The Sisters were slight underdogs, notwithstanding their Goldi-Legs punch. The boys on the opposing team—the Capital City Striders—were bigger and faster than their counterparts, which more than offset the Sisters' female edge. On balance, players and parents alike expected this game to be the more exciting contest that morning.

Electra and Christi bounded out of the van, yelling good byes almost before Doc had come to a stop in the soccer center parking lot. Having spotted their teammates, the girls rushed to immerse themselves in the enchantment of a championship game. The parents knew how fortunate their children were to be sheltered them from the harsh realities of the world, sheltered them from the T-Plague. And they hoped their children would someday look back on how magical is the moment of a championship game.

The Goldi-Legs fan club sat with their club's parent support group that was gossiping about schools and social programs, and whispering about the lurking gorilla, the T-Plague. Fortunately, there were no casualties over the summer.

Electra's club had qualified two teams for championship games. Since both were playing in the morning, there would be an early afternoon celebration at their club center. Parents had lectured players that no matter the final score, everyone's a winner when they do their best. For young children, girls understand the message better than boys. Perhaps it's coded in the Y chromosome, but boys always keep score, and Electra could tell the boys on her team would be disappointed if they didn't bring home the winning trophy.

The first game went as expected. Electra's club team, being the underdog, had trouble penetrating the opponent's defense, so most of the game played out in front of their own net. But they put up a gritty defense, blocking what must have been a record number of shots to keep the game exciting, and though the final score was 4—0, they won the admiration of the fans.

In the parlance of prize fighting, the first match could be called the wind-up because it prepared the spectators for the main event, the Sisters versus the Striders. Five minutes remained to game time, and Connie, the Sisters coach, saw pre-game jitters flitting like butterflies about the locker room. It was time to chase them away by using the right words spoken from experience.

"Huddle up in a circle and grab hands. Each of you should be proud of what we've accomplished together. Always remember, that no matter what level you're playing at, reaching the finals is as good as it gets, and that's what counts, not the final score. Put your jitters in the rearview mirror! Play with joy, for the thrill of being right here in this moment. Use your heads and play with your hearts. Make your parents, your teammates, and yourselves proud of what you'll do on the field. Let's go!" The Sisters charged out of the locker room, scattering any remaining butterflies.

The game unfolded even better than advertised. Both teams played aggressively, fearlessly on offense and defense. Both scored a goal midway through the first half. It stayed that way until a minute to go. Sisters and Striders were tiring just when Electra caught her second wind, along with a perfect piercing pass from Christi. She streaked like lightning towards the opponent's goal, able to fake past the last defender by using agile side to side push-pull footwork and scoring when the goalie leaped to defend the wide side of the net. The first half ended 2—1 in favor of the Sisters.

The Sisters, waving to their parents on the way to the locker room, were buzzing about the first half. Connie insisted they get something to drink, telling them to settle down and be ready for final instructions when she calls them to action in fifteen minutes that were racing away.

"Huddle up in a circle and hold hands. In any game you play, you never look back. You put your game face on and focus on what's in front of you. Don't think about the score, just stay centered in the action. Play with drive and determination and teamwork. Victory goes to the team, not the individual. Let's go!"

The second half was even more spirited than the first, action fast and furious from the get-go. The talented goalies each blocked four breakaway scoring attempts. Coaches yelled to their players to conserve energy, but youthful excitement wouldn't let them listen and the pace took its toll as both teams tired, allowing each to score twice. With only five minutes remaining, both teams had used up all allowed substitutions, and the game became a war of attrition, the crowd cheering both sides for their grit and determination. In a burst of last ounce energy, the Striders mounted a scoring drive that the Sisters could not defend. The score was now tied, only two minutes remaining. The crowd expected a ten-minute overtime period that would determine the last team standing.

Overtime seemed likely until the Sisters intercepted an errant pass and staged a last-ditch scoring drive. As luck would have it, the ball was mishandled by the Sisters, and then by the Striders. Then the gods smiled on Christi. She came away with the ball, spotted Electra and once again made a perfect pass. Two defenders were closing in, but Electra stutter-stepped as the first defender reached her, freezing him in his tracks. She then toe-shot the ball between his legs and caught up with it while he fell on his backside. Only one defender remained between her and the goalie. Out of the corner of her eye, she saw he was bigger and faster, but she had the angle. She was unstoppable unless he tripped her, which he did to trade an almost sure goal for a penalty kick. Electra saw this at the last second, bracing herself for the collision. It was a solid body blow that knocked the wind out of both players. Parents on both sides booed the infraction and were more incensed than the players, who by this time were gasping for breath. Both players staggered to their feet; no serious damage done.

Electra's brain seized the situation. Someone on her team would take the penalty kick, and Legs was usually the first choice. But this time she chose something different. When Connie gathered the team, Electra said she was woozy from the collision. Someone else should take the kick. And to Connie's everlasting credit, she made a decision the team would remember always. She asked her players to pick, and they picked Ruby, the smallest player. Though she was not a swift runner, Ruby had a strong leg. The Strider goalie relaxed a tad too much. Boom! Ruby's kick thundered past a surprised goalie as time expired. Final score: Sisters five—Striders four. Parents streamed onto the field, hugging and congratulating both teams.

The parents had decided in advance—win or lose—to form a motorcade back to their clubhouse where the team would change before holding a celebration party. What a joyous, raucous ride it was. The girls whooped and sang from the back seat, Jennifer wedged between and joining in the fun. The menfolk up front were as pleased as could be.

"Doc and I say you two are quite a pair. I volunteer to be your agent next year when teams come calling."

Doc added, "That was a game to remember. I hope you text Russell."

"I did, and he sends hugs and kisses to the girls. And how about this? He would like us to chaperone a pajama party tonight for all the girls. What do you think?" It was a unanimous yes vote.

The celebration was among the best in club memory. Afterwards, the girls begged their parents for P.J. party permission. All parents said yes, so the Conklin household contained six of the happiest soccer girls that night. Their youthful energy and innocence made it one they would always remember. Even late the next morning, when parents retrieved their champions, the girls were still babbling up a storm. It wasn't until the drive home that Jason noticed Electra had something on her mind.

"I never went to a P.J. party, but I know you girls must have had fun talking until the sun came up. You must be tired. No wonder you're quiet."

"It was the best night I ever had. Even better than Christmas Eve. I wish it could it could go on longer. Thank you for making it happen."Suddenly, sobs and tears gushed from their still innocent but maturing little girl.Doc pulled the van to the curb while Jason reached into the back seat and patted Electra's tear-streaked face.

"You'll have many wonderful times like this. Don't worry, just enjoy them." Electra sniffled, then stopped the tears.

Doc said, "You've grown up a lot this year. And it's normal for people, as they mature, sometimes to feel a bit sad after having a great time. You're feeling sad because you've reached the end of something you wanted to last forever. But although nothing lasts forever, there will always be something good to take its place. You'll see." Electra perked up.

"Gramps, are you sure?"

"Your grandfather's right. So, try not to worry. Let me do the worrying for all of us.That's supposed to be one of my duties."

"OK, Dad. I love you both. I understand the advice, so don't worry about me. I'll look forward to the future."

Electra would do that later, but first, she returned to the unconditional joy of the moment.She would let the future wait its turn, at least for another day.

CHAPTER 22
February 2109

"The Cause of Effects"
(Thread 2 Chapter 9)

Mo WAS UNCHARACTERISTICALLY DISTRACTED after his February think tank meeting, for not even he could find a sliver of a silver lining in the warning clouds on the horizon. He needed to put a positive spin on what he just heard so could avoid stressing his Worldstars even further. Pressure was building because the latest S-Vac formulation underperformed. That was the reason for his surprise visit this afternoon. *At least I can say the clouds are in the distance and not in the offing. There's still time to keep them from blowing in.*

Although Mo had obtained additional resources the team had asked for after Indy's death, the new lab tech and junior researchers added nothing to momentum because the senior virologist that replaced Indy, though he tried gamely, couldn't keep up with Su. Mo blamed no one, for he had witnessed the chemistry between Indy and Su, but Mo's bosses had to have results, and Jason and Adom's diligent efforts to assist fell far short of the mark. As he walked from his car to the lab, Mo mulled over Cognicom's problems.

Fifteen years and counting. All that time and effort, and so little to show. No wonder bosses are frustrated and researchers depressed. I'd be depressed too if my career had nothing to show, but I've been lucky. Mentors and cross-disciplinary assignments have kept me moving up.

And the think tank keeps my options open, no matter what storm clouds blow in. Too bad the Worldstars are bogged down, but they're smarter and I bet have options too. But the best option is to kill the T-Plague before it kills us.

Mo's visit didn't blindside Jason because he had called ahead, but even though he brought his usual selection of mood elevators, spirits were dragging. He tried small talk and safer subjects to start the meeting, but no one talked much. Mo didn't know how much good his original opening remark would do, but he tried it anyway.

"Let me give the good news first; the storm clouds are still in the distance. The world is not about to end anytime soon. But the warnings we're seeing are sobering, so we need to plan accordingly." Jason's witticism surprised him.

"Well, being damned by faint praise is better than a stick in the eye. Let's hear the latest. Maybe among all of us, we can find a path forward."

"I'm sure we can. I'll start with economic and political outlooks. I hope you like the analogy. Think of the world economy like a big balloon. The T-Plague has punched holes in different places, different countries' economies. Soaring medical costs, lack of smart people with critical skills, and decaying infrastructures are the holes. The U.S. is in better shape than anyplace, but we must contain outbreaks short-term, and must come up with better smart pills and vaccines ASAP. Next, think of national security as a big dog on a leash. The T-Plague is sapping its strength. Isilabad has not linked T-Plague and terrorist activity, but it could happen. Finally, think about citizens working jobs that require brain power. They've gone about their lives, at least on the surface, without worrying too much about the T-Plague and national security. But too many people are cognitively impaired. The nation's I.Q. is lower than it was a couple of years ago, people are becoming intolerant, and a lot of them want the Guardian Party to do their thinking. If we reach a tipping point, watch out for government instability. The Guardian Party doesn't seem to have a hidden agenda for a power grab, but who knows?"

Adom said, "My contacts tell me Americans are pragmatic and resilient, and will continue giving the Administration benefit of the doubt as long as Washington can show some progress, especially on T-Plague. Vaccines could keep enough smart people plugged into the economy. Services and infrastructure might improve. But national defense hinges on the Administration paying attention to threats. Sometimes I applaud the Guardian Party for building Healthguard and Securityguard agencies, and all—" Su unexpectedly interrupted.

"Look, I'm doing my best on vaccine development, but let's be frank. Indy and I were a special team. You guys used to call me the genius. But genius only goes so far in this arena when the clock is ticking. I love you guys. You're smart and you're dedicated, but you don't have what Indy had. I'm sorry if you think I'm letting you down." Su stopped abruptly to avoid shouting.

"You never let us down. Please keep doing what you're doing. You'll regain your mojo. Jason and I both know that."

"No, I won't unless Mo can get us Indy's reincarnation." Mo had no idea what to say next and was groping for a graceful exit as Jason soldiered on.

"Let's not go there. Mo, before you go, let me reiterate some ideas we already gave you, and we'll add a couple of new ones. First, our latest testing indicates our newest S-Vac formulation is a little more effective but has a higher probability of side-effects, nausea for the first day or two. And it looks like we can't keep the virus in remission for longer than six months. And if major outbreaks occur, the smart pill supply chain will be empty in maybe two months. That could lead to rationing, placebos dumped into the pipeline, black markets, public unrest. Take that back to your think tank."

"I got it, and thanks for the straight talk. I'll relay the message." As he escaped from the meeting, he hoped chinks in his confidence didn't show.

Jason kept the meeting going after Mo left. "Thanks to Su, we've been able to keep our Stealth project alive. She's even given suggestions to the other teams, and here's what I've been thinking.

Suppose we quit NIH and start Worldstar Biologicals. Would we be better off?"

Anger having subsided, Su answered, "No. In fact, we'd be in worse shape. We don't have the brain power by ourselves. We'd have to hire researchers like the ones Mo got us, and that's done nothing." Adom added, "Maybe down the road we can hire Mo to run the business side. His contacts and business skills would be a big asset. I've picked up a lot by being his go-to guy for meeting preparation, and then watching him in action." Jason ignored the comment and shifted subjects.

"We're doing all we can and have to keep pushing. Let's bring in the rest of our people and tell them the latest. They deserve a lot of credit for putting up with me, and I have some service award coins they can use in the cafeteria. And they're not getting a free lunch. They earned them."

"Let's run through that scenario again. Imagine you're in a car that flipped over and is on fire. Think hard about how you feel and what you do to escape. I'll record brain scan readings so we can compare your cognitive state with the others."

"Roger that, Gramps. I'm good to go!" Depending on what she was doing, Electra peppered her dialogue with pet phrases learned from favorite retro sci-fi or action adventure movies; the oldies were more sophisticated, more creative than the current batch. The "Great Dimming"—a gallows humor term characterizing how the national IQ had shrunk—was fact, not fiction. T-Plague had infected critical thinking skills in the arts and the sciences, swelling the ranks of dementia-suffering people and damaging the nation's economic, political and moral climate. America—at one time the shining city on the hill—was becoming darker.

That darkness had not yet entered Electra's personal world. In fact, she was thriving, interacting socially and thinking better than ever. For the past year, she and her grandfather had been piecing together the operating manual for her lightning brain, a sui generis, one-of-a-kind creation, and Doc was teaching her how to harness its power. She would imagine a specific task involving cognitive or physical skills, memorize how she felt and thought, and then try to duplicate the cognitive state of mind. Doc recorded neural activity scans, and together they would practice controlling the process. She was mastering altered cognitive states—mind control—so she could shift gears to match the action.

"I've got all the scans. Disconnect the electrodes and go grab us a couple of Cokes while I upload the data."

"Roger that." Doc knew many of Electra's pet phrases and expected to learn others as she matured further into adolescence. During the past year he had witnessed Electra's amazing self-directed growth, a phenomenon that had only been conjectured by neuroscientists. Not only was Electra able to put herself in different cognitive states, but she could tell her brain what she wanted to become. Since she wanted to be tall, strong, trim, and fit, her physical persona subtly developed apace. She wanted to excel in school, and her cognitive persona had exceeded that long ago. Now that adolescence had blossomed, she saw the emotional persona's darker complexity and needed to develop more empathy, because handling feelings requires dealing with people relationships. High school would start next fall, expanding her interpersonal horizons and forcing her emotional persona to go where it hadn't gone before.

Doc wasn't concerned that many of Electra's friends were more mature in the ways of the world. *She has a lifetime of people interaction ahead of her. And now that I've trained her, she'll be able to make all three personas work together. I'm glad the joys of youth have stayed with her as long as possible.*

Electra returned with the Cokes and a question. "How does my brain look?"

"The computer's still crunching the numbers. Give it more time, and I'll give you a diagnosis and prescription."

She sat next to Doc, using her smart-phone to view correspondence from her circle of mostly female friends. Doc took his time gathering thoughts after the computer finished because the output was startling. Electra had learned to control the links among her brain's cognitive, subconscious, and physical states.

"I've got the results, but before we go over them, let's make sure you understand what your brain is like. This is a review, but it's important, so pay attention.

"Your brain is like a powerful, complicated, and highly tuned dynamo, generating electrical signals that control your body, thinking, feelings, and emotions. I've been training you to control your brain, to make it run faster or slower, and to control how it handles events. Let me show you some of the brain scans." Doc pointed to images displayed on the monitor as he talked.

"Here's your normal pattern. It looks like a forest of lighted Christmas trees. And here's an image when you make your brain run real slow. Now the scan looks like a normal person's. This is what your dad wants. From now on you'll be able to fool the scanners. No one will know how exceptional your brain is. I won't need to fudge your medical records, and if Healthguard ever scans your brain, you'll appear normal as long as you shift into the correct brain state. The only way they would know how special you are is by doing a DNA sequencing test, and that's rarely done past the age of twelve because the genetic patterns are stable by then. And I have a supply of bogus DNA samples we can use in case they ask for one. Any questions?" Electra had none, so Doc carried on.

"In your case, DNA mini-mutation is still active. Your brain adapts quickly to internal or external stimuli. That's one of your special gifts. Now, look at these images. Notice how similar certain pairs are. You're able to put yourself into cognitive states that sync your brain and body. Here's the sports analogy. You can match your game face to whatever you're facing."

Electra sensed her grandfather had more to say so she didn't interrupt. *Gramps has some warnings for me. I know what some of them are, but I'll keep quiet. I want to compare his with mine.*

"You've grown remarkably over the past year. Mentally, you can think like a grownup and could handle college classes. Physically, I can almost hear you growing. You've emerged into adolescence faster than even you realize.

"It's an exciting time. I wish your father or Aunt Su had a copy of your mother's poems, because she had written several about being your age. Ask your Aunt Su. Maybe she can run through the whole poem, but here's a verse I happen to remember."

"Youth's intoxicating optimism will not be denied!
Unstoppable force, it powers that wild ride,
One-way, once-in-a-lifetime trip to boundless future.
Just over time's horizon, the other side
Of breathless dreams, nothing can circumscribe!"

"Trouble is, you're way ahead of kids your age, in a league of your own. If you're not careful, people are going to wonder why you're so much better, so different. You'll attract too much attention, and we don't want that. They might stumble onto our secret, so I've come up with a new game you can play to keep that from happening. I won't tell you the rules today. Instead, I'll tell you when we start preparing your high school study plan. How does that sound?"

"Sounds good to me. You know how I like games."

"There's just one more thing I want to say, so please pay close attention. You still need guidance from your father, Aunt Su, and me when it comes to dealing with emotions. You need to trust and talk with us. All too soon, you'll be all grown up and on your own. Whew, our training session today has been a lot of work. I'm ready for an ice cream break on the way home. And I won't tell your dad if you won't." "Deal. And when should we tell Dad about today's training results?"

"We'll tell him Saturday, before Aunt Su comes over. Do you remember she's staying overnight? And I don't know what it is, but she has something special for you." Electra rolled, then crossed her eyes.

"Of course, I remember. I'm no retard."

Su had been waiting patiently for twelve years to fulfill Indira's final wish. Jason had given her an envelope to be opened after Indira's death, the contents of which were for Su's eyes only. She did reveal to Jason and Adom some of what it contained, but kept much to herself.

Inside the envelope was a smaller one, with instructions to give it to her daughter when reaching the cusp of adolescence. Electra, mature mentally and physically beyond her years, had ventured into that world, so the moment had come for Su to deliver on her promise. She had no idea what the letter contained, but no doubt the message would be surprising. This weekend, when the contents of the smaller envelope come to light, perhaps there would be another epiphany for the girl with the lighting brain.

"Hey you Kittners," Jason called from the kitchen, "Aunt Su will be here in about twenty minutes, so please be ready. We'll have dinner when she gets here." At times like this, Jason's smart phone came in handy for coordinating cooking with guest arrivals. It was time to mobilize the troops.

All the Kittners gathered in the kitchen, awaiting last-minute instructions. Earlier in the day, Doc had gone over Electra's brain scan results, making Jason happier than if she had achieved perfect SAT scores. No longer did he need to worry about high school medical testing that might reveal her secret. He was happy to cross that off his "to-worry list," but it was replaced by a new one. Jason knew her extraordinary abilities give her great power that must be used wisely, but he didn't know how she would balance it against the emotional demands of adolescence.

"I've been coaching Electra, and I know she can handle her gifts. You don't know your daughter as well as I do. She's more intelligent and mature than you realize. Electra, tell your father the famous quote I gave you."

"With great power comes great responsibility." *I know what it means. I even know it was said by Uncle Ben in the Marvel Comics Spider-man series, but I don't care about being great. I'm only an adolescent, and I care about becoming a good person that uses my brain. I'm going to use my Mother as a role model. Everyone tells me she was practically perfect. And I'm going to start acting more grown up.*

Electra was the first to react to the doorbell. "I'll get it. That must be Aunt Su."

"Now please control your excitement. Remember to tell her you're starting confirmation classes next month. I'm sure she'll talk with you about religious matters whenever you want. And don't pester her about what she has for you. I'm sure she'll bring it up right away. She knows how boisterous you can be." Doc winked at Electra, who agreed to Jason's terms. A minute later, she brought Su into the kitchen.

"The fragrance in here is mouth-watering. I'll have to award Jason the Chef's Cap. And I'll have to teach him my secret recipe for fudge brownies."

"Maybe you should get an apron for Electra, because she helped me cook."

"Perhaps I shall, but for today, I can give her something I know she likes." Having said that, Su placed on the counter a container of brownies.

"This is just the first item I brought. After dinner, I'll surprise Electra with another. And to build the suspense, I'll say only this: I don't know what's in it, but it is for her eyes only. Now, no more hints." Electra's pledge to act like an adult had taken hold. She thanked Su, then excused herself to finish setting the table.

Dinner conversation was as lively as usual. Electra told about enrolling in confirmation classes; Su talked about her new piano. Electra didn't know much about Su's avocation because she and Su never talked about music. Electra realized she had much to learn from Su's patient guidance while navigating the twists and turns of adolescence. *And I won't rush Aunt Su away from the table. I'll practice being patient.*

"Thanks again for the super-sized batch of brownies. We have enough for lunch and dessert for the next three days. Dad, I hope Aunt Su will give us the recipe as a Christmas present. Then I can help bake them." Doc chuckled, then replied.

"If you keep helping your dad cook weekend meals like the one today, I'll get you a new apron." Electra added a clever zinger.

"I think I'm ready to handle kitchen duties besides clearing and scraping and loading the dishwasher. After all, cooking is a critical skill."

"You're right. We'll include a culinary class in your high school study plan. Your Dad and I need to sit down with you and put it together. Then we'll get it approved by the school district. And that's assuming we get you in the guided independent study high school program." Su knew Electra would graduate from grade school home track in June and asked what would be next, so Doc continued.

"We're almost certain Electra's high school placement test scores will put her in the top tier, which means guided independent study supervised by an academic team. Depending on what she selects, we would like you to be part of the team. Jason and I are on it, and with your resume, the program administrators would approve you in a heartbeat. But that'll be another conversation." Electra saw an opening, but kept her mouth shut. *Come on, Aunt Su! Gramps just provided a perfect segue for you and me to get up and go.*

"I would be pleased to be part of the team. And like you said, that will be another conversation. Right now, however, I think it's time for me to chat with a blossoming adolescent. Electra, let's continue in your room."

All through dinner Electra had behaved outwardly like a mature adolescent, though inwardly she was racing to unravel Su's mysterious gift. Tonight seemed even more exciting than Christmas Eve because Su's gift was unexpected. She led the way to her bedroom, scatter pillows already arranged on the carpet, her favorite location for Aunt Su conversations. She adjusted the lighting to an indirect glow, and after they both settled in, waited for Su to begin.

"I have something for you that was given to me long, long ago. It was given to me by my best friend, your mother." Electra felt her heart skip a beat then quicken. "I am the only person who misses your mother more than you do. We miss her for different reasons. You because you never knew your mother and would like to know all about her, and I because I loved her dearly and will never be with her again.

"Just before you were born, your mother wrote a series of letters, giving them all to your father with instructions to deliver them in person if something terrible happens to her during childbirth. Your father, your grandfather, and I, as well as your Uncle Adom suffered through the tragedy of the fire, from which by some miracle you emerged unscathed.

"Your father gave me my letter the day after your mother's funeral. On it was written 'For Su's Eyes Only.' It is a beautiful letter, one that I read once a year to commemorate my love for your mother. Some of what it contains I have shared. That's why I am your aunt and your godmother. Other parts are for only your mother and me, similar to secrets you share only with Christi." Electra was mesmerized, looking and listening with every ounce of attention. Su continued.

"But it contained something else. Something that no one but your mother and I know about until this moment. But now, you do too. It is for you." Su removed a smaller envelope from her pocket. "My envelope contained this envelope addressed as follows.

'For my Daughter's Eyes Only—When Nearing the Cusp of Adolescence.' Your mother intended for me to give this to you when I think you are ready, and that time has come." Su grasped Electra's hands before giving her the envelope.

"You should read this letter in the privacy of your thoughts. Then you decide, after finding what's inside, if or what you wish to share. I know your mother liked games. It might contain a game just for you. While you are reading it, I'm going to explain to the men what's happening. It's a special moment, it's an epiphany. I'm sure they'll be speechless. Then I'll come back in a little while to make sure you're OK. You can decide if you want to talk with us, or if you prefer to be alone." Su kissed Electra gently on the forehead, then left.

The menfolk were sitting in the living room, enjoying the companionship that follows a satisfying dinner. Eventually, Jason had something to say. "What do you suppose they're talking about?"

Doc tut-tutted, "Understanding women was never your strong suit. Electra's at an age when she needs to start talking about emotions from the female angle, so that's what they're doing. Maybe she'll want us to start calling her Electra all the time. She doesn't call me out whenever I use Kit or Kit-Kat, but she glowers at me whenever I do."

"You're the only one she lets get away with it. I've seen her snap at some of the researchers when she's with me in the lab. The older she gets, the more I worry about making her angry."

"Son, stop worrying about that and be glad she loves you and me. She'll always be on our side. It's anyone on the opposite side who should worry. I've seen the transformation when she puts her game face on and shifts gears. She'll be a formidable opponent to anyone who crosses her." Jason was about to make a reply, but changed to another topic when Su entered.

"According to Doc, you and Electra have been talking about emotional issues that concern adolescent girls. Am I right?" Su's one-word reply brought the men to attention.

"No." Su said nothing else, waiting for a response. Jason blinked first.

"I give. What were you doing"?

"Finishing the game Indy and I have been playing for twelve years."

"Jeezus," Doc exclaimed, "twelve years. How'd you keep it a secret for so long? I'll bet on you in any poker game."

Jason wanted to know, not bet.

"OK Su, you win. What's the game?"

"Do you remember the envelope you gave me the day after the funeral? Inside was another sealed envelope, for me to give to Electra when I decide she's ready. Well, she's ready now. I instructed her to read it in private and tell us what it says, but only if she wants to, and only when she's ready. After all, it was addressed to her."

"You've been holding out for twelve years? And Indy knew she would have a girl? I never would have guessed."

Doc added, "Good thing to give her time by herself. We'll hear from her when she's ready."

Electra sat perfectly still after Su left. She was trying to corral a tornado of emotions spinning about in her brain. She wanted to be as calm as possible, missing nothing and understanding everything about this once-in-a-lifetime moment. She slowly, carefully explored the outside of the envelope, discovering it was three dimensional. Something was inside besides a letter. A multitude of possibilities flashed through her brain. Electra rose to find a letter opener in her desk drawer, then sat again on the floor. The envelope was old, so she handled it carefully to preserve its pristine condition. She slowly opened at the top and removed the contents. There it was, a two-page letter written in flawless penmanship; she had never seen her mother's handwriting. And attached to the bottom of the second page was a plastic sleeve containing a small object. Electra would investigate, but only after reading.

"My dearest daughter, I know your Aunt Su has found the right time to give you my letter. She was my kindred spirit, knowing me better than your father did. Let me guess; you are just past your twelfth birthday, and you are mature beyond your years. Please thank Aunt Su for patiently following my last command.

"I am sorry I was unable to experience my life's greatest wish: the thrill of raising you, my only daughter. I know you would have blossomed into a wonderful young lady under my care, perhaps somewhat differently than the marvelous young lady you are this moment, but exceptional either way. I am certain that your father and Aunt Su found ways to bring a mother's touch into your life.

"You've seen pictures and heard stories about me. Aunt Su's will be the most thoughtful, the most colorful, but even they touch only the surface. I am sure you would like to talk with me, to get to know me better and what goes on inside. Now you can!

"Do you like games? I did, so here's a chance for the two of us to play another. I'm offering you my humble legacy. Attached to this letter is the only complete collection of my poems."

Electra stopped abruptly. *Mother's poems! I have Mothers poems!* Then she continued.

"No one has this but you, and now we can play a new game. Simply become familiar with poem titles. Then when something or someone crosses your path and catches your fancy, read my appropriate poem and compare what it says (my thoughts) with yours. If you keep doing this, you will know me better than anyone, with the possible exception of Aunt Su. Great fun for you and me! And maybe someday you'll bring Aunt Su into our game. That will be for you, and only you, to decide.

"I shall end this letter with my most recent poem titled 'I run to You' which commemorates your birth. It captures the essence of my love, which extends through our eternity. My love is with you always."

"I run through hushed stark darkness
Of cold autumnal night.
Impervious to the realities
Of approaching winter's bite.
For you are the guiding wind at my back
That brilliant shining light.
That will always bring me back to you
My thoughts aloft in flight.

Your feelings reach out across the miles
On golden eagle's wings.
And mine to you for the rendezvous
That only devotion brings.
The joy of knowing we're together
A gift bestowed from kings.
Possessing treasure for our souls
A joy that for us sings.

So my commitment is a pledge to you
That can never be undone.
I run to you until I reach
Our El Dorado's Sun.
Our treasure trove that offers us
All the precious, hard-won fun
Of knowing you are safe and warm
In a world that has only just begun."

Electra read the letter over and over, tears flowing softly, quietly. They were tears of mixed emotions: aching sadness for loss, thrilling joy for renewal. Her reverie would have lasted longer but for a tap at the door. "Electra, may I come in?" She answered immediately.

"Aunt Su, please come in." When she did, she sat down next to Electra and waited. She had waited for twelve years, and would wait until Electra said something. Electra handed the letter to Su, saying nary a word. Su read the letter twice.

"I hope you will let me play the game. And a thought just occurred. Has your father given you pictures of your mother?"

"No, and he says very little when I ask about the past."

"I'm sorry I never thought of this before. Uncle Adom was the Worldstars designated photographer. I'm sure he has cell phone videos. I'll ask him to upload them for you."

Electra wiped away the final tears and said, "Let's tell Dad and Gramps about the letter. But let's keep the videos to ourselves. I don't want to give Dad an emotional overload."

"You are wise beyond your years. Your mother would be as pleased as I am. And now, let's go tell the menfolk what you've got…"

Electra would forever remember the spring of 2109 when adolescence blossomed, crowned with the gift or her mother's poems. She followed her mother's advice, memorizing titles so she could match them with whatever caught her fancy. And as Electra did this, she painted in her mind pictures of her mother that complemented those from Adom's videos. One of Indy's verses poignantly said what she felt.

Though Time demanded she depart,
For fields far from here.
Her presence will forever thrill,
A mind's eye holds her near.

Thank you, Aunt Su, for helping bring Mother to life in my mind. I shall always remember this magical epiphany.

The "Three Queens" blossomed that spring, that being the name for a sorority consisting of Electra, Christi, and Robin. Home-schooled Electra had chosen Christi's school for social activities. Robinova Setdarova, a musically gifted classmate of Christi, had gravitated to the spirited Christi-Electra duo. When parents realized the collective chemistry, all efforts were made for group activities; the girls became inseparable.

Robinova—abbreviated Robin—played the piano. She was not as boisterous as the other two; her time was spent at the keyboard rather than on the soccer field. In addition to soccer skills, Christi was a talented singer-dancer. All were pretty: Christi and Robin the willowy blondes, Electra the black-haired, long-limbed dynamo. They were good students too, but to keep Electra's extraordinary brain a closely guarded secret, she pretended to be bright rather than off the charts.

Classmates christened them the Three Queens out of genuine admiration; the girls were unaffected by their status. They and their classmates were not yet sullied by the complexities of adolescence. When watching the class in action, the teacher hoped her students, soon to be performing at the high school level, would make the transition without sacrificing too much innocence too soon.

Spring brought the excitement of grade school graduation and high school preparation. Electra's academic team included her father, grandfather, and Su, plus a school district counselor who would approve a study plan. Her grandfather was developing it and would present it to Jason and Electra before meeting late summer with the counselor. Electra didn't know all the details, but since she had four glorious months until the start of high school, decided not to rush the future.

Spring also brought confirmation class, and the Three Queens studied together because they attended the same church. Classes met Wednesday evenings and Sunday mornings before church services. Electra always did supplemental reading after breezing through the bible assignment.

Electra's extraordinary brain made her autodidactic. She could teach herself any subject better than sitting in a classroom. The Internet supplied everything needed to stoke her insatiable desire for knowledge. She already knew philosophy and religion better than most college freshmen. She liked to skim study guides, like Cliffs Notes, to confirm she knew more than what had been explained in the books.

In preparation for a mid-May Saturday confirmation class activity—a creation of the universe debate hosted by a local community center—Electra chose to review how each person decides their religious beliefs. She knew it was done by balancing faith versus reason. Since the lightning brain placed reason ahead of faith, she leaned towards agnostics rather than fundamental belief. Her emotional persona wanted to believe God exists, wanted a higher power to watch over her, giving security and certainty, but her cognitive persona found nothing to support the fantasy. She would sometimes glance—as she was doing tonight—at written notes (she called them a "Doubter's Checklist") describing why she doubted some of what the Bible teaches.

It's illogical to think God looks like a person, but that's what people from ancient civilizations thought. I used to think that the philosophers or shamans from antiquity who wrote seminal religious scrolls were unsophisticated, but now I know better. They were just as smart as we are, but they lacked tools and technologies to figure out how the world works. They invented religion to explain the physical world. How fortunate that we have science. Neuroscience connects human thinking with the brain's neural structures, and evolution explains how humans adapt and change. From what I've read, cognitive psychologists conclude humans are genetically predisposed to believe in a god, just as we're predisposed to be afraid of snakes.

But why did theologians from antiquity invent Original Sin? According to cynics, they did it to control the faithful. One article I read claims organized religion isn't out to save souls, but rather out to grab power, and it presented evidence that more people have been killed in the name of religion than from wars.

When I go to college, I'll take religion and philosophy classes. But I can study on my own until then. I'll stick with my checklist. I bet I know more than our associate minister who leads our confirmation class, but I'll just sit and listen. I learned last year not to attract attention by showing off. And I know each person must pick religious beliefs for themselves. Some people don't want to face an indifferent Universe, so they seek comfort through believing in God. I'll never argue with their choice. I just hope they make it by careful consideration, not blindly following what someone tells them. Maybe I can use some of my checklist tomorrow when I'm with Christi and Robin.

When Saturday arrived, so did Su. She would coach a Three Queens Bible study session at Christi's house. Afterwards, the parents would order pizza, and that evening the girls would attend the debate, the results of which would be discussed at Sunday's confirmation class. But the girls had an ulterior motive for studying together. They would experiment with a carefully concealed makeup kit Christi had discovered, making for an abbreviated Bible review session. When the trio made plans for today, Christi joked that the beautiful—rather than the meek—might inherit the earth, and a little hands-on practice would improve their chances.

Su's study session wrapped up by early afternoon. When Su joined the parents in the living room, she mentioned how quickly the trio had answered all her questions. "We should be pleased the girls are applying themselves so diligently to Bible study." Meanwhile, the girls ventured into Christi's bedroom, ready to apply makeup.

Christi and Robin unpacked the kit, taking inventory while Electra found cosmetology Websites. Christi's mother had used the kit during her modeling days, and from the pictures Christi showed, Jennifer Conklin knew how to apply the goods. Electra's comment confirmed why the trio ogled the photos: "If you've got the goods it's OK to strut your stuff."

Christi volunteered to be the makeup artist and Robbin the first model while Electra studied makeup instructions. The girls rotated through roles; an hour later they were fully painted, looking good enough for a first session. Then a knock at the door silenced the giggling.

"Girls, we're ordering pizza. What pizza toppings do you want?" Without further ado Jennifer entered the room, greeted by pretty silent faces. To the trio's amazement, she smiled impishly after viewing the handiwork.

"You did a nice job. Why don't I give you some additional pointers?" "Oh Mother, would you? That would be super!"

"Let me tell your father what we're doing. We'll order one large pepperoni and one medium veggie pizza for the three of you." Jennifer realized the girls were growing up and would use this opportunity to teach them the art of makeup, while at dinner the parents would lecture on acting responsibly to handle boys' reactions.

Jennifer spent the next hour teaching tricks of the trade, illustrating by applying makeup to herself. The results were transformative, creating a Hollywood beauty and an entourage of ingenues. Because they were similar-sized, the girls changed into some of Christi's stylish clothes before launching a fashion show. Jennifer noted how alluring adolescent girls can be, and hoped the girls would remember what the parents would tell them at dinner.

Jason called out, "Pizza's here, so come and get it. We'll be in the dining room."

Jennifer said, "It's showtime before dinner, and parental advice-time afterwards." The girls bounded downstairs. The adults were already seated, waiting for a Junior Miss America Pageant, for which Russell Conklin was the first to applaud.

"You look like starlets!" Everyone agreed, but Jason added a note of caution.

"If you don't dial down the makeup, you'll give adolescent boys the wrong ideas."

Jennifer said, "After dinner, we'll talk about what the girls must do to prevent this. The women will lead the discussion and the men can tell us how healthy young lads might react." Attention shifted to the pizza, which slowed the conversation until most of it disappeared and the table cleared, after which Irena Setdarova picked up where Jennifer had left off.

"All adolescent girls want to be attractive, and the three of you are fortunate to be endowed with good looks. But don't be show-offs. That leads to jealousy among girls not as lucky as you, and often encourages boys."

Su added, "When you get older, you will realize that other aspects are much more important than looks. Like character and intelligence and personality. Jason, what would you like to add?"

"Remember this. Adolescent boys aren't deep thinkers. They're swayed by skin-deep beauty and sometimes act irrationally around girls. That's what emotions can do, so always be on guard." Christi spoke on behalf of the Queens.

"We've talked about this in our social adjustment class. And we're told to talk with parents before starting high school, because that's where the social scene shifts into high gear. Don't worry. We'll be ready to handle the situation."

Robin added, "Thank you, Mrs. Conklin, for giving us makeup pointers. Maybe my mother will let me go shopping with Electra and Christi for some, now that we know how to apply them."

"You're welcome, and I am sure your mother knows about makeup too, so she can help you now that we know you girls are ready, willing and able." That was Doc's segue.

"Speaking of being ready, it's time to leave for the debate. I'll drive. And remember to call me when you're ready for pick-up. Electra has the number."

Tonight's debate, sponsored by local church groups to stimulate parental discussion, filled a community center auditorium. The girls sat with classmates, all listening attentively to religious versus scientific explanations presented at a PG-13 level for the creation of the Universe.

Electra paid more attention to classmates than to speakers, for she already knew both sides of the debate, giving more weight to science. She had explained both sides to Christi a couple of weeks ago, even using Earth's creation to illustrate cause and effect. Electra had her ideas about Man causing Earth or vice versa, but never forced others to agree because she knew it was better and safer to let people decide for themselves. As the debate wound down, one of the panelists brought up Earth's creation to illustrate cause and effect.

"Over thirty properties of the Earth, such as its size and orbit and atmospheric percentages, are required for Man to thrive. I think this proves someone upstairs loves us very much. Well, let's have questions from the audience before we take a break. When we come back, we'll show a video about the Synoptic Gospels."

Electra was not going to ask any questions, but rather sit and listen. *The questions raised confirm what I know. Many people need religion for comfort. They're afraid of being alone in an indifferent Universe. Some people who think Man is the center of the Universe ignore the facts, while others don't. And some people who think Man is not the center can deal with the facts, while others can't. To each, his own, live and let live.* Christi surprised Electra by asking a question.

"Isn't it possible that instead of the Man causing Earth, it's just the other way around? Maybe man evolved to fit the conditions here on Earth. Isn't that a possible theory from evolutionary biology?" The combined thoughtful question and Christi's wholesome appearance drew approving murmurs from parents.

"Young lady, that's a great question, and you are very intelligent for asking it. And it connects with the Anthropic Principle, so I challenge all confirmation class students to learn about it on the Internet and discuss it in your classes tomorrow. Now let's take a break. The video starts in fifteen minutes."

The girls mingled with friends who congratulated Christi for asking such a thought-provoking question, and she enjoyed the adulation. Most were going to watch the video, but the trio had heard enough and was ready to leave. Electra called her grandfather, and they watched at the entrance for his van. Christi needed to use the washroom, so Electra and Robin ran outside to wait in the crisp air. "She's heading to the washroom. Let's surprise Miss Smarty. You stand guard outside the door and we'll greet her inside." Three boys had taken an interest in the pretty smart girl who had asked a question they didn't like. Now they would have an opportunity to discuss things in a little more depth. Christi was in such a hurry she didn't notice a fellow loitering nearby.

"Christi's taking too long. I'll go get her." Electra bounded out of the van, activating her early warning system. She had learned the lesson last year; always to be watchful. And sure enough, she noticed a boy near the washroom. As she approached, she pretended not to notice him tapping on the washroom door before walking down the corridor. *That's not a good sign.* She could hear scuffling behind the door. *Get my game face on.* Electra pushed through the door.

In a flash, the lightning brain sized up the situation. Poor Christi! One fellow had her pinned to the floor with her head suspended above the toilet while another eagerly watched.

"Well Miss Smarty, let's see if this will clear your thinking." *Time to act before Christi gets into cold water over her head.*

"Hey, you're not playing fair!" The boy standing turned just in time for Electra to score a swift kick directly into his pillbox.

"Oof," he grunted as he hit the floor, doubling up in pain. As he raised his head, Electra added a Karate back fist to make sure he stayed out of the way. *One down, one to go.* The adrenaline was flowing, but Electra controlled her emotions. When the second fellow rose to action, Electra delivered an open palm strike that crunched into his nose, unleashing a gusher of blood, and he rolled on top of his buddy. Electra grabbed Christi's shoulders, dragging her off the floor.

"Follow me!" The girls dashed out, nearly colliding with two men. "Help! Two boys are fighting in the washroom." The girls ran out as the men hurried in.

"Don't say a word about this! We'll be grounded if our parents find out."

Christi said, "I'll keep my mouth shut, but don't you think those bozos will tell on us?"

"Not likely. If you were those jerks, would you want to tell that two girls just kicked the shit out of you?"

"Electra! You just used the S-word! I won't tell you swore. I'm sworn to secrecy whenever we're on an adventure. Come on, I'll race you to the van!"

The drive to Christi's was much calmer than the washroom episode. At home, there would be ice cream and a discussion of the evening's excitement, edited appropriately by Electra. Mr. Conklin asked, "What was the biggest thing you learned tonight?" Electra purred out a pat answer.

"I learned that at meetings like this one, it's good just to listen and not attract attention. People can get the wrong idea about you, either from what you say or how you look or what you do. Christi, how about you?"

"I agree. What about you, Robin?"

"I liked Christi's question about Earth's cause and effect on us humans. We're supposed to talk about it tomorrow in confirmation class." The parents beamed; their little girls were growing up. Electra wondered what her father might say if he knew tonight's full story. *I'm not telling him. It would cause him to worry when he shouldn't. Thanks to Doc, I know how to get my game face on. And when it's on, the other side should worry, not me. And I'll keep this under wraps. It's a game I control, and I like being in control.*

As the girls hugged one another goodnight, Electra felt a new emotion surge briefly, then vanish. She didn't consider it further, for tomorrow would be soon enough to think through all that she had just learned. Electra slept soundly that night.

245

CHAPTER 23
June 2109

"Rites of Passage"
(Thread 2 Chapter 10)

Doc knew Electra better than anyone ever could. After rescuing her from a near-fatal lightning strike at birth, he served as physician and trainer while raising her with more loving attention than even her father could give. Doc knew best how to build her high school study program, which he would submit to a school administrator after making final adjustments that suited his prize student's wishes.

The program must achieve one overarching goal: develop her multifaceted abilities while guarding her secret. Doc tracked her development from day one, sharing them with no one, not even Jason, who was too distracted by work-related worries. Doc kept him informed on a need to know basis, and little was needed because Electra's academic, social and physical development were on target, thanks to Doc and the home-schooling track. With high school's rite of passage drawing near, he needed to summarize what Electra had achieved and what lies ahead, and he did so after a final brain control training session. They were sitting at the kitchen table, each sipping a Coke mid-afternoon on the last Friday in June.

"You graduated from grade school last Wednesday, and today you graduated from my brain training school. You've mastered all I can give. You're ready to take it from here. Tonight, we'll share with your dad what we've cooked up for high school, but before he comes

---

246

home, I need to give you final instructions. So, here's my address to a singular graduation class." Electra listened intently.

"You are smarter than most adults, and I believe the gap will continue to widen. And you have an uncanny ability for self-directed growth, as if you can command, within physiological limits, what you want to be. But danger lurks because you must never draw attention to yourself. You must never reveal your secret. And you must never turn your abilities unwittingly into weapons against anyone except life-threatening enemies. Furthermore, you have much to learn about emotions and empathy, both so important for dealing with others in today's complex, socially-connected world. You've left behind childhood and its unconditional joys. The future is filled with contingencies, many outside your control.

"I know all this is sobering for one just graduating from grade school, but you're much more mature than your chronological years. You're ready to deal with whatever path you take. Use your extraordinary ability to find the best way forward, to make a difference. It's up to you. Your dad and I, and also your Aunt Su, can give you pointers for dealing with people and emotions, but you'll get more and better ones when you build relationships with people you will meet."

Electra talked only to herself while Doc spoke, comparing what he said to what she thought. *Grandfather knows me well. And I wasn't aware of accidentally hurting others. He's right. Emotions are tricky. Thanks, Gramps, for all you've given me.* Electra gave him a hug when he finished.

"I'll try to live up to those high expectations. And thanks to you, I'm ready for high school. But let's give Dad only the Cliffs Notes version of what you told me. He doesn't need to know all the details." Doc smiled back.

"I agree. He would probably find something to worry about, and we don't need that. I've taught you well. We know what's best for your dad."

Doc called an all-Kittner meeting after Electra put supper dishes into the dishwasher, its rhythmic clicking and swishing delivering a backbeat fitting for his upbeat pronouncement.

"I saved the good news for tonight. I spoke Wednesday morning before the graduation ceremony with your grade school counselor Stenice Maze. As we expected, Electra's test scores qualify her for the high school home track. The official name is Career Prep Guided Independent Study, referred to as CP-GIS."

Jason said, "The education system certainly has changed for the better since I was a kid. Now there's competence-based learning and certifications that give extra flexibility for students at either end of the capability spectrum. It's cost-effective too. Students graduate faster."

"You're right. If Electra follows the plan, she can graduate in less than four years. Let me go over what I've got. It's based on her biotech career choice, and it contains enough college level credits to place her out of many courses she'd have to take in the first two years. "Of course, we'll cover the arts and social sciences. These are the basics in English, history, social studies, and languages, along with econ and comparative civilization. And we'll cover mathematics, including algebra, geometry, stats, and calculus, along with computer logic and discrete math. For science, she'll get biology, physics, chemistry, and a smattering of geology and ecology.

"We need physical fitness, but we'll keep her out of competitive sports for obvious reasons. So, you can take martial arts, personal fitness, or gymnastics classes. You'll blend right in. The classes teach basics and there's no competition. You'll meet a lot of classmates, so consider it relationship-training.

"And I've added a piano class, but we can switch that to whatever instrument Electra would like to learn. If you decide to apply yourself you'll be good, but there are many talented young musicians, like your friend Robin, so you won't be conspicuous. I recommend piano because Aunt Su can help out. Do you like what you hear so far?"

"I do. And I'll go with the piano. I can spend more time with Aunt Su."

"Good. You'll also take a couple of fun courses in cinema, culinary skills, driver training and home repairs. And now, here's the best part. Your CP-GIS study team includes your father, Aunt Su and me, plus a high school counselor. We'll find out who that is after we submit the plan. Aunt Su has already confirmed that NIH has a gifted students' co-op program, so your career path activities will include time spent with her or your dad working at their lab. Now, how about that!"

"Gramps, this program is perfect." Jason added, "Incredible. We have Electra's game plan all set for high school. And like you've already told us, she'll appear normal on all medical tests. It all looks good on paper, but let's always remember that no one but the three of us must ever know how exceptional Electra is."

Doc added something extra for Electra. "I'm giving you an assignment. I want the three of us to watch a retro sci-fi movie, 'Forbidden Planet,' and a couple of episodes from the old TV series 'The Incredible Hulk.' Please set up a time."

Jason asked, "Is there anything I need to do?"

"Yes. Please tell Aunt Su the Conklin's have invited all of us to a combination graduation party and Fourth of July celebration for the Three Queens."

"I'll do that. And I just thought of something else. Electra, now that you're ready for high school, what name do you prefer? Shall we call you Kit, or Electra?"

"Call me Electra. Kit is for a little kid, and I'm beyond that. But if I ever play sports again, maybe I'll use Kit. Kit Kittner would make a snappy name for soccer player or quarterback."

"Fair enough. Now, here's your first test. If we go for ice cream, what should we call you?"

"That's a no-brainer. Call me anything you like, as long as I can get two scoops of chocolate fudge…"

As they drove for ice cream, Jason's whimsical observation put Electra's adolescence into a family perspective. "When you get your driver's license, you'll be able to drive us for ice cream. But don't worry. I'll still buy until you're all grown up. And no matter how grown-up you get, Gramps and I will always see the little girl that's inside."

Cool and rainy Fourth of July weather didn't dampen the spirits at the Conklin party. Everyone but Jason and Russell (they manned the grill on the covered deck) moved indoors, the graduates into

Christi's room, the adults into the family room. The girls swapped high school preparation stories, most notably that Electra and Robin had qualified for CP-GIS tracks while Christi would stay in the traditional track because it fitted better her social skills and interests. Christi's test scores were far below those of her best friends, but her parents didn't worry because they knew she was bright and would do well if she spent more time studying instead of socializing. Her looks and performing talents would make her a favorite for cheerleading and other high school in-groups, and she had already been recruited for the girls' soccer team. And since her high school was conveniently located, Electra and Robin chose it for on-campus courses like social studies, personal fitness, or crafts. With a little help from Christi, the trio would be part of as big a social scene as they wished.

The parents' discussion centered around more serious issues, T-Plague always near the top of the list. Exposure risk is higher in high school because there are more students and social activities to contend with. Doc mentioned that schools have to follow Healthguard-mandated "risk reduction" policies, so most parents were satisfied their children would be safe. And Jennifer joked that high schoolers never pay attention to any lurking threats, even quoting a slogan Christi often used: Worry is for the older generation. Su knew that Jason would criticize Electra if she were within earshot and was glad he was worrying about the grill instead.

July sped by as Electra busied herself preparing for school. Her study program had been approved as soon as she and Doc selected first-year courses, and then she began downloading online study modules, which had a September seventh official start date, but Electra could begin anytime. Su and Doc convinced the CP-GIS counselor to approve advanced classes early in her program so she would earn college credits long before graduating. And finally, Jason registered her in the NIH Gifted Students co-op program, giving her access to additional online seminars and certifications. Electra was so pleased she wanted to cartwheel into the kitchen, but instead practiced adult-like self-control to contain her enthusiasm.

She and Doc went shopping early August for a used spinet piano. She didn't need a grand piano like Robin because she was just starting, and no one knew if music would become center stage. They comparison shopped online, then visited several specialty music stores before finding one that would fit nicely in the living room. She told no one she already knew from practicing on the Internet how to read music for it made no sense to show off, and when the piano arrived on a late August Thursday, she casually practiced when no could hear.

The following Saturday evening was showtime; the Kittners would watch *Forbidden Planet*, and then on Sunday an episode of *The Incredible Hulk*. Retro sci-fi flicks were among Electra's favorites, and she had watched years ago what her grandfather had selected, but she would play along when he explained connections to the movies. Games within games were Electra's specialty, and she expected high school to increase the number of unwitting players.

Doc gave a synopsis before starting the movie. "*Forbidden Planet* is a sci-fi classic that set the standard for its genre. The plot is loosely based on Shakespeare's play *The Tempest*. I want you to pay close attention to Doctor Morbius. He's brilliant, but becomes a victim of his emotions. Are we ready?"

"Yes Gramps, and I made popcorn for everyone. Here's your bowl. Oops, I forgot the Cokes. Hold on. I'll be right back."

Though the original movie dates back to 1956, it is Electra's all-time sci-fi favorite. Even by today's standards, the visual effects are spellbinding, and the sound effects keep an air of mystery and suspense always present. The plot and character development are more sophisticated than today's fare, which seem one-dimensional by comparison. Her favorite character is of course Dr. Morbius, whose brilliance is like hers. And Electra knows how to overcome the fatal flaw that ultimately kills him. *My emotional persona might someday be put to a similar test, but I'm sure I'll be victorious.* Doc wasted no time quizzing Electra after the movie ended.

"What connections do you make with the movie?"

"I guess it shows that no matter how smart you are, you need to be aware of other people and your emotions."

"Precisely. The poor Krells didn't realize that when push comes to shove, emotions will always overpower reason. Your father and I have managed to keep you as safe as possible. But in high school, you'll be in uncharted territory. Please don't be like most adolescents. Talk with us so we can help you."

"I think I know what you mean. You're giving me more independence, and I'm ready to handle it. Don't worry. I won't show off how smart or strong I am. And I can keep my brain and body in sync, so when I do something, I'm ready for action."

Jason said, "When cognitive and physical states work in tandem, the outcome is always superior. But there's a final piece to the puzzle, the emotional piece. I know how much you like to study, and you probably already know the matchup between Plato's chariot allegory and Freud's psychological model containing the id, ego, and superego. Emotions correspond to Plato's unruly horse, or Freud's id. You have to keep them under control." Electra nodded, waiting for Jason to continue.

"When high school starts, you'll begin experiencing a wider range of emotions, and even more when you go to college. Emotions are part of being human. Some are wonderful, but some are painful. Everyone needs to control them best they can. And it's even more important for you. So please, make sure you understand your feelings."

"Got it, and I got the movie too. And let me guess about tomorrow's when we watch a Hulk episode. Poor David Banner. He tries to do what's right, but when people push him too far he loses control and turns into the Hulk. I promise to stay in control."

"Your dad and I know you'll always do your best. Just remember what we talked about tonight."

Thanks to seamless preparation, Electra cruised into high school's brave new world, unlike many whose passage was rough. She thrived on CP-GIS flexibility, allowing her to work at her own pace. The assigned textbooks and automated learning units were a snap, but she kept that to herself, submitting assignments and tests only when due and scoring well enough to place in the upper decile, but not so high to attract attention. She had ample time for advanced study on topics of most interest: science, math and computers, and always made time for sci-fi and action-adventure flicks that motivated her to practice high-speed driving and martial arts by watching online videos. Electra was having the time of her life.

Her chosen career, motivated partly in remembrance of her mother and partly in recognition of her genetic para-normality, plus her father's connections, paved the way into the NIH co-op program. Several times each month she went to the lab to work with Su or Jason, talk with researchers, or study online, being careful not to overstep her bounds when talking with researchers. Besides, she had figured out how to hack into all NIH or Cognicom directories of interest, so could work in comfort on her home computer.

Electra uncovered a puzzle while hacking into directories. *The Worldstars' official project, Cognicom-S/Z for the suppression vaccine, contained hidden directories for a Stealth Project. Hmm. Dad's team is also playing a game-inside-a-game. Once I know more about biotech and Cognicom, I might be able to play along.*

Entering high school's brave new world pricked the protective bubble of Electra's pre-adolescent world, unlocking whole new vistas now that Electra had even more freedom to work on her own. Classmates showed her a world of subjects besides science and math, and she began exploring newfound feelings that came with adolescent social interaction. For the first time, she understood the difference between loneliness and aloneness. Loneliness is a lack, a feeling that something is missing, and that may cause pain. Aloneness, on the other hand is presence, fullness, a joy of being where nothing else is needed. Electra never felt lonely.

Now that Electra's increased freedom had expanded her world, she knew she must rely only on herself. *I've grown enough to stand on my own. Isn't there a poem in Mother's collection that touches on this? Yes, and how fitting for me. It's titled "The Stranger," and I can recall its verses.*

"Into this world uninvited we came.
Often deceived into thinking we're grand,
Often not knowing the place where we stand,
Nothing provided the rules of the game.

Searching for meaning the myths do abound.
Often promoted by personal cause,
Often ignoring humanity's laws,
Full of such wisdom as word-empty sound.

Remove all the blinders and so understand.
Meaning is found in your singular thought,
Contingently pointing to what should be sought,
Alone as a stranger in an always strange land."

I can handle being alone. It's part of being alive. Everyone must come to terms with being alone. But I'm never lonely. My brain takes me to cognitive states where I share my world with whomever or whatever my brain creates. The only world there is, the world I know, is the world constructed by my brain. I'll understand all this even better when I take college philosophy courses, but until then I'll enjoy my high school transition period and study some philosophy on my own.

Electra's new world brought exciting changes, but with them came a troubling awareness: the world is in constant motion, changing everything. She could feel her changes and liked what she saw, but if she were changing so were her father and grandfather. She was too close to see, or perhaps she didn't want to. To her they were like the Greek gods on high; they were constant; they would never die, but she knew this was a lie. The time would come when they would grow old and she must take care of them, but she pretended that was in a faraway future and tucked the worry away for a distant day.

Electra attended on-campus classes for gymnastics and music at Christi's school. She liked the grace and body control gymnastics taught, but had no pretenses for becoming anything but mediocre. The ideal female body type was not to her liking: too short, too stocky, or too anorexic.She learned enough to satisfy the Peter Principle made famous long ago: people rise to the level of incompetence. She liked having no pressure to excel. Events in the last six months had spurred her emotional growth, forcing her to understand why talented people are often haunted by impossible expectations. She would try her best to avoid "pitfalls of excellence."

Bi-weekly music classes were also to her liking, and on alternate weekends Su helped her practice. As with gymnastics, expectations were modest. The math-like precision of classical music resonated with the logical part of her brain, but she hadn't learned enough to know if she wanted music to play a bigger role in her life. Since there was no need rush a decision, she simply enjoyed playing tunes. Electra's social world grew much faster than before thanks to Christi, who had become fully engaged in a whirl of high school activities. Whenever the Three Queens gathered, much of the conversation focused on how demanding high school's social proving ground can be. Only Christi had all the right stuff for the in-crowd, letting her thrive in the wanna-be-cool preppy groups. She had kissed childhood goodbye, bringing with her only Electra and Robin.

The action-packed weeks rushed by, flipping the calendar to mid-December, one week before the start of Christmas vacation. Christi had inveigled invites for the Three Queens to an in-crowd party hosted by an older cheerleader. Though only a freshman, Christi's looks and with-it personality granted membership to the socially connected. The Three Queens were ready to leave from

Christi's for the party, and afterwards would spend the night at the Conklins. Christi rattled off last minute instructions.

"Don't ever again refer to us as the Three Queens. That's grade school, and we're way beyond that. And let's shit-can our kid nicknames. No more Chris or Kit or Robbie crap. Our names are Christi, Electra, and Robin. We're mingling with older students, so act mature." Robin was about to complain, but Christi talked over her.

"Don't be so sensitive. You better get used to four-letter words not found in the books you like to read." Christi would have schooled Robin further, but her mother knocked on the bedroom door. She had a different set of instructions.

"Now remember girls, no drinking and of course no drugs. I'm sure most of the kids follow the rules, but some of the older boys might push the limits, so please be careful. And call me no later than midnight. Into the car you go."

The girls chatted nervously in the back seat, then Christi spoke to her mother.

"Darlene's parents will chaperone the party, so you don't need to worry. By the way, Darlene thinks I should try out for the acting club next term. And she says Robin should be the club pianist. We'll be putting on a musical in the spring." Electra was happy for her best friends; their talents were being applauded by their peers, which at that age is heady stuff indeed.

Darlene and her parents greeted the trio at the door, then Darlene hurried them into the party area after Mr. Gustavson collected coats. Darlene pointed out prime locations: bathrooms, snack tables, mingling corner including a piano, and a dance area. Thirty guests had already arrived; most of the upper-class students would come later. The girls recognized some classmates and Christi broke the ice with the others, especially with the boys, two of them recognizing Robin. "Didn't you play the piano at the last assembly? You're pretty good. Can you play some sing-along stuff for us?" Robin blushed in her shy manner that the boys mistook for cool aloofness.

"Sure. Just tell me what to play and I'll give it a go."

"Your name's Robin, isn't it? I'm Liam, and this is Carter." Robin and her two escorts cruised over to the piano, where Robin would be for the rest of the evening.

Christi took Electra around the room as more students arrived. Christi was primed for dancing and soon paired up with one of the older boys. Electra chatted happily with a couple of talented girls from her gymnastics class who were built for the sport. The tinier of the two said, "You're pretty good for someone who didn't do gymnastics before taking the class. And your height makes you look graceful."

"Thanks, but I'm just trying to hang in there. Do you belong to a club outside of school?" They did, so the girls talked about club versus school teams. Soon a couple of boys joined the group.

"I know you. Isn't your nickname Legs, and didn't you play soccer on the Sisters team? You've grown since then. I bet you're even better now."

"I was called Legs back then, but please call me Electra; it sounds more grown-up. I recognize you from last autumn's soccer tournament."

"Yeah, I was a spectator watching my younger brother play. Are you gonna play soccer on our girls'team?" Electra had already developed pat answers for questions like this.

"No, at least not this year. I'm taking gymnastics. My parents thought it would help me adjust to my new height." As conversations continued, Electra relished the opportunity to meet new high schoolers. She glanced about, happy to see Christi and Robin in the thick of the action.

And so, the evening whisked away. It was nearly midnight when a breathless Christi rendezvoused with Electra. "What a great way to start Christmas vacation. I hope you're having a good time too."

"I sure am. I made some new friends, and now I have more contacts when I'm on campus."

"I better call Mother. Let's round up Robin first."

"Judging from the chorus at the piano, she's pretty wound up. Let's get her and go." As they walked towards the piano, Electra noticed Robin swaying while playing. Robin's escorts were still with her, standing just to the right of the piano bench.

Liam whispered to Carter, "When's that date pill gonna kick in? She drank the stuff ten minutes ago, and nothing yet."

"Don't worry. We're experimenting."Their patience was rewarded, for suddenly in the middle of a treble arpeggio, Robin listed forty-five degrees to starboard and waltzed off the bench, colliding with Liam. The boys sprang into action, propping her up on either side, steering her into a nearby room occupied by several older girls and boys. When the door closed, the lightning brain switched gears. Electra snapped instructions.

"Did you see that? Get Mrs. Gustavson while I get into the room. Do it now."

With so much activity going on, few paid much attention to the sudden exit of the piano player, so Electra slipped into the room unnoticed. Poor Robin! There she was, the center of attention, sprawled on her back with one of her escorts astride at her waist.

Her eyes seemed to spin in opposite directions as her head rolled from side to side. An attentive audience waited for an encore.

"Carter, give me the magic markers. Let's do a little body painting." Liam unbuttoned Robin's blouse, then reached for the pen, but before he could scrawl the first letter a wave of nausea swept through Robin, instinctively propelling her to sit up and throw her arms around him. A rumble issued from deep inside, like the sound of a drain pipe about to discharge its contents. Liam tried to avoid the deluge by pushing Robin and twisting to the right, but he was a goner. He ended up on his back with Robin on top—face to face—just as she heaved her Christmas cookies, along with Friday's entire menu.

"Get her off me! She's heaving her guts out! Aggghh!"Liam was screaming and gagging; the viewers were stunned into utter silence. Electra was about to take charge when two boys helped Robin to her feet. Now that her stomach had emptied and the remains of the date pill ejected, she was coming around.

"Thanks," she stuttered weakly. "I don't know what happened. That last drink didn't go down too well." Electra led her out of the room, away from the mess. Fortunately for all involved, the episode was invisible to most of the party-goers. Story-filled rumors would embellish what had happened, and as in war, the same in high school: history is written by the victors. Robin would remain unblemished, much to Electra's relief.

"You look better now, but I never saw eyes twirl as yours did."

"My stomach's still queasy. I feel bad for Liam. His sportscoat is ruined.

"Better his clothes than yours. There's hardly a mark on you." Christi and Mrs. Gustavson suddenly appeared at Robin's side.

"Child, what happened? You look terrible." Electra explained what had happened, and then let Robin speak for herself. Mrs. Gustavson quickly surmised there might be more to the story.

"I will speak to Liam and Carter. Christi, please tell your mother I will call her tomorrow. What's the phone number?"

"I'm calling her now to come pick us up. Here's my cell phone. Please punch in your number, and I'll leave a message."

The trio waited in the entryway, inventing an interim story for Mrs. Conklin. "We have to tell Mother something pretty believable, but let's not get ourselves grounded because of this."

Electra said, "Here's the scoop. We'll keep it short and simple. Robin picked the wrong drink off the table. It upset her stomach, and she started feeling better after she barfed. Sort of like no harm no foul." Neither Christi nor Robin could come up with anything better, so they would go with Electra's version of the truth.

Christi added, "Those jerks were experimenting and Robin was the guinea pig. And when the rumors spread, they'll be even bigger jerks because Robin came out on top. There's Mom's car. Electra, you do the talking."

"So girls, did you have a good time?"

"We sure did! We'll tell you all the excitement." Mrs. Conklin listened patiently, realizing a bit of cover-up was taking place, but decided not to be too judgmental.

"Hmm. Well, it's good Robin feels better now. Christi, please call Robin's mother. I'm going to drive her home. And I'll get the full story tomorrow from Mrs. Gustavson. I'll talk with you girls afterwards, and when we do I want each of you to think about what you've learned."

"Yes, Mother, and thanks for giving us some credit for using our heads." Jennifer smiled to herself, remembering some of her teenage escapades. She would make sure tonight would be a learning experience regarding caution and consequences. *Christi's high-spirited, but I have to let her learn for herself. Good thing Electra's often with her. I hope high school doesn't pull them too far apart, but it can be a rough passage for childhood friendships. Maybe Christi will have smoother sailing than I did. The tale's not yet told.*

"The Chosen Path"
(Thread 2 Chapter 11)

THE T-PLAGUE STRUCK EARLY in the year with the fury of an apocalyptic perfect storm, paralyzing two of China's largest eastern cities and overwhelming the country's teetering healthcare system. Outbreaks in San Diego and Boston were larger and harder to contain than the ones from a year ago, and although an Israeli outbreak was contained, fear and rumors in Tel Aviv were rampant. Social media buzzed about mutated virus strains impervious to smart pills while the news hyped Isilabad's recruiting campaign that called the T-Plague Allah's vengeance on the Infidels, sinking Europe deeper into a funk.

All the furor impacted Electra's world in three ways. It reduced social interaction. Although schools increased screening and sanitizing while cutting back on social events, many parents kept children out of school. It increased pressure on her father's Cognicom project to deliver an improved smart pill. And it confirmed Electra's career path. She planned to battle the T-Plague as soon as she knew enough to make a difference.

Electra prepared for battle by playing a "boot camp" training game. She studied enough biotech and math to grasp the tools Cognicom projects used, equipping her to learn more at Jason's lab or through online courses, and she pored over Su's white papers that explained the solution path for effective vaccines. She also added to her computer skills so she could hack deeper into Cognicom project files. Her brain worked at lightning speed, and in three months she had sorted through all the data, identifying where to improve the Indy-Su conjecture for a complete T-Plague solution.

For the next month Electra dashed through school days so she could focus on Worldstars T-Plague work, and her hard work paid off because now she fully understood the Indy-Su solution path, realizing it was merely a good starting point from which to make further progress. But the Worldstars had been unable to move to the next level. If her mother had lived longer, perhaps she and Su might have figured out the next step. They might have corrected their mistakes.

Electra had just uncovered three incredible blunders that not only partially canceled, but also led Su away from improved vaccines. Su failed to account for both aggressive and remissive viral states; Indy failed to find both DNA sequences that control neural-entangling nano-enzymes; Jason failed to edit completely the one sequence she did uncover. Subsequent results fit exactly what Electra predicted: the initial S-Vac and improved smart pill slowed but did not stop cognitive impairment, and Worldstars' efforts to improve the initial formulation were doomed to fail.

After diagramming the complete solution path for all vaccines, Electra sat back to contemplate what she had just accomplished. She had traced the links from virus to bacteria, and from bacteria to brain centers. The infected brain centers release enzymes that cause neural entanglement in the brain's neurons. She even knew how to develop additional vaccines only she would use if darker contingencies emerge.

Not even Su is going to understand my solution. And the other teams are lost in the R&D wilderness. I'll have to dummy down a diagram and clues I'll give to Su just as soon as she and Dad are ready.

Electra now had answers for how the T-Plague works and how to kill it. I know my solution path is correct, and I can make minor adjustments as I move ahead. My next challenge is coming up with the people and the plan to launch my vaccines.

This would pose no problem in a world inhabited by people as smart as Electra, but she was trapped in a primitive world, living with humans who were light years behind. She had to proceed cautiously, invisibly, or risk revealing her secret. She could not tell even her father, so she plotted a plan that would work with what she had: plant clues for Jason to trip over. If that didn't work fast enough, she would develop a contingency, but there was no need to do so until her initial plan unfolded. Electra began to queue up clues.

There were factors beyond R&D affecting the T-Plague storm, namely political and cultural settings. National and international politics roiled the situation; the media screamed about it daily. Talk of terrorism stirred the public and disrupted the cultural climate. Observing from the sidelines, Electra knew there was too much happening for Mo and Adom's networking to assimilate. *Maybe I can help there too. But first things first. I'll help get effective smart pills and vaccines. I'll worry about politics and terrorism later.*

Mo had recently joined the ranks of the worried because public concern was climbing as fast as early July temperatures, and T-Plague progress was dead in the water. Now more than ever he needed the Worldstars to deliver. Though he tried to project grace under pressure, his even-tempered manner was starting to buckle, putting the Worldstars on edge whenever he came to the lab for impromptu meetings. He was about to start another when he noticed an extra person in the room—Electra sitting at the conference table.

Mo remembered she participated in a co-op program and had seen her occasionally in the lab. What struck him immediately was an eerie mini-Indy resemblance. Jason had told him she was bright; Mo wished one kiss would change her into her mother so she could take Indy's place next to Su, for then progress would rise like the phoenix from the ashes. But he knew better and said to himself *What a pipe dream! Indira's an impossible act to follow.*

"Hi everyone. I hope the mood elevators I brought work, because we need to go over some serious issues. And I see we have a new Worldstars member. Hello Electra." Mo had never acknowledged her status, so Electra decided to find out where she stood.

"Hello, Mr. Solstein, and thanks for the chocolate chip cookies. They're almost as good as Aunt Su's, and they'll give me energy to keep up." *Let's see how he handles that.*

"I see you're ready to take notes. I hope you realize what we talk about stays here. And maybe you shouldn't be here. You won't understand what we're going over." *I understand more than you do, but I won't show it.* "Why don't you go back to your workstation? Your dad can tell you later what we talked about."

"Chrissake! snapped Jason. "She's not bothering anyone. Maybe she'll bring good luck. Let her stay."

"OK, OK. I didn't mean to disrespect her. I apologize. Let's start. It's not a pretty picture, internationally or domestically. The Chinese report the virus has mutated, and the smart pills they've got from us don't work. The same goes for San Diego. So, here's our first issue. What can we do to get a better smart pill for the mutation? And here's the second. What's the link between China and San Diego? Any ideas?" Electra had plenty but kept mum. *I know what to do to get a better smart pill. Compare mutated to original virus. Look at the mutated DNA sequences for changes that would put it into remission. Modify the smart pill to target the appropriate sequence. Dad should pounce on this.* Jason faced blank stares from everyone, even Su, but as team leader felt obligated to break the uncomfortable silence.

"I think the best place to start is for me to look at the new virus and go from there. Su and I will start working out a plan for this right after the meeting. Adom, how about you taking the lead for finding a connection between San Diego and China?"

"OK, but I'll need some ideas from Mo. I'll talk with him after the meeting."

Mo said, "That'll work. Let me go over some other issues. These aren't in tech arena, but they could spill over into Cognicom. The first deals with the Middle East, Isilabad specifically. They're calling the T-Plague a curse on the West against Modernity. We don't think they're capable of causing mischief, but who knows? I'm told CIA is keeping a close watch on their biotech capabilities. The second hits closer to home. Public sentiment against the Washington Establishment is growing. They want more national security and anti-terrorist protection, and they want smart pills that work. This is playing right into the Guardian Party. The public likes Securityguard and Healthguard. And they're the brainchild of the guy leading the party, David Rushman. If the trend continues, he'll make them even more intrusive in private life and government programs. Cognicom will be hit hard." Mo saw nothing but grim faces, and the next topic wouldn't make them go away.

"Let's come back to our team. What can I report back to Bobbi? Are we making any progress? Jason, the floor is yours."

"The other teams are stumped, but at least they're asking for help. We haven't made additional progress yet, but Su is working on some ideas. How about giving us another month to figure out what we can do for them? As for improving S-Vac, we've ground to a halt. Su can give you a better picture. Su?"

"Our new formulations are less effective than the old ones, and I don't know why. When we made our big breakthrough, we were able to tweak the original formulation to get improvements. But it's no longer working. My recommendation is for me to work with Jason to compare mutated versus original virus. We'll have to see where that leads."

Mo could tell he had worn out his welcome. "OK. I gotta go. Keep me posted. I have to tell Bobbi something, so I'll give her a SWAG estimate that in three months we'll know if we're back on track." Perfect segue for Electra. She knew the acronym, but asking a question might defuse the tension.

"Mr. Solstein, what's a SWAG?"

"A SWAG is an official scientific term. It stands for Scientific Wild-Ass Guess. And I know plenty of other military acronyms. Maybe you and I can talk about others when your dad lets us."

"Don't be surprised if Electra already knows them. My daughter is a clever young lady."

Clever indeed. She had already prepared a queue of clues that would lead to progress as soon as she recruited her father to play the game. With her grandfather's unwitting assistance at dinner, she would teach him the rules. Since Doc always started dinnertime conversations asking about Electra, stories tonight would include Electra's day at the lab.

"I had a neat time at the lab today. I got to sit in on my first team meeting that Mr.Solstein led, and I think I did a good job keeping track of what was going on, right Dad?"

"You were fine. He'll let you sit in on others, now that he knows the team thinks you bring us good luck. Who knows? Maybe you will." Doc smiled as she added to Jason's comments.

"Dad and Aunt Su are putting a plan together so our team can start making progress again. Please let me be your junior partner on it. I'll learn a lot and maybe even come up with ideas, just like mother's distant relative Srinivas Ramanujan used to do." Electra waited for Jason to catch up.

"Who?" Electra checked to see if her grandfather knew and was in luck when he came to her aid.

"Don't you know the story about Ramanujan and G.H. Hardy, the most famous British mathematician of the early 20th century?" "Indy told me something a long time ago, but I've forgotten.

What's the story?"

"Srinivas Ramanujan was an Indian self-taught math genius who was discovered by Hardy. Hardy took one look at some of the theorems sent to him and said Ramanujan was a mathematician of the highest quality, a man of altogether exceptional originality and power. Hardy brought him to England, where for the next twenty years he did amazing mathematics, often collaborating with Hardy. I think Electra would like to play the Ramanujan game with you. Why not let her look over your shoulder? It can't hurt." Electra was turning virtual cartwheels, all the while maintaining demure composure.

"OK, we'll give it a try in two weeks when Mo gets us a mutated virus sample. But Electra, please don't get discouraged if a lot of the work is way, way over your head. We know you're very smart, but it takes years of study for even the smartest to understand cutting edge genetic research. Promise?" Electra fought to keep her joy contained. It was like keeping lightning in a bottle, but she did.

"Yes Dad, I promise. And you and Gramps will be proud of me." Electra was becoming a slick handler of people because widened horizons gave her opportunities to practice the art of negotiation, and now she applied a cardinal rule: change the subject just as soon as you get what you want.

"Why don't you let me cook dinner Saturday? I want to practice some of the recipes I learned in culinary class. And I'll cook dinner on a Sunday when Aunt helps me with piano lessons. Practice makes perfect. Deal?"

"That's an offer I can't refuse. What's on the menu?"

"I'll tell you Friday night when we go grocery shopping, but before I tell, you'll have to make a couple of guesses." A nostalgic smile flickered when Jason said, "There's only one person I ever knew who liked games as much as you."

Electra was at the lab when Mo delivered mutated virus samples that started her game of clue. Now she could watch her father and Su in action, following like a shadow, always near but not the least bit noticeable, until she wanted to be.

"We're going to take DNA scans. Then we'll compare with the original virus. I'll show you how." Having watched before, she already knew but always took advantage of supervised training as a cover for how she learned. Jason was impressed. *She has good hands. Picks up lab techniques like lightning. Dammit! I'm getting neurotic. I gotta stop associating lightning with Electra.*

"Nice work. That'll do it for today. Tomorrow when you get here after your morning at school, we'll take a look at the computer-enhanced pattern overlays for ideas on where to go."

"I have gymnastics class tomorrow morning, so Gramps will bring me right after lunch." Electra was as happy as a New England clamdigger because she had a plan for opening Jason's mind to find her clues.

That evening, she dusted off all school work in record time, then logged into NIH DNA analytic software packages. Even skilled researchers need weeks to become proficient. Electra had mastered it a week ago, using tutorials and practicing with original virus samples. Electra knew precisely where and what to look for. As she had predicted, the mutated DNA segments differ significantly from the corresponding segments in the original virus. Two hours later she had a diagram and two clues for Jason, telling how to re-sequence the known segment and where to find the other one. She practiced what to say and was counting on Su to open her father's sometimes stubborn mind so he would trip over what should be obvious. Jason and Su would start playing her game of clues tomorrow.

Jason's tomorrow was a big failure. He frustrated himself and disappointed his daughter. After poring over comparisons for most of the day, he was at a loss for what to look for. Electra simply observed; she didn't want to rile his temper. Finally, he said, "I'm a bit rusty. Interpreting comparisons is both art and science. I'm going to ask your Aunt Su to join us tomorrow when we continue." *Perfect! Aunt Su will be better with clues. I'll clue her in when we leave so she's primed for tomorrow.*

Su was digging through calculations when father and daughter stopped to say good night. "Dad and I have done the DNA scans and comparisons, and he says I'm catching on. And maybe tomorrow, you could help us with some of the interpretation, right Dad?"

Jason smiled wearily. "Right. Su, I'm not as quick as I used to be on pattern analysis. We could use your help."

"I'll be happy to help. That's how Indira and I did some of our best work. Let's think of Electra as Indy's helper." Even Jason, who made a career of denying his emotions, welcomed a bittersweet burst of nostalgia. Electra smiled sweetly, so pleased that Su was now in the game. Round two awaited.

No on-campus classes got in the way, so Electra sat at Jason's workstation the following morning while Su helped him review yesterday's scans. She needed time alone to sift through the data, so they decided to reconvene after lunch, giving Electra time to consider tangential issues. The one that intrigued her most was the Worldstars stealth project.

She had already pieced its history together. It was launched soon after the S-Vac project started, and it separated NIH from Worldstars independent study. They were banking on breakthroughs to launch Worldstar biologicals. The Indy-Su Conjecture was impressive because it gave a first-order solution by integrating quantum biology into biotechnology. But not even the brilliant Indy-Su combination was going to take it much further because they didn't see the way forward to second-order and beyond. It would take more collaborators more years to find the mistakes and move ahead. Or it would take the brain of one exceptional creature: Electra.

The sensation of aloneness made her shiver. Once again, she knew going forward to rely only on herself. It was exhilarating—she was beyond the pale of mere mortal intelligence. It was sobering— she had outgrown her father and Su and everyone else. She realized the same would happen for her physical and emotional personas as well, and it was vaguely troubling, but now was not the time to consider further, so she dismissed the thought.

Jason glanced up and noticed Electra self-absorbed in thought. "Don't be discouraged. We'll get together with Aunt Su after lunch and figure something out." Snapping out of her reverie, Electra walked over to Jason.

"Aunt Su and you will know what to do, and maybe I can help. I'm starved. Can we go to the cafeteria now?"

"Sure thing. And let's tell Aunt Su you're cooking dinner Sunday when she comes over to coach your piano practice."

Lunch worked its mood elevating magic, bringing out a cheery change-of-pace conversation. Jason mentioned how mature Electra is becoming, and how much she's learning about biotechnology. Su talked about the tiramisu she would make, a perfect dessert for the lasagna Electra would bake. Electra said she planned to take an advanced culinary class next year.

Jason and Su were much sharper after lunch. Electra listened as they exchanged ideas, realizing again how smart they are when compared with their associates. She was looking for the right moment to drop her clues, and it came after two hours of give and take.

"I see what you're driving at, but it's different than I thought. Let's ask my clever daughter what she thinks. *Bingo. Time for show and tell. Be convincing. Be modest too.*

"Well, I've paid attention and done my homework, and I have a hunch. Maybe we should be looking at a different sequence and pattern." Electra pulled out a diagram she had sketched last night and described her hunch, using a simplistic approach for why it might work. Twenty minutes later she was done. Though Jason was still nibbling, Su had taken the bait.

"Your mother would be proud of you. That's just the kind of intuition she had." Su rubbed Electra's head then said to Jason, "Let's think about it over the weekend, and we can reconvene Monday. We'll clue in the rest of the team just as soon as you and I have the particulars."

"You'll have to show me how this all works, but if gets us moving again I'll cook dinner for all of us next weekend."

"Dad, I'll settle for a pizza and ice cream." The meeting ended, as did lab work for the week.

Su came Sunday to coach Electra's practice session. After only nine months of lessons, Electra was playing pieces considered advanced for even a second-year student. Su listened attentively as Electra raced through a medley, then asked her to stop.

"I'm impressed with how well you read music in the short amount of time you've been practicing. You certainly play all the right notes."

"Thank you." Electra was good at reading body language too. Aunt Su had more to say.

"Playing the right notes or keeping time is important, but music has another dimension that's even more important. And it's missing when you play. You don't feel the music. Instead, you're pounding on the keys. Many young musicians are the same. They haven't had enough real-world experience to get in touch with their emotions. I know you've grown a lot since starting high school, but more emotional growth awaits. Please don't be upset. I'm giving you constructive criticism."

Su's comment resonated. Electra knew her emotional persona was the slowest to develop, as if her brain were holding emotions in abeyance. "You're right. I don't feel the music the way you do. You play with such feeling, as if your soul is singing the notes. I'm not there yet."

"You have such wonderful insight into most things we talk about. Your emotions will come out when they're ready to show themselves.

———

And when they do, I think you'll become more empathetic. Right now, you sometimes ignore how other people feel. But frankly, I think you're much better off with a late arrival. Once adult-type emotions emerge, you'll be an adult for the rest of your life. And let me make another observation. You probably like studying practical subjects, like history or psychology or sociology, but might not like studying art or literature as much as science or math. Am I right?"

"Yes. How'd you know?"

"I can think of two reasons. Some people have artistic talent programmed in their DNA. I had childhood friends who could paint or play music almost as soon as they could walk and talk. Mendelsohn and Mozart wrote symphonies before they turned ten. But I don't think you're built that way. You're rational rather than romantic. And here's another reason. Appreciating fine arts requires connecting to your emotions. If you read the biographies of great artists, you'll find many of them deliberately pushed to the emotional limit, claiming they learned how to feel not by reading or thinking, but by doing, by living life to the fullest." Electra was at a loss for words, but Su knew what she was thinking.

"I imagine you think that because you're exceptionally smart, you can be good at whatever you want. Well, there are more types of intelligence than linguistic and numeric. Why don't you search the Internet for an article describing the nine types of intelligence summarized by American psychologist Howard Gardner back in 1983? Start there and see how his ideas branch out."

"I will. Aunt Su, how do you know so much?"

"I'm older than you, and I've studied neuroscience and cognitive psychology. At the rate you're going, in a year or two I won't be able to keep up with you."

"You know a lot about art and music too. Do you think I might have artistic talent that'll show up later?"

"It's possible. As you experience more of life through relationships with others, it might emerge, along with more empathy. But don't rush to grow up. Once it gets here, you're stuck with it. Do you remember this verse from one of your mother's poems?"

"I curse the loss of innocence,
Replaced with adult views.
Skepticism—indifference,
The path becomes so hard to choose."

Electra nodded, waiting for Su's interpretation. "Your mother knew the innocence of youth provides unconditional joy, which adults can never reclaim. So, just enjoy the now, when you are untroubled by adult-like experiences and emotions."

"I'll try. And I'll try to put more feeling into the notes as I learn to feel the music. When I read mother's poems, I see how well she understood feelings. Do you think Mother was especially empathetic?"

"Yes, and unlike me, your mother was much more demonstrative."

"What about Dad? I think he ignores feelings."

"Men are not attuned to emotions. They just don't have them as women do. You'll have to make comparisons for yourself when you get to know more young men. Whew. Let's talk about lighter topics. Tell me about supper."

"Please compare my lasagna with the last lasagna you had at an Italian restaurant. Gramps and Dad say I'm becoming a good cook. You have even better taste than they do, so your opinion's worth more." Though Su preferred letting others be punsters, she too could play with words.

"If your Uncle Adom were here, he'd probably try to say something clever, like 'I'm in flavor of that.' Let's check what your father and grandfather are cooking up…"

Electra's first high school year ended in June and she scored near the top on all tests, but not so high to call attention. Happy with her freshman year academic learning, she was even happier with emotional learning achieved by face-to-face contact with classmates. On the last official school day, she mulled over what she had learned about herself. Electra, a master of bullet point summaries, jotted a list even though she could picture it in her brain, and when finished scribbling reviewed it.

Even though I like to plan for the future, I'll try to enjoy the present, but I must embrace change because the world's always in motion, which often leads to problems. And I must rely only on myself for deciding what's the best course of action by finding a practical solution. I'll remember to avoid paralysis by analysis.

Many tricky issues are caused by people relationships because I have to deal with other people's emotions which I can't control, so I'll have to be more empathetic and patient. And I'm learning how to work with people or work around them.

I can put into my own philosophy some of what I learned about myself this year. Each year I can add to it, especially in a "rites of passage" year. There are many rites of passage on the path ahead. I recall a poem Mother wrote that covered it:

Our one way only odyssey
The path that we are on.
Made up of many passages,
Emerging when running along.

At first, we run fast as we can,
To reach a stage-end prize.
We're thrilled, but then we speed away,
As another greets our eyes.

But soon enough we realize,
The passage not always fun.
And now the truth reveals itself,
Lento—enjoy the run.

Victory is not laurel-bound,
Instead within the race it's found

So far, my passages have been fun, but perhaps some in the future aren't. Mother must know better than I. She had the mind of a scientist and the soul of an artist. Too bad I lack artistic ability, but at least I can enjoy studying the fine arts. I learned last year there's more to school than math and science and computers. And I also learned not to compare myself with others. Compare myself with what I need to become.

I'm going to make a summer project of studying religion and philosophy, and I'll make a diagram showing how they're connected. It'll help me now and in the future.

July and August would be Electra's first post-childhood summer vacation in her expanded world, and she could keep doing most of the activities she started during the school year. Childhood joy lost was offset by adolescent relationships gained.Doc or volunteer mothers chauffeured her to safe (low T-Plague risk) gatherings whenever too far for biking. Jason took her to the lab once a week while on other days, when not with Christi or Robin, she studied or explored online. Electra was not old enough for a part-time job, but even if she were she would have to compete to get one because automation kept cutting into the supply of low-tech jobs while the T-Plague kept swelling the ranks of low-tech job seekers.

Electra mapped out her second-year class schedule, choosing from the master plan created last year. Some of the courses were open to all students, but others, such as physics or pre-calculus, required she pass a qualifying exam, so she scored high enough to get in but not to stand out. Jason was relieved that his assistance wasn't needed because S-Vac project work monopolized his time. When asked to review the schedule, he told her that today's flexible educational system is tailor-made to keep her secret hidden.

As summer wound down, Electra wrapped up her potpourri study of religion and philosophy. Tonight, she was sitting at her home computer, viewing the printed flowchart she had just constructed by combining the two and dividing chronologically by period or philosopher. *This is my summer's magnum opus. I have diagrammed a unified religion/philosophy structure. I can refine it when studying at a deeper level, grouping by period and subdividing by theologian or philosopher, but that would make for too much detail and too cluttered a picture. I'll come up with a better diagram when I study these subjects in college.*

This summer marked a decline in the amount of time Electra spent with her grandfather, but Doc didn't worry about it. *She's matured so quickly and behaves so much like an adult. I predicted this would happen. She only needs me to chauffeur her about, and she'll need me even less when she gets a driver's license next year. I'll tell Jason we'll buy her a car sooner than we thought. All this makes me feel old. My little girl is growing up. Well, I think I'll look in on her. She's been so studious all day. I wonder what she's been thinking about? I'll get us a Coke and we can talk.*

Electra could tell from the steadfast footsteps her omni-parent was coming. "You've been so focused today, I thought you might like a Coke break. Whatever you're working on, it'll go better with Coke. And here's a fact you can tuck away in your brain. I forget where I heard it, but Coca Cola is still the world's most recognized brand. Even I've been brain-washed by advertising. The slogan 'Things go better with Coke' sticks with me."

"I can use one. I've been so busy I forgot I was getting thirsty. Would you like to see what I've been working on? You'll be the first person to know what I've come up with."

"I sure would. Why don't we go the kitchen and you can show me what you've got? And you can grab a cookie." As they strolled to the kitchen, a calming security that Doc always brought to Electra came along. Once seated at the table, Electra showed Doc her magnum opus diagram.

"I want to know more about religion and philosophy. It'll help me understand better how everything I'm now studying or doing fits together, and even more so when I go to college. So, I made it my special summer project. Take a look at my summary flow chart." Doc knew he was in for a surprise, and one glance confirmed Electra had taken her work to a level far beyond what Sunday school or church services could teach.

"When I was in college, I studied religion and philosophy. That was a long time ago, but I still remember it pretty well, and I go to church regularly. But church services stay at a simpler Bible-like level, and I can tell you why. People are too busy or indifferent to confront the kinds of issues your flowchart points to. I can hold my own in most discussions, but I can't follow what you've put together. You better walk me through it."

"It's like this. Now, remember, what I've put together would get perhaps a C from a college professor because my diagram combines and simplifies, but it gives me a model for how religion and philosophy relate. Religions fall into two groups. Cyclic when they have a holistic repeating pattern of birth-death-birth-death going on forever, or linear when they have one God who gives salvation to sinners as they move through a linear birth-living-death-heaven-or-hell pattern. People struggle with religion or philosophy because they have to balance faith versus reason. And as you scan down the page, you can see how man's better understanding of the Universe works; that's represented by the arrows coming in from the left, shifting the balance towards reason."

"OK. I can follow that. You're saying advances in science and technology give us better tools to explain what we observe empirically. We no longer rely on myth or superstition, which are the forerunners of religion and faith. Keep going."

"Look on the far right. We've gone from Theism—that's where God works to make our lives better—to Deism—that's where God works to redeem us by setting up a clock-work Universe and then withdrawing from our experience—to Irrelevance—that's where God doesn't need us and vice versa. Now look again on the far left. As you scan down, you see a smooth flow from faith towards reason, from spiritual to secular, from revelation to observable phenomena. But then along comes the failures of the 20th century: world wars, power struggles, pollution, degradation of the environment, and so on. That leads to a post-modern backlash: God is dead, pessimism, rejection of religion and morals, and power struggles come to the fore. All depressing stuff. That was the state of religion and philosophy late in the 21st century."

"OK. I follow that too. So, how did we go from there to the present? And please, tell me where we are today."

"It's like this. DNA and neuroscience came to the forefront, providing factual foundations that show man is predisposed to certain beliefs or behavior. Leading theologians or philosophers united Neuroscience with best of Rationalism, Empiricism, and Materialism, leading to what is today labeled the Neuro-Sci

Synthesis. It ends the debate between faith or reason, God or atheism, good or evil. It suggests that God or the Universe or Absolute Truth is unknowable. The human mind, subject to error, can't prove or disprove God's existence. So, Neuro-Sci Synthesis leaves room for God. Each person chooses faith or reason, whichever matches their pre-conditioned neural patterns. Believers, agnostics and atheists all have a place. That's where we are today."

"OK. I see where we are, but where do we go from here? I don't think the religious debate is over. Look at the controversy between Isilabad and Western civilization."

Electra said, "From what I know about the history of religion, conflicts between religion, kings, and the people hinge more on power, control, and economics than on spiritual beliefs."

Doc agreed. "Yes, there's a quote about more people having been killed in the name of religion than from all else combined, which means rulers hide behind religion to hide their intentions. That's a whole other subject, but let's not talk about it tonight. My brain's getting tired. I like your flowchart, but it leads to additional questions. Let's stop here, but before we end, please explain two terms on your flowchart. What is 'Subjective Bypass'?"

"It's the direction early Enlightenment philosophers took when scientific thought came to prominence. Before then, philosophers were polymath thinkers possessing wide-ranging knowledge. And they did more than sit and think. For example, Roger Bacon, the father of empiricism and scientific inquiry, was attorney general and chancellor of England. But the rise of science raised the bar for understanding mathematics and logic. Many philosophers didn't know enough about math to study external phenomena using science, so they relinquished the high ground to scientists, retreating inside university walls or their heads. That's where they are today. Scientists became explorers of the natural world. Philosophers turned inward, studying the meaning of words and paragraphs instead of the physical world."

"I get it. They took the wrong intellectual path. Now, I see the sentence 'Turn to the Subject' on your flowchart. What does it mean?"

"It's all about early Enlightenment philosophers replacing Church authority with individual autonomy, and it ultimately led to the rise of humanism, where people work together to make life better rather than waiting for divine intervention that will never come. There's more to it, but I have to study more before I can give you a better summary."

"I've heard enough. You know what you're talking about. How do you plan to use your flowchart?"

"I'll use it to explain my position whenever I discuss religion and philosophy with other people and—" Doc stopped her right there. "Whoa. You're about to enter a discussion danger zone. Never talk to strangers about sex, religion, or politics. People's minds are already made up. Discussions would become heated and people would talk past one another, not to one another. There's only one person besides me you could show your flowchart without causing a ruckus. Who do you think it is? And I'll tell you right now, it's not your father. He has no interest in religion."

"I wasn't going to pick Dad either, but for a different reason. He's too focused on his S-Vac project. I wouldn't want to interrupt him. I'd pick Aunt Su."

"Correct. She's open-minded and has your best interests at heart, just like I do."

"I'll be careful what I say to strangers. I don't ever want to criticize another person's beliefs. It's important they pick what they believe for good reasons, but it's their choice. I'll remember your warnings if I ever get into a religious debate."

"Good. You make me feel like I'm still needed, at least a little. I guess I can still help you deal with people, but pretty soon you'll have mastered that too."

"Please, don't say that. I'll always need you and Dad."

"It's getting late. I'm going to bed. You should too. Give your brain a rest."

"That's more good advice. See you in the morning."

As Doc trooped away, Electra thought about her grandfather while tidying up the workstation, preparing for tomorrow. *Grandfather's aging. Gray hair turning white, steps slowing, shoulders drooping. But his brain's sharp as ever. It's painful to think, but someday he'll be gone. I'll do all I can to push that day far away. The time's coming when he'll need more help, and I'll be there to take care of him.*

Electra slept soundly. Meanwhile, the lightning brain worked subliminally, preparing for whatever path it decides to take. And it knew Electra would want to come along, for it would share all that was needed for Electra's cognitive persona to enjoy the journey. Even though Electra might travel alone on a road less traveled, she would never be lonely; she would always be engaged. The lightning brain would see to that.

CHAPTER 25
September 2110

"Changing of the Guard"
(Thread 2 Chapter 12)

HEADLINES SHOUTED "T-PLAGUE ATTACKS Guardian Party: Rushman Struck Down!" Washington gasped and the nation held its breath because David Rushman, the Guardian Party's iconic leader, might be out of action permanently.

Rushman had been the real deal, a patriot holding military and political credentials the public respected. Not even DC dirt diggers could find chinks in his armor. He had dedicated himself to rebuilding America's flagging security and healthcare systems, carrying out what people wanted, often at odds with the Washington Establishment. Considered a statesman rather than a mere politician, his ethics filtered into the core of the Party, keeping his aggressive lieutenants in check. The public backed him bigtime, and if he ran for president, the Guardian Party might sweep to power. But these hopes were as dead as a terminal T-Plague victim if Rushman didn't recover.

The Party's Inner Circle was holding an emergency session soon after the news broke, led by Rushman's heir apparent Jared Gardner, an assertive second term representative from California. Smart, charismatic, and certain he knew what was best for the county, he planned to follow Winston Churchill's advice: never let a crisis go to waste.

"I just got the latest report on David's condition. We don't know where he picked up the mutant virus, but it's put him down. He's now in ICU getting massive doses of smart pills. It's too soon to tell how long he'll be sidelined, but we better plan for the worst-case scenario. I'd like opinions."

Everyone at the table wished David a speedy recovery but placed the Party ahead of the person because there was a man in the room groomed for leadership: Jared Gardner. Last summer, the Inner Circle privately bought into his plans for increasing Party clout. Though he cloaked his conceit in a show of false modesty, he and the Party leaders believed fate had picked him for greatness. Jared gave credit to the past but quickly charged ahead.

"All of us owe much to David.He's championed our cause.He's mentored me, allowing me to grow into the leader who can pick up where he left off.We have a great organization thanks to all our collective efforts, so let's use this changing of the guard to become even stronger.Here's my plan."All eyes focused on Jared,revealing his time to lead had come.

"First, our media spin doctors will blame the current Administration for failing America on national security,healthcare, and infrastructure.If a leader like David Rushman can't be protected, then what about the man or woman or child on the street? This message should help in November elections.

"Next, we'll push for harsher steps to be implemented by Healthguard and Securityguard.We're the party that created them, and the public likes how they tie in with what they fear mightily: T-Plague and Terrorism.

"Then we'll get inside the NIH tent.We have to know the inner workings of Cognicom.Our covert operation team hasn't planted a mole yet, and if our Invisible Man can't do it,we'll replace him and his Invisible Hand.We don't want excuses; we want results.

"Finally, we'll start rumors Isilabad is about to unleash terrorist attacks using T-Plague as a WMD. We can say Muhammad's followers created germ warfare." Jared had more to say, but one of the public relations people interrupted.

"Let's get the facts straight because social media checks what we say.The Greeks and Romans invented germ warfare.They used to catapult plague victims over enemy fortifications. Let's say this: Islam learned long ago from the Greeks how to spread terror using germ warfare."Jared liked what he heard.

"Promote that guy. He knows what to say. And I'm glad he's blaming the Greeks instead of the Romans. I like how Caesar controlled his subjects." The Inner Circle was onboard so Jared ended the meeting fifteen minutes later.

"Fasten your seat belts.Our race to the top is about to accelerate, and trust me when I say I know what's the best way to get there. We'll reconvene in a month unless I call a meeting sooner."

Mo never ran scared, but today he was running hard to stay ahead of a tidal wave about to crash over Cognicom projects. Recent meetings had given him a laundry list of bad news.He read again his handwritten copy as he drove to a lunchtime meeting where he would tell Jason what to do so the Worldstars could stay above water.

Jason won't like my criticizing the team.He'll say the latest smart pill doesn't work because the mutated virus is tougher. I hope he realizes the public's patience is wearing thin and our economy could spiral downhill, just like China's. And thanks to the Guardian Party's news bulletins, people are blaming Washington for Cognicom's failure and are starting to believe the rumors that Isilabad is turning T-Plague into a WMD. And I hope I can convince him not to worry about researchers becoming targets. There's no reason to be paranoid.

Jason arrived before Mo at the Home Base private dining room, accompanied by a feeling of déjà vu. *I was here for lunch 17 years ago. What a happy day that was. Indy was alive to share our contest victory. How different today's lunch will be. Mo says he's the bearer of bad news, but has a contingency plan. The pressure's getting to him too. He just walked in, and he's not smiling. Well, it's my turn to buck him up.*

Mo headed to the table after Jason caught his attention. *Jason's smiling. Good. He's been so edgy lately. I hope he can handle the news.* Mo sat down, wasting no time getting to the point.

"You got here first.Well, you had fewer miles to drive, and I drove slow because I was checking the list of items we need to discuss. I apologize for being so direct, but Cognicom's in a tough spot, and if my plan doesn't work we're SOL. Take a look at what we have to deal with." As Jason read, Mo considered ordering something stronger than a Coke, but changed his mind by the time Jason finished. Jason's expression was better than expected.

"I can see why you weren't smiling when you sat down. It's better that Adom and Su aren't with us. There are bullet points that would upset both of them. But let me talk you through what we're doing that can help."

"Good. I'll add them to the plan."

"Su and I already know the mutated virus is worse, but here's some good news. She and I have an improved S-Vac and smart pill. She corrected a couple of mistakes we made, so we're finally making a little progress. And she thinks the corrections will carry over to I and R-Vac."

"Excellent. That addresses the first two bullet points. What about the others?"

"Why don't you have Adom brainstorm them with you? He's done it before, and I think he likes checking the political side. And I know the last two bullet points will get his attention. And maybe you can ask Su to help out on the others." Mo shook his head no.

"It'll work for Adom, but not for Su, and here's why. She's being promoted to tech lead for our team, and you're being promoted to tech lead for the other two. The current leads are being demoted and will report to you until they're reassigned. You should be able to guess the reason."

"Are they scapegoats?"

"That's it, whether or not it's justified. We're the only team that made at least a little progress, and I told Bobbi you and Su are the reasons why. That's why you're being promoted, but with the promotion comes even more pressure."

"I can handle it. I'll help Su with the political angle, and she'll help me with the formulations. And I forgot to mention that Electra's helping Su. She has a knack for playing hunches that Su can use." Mo finally had something to joke about.

"I knew that would happen. If I hadn't come to her defense at that first meeting she attended, you would have kicked her out, and if you did that, you'd be in big trouble. I don't ever want to make Electra angry." Jason smiled as he nodded in agreement.

Jason recapped his lunchtime discussion at dinner and, as always, Doc offered common-sense advice.

"I'd be careful. Now you have two headaches instead of one. All the senior researchers are going to resent you, and you could be benched if you can't jumpstart progress."

"Su and I think the corrections we made carry over, so I think we'll finally see progress. Besides, the change will do me good. Adom too. And Su gets to study more. She'll go to additional seminars and learn new techniques. And what she learns will help me too."

"I hope it works. At least you're smiling. You've been too grim lately. Just make sure you don't burn out or blow up out by working too hard."

Electra liked better than Doc the news Jason had brought home. Since Jason was handling other teams, she could drop the clues for Su, who was more fun to work with. She would find them faster and share with Jason. Meanwhile, Su would show Electra additional biotech procedures. Electra had learned a month ago how to use cryo-electron and atomic force microscopy (AFM), as well as their successor scanning devices, for mapping the structure of DNA or its editing enzymes. After that, she had learned CRISPR/CAS9 and related methods for unzipping DNA to snip out and then insert sequences needed to make genetic modifications. Electra would tell Su about upcoming MAGE and CAGE seminars that teach the latest methods for largescale genetic segment transfer across different genome types, and Su would teach her all she had learned from attending.

Every so often Electra would become frustrated that it takes Jason or Su so long to understand her clues. That's when she invented a Dream Team of researchers as smart as she. *Just think how much and how fast I could get things done if Dad and Su weren't so slow.* But then she would scold herself. *I must be thankful for my extraordinary abilities and appreciate the best in others rather than criticize. And when I get to be an adult, I can step out of the shadows and show the world what I can do. Right now, time is working for rather than against me. I wish I had Mother's empathy. She knew how to find the best in everyone. She wrote a poem titled the Triple Crown, and it helps me handle frustration. It tells me to enjoy the present and give thanks for what I have. Time to recall it.*

Am I where I want to be?
Engaged in what I want to do?
With those who love and care for me?
With joy of Youth still strong and true?

It's not like that past early years,
To search for meaning in my life.
Some paths may lead to bitter tears,
The journey's often fraught with strife.

This crown is sought by everyone,
It's oft beyond the outstretched reach.
I hope to earn while in the sun,
Appreciate, and Life will teach.

Electra was sure Mo's plan would work, for she could work from the shadows to help make it so.

Electra basked in the warm September sunlight as the school year started. Her schedule was working as planned, giving plenty of time to balance high school and Cognicom work. *What wonderful serendipity! I get to be student and teacher at both places.* Today, the last Saturday of the month, Electra was at Christi's, helping her with a course feared most by high school sophomores: geometry.

Christi was bright but preferred social activities rather than school. Her parents told her she needed a solid education to support whatever career she would choose, but she disagreed. She had her sights set on the performing arts and didn't think she needed a college degree because her singing and dancing talents would take her there. Christi was mature beyond her years, possessing looks and personality that extended her social world, a world that included the opposite sex. That evening she and Electra would explore further.

"I still don't get it. What's so important about proving facts about triangles, so I know when they're congruent? It seems so irrelevant. How will it help me get a job?" Electra knew the answer to a question often asked.

"If you become an entertainer, you won't work with triangles, but you'll still need to think. And geometry is your first math course that teaches you how to think logically. No matter what you do, you need to apply logic. So, don't blow off geometry."

"I'm getting all tangled up in the jargon. You're going to have to explain again what Side-Angle-Side, Angle-Side-Angle, and Side-Side-Side mean." After spending the next hour drilling congruent triangle theorems into Christi's pretty head, Electra could tell from Christi's frown she was tiring.

"I get some of what you're saying, but this stuff is hard. It's easy for you because you're smart. But I'm getting twisted up by the different side-angle combination stuff. Why aren't you teaching me about Side-Side-Angle?" Christi's question stopped Electra cold, forcing an Electra-only private conversation before answering.

Huh? I never thought about it. Christi just found something that's not in the book.

Maybe I'm not so clever after all.

"You've stumped me by thinking outside the box. I never thought about Side-Side-Angle. Tell you what, I could surf the Net for the answer, but I'd rather work it out on my own. It's a matter of pride. And you've taught me a lesson. Sometimes I get lazy and don't look outside the book." Christi was genuinely surprised.

"This is a first. I can't believe you don't know the answer. Well, you'll figure it out, and then you can tell me. But let's switch subjects to something I know all about. I'll tell you about our new plan for tonight."

The original plan—going to a movie after having supper at home with her parents—changed to a double date when Gary, a college-bound senior on the soccer team, called early in the week. Christi's new plan also stretched the truth so her mother understood why she didn't need to pick the girls up afterwards. Electra liked what Christi had come up with and was ready for final instructions.

"And after the movie, Gary will drive us somewhere. His soccer buddy Bill will be your date. I told Mother your grandfather would pick us up. Mother doesn't know we're meeting two boys at the movies. And I told her I'm spending the night at your place. Can I do that?"

"Of course, you can. I'll play along if your mother asks, and I'll call Gramps so he knows what's going on, but I won't mention the date part. And I'll tell him not to pick us up unless we call him after the movie. So, if your mom checks us out by calling him, we're copacetic."

"Good good good. And when you get a car next year, we won't have to worry about parents driving us around."

"I wish you had told me before I came over about going out on a date. Do my clothes look OK?"

"You look fine and before we leave, we can put on some makeup. This is gonna be a night to remember. Mother's calling. Pizza's here just in time. I'm hungry, are you?" Electra agreed on all counts.

The thought of socializing that evening and making new friends excited Electra, but making out in the back seat was even more to her liking. Though not as fast as Christi's, Electra's hormones had awakened last spring. Su had already diagnosed the condition and convinced Jason that Electra was ready to meet boys. She also gave a summary sex education class in which Electra heard much the same as at school: modern cultures acknowledge sex is a survival instinct that must be obeyed, so adolescents need to learn by experimenting sensibly when old enough. Like adolescents everywhere, Electra didn't want to talk to her parents about sex. Parents or relatives occupy a special place, one that is never connected with baser instincts. Su's class was mostly review because Electra already had a master sex education teacher: Christi.

Gary waved to Christi as soon as she entered the lobby. "There she is. Wow! Christi looks hot to trot. And that must be her friend Electra. How does she look to you?"

"OK, but sort of serious. Are you sure they're only sophomores? They look older. But if they are that's all to the good. They'll like our change of plans, and they'll know how to handle our car-party goods. Where'd you put them?"

"Rum and cokes are iced in the trunk. Weed's in the glove box, and I've got condoms in my pocket. Here's your supply." Bill stashed them in his pocket before the girls approached. Gary made the introductions.

"Christi, you look totally hot. This is my friend Bill. And you must be Electra. I'm Gary." Electra smiled, letting Christi do the talking.

"I'm surprised there aren't more people. This is the film's first weekend and the critics gave its special effects high marks. Well, we'll cruise through the ticket line that much faster."

"Bill and I have a better idea. Let's skip the movie and go cruising in my car. We know just the place." The girls liked the idea, so the four hiked to Gary's car, placing Christi up front, Electra and Bill in back. Gary did most of the talking while Electra did most of the thinking.

The guys are looking good, and the park seems safe. Bill's babbling is harmless, and there's no harm in sampling the goods. And I'll keep an eye on Christi. Gary knew all the right moves, and Bill followed along. They started with rum and cokes that loosened tongues and inhibitions, then graduated to smoking marijuana while Gary paraded his knowledge of recreational drugs.

"Do you know that marijuana has been used for 3000 years in rituals and medicine? And do you know that most rum is made in the Caribbean and is part of island culture? And back in the 1800's, British sailors were given a daily ration." Christi was drinking in more than the words. Hers were beginning to slur.

"Izzat so? No wonder I like it. Pour summore." Gary was happy to oblige, pouring more and lighting another joint. Meanwhile, the couple in the back seat had moved to other activities. Electra observed all from her perch, participating too.

Bill has nimble fingers. And he's very careful with my buttons. Up close and in person is better than books for learning about sex. I'll stop him just before he gets my blouse off. That'll be enough for tonight. And next time, we'll go from there.

Action in the front seat was proceeding at a faster pace, not because of Gary but because of Christi. The more she consumed, the hungrier her appetite for the opposite sex. Gary was getting more than he bargained for. Suddenly, Christi bolted upright and ripped off her blouse, crushing Gary's face between well-formed breasts. She threw back her head and trilled to the melody of a popular opera fantasy a lyric she improvised:

> "Roll me a joint and then pour me summore,
> Then get ready get set Eddy go rock steady on the floor."

Then she leaned forward, preparing to devour Gary's lips. Poor Gary had nowhere to go; Christi had him pinned to the door, but another primal instinct came to the fore before she could lock on. Christi's stomach gurgled a brief warning, then spewed forth a generous portion of the day's menu. Chunks of mushrooms and half-digested sausage cascaded onto Gary's head, then streamed down his chest. That did it; the flow goaded Gary to action. He pushed Christi off and screamed.

"Aagghh! She just hurled half a pizza on me!" He escaped out the driver-side door just before throwing up. The sight, sound, and smell from up front cooled back seat activity. Bill and Electra bailed out before they became collateral damage, then rendezvoused to pull Gary off his knees. Electra surveyed the mess before offering advice.

"It could be worse. Only Christi heaved in the car. Let's do this. We can use the melted ice from the cooler to clean up Christi and Gary. Then we can wipe off the front seat and get out of here. Do you have a towel in the trunk?" Gary staggered to the trunk where he gathered cleaning supplies; Bill and Electra moved to the passenger side to extract Christi. She was able to stand, but had little to say, watching mutely while the others scrubbed away the debris. Afterwards, Gary drove to Electra's. The only words spoken were Gary's when he walked them to the front door.

"Let's make a deal. I won't breathe a word about tonight if you won't." Christi didn't want to talk, so she nodded, and Gary hurried to the car, promising to himself never to see her again. Electra grabbed Christi by the arms, trying to shake some sense into her.

"Doc is waiting up, so let me cover for us. If he asks about the way you look, I'll say the pizza gave you an upset stomach, and you ripped your blouse on the sink faucet while washing away some of the glop."

"I still feel woozy. Doesn't rum stay in your stomach longer than other liquors? All I wanna do is sleep. We can talk tomorrow."

"When we do, you'll have to tell me what got into you. It looked like you were gonna suck his lips off."

"I'll tell you when I feel better. But let's go in and fake our way past your grandfather."

The girls passed Doc's inspection, and Christi was asleep ten minutes later, giving Electra quiet time to sort through the night's excitement. *Playing around with Bill was fun. I like the feelings his touch brought out. I didn't see Gary doing anything different, but Christi sure got into it. I'll learn more about it from her. Now I'm just gonna lie here and let my brain wander. It'll talk to me when it's ready.*

The lightning brain snapped awake at sunrise, telling Electra how to solve yesterday's geometry problem. *Now I see the Side-Side-Angle proof. It's so simple. I see how I can construct two distinct non-congruent triangles having two sides and a non-included angle equal. How come I didn't I see it before? The answer flashed in an instant. I got it. It's all about brain states and cognitive control. Doc helped train my brain so I can switch mental states when I concentrate. Both Christi and I were concentrating on sex instead of triangles yesterday, but my brain switched back to math when I fell asleep, and it worked out the answer. It's what makes me special. For me, there's never a changing of the guard. It's my changing of the cognitive state that sets me apart. And I remember Doc's warning. I have to practice brain-state control when emotions come into play so I can handle the situation. I guess I can practice on other dates. Aha! Not only is sex fun, but it's also good practice. I'm ready for more.*

CHAPTER 26
March 2111

"Run for Nurse"
(Thread 2 Chapter 13)

THE MUTATED T-PLAGUE STRUCK Washington late February, converting anxiety into widespread panic that canceled public events, closed schools, and overloaded hospitals. The public didn't need media or Guardian Party bulletins to identify the cause. The Washington Establishment had brought a pox on more than just its two houses.

This time the T-Plague crashed directly into Electra's private world: Christi became a victim. Jennifer Conklin called Jason at seven a.m. Saturday to relay the grim news. As soon as Electra heard, she insisted they go to the Conklin's because something must be done to rescue her best friend.Doc drove, taking control of the situation as soon as he saw how helpless Christi's parents were.

"Where did she contract T-Plague?" Jennifer shook her head. "We've been trying to backtrack where she's been the past week, but with so many places and so many cases we can't figure it out. Might have been at school, or it could have been at dance class or the mall."

"What hospital is she in? Has her condition stabilized?"

Russell replied, "Good Shepherd. We rushed her there yesterday evening. It's the closest T-Plague treatment center, but it looks like a war zone. The staff can't handle the load. Patients are stacked in hallways, and the nurses are running every which way. It took all my clout to get her into a semi-private room. She tested positive for the mutated strain and I don't know her condition. We're going back as soon as I know what to do."

As she listened, Electra felt a jarring sensation in her head, as if the lightning brain were shifting gears. Suddenly, she knew what to do.

"We can't wait. I need to see Christi. Please take me to the hospital now." Her expression ruled out further discussion. Fortunately, Doc agreed.

"Russell, she's right. We don't know what care she'll get today. Why don't we all go? I'll follow in my van."

"Good idea. At least we have enough masks so we can see her. We kept ours, and I have some extras. I'll get them for you."

"Electra, you ride with the Conklins. We'll go as soon as Russell gives us our masks."

The ten-mile trip sped by as the convoy ran red lights on eerily quiet streets, giving Russell just enough time to tell Electra what treatment had started. When they arrived, the overflowing parking lot warned that helter-skelter had replaced standard operating procedures. One look is all it took for Electra to issue orders.

"Dad and Jennifer better stay in the car. I'm going in with Gramps and Mr. Conklin." Jason was about to intervene but thought better. He had never before seen the look in his daughter's eyes. Better let this play out. His words weren't necessary because Doc spoke first.

"Russ, Electra's right. The three of us can handle it."

Once inside, Doc didn't ask permission; he pushed through to Christi's room. As soon as she saw Christi, a heart-rending wave of emotion swept over Electra, stabbing her in the chest. But even with tubes drip-feeding medications into her arms, she was still beautiful to Electra, as if she were a sleeping beauty awaiting serendipity's kiss to awaken her, to bring her back.

"Christi, Christi, it's Father. Can you hear me? Electra and her grandfather are here with me." Christi's eyes fluttered briefly, along with a fleeting smile. She didn't speak, but slipped again into sleep. Just then a nurse entered, and Russell started grilling her.

———

"I am Doctor Russell Conklin, Senior Medical Director at NIH. This is my daughter. What can you tell us about her condition?"

"We're still trying to stabilize your daughter. She has a severe case." While the nurse was fully occupied, Electra scanned Christi's medical set-up and charts, then ducked unnoticed into the corridor to locate nursing stations and supply rooms. She watched the nurses, who for the most part were volunteers from area hospitals, all wearing different uniforms and improvising what to do. She saw none from her grandfather's clinic. Electra ducked back into Christi's room just before her grandfather ended the discussion.

"Thanks for sharing with us. I know you're doing everything possible. Is there anything we can do to help? We'd be happy to stay with her, like an extra caregiver." The nurse was too tired to smile.

"I'm afraid not. With all the commotion swirling about you'd be in the way. And in her sedated state, it wouldn't help. Maybe in a day or two when she stabilizes. And then it would be good to take her home. Why don't you come back tomorrow?"

Electra noted the hospital layout on the way out, making comments only to herself. *This place is a disaster, and that'll help me. I won't have to put up with bureaucratic red tape.* Doc spoke first when they gathered by the van.

"Good thing you two stayed here. It's bad in there, but Christi's getting all the care they can give her. She's still in a semi-private room. They're sedating her until her condition stabilizes. According to the nurse, she has a severe case."

"Doc, you've been a brick. Now it's my turn to do something. I'm calling our family physician to let him know what's going on. He can't do anything today, but I'll ask him to check her condition as soon as she stabilizes. Jenn, do you have his number?"

"I have it at home. We'll call from there."

Doc said, "Russell, please call me when you hear from the hospital. There's nothing else we can do until then." Jason hugged Jennifer before they drove away, but it did little to calm her.

Electra sat stonily silent on the drive home, and her companions weren't surprised because the morning had been traumatic. They would be surprised, however, just as soon as they returned home because the lightning brain was charging ahead, preparing the next steps for rescuing Christi, steps Electra would reveal to no one. She had places to go and things to do. She spoke as soon as Doc turned off the engine.

"Gramps, please let me borrow your van. I'll get my driver's license. I have errands I need to run." Doc was about to give her the keys when Jason cut in.

"Wait a minute, Electra. You're upset. You need to settle down. Tell us where you're going and why?"

"No, not right now. Later." As she took the keys and started walking towards the house, Jason grabbed her arm, a gesture meant to protect his daughter from doing something rash. He would have done differently had he known what was emerging inside the lightning brain.

"Wait a minute. I can't let you go off like this." Electra grabbed his hand, forcibly removing it.

"Electra! Stop squeezing! You're hurting my hand!" Jason saw an odd intensity in Electra's eyes that frightened him. He didn't understand that his daughter had crossed over to an altered state.

"I love you and Grandfather more than anything, but even you two don't know who I am or what I can do. Please don't get in my way. Don't make me angry. You won't like me when I'm angry." She said this dispassionately, her cognitive self still in control. They let her go without saying another word.

It took five minutes to gather what she needed, then she hurried to the first destination, her grandfather's clinic. Because the staff knew her well, she was able to come and go without being stopped, today being no exception. She knew where to find a nurse's uniform, shoes, and I.D. badge. She also took from her grandfather's examining room a handful of injection syringes and antiseptic wipes.

Now she rushed to the second destination, her NIH work-study lab. It was open twenty-four seven because Cognicom researchers could work any shift, including weekends. Because she had a security badge and knew all access codes, she dashed inside and the two lab techs present left her alone because they didn't know her well. She took four bottles each of her latest powder and tablet formulations, a set measuring spoons, two bottles of sterile suspension fluid, and enough containers to hold what she would mix at the hospital.

Twenty minutes later she returned to the van, ready to change into the nurse's uniform. Intermittent sunlight helped warm the cool and blustery morning air, making Electra's change of uniform less chilling. She put all items into a medical bag, then raced to her final destination, Good Shepherd Hospital, where her plan would unfold.

The plan was simple in theory—treat Christi with improved smart pill formulations—but implementation required ingenuity. Electra would play the role of a volunteer nurse summoned to help handle patient overload. She would bypass notifying any supervisor because the hospital was operating in chaos mode; she would blend right in, stationing herself in Christi's room so she could inject massive doses every four hours to arrest the viral infection and stabilize symptoms. She would remove sedation from the treatment schedule, and as soon as Christi regains consciousness, Electra would call Russell Conklin to take Christi home immediately. Then she would gather all her supplies and disappear like a whisper in a windstorm.

Not a shadow of doubt clouded the lightning brain. *Of course, my plan will work. I know my vaccines are effective. And I know how to take control.* Problems could arise if the hospital staff becomes suspicious, but she was ready to deal with that. She would stay at bedside or hide in the bathroom; she would become assertive if another nurse came in, bullying her if necessary, and she would walk the floor once every two hours to uncover possible snags. If anyone questioned why she was there, she would tell them to call a Dr. Russell Conklin at NIH, who had authorized bedside care for this patient. And she would rely on her lightning brain to handle whatever else might come her way.

It was high noon when Electra pulled into one of the few remaining parking spaces. The crush of people would provide extra cover getting in. According to her calculations, Christi would be stabilized and conscious in about sixteen hours. That meant four injections and one oral treatment before calling Russell. She must also call her father at a time still to be determined. Just before leaving the van, Electra gathered her thoughts, using her incredible powers of concentration. A strange calmness and clarity clicked into her cognitive and physical states as the lightning brain shifted gears. She was wearing more than a game face, for the lightning brain had zoned into the task at hand. Electra put on her safety mask and gloves and strode purposefully, confidently towards the entrance. It was time to act.

Electra breezed right through the reception area. Much later, she would joke to herself that a gorilla would have gone unnoticed, but no time now for kidding. She marched through the crowded stairwells and corridors to Christi's room, arriving just as the shift nurse was about to enter. The badge said Rosa; she looked exhausted, stressed to the limit.

"Hello, Rosa. I just came on duty to start with this patient. Why don't you give me the chart and meds tray and I'll carry on while you go to your next patient."

"Oh, would you? I'm finishing up a twelve-hour shift and am dead on my feet. This is my last patient before going off duty."

"Before you go, what can you tell me about, um, Christi Conklin? Has she stabilized?"

"No, not yet. She's still running a high fever and does nothing but sleep. I think sedation is wrong, but that's not my call."

"Thanks for the update. I'll take it from here. Go get some rest." Electra entered the room, making sure the partition screened Christi's side. The medical set-up had not changed from earlier in the day, so she knew to arrange supplies in the bathroom, lining up syringes, bottles, and measuring spoons. Next, she set out powdered smart pill formulation and suspension fluids. Her lab techniques were flawless; she prepared the first mega-dose, loading it into the first syringe. Then she went to Christi, still beautiful to her, still asleep to the world.

Electra found a forearm vein and injected the dose on the first try, then examined the tray and chart taken from Rosa, crossing out sedation instructions. After that she spent the next two hours measuring, mixing and loading. All syringes were now set. The only thing left was for Christi to regain consciousness before sunrise on

Sunday, nearly twelve hours away. It was time for Electra to play a waiting game of blending in, staying unnoticed. That suited Electra, for she could rest while sitting next to Christi as the lightning brain kept thinking.

One nurse did come in, making the rounds for the other patient in the room. Electra ignored her by adjusting Christi's monitors. After the second injection, Electra walked the corridor again, witnessing blunt testimony to the damage T-Plague was inflicting on hospitals, which today was to Electra's advantage. She was as invisible as an air molecule.

Electra's plan unfolded neatly through the night. No shift nurse would check because she had already removed Christi's chart from the rounds list kept at the nurses' station. The waiting game continued until five a.m.

Electra was sitting in semi-darkness next to Christi when she detected a stirring that jolted her like an electric shock. She leaped to her feet, peered intently.

"Christi, can you hear me? If you can, nod your head. Don't try to open your eyes just yet." A couple of seconds passed, then Christi nodded.

"Try to open your eyes. Don't try to talk yet. You need to drink some water first." Electra could tell by Christi's breathing she was coming to. A couple of seconds later, her eyes blinked open and closed, then stayed open.

"Let's get you sitting up so you can drink." The combination of Christi's slender build and Electra's well-concealed strength made that easy. "Now drink slowly. Let me do the talking. Your T-Plague condition has stabilized. You are no longer contagious. Your fever has broken. You must go home as soon as possible. You are not safe in this hospital. I am calling your father to come pick you up. Do you understand what I just said? Nod your head if you do." Christi nodded; Electra stepped into the bathroom to dial the Conklin's number, praying someone would answer. After the seventh ring, a sleepy Russell Conklin answered.

"Hello, this is Good Shepherd Hospital. Christi Conklin has regained consciousness. Her condition has stabilized and she is no longer contagious. You must take her home immediately. It's not safe for her to stay. Bring the gentleman who was with you yesterday in case you need help taking your daughter home. Do this immediately. Just come to her room and get her out as fast as you can. Good bye."

Electra then dialed home, again disguising her voice. "This is Good Shepherd Hospital. Christi Conklin must be discharged now. Call Doctor Russell Conklin immediately. He needs your help and will give you the details. Good bye." Electra packed all supplies and was ready to leave, taking with her all charts. Christi was barely aware of what was happening and could barely talk, but she needed to say something.

"Hey, don't I know you?" she whispered hoarsely. "Why are you doing this? Tell me." It took all of Electra's self-control to ignore Christi's pleas. Without looking back, she said, "You'll be fine as soon as your father takes you home. Good luck." And then she vanished.

Electra marched down the stairway to the first-floor entryway. *Be confident. Take command if someone stops me. Keep moving.* She was on high alert when she noticed two security guards glancing her way. *Don't look back. Just weave through the parked cars and get to the van.* Sunrise was two hours away so she had the cover of darkness, but she heard footsteps echoing behind.

"Oh nurse, I need to talk to you."

Electra kept moving, snapping back, "I'm off duty and need to report to my assigned hospital. I don't have time now." Electra kept walking, but the guard started running, grabbing her arm when he caught up.

"Hold on! You're not supposed to be here. You've got some questions to answer. Come with me." That was his first and final mistake. Electra whipped around, wrapping her arm around his, using it to pull herself against his body, immobilizing his arm while gaining leverage. She snapped his head backward by striking an elbow to his mouth, stunning him, followed with another elbow to the side of his head. He was out cold after his head slammed into the pavement.

Electra didn't bother looking around. She took the guard's badge and weapon, then ran, ducking and weaving among vehicles. She spotted a security alarm and pulled it. Someone would find the guard, causing more commotion that would cover her escape.

She dived into Doc's van, driving out of the lot slowly, not turning on headlights until clearing the lot. Then she accelerated, zigging and zagging down alternate streets to elude any pursuers. There were none. Five minutes later, she was on a familiar road home.

I've done it! Mission accomplished. Russell and Doc should have Christi home soon. It was not yet seven o'clock and street traffic was non-existent except for two cars in the distance speeding towards the hospital. Electra pulled into a driveway and waited for the cars to pass, recognizing both: Conklin's car first, closely followed by her father's. Christi would soon be in safe hands.

A wave of euphoria swept over Electra. For the first time in twenty-four hours, she could stand down; she could smile again. She needed to let her emotions run free. Suddenly, an intense pang stabbed her chest, making her sob so violently she couldn't breathe. Her emotions ran wild for two minutes before she regained enough control to finish driving home.

Electra sat in the van until she figured out what to do, at first not knowing what to think. And then she felt her brain shift to another state, once again accompanied by a calming clarity. *I know precisely what to do. First, I'll apologize to Father and Grandfather. They need to know the new order. Then I'll be Christi's caregiver for a couple of days to make sure she's recovering. And then I'll sort through everything that's happened. It's another epiphany. My plate's full.*

All Saturday Jason had felt like a character in Becket's play *Waiting for Godot*, waiting for a call from his daughter that never came. He did receive a routine text from Lab Security informing him that a researcher on his team had come and gone, but there was nothing else until an enigmatic Sunday morning wake-up call, followed closely by Russell's.

Had Electra behaved this way even last summer, Jason would have worried himself to a frazzle. But not now. Saturday morning's confrontation told him that Electra had crossed over into a different state of awareness. She was ready to stand alone, stand on her own. Doc understood even better than Jason.

"We've known for years this day was coming, but you haven't noticed the changes taking place in your daughter. You've let your job consume you. Think back when we discovered she's a genetic freak. We pledged to protect her, to prepare her for what's to come. You hit on the idea that I teach her how to control her brain, and that's what I did. You haven't spent enough time with her to realize how smart or how emotionally mature she is. Yesterday's trauma jolted her to action. Electra has unleashed herself into the adult world, and neither will ever be the same again. But don't worry. She's in control, not us. We did what we were supposed to, so let her go. She'll let us know what's going on."

Both guessed that Electra played a role that culminated in the call from Good Shepherd, but said nothing to Russell. Their convoy encountered no obstacles and when arriving, a parking lot kerfuffle added to the disorder. They charged in, ready to bully their way through, but nothing of the sort was necessary. Russell swept Christi into his arms, and they dashed out, talking to no one. Doc helped Jennifer put Christi into bed, and before Jason drove them home, Doc promised to call later.

Electra showered when she came home, ate a hurried breakfast, then waited in the living room for her father and grandfather. She knew what they would ask and was preparing her answers.

"Living room lights are on. Electra's home. Let's go listen to her story." Jason nodded as they hurried to meet their erstwhile adolescent. Then they sat and listened while Electra filled in the details, first apologizing for her behavior.

"I'm sorry for not explaining my actions yesterday morning, but I didn't have time and I hope you understand. I love you, Dad; I love you, Gramps. Always remember." Electra proceeded to explain what she had done, looking sad afterwards, as if something precious had slipped away. Doc knew what to say.

"Your father and I knew this day was coming, and ever since we discovered how extraordinary your brain is, we've been doing all we can to get you ready. Well, it came yesterday, and you showed you can handle whatever comes your way. Our job's done.

"I know why you look sad. You're in the adult world now and ready to run all on your own. You've left behind the innocence and wonder of childhood, and that's just the way it is. You're trading it in for a better understanding of the human condition. It's a rite of passage everyone has to make, whether you want to or not. And unlike most people, you're fully equipped to handle it."

Jason added, "I'm sorry I haven't been as close to you as I should have been. I don't have the empathy that your mother did, or your grandfather does. One of the reasons your mother wanted you was to complete her life, to experience life to the fullest. Now you're ready to do the same." Electra wiped away a silent flow of tears, not yet ready to reply.

"Your father's right. You're ready. Just follow your thoughts and feelings. And please, let us know what's going on. Maybe we can give you a point of view you hadn't considered. And always remember to keep our secret. So, let's cheer up and figure out what to do next. I think we should go see Christi." Doc's words snapped Electra back to right now.

"You're both right, and why don't we do this. Let me stay with Christi the next couple of days. I'll be her caregiver. You be her physician. And we don't tell anyone what I did. Christi was too out-of-it to recognize me, so I'm in the clear."

"Yes, I should be her physician for this episode. I know the facts and how much to say. I'll call Russell right now, and then we'll visit in two hours."

Russell Conklin was deeply troubled by what he had witnessed during the last two days; America's medical system can't handle the T-Plague. This was his wake-up call. Until now, he had been too insulated from the ominous realities looming. No longer would he be a bystander.

I was wrong about the Guardian Party. They're not a misguided offshoot of some ultra-conservative America-first group. They're pushing to do what the Washington Establishment can't or won't. They're facing up to T-Plague and terrorism. From what I just lived through, Washington's wrong when they say our nation's infrastructure is in good shape. And it refuses to acknowledge rumors about Isilabad working to weaponize the T-Plague. It's time I get involved. I know some people who might feel the way I do. As soon as Christi's feeling better, I'm going to make some calls.

"Russell, the Kittners are here. Would you please answer the door?" Jennifer was busy with Christi, so Russell let them in.

"It's time for me to check our patient. I want to take some blood samples and scans so I can confirm Christi's on the road to recovery. And Electra wants to be Christi's caregiver for the next couple of days, which will be a big help for you and Jennifer. How does that sound?"

"Doc, that beats our goddam healthcare system like a drum. I can't thank you enough."

"Wait until you see my bill. This is worth two Sunday dinner invites. Now let's go see Christi."

An amazing transformation had taken place. Christi was indeed the awakened sleeping beauty. Jennifer had bathed and washed her hair, then put her into usual sleep wear, even applying makeup. Russell let Doc explain care regimen for the next couple of days. Test results and Christi's resilience would determine the rest.

Doc took Jason with him to help analyze the samples, leaving Christi in Electra's care. Electra walked her about to shake off the effects of too much bed rest, then prepared a lunch of bananas and oat meal, followed by Internet surfing until Christi tired. Electra tucked her into bed, making sure she took her medicine. While Christi slept, Electra was happy to sit nearby and let the lightning brain sort through everything that had happened.

I'm happy with my physique. It's what I want to look like: trim, slim, fit, and tallish. And my self-defense training paid off. If someone challenges me, they'll be surprised. I'm happy with my brain control too. I'm able to synchronize cognitive and emotional personas with my physical self when I switch states. I just have to put my game face on and focus.

Christi was still asleep when the downstairs phone rang. Electra guessed it was her grandfather calling, so she positioned herself to eavesdrop, hearing everything she had hoped for. Christi was in remission and no longer contagious. Russell and Doc agreed he should be her physician, telling no one about the bullet Christi had just dodged. They did not want Healthguard snooping around, probing into her recovery. Electra would be caregiver for the next two days.

Monday was recovery day at the Conklin's. Christi was up and in motion, still a bit pale but gaining strength. Russell went to work and Jennifer caught up on all the neglected chores while Electra tended to the patient. When Robin visited that afternoon, the trio chatted up a storm; recapping the harrowing events was an elixir.

Jason and Doc retrieved Electra after dinner. Christi was safely on the mend, no longer needing Electra's personal touch, so Doc left instructions for the rest of the week. Christi would study from home and have Electra visit every other day. When Christi kissed Electra goodbye, both girls flushed from an emotional surge that went unnoticed by the adults. Jennifer hugged all the Kittners before they left, thanking them again.

"You, Doc, and Jason are miracle workers." Electra smiled, then deferred to the men.

"Gramps, Mr. Conklin, and my Dad are the heroes. They got Christi out in the nick of time. That place was chaos city, not a bit pretty. Christi, I'll be back on Wednesday. See you then."

CHAPTER 27
June 2111

"The Competitive Landscape"
(Thread 2 Chapter 14)

Mo LIKED THE FINALITY of sports, often using competition as an analogy for what careens through life. When asked about Cognicom projects, he would compare them to a heavyweight bout in which his side is taking a pounding. Each outbreak starts another round. At the end of each round, the project teams stagger to their corners, barely regrouping in time for the start of the next, but still able to come out swinging.

That's why he picked this afternoon's paintball outing for a Cognicom team-building session. It promised to be a fun-filled afternoon that would bolster camaraderie and boost flagging spirits. The researchers would self-select into three teams that would battle to win the war by eliminating all opponents on other teams (splattering an opponent with two paint balls constituted a kill). The battle would be waged at an outdoor amusement park that staged a variety of corporate events. The business leads would accompany the referees who controlled the competition, and afterwards, Mo expected everyone would be in a rejuvenated frame of mind so that his after-dinner remarks wouldn't churn stomachs.

Mo had come through a whirlwind round of meetings, coming away with only one ray of optimism: there had been no major domestic outbreaks since early spring. Other than that, results were bleak. While sitting in the car, he glanced at the bad news bullet points.

China can't contain outbreaks, and though Europe can, it reports more than before. And we hear rumors of corporate espionage going after NIH data. Our researchers probably know about this because the media hypes all the bad news, including Washington's political intrigue surrounding the Guardian Party.

I won't talk about any others. Even today's sparkling weather and the fun-filled game might not be enough to jolly up my researchers. Too bad, but the show must go on. It's time to chat with the refs so we can get started.

Mo's good intentions started unraveling the minute team selection began because instead of dividing into inter-project groupings, each team stayed together. Unbeknownst to the managers, I-Vac and R-Vac researchers had allied to destroy S-Vac, which until recently had been run by Jason. His abrasiveness had created permanent animosity which, thanks to the halo effect, spilled onto S-Vac. Su, Adom, and their entire S-Vac support team became plastered with paint, and though fast on her feet, Electra too was hunted down. What should have been fun became nasty piling on, and when Jason was "assassinated" by several seniors on his new teams, Mo had to stop play before the game became a fistfight.

Not even Mo's after-dinner abbreviated pep talk could repair the damage, and when the teams divided into discussion groups, he didn't have the heart to discuss his bullet points. He simply gave a copy to Su, asking her to jot down comments, and then left. Adom saw Mo's frustration and walked with him.

"You did your best, but you can't control everything or everyone. I'm sure you had something positive to say. Why don't you tell me, and I'll help you come up with something that'll be even better." When Jason spotted them and joined, Mo handed out copies of his bullet points.

"After today's fiasco, please keep this to yourselves. Adom, tell Su to add to this any items she can think of, and you two do the same." Mo talked just long enough to point out the grim realities approaching, then Adom spoke.

"Since I'm the one who's always talking about threats, how about if you let me work with you on the political and espionage angles. Su can fill you in regarding progress she's making on her latest S-Vac. It's not much better than the current formulation, but at least it demonstrates progress." Jason cut in before Mo could reply.

"I'm partly to blame for what happened today. I apologize for pushing a couple of the seniors."

"Don't apologize to me. Apologize to your teams. I thought you'd become a better people manager, but you've slipped. Are your new teams making any progress?"

"No, but thanks to Su I see a way forward. And until today, I thought team morale was better. Most of my researchers are working weekends."

"Everyone working weekends? Maybe you're pushing them too hard." Jason had no reply other than to shrug his shoulders.

"Let's all go home and sleep on it. I'll talk with Su tomorrow." Electra rode home with Jason, feeling sorry for her father.

He was trying so hard but getting nowhere. She wanted to say something to help ease his frustration, but she knew when to leave him alone, so they drove in silence.

Electra kept watching and listening after the disastrous paintball outing, adding to what she already knew. She tracked Su's S-Vac progress and planted another clue to make the next S-Vac release better. And she spied on Jason's I-Vac work. Su had helped enough to make a little progress, and Electra would plant an I-Vac clue. She also formulated samples of her superior vaccines that only she knew about. Only Electra would decide when and how to use them.

Spring blossomed that year as brightly as Electra's social world. Now that Christi had fully recovered, the two became closer than ever. Christi found plenty of activities to fill Electra's social calendar, and they invited Robin to join whenever she took time away from studies or piano. That happened infrequently because she usually preferred learning more about music than about the opposite sex.

Electra's social whirl taught her up close what poets had always known: sex and love are closely related but different. Electra knew from reading that they trigger the strongest of all human emotions, always trumping reason. Contemporary neuroscience and psychology explain why, and Electra could feel the hormonal effects. Thinking about sex excited her, and she wanted more hands-on experience to compare feelings towards girls with those towards guys.

Electra always studied anything that interested her, so she knew about the relative strengths and weaknesses inherent in both sexes. *Men are supposed to be straightforward and rational, although dull, insensitive, and too often controlled by their lower head. Women are supposed to be thoughtful and caring, but a jumble of emotions clutters logic. I'll have to explore all this and more.*

Love and sex also connected her with religious teachings about the Seven Deadly Sins. Her study went far beyond the Bible, and she had read about emotions accompanying the worst aspects of being human. She had learned firsthand how to handle the deadliest: Pride. She would never assume she was "better than everyone" nor claim she knew what was best to do without thinking things through. And she was confident her pragmatic, rational nature would deal with four others: Envy, Greed, Gluttony, and Sloth. That left two she connected with love and sex: Lust and Wrath. She had an uncomfortable feeling they might overpower rational thinking when unleashed in a crisis, and if that occurs she would simply trust her lightning brain. There was no other choice, so she stopped worrying about it.

Christi's high school sponsored one final dance before spring term ended, the School's Out Jamboree, to which she invited Electra and Robin. It was a popular tradition, attracting an assortment of Jennifer Conklin-approved boys in case the dates arranged by Christi fell through. The trio would meet them at the dance, and afterwards sleep at Christi's, much as they did in their Three Queens sheltered childhood. Still, they led charmed lives insulated by their parents from most of the ugliness swirling about.

All three had blossomed, but in different ways. If they were competing in a Junior Miss America Contest, Christi would qualify for the final round. She had talent, looks, and spirit, flashing a sparkling personality when performing. And thanks to Electra's warnings, she was not jaded; she kept her one-on-one encounters with the opposite sex within bounds. Robin might qualify for the final round. A prodigy on the piano, her high-cut European features and thin-boned physique projected a subtly exotic appearance, while her inherent shyness came across as a sophisticated cool reserve.

Electra's bloom was hard for others to see, for she hid her talents. She did not want to appear exceptional in any way, so she "dummied down." She made herself attractive enough and smart enough, and she had learned to resist the temptation to show off. Hiding in a crowd was easy with her two best friends because they became the center of attention. Electra was not envious; she was pleased for them.

High spirits ruled on that last Friday evening in June. Jennifer gave last minute instructions before dropping them off. "Christi, call me when you're ready for pickup. And be aware of your surroundings. Watch what you drink and who you dance with."

"Oh, Mother!" We learned that lesson two years ago. We're good to go!" Off they went to meet the guys.

The boys met Jennifer's standards that Christi had to live with. They had to be good students possessing adequate social skills, good manners, and good sense regarding drinking, drugs, and sex, the last being Jennifer's primary concern for her adventuresome daughter.

Christi's date Daniel, a senior on the basketball team, had paired Robin with his friend Erik. Electra chose Hector, who had been her partner in drivers' education and auto repair classes. Erik texted Daniel late that afternoon he would miss the dance because of food poisoning. Daniel, who would be the group's social facilitator, announced the change when the group rendezvoused.

"Yo, everyone. Hey, Robin, I'm sorry, but Erik is a no show. He has a case of food poisoning, but that's better than you-know-what. Anyway, no problem. There'll be plenty of guys."

Christi added, "With Robin's looks, she can pick and choose. Come on, let's hit the dance floor." Christi and Daniel peeled off to dance, leaving the others to enjoy the scene.

The large turnout had its share of boisterous fellows. Evidently, T-Plague concern had lessened; the dance would be safe, and adolescents know they're immortal. Roberto, a friend of Hector, took Robin to a group gathered at a piano while Hector and Electra mingled with fellow students, chatting about vacation plans, and then joined the dance floor action. The trio and their partners were happily engaged.

Where'd the time go? It's after eleven. Time to call it an evening and call Mother, so I can tell her how responsible I am. Christi rounded up everyone except Robin.

"Has anyone seen Robin? I thought she was dancing with you." Roberto said, "Two guys I've never seen before muscled in on me. There they are, by the parking lot door." Roberto pointed to where Robin and two fellows were about to exit. Electra's early warning system activated.

"Christi, let's go collect Robin. We'll meet you guys at the main entrance." The duo started weaving through the crowd towards Robin and her escorts but got there too late. Electra's warning system elevated.

"They can't be too far ahead. We'll find her in the parking lot. Let's split up. Yell out when you spot them. I'll do the same." The gravel and dirt lot had lot poor lighting, and on this now windy overcast night it might be hard to find Robin.

Electra dodged down one lane, then up another. No luck until she heard a muffled scuffle and ran like lightning towards the sound.

"Help! Hey, leave her alone before I get the chaperones!" That didn't bother the fellow; he had already shoved Christi to the ground before turning to face Electra.

"Hey yourself! You better walk away if you know what's good for you. And take her with you!" Then he made the mistake of kicking Christi, for he had just exposed himself to a soccer-kick into his privates, delivered with gusto by Electra. He dropped to his knees, clutching his groin as he slowly toppled forward, like a tree that had just received its final axe-blow. Electra calmly grabbed him by the hair when he reached forty-five degrees and bashed his head into the car's rear quarter panel, the impact sufficient to shake up the back seat. He fell to the dirt, motionless.

Electra stepped over him, peering inside where she saw the other fellow astride Robin. When he turned to face Electra, she saw Robin was holding her own. Gouges on his cheeks looked like garish fertility rite markings. Electra could see that he was learning a painful lesson at Robin's hands, and an odd thought flashed in her brain. *Playing the piano gives Robin strong fingers. I'm gonna keep practicing. Even if I don't get any better, I'll get a stronger grip.* Electra returned to action, grabbing his hair and pulling backward. He tumbled out like a bag of golf clubs, limbs scattering in all directions. Electra made sure he stayed down by kicking him twice, then pulled Robin out. By this time Christi was on her feet and fighting mad.

"That asshole splattered mud all over the front of me! And dammit, my pantyhose ripped. He's gonna pay for this!" The trio clustered above their victims, who were just beginning to stir; a gleam came into Christi's eye.

"Let's take their wallets. They owe us big-time." Electra glanced around. So far, the struggle had been brief and unobserved. Robin rose to the occasion.

"I think these bozos should drive us home unescorted. Let's borrow their car. Who has a driver's license?

"I do," Electra chirped brightly. "I'll ask to borrow their car. Robin's new friends were able to sit up, so Electra grabbed the fellow who was nearer.

"Stop! You're gonna crush my windpipe."

"Give me the keys to your car. When the cops call, tell them you let us borrow it. We'll leave your wallets when we dump your car and take just enough money to cover the damages. And if you cause us any trouble, you'll regret it. I'll know from your driver's license where you live." Silence confirmed the agreement, so the girls grabbed the wallets, then piled into the car; Electra gunned the engine, and they raced out of the lot. Five minutes later, they were settled enough for Electra to snap out commands.

"Christi, call your mom and tell her we're getting a ride home. Then call Daniel and tell him the same so he knows where we went."

"Will do." Christi made the calls, and then asked Robin to explain.

"How'd you got mixed up with those guys? And by the way, nice job with your nails."

"I'm so sorry, but they seemed so nice. They were into music and were going to give me some thumb drive recordings. You two are always bailing me out of bad situations. I've got to do better picking guys." Electra's warning system was standing down; she was able to relax.

"We gotta figure out why you have such bad luck with fellows, so let's do this. Robin, draw up a list of the reasons why you like boys, and another list for why you don't. Christi, you make a list of what to look for in a guy, and what to avoid. Then we'll talk about them and see what advice we come up with."

The trio had reached the end of the night's unexpected ride. Electra parked the car a couple of blocks from the Conklin's, and while walking, they rehearsed a story for Jennifer. It would be another all's well that ends well tale, suitably edited for adults.

Summer came and went uneventfully compared with winter and spring. There were no serious T-Plague outbreaks at home or abroad, but Cognicom projects continued struggling. The dog days of summer trudged by for S-Vac because Su's progress was slower than expected, and Jason's I-Vac took one step forward then three-quarters step back. R-Vac was the worst: suspended in no-motion. Electra observed it all, concluding no additional clues would be given unless public panic accelerated the government's downward spiral.

By comparison, Electra's summer danced by. She was already working on third-year classes and would have enough credits to graduate next June at the age of fifteen. That was nowhere near the record, so she didn't worry about being noticed. She scored well enough on SAT exams taken in July that would combine with a near-perfect grade point average and impressive extra-curricular activities to gain admittance wherever she applied to college. George Washington and Johns Hopkins universities were her top picks because they were close and offered excellent biotech programs. She might want to live on campus for its social experience, but she would make that decision as the final school year unfolded. In the meantime, she would polish off whatever she needed or wanted to study.

This was the summer Electra raised her sights beyond biotechnology to focus on physics. Su had mentioned that quantum biology uses the more elementary principles of modern physics, such as tunneling, a phenomenon observed in many intra-cellular chemical reactions. Certain reactions take place because low energy electrons or other reactive components tunnel through high energy barriers rather than climbing over. She skimmed college level physics books and even completed for credit an online Philosophy of Physics course that provided a big picture of the "King of Sciences."

In the first week's lecture, the instructor provided an apt quote from the 18th century mathematician Carl Gauss: "Science is the King of Philosophy, Mathematics is the Queen of Science, and Number Theory is the Queen of Mathematics." The instructor added that physics is the king of sciences, emphasizing that to use physics a research scientist must master the more difficult elements of its mathematical vocabulary, including advanced calculus, differential geometry, abstract algebra, and tensor analysis.

The instructor used clever examples rather than equations to make the topics come alive, using Karl Popper's famous article, Science as Falsification, to illustrate how science distinguishes itself from all other areas of learning. Science is the only discipline that uses observable phenomena to verify or refute a theory. If you can't test the underlying assumptions, you aren't doing science. The instructor explained a little-known principle from logic, the Explosion Principle, that proves anything can be concluded once a contradictory assumption is asserted. He then showed how classical physics, known as Newtonian physics, breaks down at the extremes, very big or very small or very fast, and then said not to worry, because classical physics approximates accurately everything we see in the everyday world.

But in a subsequent lecture, the instructor explored paradoxes that appear when looking at extremely small or extremely large objects—atoms or galaxies. Classical physics can't explain what happens at these dimensions so we must enter the brave new worlds of Quantum Mechanics and General Relativity. The holy grail for physicists is a set of equations that explains all phenomena over all dimensions. Then he pointed out how all modern theories about the Universe—Unified Field Theory, M-Theory, String Theory, and their successors—are simply leaps of faith because their assumptions can never be verified. He even explained a fantastic faster-than-light conjecture: use black holes to fold space and tunnel to a distant galaxy faster than light could get there. And he made an argument that time exists only in our minds: it is nothing more than atomic vibrations that only humans use to order events so they agree with cause-and-effect. But then he stumped everyone by showing cause-and-effect reversal in accelerated reference frames. A handful of respected scientists could reconcile why this is so, but because these examples were mental exercises impossible to observe, the instructor concluded that most theories used to explain high energy physics could not be tested, making it difficult to know if the theory led to valid conclusions. Electra stored all she learned and would explore more about physics and its connections with bioscience when she needed it.

This was also the summer Electra convinced Jason she needed a car. Although inter-city self-driving trucks are now in use, computer-controlled public transportation streets and self-driving intra-city cars are still in the future. America's love affair with cars continues. Gasoline-powered internal combustion engines are still important because the auto industry had increased engine efficiency while engineers still battled with electric battery energy density, fuel cell durability, and safety issues (lithium batteries spontaneously burst into flame if the metal is exposed to air). Though engineers are convinced technological breakthroughs would make electric vehicles cheaper and hydrogen-powered engines would become a reality, cynics used the same quote they had been using ever since the first hydrogen bomb: the future of fusion reactors for power generation would always be forty years away.

That quote did not apply to Electra's driving future; she already had a full-privilege driver's license because she had passed driver's education and vehicle maintenance courses. Having her own car would give her greater flexibility getting to or from the lab, eliminating the need for being chauffeured, so Jason would help pick a low mileage, inexpensive hatchback in good condition. Electra had been fascinated by cars ever since watching action adventure chase scenes. She had taken online car handling courses, but to date had never tested on the road her race-car driving skills. The closest she came was the go-kart track, where she reveled in the thrill of a race. She could lap the field but usually held back to keep opponents in the game. She knew that showing off behind the wheel could be hazardous for a number of reasons. Her friend Hector paid the biggest compliment he knew when he said she drove like a guy. He would never know why.

As in everything she did, Electra thoroughly researched cars before making a decision. *Ford Motor is my kind of car company. Proud of its American heritage, it builds high-performance models that racing enthusiasts love. And it's a smart survivor, the only American car company that steered through last century's Great Financial Meltdown without a government bailout. I'll get a retro-remake of the iconic Ford Fiesta. It won Hot Hatchback of the Year honors a couple of years ago.*

Electra continued taking piano lessons at school that autumn, knowing full well music was not her calling. She knew theory and played all the right notes, but didn't feel the music. How different for Robin, whose fingers and emotions were attuned to the piano. A gifted musician aspiring to a concert pianist career, Robin faced a major challenge. She needed to control her high-strung nerves when facing an audience.

Robin's teacher had submitted a recording that earned Robin a spot in a prestigious East Coast young pianist's competition, and in spite of a bad case of nerves, had qualified for the round of sixteen to be held the second week of November in Bethesda Maryland's Strathmore Music Hall. Five finalists would be selected by playing in front of a judges-only panel, and winners determined on the concluding Saturday by performing in front of a live audience Beethoven's twenty-third piano sonata, appropriately named The Appassionata, a perfect choice for Robin because her emotions throbbed with a passion for music.

Electra gave herself an extra October music assignment: teaching Robin how to handle high-strung nerves. Once a week

Electra would watch Robin practice the sonata, comparing Robin's technique with instructions written in the score. Robin's play became flawless, impressing even her music teacher who gave some credit to Electra's coaching. It was now time to soothe Robin's performance nerves once and for all. Saturday before competition week would be the right time, Christi's bedroom the right place, so after ordering pizza the trio sequestered for a final practice session. Electra dived in when all were comfortably sitting on floor pillows.

"Christi, you're a great performer in front of an audience. Why don't you tell Robin how you handle nerves?"

"I love the spotlight. I can't wait to get out there and strut my stuff, because I know I've got the goods. I guess it's just part of my social DNA."

"Fair enough. You're not high-strung like Robin. What advice would you give her?"

"Try to forget about the audience, and just do your own thing." Robin looked exasperated.

"I try, but I can't seem to. Some musicians take propranolol to steady their nerves before they play, but I don't want to go that route." Electra queued her ideas and let them roll.

"Let's start with what Christi said. Instead of trying to forget about the audience, I want you to picture the audience for what they are: nothing but a bunch of naked apes all dressed up and sitting down. So far so good. Now I want you to think about your music talent. You can feel the music. That's something I can't do. Few can. You can make the notes flow from your head to your heart to your hands when you play. So, before you start playing, take a deep breath and concentrate on that flow. Still OK?" Robin nodded yes, so Electra delivered the most important piece of advice, a gift from Indira.

"I want to recite one verse from a poem written by my mother. It's the first verse from a poem called 'Vanishing Point.' It goes like this,

'Are you among the fortunate few—
disappearing into the present?
Abandoning past and future—
if but only for a moment.
If so then you are truly Tuesday's Child,
Full of grace—radiant with the joy of being.'"

Electra paused for impact, then continued. "Her message is this: if you love music the way you do, you simply want to lose yourself in the moment of your performance. Feel the music. Become the music. Let that be your reality while playing. You do that, and you'll never be bothered by nerves again. Between now and the competition, I want you to think about it. Take some quiet time and let my mother's poem sink in. And I'll be with you at the competition to help you remember. Christi, don't you lose yourself when you're performing?"

"I never thought of it quite like that, but you're right. It's like I'm in my own world when I'm onstage. Robin should zone in to that."

"I will, and Electra, please be there for me."

Christi said, "Let's call a timeout. I'm ready for something sweet. Let's see what mother has for us in the kitchen." The trio skipped to the kitchen, then to the family room to watch a movie. Later, they returned to the bedroom to spend the night chatting about a future framed by "why not?" rather than "why?"

When Electra called mid-week, she heard a more relaxed and upbeat Robin. According to her teacher, she might be among the five finalists. Robin's mother

Irena called Jason Thursday evening with the good news: Robin was among the finalists. That sparked an impromptu Friday night party hosted by Christi's parents.

Robin glowed at dinner like the candles on the table. According to her parents, the top three would receive cash and scholarships to elite music schools, along with accolades for winning a storied piano competition that would set the stage for the next four years. That in itself could jangle anyone's nerves, but not tonight, for Robin had disappeared into the joy of this evening.

Saturday plans were made at the dinner table. No matter where Robin places, she's still a winner, and the Setdarova's would make dinner reservations at a restaurant near the concert hall. Electra would drive to and from with Su, who had also helped Robin prepare. The week had been tiring as well as exciting, so the celebration ended early. Electra hugged Robin and gave her final instructions.

"Remember what we talked about. I'll see you backstage Saturday to check you out before you perform. I'd say break a leg, but that's too trite."

"You can say that to me when I'm dancing, but for Robin, how about break a finger?" Robin smiled as Christi hugged her too. The parents gave their goodbyes and everyone departed.

Saturday morning was typical for mid-November. Temperatures near forty, sunlight punctuated by windblown darkish clouds scudding across the sky. No one knew what today's weather would bring; the same could be said for today's competition; excitement was in the air. The recitals would start at two, lasting for three hours, after which winners would be announced at five-thirty, followed by winners' encores at six.

Su picked up Electra at eleven, which gave plenty of time to be with Robin. By luck of the draw, she would be the final performer. Electra liked that because not only would Robin's performance bring the competition to a close, but if she played her notes right it might bring down the house. When they arrived, Electra went directly backstage where Robin and her parents were huddling. As already agreed, Robin wanted only Electra with her beforehand, so all but Electra took their places in the auditorium.

"Are you going to listen to the other performers?"

"Nope. Aunt Su will let me know what they're like. I have an idea. Let's duck out the back and take a quick walk to check out the area. We've never been to Baltimore. The fresh air and exercise will be good for you. Then we'll come back and make final preparations."

"Good idea. I want to release some of my excess energy."

The girls walked briskly for about a half hour, looking in store fronts and sharing comments about passersby. It was now three-thirty; time for final preparation. Robin changed into her all black performance gown, its understated elegance making the ashe-blonde thin and light complexioned Robin all the more striking. She stretched and flexed and splashed some chords across a practice keyboard; she was ready for Electra's final words.

A knock on the door. "Five minutes, Miss Setdarova. Do you need anything?"

"I'm all set. Knock again for me to come out."

It was game time. As they stood by the door, Electra holding Robin's hands, smiling brightly while gazing intently into Robin's eyes, a jolt of emotion surging through both.

"This moment is as good as it gets. Make the most by enjoying it to the fullest. Winning or losing doesn't figure in. You're already a winner and always will be. Just remember to let the music flow out of your head, heart, and hands into the keys. Disappear into the music. You'll be great." The knock came, whisking Robin to the stage. Electra ran to sit by Su.

"So, there you are. How is your protégé?"

Electra whispered, "I think she'll be on fire. How have the other performers done?"

"One was outstanding, one excellent, one good, and one faltered a tad. But considering how pressure-packed the competition is, they all did fine. Quiet now. Here's Robin."

Light applause greeted Robin as she took center stage, glancing at the audience. Electra caught her eye and did what any serious music lover would do: stuck out her tongue and made an ape-face. A hint of a smile flitted across Robin. Then she composed herself, placing folded hands on her lap, closing her eyes, and summoning inner strength before striking the first key.

From the first notes that hinted at the composer's emotions, Electra knew Robin had vanished into the music. Through the allegro, through the scherzo, she played effortlessly, flawlessly, with all the feeling called for. Then came the glorious third movement—the presto—requiring power, speed and dexterity. Robin was ablaze, notes cascading in torrents. The audience momentarily gasped, and Su pointed to the overhead monitor that displayed the pianist's fingering. "Goodness, Robin's just crossed over. Right hand playing base, left hand playing treble. Few pianists master this, but if judges consider it grandstanding, she'll be penalized." No one knew that when Robin became one with the music, instinct chose which clef to play with which hand.

Robin's fingers danced over the keys, closing her performance with powerful trills and chords. As the last notes faded, Robin sat motionless for several seconds more, suspended by her emotional high, then rose to acknowledge the applause and glided off the stage.

"Ladies and gentlemen, we have heard five outstanding performers this afternoon. We will announce the three winners at five-thirty. And please remember, everyone who performed today is indeed a winner." The lights came up and the announcer came down to join the judges.

Electra decided to stay put for Aunt Su's comments. "Robin's performance is among the best that I've heard live for that piece." Did you know she could cross-play?"

"No. I never knew about it until you told me."

"The judges might penalize her. Competition judges frown on overstated fingering techniques. We'll just have to wait and see. Let's find the rest of her fan club and see what they think." Christi and her parents were with Jason and Doc. Robin's parents were waiting backstage, undoubtedly more nervous than their daughter. Su joined the adults while Christi took Electra aside.

"Whatever you did to Robin, you have to do to me before I go onstage. She was totally hot!"

"All I did was tell her to vanish into the music. Pretty much what you and I told her last week. And I'll be backstage with you whenever you ask."

The lights dimmed, calling everyone back. Five minutes later, the announcer strode to the microphone.

"Ladies and gentlemen, I need to clarify one of the competition rules dealing with what is sometimes referred to as grandstanding. Contestants are penalized for deliberately using exaggerated fingering. As you witnessed, our last contestant used a cross-over fingering technique, which is as difficult as it is flamboyant. However, we have reviewed the video and talked with the contestant. It is the judges' decision that the cross-over was done instinctively and not deliberately, so the contestant was not penalized." The announcer waited for the murmuring buzz to subside. "And now, we will announce the three winners. Third prize is awarded to…"

Electra compared the results with Su's predictions. Third place went to the contestant Su rated excellent. The judges must have listened for slightly different qualities, but Su nodded in agreement. Judging in the fine arts, after all, is a subjective call. He was a tall, curly-haired fellow who could have been close to the maximum contestant age of seventeen, and he looked relieved. After handing a plaque, the announcer directed him to wait on stage. "Thank you very much. And the second prize is awarded to…" Second prize went to Su's second choice, a serious girl of medium build who was perhaps sixteen. She too looked relieved and gave a slight bow to the audience. The applause subsided; whispers of anticipation rustled through the concert hall.

"And first prize for this year's contest is awarded to Miss Robinova Setdarova." Robin walked quickly, gracefully to accept her plaque. All three winners bowed to the audience, then exited. "Ladies and gentlemen, thank you again for being a most appreciative audience.

There will be encores from our winners starting at six o'clock. We welcome all of you to stay. Until then, please enjoy the refreshments in the lobby."

"Aunt Su, you sure know how to pick em. Can you do that with horses?"

"Yes, I can. When you become rich, we'll go to Pimlico and win you a small fortune. And the secret? Start with a large one." Aunt Su could surprise by expressing her wisdom in clever ways. The contrast between her facial expression and the content of her quote always provoked smiles.

Robin's entourage gathered in the lobby, chattering happily while sipping wine as the minutes ticked away unnoticed. Soon the lights dimmed, summoning the audience. The competition's host spoke as soon as the audience settled.

"Ladies and gentlemen, our three winners will each perform an encore to award you for being such a great audience. The order will be our third-place winner, Mr. Sidney Clayton, followed by our second-place winner, Miss Beverly Di Carlo, and then our first place winner, Miss Robinova Setdarova."

The winners played with exuberance now that they were free from the pressures of competition. Sidney played two Chopin pieces—*Spring Waltz* followed by *Butterfly Etudes*. Beverly played Beethoven's *Turkish March* and then *Mozart's Rondo Alla Turca*. All were audience favorites and were applauded loudly. Now came Robin.

She played the first movement of Beethoven's *Moonlight Sonata;* its hushed, dream-like melody provided striking contrast to the energetic pieces just performed. After the applause, she was about to play her second selection but stopped before striking a note. Turning to the audience, she asked, "What would you like me to play?" Whispers rustled again, then a burly voice spoke.

"Miss Setdarova, how about playing the Horowitz transcription of *Stars and Stripes Forever?* The media doom-and-gloomsters are wrong. America's number one and here to stay." The crowd seconded his sentiments and Robin went to work. The Horowitz transcription is noted for its fingering and fireworks, and Robin played with flair. Thundering final chords brought forth bravos, a fitting end to an outstanding competition.

Su and Electra welcomed the three-block walk to the restaurant, letting them stretch their legs after sitting for so long. And a short stroll after dinner to the parking garage would be a pleasant way to conclude the day.

Robin was the center of attention, flanked by her elated parents. The conversation bubbled as pleasantly as the champagne, which the trio was allowed to sample. When asked if this was their first taste, the girls were coy in their reply, Christi saying that nice girls don't talk about such things. Though Jennifer knew otherwise, she kept their secret.

All too soon the evening ended. Jason offered to drive Su and Electra to the parking garage, but Su said the night air would make the walk enjoyable, so he and Doc drove on. It was now after ten; streets and sidewalks were deserted. Electra was about to ask Su if she had entered piano competitions as a teenager in Beijing, but the lightning brain's early warning system intervened. It detected a car idling in the shadows, no lights on, and it escalated to the next level when two men exited the car and began following.

"Let's walk a little faster. Don't look back, but I think we're being followed." They were a half-block from the garage, and if they stepped up the pace, they would enter before the strangers caught up. They did, and when reaching the elevator, Electra punched the up button. If they could enter the elevator before the followers arrived, they would be safe. Electra looked at the elevator indicator display; it signaled a stop at the fifth floor, descending from the top. She could hear clicking heels approaching, and Su looked puzzled, so Electra spoke quietly.

"If people get off the elevator, we'll walk away with them. Whatever happens, don't get on the elevator with whoever's following us." She glanced again at the indicator. Three, two, one. The heels arrived just as the doors opened, revealing nada. Electra shoved Su in and yelled "Go!" then pushed the closer adversary into his partner. The doors closed and Electra dashed for the stairs. She was faster than her startled pursuers and reached the third level in the lead, but the door was locked. She could hear pounding feet approaching, so up the stairwell she flew. But no luck on level four. By the time she reached the top her lead had grown, but level five's door was also locked, so Electra was trapped. As the lightning brain raced through options, Electra felt a sudden jolt as her brain shifted gears. She became calm, focused.

Like a long jumper's leap, she launched herself from the landing, feet forward, and arms flung back. Gravity added velocity to her downward arc, and as her feet collided with the leader's chest, the impact thrust him backwards into his partner. Both tumbled down the stairs like a pair of circus clowns, coming to rest against the wall at the back of next landing. Electra landed on her feet, springing past a pile of arms and legs. She stopped to pick up a cell phone that had clattered out, then dashed down the stairs, never looking back. She knew where she was going.

She streaked out the garage entrance and onto the street, running in the direction Su would drive. She would run until she could call for help. She heard no footsteps or engine behind her, so she focused on the road ahead, spotting flashing lights in the distance. *Su must have called for help.* Electra startled Su and a police officer when she stopped at Su's rolled-down window.

"Electra! Thank heavens you're safe!" No time to waste, so Electra rattled off the situation. The officer radioed for backup and sped away. Electra jumped into the front seat and was still catching her breath when Su asked how she escaped.

"I ran up the stairs, and they couldn't catch me. Let's go before we have to talk to more police." They drove in silence towards an I-95 entrance ramp. Electra waited until Su had them pointed south towards DC before talking.

"What have you heard about security leaks or threats about researchers being targets? I think those jerks were after you."

"Nothing. Maybe the police will learn something if they catch them. The officer rushed away before I could give him my name. I better call when we get home."

"No. I have a better idea. Let's report this to Mo. Let him follow up. If anyone knows about security threats, it'll be Mo." They drove most of the thirty-nine miles in pensive silence, glad to have dodged an unpleasant encounter but unsure why Su might have been targeted. *I'm not the target. Su is, but why? Was it random or intentional? Is it Cognicom related?* Electra dialed recently called numbers made on the cell she had confiscated. No answers or recordings until the fifth; then she connected with a heavily accented male recording: "Allahu Akbar. Leave your name and number." Electra snapped the phone shut, then turned to Su.

"I think I know who's looking for you. We have problem…" Su's post-midnight call shocked Mo awake. He conferenced Adom and Jason onto the call, and they reached a unanimous decision: Su would drive Electra home immediately and then stay temporarily with Adom until Mo figures out if Cognicom researchers are targets of some as yet undetected adversary. Mo would work his network as soon as he talked with Bobbi.

Two hours later Mo knew more than the Baltimore police. The police knew nothing beyond the dispatcher's recorded call. No suspects had been detained. They didn't even know Su's name, nor did they want Mo to call again, and he'd be happy to oblige. He left a message late Sunday morning, giving Bobbi a summary of what he'd discuss in her office first thing Monday, then talked with Adom after deciding who he'd call Monday afternoon.

Su's encounter baffled Bobbi too. She would ask her boss to set official security guidelines which Mo would circulate among all Cognicom teams, and she told Mo to alert all business and tech leads immediately. Mo spent the rest of Monday tapping into his network but came away as bewildered as before, so he expanded the call radius, contacting an ex-CIA field agent he met at an Air Reserve training weekend last August. Success at last. Though he hadn't a clue why Su had been followed, the fellow promised to contact his network and report back anything even remotely related, and he could find someone to pick apart the cell phone Electra had picked up. He, like Mo, was disgusted with the Administration's fumbling in the face of worsening crises, labeling the man in the oval office an empty suit doing nothing but spouting empty speeches, and he shared Mo's concern that the Guardian Party or another opposition group might step in if conditions continue spiraling downward.

Mo was turning out lights in his office late Friday afternoon when his cell phone beeped. An unfamiliar voice said, "Hello, Mo. I heard about the excitement last Saturday, and I have an idea that might help both of us. I know a place we can talk. From what I've heard, you might be our kind of guy, but I don't know if you're game for what I've got. What do you say?"

"Where can we meet?"

Late Saturday night a call came to the Invisible Man from the Invisible Hand. They are another reincarnation, predecessors having been terminated for lack of performance. These successors know better methods for obtaining results, and their futures depend on meeting expectations.

"This is the Invisible Man."

"This is the Invisible Hand. I have made contact with suitable moles and will confirm as soon as they are in place and operational.

"Good work. Make sure they ferret out info and finger primary targets."

"I copy."

"Good. Call again as scheduled."

After the call, the Invisible Man started to make a mental list of next steps. No matter the collateral damage, he would be prepared to step on whatever or whoever gets in his way. And there would be no footprints, only confusion.

CHAPTER 28
February 2112

"Blow-Up"
(Thread 2 Chapter 15)

ELECTRA TURNED FIFTEEN TODAY, but poor Jason couldn't celebrate with his family because he was trapped today and tomorrow in offsite emergency Cognicom sessions. Vaccine progress was just like Jason: stuck and going nowhere. Combine that with political instability and terrorist threats, and the researchers understood why they had to come up with new approaches. The pressure kept building to get effective vaccines because any sign of progress would shore up the public's flagging confidence in the government.

Jason's hit a rough patch at work, but we can't put Electra's life on hold, so she and I will hold our own party. So much has happened to us since she was born. No wonder the years flash by. I used to be her omni-parent, helping her in ways Jason couldn't. Now she's outside my comfort zone. She knows what's best so I'll give her all the freedom she wants. But it's good we stay connected. She still needs me to help stay centered.

When Electra exploded into Doc's life, he needed her as much as she needed him. She filled a gaping crater that opened the day his home went up in flames that consumed his wife and de facto daughter-in-law. Over the years, he had become Electra's best friend and vice-versa because he possessed a loving empathy that gave Electra exactly what she needed to thrive while growing into adolescence. Then suddenly, events catapulted her into adulthood, changing their relationship and putting Doc on the periphery.

Doc mused *She still has the fresh appearance of a mature and tallish adolescent, but concealed within lurks extraordinary power, ready to be tapped whenever she decides. Kids today are expected to mature as fast as their abilities allow and conditions dictate. It was different when Jason was growing up. Adolescents back then were stuck in an inflexible education system that kept them too dependent for too long. Our society's approach is better now. Those adolescent years are no longer a troubled wasteland. Teenagers need to get past them as quick as they can so they can grow up and into something. Just look at Electra. Already driving, graduating in June, accepted into a college work-study program. She's a fully-functioning adult. And all because she was ready to handle the load. America's much more progressive and pragmatic than the rest of the world. I hope the T-Plague doesn't set us back too far.*

Doc wanted to chat about Electra's plans, not that she needed guidance but because he wanted to know where her plans would take her, and he didn't know how much longer she would confide in him. He was eighty, and although his mind was sharp, his health was on a downward slope, made steeper by his mild heart attack three years ago. He was controlling with low dose beta blockers congestive heart failure, a chronic condition for many his age, and he was forestalling further deterioration by exercising occasionally, but he was beginning to experience kidney and liver complications. Doc didn't worry about dying, but worried instead about living each day to the fullest, wishing to exit while in action. Taking care of Electra had allowed him to enjoy each day; now he hoped just having her around would do the same.

"Happy birthday, Electra. Years ago, it was sweet sixteen, but for you, I'm calling it festive fifteen. And here's my special gift." Just before slicing the cake, Doc handed her a card, and even though older now, opening cards or gifts thrilled her. She read the card aloud, kissing her grandfather before checking the contents.

"This is grand. Hector and I will put it to work right away." Doc had given her a generous gift certificate redeemable at a nearby auto shop, knowing she had big plans for her humble hatchback.

"Now, just be careful. No driving tickets because you'll need your license even more after you graduate. How are plans shaping up?"

"Thanks to you and Dad, the road ahead looks smooth all the way through college. I picked DC's George Washington University where I'm enrolled in a biotech career-study program extending the NIH co-op program I'm in now. And I won't live on campus because I can socialize all I want when there and then come back here for my serious study. And by living here I can keep my eye on you and Dad. The only bump in the road might be the T-Plague, and as everyone says, we'll just have to wait and see."

"How about Robin and Christi? Will they be graduating in June?"

"Robin's plan locked in place after she won last year's piano competition. She'll have enough credits for high school graduation next year, and then she applies her scholarship to the Curtis Institute in Philadelphia. She could go anywhere, but Philly is close and Curtis is highly regarded." Gramps nodded.

"She's a lovely, innocent young lady, not nearly as wise in the ways of the world as you or Christi. It's good that you two look out for her. Now, what about Christi?" Electra would have to provide an edited version because Christi's current calling centered on the opposite sex and the performing arts. Her activities often exceeded PG-13, also exceeding Doc's acceptable level.

"Christi's very social-minded, so she won't have enough credits to graduate until she's eighteen. She spends a lot of time taking voice and dance lessons and she's talented, but not anywhere near Robin's level. Her folks encourage her to study for a profession if or when her performing career fizzles. She says she'll be a cosmetician if she can't cut it as an entertainer. Since Christi at least has a plan, her mom's letting her follow it for the time being. We'll have to stay tuned, because that plan's gonna change."

"I'm glad you'll be living here after you graduate. It will be good for you and me, and good for Robin and Christi because you mean a lot to them."

"And all of you mean a lot to me. Hey, this birthday cake with all the buttercream roses is best ever. Maybe there'll be a piece left for Dad when he gets back Friday."

"Tell you what. I'll cut off several pieces and set them aside so you and I can take care of the rest. The frosting and roses will pick him up after all the hubbub he, Aunt Su, and Uncle Adom are going through this week. I hope they can figure out what to do about T-Plague vaccines."

Adom and Su hadn't figured out what to do about the T-Plague, but they did figure out where Su should live. Her temporary living arrangement with Adom became permanent. After she and Electra had been mysteriously followed, Su leased her condominium and then moved her piano and enough furniture into Adom's three-bedroom apartment to make it look lived-in. Like many bachelors, Adom kept possessions to a minimum for maximum flexibility. He said he would buy and furnish a place when he was ready to make a commitment, but until then didn't want furniture getting in the way. Neither Su nor the additional furniture were in the way. She and Adom had a comfortable relationship.

When they were younger, there had been hints of romantic interest, but it evolved into something better—platonic friendship. Over time, Su's subtle suggestions helped Adom become a more thoughtful, sharing person even though he was never able to commit to serious relationships. Though he half-joked his DNA contained the bachelor gene, he was serious about being more responsible, so he offset self-centeredness by helping Middle East immigrants adjust to life in America, which in turn helped him find new interests by networking into other cultures.

Adom used his network to help Mo check the public's pulse on the Middle East or politics at home. For obvious reasons, Su could not come to any Middle East events Adom attended, but her friend Kayed often did. Adom did find anecdotal links between Islamabad and T-Plague, but they weren't sufficient for Mo to take to the next level. Why Su had been followed remained a troubling puzzle.

Winter transitioned to spring and spring to summer, meshing seamlessly with Electra's plans. She wrapped up high school, skipping graduation ceremonies that are optional for guided-study students, and she officially started her collegiate work-study program because it extended the one she had in high school. She would continue working with Su and now earn a token salary. Su assigned her harder tasks which Electra pretended were challenging but in fact were child's play. That fit her plans too. She spent most of the time working on her own vaccines or hiding clues for Su.

Su found most of them without additional prodding and made marginal S-Vac improvements or assisted with Jason's I-Vac. Jason's R-Vac team had no idea what to do and Electra couldn't help because even with Su's assistance, Jason was stretched to the limit handling I-Vac, so Electra would defer planting R-Vac clues until Jason could deal with them. Meanwhile, she studied ahead for first-semester college courses while working at the lab.

If I could chat with Mother, I'd say the last verse of the famous Invictus poem summarizes how I feel about my first year in college.

> *"It matters not how strait the gate,*
> *How charged with punishments the scroll.*
> *I am the master of my fate,*
> *I am the captain of my soul."*

I plan to be in control all the time, and we'll see if I'm smart enough to make it so.

Where are you, Electra? Come on, get here. We have places to go and things to do. So fussed Christi as she waited for her ride on a gorgeous mid-August early Friday evening. Christi had two tickets to a midnight closed circuit showing of a live West Coast new century music concert. The younger crowd, unlike the older folks, still flocked to social events, ignoring the T-Plague, and would reply to parental warnings that every generation has a cadre of young invincibles created by youth's intoxicating optimism.

Christi's social world was in full bloom because of her looks, talents, and hormones. Within the last year, her interest in the opposite sex had gathered urgency, which like many in her generation led to sexual encounters of the closest kind. Modern cultures recognized the necessity and condoned it as long as activities stayed within bounds. Christi was eager to experiment more, maybe with the same sex or with older fellows for added excitement. And some of her adventuresome friends said she should sample recreational drugs to see if they enhanced onstage or under-the-covers performance. Not even Electra knew about one of tonight's activities that Christi had concocted.

Electra rolled into the Conklin driveway at eight; Christi dashed out of the house and into the passenger seat, excited for the night to take flight.

"Golly dolly, glad you're here. Why so slow? We've got miles to go." Electra reached across to give Christi a hug and calm her down.

"Traffic was heavy, but I'm not that late. We don't have to be there until midnight. That's over three hours, so let's stop for a snack and catch up on the latest." Christi flashed a wicked grin.

"Let's take a detour that might be uplifting. How about helping me get some mood elevators? Peter from my theater group gave me a safe contact, and I arranged to meet him tonight. Please? Please?" Christi's impersonation of a panting dog begging for a bone forced Electra to smile.

"You've been angling for this for over a month, so I guess it's better I help you rather than one of your artsy-flighty friends, as long as the stuff and the drop zone are safe. Is his stuff clean? And where are we supposed to meet your so-called elevator man?"

"It's clean, and I'm only buying the tame stuff, so not to worry. I'm supposed to meet him at ten o'clock at the Forest Trail Park Center restrooms. Do you know how to get there?"

"No, but let me bring it up on my GPS." As they viewed the screen, the lightning brain memorized alternate routes. "I've driven in the vicinity before. It's rural once we're off the Interstate. It's about a forty-five-minute drive. You sure about this?" Christi encored her panting performance, so off they drove.

The sunset drive set a mood of excitement as the shadows deepened. The new moon wouldn't rise until well after midnight, so darkness rolled in as they drove on this warm and windless night. The well-paved roads leading to the park were tree lined, winding, and had little traffic, so though not lighted, they were fun to drive. Darkness had fallen by the time Electra drove through the entrance. When approaching the center, which was a mile inside the park,

Electra noticed a car stationed at the start of the parking area, while the only other car was waiting a hundred yards further, near the restrooms. Electra's early warning system signaled to watch out for both. When Electra parked next to the car by the restrooms, its driver rolled down the window, muttering instructions in a deep voice to enter the ladies' restroom.

Christi whispered, "You better come with me." Electra shared Christi's growing excitement.

"Sure thing. You do the talking when we get in and act cool." No lights anywhere, and since not even a sliver of a new moon showed itself, the girls slipped into darkness as they stepped gingerly towards the rendezvous. As soon as they entered, the lights switched on, temporarily blinding them. As their vision cleared, the elevator man came into focus: average looking and stubble-bearded, a little over six feet and wearing a windbreaker. He didn't waste a moment.

"Which one of you called?"

"I did. A friend of mine said you could be trusted."

"Hi ya, babe. My name is Stoney, and yeah, you can trust me, but only when I'm pregnant." He revealed a small caliber pistol and said, "Why don't you show me the money?"

Electra edged closer while Christi fumbled for the bills in her pocket.

"I was told I could get six Ecstasy hits for sixty dollars."

Stoney smirked then said, "Yeah, that's the starting price, but now we'll negotiate. Why don't you show me what else is in your pants?" Christi didn't understand at first; Electra did but kept her mouth shut. When Christi didn't answer, Stoney pointed to Electra. "If you're shy, we'll start with your friend. Suddenly, Christi knew what was coming, so she walked up close.

"Go screw your bozo friend in the car!" Then she threw the bills in his face while kneeing him in the gonads. Stoney was caught off guard, and as he doubled up in agony, Electra delivered a kick flush on his Adam's apple. He landed on the tile floor, gagging for air, unable to talk while his pistol skittered noisily towards Electra. She lunged for it, then yelled.

"Get your money and let's go!" Christi grabbed the bills and Stoney's satchel. Electra grabbed Christi's arm and barked, "Walk fast but don't run. Get into the car and lock the door. If the guy says anything, let me do the talking." Stoney was still gasping as Electra placed a final kick between his legs just before turning out the lights.

As they slipped back unnoticed, the other car's lights came on when Electra started the engine. The deep voice called out, "Hold on until Stoney says it's OK to go."

Electra rolled down the window and snapped back, "He said we're good to go, so adios." She put the car into reverse, using only parking lights while backing up, then drove forward into the park, away from both cars. She knew where the winding drive led and thought it would better to drive out a different way, so she flipped on the headlights and continued driving slowly.

"Make sure your seat belt is good and tight. Hey, nice self-defense move in there. I'm proud of you. Where'd you learn it?"

"From watching all those action-adventure flicks with you. What are we waiting for? Let's go."

"In a minute. I just want to see which way Stoney's going." Suddenly, she saw in the rearview mirror two sets of headlights blaze on, and in the distance could hear tires squealing and engines thundering towards her. Electra calmly pushed several buttons on the dashboard, then punched the accelerator, converting her humble hatchback into a little beast that roared to life, it's high performance exhaust pipes screaming in response and the over-sized turbocharger howling as it spooled toward six digits. Electra had transformed it into a stealth street racer, which her mechanic-friend Hector said would blow the doors off anything, even a police Elite SWAT Cruiser.

As Electra ran through the gears, the lightning brain switched to an altered state where brain and reflexes are one. A thrill swept through her, keeping pace with the start of her first high-speed road chase. Hector had told her to practice handling the little beast so she could keep it on the road. Tonight, she would do that again, but the stakes were higher because the pursuers were playing for all the money and drugs stashed in Stoney's satchel.

Electra let the pursuers get to within a car-length because she wanted to watch them in the rearview mirror while playing with high-performance options, and when she was satisfied she could control the car, she would take it to the next level. She nimbly braked and drifted through the curves while the pursuit cars careened sideways, nearly crashing into one other. Christi was too terrified to scream, and instead just clung to whatever she could grab, trying to survive the ride of her life.

As she raced to the park exit, Electra needed to turn sharply to the left. She heel-toe shifted into the turn, rear tires drifting but under control, losing little speed. The pursuit cars couldn't handle the turn and spun out, banging into each other. Electra was not finished playing, so she slowed to let them rejoin the chase and then accelerated. The hatchback performed like a thoroughbred. It shifted, drifted, and cornered as if on steroids. And it was, because Electra fed it only 100-plus octane gasoline. The pursuit cars were high-performance modified, but neither cars nor drivers could match what they were up against. Only one turn to go, and then they would be on a straightaway where Electra would finish with a flourish.

As she blew out of the final curve, her pursuers zigged and zagged, almost driving off the shoulder. By now, Christi had snapped into the thrill of the chase, paying attention to what Electra said or did.

"Hold onto your derriere. I'm going to kick in the nitro system." Electra hit its arming button, then floored the accelerator. The hatchback leaped forward, and Electra countered the torque pull to the right. Both tach and speedometer whirred to redline; headlights in the rearview mirror faded to black. This little beast could fly with the fastest. The girls vanished into the darkness of the night.

Although her lead was insurmountable, Electra changed routes in case Stoney chased further. By the time she was back on the Interstate, Electra had down-shifted her brain to a more normal state.

"Jeez Louise, where'd you learn to drive like that?"

"Watching action movies and online race-car driving videos. You have to keep it a secret, just like I'll keep my mouth shut about tonight's trip." Christi nodded in agreement. Electra changed the subject.

"I'm worried where you're heading. Why the interest in drugs? You're playing with fire. I must sound like your mother, but what's going on?"

"I want to find out if they'll help me perform better. Everyone tells me how good I am, but let's face it. I need to kick it to the next level, or all I'll ever be is an amateur. Psychologists have done surveys of top athletes and performers, and way over ninety percent say they'd take a long-term risk for a short-term gain. I have to know if I can cut it with drugs. You're the only one who knows what I'm trying, so please help me find out. I need you to keep me in bounds." Electra concealed the emotional jolt that just hit.

"OK. It's better I help. But what about all these guys you're suddenly interested in?" Christi sighed, then spoke.

"We've been best friends as long as I can remember. I tell you things I don't tell anyone else. We both know what sex is all about, and how males and females handle it differently. My sex drive runs at a higher RPM than yours. Sometimes my hormones make me feel like screaming."

Exciting yet frightening emotions surged through Electra. *Calm down. The urge will subside. Change the subject and lighten up.*

"I'm a bit slower on the hormone uptake than you, but believe me, I know what you mean. Sometime we'll compare notes, but tonight let's focus on the music. Are you still game for the concert, or have we had enough excitement for the evening?"

"Are you kidding? I'm totally energized by the chase, and it's only eleven. Let's grab a snack and dash to the concert."

"Fair enough. I know a snack place close by…"

Labor Day weekends always remind me of new school year preparations, and I have two sets to remember: Jason's and Electra's. Jason always needed a lot of help from his mother, but Electra takes care of it all herself. We talked on her birthday, but she hasn't said a word since then. I think I'll check in to see what she's planning.

Electra was reviewing at her home workstation all the directories that contained e-books and syllabi for first term classes. Though professors had not yet loaded presentations or assignments, she felt adequately prepared because she had already read chapters covering the first half of most courses. She was about to watch a movie when she heard her grandfather approaching, so instead she pulled a chair for him close to hers.

"Mind if I join you? Your dad's been at the lab all day, and I haven't seen you since breakfast, so I thought I'd come talk with you to make sure my voice still works. How does it sound?"

"Your voice always sounds good to me. Please sit and talk. I've been looking at the course outlines and textbooks for the fall term. That's not very exciting, but I do have something I'd like you to see, and in fact, you'll be the first." Doc settled into the chair before he replied.

"Well now, I'd like to see it. Is it something I'm familiar with?" "Yes, it is. A couple of years I ago I showed you my summer

project magnum opus diagram illustrating how I organized religion and philosophy. Well since then, I've studied philosophy at a deeper level, and I'd like to show you my detailed bullet point summary that covers only philosophy. Let me open the document."

"Doc studied it for a minute, then said, "Let's pretend I'm giving a lecture as I read it. That way, you can make sure I'm interpreting it correctly, and you can step in when I need help."

"Good idea. You start, and I'll talk when you want me to." Doc read carefully for another minute, scrolled to the top, paused to organize his thoughts, and then began.

"What we have here is your more advanced summary that extends your previous work. And you won't include the holistic and rather static Oriental philosophies because you like how you covered them before. We'll be updating only Western Philosophy." Electra nodded her approval; Doc continued.

"I like how you've categorized all branches of philosophy under the two most important: Metaphysics and Ontology. These are the battlegrounds for answering all the big questions about reality and being. And I like how you've placed the hard and soft sciences underneath Epistemology,because that's where we wrestle with the limits of knowledge. And now, we're ready to give a chronological summary." Doc scrolled down to continue.

"I'm familiar with the starting point, the Greek philosophers Socrates, Plato and Aristotle. They developed two views of the world, Idealism and Materialism. I think the names are self-explanatory, so I'll move on. And I'm familiar with the Religious Philosophy of St. Augustine, who reconciled Christianity with Greek philosophy, and with the Medieval Philosophy of St. Aquinas, who reconciled St. Augustine with Ptolemaic Earth-centric solar system and Aristotelian biology. But you better take it from here. The chronology gets complex and I don't follow what you've got."

"You get an A-plus for your part of the lecture, and I'll take it from here." Electra scrolled a bit further before she started.

"Renaissance philosophy comes next, and that's when Francis Bacon developed the scientific method for investigating the material world. That led to Descartes' Rationalism and Mind-Brain duality, and Hobbes' Social Contract Theory. As science grew further and ushered in the Enlightenment philosophies of Bentham's Utilitarianism and Kant's Theory of Reason,religion had to retreat. All that paved the way for Hegel's dialectical world view which leads to history ending when Liberty,Freedom,Democracy, and Progress all come to the fore."Doc interrupted before Electra could continue.

"It sounds clear in hindsight, but there must be more to it than that. I bet you could take an entire course on any of the periods."

"Yes, you could. I'm simply presenting a thorough overview from which you can jump into whatever period or philosophy you want. And when we get to the 20th century, modern philosophy fragments into numerous schools and specialties, all caused by scientific findings in Evolution, Neuroscience, Relativity and Quantum Mechanics. And then along come the World Wars, which derail all extensions of Rationalism. Existentialism, Analytic Philosophy, and Deconstructionism drive nails into modern philosophy's coffin, claiming both God and Philosophy are dead. That's the legacy of post-modern philosophy." Electra didn't have to wait long for Doc to catch up.

"That sounds awfully grim. I hope there's a happier ending."

"There is. Some of the more resilient and optimistic philosophers at the end of the 20th century regrouped to conclude that the death of philosophy is greatly exaggerated. By the way, that statement pops up all the time in philosophy articles. It is patterned after Mark Twain's quote: 'The reports of my death are greatly exaggerated,' so he gets credit for saying it first. Anyway, let me wrap up the happier ending. Are you ready?"

"Yes, but I'm running out of mental energy, so please take it easy on me."

"Here's what they did. They salvaged philosophy by synthesizing the optimistic and pragmatic contents of the major post-modern branches, scaling back Rationalism's reach, adding the findings of Neuroscience, resurrecting some of Emergence theory, and keeping the provable pieces of high energy physics. And since then, 21st century philosophers have extended it so mankind is not left drifting aimlessly. There is purpose to Philosophy, to the Universe, to Life, and to Civilization. I'll state only one, but it's the one most people want to hear. The Purpose of Life is simply to survive and to go on living." Electra stopped there, waiting for Doc's rejoinder which came soon after his quizzical smile.

"All that effort by great thinkers through the ages leads to a pretty obvious purpose. I guess that's why I remember you saying that when it comes to philosophy, it's better to stay at the shallow end of the subject. Well, after all that, I'm going to the kitchen to start dinner so we can eat to survive. And thanks for taking the time to explain what you've been thinking about. Please, let's do this more often."

As Doc rose to leave, Electra said, "When you and I cook, we don't just survive, we thrive. I'll join you in a minute." As Doc padded away, an emotion pinged, to which she pleaded guilty. *I've been too wrapped up in myself. I need to spend more time with Doc. I'm trying to be more empathetic and less self-centered, but I still have a lot to learn. Doc's my best friend, but because we're so close I too often take him for granted. That's going to stop right now. And the same goes for my father.*

Doc and Electra had dinner on the table by the time Jason came home. He showed the strain from working the entire Labor Day weekend, but Electra knew that's what he wanted to do. She didn't say anything, instead letting her hug speak for her emotions. And then she hugged her grandfather, who said, "Your daughter is a deep thinker, and she taught me more about philosophy this afternoon." Electra replied, "Yes, but the two of you have taught me what's even more important. And that's my love for both of you. Dad, please tell us all about your day, and then Gramps will tell you about what he and I have been doing. I'm all ears…"

September brought the start of Electra's collegiate career. For most freshman, it brings trepidation regarding an uncertain future, but not for Electra. Having transitioned beyond adolescence while in high school, she already knew what to expect. She breezed through reading and homework assignments, using what she learned to point towards advanced study, and she expanded her social network, enlarging the pool of datable males.

By comparison, Electra's Cognicom work was problematic. Even though she had effective vaccine formulations, virus mutations forced her to make modifications. Electra had a good handle on the biotech piece, but less so on ethical dilemmas that emerged. *I could give Su my clues rather than hide them, but what's the tradeoff between helping the other teams and protecting myself? I could show the other teams what to do, but how do I know that's best for them? Should I be playing God by assuming I know what's right? Am I tampering with the future? And how far do my responsibilities go? Aren't people responsible for themselves? They can use their own free will. But does anyone have free will?*

These questions piqued Electra to learn more about ethics, which she did by self-studying more about that branch philosophy. She learned that ethics is the most accessible branch of philosophy, for unlike metaphysics or epistemology, people deal with ethical issues every day. She mastered ethical systems and analytic frameworks, concluding that all ethical systems can be placed in one of three categories: care-based, rules-based, or ends-based. And she went beyond the textbooks by integrating neuroscience principles and relativism, concluding that most professional philosophers think about unanswerable questions well past the point of diminishing returns. *It's silly to look for nuances that human nature would ignore anyway. I know when to say when, and I don't have to seek permission or ask forgiveness. I can trust the lightning brain to make decisions, and I can live with the consequences. But I must always remember my limits. Although I might have a god-like intelligence compared to mere mortals, I'll never understand ultimate reality. Some phenomena are inaccessible, even to me. And I'll never know all the consequences for my actions. Mother's right when she quotes the Buddhist monk. Perhaps is an answer that always fits.*

Sitting in classes containing male students heightened Electra's desire to learn more about relationships by trial-and-error. *Learning by reading is easy because I'm in control and my brain absorbs it all. Learning about relationships is harder because I'm not in control. I have to depend on another person, and it's hard to know what's going on inside another person's head. I need to be more empathetic, and that's what relationships will teach me.*

T-Plague consequences hit Jason hard that autumn. Su did her best to help, but he was beginning to crack under the pressure, becoming short-tempered at the lab and irritable at home, forcing Electra to steer clear of her father on anything T-Plague related. *I'm glad I'm working with Su. I can find out from her what's going on with Dad.*

Electra picked an appropriate Friday to enquire. "Aunt Su, how's Dad doing on I-Vac?"

"I'm sorry to say, not very well. He's between the proverbial rock and hard place. The rock is the T-Plague, and the hard place is NIH demanding results. I wish I could give him something."

"Dad's so stressed out I have to be careful what I say to him. I've been looking into some research papers for one of my biotech classes and I came up with an idea that might help. When you come back from lunch, may I sketch my idea?"

"I'd love to see what you have. Your last couple of hints worked for me. I'm having lunch with Adom and your father, but I won't mention it to him. I'll be back in about forty-five minutes." Electra made copies of what she had drawn last night, giving them to Su and explaining how she came up with it.

"I think you're on to something. I'll research it over the weekend, and if I still think it's feasible, I'll show it to your father next week. You get extra credit from me for today, so as you like to say, you're good to go for the weekend."

"Thanks, and I will. And I'll say bye to Uncle Adom on the way out." Adom's workstation was close by, so she passed that way.

"Hi, Uncle Adom. Aunt Su's giving me time off for good behavior, so I'm leaving early. How are things with you?"

"Hi there. Do you remember the sergeant's saying in one of your sci-fi thrillers? 'Every march is a parade; every meal's a banquet; every day's a payday.' Well today's not quite that good, but it's been OK. How's school?"

"Going well, thanks. Science and math are always fun, and I like the comparative civilizations course almost as much. I'm doing a paper on Islam. Haven't you met a lot of people from the Middle East? Do you suppose I could interview a couple of them? I could compare what they say with what I read in current articles."

"Sure, and your timing is spot-on. I'm invited tomorrow for dinner with Devra and Deron Sarkia. They know a lot about current events in Isilabad. He's a pharmacist, and she works for a community daycare center. I'll call Devra, and I'm sure she'll be happy for you to join us. I'll pick you up so we can drive together."

"Thanks a bunch. And I'll be well prepared. I already know how to say goodbye in Arabic, so Alaykum al-Salem." Off she went to start the weekend.

Adom had met the Sarkias six months ago while doing volunteer work. They liked how he respected Islamic traditions and they were willing to talk with him about Middle East trends. They also appreciated his honest answer when asked why he wanted to talk; he was looking for a connection between Isilabad and possible T-Plague terrorism.

In preparation, Adom learned enough about Islam to make himself useful. He understood its Five Pillars: declaration of faith, daily prayers, fasting during Ramadan, charity and assistance to the elderly, pilgrimage to Mecca. He knew its history and sects, and could accept some of its principles, at least the ones shared among major religions, but he thought other beliefs were incompatible with life in the 22nd century. When he talked with his Middle East friends, they told him more than they told other Westerners because they respected how he had made an effort to understand their culture.

The Sarkias liked Electra the moment she arrived. She used customary Islamic greetings and acted like a perfect guest, recognizing and complimenting what was served, asking only safe questions, and knowing what topics to avoid. Adom wasn't quite as diplomatic as Electra. She hid her chagrin when Adom asked a politically incorrect question: why do so many intelligent Muslims cling to worn-out religious beliefs?

"That is a question we are often asked," Deron replied patiently, "and if you look at any religion, the question applies. Devra and I came to America because we want to live in a modern society, but we left behind many friends who seek the comfort found in tradition, even though so many traditional beliefs are misguided. And like many religious leaders, I fear those in Isilabad use worthless beliefs to manipulate their people so they can stay in power. These extremist beliefs become an addiction for a small but radical group, and for hundreds of years that group has fomented terrorism. How much do you know about comparing Islamic beliefs with those of Catholicism?"

"I never gave it much thought," replied Adom. "And I apologize if I insulted you."

"You didn't because I know your question is well-intentioned. And I enjoy debating religion, so let me give you a summary comparison." Electra was all ears. *Thank you, Adom, for asking what you shouldn't have. And thank you, Deron, for telling us Islam's story.*

"Let me trace Catholic beliefs, starting with 4th century's Saint Augustine, the patron saint of the Catholic Church. He emphasized faith over reason. That carried all the way to 12th century Saint Thomas Aquinas, who attempted to reconcile faith and reason. His teachings gained traction and were used by Martin Luther's Reformation that led to Descarte's Enlightenment. Kant took that as far as he could,leading to modern religion concluding God is unknowable to human experience. Then along comes 20th century disasters, causing doubt and pessimism that led to 21st century depressing post-modern religion and philosophy. Some people turned away from the facts, while others turned back to fundamentalist beliefs, but many turned to a Neuro-Science Synthesis that combines scientific findings with adjusted expectations for what reasoning can do. The result is today's ecumenical religion that has room for both faith and reason sitting in a DNA context. You're a PhD in biotechnology. You should understand this."

"I follow some of it. And will you now trace Islam for me?"

"Yes. Islam shares the same heritage as Catholicism. It starts with Judeo-Christian beliefs. Muhammed adapted them to create Islamism and liked faith more than reason, just like Saint Augustine. That lasted until Averroes, a Spanish Islamic polymath and contemporary of Aquinas, did the same as Aquinas: reconciled faith and reason. But Islam's rulers disagreed and returned to faith-based beliefs championed earlier by Avicenna. And unlike the West, the Middle East remains mired to this day in fundamentalist beliefs. It is hard for Muslims, even those who understand and want the modern comforts technology brings, to abandon centuries-old beliefs. These beliefs have become memes, also known as socially transmitted cultural genes. Even I cling to some. Electra, I hope you've been taking notes for your paper. A college course should be a safe place to make comparisons."

"I have, and I'll have to study more before I give my presentation. Thanks for pointing me in the right direction."

"You are welcome. And now I'll give Adom once again the answer to the question he's always asking. Don't look for Isilabad to weaponize T-Plague. They don't have, nor can they get, the expertise or tools to do so. Look instead at America's homegrown terrorists or sleeper cells."

Adom told Mo the following week that he was unable to find any link between T-Plague weapons and Isilabad. Mo agreed, making an election prediction. "Whether or not the Guardian Party is leaking rumors, watch out after the elections. Securityguard and Healthguard are going to push for more surveillance and mandatory testing. Cognicom projects will be pushed even harder to get results."

The election confirmed Mo's forecast. The Guardian Party was ascending to America's plurality party. Pundits claimed it could make a run at the White House in the next election, even suggesting its aggressive leadership was making plans it could trigger sooner if the country went past a tipping point.

The public wouldn't believe the worst, but some of the moderates in the Washington Establishment realized they better counteract the Administration's destabilizing, directionless drift. That was the backdrop for a meeting attended by a tight network of high ranking officials coming from varied government departments. It had been organized by a clandestine steering committee of the recently formed Government Opposition Group. The chairman set an ominous tone.

"Thanks everyone for getting here on such short notice. All of us know there's a crisis brewing, and if we don't take charge of our government's future, the situation could blow up in our faces. We all know the public is fed up with the string of lead-us-nowhere politicos they've elected, starting at the top and going down to the bottom of the totem pole congressman. So, here's what I propose.

"First, we recruit more movers and shakers into our Opposition Group, so we have a critical mass of clout. It better include high-ranking military personnel from Joint Chiefs of Staff or their direct reports. And it better include NIH people so we know what's going on in all those dark T-Plague projects. Then we set up a covert operations organization, like the CIA has. We better know what's going on in the current Administration and the Guardian Party. Let's get busy recruiting top guns and setting up covert operations." Marching orders were issued and grim-faced people filed into the darkness of that late November night.

It was good the Holidays were only two weeks away, for Mo had almost surpassed his annual quota of meetings. He decided not to attend any remaining Cognicom sessions, instead turning them over to Jason, Su, or Adom. He even replaced the meeting scheduled for the three of them with a dinner chat after an afternoon skate on the Washington Mall. Adom would handle the driving, Su would pick the restaurant, and Jason would lead the discussion while Mo would sit back and listen.

The outing exceeded everyone's expectations. They chatted happily afterwards, their table insulated by a wall of white noise constructed by the buzz from surrounding tables.

"I never realized what a great analogy skating makes for a project team. You gotta keep moving, or you fall on your fanny. You gotta help one another. And you gotta be ready to change direction. And it's a first for me. First time I'm better than Adom at a sport."

"You surprised everyone. You managed to stay vertical, thanks to your lower center of gravity. I'm lucky Su's a good sport. She kept picking me up after I kept dragging her down. Sort of like what I've been doing at the lab this year."

Su replied, "After today, I'm sure next year will be different for the three of us. Mo will plug you into other networks, I'll come up with better ideas, and Jason will energize his teams. And as for Mo, he'll keep doing what he does so well. He'll keep us out of harm's way."

"Thank you, Su. I plan to use that kind of cheery summary at all our meetings next year."

Electra's Holiday breaks at college and Cognicom coincided, so she penciled on her social calendar enough to keep her happily engaged until January. This Sunday she would take her grandfather to an early afternoon multi-cultural Christmas concert. The two of them were talking about this at breakfast when Jason hustled in.

"I wish you'd take the day off and come with us. The change would do you good. Aren't you gonna have breakfast?"

"I'll grab something at McDonald's and take it with me. Trust me Dad, I know what I'm doing. Su gave me some good I-Vac ideas, and we're doing a pilot run today."

"OK, but just be careful not to explode from too much T-Plague pressure."

"I won't. And after skating with Mo, I feel good about next year. I'll go back to my original proclamation, we're kissed by the sun. It's time to run. Enjoy the concert and tell me all about it tonight."

"How did you like the music?" Electra was driving after the concert to a favorite restaurant and wanted to compare Doc's picks with hers.

"I'm sort of a traditionalist. I liked the old English carols the best, especially "Once in Royal David's City." But the newer carols were enjoyable too." What did you like?"

"I like the French and Spanish carols, but all cultures have music and singing that fit the occasion. I enjoyed all the selections." Just then Doc's cell phone beeped. "Hmm, I don't know what this could be." Doc punched the connect button.

"Hello, this is Doctor Justin Kittner." Out of the corner of her eye, Electra noticed a sudden change in his expression just before he started yelling.

"Jeezus! Jeezus! Jeezus!" Something was terribly wrong. Electra pulled to the curb and waited for Doc to finish. The tone of his voice switched from frenzied horror to metallic.

"Yes, I'll call back." When Electra looked directly at her grandfather, waiting for him to say something, she saw a grimace of shock-filled disbelief.

"That was Security from Jason's lab. There's been a terrible accident. Jason just blew himself up…"

CHAPTER 29
December 2112

"The Next in Line"
(Thread 2 Chapter 16)

Doc's SHOCKING WORDS JOLTED Electra's lightning brain into an elevated state, instantly telling her what to do. "Please repeat exactly what Lab Security said." Doc stuttered out all he remembered. An explosion in Jason's lab breached containment systems, forcing a lockdown controlled by a Healthguard hazards team. No casualty reports, but the entire wing housing Cognicom was contaminated. Doc even recited the number to call for updates.

"Give me your cell phone. I'm calling Mo." He answered on the third ring.

"It's Electra. There's been a bad accident at Jason's lab. Cognicom wing is contaminated. Healthguard hazards team locked down the entire facility. Get to our house ASAP. I'm calling Su and Adom." Then she called Su, rattling off the same, adding, "I just called Mo. He's on his way. Please call Adom and get here ASAP. Electra ended the call and gave back the cell phone as she focused on her grandfather.

"Let's not jump to conclusions. We'll get everyone together and decide what to do. Tell me again Security's number." Doc mechanically repeated the number, which to Electra's relief matched what he had said before. As they drove in silence, the lightning brain was already developing a set of contingency plans. Before picking one, Electra would talk with her team and then call Security.

An hour later everyone was in the living room listening to Mo, who was floundering for what to do. "I, uh, I think we should wait until Security calls us before we do anything. Maybe I should call Bobbi. She'll know more." Electra had heard enough. *Mo should step aside. It's time for me to speak up and lead.*

"Security won't tell Bobbi any more than we already know. She'll expect you to figure something out, so let's sketch a plan and start following it. And since Security hasn't called you, call them and tell them what we're doing. See what they're saying now." Mo snapped to attention and made the call.

"Hello, this is Moses Solstein, Senior Business Manager at NIH. I'm in charge of all Cognicom projects. What can you tell me about the accident?" Mo listened carefully, taking notes and ending the call a minute later. "Thanks for the update. I'll meet with the hazards team first thing tomorrow morning and explain what we're planning to do." Mo disconnected the call, then recapped all he had been told.

"The hazards team recovered three badly burned researchers, Jason and two others from his team. A Healthguard medical squad has them. All persons that were inside have been placed under quarantine. That's the story." Everyone but Electra sat is stony silence, minds unable to focus, emotions unable to cope.

"Let's do this. We'll give everyone a turn explaining what to do. I'll take notes and put together a plan for Mo to approve. Before we leave tonight, we have to have marching orders. So, take a minute to think while I order some pizza. Doc, would you please get soft drinks and make coffee?" Electra and Doc went to the kitchen while the others stared at the carpet, trying to snap out of a surrealistic brain freeze. By the time Electra returned, thoughts were finally flowing, and by the time pizza arrived, Electra had jotted down the best ideas.

"Let's take a break. When we get back at it, I'll summarize a plan." Electra scribbled out not one but two, adding to her ideas what others had given. *No one came up with much I didn't think of. I'll walk them through my first choice. If Mo hears something different tomorrow, we can change it.* After Su helped Electra clear away the plates and glasses, the discussion continued.

"Here's what's next. You remember the saying, hope for the best but plan for the worst? Well here's our worst-case scenario. Jason and the researchers are dead. Lab badly damaged. The media knows about the explosion and makes it headline news. Guardian Party has insider information and spins it to make the situation worse. Any assumptions anyone wants to add?" None came, so Electra continued.

"For safety reasons, Healthguard will cremate the bodies immediately. We'll hold a remembrance ceremony at home for Father in a couple of days, after the commotion settles. No church service because he wouldn't want one. Grandfather, do you agree?" The best he could do was nod mutely.

"Su, your current assignment is S-Vac, but Adom will be promoted to be its tech leader. You'll take over for Jason, getting replacements for the researchers killed in action after you figure out what caused the explosion. So now you handle I-Vac and R-Vac. Mo, you ditch the bus-admin managers for I-Vac and R-Vac. You should manage all projects. Take the dollar savings and staff up R-Vac. And depending on the damage report, you might have to relocate I-Vac. Mo, can you handle all this?"

"Yes, let's go with your plan." Electra had more to say.

"That's only part of it. Let's talk about the media. This is gonna be national news that'll give the Administration a black eye. NIH has to spin the story so Jason and his people are not fall guys, but instead heroes. Mo, you have to get NIH public relations people to say his team was about to release an improved smart pill. That will buy time and sympathy, but the Administration better act fast or they'll get killed in the next election." Electra paused for everyone to catch up, then proceeded.

"Let's think about the Guardian Party. They'll spin the story to get more support for Healthguard and Securityguard. And watch them connect some dots to link T-Plague with possible terrorism. There's gonna be a backlash against Muslim groups. I expect the Guardian

Party will buy media time to get their message out. Anything you want to add?" Nothing but grim silence.

"Mo, you've got a tough job. You better use your network to lobby hard so Bobbi's bosses buy in.But she'll give you high marks for taking charge of what's becoming a dangerous game.Call Bobbi right now, so she knows what you're doing."

That was the plan. It was hard for everyone to digest so much so fast, so Electra looked for a softer end to the evening."It's late, and we're all tired. And like Mo often says, the sun will come up tomorrow, so let's stop and reconvene here tomorrow afternoon at four. Mo should have more details by then."

No one said much on the way out. After everyone left, Electra walked to where Doc was still sitting passively and hugged him.She could feel heaving sighs as he whispered,"All gone, all gone. How can you be so coldblooded, so emotionless?" She was taken aback, but recovered to say, "Gramps, we both need to let our emotions come out and grieve.That'll happen when the shock wears off,but that won't happen tonight. We're doing the right thing by dealing with tomorrow.I'm sorry you think I'm cold-blooded.I'm not,and when you feel better, you'll know."

Electra was unable to sleep; the lightning brain was working through everything that had happened. She sat light outs in the living room,completely alone.Doc was upstairs,finally asleep.She could hear his fitful breathing, which for a time comforted her, knowing with certainty that at least one of the only two people she loved was still alive. She loved her father and grandfather unconditionally, intensely. Her father was her alpha, her omega. From him alone spun the continuous thread of her existence.The lightning bolt—the Brahma and the Shiva of her two worlds— had jolted her into her present. Her past contained her birth, her mother, and her grandmother,all irretrievably erased from memory. Her present emanated from her father. She saw him etched in the flash of creation, outstretched arms pulling her to safety. She did not know what she would do if he were dead. She would have to figure out later how to handle the loss.

What she did know was this: if her father had indeed died in the explosion, then she was responsible.She had provided the clues which led him to the lab today. She had played the role of an all-knowing parent,god-like in understanding what is best,and it had caused today's catastrophe.If her father were dead,she would have to live with the consequences. But it made no sense to extrapolate further because her father might still be alive. As she clung to that hope, sleep finally came to the lightning brain.

Mo bolted upright after a fitful night's sleep. *What a horrible dream. No wonder I feel dreadful.* Then he realized today would extend yesterday's nightmare.He forced himself up and out because he had to face today's daunting challenges.

While driving, Mo thought long and hard about last night, about Electra's plan, about Electra. At first, his pride goaded him. *What do they think of me now? Compared to Electra,I was as useless as tits on a bull. Then his pragmatic side kicked in. Electra's plan covers everything I can think of. It bails me out. It's a gift, so just use it. If I don't, I'll have to run for the exits to beat the crowd.* Coffee helped lift his spirits further. He was ready to meet the hazards team.

Mo saw immediately how bad the situation was:access cordoned off, clean-up barely begun. Mo's badge gained entry to the haz-team van where he found the person in charge and came right to the point.

"I'm Mo Solstein, NIH manager for Cognicom projects. I was told to come here first thing this morning. How are my people and how bad is my lab damaged?"

"Sorry, but I have bad news. Your three researchers are dead. We had to cremate the bodies. Here's the number relatives can call to retrieve the ashes."Mo tucked the note in his pocket while the haz-team leader rattled on. "As soon as decontamination is done, your people have to go in with ours to figure out what caused the explosion. Be here tomorrow morning by eight. And we're closing the facility until January." Mo pushed his luck by asking one more question.

"How do you think the media will handle this?"

"Are you kidding? They're gonna crucify the NIH.Healthguard P.R. is holding a press conference as soon as we give them our report.

There'll be repercussions for your teams. I've told you what I can, so that's all until tomorrow morning."

"Thanks for briefing me. I'll come back then with some of my team."

Mo drove to his office where he would keep busy writing a status report and placing calls until meeting with Bobbi. Two of the researchers he contacted volunteered to help inspect the lab. He had everything in order, and after presenting his plan, Bobbi looked relieved.

"This is just what I need. How'd you put it together so quickly?" "I met with Su and Adom yesterday, and we're meeting again later this afternoon. I'll report back to you after tomorrow's inspection."

Mo had just enough time to drive to Electra's for their 4 p.m. meeting, and while double-timing to his car, it dawned that he had already put Jason in the past tense. *But that's how life plays out. The present and the future are for the living. We have to move on. As he drove, he considered who should run the meeting. I should, but will Electra let me? She ran the show yesterday, and I saw how formidable she can be. But she knew what to do and I didn't. I'll sit back and let her set the tone.*

Electra knew that her father was dead. Mo would have phoned if the news were good, but he hadn't; her worst fear had materialized. The meeting would be brief because Mo already had the worst-case scenario. It was time for him to lead. Adom and Su arrived together, followed closely by Mo. No one talked until everyone gathered in the living room, and Electra wasted no time.

"I want to apologize to everyone for my behavior yesterday. It wasn't my place to take over, but I needed to spell out what I thought was the best way to go. And it's time for Mo to take command, but before he starts I'll break the worst of it. Jason is dead. Mo would have called me if the news were better. But this is not the time to grieve. Let's hear from Mo what he needs us to do." She nodded to him and he started in.

"I'm sorry to confirm our worst fears, but Jason and two other researchers died as a result of the explosion." He handed out copies of the plan, then recapped what he had learned that morning. "So that's it. First thing tomorrow I go back for onsite assessment.

Adom, would you be willing to join us?" Adom said nothing but slowly nodded yes. "The lab won't reopen until January. Let's meet Wednesday morning in my office so we can plan for our first month back."

Su said, "Adom and I will be there are nine. Electra, will you want to join us?"

"No, you won't need me. Besides, I need to take care of personal matters." Since there was nothing left to cover, Mo ended the meeting.

"We all have our marching orders so let's be on our way. See you Wednesday."

Electra had only one person left to deal with, her grandfather, who remained sitting like a stone. "Gramps, come to the kitchen and talk with me while I make us supper."

"OK," he mumbled, but said nothing else. Electra peppered him with small talk, gradually bringing him out of his stupor. He helped clear the dishes, paying attention to what Electra said.

"I've been thinking about what you and I need to do. Why don't you start calling the people you want to join us on Saturday for father's remembrance? We'll make it a buffet starting at three. I'll order the food, and I'll make arrangements for placing ashes in the burial vault. When you're ready, will you want me to help put Dad's things away?"

"Yes, but not until I feel better."

"Would you like to watch a movie with me? When you get tired, we'll turn it off and say goodnight." Doc tried to smile.

"I know you're trying to cheer me up and it's helping, but I feel like having time to myself, so let's say goodnight." Doc shuffled to his bedroom upstairs. Electra adjourned to the living room, retreating into her brain's fortress of solitude.

She thought about the rite of passage suddenly thrust upon her. According to a philosopher she had read long ago, we become adults only when both parents are dead. *I'm the next in line. No one's standing ahead of me at the grave. Though it hasn't sunk in, I know Dad's gone. That leaves only one person I love, Grandfather. And any remnant of childhood is gone too. I've permanently crossed over into the adult world.*

She thought of her mother's poetry. *Didn't Mother write a poem about great sorrow, great loss? Yes, she wrote a trilogy, the first dealing with grief. I can recall the first:*

> *"A dreaded darkness fills me to the core,*
> *I grope for bearings to help pull free.*
> *My pole star lost, I have been tossed and alone now must cross,*
> *This leaden, deadened, mirthless sea."*

The first verse was spot-on, capturing her feelings. Electra turned to the second:

> *"The harboring lights of my once carefree youth are gone,*
> *Through no one's fault save that of unrelenting Time.*
> *And though often told that this loss would unfold,*
> *No preparation could soften or lessen or put in remission,*
> *This grief I am feeling that sends my soul reeling,*
> *This loss of the precious that cuts to the bone,*
> *This loss of the priceless that's all mine to own."*

Once again, words and feelings were as one. Her cognitive persona was prepared, but not so for the emotional one. Finally, she recited the last verse:

> *"But stop to remember light comes back in view,*
> *When Love of the child burns bright and cuts through*
> *The fog of gloom.*
> *My Spirit restored to be happy again?*
> *I numb and dumb wait for the if and the when."*

The best Electra could hope for was in the last line.Something would trigger an outpouring of grief, the first step in a healing process. *I don't know when or what,but something will bring it on.No sense worrying about it. I'm going to bed.*

As she walked past her grandfather's closed bedroom door, she heard him sobbing; that sound pulled the trigger. She knocked and said she was coming in. There he was, sitting in a chair by the window, looking so sad, so lonely. She rushed to hug him, her sobs joining his. They stayed that way for a minute, emotions and tears flowing, an overdue catharsis. As her tears subsided, so did the stabbing pangs of grief, and she wished the same for her grandfather as she regained control of her emotions.

"Gramps, why don't we sit and talk about Father?" For the next two hours, they did just that.

Later in bed, Electra traced an analogy between her mother's death and her father's. When her mother died, her father found meaning and purpose for living by taking care of Electra. That pulled him out of a deepening depression. For Electra, caring for her grandfather would do much the same. That thought gave her a peaceful stillness, allowing her to sleep. She would awaken with grief in remission, able to handle week-ahead duties.

Keeping busy helped Electra keep depression at bay. She arranged for Saturday's buffet, helped her grandfather contact Jason's close circle of friends, and placed her father's ashes in the family burial vault. She dealt with Cognicom by reaching out to Mo, who thanked her again for all she had done, complimenting her for understanding the political climate. The only glitch came from NIH public relations, which released too much information about those killed. Names, photographs, biographical sketches, and next of kin names appeared in the media, but her grandfather hadn't been contacted, and she hadn't been mentioned.

Saturday's remembrance buffet was bittersweet. Everyone shared lighthearted memories of Jason, but underneath lay the melancholy fact that Jason had been cut down in the prime of life, one full promise, some success, and much struggle; he should have lived longer and been happier. While Electra talked with everyone, she noticed Mo and Russell Conklin conversing quietly. Though they had never met, they talked at length.

Talking with close friends helped Doc handle his grief. He was ready to accept what fate had sent and was taking first steps beyond his second personal holocaust. Electra and Doc were glad when Saturday evening came and all the guests had departed. They spent the rest of the evening putting Jason's belongings away.Electra did the packing while Doc provided commentary, separating special items for Electra to keep. It was good they do this now because it added closure to a somber rite of passage.Jason would want this for Doc and Electra,just as Indira had wanted it for Jason.

They were nearly finished when Doc found a sealed envelope tucked away in a desk cubbyhole. "Look what I just came across.An envelope addressed to you and me from your father.Why don't we open it now?"Electra remembered stories of the surprise envelopes left by her mother.

"This is the right time,so why don't you read it to us."He carefully peeled back the flap.

"There's some sort of key in here with a letter.I bet it'll explain the key. Here goes."

"Dear Father,

You know me better than anyone, so it's no surprise when I say I never liked talking about my feelings or emotions. Indira told me that emotions are the body's physical response to events, while feelings are the mind's. And she said the brain and mind are one.Well, however you look at it,talking about them always embarrassed me,and that's the way it is.So,I am expressing them in this letter,which I hope you are reading with Electra at your side. I'm trying, but it's hard to find all the words to express the depth of my love for both of you.

"Dad, thank you for all you have given and have done for me.If I had lived to be a hundred, I would still owe you. And thanks for helping me raise Electra.You have been a better parent to her than I was, and I know she loves you deeply. When you and our lawyer read through my will, you'll see she is the beneficiary.

"I might say that you should keep watching out for her, but we both know it's the other way around,so Electra,please take care of your grandfather in my absence.

"Electra, I am sorry I was so reticent whenever you would ask about your mother, but the subject was too painful and I did not want my feelings to go there. Your mother gave me an envelope to open after her death. In it were instructions for me, as well as envelopes for your Aunt Su and Uncle Adom. One of my instructions was to pack up her belongings while holding my own private remembrance, and then go on with my life. I followed her wishes and never looked back. When I put her belongings away, I sorted out the ones I thought you might like to have some day. Among them are your mother's favorite scarf—a gift from me when I learned she was pregnant—and a pair of earrings—a gift from her parents when she left for college. The scarf's motif always reminded me of a stylized heart. The earrings are shaped like lightning bolts and must have been selected to symbolize your mother's middle name Jaswinder, which in Indian mythology is the name of the lightning bolt possessed by the goddess Indira. You'll find a key in this envelope for a safety deposit box at our bank. The box contains what I sorted out. I hope that in some small way it will make up for my silence. Maybe you could show them to your Aunt Su. She will help you connect them with your mother.

"You will also find some handkerchiefs and other jewelry, a couple of photos, and a couple of unopened letters that arrived the day you were born. (Your mother once called me out for opening her mail; I pledged never to do that again. You decide if you want to open them). You probably think it's not much, but your mother didn't hold on to possessions or the past. She told me that when she came to Boston for college, she was leaving her old world behind. The photos are of her friends in America, not of her parents or childhood.

"You both know I never believed in an afterlife, so I won't pretend my spirit is hovering above, waiting to hear from you or vice versa. I remain alive in your memories. Keep them as long as they give back to you the love and comfort I received from both of you.

"Let me depart on a lighter note. I hated rituals or services, so I hope you didn't hold a wake or funeral. If I knew ahead of time you were, I would have come up with an excuse for not attending.

Love to both of you always…"

Electra and her grandfather were at a loss for words until a whimsical smile crept across Doc's face. "Jeezus, in his entire life your father wrote me maybe five letters. He saved the best one for last. I think you should keep it for us." Electra read it aloud once more, then carefully put it back in the envelope.

"I'll keep this with the letter from Mother. And on Monday, I'll check out the safety deposit box, but I won't go through the contents until I bring them home so we can look at them together." "I have an even better idea. Let's look at them when your Aunt

Su comes over. You and she can decide the best time." Electra agreed; now they had another reason for another day.

Su and Adom had Cognicom teams back in action by the end of January, letting Mo absorb as much of the pressure as he could. Electra's collegiate world spun forward, but Doc had to adjust to a new normal because Jason's death took a heavy toll. It sapped his strength, forcing him to cut his medical practice and making him a dour old soul.

Electra adjusted her world accordingly. She ran the household and handled more caregiving for Doc, but still fit in outings with Christi,whose flair for clothing and cosmetics spruced up her best friend.The latest makeover created just what Electra wanted. She looked good enough; she looked older; she blended right in. No one would notice her.

Two events punctuated February, the first a phone call from the Invisible Hand to the Invisible Man. Its sign-off was ominous.

"Your assignment now is to drill deeper into Cognicom. Look for anything we can use to advance our cause. Do you copy?"

"Copy that."

"Good. Call me again at the scheduled time."

The second event, a meeting held by Project Death Shield, was equally ominous.This project, a CIA covert operation set up ten years ago to monitor T-Plague impact on the political climate, had never done much. Its standing orders were observation, not interdiction. It had been a place for new recruits or those cycling down, and had never uncovered any T-Plague related links to terrorists or opposition groups. But that could change. Current events frightened the Washington Establishment. The man in charge was about to give his team new marching orders.

"Head honchos up the chain of command need us to deliver on terrorist or opposition group linkage to T-Plague. November election results and the DC lab explosion have made them nervous. We've got a bigger budget. Let's use it to get more eyes and ears placed where they'll do the most good. Let's use it to interdict, interrogate, interrupt, or terminate when appropriate. There's T-Plague smoke out there. Let's find the fire."

A tangential event occurred in Texas. Hudson Haller had decided to call a classmate from years ago because news headlines reporting the December NIH lab explosion mentioned the name Jason Kittner.

Hud considered himself a good ol' boy, possessing a broad-brimmed personality and Texas-sized boots able to span multiple businesses with a single bound. He needed only three fingers to count his passions: bio-tech R&D, oil and gas, and the game of poker. He had grown up in Austin, the only child of Hollis Haller, a self-made millionaire. Hud loved the oil business his father started sixty years ago. He was big and strong enough to work on one of his father's drilling rigs while in college. His father wanted him to join the business, but that would have to wait until Hud scratched an itch for success on his own. Not only was he ruggedly good looking, but he was intelligent too, possessing the pragmatism of an engineer and the instincts of an entrepreneur. He earned a master's degree at MIT in bioengineering, then worked for ten years in the corporate world before launching a biotech company specializing in DNA R&D.

Venture capitalists wouldn't fund him, but his father—a gambling man like his son—put up the capital on one condition: headquarter the company in Austin so Hud could run the biotech company and help run H&H Energy Partners. Hud came back to Austin and launched H&H DNA Partners as fast as he could. That was ten years ago, and today both privately held companies were in the black.

When the T-Plague surfaced over twenty years ago, Hud thought it would be brought under control quickly. Instead, the virus became an incredible challenge. After all the time and money spent, successful vaccines eluded all players, and the only one with even a glimmer of success—NIH's smart pill—was fading. Any company that could develop effective vaccines would own the biotech world. Hud dreamed of doing that, but hadn't a clue for what to do.

The deadly DC lab explosion made national news, reporting the name of someone he knew in graduate school: Jason Kittner. He knew the roommate better, Adom Ola, and through him had become friends with a group of talented grad students nicknamed the Worldstars. He recalled them all. First Adom, the clever, handsome, carefree guy women went for. Then Jason, a square-built sort of plodding drone who in fact was even smarter. Then Su, petite, reserved, and enormously smart. Finally, he recalled Indira, peerless, practically perfect Indira. She had it all: intelligence, looks, personality, and social graces. And she was so genuine everyone liked her immediately.

Hud had kept in touch with Adom for several years after graduation. He was pleased they were doing well at NIH, and was saddened when he learned of Indy's horrible death. Now Jason Kittner dies before his time. Hud decided it was time to call Adom.

<hr>

CHAPTER 30
June 2113

"The Monster from the Id"
(Thread 2 Chapter 17)

T-Plague outbreaks retreated, and by Memorial Day the nation basked in a temporary sense of security that grew as the days advanced towards the summer solstice, even though the cumulative number of cases grew. NIH tracked the data that trended to dire conclusions: healthcare infrastructure overloaded, too many cognitively impaired survivors, lawlessness on the rise, quality of life and GNP declining.

Some segments of the economy appeared normal, but statistics revealed declining worker productivity. America's high-tech, knowledge-worker-driven juggernaut needs smart people, and the T-Plague was eating into the supply as well as into the nation's infrastructure. Power and communications grids failed too often and were out too long. Some roads and bridges were beginning to look like those of a third world country, and air traffic, though not impacted yet, might suffer disruptions like those in automated interstate trucking or rail traffic. And if Internet disruptions joined the trend, people would be impacted at home because the "Internet of Things" wired household appliances into the Web. Public anger lurked just beneath the public's awareness, ready to break through at the slightest provocation from unsettling events or media hype.

Electra continued shadowing Cognicom projects, snooping unobtrusively. Researchers would talk with her because she seemed pleasant though not of much value. All project teams were stressed to the limit and getting nowhere, and rumors of NIH farming out research to private companies added to their worries. *I could cure their worries by giving them my vaccine formulations but I won't. I learned a bitter lesson when Dad blew himself up, so I'll give only Su my clues.*

Electra's college career posed no stress. She mastered all upper-level courses, carrying course loads allowing her to graduate next spring. She deliberately throttled back on-campus socializing but continued dating when the right fellow caught her fancy, sometimes matching Christi with suitable classmates because she had outgrown high school boys.

Electra's emotional growth spurted again when she became her grandfather's caregiver. He had slipped further since Jason's death and needed assistance getting up and moving in the morning. One Sunday morning, after getting Doc up and settled, a sudden emotion pinged. *Doc's gonna need a lot more help as he pushes towards ninety, and I'm ready, willing, and able. I get such joy taking care of him. It only comes from giving unconditional love to someone who needs help. How could Mother write such moving poetry about love? How did she manage to understand so much while so young? Her empathy is way beyond mine.* Electra recalled a relevant poem:

<blockquote>

Please take the love I give to you,
Though your years are ahead of me.
It's there I found joy does abound,
When caring set me free.

The World may wonder what's wrong with her,
From this Muse, she will retreat.
Time will show for all to know,
You make my life complete.

</blockquote>

So I'll be with you and care for with you,
Across the many-a-mile.
I will ensure love shall endure,
My reward's your eternal smile.

Su told me Mother considered Father her work in progress and took good care of him. Father was fortunate. And how different my world would be if there had been no lightning bolt. But it struck and I'm here, and Indira and Jason are gone. All this is neither good nor bad. It's reality. So, I'll keep moving forward and make my own meaning for living.

Electra considered Christi her work in progress. Poor Christi was struggling with two intertwining issues: the opposite sex and an acting career. She liked dating older guys she met in performing arts classes or at auditions. Getting dates was easy, but getting to the next level in an acting career was hard. Even with Electra's counseling and Robin's coaching, she was falling behind.

Robin and Electra went to all contests Christi entered, and each time they drew the same conclusion: Christi was good but not good enough to make it as a professional entertainer. She had the looks but not enough talent. Aspiring performers have to be ruthlessly self-centered and exceptionally talented to make the cut, and Christi didn't possess enough of either, but she wouldn't listen to Electra. Electra came up with a different approach she and Robin would try after Christi's next audition.

Electra was the designated driver on that audition Saturday in July. She picked up Robin, and while driving to fetch Christi, they discussed Christi's situation.

"We've listened to a lot of Christi's auditions, and I think she's kidding herself. She's good, but many of the girls are better. I've told her that. She better pick another career, but she won't listen to me. Maybe she'll listen to you because she respects your musical ability."

"Maybe you're right. When I went to the music career orientation session, I got to watch many first-year voice and dance students. It's amazing how much talent is out there. Sometimes I wonder if I'm good enough to be a professional pianist."

"Don't worry. You have boatloads of ability. Just keep doing what you're doing." Robin smiled but didn't comment further. Electra added, "So today after the auditions, let's stop for a snack and then you tell Christi. Better to hear the truth now, rather than go on kidding."

Robin sighed, then said, "Yeah, but if Christi starts pouting you back me up."

"Will do. The two of us should be able to talk some sense into her pretty head."

Christi was already waiting outside, so she dived into the back seat, and the trio charged off to the audition.

"Attention, handlers. Today let's take it to the next level. I want to impress the promoters because they have a lot of pull and can help me move up."

"I hope you worked on what I pointed out the last time I played for your practice session. Voice control and range need some tweaking…" Electra listened as Robin talked about technique, offering suggestions for today. Christi said she was ready to strut her stuff.

The audition lasted five hours, four performers each hour. Christi would be the thirteenth, and Electra was surprised how quickly the time went. Robin made occasional comments; soon Electra knew better what to look or listen for. Christi performed three songs, one of which required interpretive dance. Electra thought it was all good, but afterwards she could tell by the look on Robin's face that was not the case. She glumly whispered, "Christi's subpar compared with the others. Timing and some of the notes are off." Electra nodded but couldn't comment. They listened to the remaining performers, then went back stage to retrieve a crestfallen Christi.

"Don't tell me. I already know. I stank out loud today. They'll call me in a couple of days with the bad news." Robin tried to cheer her up.

"We all have our good days and our bad days. Let's get something to eat and talk it over." Christi forced a smile and off they went.

For a Saturday evening, Electra thought the restaurant should have been busier. *People are worried about T-Plague exposure, even though outbreaks have subsided. I wonder how much damage the T-Plague will do to the economy if outbreaks spread again.*

After the trio ordered, Christi said, "Let's face it. I didn't have it today. What do you think I should do?" Robin glanced at Electra, took a deep breath, and then plunged in.

"I don't want to hurt your feelings, but you asked me, so I'll tell you. You're usually better than you were today, but from all the listening I've been doing, even on your best days, the competition's better. You've been in overdrive for the past three years, and I think you've maxed out."

"Electra, what do you think?"

"Robin knows more about performance stuff than I ever will. When I listened today, I thought you needed to be better, and today the competition was tougher than ever. So maybe it's time to change course, but look at it this way. You gave it your best shot and had fun doing so. That's what counts. You'll find something else that's even better."Christi shrugged, saying nothing, so Robin jumped in again.

"Electra's right, so think about it. You can find other things you'll like doing."

"Like what? I'll have to think about it later. But not now. Let's eat instead. Here comes the food, and I'm starved."

Electra didn't call Christi the following week, figuring it was better for her to digest the audition results first. She expected Christi to call her or Robin when she was ready, so Electra called Robin to check. She hadn't heard either and said Christi probably went with her parents for a vacation week at the Jersey shore.

Electra used spare time that week to study politics and political party history because her next endeavor would be in the political arena. When school starts in September, she would earn guided independent study credit doing Guardian Party volunteer work at National Headquarters, at the same time digging for hidden agendas. *I'll start at the top and work my way to the bottom.How's that for unconventional wisdom? And I'll chat regularly with Doc. Unlike Dad, he's social-minded and follows politics. Maybe that'll get him out of the doldrums. I'll start talking politics with him right away.* Every day that week she hurried through chores to carve out extra time for Doc, and it worked. Doc started watching the news again, and Electra learned from his hands-on experience because years ago he too had been a volunteer.

She and Doc had just settled into the living room after supper on Saturday when Electra answered a call from a worried-sounding Robin.

"I think Christi's heading for trouble. Drive to my place as fast as you can. Call me from the car and I'll explain. Hurry." Electra explained to Doc what she had just heard.

"That's Robin. She says Christi's in a jam. I better go."

"You three have been close friends for years.It used to be Christi and you watching out for Robin.Now it's Robin and you watching out for Christi. Is it serious?"

"Robin didn't give me any details. I bet it has something to do with last weekend's audition."

"You don't need my permission to go, but please call me if you run into more than you can handle."

"I will." Doc's sincerity touched her to the core. She hugged him, then dashed out the door.

As instructed,Electra called Robin."Here's what I know.Christi called me twenty minutes ago. Last Thursday, one of the concert organizers called her.She thought it would be one of those standard flush calls, but no.The producer liked her looks and was thinking she could play a different role.They wanted her to audition again. They're picking her up this evening,and I think she needs someone to go with her, but I didn't tell her that. She'd blow me off if I did. What should we do?" Electra could feel her brain shifting gears.

"We'll drive to her house and just drop in. If they've gone somewhere, we'll call her cell phone. If no answer, we'll call her friend Peter. He might know where she is. Or we could track her cell phone location.What's Peter's number?"

"I don't know it.I don't even know his last name.We're screwed and so is Christi if this goes badly."

"I sure hope not." Electra completed Robin's sentence to herself: *in more ways than one. Better hurry.*

Dusk was descending when Electra parked in front of the Conklins. *The garage door is open. I'll bet that van belongs to the concert organizer. Let's check it out.*

"Let's try the garage entry to the kitchen. Follow me and keep quiet until we know what's going on." Electra peeked into the van, but saw nothing unusual. The garage was spotless, everything in its place, tennis rackets hanging on the wall next to a set golf clubs. *The Conklins keep everything they own so neat, clean, and under control. Too bad they can't do the same with Christi.*

The door to the kitchen was unlocked. No lights or sounds attracted their attention, but Electra heard muffled voices coming from upstairs as they approached the stairway.

Electra whispered, "Follow me and keep quiet." The deepening dusk enveloped the duo as they crept Indian file up the stairs, stopping at the top, locating the sounds coming from behind the closed master bedroom door. "Wait by the stairs until I check things out. Come in if I say it's OK, and get out fast if I tell you to run. Get out through the garage and don't slam the doors closed; I'll be right behind." Robin nodded, so Electra stepped to the door. She listened, detecting a female giggling while two men talked, but didn't hear Christi.

"My, isn't she pretty in the buff. Donna, you've got a great girl toy. Too bad she's not awake to enjoy the show." Electra heard all she needed. *Uh-oh. It's time to crash the party.* Electra flung open the door, entering just far enough to see the sights: Christi completely naked, hands tied to the headboard, all set to become a porn queen. She had been drugged, head flipping from side to side and lips mumbling incoherently. Her part would not require much speaking. A thickset clod was adjusting a video camera, assisted by a partly dressed fellow, while a young girl wearing only a black bikini thong and stilettos was arranging Christi on the bed. Lights on, camera and action were about to roll. Electra launched into her show-stopping cameo appearance that froze Christi's helpers like wax statues. Electra had only one line, which she shouted out convincingly.

"Run Robin, run!" Electra slammed the door and bolted down the stairs. Robin was already out of the garage, racing towards the getaway car poised in the dim glow of a distant streetlight.

Electra stopped to listen after slamming the garage door.Clunk, clunk, clunk, thud. Sounds of the clod tumbling down the stairs, followed by a grunt-muffled scream. Then she heard lighter feet coming down.

"Mick! What's wrong?"

"I broke my ankle! Stop them!"

Electra stood by the light switch, armed with a carbon fiber racket. She flipped the switch as soon Mick's partner rushed into the garage, the glare startling him. Electra delivered a two-handed forehand with the racket edge into his Adam's apple, followed by another to his gut, doubling him over. She ended the match with an overhead slam to the crown of his head, the broken-stringed racket now collaring his neck. *He's not jumping over a net anytime soon. Let's deal with the clumsy clod.*

Electra armed herself with a golf club. She flipped a light switch near the stairway and spied her opponent at the foot of the stairs, clutching a broken ankle. Electra's anger,though building,was still under control. She hissed venomously, "Why don't I putter you with this? Might make a nice video posting, asshole."Mick was in no position to argue.

"Please, don't call the police. Let us go, and you'll never see us again. I promise, we won't repeat this stunt."

"What kind of drug did you give her? She looks out of it." Mick's broken ankle couldn't support any weight when he tried standing. He grimaced when answering.

"Two Spazz tabs. The effects are already starting to wear off." *Christi's parents will go ballistic if they find out what happened. We better keep the cops out of it.*

"Here's what we'll do. I'll get your girlfriend to load you and your buddy into the van. I'm gonna keep your video set-up. If I hear even a rumor that you're back in business, you won't be for long."There was no disagreement. Electra ran upstairs, brandishing the golf club.

The bedroom action had ended even before it started. The young girl had untied Christi and was helping her sit up, using a washcloth to clean her up because the drug had made Christi nauseated. Electra's anger dissipated as soon as she saw the frightened look on the girl's face.

"It wasn't supposed to happen this way. It's my first time and I swear my last." Tears crowded out any additional words.

"Why don't you get dressed. I'll handle the cleanup." Electra heard Robin approaching, and when she entered the room Electra said, "Why don't you take care of Christi. I'll help Donna load her buddies into the van." Donna dressed as fast as she could, collecting all belongings except for the video equipment. Then she and Electra loaded Mick into the van. The other fellow had recovered enough to put on clothes that Donna gave him.

Electra felt sorry for Mick's unguided accomplices, She fought the urge to give advice, remaining silent as they drove away. *I'm older than Donna and could give her advice, but I'm not going to meddle where I don't belong.* As she turned to walk upstairs, a contradictory thought flashed in her brain. *But Robin and I are interfering in Christi's life. What's the difference?* Suddenly she knew the answer. *I can't spend my life being only an observer. I have to participate. I must rely on my brain for knowing when to act. Tonight's the night to help Christi.*

By now Christi had regained her wits as well as some clothes. Robin helped her off the bed,   wrapping her in a robe while Christi examined the video equipment and shook her head in disbelief. "What a sucker I've been," she said glumly. Electra smiled as she held her by the shoulders.

"No serious damage was done, and Robin's got you back on your feet."

"I'm still groggy. Let's go sit in the family room. What are we gonna do with the video equipment?"

Robin joked, "Let's make movies of guys acting out women's fantasies." Christi grimaced at the thought. "No way. I'm changing careers."

It was nearly midnight; Robin and Electra called home so their families wouldn't worry. They would spend the night with Christi, and since the adrenaline rush still powered the trio, the girls needed something to do.

"Let's go for a drive and talk about Christi's new career. Electra drives, I talk, and Christi listens."

"Good idea. Robin and I will be career counselors. By the time we're done, we'll have you pointed in the right direction." The trio cruised for a couple of hours, looking for what might be good for Christi. Christi reluctantly agreed to consider college or certification training, and perhaps a cosmetics or fashion design career afterward.

"My parents will be glad my performing career's in the rearview mirror. It's a tougher life than I thought. I gotta turn the page to something I can do." Christi remembered a haunting melody from a classic rock song describing a performer's brief, lonely life on the road and she softly sang its lyrics while Electra mused to herself what an appropriate metaphor for much of life. She silently recited a Shakespearean quote from Macbeth expressing a similar sentiment.

> *"Out, out, brief candle! Life's but a walking*
> *shadow, a poor player that struts and*
> *frets his hour upon the stage and then is heard*
> *no more. It is a tale told by an idiot,*
> *full of sound and fury, Signifying nothing."*

There must be a receding sequence of similar expressions extending from here through the mists of antiquity. But enough philosophical musing for tonight. It's making me depressed.

"I'll drive us back to Christi's. It's time to rest up for tomorrow. And we're sworn to secrecy. Your parents will never know what happened."

Robin nodded, then said, "Do you remember when Christi dumped our Three Queens nickname? Well, whatever we call ourselves, we'll always be ever the best of friends. I'm counting on the two of you to bail me out whenever I get into something over my head. And though you haven't needed us yet, Christi and I are there for you." Electra nodded, but kept her thoughts to herself. *It will sound like bragging if I say I won't need help, but I shouldn't need any because I'm strong enough to stand on my own as long as I keep my brain focused, and I stay in control. That's what I plan to do.*

September came cool and rainy, but that didn't dampen Electra's enthusiasm for the start of her third year at GWU. It would be her last as an undergrad since she would have enough credits to graduate in June. Then she would pursue a GWU biotech graduate degree because she could stay in the Washington area, taking care of her grandfather while working on a joint NIH-GWU research assistantship from where she could continue spying on Cognicom. Acceptance was virtually guaranteed because her excellent grades and test scores placed her near the top, but not so high to attract undue attention.

Electra's political science professor approved Guardian Party volunteer work for part of a guided independent study course, and in early October he helped arrange an interview; even volunteers were vetted to confirm they had what was wanted. She hoped they wouldn't link her last name with the NIH lab explosion, for that might raise questions. That didn't happen and the interview went smoothly, which meant Electra would become a volunteer pending a routine background check. Clarence (the EMT from Doc's clinic) and the poli-sci professor were suitable references. She would attend an orientation session a week from Saturday, watching a video and meeting department heads. After leaving the interview, she briefly toured the building, coming away impressed with what she saw and overheard. Everyone appeared energetic, competent, and committed to the party line. That night at supper, Doc supplied more political insights.

"You're going to learn a lot about the inner workings of politics. Just like anything, what goes on inside is much different than what you see from the outside. From everything I've been hearing, the Guardians are looking out for the public's best interests. Media hasn't found a shred linking them to rumors hyping a power grab or some hidden agenda. And the orientation session speakers wouldn't tell you about that either. So just keep your eyes and ears open. Check if what you see or hear agrees with what you think. I like them better than the other parties, and lots of people feel the same way."

Electra replied, "I'll be interested in what they tell us about membership growth, and what sort of connection the Guardians make with T-Plague."

"I like how you've connected school, volunteer work, and your Cognicom work-study program. You're covering all the bases."

"I'll tell what I hear after orientation…"

Electra would tell no one else what she was up to, instead following standard military protocol: provide information on a need to know basis only. She would share as little as possible with Cognicom or the Guardian Party, keeping a low profile and blending in. She would be as bland as melted butter.

Whenever at the lab, Electra saw firsthand Cognicom projects in disarray. Although Mo did his best to get whatever Su or Adom needed, nothing moved progress forward, and rumors about moles burrowing in brought out the worst in Adom, who had inherited Jason's penchant for worry. He complained that many researchers fretted about safety issues or identity leaks, letting Mo know how he felt.

"So not even you can figure out who might be planting moles. I don't like it when you tell me they could be working for the CIA or the Guardian Party or that shadowy Opposition Group. How about adding Middle East terrorist groups? And maybe there are multiple moles. No wonder morale is at a record low."

"Come on Adom, buck up. At least be positive when talking with your team. Let's go chat with Su and find out how worried she is about safety."

"Are you kidding? Su worries about one thing only, making vaccine improvements. Too bad I'm not much of a help for her."

Electra didn't worry about safety or moles because she operated below everyone's radar, but she would like to uncover them. Everyone but Su or Adom were possibilities. *Could Mo be a mole? I like him, but I don't know. He's got character and respects traditional American values, and he's concerned about the country's direction. But who would he work for? I better keep him at arm's length.*

Electra arrived on time with fifteen other recruits at the Saturday morning orientation. Introductory remarks painted Guardian Party member characteristics: ages between 30 to 70, concerned about terrorism and T-Plague, mad at the government, and didn't think the world was a kind or gentle place.

A rousing video tracing party history followed the speakers, emphasizing the Party's principles. Patriotic theme and supporting evidence were moving, highlighted by David Rushman's T-Plague-induced downward spiral into senility dramatizing why America needs the Guardian Party more than ever. It concluded with a call to action for all patriots: become a volunteer to help guard what makes America great, because today's harsh times demand harsh measures that only the Guardian Party can implement. Electra liked what she heard. *What a powerful message backed by facts. Any misinformation spread by government or media about the Guardians is going to backfire. Anyone would be motivated to join, including me. But I'm looking for more than volunteer work. I'm looking for moles and hidden agendas, and this is the place to start digging.*

All recruits stayed and Electra was directed to Burton Burhanz because he had reviewed her application earlier and liked what he saw.

"Good morning, Electra, and thanks for coming. How did you like our orientation video?"

"It's a powerful, patriotic message. It makes people want to join and help fix our problems." Burton beamed, then continued.

"Right you are, and since you're still in school, we thought the best way for you to start would be working on fundraising and recruiting at our headquarters location because it's so close to campus. Our state-of-the art computer network will make your work easy, and we have a great training session to get you up to speed. And we can plan your work schedule around your class schedule. Do you think this will work?" Not even Electra could have planned it any better.

"Mr. Burhanz, that should be OK. I think my skills are what you're looking for in volunteers, and what I learn will earn me a good grade in my poli-sci course." *I've said enough to hook Burton. I can make his people unwitting players in my hunting game.*

"Well then, how about we arrange for you to attend a training session where you'll meet your supervisor and learn how to use our computer system? Would you be able to pick a date now?"

"Is next Saturday available? If so, I'll take it."

"Yes, it is. And after you complete the initial training, you'll come back a month later for additional training. So, if there are no other questions, we'll see you next Saturday."

That night at supper, Electra reported to Doc all the details of the day.

"I'm happy for you. What you'll be doing sounds interesting, and it sounds like you'll be part of a with-it group. You'll be busy too. How will it fit in with your class and lab schedule?"

"I can plan it around both. And I like keeping busy."

"Yes, you thrive when you're multi-tasking. I'd say you'll be happily busy for the rest of the year."

"Agreed, and there's always time for you and me to have fun. How about we watch the latest action-adventure flick tonight. Doc chuckled.

"I'll answer in terms you like to use. Copy that."

Electra's October and November danced by, keeping her as happily busy as Doc predicted. Everything in her personal world was under control. Thanksgiving came and went uneventfully, and Electra pointed for a follow-up training session that would be held a week from Saturday. She would use it to learn more about the Party's computer system so she could burrow deeper, but she needed to be careful, because hunting for agendas or moles could become a most dangerous game. *Long ago I read a story with the same title. It had a happy ending because the hero escaped from a pack of pursuing hounds by leaping onto the back of a truck so he no longer left a scented trail. In my game, terrorists or aggressive covert operation agents replace the hounds. My story will have an even happier ending because I'll never leave a trail. I'll stay invisible.*

December blustered in, bringing gloomy intermittent snow showers that contrasted sharply with the upbeat climate found at the training session. A youthful Gretchen Tomlinson greeted Electra, explaining she's a full-time Guardian Party supervisor. Six other volunteers, two each in their thirties, forties, or fifties came that day for training. Gretchen patiently explained advanced techniques for using proprietary network and software tools. She then illustrated how to retrieve call scripts and contact lists, and then how to select the best targets. It was a lot to learn in only three hours, and all the trainees struggled. Electra, however, mastered it all but kept that to herself. Gretchen complimented everyone as she ended the morning session.

"Let's break for lunch. You have all afternoon to practice here. And your training manual presents everything we've gone over, so take it with you and study it so you can logon at home and practice. Are there any questions?" One of the older trainees voiced a concern.

"I wish my computer skills were better. Will you fire me if I don't catch on faster?" Gretchen laughed and had a reply she used often.

"I hear that from a lot of our more mature trainees. Don't worry. You'll catch on with practice. And if you don't feel comfortable with what you're doing, you can transfer to another department. We have many volunteer positions. Some of our volunteers are so dedicated they become regular employees. You can go as far as your ability and interests take you here at the Guardian Party." Electra was impressed. *These Guardian Party people are good. And as I observed before, they're committed to the cause.*

Gretchen gave each trainee a cafeteria voucher and invited everyone to join her for lunch. The four oldest trainees said they were tired and left, but Electra and the youngest two stayed, listening to Gretchen's cheery description of life at headquarters. It was clear she knew something about each trainee's background, which added a personal note to the conversation. Electra didn't ask questions, preferring instead to listen carefully to all that Gretchen mentioned. There would be plenty of time to ask questions once the lightning brain decided how best to use her.

Electra stayed for several hours that afternoon, exploring the Guardian Party network and probing for ways to hack into the system. Over time she would "borrow" login I.D.'s and passwords; by three o'clock she had accomplished enough and decided it was time to get home and prepare supper for Doc. Not only would she prepare the meal; she would also cook up an entertaining story about today. She always enjoyed sharing the day's events with her grandfather, and as she drove home, a recurring emotional ping touched her. *I'm lucky to be Doc's caregiver. It feels good to be needed. I hope I can do it until he's a hundred.*

Electra parked in front, using the front door for a shorter route to her bedroom where she would deposit items brought from the car.

"Gramps, I'm home and I have a great story to tell you at supper." She heard no response. *He's in the kitchen and didn't hear. I'll go there after stowing my stuff.* Still no grandfather. Then she saw the kitchen door open and Doc's coffee mug spilled on the floor, coffee brewer on but most of the coffee gone. Electra sensed something unexpected had happened much earlier; the lightning brain shifted to a higher gear. She was about to check the garage when her cell phone beeped, flashing a number she recognized. Su was calling. "Hi Aunt Su, I just got home." Electra listened for only a couple of seconds before interrupting Su mid-sentence. "Stop talking and listen to me, then do exactly what I tell you to do." Su had just blurted out that Doc had been kidnapped.

Electra was waiting in the living room for Su to arrive. Her instructions to Su had been crystal clear: don't say anything to anyone, drive here immediately, and call me en route. Minutes later Su reported the full story. A strange call had just come from a heavily accented voice. Doc was being held ransom until she delivers T-Plague virus culture, handling equipment, and instructions for growing more. She would be given further instructions later but no second chance. If she did not give them what they demanded, Doc would be executed.

Electra launched her plan as soon as the call had ended. She changed into all-black winter running gear, parked her car several blocks away, then ran back home to pack what she needed. Out she ran when she spotted Su's car approaching. It was seven, and Electra was primed for action. She jumped into the passenger seat and after a terse greeting told Su to drive on. Five minutes later, Electra told her to stop.

"Let's wait in the strip mall for the call." Su pulled over, then waited for Electra to tell her more. "When the call comes, make sure you repeat exactly what they say before disconnecting. Ask for a call-back number. Ask to speak to Doc. And make sure they believe you when you say you're alone." Su nodded.

"Once we have the exchange location, I'll punch it into the GPS. I'll bail out a mile away. Wait ten minutes, then drive to the site. I'll find cover close enough to watch. If you get there before the kidnappers, wait in the car. Follow their instructions when they arrive. Make sure you leave your keys in the ignition and carry your cell phone." Su nodded again.

"Now, here's what to expect. There'll be two cars. Two bad guys in the first; Doc and another in the second. The guys in the first car will call the shots. Tell them you want to see Doc. Then, give them just the virus culture. They'll want you to prove it's the right stuff. Did you bring a test kit?"

"Oh my God, I forgot."

"Don't worry about it. One of the bad guys has got to be a biotech type and should have brought one. He might even do the test. Just play along." Electra paused for Su to settle down, then finished. "When they're satisfied, tell them to release Doc and you'll give them the rest of the stuff. If they refuse, give it to them anyway and hope for the best. I'll be close enough in case something goes wrong."

Su stuttered, "What could go wrong?"

"That's for me to deal with. Your job is to do what I just said. If they tell you to do something different, just go along with it. I'll take it from there. OK?"

Su took a deep breath and said, "Let me sit and run through it again. Then I'll say if I'm OK." A calming awareness began flowing through Electra's brain as physical and cognitive personas merged. Su clicked back to attention, announcing she was set, no need to rehearse further. There was nothing to do but wait. Electra didn't want to talk, so she turned on the radio, hoping it would help Su stay calm. Electra used the time to plan for several contingencies, and when the call came two hours later, she felt ready.

"This is Doctor Chou." For the next two minutes, Su listened to instructions. Then she said, "I don't know where Memorial Park Field House is. Please give me directions so I can get there by eleven. And please give me a number to call in case—" The caller abruptly disconnected. Su was at a loss for words, but Electra knew what to say.

"They told us enough. Let me drive." Off they sped to an uncertain engagement.

Electra was hiding fifty yards from the field house when Su's car arrived first, parking lights on and the motor running. They were in Orchard Grove, a sparsely populated distant suburb whose streets were deserted this time of night. Only one bulb glowed dimly at the field house entrance, thirty feet from Su's car. The unlit drive into the park ran for a quarter of a mile, enough distance to give Electra a minute's warning when other cars approach. The cell phone glowed 10:54, and Electra began to worry. *What if they deliberately come late? What if they run Su from place to place? What if they force Su into their car and drive off? What if they call Su again? My contingency plans are incomplete.*

Panic began to paralyze Electra. She felt pounding in her chest, shortness of breath. And suddenly, the lightning brain shifted to a higher gear. *Get with it Soldier! This is not a drill! Think. You know what to do if plans change. Let the lightning brain take charge.* A thrilling clarity replaced panic as Electra strapped her game face on.

One set of headlights appeared, then another turned into the drive. Electra's adversaries were about to engage. As they approached, long-anticipated excitement welled up from the subconscious. She trembled with a desire to act as she crept forward, concealed by a dark blanket.

Two cars parked adjacent to Su, who was the first to walk to the field house, soon followed by two men, the bulky one measuring six feet, the medium built fellow an inch or two shorter. Both were dressed in light coats although the temperature this windy, overcast night hovered near freezing.

Electra crept closer, knowing all eyes were on the field house, and she was close enough to hear angry words. Suddenly the bulky one punched Su, crumpling her to the ground.

"You are stupid and weak!" he shouted, then kicked. "We should kill you both for not bringing a test kit!" His accomplice spoke Arabic before jogging to the car. *That's the biotech guy.* The bulky thug dragged Su to her feet, pushing her towards her car from where she took her satchel containing what they wanted. Then he pulled her to his car, shoving her into the front seat. His accomplice was already sitting in the back.

Electra's brain raced through the unfolding contingency. *If they drive off with Su, I'll call the police. They can track Su's cell phone. Then I'll join the chase using Su's car. If they stay put to test the virus, I'll wait for results.*

Ten minutes later, the car's rear door opened. The biotech guy opened the passenger-side door, cursed and pulled Su out, sprawling her onto the frozen ground. He ran to the other car, growled instructions, and then ran back. As soon as he got in, the car drove slowly away. Electra trembled again, not from panic or fear but from an adrenaline rush.

Su's car blocked Electra's line of sight, so she crawled furiously to where she could see, but before she could the driver of the remaining car pulled Doc out of the back seat, threw him to the ground and pulled a gun's trigger twice, the whip-cracking sounds cutting the night air. The terrorist had just executed Doc, and Su was next in line.

Electra's adversary never knew what hit him, never heard her swoop in from behind and snap his head backward, tumbling him to the ground. Pouncing on his gun, she pressed it against his temple and hissed, "Tell me where your friends are going if you want to live."

"I don't know. They're waiting for me at the park entrance. I'm supposed to follow them—"That was all Electra needed to know. She grabbed forward, twisting his head with all the torque her fury could generate. A crisp snap signaled a broken neck, the sound filling Electra with glee. Then she rifled the dead man's pockets, coming away with a wallet and cell phone.

Su struggled to her feet, unable to speak. Electra kept shaking her until she could talk. "Su! Listen to me! Doc is dead, and so's the bad guy. Get in your car and drive home. Call the police in twenty minutes. Use the dead guy's cell phone so they can't track the call to you. Tell them you heard gunshots when you drove by the park. Don't give them your name. Don't tell them the bad guys contacted you. Don't tell them we were here. Do you understand?" Su grimaced, then spoke.

"My God." Su could think of nothing else to say, so Electra shook her again and rattled off more instructions.

"Go home and get ready just in case the police track you. Tell them you were driving home after visiting friends. Tell them nothing about being called earlier. Do you understand?" Su was beginning to come around.

"Yes! Stop shaking me."

"I will call you tomorrow when I can. Now wait five minutes, then go." Electra pulled Su to her car.

Su stammered, "What are you going to do?" "Don't ask," was the abrupt reply.

Su stayed put while Electra dragged the dead man into the passenger seat of his car. Before Electra drove away she retrieved all her gear, then fired the pistol one time. Su watched in disbelief. *Who is this creature? Can it be the Electra I thought I knew?* Su was in no condition to think any further than her five-minute countdown, so she let her mind go blank.

Electra drove away slowly until the lightning brain fully adjusted. Her anger and fury morphed into an even deadlier combination, an all-consuming wrath never felt until this moment. She could feel it surge from her subconscious, turning her emotions into an unstoppable force overpowering her rational self and fusing with her cognitive and physical personas into a single identity. It was raging unloosed in an ecstasy beyond orgasm, lusting for blood— even its own. It was the Monster from the Id, but not some mindless beast. It was the lighting brain in full control, wielding all its powers. Electra had become her Monster. And it knew what to do.

Electra drove faster, flashing headlights as she approached the other car. The lead car accelerated away; she followed four car lengths behind until the road straightened on a rural stretch. As the lead car accelerated to sixty, Electra made her move.

She veered into the left lane as she floored the accelerator and rammed into the rear of the lead car, spinning it out of control, then she slammed the brakes to avoid colliding again. The driver brought his car to a stop facing backwards. He gunned the engine, tires squealing, and raced past Electra. Electra spun tires as she drove in reverse and did a 180, then shifted into forward and punched the accelerator. She was driving with a fury the other driver couldn't match and overtook her adversary as they entered a twisty section of road. The lead car had to break, but not so for Electra. She floored the accelerator and rammed again. The other car spun crazily out of control, its center of gravity beyond its tipping point. It rolled onto its left side, tilting off the road and down an embankment, coming to rest on its roof near a stand of trees, motor running and headlights cutting through the darkness. Electra screeched to halt, grabbed a pistol, and raced to the car. She tried to open the door but it wouldn't budge, so she smashed the passenger window. Both terrorists were upside down and strapped inside. Electra got on hands and knees and screamed.

"Give me your cell phones and wallets if you want to live!" They struggled to obey. "Faster!" she screamed again. A look of naked terror etched on their faces thrilled her. When they gave her what she wanted, she screamed yet again. "Who sent you? Who are you?" As soon as the driver uttered Allahu Akbar, she had heard enough and shot him once in the side of the head. Blood splattered the biotech minion who was numb with fear. Electra grabbed him by the hair, pulling his head out the window.

"Where are you going? What's the location?" His terror-filled eyes answered. He didn't know. Electra snarled, "Last question. Where's the virus sample"? He motioned towards the back seat. Electra smashed the rear door window, saw the satchel but couldn't reach it. She shoved the biotech's head back into the car. He stammered, "Please! Let me—" Electra fired a bullet into his head, then finished his sentence. *Live in Paradise!* Her blood lust was insatiable.

She ran up the embankment, removing her belongings from the car, placing them with the items she had just collected. She leaped in, drove in reverse to gain distance, then careened down the embankment, crashing into the overturned car, the collision locking the cars together. Then she raced back to her supplies, ripped the blanket in two and ran back to the wrecks. She lit each blanket half and threw them into the front seat of each car, watching until satisfied. She fired one bullet into the overturned car's gas tank, then ran up the embankment for the final time. The tank erupted into a fireball, spreading flames to the second car. Electra had seen enough. She threw everything into a backpack and backed away, waiting until the second gas tank exploded, sending a second fireball high into the sky. She looked and listened. She saw no traffic; she heard no sirens. Then she started running, faster and faster towards the shelter of home. As she vanished into the blackness, a fantastic image streaked through her brain. She was shredding her clothes, running naked through deserted streets at midnight, howling at the Moon, all her desires unleashed.

Electra ran past her aerobic threshold, running faster than her body could clear lactic acid, forcing her to walk. She had detoured onto another road less traveled, and could hear faintly in the distance a siren's pulsing wail. Her cognitive persona regained control, forcing the Monster back into the subliminal, then geared up for the long run home. As she settled into a sustainable pace, her rhythmic stride focused her worldview onto one event: tonight's epiphany. She needed to sift through all that had been revealed.

Doc's dead but I'm too numb to feel the loss. I'll have to grieve later. How did terrorists link Doc to Su? Perhaps through Su when we were followed. Perhaps through Jason when he blew himself up. Am I to blame? No. It is what it is. Suddenly, an odd thought stopped Electra dead in her tracks, a quote attributed to Japanese commander Yamamoto after Pearl Harbor: "I fear all we have done is to awaken a sleeping giant and fill him with a terrible resolve." *I shall avenge the execution of the only person I love. I saw tonight the power of the three emotions I cannot control: love, lust, and wrath. They overpower anything standing in their way. It thrills and frightens me. I become my own Monster from the Id, not mindless but fully aware, fully committed to the lightning brain's commands. I must obey, and I shall never question what actions it directs.*

Electra resumed a near-marathon trek. Each mile increased the flow of endorphins, adding to her focus. *Now I see why an inaction decision trumps armchair moralizing. Ethical relativism trumps deontological rules for right and wrong. My brain makes the right call. I alone am the judge of my actions.*

I learned tonight why I'll never again panic or fear for my life. My brain can switch gears to altered states that fulfill my prime directive: to survive and to go on living.

Another thought crossed her cognitive path. *What about people I care about? People I love? Obligations to them impinge what I can do. Love is a double-edged sword. It connects me. Provides a sense of belonging. But it makes me responsible for others. If I withhold love, I don't have to worry about anyone but myself. Perhaps I don't need love. Maybe I'm stronger when alone.* Another sudden thought jolted Electra's brain but vanished before she could grasp it, leaving her with an uncertain feeling. *I'm missing something, but I don't know what. All I know for certain is that Grandfather's dead.*

The feeling dissipated as distance and time ticked away to the tempo of her stride. She zoomed out to find only six miles remained. *It's time to plan for what to do next. When I get to the car, I'll change clothes then drive home. Then I'll call the police if they haven't tracked me down. Then I'll shower and eat breakfast. Then I'll go to the morgue. Then I'll call Su.*

Electra, soaked with sweat and unable to run another step, reached the car at three thirty-four, having averaged just under eight minutes a mile on the twenty-five-mile journey. *I hit the wall; I'm out of glycogen and had to walk. I thought I was in better shape. I'll worry about it later.* She toweled off, then changed clothes and drove the two blocks home. *No cops. Good. I'll put all my stuff away, check voice messages, then disable cell phones' GPS tracking. Then I'll call the cops after I rehearse what to say.*

Forty-five minutes later she called the police. After four transfers, the connection went dead. *They're clueless. I'm way ahead of them. If they don't call me back, I'll call them, then I'll call Su. But I've gotta shower first and eat breakfast.*

Electra sat for twenty minutes under the showerhead's pulsating stream, loosening some of the stiffness and soreness, cleansing away some of the ugliness that had violated her world. Afterwards, she wrapped herself in a thick cotton robe, gobbled enough cereal and muffins to quell her appetite, swallowed four aspirin, and considered what to do next. *I'm still too wired to rest. I'll call the police again.*

This call went only a little better. She learned the police had been contacted in the last twelve hours by many people reporting missing people and had recovered one or more bodies matching Doc's description (they wouldn't say how many or where). The name Justin Kittner was not on a person of interest list, so the police would not contact her unless there was a good reason. *I don't know if Su got through to the police. Maybe they haven't found Doc's body. I'm glad I didn't tell them about the broken mug in the kitchen. I don't want the cops poking around. I better call Su.* Su answered on the first ring.

"I've been waiting for your call. I did just what you wanted. I told the police only what you told me to say and hung up. I don't think anyone followed me home or tracked the call to me."

"Good. I called the police too, but I couldn't find out if they found Doc's body yet. I'll call them later this morning. And don't tell Adom anything until you and I talk in person."

"It's good that Adom and Mo aren't back yet. I need to talk with you too." Just then Electra's phone beeped for an incoming call. "I'll call you again later this morning." She disconnected Su and answered the other call.

This time the police knew more, matching more of what Electra knew. They asked her to come to the medical examiner's morgue to identify a gunshot victim matching her grandfather's description. She memorized the address and agreed to be there at eleven. Then she called Su one more time, arranging to visit after leaving the morgue.

Electra's cell phone flashed six a.m. when she crawled back into bed, but was unable to sleep. *I'll lie here and focus on getting rid of the lactic acid in my legs, and I'll use the time to plan the week ahead. Three hours later she summarized what she would do. I'll make calls from the morgue to my family's funeral parlor and church to arrange for a Wednesday morning wake and afternoon funeral. I want the body cremated before the wake. I want grandfather's friends to remember how he looked when alive, not as a corpse. I'll start calling his friends tomorrow.*

Electra could tell by flexing in bed that her leg stiffness had worsened. *Time to get up and do some stretching and sit-ups, chin-ups and push-ups, then eat another breakfast before heading to the morgue.* Unfortunately, her brain was ahead of her body, for Electra couldn't handle an exercise session. *I'm stiff all over. My body feels as if it belongs in the morgue too. My thighs feel like pin cushions. I might have to walk backwards down stairs to keep a million pin-prick sensation at bay. When my life settles down, I better pick up the pace of my workouts.*

Electra limped to her car after eating another breakfast, requiring extra time to fold herself behind the wheel before driving off, trying unsuccessfully to jolly herself into a better mood. She entered the morgue feeling as it looks in movies—lifeless and grim. A pungent odor mixed with a tinge of sickening sweetness hung in the air, and it combined with the stress-filled aftershock of last night to overwhelm Electra. She fell to her knees and vomited noisily, frightening a sympathetic guard who helped her stand.

"You're whiter than a cadaver. Let me take you to the lounge so you can lie down."

"No, I'll be OK in a minute. I'm so sorry for the mess I made." "Don't you worry. I'll take care of it. Where are you heading?" "To the counseling room so I can view my grandfather's body.

He might have been a gunshot victim."

"I'm sorry to hear that. Come on, I'll get you some water and then take you there."

The morgue attendant was as consoling as possible, explaining what they would do.

Electra chose to view her grandfather's body in person rather than through remote cameras. She accompanied the attendant to the storage area, spending all of fifteen seconds identifying the body because that was all the time she needed to store the visual reminders of her grandfather's corpse. The attendant escorted her back to the counseling room for her to sign the requisite forms, after which she placed two funeral arrangement calls. Nothing else needed doing, so she thanked the attendant, steadied herself, and walked away, never looking back.

The ugly part of my day is over. Time to call Su and start living in my new world. After the call, she sensed her brain shifting to a better state, kindness replacing callousness, empathy replacing indifference. Her leg muscles were beginning to loosen, and a better emotional persona resurfaced.

Su was beginning to feel better too, having regained her bearings after last night's horror in the park. She was certain the police couldn't connect her to Doc's murder, and that was one less worry, but it was replaced by a bigger one.

I witnessed an Electra biofield transformation last night. Will Electra return to her normal self, or is she now a different creature? And I shall never ask where she went or what she did when she drove away. Those are dead subjects. Electra better lead the conversation when she gets here.

When Su opened the door, she recognized an Electra who was still recovering from the gruesome events of the last twenty-four hours. Su gave her an arm's length hug, then took her to the kitchen for a late lunch, ladling out homemade vegetable soup served with salad and fresh-baked rolls. Although neither was hungry at the start, conversation and companionship helped improve appetites the longer they were together.

"I don't think last night will be reported on the news. There's no reason for the police to say anything to the media because they have so little to go on, and no one saw anything.I hope it stays that way." Su nodded slowly in agreement.

"I hope no one learns much about your grandfather's death. It would serve no purpose."

"I agree. I went to the morgue this morning, and while there I made funeral arrangements for Wednesday. I'll tell anyone who asks that grandfather died of a heart attack while he was at a park, and I don't know why he was there. That's all I'm going to say." *Time to change subjects.*

"I almost forgot that next Sunday is Christmas Eve. Maybe that'll cheer me up.And the last thing I want to do is hold any sort of remembrance celebration for Grandfather because it just doesn't fit with my mood. Maybe next spring, sometime after Easter, but not now."

"Would you like to spend Christmas with Adom and me? We'd love to share it with you."

"Thanks for the invite, but I don't know. May I give you an answer after the funeral?"

"That's fine. You look tired. Why don't you go home and take a nap? And take the brownies I baked. I'll also pack you a container of soup, along with some rolls. Soup always helps settle a stomach." Su's kindness brought only a hint of a smile.

"I'll take your advice and a goodie care package too. Thanks to you, my spirits and stomach are feeling better."

Electra paced herself the rest of the weekend, taking breaks between household or funeral-related chores. *Keeping busy is how I'll keep depression at bay. And I'm going to step up my exercise program. I've been cutting too many corners. But at least I don't belong to the 75 percent who add the "freshman 15" by the time they graduate.*

When Monday came she followed advice that works wonders for dealing with life's dreaded obligations: don't dwell on them, just do them. By Wednesday she had secured all interment arrangements and had concluded death notification, banking, and legal matters. A hundred people came to the wake, people who knew Doc from the clinic or church. Electra knew only a handful, but everyone shared consoling stories. Only a handful attended the funeral, which was to her liking because she wanted it to be a family affair. Christi, Robin, and their parents, Su, Adom, Mo, and Clarence, Doc's stalwart EMT, were there. Su's dinner invitation helped put a period at the end of a terrible chapter in her life.

Electra turned the page the next day, immersing herself in Guardian Party work where she was secretly burrowing into organizational, Email, and network structures to locate confidential information that might reveal what she was looking for. She had already stolen user I.D.'s. Her digging had just begun, but she knew snooping would work and was satisfied with how much she had already accomplished. She was following the advice given at a software development seminar: learn only enough to achieve your goal and move on, adding to it when needed. But when she glimpsed the incredible power available through computers and the secrets hidden in shadow-Cyberspace, she turned her efforts into a self-directed "Network Security and Hacking" course in preparation for software-related projects that would become part of graduate study. All thesis topics Electra had proposed would require advanced computer technology.

Electra used the day before Christmas Eve to go shopping at three malls. Traffic was heavier than she expected, holiday cheer evidently suspending T-Plague exposure concerns. She bought token gifts for Su, Christi, and Robin, then drifted in the crowd, window shopping on the way to her car. As she was driving home, she decided to pack up Doc's belongings on Christmas Eve. She had extra boxes and would store them next to those packed a year ago for her father's.Before dinner she called Su to accept Christmas Day's dinner invitation, then left messages for Christi and Robin, announcing she would visit Christmas Day to deliver presents.

Most families bustle through Christmas Eve preparations, adding excitement and anticipation to a timeless tradition, but not Electra for she was alone, having finished a lazy Christmas Eve day at home. She planned to stay home that evening because she had outgrown the need for ceremonies, which are useful only when sharing with loved ones,and Electra's list of people she loved, except for perhaps Su,was empty.She made quick work of packing Doc's belongings, setting aside a couple of keepsakes she put with those of her parents. She found no sealed envelope, which came as no surprise because her grandfather gave of himself completely and willingly while alive.

But Electra did find an added sense of closure that afternoon because she realized grieving for her grandfather could now be placed in the past tense.The past week,a passage to another phase in her life, had not been as painful as she had thought last Sunday. *A good night's sleep will bring back my enthusiasm. I'll have a brighter outlook when I awaken tomorrow.*

She entertained herself after dinner by switching among televised cathedral services or classic Christmas movies but became restless. Watching alone made her vaguely depressed so she followed her own advice and went to bed early so she would be fresh for her traditional sunrise run on Christmas Day.

"Electra? You are ready to know who and what you are, and perhaps what you will be? Awaken now and talk with me." These enchanting words entered Electra's consciousness and brought her out of a deep sleep, rousing her to a sitting position. Yawning and stretching, Electra rubbed her eyes and wondered *Why is the lamp switched on? Did I forget to turn it off? The nightstand clock glowed one o'clock.*

"Electra. I am here. Please come sit next to me." A lilting voice snapped Electra to attention. As she turned toward her bedroom chairs, she saw a shimmering apparition gracing one of them, the ghost of Indira, the mother she never saw in life but recognized immediately in spirit. Electra was unable to speak; she stared in wonderment.

"Yes, my daughter, you have known me for several years. Now come sit by me so I can explain more." Electra obeyed her command.

"You and I are kindred spirits in appearance and in thought. Even though still so young, you are superior in many ways, and if you pay attention, you will improve where you must." Electra was finally able to stutter a few words.

"Mother? Am I dreaming? All this seems so real." Indy laughed lightly and replied,

"My precious daughter, of course you are dreaming! Dreaming is part of being human, part of how the mind and brain are one. But for you, dreams are intense."

"But why haven't you come to me before tonight?"

"Because you were not ready until completing your latest rite of passage. That is why your lightning brain summoned me. It encompasses all of your reality, the physical, the cognitive, the emotional. It has chosen me to be your Muse, your inner voice that is with you always. I am alive in altered states of your neural connections. Your brain will summon me, like tonight, when needed." Suddenly, Electra understood all that Indy had spoken. She marveled at this extraordinary gift from her lightning brain.

"Will I be able to know the future? Will I know the answer to life's mysteries?"

Indira smiled wistfully.

"No. Powerful as your brain is, many mysteries will always be inaccessible. I cannot tell you the future, because your brain does not know. Your brain does not know if a purpose or guiding force drives the Universe. But through dialogues with me, you have reasoning powers beyond those of—as you refer to other people— mere mortals. You will know how to make the best of whatever comes your way. But remember this. Emotions shall always challenge you because you cannot completely control them. They depend on relationships with others. Perhaps you think you don't need love. But perhaps you will someday want love. You'll have to decide, and it won't be as easy as solving a math problem." Indira continued before letting Electra speak.

"I have spoken all I wanted to and must say goodnight, but remember, I am always with you."

"Mother, don't go! I need to know more about you. Please tell me more."

"Very well. I will tell you what you should do. Read my poems again. Talk more with Su. Adom too. You are clever, so build on that."

"May I ask you one final question? Please tell me if I'm choosing the right path."

"Tell me your choice, and I will answer."

"I want to connect neuroscience and biotechnology with artificial intelligence and nanotechnology. I want to figure out cognition at the cellular level, what thinking is and how to make humans better. And I want to defeat the T-Plague, but all the while I have to hide the secret that I'm a genetic freak. The best I've come up with is leaving clues for Su. Am I doing what's right?" Indira smiled.

"My answer is that of the Buddhist monk: perhaps. You have great expectations and abilities to match, so never be discouraged when obstacles arise, but you must allow your empathy and patience to grow. As you do that, you will begin to treat others less as means to your ends and more as individuals deserving dignity and respect. And if you decide to seek the love of others, you must care for them more than yourself, and you must learn to be more giving and less self-centered."

Electra was at a loss for words. Her lips struggled to form syllables but none came, so Indira filled in for her after a melancholy shake of her head.

"Your grandfather was the only person who could give you such advice. Now that he has departed, you must rely on your inner voice to keep yourself centered, and that is one of the reasons your lightning brain has conjured me. I am your inner voice. I am with you always. And though your future is unknown, one thing is certain. I will always be here for you."

Indira's apparition vanished like a mirage, shimmering as it receded to an indistinct horizon, suspending Electra in space and time. Electra sat in her chair, completely absorbed in her thoughts. She sleepwalked back to bed when the lightning brain told her to rest for the coming Christmas Day.

Electra awoke to glorious sunlight streaming into her bedroom. She felt alive, filled with tidings of joy. As she stood, stretched and walked to the window, all of last night streamed through her brain. *Mother's visit is my personal Christmas Carol. I shall never share it with anyone but my inner voice, but I can use Mother's gift to give back to others. And I'll never doubt myself again. I'll never imprison myself like the doubter in one of Mother's poems.* Electra recited it aloud as she prepared to run:

> For those who have conviction and faith,
>   Their journey sure their sleep secure.
> Compared to me doubt comes as wraith,
>   Haunting this life I must endure.
>
> I curse the loss of innocence,
>   Replaced with jaded adult views.
> Skepticism—indifference,
> The path becomes so hard to choose.
>
> But while I'm trapped by my own doubt,
>   I will not quit I carry on.
> I'll strive for more convincing thought,

Perhaps I will break free anon.

Electra had broken free and was now on her chosen path, ready to discover whatever awaited, and her mother would be with her. Though she had arrived as the Ghost of Christmas Present, Indira would remain in Electra's present and future, a Muse and constant companion. Electra would never be alone.

CHAPTER 31
March 2114

"Dodging Bullets"
(Thread 2 Chapter 18)

THE INVISIBLE MAN RECOGNIZED the caller's I.D. *The Invisible Hand is making an unscheduled call. It must be important, so I'll take it. His head is on the chopping block, and so is mine if we can't deliver.*

"This is the Invisible Man. Identify yourself."

"This is the Invisible Hand. My NIH mole just reported a breakthrough we've been looking for. Here are the facts."

The Invisible Man listened intently, scribbling notes as the Hand relayed good news. When the Hand finished, the Man sat perfectly still, momentarily stunned by his incredibly good luck. Then he snapped back, composing his thoughts, and then replying in a dull monotone voice.

"This might do. Tell your mole not to contact the target. We'll do that from Headquarters. Contact me at your regular time."

After terminating two previous moles for non-performance, the Hand's third NIH mole finally touched someone who might be an unwitting Cognicom "leaker." The name: Electra Kittner. Her low-level Cognicom job and Guardian Party volunteer work made her ideal. *This is just what I've been looking for. I know someone who can convert her into an unsuspecting source of inside information.*

Since the year began, Electra approached everything with renewed purpose and determination, though she hid them under a cloak of sadness worn because of Doc's death. Her inner voice reminded that some good might come from the tragedy, for perhaps she could do something that would exemplify the Buddhist monk's universal answer.

Only an obituary mentioned her grandfather's death, and on the same day the paper ran a sketchy story about a two-car fatal crash. Only Electra would ever know the cause of the crash or its connection to Doc's execution. The police never contacted her again because they hadn't a shred of evidence regarding Doc's murder.

Electra continued helping Cognicom by brainstorming once a month with Su, after which she would then plant additional clues. Su was able to find them but often took longer than Electra liked. Keeping Su on track became a challenge, for even the great Su struggled with what Electra considered "back-of-the-envelope" calculations, so Electra found clever ways for Su to find the clues. But even though Su delivered some progress, the pressure on Mo ratcheted up faster than vaccine improvements because his bosses needed faster results to calm a growing political storm, a furor Electra was not prepared to engage. *Mo knew the game he was getting into. He's swimming with the sharks and it's not time for me to jump in. He's on his own.*

Although she didn't need to stay in the DC area now that Doc was gone, Electra decided to accept the GWU grad school research assistantship. Doing so made sense because she could take care of the house and combine thesis research with continued work on Cognicom projects. The university confirmed mid-March that she had been accepted into her chosen program and would coordinate with NIH—thanks to Mo—how to include NIH project work into her assistantship.

Electra had to meet with an appointed research advisor to outline what thesis topic she would pursue. Professor Ravenhill, a plucky middle-aged bioscientist, whose appearance matched that of a typical academic type, invited her to his campus office late March.

"Hello, Kittner. I have reviewed your transcript and Graduate Record Exam scores, and I see that you are qualified for our program. According to some of the professors who taught you, they applaud your hard work, but I have some reservations. Frankly, we have accepted a number of students whose grades and test scores are better than yours, and none of them have chosen a thesis topic as difficult as what you've picked. Would you please explain why you think you can do a thesis on consciousness? Don't you realize how controversial it is? Since I will be advising you, I don't want you to come a cropper. Failure would make me look bad and terminate your biotech career aspirations."

Electra had been planning for years how to answer this question. She even kept a document titled "My Thesis Planning Notes" that detailed what she would do and why she was uniquely qualified to do it. But she would never share it with anyone. She would explain to Professor Ravenhill only a dummied-down version to keep him from following her too closely.

"I have always been fascinated by the human brain. It's supposed to be the most complex object in the universe, and understanding cognition is the holy grail of neuroscience. I'm young and full of energy, so I'd like to take a shot at it. People tell me I have a knack for combining disciplines, and I have a good background in what's needed. I understand DNA and genetic engineering, nanotechnology, computers, and artificial intelligence. And once my PhD program starts, I'll carve out a specific topic I can focus on."

"Yes, yes. That sounds good, but you need to master four separate disciplines, tying them all together with advanced mathematics. No one's smart enough to do that. You'll have to be exceptionally lucky to come up with a contribution worthy of a PhD. But, tell you what, I'll let you try, even though I don't think you'll get anywhere. And I'm not going to waste my time watching you on a fool's errand. You can work on your own until you get frustrated and give up. If you do that soon enough, you can pick another topic and continue in the program. But there's a seven-year time limit."

"I'll follow your advice. Thank you for letting me try. I'll do my best."

"Very well. Be on your way. Come see me in the fall when you register for courses."

As she left his office, another pet saying flashed into the lightning brain. *I love it when a plan comes together.*

As Electra drove home, she compared the beginning of her relationship with Professor Ravenhill to that of a Nobel Prize-winning physicist from a hundred years ago. Early in his career, he had been highly recruited because of his reputation, and the advisor he picked called him aside after working together for a couple of weeks. But instead of being lavished with compliments, his advisor criticized him, saying there were better candidates. At first, the young physicist was devastated by the remarks, but then realized how fortunate he was to have an advisor who wouldn't hold back the truth. From that moment forward, the young physicist raised his level of excellence, eventually reaching the pinnacle of success. *I'm glad to have Professor Ravenhill for my advisor. He'll always tell me exactly how he feels, so I'll know if I'm telling just the right amount about what I'm doing. It's another Goldilocks game, not too much or too little, just the right amount so I keep my secret hidden.*

Electra had plenty of time to burrow into Guardian Party public relations classified files while doing volunteer work. She had just arrived at Guardian Party headquarters on an Early April afternoon when Gretchen motioned her into an unoccupied office. *Hmm, are they on to my snooping? Did I trip a security violation switch? If so, I'll plead ignorance and stay alert.* The chair was uncomfortable, but Electra didn't squirm as Gretchen started talking.

"We at the Guardian Party value our volunteers and always do our best to honor their wishes and privacy. We hope you like working with us because we appreciate how well you fit in. The happier you are, the better for all of us. That's why we like to know more about our people. And we just learned of your terrible tragedy last Christmas. Please accept our condolences." *So that's it. She's been snooping into my background. Let's see where she takes us.*

"Thank you. It was a shock, but I'm adjusting."

"We didn't realize that you worked on a Cognicom project. That must be exciting. How do you find the time for volunteer work?" *Aha. She wants to talk T-Plague.*

"Well, I just do some basic admin work. It's rather routine and doesn't take long. I like the work here better."

Gretchen smiled then said, "I'm glad you do because we'd like you to become more active. How would you like to join our current events discussion group? Its members meet twice a month to talk about what they're doing or what current events have caught their attention." *You can keep talking, but I know what my new role would be, Electra the leaker. I can make it a big win for me and keep you happily misinformed about what's actually going on.* Electra answered as soon as Gretchen finished.

"I'd like to join. I might not have much you'd consider interesting, but I sure would like to know what's going on."

"Wonderful. We'll make arrangements for you to come to the next meeting. If you would, please give me a list of days and times that work for you."

"How about next Wednesday?"

"Fine. That's when the next one is scheduled. Well now, I have to run to a meeting, so you and I will talk again next Wednesday. And on behalf of our Guardian Party, thanks for working with us." Electra got up to go.

"Thanks for the opportunity. If you need me, I'll be making fundraising calls." *And I'll keep digging where you don't know.*

Su was sure of one thing: Electra's "bio-field" had shifted abruptly to a different Electra on that horrid night last December, but the next day it had shifted back to the Electra she knew. Like most scientists, Su followed a materialist philosophy that claims matter is the fundamental substance in Nature, equivalent to energy and controlling all phenomena, which means atoms and molecules cause consciousness and emotions. Just as gravitational or electromagnetic fields emerge from clumps of atoms or charged particles, just as water waves emerge from Newtonian physics interaction of water molecules, just as sound waves emerge from the movement of air molecules, or just as organs emerge as the composite of cells, so must an organic phenomenon emerge from each brain's grand canonical ensemble of billions of cells and trillions of synapses, creating a bio-field that interacts with everything found in Nature and constructs cognition, emotion, intelligence, and self-awareness.

Other forms of life have emergent interactions that are obvious, while others might be so elusive that Nature's secrets might never be accessible to humans. Consider birds navigating by magnetic fields, sea creatures glowing or defending themselves by using electric currents, or insects thriving in their deadly biochemical world. The list is endless for primitive life forms; it must be even more fantastic for the human species, even though it is just beyond man's ability to comprehend. Just as it is impossible to capture lightning in a bottle, so is it impossible to capture a physical entity called the mind and separate it from the brain. Physicists readily admit that it is impossible to store a phenomenon caused by a field interaction.

Such are Su's conjectures that she shared with no one. They were too esoteric, too subtle for others to grasp. Compared with Su's rapier intelligence, most people are dull blades, except for Electra where the comparison reverses. *I'm disappointed it takes me so long to understand her, but Electra's becoming more patient, more empathetic. I don't believe in the spirit world or reincarnation, but if I did Electra would be Indira's reincarnation. She rekindles feelings I had only when Indira was alive.*

On a mid-April Saturday morning, Electra would soon be at Su's. The two would work in privacy because Su had pushed Adom out the door fifteen minutes ago so he'd be on time for his African immigrant volunteer work. She hurried to the front door when hearing a knock, anxious for Electra to explain vaccine solution paths.

The duo worked at the kitchen table for two hours. Electra brought with her two sets of diagrams complete with biochemistry formulas and equations: one for Su's I-Vac project, the other for Adom's S-Vac. Poor Su had to struggle through two separate solutions that were built on extensions to theories she barely understood. Electra sensed Su's frustration and changed course.

"Let's take a break and do some role reversal. Do you remember the original sci-fi flick *The Day the Earth Stood Still?*"

"I'm not as much a sci-fi aficionado as you. I remember it vaguely, so please refresh my memory."

"The black and white original is even better than the remake. It's all about a visitor from a super-smart world who comes to warn Earthlings they must become peaceful, or Earth will be destroyed.

He wants America's smartest scientist to get the message across to world leaders, but first he has to prove to the scientist that he's for real, so he corrects a mistake the scientist made in an enormous formula written on a blackboard. Well, I'm going to role-play both parts using my own twist of humor. See what you think."

Electra's performance lasted nearly ten minutes, containing dialogue and gestures that proved to be hilarious. Su could picture a study session pitting a crabby old scientist who thought he knew it all against an impatient, arrogant space visitor who considered the human race inferior. Both characters had sarcastic wits that made for a clever ending. Scientist and alien become best friends forever and decide to engage caffeine lovers in a spirited debate at a local coffee shop about orders of infinity. And they're booted out the door because only mathematicians or philosophers worry about infinity.

"Bravo! That was priceless. I wish I had recorded your performance on my smart phone. And I get it. With a little more coaching, I'll play the scientist part better."

"You're a quick study, so I know you'll be able to explain to Adom what his team needs to do."

"I'll do just that, but I want to think through all you've shown me before I talk to him. And now, let's have lunch. You can sample my new double fudge brownies. And I found some photos you haven't seen before. We can look at them after lunch."

"Perfecto. You are the brownie-meister." The brownies were among the best ever.

On the drive home, Electra thought about her special relationship with Su while basking in the morning's afterglow. *Both of us keep feelings to ourselves. And we're subtle and nuanced, so it's easy for us to know what the other's thinking.* She recalled a recently intercepted Guardian Party public relations memo that cleverly summarized how to keep messages private:

> "Don't write if you can talk.
> Don't talk if you can whisper.
> Don't whisper if you can nod.
> Don't nod if you can wink."

Electra and Su were able to take this to the next level:
"Don't wink if you can think."

Electra didn't tell Su the darker side of the sci-fi flick. The visitor is killed by soldiers but is brought back to life by his indestructible robot. His stern warning finally crashes through to the world leaders and there is hope the Earth won't be destroyed. Electra preferred not to bother Su with analogies.

A sudden emotional twinge struck her. *I care more about Su than maybe I should. Now I have to watch out for her too. What'll I do if I accidently put her at risk? I don't know. I'll have to let the lightning brain figure it out.*

As Electra's undergraduate career drew to a close, she took a course that became one of her favorites, Science Capstone, a series of weekly lectures providing perspectives on how scientific findings fit within a broader context of other academic disciplines or society. In an early lecture, the instructor included additional topics Electra found especially relevant. "The Science of Religion" session discussed why modern theologians grudgingly accept Darwinism, and why they finally have the right cause-and-effect relationship: Earth's characteristics caused Man and not vice-versa. The same can be said for the Second Law of Thermodynamics. For too long, theologians pointed to this law, which says entropy (a measure of disorder) always increases. The instructor posed a question often raised by theologians: if this were so, how could Life appear on Earth if not for God? Living organisms exhibit much order, such as cell walls and distinct organs, and this decreases entropy. He answered the question by explaining that Earth is not a closed system; entropy on Earth can decrease as long as entropy somewhere else in the universe increases.

Another lecture described the current state of high energy physics, comparing it to the conditions in 2015-2017 when scientists detected the Higgs boson—referred to as the God particle. When it was discovered, hopes ran high that it would confirm a Unified Field Theory equation which would explain how all forces in the Universe arise. The equation looked promising, but subsequent projects (Dark Matter Probe and the Electron International Linear Collider) failed to replace String Theory and its 11-dimensional representation of the Universe. Furthermore, none of the 21st century models could handle the conjecture that time does not exist, but is merely a mental construct that allows events to be ordered. Today, physicists hope once again another new theory will point them in the right direction. The speaker was candid, pointing out that such hopes have often recurred and suggesting that high energy physics is no longer a science but a religion because it is based on faith alone; no observable events or experiments could verify or falsify competing theories.

Electra's favorite lecture explored how current inter-disciplinary research in neuroscience, nanotechnology, and artificial intelligence is paving the way to a promising future. The speaker connected these developments with two classic books: *1984* by George Orwell, and *Brave New World* by Aldous Huxley. Orwell worried that too much computer-generated information controlled by a ruthless government could lead to totalitarianism. Huxley worried that psychotropic drugs and genetic modification might destroy the fabric that makes us human. Yes, these are risks, but the United States must not fall behind China's R&D efforts. And the speaker closed his talk by mentioning legendary physicist Richard Feynman, who said that there's plenty of room at the bottom—the cellular level—to make original contributions. He and many brilliant 20th century scientists foresaw much progress awaiting those who were able to combine the three disciplines showcased in the speaker's talk. Electra had already picked them for her graduate thesis.

She respected the instructor's balanced assessment of technology's promises. One of the later lectures struck a cautionary note regarding the future of technological progress. Human nature evolves too slowly to deal with paradigm-shifting breakthroughs. We should expect lifestyles a hundred years from now to be recognizable because mankind's hierarchy of needs from lowest to highest—Physical, Security, Social, Esteem, Self-Actualization— is timeless. What will be different is the array of new hedonic, entertainment, or time-saving products and services made available thanks to two driving developments: computer chip-based artificial intelligence and DNA-modifying neuroscience. Many of the prototypes hyped in futuristic publications or videos will become a reality because the military is building advanced weapons systems incorporating these concepts, but even these must abide by the laws of physics, so we shouldn't expect time travel, wormholes, or aliens to arrive soon. And in the long-long term, mankind must decide what to do if it wants to preserve what it means to be human. Futurists are thinking about that now, even though decision deadlines are as far out as some of the conjectures. The instructor ended his talk pointing to a troubling possibility: machines won't take over the world and terminate homo sapiens in the next hundred years, but humanity could pull the plug on itself if nations don't cooperate.

Graduation from college is a major milestone for most students. Not so for Electra, but she pretended anyway because Su and Jennifer had arranged a graduation party, inviting Christi, Robin, and their parents, plus Adom and Mo. All of them wanted to come to the graduation ceremony, which meant Electra would be obligated to march wearing cap and gown and sit on an uncomfortable folding chair propped up on rain-soaked grass while listening to dull speeches. So much for pomp and circumstance. But the party would be worth the wet shoes. There would be a luncheon at an elegant restaurant before the late-afternoon ceremony, followed by cake and conversation at the Conklins.

No wet grass dampened any of the graduates because the early June weather cooperated, and the Conklin's get-together put an exclamation point on the day. It pleased Electra that her friends liked one another, especially Mo and Russell Conklin. Electra and Su chatted at length with Christi and Robin, catching up on latest adventures. Robin was doing well at the Curtis Institute, while Christi—with her mother's guidance—would graduate next year from high school, after which she would attend DC's Fashion Design Institute. Jennifer used Electra's graduation to show Christi why college degrees or vocational certifications matter.

"Look at all the talented women in our group. They are using education to build bright futures."

"Yes Mother, I learned the lesson. And don't leave yourself out of the discussion. Do they know about the certification programs you plan to take?"

Electra asked, "Are you going to build on your nursing background? You have lots of options. And now's the time to do it, now that you don't have to worry about Christi running off on some rock star tour."

"I'm planning to combine nursing with nutrition and fitness counseling, and I'll work with a couple of local clinics. And today, with all the appetite-suppressing drugs and surgical procedures, I can tell people how to get fit and look good, especially when I include proven weight-loss diets and exercise programs. And if NIH or someone comes up with T-Plague vaccines and treatment, I'll add those survivors to my client base." Adom continued talking about Jennifer's last observation.

"Hey Jenn, not to worry about the T-Plague. Thanks to Su, we're finally making some progress." Mo and Russell heard Adom and they too joined in, with Mo only half-joking.

"Adom's right, but he's not allowed to say anything else. We're all sworn to secrecy about what we're doing. If he does, Russell and I will have to muzzle him." Electra detected a hint of tension in Russell's expression, so she redirected the conversation.

"That won't help Adom much, because he's busy talking with all the folks in his newest volunteer project. Why don't you tell us what Su lined up?"

"You all know me. All I need is a little prodding from Su to get moving. After my volunteer work with the Middle East group sort of petered out, she lined me up with an African immigrant group. She thought my Kenyan heritage would give my volunteering more staying power, and as usual, she's right. I like what I do and the people I meet. Mo, since we're all playing show and tell, why don't you tell us about your latest air reserves stuff?"

Mo never bragged or talked much about himself, but this evening he saw no harm talking about his hobby because he was among friends. "Flying is my one big passion other than my career. I flew helicopters when I was in the Navy, and have been doing so in Air

Reserves ever since. The latest military choppers are unbelievably sophisticated, many needing dual pilots, one for flying and the other for weapons control. I was recently selected for advanced training on dual pilot choppers. And choppers are best for me. I meet the age and fitness standards. I plan to keep flying until I get too heavy for lift-off, and that's a big motivator for me to exercise.

Russell said, "Mo, I know you have a lot of hidden talents, but I didn't know you were still active in Air Reserves. You're a surprising fellow."

As evening shadows lengthened, Jennifer called for everyone to gather at a table holding graduation cards and gifts. Su spoke for everyone.

"I know that Electra has learned a great deal during her college years, but I think most of the credit goes to Electra, not to her professors. In fact, I believe her professors could learn a lot from her. She has great expectations, and someday she will electrify the world. May serendipity allow us to be there when she does." Russell opened more champagne, then proposed a toast.

"To Electra and the women with us tonight. May their futures be bright."

Electra added, "And to all the men in our lives, past and present."

Grad school plans kicked off immediately. Although courses would start in September, the research piece started in July under Su's supervision because her assistantship extended NIH activities that had been part of her undergraduate program. She worked several days a week at Su's lab, which left ample time for socializing or working at Guardian Party headquarters. The combination seemed too good, which triggered a message from her inner voice. *No matter how much you wish, you cannot make good times last. And no matter how bad the situation, you can always make it better. Focus on now and enjoy each moment.*

Electra used some of her extra time to study ahead in computer science related areas because they would be needed in her graduate degree focus area. Her brain effortlessly handled abstract thinking, so she simultaneously devoured and applied what she learned when creating novel computer hacking apps. She saw in herself personality traits shared with those attracted to Cyberspace. *Cyber-people are smart and logical, possessing tremendous powers of concentration, thriving in a virtual reality under their control, avoiding others when they want to be alone. They prefer a solipsistic existence inside their brain, a much safer place than the three-dimensional world swirling about. How remarkable that technological progress has created a Cyberworld of opportunities for a whole group of people who until recently were misunderstood and underappreciated. Lots of autistic people have found a place in Cyberspace.*

Today Electra was in Cyberspace not to avoid others but to hunt for moles, working on Guardian Party fundraising while constructing a mole hunting license. Though hacking into Guardian Party computer networks was not what her boss Gretchen expected, Electra rationalized hiving off time for hunting. *Companies know people do personal tasks, like shopping or texting friends, while on the job. The smart companies make it easy for employees to do it quickly and get back to work. And hunting for moles isn't hurting the Guardian Party.*

By late afternoon, Electra completed the license and read it one more time. *This will work when I start hunting for moles later this week. It keeps track of where to look, what to look for, and how to hunt them down. I have a lot of rails to track, but I've got my hunt organized. And everyone except Su and Adom are possible moles. Electra's inner voice pointed out an obvious target. I match the mole characteristics! Good that no one else is hunting on my license. And if anyone is looking for me, I know how to stay invisible.*

Electra used some of August to refine her own school of philosophy. The past year's experiences added hands-on understanding to what she had already studied. *I know enough about major philosophers and philosophies to grade the current crop. Postmodernism and most of its successor philosophies get a failing grade. They merely impersonate what philosophy should be. And most philosophers today have relinquished to scientists the premier role for explaining the natural world. Instead of embracing new tools of science and mathematics, philosophers have taken a subjective bypass into their private worlds of contemplation, shutting out obvious facts they don't like. Nothing they have to say helps a person get through the day.*

The current crop of philosophy professors never struggled through Kant's convoluted sentences or grappled with Wittgenstein's opaque writing. They're tucked away in academia, proclaiming ethics without ever holding a job that got their hands dirty. Wait until the T-Plague or terrorism crashes through their ivy-covered walls. Then let's see how they handle ethical dilemmas. At least I know how to balance the equations and can live with my decisions. I'll rely on facts and reason rather than falling through a faith-based infinite regress leading to a non-existent prime mover, or even worse, into a nihilistic void.

Like most post-modern philosophers, Electric knows the universe is indifferent to Man. Man is not the center of the Universe; there is no grand purpose waiting to unfold. But unlike most, who sink into gloomy doubt or inaction, she embraces a pragmatic view to life's unanswerable questions. Her philosophy seeks meaning in our biological prime directive, which is simply to go on living by balancing our primal needs with our higher aspirations, accomplishing worthwhile goals that each person must select. Her philosophy would command a person to think deeply enough to "Know Thyself"—a famous quotation inscribed on the Temple of Apollo at Delphi—but not so deeply that one can't find a way back to the surface.

She even gave her brand of philosophy a whimsical name, a name only a philosopher would admire: Neurosci-Extended Deconstructed Emergent Post-Pragmatism. The recipe is simpler than its name. Take those rational elements articulated in Kant's *Critique of Pure Reason* that were extended to produce Pragmatism, and adjust according to the limitations deduced by Deconstructionism, then add elements resurrected from Emergence Theory. Next, account for the limitations of high energy physics, the implications of neuroscience, and apply commonsense reason, the end result yielding a philosophy that offers helpful, optimistic advice that can guide one through life.

Electra never forced her philosophy on anyone. She neither debated nor criticized what others believe, but always respected other views, especially when the person holding them wasn't blindly following an obsolete ideology. She kept her philosophy to herself, always ready to improve it whenever reasonable facts come to light.

Electra followed her own advice by spending only enough time on philosophy so she would be ready for the fall term. As Labor Day approached, she was set to charge into September and through another passage on her journey to an uncertain future, but a future she would try her best to control.

October's T-Plague outbreaks in New York, Washington, and Los Angeles, blew away September's optimism, puncturing the calm and stressing testing centers to the limit. The media reported that windows in several New York medical centers had been smashed, fueled no doubt by rumors that dispensaries were restocking smart pills with placebos. All the bad publicity increased black market demand for smart pills and kept doom and gloom blogging sites buzzing.

Once again, an outbreak crashed into Electra's world; Su had contracted the T-Plague. Adom took her to the lab's testing facility after she collapsed at work. Fear of another containment breach gripped the facility, but a Healthguard Hazards Team confirmed that hadn't happened, so the lab remained open. Only a handful of researchers knew Su was assigned top priority treatment at an NIH intensive care unit, because if she didn't recover quickly, Cognicom progress would grind to a halt.

Electra shuddered when Mo told her the news. Even top priority treatment would be inadequate because available vaccines or smart pills didn't work. *I need to do for Su what I did for Christi, but I'll use my advanced formulations, and I'll get help from Mo and Adom if I can get them to play along.* She cornered them in a conference room and made a suggestion Mo had to run with if he wanted to keep Cognicom running.

"If Su is out of action, so is Cognicom, so let's do this. Why not treat her with experimental vaccines?" Mo liked what he heard but didn't know what to do, so he asked Adom for advice.

"I haven't a clue how to make experimental vaccines. I've simply taken Su's instructions and given them to my researchers." That wasn't what Electra wanted to hear. *This conversation is going the wrong way. It's time for me to point Mo in the right direction.*

"I've been working more closely with Su than Adom has, and I've compounded her experimental vaccines. If you can set me up as her caregiver, I can sneak them in."

Mo asked, "Will they work? Are they safe?"

"Yes, on both counts. Su says they're ready to go. But we have to act before the virus causes too much neural entanglement."

"So, how should we proceed?"

"Let's try this. Use your clout to place me as her twenty-four seven caregiver. Tell them she's the only person able to keep Cognicom moving forward, and I'm her research assistant she wants at her side to relay to Adom what the teams must do. I already know caregiver protocols and can play along with the ICU nurses. You can move her home as soon as she's no longer contagious, and Adom can take over for me." Electra waited for a response, guessing Adom would want to jump into the fray, but she was wrong.

"We can't do this. It's too risky. We could get sick. What if the stuff doesn't work? We could kill Su. What if we get caught? We could lose our jobs, even go to jail." Mo looked disgusted.

"For Chrissake, Adom! When are you going to show some backbone? You live with Su. Electra, are you sure the stuff will work?" "It will, and it's up to you to convince Adom to play along or step aside." Mo took a deep breath to settle himself.

"I hope you want to pitch in, but if you don't, I'll come up with documented reasons to fire you immediately for cause."

"OK, OK. Jeez, you know I love Su. I'm sorry I'm such a coward sometimes."

"Uncle Adom, you're not a coward. Let's do all we can to get Su back."

"She's right, Adom. Come on, let's get our plan in motion. Electra, we'll phone as soon as we're ready to get you into ICU. Better get your supplies and write down instructions for Adom. We're outta here."

Electra was ready and, while waiting for Mo's call, had made all preparations, so the odds should be in Su's favor. *Mo's diplomacy and Cognicom Senior Manager clout can cut through any red tape. I'm glad*

Adom answered the call when Mo read him the riot act, and I can handle the nurses. Ninety minutes later, Mo's call came through.

"Mo here. We're all set. We're coming to get you." While adjusting her game face Electra's inner voice spoke. *Congratulations. Another plan's coming together.*

In retrospect, Su's rescue mission was more stressful in planning than in execution. Once Mo and Adom were onboard and in action, the plan unfolded to perfection. ICU welcomed any support Mo could commandeer and were so overloaded they let Electra handle Su by herself. It was much easier this time to perform caregiving because she didn't have to hide what she was up to. The nurses knew her role and gave all the support she needed. Su was conscious most of the time, drifting into fitful sleep rather than coma. She was released two days later to home health care administered by Adom and supervised by her regular physician, and she was back in action late the following week.

Thanks to Electra, Su had dodged what might have been a brain-numbing bullet. But Electra was not in the clear just yet. Thanks to Healthguard's intrusive new regulations, anyone working at NIH labs who came in contact with anyone contagious had to undergo testing before coming back to work. This included brain imaging and DNA testing. Her grandfather warned years ago that Electra's extraordinary brain would remain undetected in all testing except the one for DNA. Given the high security level maintained at all NIH labs, there would be no exceptions, not even for Electra, so now she needed to devise a plan to avoid a bullet aimed at her.

Electra decided to call Zeta Lab's testing facility to find out what she was dealing with, confirming its location and the name of its technician, a fellow named Joe Miese. According to the "On the Go" section in a recent NIH newsletter, she learned that Joe had won a Labor Day dance competition. She would call him after checking his background, looking for a way to recruit him into a new game aptly named "Fool the Tester." *I know how to rig the game. Substitute a bogus blood sample for the one Joe takes. I'm glad I saved the ones Doc used when faking my test results. Let's find out how Joe can help. I can use my hunting license to practice hacking while checking him out.*

Electra hacked into the lab's H.R. files, confirming what she had heard; companies share more data about its employees with cooperating government agencies or social media sites than is widely known. Twenty minutes later, Joe's profile emerged: college biology major (3.2/4.0 GPA), had worked at the lab for three years (average employee ratings, needs to reduce days missed), hobbies include dancing, fitness, and tennis. Judging from a photo and personal profile, he was a good looking, dark haired, six feet one-inch guy sporting an athletic build.

Next, she confirmed using social media what she thought: Joe likes females. Comments posted by ladies he dated joked about great moves on and off the dance floor. Electra had all she needed for her first move. She called Joe that afternoon, telling enough of the truth to get a pre-test appointment the next day.

Electra checked her appearance before meeting Joe. When she wanted to, she could look subtly yet provocatively sexy. The mirror on the wall reflected an Electra that would catch the eye of any guy. She was ready to be a flirtatious teaser.

Joe jumped to attention when Electra walked in and cast her line. "Hi, is this the place to come for the scanning and DNA testing?"

"Yes, it is. You sure don't look like the next person on the list. You can't be Rex Gilmore." Electra grinned pertly.

"Oh no, my name is Electra Kittner. I called you yesterday, and you said to come in at this time, and you'd show me what you'll do to me." She coyly leaned against the counter and asked, "It won't hurt, will it?" Joe could feel a hormonal jolt that spoke hello, you sexy thing. "It won't hurt at all. For the brain scan all you do is wear a helmet with built-in electrode sensors. Won't take but five minutes. Then I'll draw a blood sample—no pain because I have great hands—and you'll be on your way." Electra needed to see where the samples were stored.

"Do you do all that here?"

"Sure, let me take you into the testing room so you can see for yourself." Joe walked her to another room which contained a sink, scanner equipment, patient examining table, and a desk with chairs.

Off to the right was a locked room where Electra thought he would keep the samples refrigerated until being tested.

"Here's where we do it all. Want to try on the helmet?" "Thanks, but not now. It'll mess up my hair." Will you really test my blood when I'm here? That sounds sort of creepy." Electra rolled her eyes and smiled coquettishly. Joe had taken the bait and was hooked.

"Oh no. I'll put your sample with all the others, and another lab technician will do the testing. Let me show you where we put them." He opened the room using his I.D. badge, and it was just what she thought. It contained a large refrigerator containing racks to hold samples and supplies. Perfect for her plan. She knew enough and was ready to make her exit.

"Thanks for the tour. I feel much better now that I've met you. I'm always kind of nervous when I first meet someone." Joe put his arm around her shoulder as he walked her towards the door.

"Don't you worry, I have great hands. And if it hurts I'll buy you dinner. Hey, how about we go out afterwards? I'll make you my last appointment, and I know a great place for Friday night. Come back tomorrow at six."

"Dinner sounds nice. Is what I'm wearing OK?" "You look great, just like that."

"Well OK, it's a date. See you tomorrow."

Electra wore sexier clothes and more makeup the next day just in case Joe had second thoughts. Then she packed her shoulder bag with everything needed to guarantee getting test results she wanted. One final glance in the mirror and off she went.

Electra deliberatively arrived five minutes late so Joe had time to prepare. He had already closed the blinds and locked the door, so she tapped lightly. He immediately opened the door.

"Come on in. I'm all set and hope you are too. Let's go into the testing room." Joe was all business during the procedures. *This is a snap. His scanning equipment is the same as Doc's. And he does have good hands. I didn't feel a thing when he took the blood sample.* Joe finished labeling the sample, then showed Electra where in the refrigerator he placed it.

"And that's a wrap. How about we head out for dinner first, dancing later? I'm hungry." Electra grinned mischievously when Joe took her hand.

"You do have great hands, and if you're hungry, how about an appetizer before we leave?"

"I'm always hungry. What would you like to serve?" Electra slowly pulled away.

Well, I'm sort of hot in these clothes, so let's play a game. You let me get more comfortable by myself, and you do the same. I'll let you know when to come in."

"I can handle that. Call me when you're ready." As soon as Joe closed the door, Electra removed from her bag what she needed to mix two glasses of a popular mood elevator drink, adding a date knockout drug to Joe's. Then she stripped to nothing but an unbuttoned blouse and bikini thong. Electra was ready to play and ready to stop when Joe had enough. While sitting on the desk and coyly crossing her legs, she called out to Joe.

"What's keeping you? Come on in."

Joe came in ready to play, wearing only long pants and an unbuttoned shirt. To enhance the experience, he had already popped a couple of sex pills, the kind Christi had been given several years ago. Joe could already feel the effects when he reached for Electra.

"Not so fast, big boy. Let's have a mood elevator warm-up." My party friends say Parti-Play is a great icebreaker."

"I can give you something better. I just popped a couple of pills. Want to try one?" Warning signals went off in Electra's brain. She wouldn't take any because she didn't know what the interaction between pills and knockout drug might be. She would watch and wait, so she declined his offer but continued smiling as they clinked glasses and drank.

It took nearly five minutes for the interaction to take effect. By that time, Joe had placed Electra on the examining table and was removing the rest of his clothes. He was so focused on Electra's stunning body he was unaware of his fuzzy thinking and loss of coordination. Suddenly, while trying to remove one foot from his slacks, Joe's world tilted backwards and he toppled to the floor. Electra leaped into action.

Her first concern was for Joe, so she checked vital signs: pulse elevated, pupils dilated, but he wasn't hyperventilating. He wasn't in trouble, so she raced for his employee badge, then removed a bogus blood sample from her bag and swapped it with the sample in the refrigerator. Then she retrieved his clothes, removed all evidence of her being with him, and after getting dressed, soaked a cloth in cold water to revive Joe. Ten minutes later Joe was able to sit up and talk, though he sounded like someone coming out of a drunken stupor. His thinking was muddled, but with Electra's help was able to put on his clothes. She could tell from his mumbled answers to her questions that Joe couldn't remember what had been going on, so Electra ended the game. She pulled the room's emergency alarm and vanished before security guards arrived.

Electra drove home in satisfied solitude, glad to have today's excitement over. Since she knew Joe's cell phone number, she would call him tomorrow, filling in whatever memory gaps needed plugging. *No matter what he remembers, I'm in the clear. I like Joe, and since I can go back to the lab next week, I think I'll visit him. Under different circumstances, we could play different games. And perhaps I'll flip a coin to see if he wins.*

CHAPTER 32
November 2114

"Drilling into Danger"
(Thread 2 Chapter 19)

ELECTRA'S FIRST TERM IN graduate school proceeded according to a plan her advisor thought he directed but was actually controlled by Electra. Professor Ravenhill had approved all her courses but warned that he would spend no time advising until she picked an easier thesis topic that better suited her ability. *That's just what I want. He's out of the way and won't meddle. I have complete access to his state-of-the-art lab equipment that rivals what I have at Cognicom, and I have a work station in an office occupied by me and three other grad students who've been working for Ravenhill for four years. They're nice enough, but since we have little in common they leave me alone.*

Electra worked whenever she wished, and since no one intruded, by the end of November she had hiked far into the details of her thesis, telling no one about her breakthroughs.

Though first term courses were a breeze, she pretended otherwise to fit in with the other students, who needed to form survival study groups, and she joined several that invited her. They taught her more about professional relationships among peers, and she taught them enough to follow the textbooks. And she also witnessed firsthand how difficult mathematics is, even for the best students.

Electra had begun college-level study while in high school, and in preparation read cognitive psychology's gold-standard book:

Thinking, Fast and Slow. The Nobel Prize-winning author Daniel Kahneman explained that evolution had equipped man to think fast (intuitively),but not slow (logically and rationally).As a result, even the brightest are intimidated by numbers and struggle even more today than a hundred years ago because today's technological advances require at the graduate level superior mathematical skills. Not so for Electra. Her neural circuitry let her cruise through the most advanced subjects in math and science.

Electra didn't need to take any computer science courses because she treated computer programming as a tool she could learn on her own as needed. She would need advanced computing algorithms for dealing with DNA-related biotech research and its artificial intelligence interfaces, and had already scoped out her beyond-state-of-the-art programming techniques, so she audited a graduate computer science course, sitting in the back and keeping quiet, simply gauging how far ahead she was. Neither she nor the students liked the arrogant instructor, but at least he did cover the latest developments in quantum computing.

It was clear to Electra that quantum computer hardware far exceeded the latest software techniques. Its deep-layered matrix of supercooled parallel-processing microchips could store 0 or 1 "qu-bits" in spin states of individual atoms, and it used quantum mechanical superposition, entanglement, and tunneling principles to push computing speed limits beyond what the National Institute of Science and Technology had thought possible. *This fits me to a T. I can use existing hardware, and all I have to do is use my math skills to write better programs. And since I know math cold, I'll use my superior programming techniques to write apps that are better than anyone's.*

Electra decided to audit one more lecture near the end of the term. By that time over half the students had dropped the course, and those that remained had been so thoroughly dissed by the instructor that Electra decided it was time to teach him some humility. As he concluded his lecture, smirking that anyone who knows what a number is should have no trouble working the homework, Electra raised her hand.

"Yes, you in the back. What's your problem?"

"It might help the class if you gave us a definition of what you mean by number."

"Are you trying to be funny? Everyone knows what a number is." *He took a bite out of my favorite apple. Let's see how he likes the rest of it.*

"Actually, the mathematical definition is rather precise. A number is a member of a well-ordered set in which each element equals the set of its strict predecessors. But perhaps you prefer the looser definition computer scientists use. A number is simply an object that has properties and operations. In either case, could you explain how we extend this definition to obtain rational or real numbers?" *That'll put him on his heels.*

"Uh, I'm not sure. Where are you going with this?"

"I simply want to point out that you can use equivalence classes and Dedekind cuts to go beyond the counting numbers. In fact, we can extend numbers into the domain of the hyperreals. Just think, there are classes of numbers smaller than any real number but greater than zero, and there are also classes greater than any real number but less than Omega, which I'm sure you know is the symbol for the first order infinity. But I forgot. Computer scientists like you have brains that never deal with infinities. After all, computers, no matter how complicated you make them, are still finite state machines. I apologize for asking the question, but maybe you can clarify your understanding for us next week." *I can tell the students like to see him squirm, but I'll stop grilling him. It's time to leave.* Electra disappeared before anyone saw her get up and go.

December 21st was Electra's last day working at Guardian Headquarters until January because it would be closed for the holidays. She was very successful that afternoon, obtaining donations from twenty new members. Too bad her mole hunt was not as rewarding.

Electra's search through Emails and organization charts revealed nothing useful; maybe her search criteria needed modification, or maybe she needed to tap into different Email directories. She hadn't come across any trail that might lead to hidden Guardian Party agendas, so she would have to drill deeper elsewhere. As she powered down her workstation, she rehearsed what to say at today's current events group meeting that Gretchen would lead.

Electra listened patiently as Gretchen went around the table, asking each person to share what events or topics might help the Party build on momentum gained from the November election. Gretchen smiled when it was Electra's turn, knowing how well Electra was fitting in and thinking what a dedicated volunteer she had become.

"You always have interesting things to tell us. And I'll bet there was lots of excitement at your lab when some of your associates contracted T-Plague. How are things going there now?" Electra was surprised, but didn't show it. *They've got a mole burrowing close to Cognicom because the lab scare had been hushed up. I better change my script.*

"Hi, Gretchen, and hi everyone. Wow, we had a real scare at the lab a month ago, but things are pretty much back to normal. I don't know all the details, but I think one of the team leaders came down with T-Plague. From what I hear, the teams are finally making a little progress again. Maybe I can find out more and tell you at our next meeting. And Gretchen, I was thinking that all the stuff our group comes up with might be helpful to our public relations department. Why, when I read or watch their campaign promos, I see how they connect with current events hitting the public. So, maybe I could be our liaison. I could put together summaries after each meeting and go over it with P.R. people." Electra paused, waiting for Gretchen to bite.

"That's a great idea. Too bad our P.R. group isn't at this location; if they were, you and I would talk with them right now. They work at our building that houses Securityguard departments, so here's what we'll do. After the Holidays, I'll set up a meeting. They'll know how to fit you in."

Gretchen talked with Electra afterwards, making arrangements for visiting with P.R. As Electra drove home, she marveled at how useful the meeting had been. *Someone in P.R. must be connected to Party leaders. Drilling down there should take me up the organization chart, and that could lead to people who know about hidden agendas.*

And I'll be closer to Securityguard. I'll burrow there to locate their covert operations. Good hunting on both counts.

Electra's holiday break gave her more time for routine chores. Household maintenance gave her pleasure, for she considered herself the custodian responsible for any and all repairs she thought its owners would want. The house belonged in spirit to her father and grandfather. She decided not to redecorate but instead to keep it meticulously groomed so the house would be ready for their return. It was only a game, but it was dedicated to their memory. No one but her inner voice kept score.

Electra's inner voice is Indira, her constant companion she can talk with whenever she needs guidance. Sometimes in dreams, the lightning brain would create vivid images and dialogues, though none as dramatic as the "Christmas Carol" visit last year. She trusted her brain to know when a reprise would be needed. And always, her inner voice gave comfort and joy.

Electra used the break to drill into the cell phones she had taken from the terrorists last year. She hadn't forgotten about them, but until now hadn't made time to take them apart. All the while, her terrible resolve for vengeance smoldered subliminally.

After a Sunday morning run, Electra started picking the phones apart, building a list of numbers to call. Then she hacked into cell phone databases, matching name and address with numbers. She would start calling once she developed a conversation script. *I'm done with the phones. I'll make them Mo's anonymous Christmas present. He and his CIA contacts might like to pick them apart too.*

Electra's social calendar bustled during the Holidays. She spent Christmas Eve with Su and Adom, Christmas Day with the Conklins, and shopped the malls with Robin the week after, even going to a New Year's Eve dance party with Joe, her newest addition to a select list of males she used for keeping hormones balanced.

Even during the gaiety of the season, the public felt T-Plague undercurrents swirling about. People noticed—especially for

service industries—that when employees in T-Plague remission return to work, they aren't as sharp as before. They worked slower and made more mistakes. The doom and gloom blogging sites trumpeted decreasing service and increasing infrastructure failures, most apparent in power or communications networks. Website comments highlighted the public's frustration and hopes that next year the Administration will make things better.

As she did every New Year's Day, Electra drew up plans for the coming year, readying them for school, Cognicom, and volunteer work. It was only for her social world that the darker, more dangerous aspects of current events made planning difficult. *It's time to limit social activity a bit. I don't want anyone to detect my freakish secret. And I don't want to worry about other people. Things will look better once we get rid of the T-Plague, but until then I have to watch my step when navigating my social world.*

Electra wasn't the only one making plans that New Year's Day. So was a person known only to select members of the Opposition Group, and then known only by the codename Mrs. T. After months of indecision, its steering committee finally appointed someone to build a covert operations group, a person codenamed Mrs. T.

Today she expected a call from the Bad Boy, a codename for her field contacts handler. The call would be brief because all she needed was to let him know he was good to go for what he must accomplish quickly.

"This is Mrs. T. Please identify."

"This is the Bad Boy, ready for instructions."

"We need you to place your moles as quick as you can at our top targets. Tell me what they are."

"Current Admin, CIA, Guardian Party, NIH."

"Good. Burrow as close as you can. We need to play catch-up, so play fast but not loose. Do you copy?"

"Copy that."

"Good. Call again as planned. Over."

Nor were they alone. The new leader for CIA's Project Death Shield—Elliot Spitzdieck—was fabricating a story to tell his team at next week's meeting. They knew he and his handpicked replacements were coming in to shake things up and to mold them into an aggressive high-performance team that would infiltrate deeper into top targets: Opposition Group, Guardian Party, domestic terrorist sleeper cells. T-Plague fallout had increased the urgency for team members to deliver, and if they didn't, their heads would roll. Elliot grinned to himself. If he delivers, opponents' heads would roll.

Electra charged through January. She dropped clues for Su, found several solid leads from the cell phone list, and heard from Gretchen that they would meet in February with the P.R. department. Her inner voice commented that at this rate, she could do her new year's planning for next year in six months. Mo's early February meeting added to the momentum.

"Looks like we're moving in the right direction. Su, would you please summarize what we need to do to keep progress moving?"

"It's time you turn both S-Vac and I-Vac projects completely over to Adom. We have pretty solid solution paths under way. Let him shepherd them along. Assign me tech team leader only for R-Vac. And when you do, please make Electra the R-Vac data collection clerk. And please do not share with anyone details of my or Electra's background. No one needs to know."

"Fair enough. Adom, will you be able to handle two projects?" Mo thought he could because Adom's backbone and commitment had strengthened ever since Su had recovered from the T-Plague.

"I think I can, and Su is still my number one consultant when I need a push."

"Good. I'll let the R-Vac team know immediately. I'll tell the H.R. department to put the current tech lead and data clerk on the bench. Electra, will you be able to handle more data collection duties? You'll have to go through more training." *Of course I can, but let's not overplay my hand. I'll nod and speak slowly.*

"I think I can. Maybe I can find some data Su can use." Enough said. Mo ended the meeting.

"I'll let you know when you can get a workstation in the R-Vac lab. And I'll get you slotted into training. By the way, I'll end the meeting with a bit of a mystery. Someone sent me a late Christmas present, three cell phones with a cryptic note telling me to have the CIA check for terrorist calls. I'll tell you if they find anything, but please keep quiet about this. Well, that's all, so I'm off to brief Bobbi."

That evening, Electra followed up cell phone leads by surfing the Web for a cross-referenced local Muslim center. What she found looked promising, so she would drive by in preparation for visiting. Later that week she surfed the Web to learn more about Islamic centers.

Muslims often refer to them as masjids or mosques, and they are controlled by an Imam who is usually a prayer-leading, self-proclaimed teacher of the Muslim faith. She also researched the role of women, discovering that the popular image of control and oppression are antithetical to Muhammad's teachings. Historians argue that male-dominated power struggles corrupted women's roles to satisfy political agendas, and although today some mullahs proclaim that women have a rightful role, Islam remains a patriarchy. Electra doubted a rational woman of Modernity would find Islam a kinder and gentler place. *I better learn about Muslim women dress codes. If I'm gonna visit, I better dress the part.And I better learn about Islam's attitudes towards women.*

Surfing the Web taught her what she needed. She learned that hajib is the name given to Muslim women garments. It may refer to clothing that covers the entire body; other times it may refer—like a veil—to just the head and shoulders. Many modern Muslim women find a full-length hajib too restrictive, whereas traditionalists consider it protection from modern influences. *Well, whatever fits. I'll drive by the New World Islamic Center to see what the women wear. According to the Website,community meetings are held Tuesday and Thursday evenings between the Mahgrib and Isha prayers, so I'll get there between late afternoon and mid-evening.*

Electra watched an online video presenting a "women's role in Islam"debate, which convinced her that no modern women would want to live in an Islamic state. The moderator kept the debate even-handed, but the facts presented backed the pro-Islam debater into a corner he couldn't escape. Islam is androcentric. Religion and politics (they are one and the same because Islamic states are theocracies) are dominated by men. Women are considered possessions to be controlled by men so they can fulfill their family role. Divorce laws are stacked against women, and unlike polygamous husbands, women are severely punished if they are unfaithful. Most abhorrent is the practice of female circumcision (female genital mutilation or cutting), for which there is no medical reason. *When it comes to Islam, I have to agree with the Guardian Party. It is not a kind and gentle place for women.*

Electra's Thursday evening drive-by showed her more about the Center. She had no trouble finding it, a converted two-story storefront located in an older, lower middle-class neighborhood, but she had to wait for nearly an hour to observe what women wore. She drove through the alley on the way home, noting a rear door and second story windows. I'll come back next week, and I'll order on the Web some clothes that'll make me blend in. Online shopping is a breeze, and drone delivery makes it so easy to get what I want.

A week later Electra went to the Islamic Center meeting. Her plan was to case the place: locate imam offices or work areas that might hold computers or files, then eavesdrop on the imam. What a complete failure the evening turned out to be. The women were separated from the men, so she had no chance to listen to the imam's conversations or steal his cell phone. And although she did learn from her greeter that the upstairs offices had the latest technology— Electra guessed she meant computers and copiers— they were off limits. She would need a different approach for drilling into the center.

The March Manhattan terrorist attacks caught all law enforcement agencies flat-footed. Three groups sprayed T-Plague virus onto subway commuters during an evening rush hour. Scores of people tumbled onto the rails; some were electrocuted; others were struck by onrushing trains, and too many were trampled to death as crowds rushed for the exits. Even police and security guards ran from the attackers for fear of being doused with deadly virus. It took nearly two hours for the police to stop the attackers. All but two were shot dead, and follow-up tests concluded the worst. This was not a dress rehearsal; the attackers used live virus.

Media reports didn't need to hype the March Madness story because videos graphically depicted the mayhem. Pro-Isilabad terrorists were on a suicide mission, and it didn't matter to them if they were shot dead or died later from T-Plague. Several carried letters proclaiming this was the start of a new offensive that would unleash a curse on the Western Infidels.

Government emergency response teams sent to the attack sites looked inept and leaderless, tripping over one another and taking too long to get control. The few reporters covering the disaster glumly reported that they could never remember a Manhattan disaster not swarming with reporters. No one wanted to get near for fear of being infected with T-Plague.

Mo called an emergency meeting first thing the morning after for all Cognicom projects, looking frazzled because he had been up most of the night.

"OK everyone, please listen up. Thank you for getting here so early. NIH and CDC are in the crosshairs. I won't go into all the details; no time for that now. Right now, all you need to know is what will happen in the next couple of hours. Healthguard and Securityguard inspectors are going to search our labs for T-Plague leaks. They're looking for a virus supply that terrorists tapped into. All our projects keep samples, so they'll be auditing our storage facilities. I want all tech leads, tech assistants, and bus-admin leaders to stay. Everyone else is dismissed for the day."

Electra ducked out before anyone noticed, a tingle of fear racing through her, not for herself, but for Su. *Su must have stolen a virus sample when we tried to save Doc. I'll bet she never replaced it. I didn't think of it either. I'm fallible after all, but let's not dwell on it now. I've got to plant a bogus sample before the inspectors come.*

The corridors were deserted because she was the first out, so no one saw her sneak into Su's lab carrying a fake sample holder. She guessed the inspectors would audit by simply counting, so she would place it and be out in less than five minutes, more than enough time to escape undetected.

Electra worked at lightning speed and was ready to sneak out when she heard footsteps approaching. Trapped, she ducked inside a tiny storage closet just in time, overhearing familiar voices, those of Adom and Su. Adom was doing most of the talking.

"When the inspectors search, they'll find you're short one sample. They'll start asking a lot of questions, and you're going to be a suspect unless we come up with something to say. How about this. When they catch the discrepancy, I'll tell them I borrowed one of your samples because I needed it for prepping the lab that I just took over, and I forgot to tell you. I hear them coming, so just act surprised and let me do the talking."

Electra could tell from the inspectors' voices they were in a hurry. Two minutes later, the inspectors said the counts checked; the group headed to another location. Receding footsteps told Electra it was safe to come out.

Electra celebrated the narrow escape by stopping for a Coke and a lemon-poppy muffin on the drive home, taking time to savor the morning's excitement. *I don't know if Su will mention anything to me, and I'm keeping my mouth shut. And good for Adom. He's becoming the guy Su always knew she could depend on.*

After exercising, Electra spent the rest of the day working on her home computer, keeping one ear cocked to news she had playing in the background. Reports trumpeted the enormity of the attacks. Isilabad terrorists had declared war on the United States, and New Yorkers had retaliated by vandalizing several area mosques. Pundits were quick to make comparisons with the 911 disaster from the previous century, stunned that this time T-Plague virus rather than fuel-laden airplanes had become the WMD. These kinds of attacks would be hard to thwart because the virus was portable, easy to conceal, and impossible to distinguish from a bogus spray. Experts were shaking their heads when asked what to do. No one knew.

But Electra did. She would use current confusion to cover breaking into the New World Islamic Center tonight before the situation spiraled out of control. She rehearsed her plan while changing into the right disguise, then packed what she needed.

She parked on an adjacent side-street near the alley, just in case she needed to make an emergency getaway. Dressed in a hajib, Electra blended in with a worried crowd and stood next to the Imam, who of course ignored her. He only wanted to talk with the men clustering about him who were complaining noisily about imminent Muslim backlash. Their Center could be vandalized by misguided patriots. That was fine with Electra because it would explain tonight's break-in.

She moved in the Imam's wake as he barreled into another men's group that asked if there might be Washington terrorist cells. His reply put Electra on notice.

"My faithful, who knows what Allah will command, but followers of Islam should cheer if the Mighty Satan were struck in the midst of his sanctuary. But I am only a conduit for the faithful, for the committed." *I don't like what I'm hearing. I better drill deeper into what the Imam is doing.*

The crowd thinned as 10 p.m. approached, and Electra began working on the next part of her plan: a break-out, not a break-in. She was already inside and would hide until the Center was locked for the night. She picked the ladies' bathroom, standing atop a toilet seat until everyone was gone.

The Center was lights out and locked by ten-thirty. She listened at the door for five minutes hearing nothing, so she drew her flashlight and walked out. She took the stairway to the second floor, then hunted for the Imam's office where she might find a computer or files. She found it at the end of the corridor and used a lockpick to get in.

The office contained two chairs, a desk, and a computer. Behind them, a locked credenza stood against the alley-windowed wall. Checking the closet, she found only a couple of men's robes and women's hajibs. She checked the pockets but found nothing of interest, so she investigated the credenza, once again using her lockpick.

Electra struck gold when rifling through a file labeled CELL ACTIVITY. *Why would he keep such sensitive information in hard copy? I know why. He's afraid of someone hacking into his computer.* She dashed to find a copier, made copies of what she wanted, and was back in the Imam's office ten minutes later. She replaced the file, locked the credenza, and then picked the lock of the desk drawer where she found the Imam's back-up cell phone. Electra was striking it rich tonight. She took the phone, locked the drawer and was ready to inspect the last item, the desktop PC that she turned on.

Eletra knew how to hack into its registry for passwords and hidden files, but it would take too much time. *The file and cell phone should do, so let's go.* She flipped off the lights, locked the door, and glided to the stairway, ready to descend when she heard a dull thunk as the first-floor entry door opened. Electra froze in her tracks at the sound of two male voices. The lightning brain shifted to a higher gear.

"Now it's payback time. Let's start down here and work our way up." The second voice replied, "We won't torch it this time, but if they don't shut down we'll do that on the next visit."

Instead of panicking, Electra looked for another escape route. She crept back to the Imam's office and focused on what was there. Suddenly, a calm clarity swept into her brain. She was wearing an all-black running suit underneath her hajib, so she peeled it off, then removed robes and hajibs from the closet. She used a knife to slit and fit them together, forming a bedsheet-like rope she would use to climb down from the window. She hurried to the credenza and anchored the rope, then tried to open the window, but it was double-paned and couldn't be opened. *Not a problem.* Electra calmly unplugged all PC connections and hurled it through the window. CRASH! The window shattered into large shards. Then a loud BANG! echoed in the alley as the PC bounced on the pavement. *A rather blunt way to hack a computer, but I can't be picky.*

She cleared the large glass pieces remaining in the window frame, fed the rope down, pitched all she brought out the window, then out she went.

"Someone's upstairs! Let's get 'em!" The two visitors ran up the stairway to find a corridor of closed doors. "Damn! Where'd the noise come from?" yelled the first intruder.

The second ran down the hall while yelling back, "I think it came from the end. Shit! The door's locked!" The two brutes kicked the door, finally breaking it open. They ran to the broken window hoping to spot someone fleeing, but only a vacant, dimly lit alley greeted their eyes. Whoever had been there had disappeared into the night.

Electra stopped when she was in the clear to make one call.

"I want to report an in-progress break-in at the New World Islamic Center. Hurry, and you'll catch them." That was all Electra told the 911 operator, but said to herself after disconnecting, *Good. The Imam's cell phone works. The police can trace the call to him, and won't he be surprised.*

Electra was too wired to sleep, so she decided to work through the night. Before starting, she took a quick shower, changed into sweats and had a bowl of cereal followed by chocolate chip cookies spread with peanut butter. She started playing background classical music—it helped her focus—and then began drilling into what she had brought home.

First up was the cell file, from which she constructed a list of names and phone numbers, and then she put in chronological order the scribbled meeting notes. She skimmed enough to conclude the Imam communicated with terrorist-leaning faithful. *I'm so lucky CIA hacking is so good it frightens terrorists into keeping a paper trail. Whoever said computers will eliminate paper never talked with them.*

Next came the cell phone. She disabled GPS tracking and jotted down its call history. *Tomorrow I'll call these numbers and the ones on my other list to see what turns up.* Finally, she turned to the PC, which though dented still worked. *I can hack into it, but I'll go with the file and cell phone info first. And maybe I'll give it to Mo. He can have his CIA buddies hack into it. They're almost as good at hacking as I am, so I'll throw them a bone.*

It was now four-thirty. Electra had done enough, so she went to bed, but as she drifted into sleep, the lightning brain was already considering next steps towards other objectives. Wrath and vengeance for her grandfather's death continued to smolder; Electra would not be denied.

Lab researchers were back to work on Friday, but little work was done because the place was still buzzing about yesterday's inspection. Electra steered clear of the conversations, instead burying herself in thesis-related study. Neither Su nor Adom came to her workstation because they were still entangled in the inspection aftermath. Electra knew more than anyone about Su's sample accounting but would act surprised if the topic were ever mentioned.She left mid-afternoon to exercise,watch the news,and then trek further down a Cyber-trail, looking for terrorists.

Friday news talked non-stop about the terrorist attacks and related events, including two of particular interest to Electra: local mosque break-ins,and a Guardian Party prime-time announcement that evening. *I'm glad Gretchen pushed back our P.R.meeting.I'll have a lot more to talk about when I chat with them.*

Electra guessed correctly that Jared Gardner would speak, because ever since seizing the Guardian mantle of leadership, Washington insiders whispered he would do anything for his party to seize the government while he seized the Oval Office. But his public image and approval ratings belied all this because he connected with everyday people.He was good looking and assertive in a statesman-like way, intelligent, and spoke authoritatively. He projected unselfish patriotism, putting God and country ahead of himself or his party.For people in his camp,he was charismatic; for those opposed,he was formidable,projecting vitality and an image of a leader much younger than his late-fifties calendar years. Even the most astute political analysts hadn't a clue what his message would be until he began speaking to a national audience.

"Good evening to all Patriotic Americans. Just like you, I am appalled and enraged by the Manhattan terrorist attacks. Words cannot express the depth of my sadness or condolences for the

victims and families. I would like all of us to pause for a minute in silent prayer to remember them." A minute later, Jared looked directly into the camera and continued.

"We have just been hit with a declaration of war, and as I stand here tonight I declare the Guardian Party will lead our country's efforts to destroy our enemy as we guard America's safety and health. "We shall take the fight from Manhattan to the Middle East. They shall pay with their own blood. Our Allies are welcome to join us, but the time for diplomacy is long past. The world is not now a kinder and gentler place; it is treacherous and dangerous.

America must act!

"And we must take the fight to Washington DC so you, the American people, can convince or replace those who have no backbone, those who are unwilling to act in our and in our country's best interests. Tonight's not the time, but soon I will present evidence of the current Administration's deliberate blunders and double-dealings that have put all of us in harm's way.

"Tonight, I ask all patriotic Americans to join us in fighting for what is best for our nation. Please join the Guardian Party and me to wipe out the enemy of Western Civilization, to strengthen America's health and safety networks, and to renew the pledge to keep our country the greatest nation forever by guarding what makes America great.

"We have no time to waste. Elections may be too late, so act now on our call to action. With your support, we can change the Washington agenda. God bless all patriots."

An American flag replaced Jared's closeup image, while God Bless America played softly and a screen crawler at the bottom displayed phone numbers or Websites to contact for making donations or commitments to volunteer.

Electra came to a halt during the broadcast, for the address had been political dynamite delivered with explosive power. Afterwards, she flipped among stations to gauge its impact. Jared's words and delivery surprised even the sharpest commentators. The Administration had just taken heavyweight body blows and would need to regroup. *I bet Mo's networking to the max tonight. He'll have a lot to say tomorrow, and if he says too little, I'll ask for more.*

Not surprisingly, the week's events had swamped Cognicom. Although emergency meetings filled with dazed administrators sucked up most of his time, Mo survived better than most, defending his people and offering suggestions, but he still came away with information overload. He had just enough time to grab a sandwich for himself and snacks for his Worldstars team before hustling to his last meeting of the week. Mo put the mood elevators in the middle of the conference table, and after everyone traded greetings while picking a snack, he dived right in.

"I can't remember any Friday in my working career that I wanted to kiss goodbye as much as this one.Reminds me of a joke my Dad used to tell about business.Whenever any of his friends asked how business is going he'd say business is so good I could puke." The ironic comparison cut the tension; even Su giggled.

"But seriously, we came out of the inspection in pretty good shape.First off,no Cognicom team is a suspect for supplying virus to terrorists.All project teams passed Securityguard audit."Electra glanced at Su to gauge her reaction and saw only a poker face.

"Of course,the other labs that have virus samples were inspected,but we'll never know the results.Security levels have never been this high. No information is shared,and everyone's afraid to talk,for fear of being caught by a mole." Adom's tone matched his chagrined expression.

"You mean moles, don't you? Several groups are supposed to be targeting us,including the Guardian Party,the Opposition Group, and even the CIA."

Su added, "And if we want to be paranoid,how about Isilabad or rogue pharmaceutical companies out to steal our secrets?"

"My network doesn't think Isilabad or private companies have the smarts to infiltrate NIH. Let me get back to how the week impacts us.We need to deliver ASAP improved vaccines and smart pills. Su, what do you need to make that happen?"

"We need to cut through the safety and efficacy testing red tape. If the FDA lets us launch new formulations with less testing, we can do it for I-Vac, S-Vac, and the smart pill. But I make no promises for R-Vac.I haven't been team leader long enough to have a viable solution path. And remember, the new formulations are only marginally better."

"I'll take this to Bobbi and tell you what comes back."

Electra waited patiently for Mo to get to the political fallout reported by his network. Fortunately for Mo, he was ready to tell what Electra wanted to hear.

"I hope everyone listened to Jared last night. I did, and so did everyone in my network.That was one hell of a political bombshell. The Administration is going to have a tough time handling all the implied accusations. And if Jared comes up with hard evidence, there'll be political bloodshed not seen in Washington since the last impeachment."

Su added, "I've been following Jared and the Guardian Party more closely during the past year. I must say his message and delivery are convincing, especially when you look at how inept the Administration has been on tough issues, T-Plague, national security,healthcare,the economy,international relations,you name it. Jared seems to be impregnable. Adom, what's your opinion?"

"I agree. His message resonates with the public as long as his critics don't stumble over a hidden agenda. And if he has evidence of a government cover-up or double-dealing, that'll inflame the public even more. I hope all the unrest is contained to the ballot box. Mo, what do you think?"

"The Administration's P.R. spin on Jared's call to action is for the public to support the government, and no one knows what it'll do. But my network thinks Jared's speech is a warning that bigger steps must be taken immediately by the man in the Oval Office and the Washington Establishment. If they don't, the Guardian Party will, and maybe take them before the elections." Electra prodded Mo with a question about how Guardian spin against the Administration might sound.

"Excellent question, and my network's been thinking about that too. Here's a laundry list of guesses. Maybe the Administration's been selling smart pills to other countries instead of keeping our domestic pipeline loaded.Maybe there's a private supply of stronger smart pills that the Administration gives to the chosen few.Maybe they've deliberately sabotaged our efforts for improved vaccines.

Maybe they're afraid of the rest of the world, or afraid of war against Isilabad. Maybe they'll push to expand government snooping into our private lives. Maybe they just don't understand how the world works today, but it's not kinder and gentler out there. Maybe they can't deal with domestic terrorism or rebuilding infrastructure."Mo stopped because he needed to catch his breath.

"That's quite a list," Electra said. "I hope the Guardian Party can't prove any of it." She stopped there, waiting for comments, and

Adom spoke first.

"If any of this is true and the Guardian Party can point fingers at the Administration, they could win the next presidential election. And maybe the public won't want to wait.I hope none of this comes crashing down on our heads."

Everyone was tired of talking, so Mo ended the meeting. "I don't think we need to worry just yet about the government collapsing or secret agents hunting us, but this week has sent a bunch of warnings. Things should settle down over the weekend and look better on Monday. Let's go home and recharge."

First things first for Electra on Saturday, which meant an early morning workout that energized her for the rest of the day. After breakfast, she checked bathroom cleaning and downstairs vacuuming off her to-do list, clearing the way to hunt further along the terrorist trail.

She pulled out telephone lists that would serve up targets and found eight overlapping numbers to call first. By eleven thirty she had rehearsed her call script well enough to begin. The first call went unanswered, while the second,though unanswered by a person, returned a personalized recording from a deep-voiced Middle East male. An actual person answered the third call, but his accent was heavy,and he mashed his words. He seemed dim-witted,unable to understand the purpose of the call. Electra hung up while he was fumbling for what to say. *This guy is too retarded to be a terrorist. He'd have trouble pushing a button to blow himself up.* The fourth call landed on a disconnected number,but the fifth found what she was looking for so she launched into her script.

"Hello, Mr. Kassab. I work for your wireless service provider. I am calling to offer you a free gift, the newest smart phone we just switched to. You were selected at random from our subscriber pool. If you provide me with a mailing address, we will rush your new cell phone to that location. Then all you need to do is call the number listed in the letter to activate the phone. How does that sound?" Electra's reply defused his skepticism.

"No sir, the offer comes with no strings attached. As the letter explains, a representative will call you in six weeks to find out how you like the phone's latest features, and to explain how they fit perfectly with our additional services. At that time, you will have the option to sign up for these new services. Whether you do or you don't, you keep the new phone. May I please have your full name and mailing address?"Khalik Kassab provided everything asked for.

"Thank you, Khalik, for being a valued customer. Your phones should arrive no later than Tuesday. Have a great weekend."

Electra knew the scam would work once she could talk with someone who had half a brain cell, because everyone loves to hear the most seductive words in advertising: free gift. Before delivering, Electra would insert a microchip that would automatically conference in her backup cell phone whenever Khalik uses his phone, and it would automatically send GPS tracking signals Khalik could not disable. Electra would be able to follow him as long as he carried the phone. *Mission accomplished. I'll let him lead me to others. And if he's a wrong number, I'll look for others to scam.*

Electra went to her favorite mall that afternoon to buy his gift, picking up a shipping box and labels on the way home. By the time she was ready for supper, she had the phone prepped and packed, ready for Monday delivery. She treated herself that evening by watching a Star Trek rerun. Star Trek—her favorite sci-fi series— was the best for projecting scientific facts into storylines, but viewers still had to suspend common sense or disbelief. *Warp drives and wormholes exist only in the far-fetched world of high energy physics, which has conjured its way into a black hole from which it might have trouble emerging. And I don't think that advanced alien civilizations would have to struggle with the same ethical dilemmas plaguing Earthlings. I can't imagine that polluting a neighbor's planet with anti-matter would lead to intergalactic war, but like Trekkies everywhere, I'll play along and enjoy the multi-series worlds.*

Tonight's episode came from Star Trek—the Next Generation and featured a young woman who had recently learned she came from the Q Civilization,an all-knowing race that exists in another dimension. She wants to relinquish her extraordinary powers so she could live among Earthlings, but she would be treated badly by her people if she does. At the end of the episode, she decides to go back to the Q-World because that's where she belongs. A whimsical thought popped into Electra's brain. *I like the Q-People. They're perfect candidates for my Dream Team. And that young girl is silly to give up her powers just because she wants to experience human emotions.* Suddenly, another thought jolted Electra, coming from her inner voice. Indira had something to say.

"Do you realize the analogy between you and the young woman? Your situations are related, but yours turns hers on its head."

"I've seen the episode before, but never made the connection. Let me think it through and explain it back. I got it. She wants to ditch her talents so she can enjoy more human emotions, but if she does the Q-People will treat her badly. I'm the opposite. I want to use my talents, but I'll be treated badly if people find out I'm a genetic freak."

"You are correct. And you should have more empathy for the young woman. Your emotional persona needs to grow further. That will come only through relationships with others."

"Mother, please tell me what I should do to make it grow."

"No, my dear. Wisdom comes from experience, not from reading or being told. But here's a clue for what you should do. Study post-Jungian psychology, which extends through neuroscience Freud's sex-laden Id, Ego, and Superego constructs, partitioning the Superego into a Collective Unconscious that represents culture's demands and constraints on the Ego, and the Shadow. Look to Jung's Shadow concept because it contains your personality traits that you think are bad, but they can actually help you when used properly. Perhaps you have been suppressing aspects of your personality that in fact you need to make your emotional persona grow."

"I don't think I will ever grow to match your level of empathy or understanding. Su told me you were considered a practically perfect person. I'm sorry I can't match your excellence."

"My dear, never doubt yourself, and never compare yourself with other people. Compare yourself only with what you want to become. And I too had flaws, but I kept them hidden. No one ever found them, but then no one is as clever as you. Perhaps you will discover my imperfections. And remember this. In some cultures, an imperfection is a mark of beauty. But enough musing. It is time you rest for tomorrow..."

That night in bed, Electra thanked her lucky stars for today's success, but then recalled one of Doc's aphorisms. *Luck is just another name for hard work. It's up to me to make my own luck. And you also taught me it doesn't matter whether I have good or bad luck. What matters is what I do with it.* Another saying drifted in as she descended into sleep, one from the Bible: Vengeance is Mine. That was an ethical issue Electra had already resolved. It belongs to me. I shall avenge my Grandfather's execution. Electra slept soundly.

Thanks to her weekend work, Monday was another lucky day. She sat in the back of the lab's auditorium, impatiently listening to Mo drone on about additional procedures slapped in place by Securityguard, then ducked out to deliver Khalib's gift, and afterwards headed to campus. *Whenever he calls me, I'll activate the phone. Then I can listen in and track him down when the situation presents itself.*

Electra devoted Monday afternoon to thesis-related planning work by putting finishing touches on her Thesis Conjecture list. She revealed to no one how much was already done because everyone left her alone, considering her an unremarkable first-year research assistant who earned good grades by studying hard.

Electra's thesis probed into the neurobiological basis of cognition, or in simpler terms, how humans think. It's a question that philosophers have been asking for thousands of years. Only since the Renaissance-inspired emergence of scientific reasoning have researchers been able to grapple with this puzzle, and only technological advances in the last fifty years have given them the tools to probe deep enough to connect individual neurons with emotional and cognitive brain states.

Electra expected to make important contributions because her brain was beyond those of mere mortals. She would keep much of her work secret, revealing just enough for advisors to approve her thesis, but she would dummy it down so they could understand it. She would start with a mathematical analogy. When set theory was invented over two hundred years ago, mathematicians struggled when using it to understand infinity. They could approach infinity by putting all the natural numbers in a set and counting them 1,2,3,4, and so on. If they did this, and if infinity exists, then the limit of the sequence—the completed infinity—exists. *My thesis will prove my conjecture that consciousness is like a completed infinity that emerges from the billions of brain cells and trillions of inter-neural connections forming interrelated associative patterns once the human brain contains a critical number of neurons and connections. I'll narrow my focus to the easier problems associated with consciousness: how does the brain process information, and what physical properties distinguish conscious from unconscious states. Because I can observe and measure events associated with the easier problems, I can test my conjecture, which means I'm doing science. The harder consciousness problems are not testable, so I can't use them in a science-related thesis. They'd be fair game for a philosophy-related thesis, but I'm not going there.*

And I know how to test my conjecture. First, I'll map the brain's neural structure using a modified T-Plague vaccine solution path to make a drug that will bind with neurons associated with cognition. Then, I'll "turn on" a critical number of neural connections to create a conscious state. And then I'll measure the brain's emotional responses for this conscious state, comparing them to a reference standard.

What I'm undertaking could last a lifetime of extended research if I become a professor or launch a biotech company like our wished-for Worldstar Biologicals. And I'll combine neuroscience with nanotechnology and artificial intelligence to go where no one but I can go. I know how to build a "biological computer" using recently discovered macro-molecules that are like tiny machines in living cells. I know how to make Boolean logic circuits with them, and they're the building blocks for digital computers. And I have a model of the brain's memory, similar to a relational database, using associative memory concepts linked to the brain's medial temporal lobe. This is going to work. I love it when a plan comes together!

Electra preferred the R&D world she controlled rather than the darkly uncertain three-dimensional one swirling about. She never tired exploring cerebral landscapes. The only frustrating part would be explaining a dummied down version of her thesis to her advisory committee or other academic associates. *I'll simplify for them by using Occam's Razor. Albert Einstein had the same challenge. I remember one of his quotes:*

"Everything should be made as simple as possible, but not simpler."

And I'll make a game of it by explaining my ideas in a way my advisors will understand, but only if they break a serious intellectual sweat. I'll teach them some humility when they read my thesis. It's bad for them to have puffed-up egos, which seems to be a chronic condition tenured profs share with some of those NIH senior researchers. And for Professor Ravenhill's benefit, I'll give him credit for pointing me in the right direction, and I'll pretend my intuitive guesses were lucky. Indira chided from the shadows.

"Don't be proud. Be thankful for your gifts and show empathy towards the people you work with. Though they aren't your Dream Team, they're they best you can get."

"I'm sorry, Mother. I'll keep reminding myself to be patient with others."

Electra was so engrossed in her thesis she had lost track of time. It was nearly seven when a cell call intruded, and her brain switched gears when she recognized the ring tone. Khalik's calling! Electra guided him through key strokes to activate the phone and confirm it is working properly. Khalik and his new phone were now ready for unwitting terrorist reporting. She allowed herself a couple of minutes to savor the day's successes, then left for home. *I'm not worried about the game becoming dangerous. I'll know what to do whatever comes my way. And I'll be able to take care of it by myself. I'll make sure the few people I care about are in the clear. My adversaries won't know what's about to hit until it's too late. Good for me and bad for them.*

CHAPTER 33
May 2115

"What Bloody Messes"
(Thread 2 Chapter 20)

"I HAD TO BRAG about all you've done to get our P.R. department interested in you, so let's make the most of our meeting." Gretchen's words sounded more like a challenge than encouragement, but as the two marched into a nondescript DC office building housing the Guardian Party's Public Relations Department, Electra was ready. "I know the P.R. people don't want us to waste their time, so I have a story they're bound to like. You will too." Gretchen signed in at the reception desk, and a couple of minutes later a senior manager escorted them into the elevator.

"Hello. I'm Theodore McNamara, but please, call me Teddy. Gretchen has been singing your praises, so you must be something special."

"Hello Teddy. Gretchen is very generous with her praise. I hope what I say meets your expectations." Teddy smiled as he replied.

"That's why you're meeting with my people. You'll find they're friendly, professional, and competent. Maybe you have what it takes to join us. I'd like you to explain to one of my media teams what you have in mind. Here's our stop. We'll go to the conference room. It's second door on the right. Follow me, please." Teddy ushered them in, then left to collect his team. Gretchen's nerves were showing and Electra played along with her. Two minutes later, Teddy and five team members—two men and three women—entered. Electra liked what she saw. *Their stylish business-casual attire is fitting for P.R. types. They're youthful and energetic, and they sure look smart. I'll tailor what I say to match as soon as Teddy's ready.*

"Hello again. As I mentioned on the elevator, I'm Teddy McNamara, and I lead several P.R. teams. Gretchen, why don't you tell us why you think Electra's idea might fit here, and then she can tell us more." Gretchen glanced at Electra for moral support, then smiled at Teddy and spoke.

"Thanks for meeting with us, so let me give you the background. Electra's been a volunteer for nearly a year, doing a great job for us in fundraising and recruiting. But that's not why we're here. She's bright, inquisitive, and has a good understanding of T-Plague basics because she works on a project that is battling it. Late last year she joined our current events group, which meets twice a month to sort through items of pressing interest. Electra came up with the idea that she could summarize findings and show them to you. Electra, why don't you take it from here." Mention of T-Plague brought the audience to attention.

"Thanks for the compliment, Gretchen. I have a part-time data handling clerk position on an NIH T-Plague project. I talk with the researchers, so I usually know what's going on. I also follow current events, something every young person should do because we need to know what's facing us. And with all the turmoil in the world, I find the Guardian Party message appealing. That's why I volunteered last year and why I'm part of the current events discussion group." Electra paused to check the audience; all eyes were riveted on her.

"Between what I watch on the news or learn at the lab, I see lots of opportunities to connect what's going on with Guardian Party recruiting messages or press releases. I'm pretty good at collecting and summarizing information from what I read or from what people say, so I thought maybe I could write this up for you." *I'll stop here to judge their interest level.*

Teddy looked around the table, then asked one of his female staffers to speak for the group. A pert, brown-haired, youngish lady followed up.

"I'm Zoe Vargas. I like what I hear so far. Tell me more about your writing skills, and your T-Plague work." *Nice vetting questions. I like the way you look, and you'll like my answers.*

"Hi Miss Vargas. I've had a lot of practice in my degree program and data collection job preparing summary reports. I've been told my writing is crisp and thorough. And regarding T-Plague, if I knew what information you might be interested in, I could ask around to find out. Of course, the researchers won't tell me too much because they think I won't understand or it's too confidential. But I'm good at reading between the lines." Electra could almost hear synapses snapping in Zoe's brain when she looked at Teddy.

He looked at Gretchen before he said, "I think we have an opportunity for Electra. But that means she would be transferred here. Are you willing to let her go?"

"If you think she can help, of course. Electra, thanks for all you've done for my department, but you should move on."

"Then it's settled. Electra, if you agree, you can transfer immediately, reporting to Zoe. Are you interested?" Electra's inner voice whispered a warning. *You're about to play the dangerous counter-intelligence game. Be careful when planting P.R. misinformation or looking for hidden agendas.*

"I'd like to give it a try. Gretchen, thanks for all you've done for me, and Zoe, I'll work hard." Teddy was ready to move on.

"That's a wrap. Gretchen, thank you for giving us Electra, and Zoe, why don't you take her around to get her settled. The two of you can arrange hours."

Zoe whisked through a ten-minute tour of the office, then arranged for a full day's briefing next week. While Zoe talked, Electra sized her up. *I like her. She's smart and snappy and doesn't waste time. I'll make a game of helping her while I'm helping myself to whatever info I can ferret out.*

Electra marveled on the drive home how different the trajectories of her external and personal worlds. While the external world was spiraling downward under the weight of terrorism, T-Plague, and political intrigue, her personal world was ascending everywhere: thesis, vaccine formulations, Guardian Party work, and terrorist tracking were all pointing up. Even her social life, which she carefully limited, had possibilities. This coming Sunday evening would be date night with Joe, who would meet her for dinner at a trendy casual restaurant on the outskirts of DC and then take her club dancing.

Electra's different personas enchanted Joe. On some dates, she was a tease, inflaming his passion, but on others she seemed aloof, inscrutable, melancholy, like a distracted philosopher. That was just part of what fascinated him, for he never knew what to expect. But he always liked what he saw, especially her practically perfect body. Joe didn't know what she might reveal tonight, but he was hungry to find out.

Before driving to the restaurant, Electra checked the gear she always kept in the trunk. Tucked in a gym bag were a jet-black SWAT uniform, mask and gloves, rope and tape, medical supplies, and a selection of weapons (knife and small caliber pistol) from her personal arsenal that she had confiscated or purchased anonymously in shadow-Cyberspace. She usually packed a small caliber pistol, but occasionally she would take her most advanced weapon, a Traser she took several years ago from a security guard. A Traser is a dual tranquilizer and electric stun gun. The model she has could be dialed from mild stun to lethal charge and stores enough energy to fire six rounds. Police departments and SWAT teams often use a Traser as the weapon of choice because it could preserve the victim. Electra knew how ruthless agents could be. *Better to have the suspect live now so they could tell all they know, and then terminate later. I vow to stay below their radar.*

Joe arrived at the restaurant first. He was one of her favorite girl toys—a term she shared only with Christi. She arrived five minutes later displaying a cheery mood because of recent successes, and had already decided Joe could sample more of her delights at his place after dancing. They were about to order when a call came in on Electra's backup cell phone, so she excused herself and left for the ladies' room. *Let's hear what Khalik is talking about.*

"Khalik, let me repeat. Tomorrow morning is strike time. Be at our staging area tonight at eleven for all details and supplies. Front door will be unlocked. Proceed to basement."

"Yes, Wahid. Allah is great." The conversation ended abruptly. After weeks of listening to unimportant calls, tonight's message announced an imminent terrorist strike. The lightning brain shifted gears as Electra hurried to her car, texting Joe before she drove off that she had to deal with a home security alert. Her cell flashed 8:22 as she pulled out of the parking lot on that overcast evening.

Electra began tracking Khalik's cell phone coordinates while driving, but she stopped in a secluded spot to change into her SWAT uniform, driving from there towards an intercept location. Cell phone coordinates started moving in a zig-zag pattern which she had no trouble tailing at a safe distance. By 10:45 they were stationary. *Time to find the building and sneak in.*

Five minutes later she drove past the coordinates that put her in a working-class DC neighborhood. Electra parked several blocks away, then jogged back in the shadows. She identified four suspect houses, observing from a shadowy distance. At 11:15 she guesstimated all the terrorists would be assembled. *How many? Three, possibly four, but no more.* A cluster of cars near one of the houses would have pointed to her first choice, but a bluish glow of a TV monitor told her no, so she went to her second pick. Excellent choice; the door was unlocked. Electra crept in, silently closing the door behind her, listening for directional clues. She heard nothing, but as her eyes adjusted to the darkness, she tiptoed around the first floor until she found steps to the basement.

As she silently descended step by step, she could hear muffled voices. It was pitch black, but a strip of light coming from beneath a closed door led the way. Once outside, she listened with ears as sensitive as a cat's, making out heavily accented raspy voices.

"The three of you have been honored to carry out our first T-Plague attack in the Infidel's capital."

"Wahid, why has it taken so long? We have been ready for months."

"It took us long to obtain a virus sample. Our first attempt last year met with failure. The fools we sent killed themselves in a car accident before they could deliver the sample, but at least they executed one of the targets. The cell in Boston sent us enough virus to make our attack. Each of you will contaminate crowds at Metro stations during Monday morning rush hour."

Electra had heard all she needed. This was the cell she had been looking for, the cell that had murdered her grandfather. The voices confirmed there were three suicide terrorists awaiting Wahid's instructions. A sudden clarity filled the lightning brain as cognitive and emotional personas united into one. Her entire body tingled with strangely exciting yet focused emotions as her smoldering wrath began breaking free. *My Monster from the Id is about to take control! I can taste my lust for revenge, for blood. I'm primed for action. The lightning brain will decide what to do.*

Electra drew a pistol, then slowly, quietly opened the door; she was a masked, all black messenger of death framed in the doorway. She said nothing. None of the terrorists were facing her way, concentrating instead on what Wahid was showing them on a desk that was twenty feet inside the room and pushed underneath a window. A minute elapsed before Wahid sensed something was amiss. When he turned towards the door, Electra entered saying nothing, stopping when just inside and closing the door. The others turned as well, faces showing surprise mixed with incipient fear. Wahid's expression turned to anger, and he spoke harshly.

"Who are you? What do you want?" The masked specter threw sections of rope at the feet of the closest terrorist, then spoke deliberately and slowly, pointing a gun.

"You. Tell all to lie face down. Then bind legs first, then arms. Do it now." One of the terrorists reached for a weapon, trying to shield himself behind another, but Electra was quicker, shooting him in the head, his blood splattering the others as he crashed to the floor. Expressions turned to naked fear, and they obeyed her commands.

Wahid stuttered, "Who sent you? Why are you here?" The specter did not answer. When the terrorist doing its bidding completed his task, it threw him a roll of duct tape.

Now, tape their mouths shut. Wrap it completely around their heads. He looked wildly at the specter, fear-induced sweat pouring from his forehead.

"But, but…" he stuttered, but no other words came forth. A bullet shot past his ear.

"Do it now!" He complied.

Electra's wrath had reached a tipping point. Her Monster was breaking through from the other side, and once unleashed, it would be in command. But suddenly, her cognitive persona wrestled control away. *Get with it Soldier! This is not a drill. Avenge your grandfather's death, but do it smart. You don't need to kill them all. Let them suffer by living. Turn them over to the police. They'll do your work.*

Electra bound and gagged her helper, then made a final check. None of them would be going anywhere soon. She stepped back to view the scene, deciding to make a better arrangement. She lined them up face-down and side-by-side, then collected her supplies, adding to them two guns and cell phones found on the terrorists. She packed everything into her satchel except a cell phone because she would use it to call 911.

"Hello, I want to report an aborted terrorist attack. Track this cell phone and you can pick up the bad guys. I'll leave the connection open to make it easier. Good luck." With that, she tossed the phone on top of the dead terrorist and moved towards the doorway. Soon she would be out and on her way to the car and to safety. And then, from upstairs came thunderous crashing and smashing.

Electra knew in an instant what was happening. *This terrorist cell has been under surveillance, and a SWAT team is moving in for the kill. They'll kill me too because I look like one of the bad guys.* The lightning brain switched gears for evasive action.

The SWAT team had to search upstairs first, giving her less than two minutes to get out. She locked the door and turned off all lights, then raced to the window, trying to open it after ripping off the curtain. No luck; it was bolted shut. Enough light was coming through the window, so she pulled a drawer from the desk and used it as a battering ram. The noise upstairs masked the crashing sound as she smashed the glass. She pitched her satchel through the jagged opening, then sprang through it with all the agility her adrenaline-charged body possessed. Electra was out and undetected. She grabbed her satchel, paused just long enough to get her bearings, then raced into the night, into the darkest shadows, like an invisible bolt of lightning.

By the time Electra reached her car, the taste of blood was in her mouth. It was her own. She had severely gashed her left cheek and arm on the fragments stuck in the window frame. Though she had no time to look at the damage, she knew instinctively from the amount of bleeding the cuts were deep and long. The blood was not pulsing out, so she hadn't sliced an artery, but she had cut into deep tissue and veins, and she knew she was in trouble. She hurriedly wrapped a towel around her damaged arm and secured it with gauze strips. The towel soaked through immediately, so she wrapped it with duct tape, and if the pressure from the wrap didn't stanch the flow she would do it again, and keep doing so until the bleeding stopped or until she reached a medical center or until she was dead from loss of blood. *No time to worry about the bloody mess. Just do it.*

She could do nothing for the cut on her cheek because too much blood was flowing for tape to stick, but at least the blood was not running into her eyes. It was time to seek help. She weighed her options as she drove away, slowly at first in case the sirens pulsing in the distance were looking for possible accomplices. She checked her left arm; the flow was less, but she still had a medical emergency on her hands. *Damn! I never thought about needing medical help. Where can I go? The answer flashed immediately. My best hope is grandfather's clinic. I have to get there before losing too much blood, before losing consciousness, and I'm beginning to feel light-headed. Come on, focus.* She would be on the Beltway in ten minutes, and from there it would be a twenty-minute trip.

Clarence always had a special fondness for Electra. He was there that terrible day eighteen years ago when Doc rushed her and Jason to the clinic, through the teeth of a blinding thunder-snowstorm. He remembered her that day, a lobster-red newborn that somehow managed to pull through that fiery, near-fatal disaster. He remembered as she became a lively child, Doc's constant companion.

And he remembered her maturing into a more reserved, unassuming adolescent who was reluctant to display her considerable talents. And now she's a competent, young adult on her own after the tragic deaths of both father and grandfather. And this minute she needed skilled medical attention. Lucky for her, she was his only patient.

Electra sat quietly on an emergency room examining table, stoically waiting for Clarence to return with the damage report. He had to cut off all her upper body clothes to avoid aggravating the wounds. Two deep gashes on her left arm still dripped blood: one on the forearm, barely missing bone and tendon, the other extending upwards from her elbow. The two-inch cut on her left cheek reached the bone. Though deep, the cuts were clean, relatively easy to sterilize, and temporary bandaging would hold until suturing.

Clarence was most concerned with the loss of blood and the possibility of scarring. Cuts this long and this deep usually leave scars unless treated by a plastic surgeon who knows the art and science of subcuticular stitching beneath the skin's surface. As soon as he had stabilized Electra, he telephoned the newest doctor on the clinic's staff. Help would be arriving shortly. Electra looked passively at him as re-entered the emergency room. *He's not smiling, but Clarence never does.*

"Reinforcements are on the way. We'll have you patched up shortly. Tell me again, what happened?"

"I was trying to fix a basement window, and I got careless. I had the stepladder propped against the wall but I slipped, falling through the glass. I thought I could patch myself up, but it was worse than I first thought, so I came right over." Though skeptical, Clarence accepted the story at face value.

"Sit here while I gather supplies for the doctor. Better yet, lie down." Clarence hustled away after helping her into a prone position. Ten minutes later the E.R. door swung open. Clarence entered first, followed by the doctor, who spoke as soon as soon as Clarence helped Electra sit up.

"Hello, Electra. My name is Doctor Rihanna Antar. I came as fast as I could." Electra, pale from shock and loss of blood, stared mutely. Dr. Antar spoke again after her probing fingers carefully removed bandages and traced the contours of the cuts.

"Let me examine further." Electra peered back at a medium height and weight woman from the Middle East, perhaps forty years old. She struggled to find something to say, finally asking, "What kind of Muslim doctor are you?" Rather blunt, but Dr. Antar handled it with aplomb.

"Don't worry, young lady. I am fully trained in Western medicine. I interned at Johns Hopkins." Electra's brain started functioning a little better.

"I'm so sorry. I don't know why I said that."

"From the quantity of blood you've lost, I'm surprised you can sit up and say anything. Clarence, please help me get her lying down again."

It took only a minute for Clarence to lock the table in a fully reclined position, then cover Electra with a bedsheet. Dr. Antar guided her left arm atop the sheet so she could examine the gashes further; five minutes later she was ready to describe treatment.

"Clarence did a fine job sterilizing your wounds. We should be able to keep them infection-free. But I can see why he called me. These are rather nasty cuts that might leave significant scar tissue, and for a young lady like yourself, we don't want that. You have such striking features." The doctor's fingers carefully traced the cut on Electra's cheek.

"I'm trained in plastic surgery and have treated cuts like yours. My suturing techniques will leave as little scarring as possible, but I cannot promise how your scars will appear. In some cultures, an imperfection is a mark of beauty. But enough talking, we need to suture now, while inflammation hasn't widened the cuts. We'll suture your cheek first. Then we'll take care of your arm. The suturing will be easier there. Clarence will hold your head perfectly still. And he will strap your arm when we suture it. We'll use a local anesthetic, and I would suggest we give you a pain killer also. Are you ready?"

Electra was paying close attention. Scars weren't her concern, but being sidelined was. "How long will I need to cut back on exercising? I like to lift weights and run."Dr. Antar stroked Electra's head before replying.

"It depends how quickly you heal, but you should restrict motion in your left arm, at least until we know the stitches are holding. We'll want you to come back Wednesday so I can check progress. Until then, please, no heavy lifting or twisting your left arm. Do you want a pain killer?"

"No thanks. I'll be OK with just a local anesthetic." Electra closed her eyes and rested while Clarence and Dr. Antar made final preparations. Five minutes later Clarence was holding Electra's head perfectly still, retelling stories from long ago about her grandfather. Dr. Antar finished the cheek, then proceeded to the arm. Electra's brain stood down. The rambling stories Clarence told of her past and of her grandfather stirred a connection between her emotions and music, bringing an iconic rock song from years ago into her head, the words and melody carrying her away. She felt safe and secure in sure hands, falling asleep before Dr. Antar finished.

"We should let her rest. I hope her skin color improves. Why don't you check vital signs?" Clarence reported back a minute later. "Pulse is slow and pressure is low, but temperature and respiration are in the normal range. I'll go fetch a pillow." When he returned, Dr. Antar was keenly observing Electra, who was still asleep.

"She's not beautiful in a classical sense, but high cheekbones, thin nose and wide-set eyes make her striking. And what expressive eyes she has when awake. Shakespeare said the eyes are the windows to the soul. From what little I saw, her soul houses great awareness. And she's a practically perfect physical specimen. Excellent muscle tone and definition for such a fine-boned build. That should help her recover quickly. How did she get so fit?"

"I don't know. Too bad you never met her grandfather. Doc Kittner took great care of her. She was with him a lot when she was little. Whenever I asked him how she was doing, he'd say she was always thinking good thoughts and drinking V8 vegetable juice. I guess it worked."

"It looks like it did. Well, my work is finished. Can you sit with her until she wakes up?"

"Yes. Go home and get some rest. I'm off tomorrow, but I'll see you Tuesday second shift. And I'll remind her to come back Wednesday evening when both of us are here."

"Good. And write her a prescription for pain relievers if she changes her mind.

See you Tuesday."

Clarence sat with Electra until she awoke a half hour later, feeling and looking better. "I'm sorry I've been such a bother, but thanks to you and Doctor Antar, I'm ready to go. When should I come back?"

"Wednesday, 7 p.m. will work. Have you changed your mind about the pain relievers? I'll give you a prescription if you like."

"Thanks, but no. I'm OK without them. Gramps always said it's better to be under rather than overmedicated, and feeling a bit of pain keeps me in touch with how things are." Clarence elevated the table, making it easier for Electra to stand.

"Let me find something better than a bedsheet for you to wear home." He rummaged around and came back with the top of a nurse's uniform.

"Thanks. I sure don't want to get arrested for indecent exposure. But at five in the morning, no one would see." The two of them managed to get the top fitted without stressing the stitches. Clarence made one final check, patted her on the head and off she went. Then he mused about the night's excitement. *I'll never know what really happened, but maybe it's good I don't. And I'll keep her treatment off the record. I'll remind Rihanna to say nothing.*

The eastern sky was beginning to lighten when Electra reached home. Today she would call in sick, for she needed a day to recuperate. After leaving a message, she stripped completely, took a warm sponge bath and ate breakfast, finally crawling into bed just before her brain summoned her into a deep sleep that would begin the healing process. She was too tired to recap all that happened in the last twenty-four hours. That would happen once she returns to action.

The SWAT team leader was finishing his report Monday morning when his supervisor walked in. "Hey, I heard your raid last night was a piece of cake. All the heavy lifting was taken care of before you got there. What gives?"

"Damnedest thing I ever saw. All the bad guys were bound and gagged, neatly arranged in a row, except for one shot dead. And we've got the goods. All sorts of terrorist cell info, plus actual T-Plague virus. We'll interrogate them further, but they claim they didn't do anything illegal. They were just meeting to talk about helping one another look for jobs. They claim that one of our people broke in and, get this, terrorized them. Whoever it was had on a SWAT uniform, said very little, and called 911 just before our team arrived."

"Did your guys see anyone? Any fingerprints?"

"Nope. Whoever it was disappeared without a trace. The only thing we recovered was some blood on the window, which we assume is from our helper. We'll check out local hospitals, and I guess we could do a DNA match. Who knows? Maybe something will turn up." The supervisor scratched his head.

"We've turned this case over to the Feds because it's a clear-cut case of terrorist activity. Is it possible last night was some sort of argument between two terrorist cells? Maybe the Feds have a theory like that." The team leader shook his head.

"We've been working with them on surveillance, and they never said anything about infighting. Maybe they'll tell us more, but I'm not counting on it. All agencies have become paranoid about leaks. We'll learn more from the media. They're all over this story, playing up some sort of vigilante angle. Too bad we can't gag them on this one, but it's too late."

"All kidding aside, you guys earned your pay last night. Nice work." The team leader's final comment had a ring of truth.

"Whoever got there before us sure did nice work too. We could use more volunteers like our mystery helper."

Electra's R&R day turned out to be just what the doctor ordered. When she awoke after ten hours of uninterrupted sleep, she felt no more dull throbbing from the cuts and was surprised when peeling back a bandage by the extent of healing. Some sections were almost closed. No inflammation, discoloration, or plasma discharge marred what she saw.

When I was a kid, Doc often said how fast I mend, as if my brain were willing it to happen quickly. I'm conscious of only a tiny fraction of what's going on inside my head, but I can tell the lightning brain's been busy. No wonder I'm famished. I need protein to rebuild tissue and blood. I also need a symbolic cleansing to wash away last night's grime. Electra did that carefully, keeping all bandages dry, then prepared a three-egg bacon and cheese omelet she devoured with two English muffins, giving a contented feeling that comes after a satisfying meal. Now she was ready to satisfy her curiosity by watching the news.

Lead stories reported a foiled terrorist plot. Electra surmised there must be a mole somewhere in whatever organization raided last night because the press had access to details that official channels would never release so soon: names, links to Isilabad, Metro station targets, assistance by an unknown vigilante. Person on the Street interviews confirmed fear and Muslim resentment were growing.

One reporter said that too much paranoia might lead to backlash, such as attacks on minorities, random acts of violence, or other rips in the nation's moral fabric. His summary called them ominous warnings that "the Great Dimming's" day of reckoning might be on the horizon, blaming the T-Plague for hollowing out the nation's I.Q. and its respect for minorities. Electra agreed.

I need to be ready when the external world's nastiness spills into my world. Who are my enemies? I think I'm below their radar but I better track them so I know what I'm dealing with. And I'll deal with them harshly. It's a matter of my survival.

And whose side of the political equation should I be on? Not the Administration or the Washington Establishment. They're out of touch with reality, living in their kinder and gentler fantasy world. What about the Guardian Party or that shadowy Opposition Group. I need to know more about each of them. And I can find out by visiting a favorite place, Cyberspace.

Electra's injuries healed quickly, and Christi's cosmetic artistry transformed what remained of the cut on her cheek into a subtle beauty mark. Fully recovered by early July, Electra didn't miss a beat. She maintained her balance on the Cognicom tightrope, furnishing the right number and types of clues to keep progress creeping forward, but nothing that would bring her under scrutiny. And although Healthguard and Securityguard imposed additional regulations, she remained invisible. No one noticed her and she set her own schedule, confirming details only with Su.

Electra used her Guardian Party P.R. work to hack deeper into confidential data. She was invisible when hacking because she knew how to avoid intrusion detection alarms, and always borrowed user I.D.'s and passwords. In return, she began supplying reports to Zoe that included Cognicom tidbits.

Electra's summer social calendar included just the right amount of dating. She took Joe to the Conklin's combination Christi graduation party and Fourth of July cookout. In addition to cosmetics, Christi had a flair for clothing, either when wearing or designing, and had won a partial scholarship for her minority women's styling concept which she had already demonstrated by adapting contemporary American tastes to traditional Middle East headscarves and burkas. Electra asked her to make two that she would give to Dr. Antar as a thank-you for stitching her back together. Christi promised to have them ready by Labor Day.

Electra wasn't the only one who had been damaged as a result of the foiled terrorist plot, but unlike Electra, Elliot Spitzdieck had no idea if he would ever recover. Before entering the section chief's office, he did know he was about to be read the riot act, and he had no place to hide or excuses to offer.

Elliot, a brutal and tough-as-nails field agent team leader, had the looks, personality, and resume for his now-precarious position. He had carved out a career in government intelligence, was fully committed to making America safe, and had alternated between staff and field assignments. Now in his late forties, he was convinced he had earned the right to manage a team because he knew better than his superiors what needed to be done. He took no prisoners or excuses and could man up to anything, but none of his previous predicaments matched the mess caused by the "DC Terrorist Debacle," a disparaging tag pinned on his team. The section chief was not about to mince words.

"You were assigned to turn Project Death Shield around, not into a farce. And what happens? Your team is clueless how terrorists got their hands on some T-Plague virus samples, and you're on the sidelines when some vigilante rolls up the DC Metro attack. We don't know who leaked what to the media, but it became a bloody mess. They crucified the Administration, and we'll be thrown under the bus if you can't deliver." Elliot stared straight ahead, seemingly unaffected by the grilling. While glaring at Elliot, the chief thought *At least this Spitz-dickhead can handle abuse. Good, because there's more.*

"I don't give a rat's ass for our current Administration. It's weak and worthless and will fall, maybe before the next election. But I do care about the agency and my career, and I damn well don't want either to fall with them. You have one more chance to get results. I don't care what changes you make on your team, or what steps you take. I don't want to know. The blame trail stops with you. If you're team delivers, you stay. If it doesn't, everyone gets the axe and will be exposed as a rogue, out-of-control operation. Find out what's happening with Cognicom projects and vaccines, and how some of their virus samples got lost.Get inside the terrorist planning loop. Will you do that?"Elliot stood at attention, staring straight ahead and saying only two words.

"Yes, sir!"

CHAPTER 34
November 2115

"The Love You Make"
(Thread 1 Chapter 3)

"So, THAT'S WHAT THE Administration is doing! It's selling the public down the river, and we have to let people know."

Zoe's reaction to Electra's deliberately exaggerated rumors couldn't have been better because Electra planned to keep the Administration and the Guardian party off balance and at odds. Cognicom researchers, increasingly intimidated by Healthguard and Securityguard, didn't trust the government, so they whispered vague rumors that Electra's invisible snooping intercepted, three of which she would use: the Administration is secretly selling smart pills to China; it is restocking with placebos; it is giving improved smart pills to the chosen few.

"Now remember, I can't prove any of this, but if it will help, I'll look harder."

"Do so, but please be careful. Don't attract suspicion. What you've just given me is more than enough to spin into a damning press release that'll hype public concern and make us their only choice for making things right. And I believe that's what Jared and the Party are."

Electra couldn't disagree because she had uncovered no hidden agenda, and her opinion of Jared and his Guardians climbed while the public's opinion of Washington sank. Other than Securityguard and Healthguard's sometimes harsh and intrusive style, the public agreed with Jared, and many people cheered how the agencies conducted business because a rather mean-spirited public attitude prevailed, placing its health and safety ahead of human rights or longer-term political considerations. People didn't want to know what the Party did to protect them as long as it delivered what they wanted.

"I have to run, but we'll see you at our next meeting. And please keep bringing me summaries of the current events meetings. Next year, I think we'll have bigger P.R.responsibilities for you."Electra flashed her humility-filled smile.

"I'd like that if it works for me and for you. I'll be at my workstation if you need me.Otherwise, see you at the next meeting." For the rest of the afternoon, Electra burrowed further into confidential files while assisting a member of Zoe's team spin another press release. On the drive home, she thought about her good fortune, comparing hers to Washington's, which made her look like a lottery winner. She was exceeding all her expectations, and her Guardian Party P.R. work was helping to make it so, particularly since working for Zoe. She was pleased that Zoe trusted her, making it even easier to burrow into sensitive Guardian files. Thanksgiving came and went, but T-Plague related news reported nothing to be thankful for.There were no new outbreaks, but insidious side effects grew: victims hollowed out mentally or morally, random acts of violence, public services slow and shoddy, power and communications outages spreading. The public's outlook withered while its resentment towards the Administration or Middle East minorities grew. Dickens wrote in A Tale of Two Cities that it was the best of times,it was the worst of times.Electra would shorten it to the worst of times.

Electra brought Christi to a mid-December late Sunday afternoon dinner with the Antars, an occasion to give Dr. Antar the head scarves Christi had finally finished. After viewing online menus of Middle East restaurants, Electra had selected one not far from where the Antars lived and she planned to order falafel patties, lentil soup, and salad served with pita bread. Electra drove while Christi gossiped.

"I've never had Middle East cuisine, but I'll order what you do. I'm sure I won't be sorry. But I am sorry it took me so long to finish the scarves."

"Not to worry. I'm sure Doctor Antar will like them."

"I hope so. My fashion instructors think they're good, and they're hard to please."

"Let me tell you more about Doctor Antar. She stitched me up when I fell through the basement window. If it weren't for her, my scars would be much worse. In addition to being a plastic surgeon, she's a totally modern woman. Both she and her husband are more interested in American lifestyles than Islamic traditions. Her husband's name is Safwan, which means rock, and she says he's her rock, her source of security. He has an accounting practice that handles local businesses run by Middle East immigrants. Doctor Antar's first name is Rihanna, which means fragrant flower. The last name Antar comes from a hero found in Arabian mythology. You might say she's my heroine because she saved me from some bad scars."

"The scar on your cheek makes you look sexy. It looks like a dueling scar. It's subtle and adds a sense of mystery. Don't put so much of my cosmetic lotion on it."

Even Electra had a tiny smudge of vanity. "You think so?"

"I do, and Mother thinks I could be a first-rate cosmetician. She tells me I have an eye for beauty."

"Tell me about it later. Hey, what luck. There's a parking spot a couple of doors from the restaurant."

As they entered the restaurant, Electra spotted Dr. Antar, so the girls hurried to the booth.

"How wonderful to see you. And you've brought your singular friend Christi. I'd like you to meet my husband, Safwan." Electra knew Middle East greetings.

"Ahlan," she replied, then shook Safwan's hand and lightly kissed Rihanna's cheeks.

"If I ever have a Website, I'll feature my handiwork by showing pictures of you. Your scars have healed nicely. Christi, don't you agree?"

"I sure do, and I think the cheek scar looks totally sexy."Electra couldn't keep from blushing. *Better change the subject, and fast.*

"Christi has some items for you that we think are sexy too. I commissioned her to make them. She's a fashion designer, and her instructors gave her high marks for her work."It was Christi's turn to blush as she presented a festively wrapped package.

"May I open it now?"

"Well if you don't open my thank you gift, I will." Dr. Antar carefully unwrapped her present, then exclaimed how beautiful the headscarves are. Christi explained how she came up with her Middle East women's fashion concept,and Safwan told her there's a growing market for the type of clothing she's developing.

"You mean I could start a business with this? My parents will be happy to hear.They'll be pleased I have career potential."

Rihanna asked Electra to model one. "It looks elegant. I want you to keep one so you can wear it every time we get together. Safwan, which one should she keep?"

"The one she's wearing. The dark blue with the green and red geometric accents is very becoming." Electra was happy to accept.

"It's good I'm wearing it. It hides my blushing."

The rest of dinner conversation touched on a variety of topics: something about plastic surgery, something about accounting, something about current events. It was nearly seven-thirty when Electra glanced at her cell phone display. Everyone would have a busy Monday, so it was time to say goodnight.

Electra insisted on picking up the check,and not even the strong hands of a plastic surgeon could wrest it away.As they left,Electra joked that Christi would buy the next time because she would be wealthy from all her Internet sales. Electra's car was closer, so the Antars walked on from there.

"I like Doctor Antar.She's quite a role model.And her husband thinks I can be a fashion designer. Maybe I'm on my way."While Christi settled into the passenger seat, Electra's eyes followed the Antars because she spotted in the darkness two thuggish types moving towards them. Electra's warning system elevated and she watched until the Antars pulled away. *Better follow them to make sure they're safe.* The thugs had disappeared, which might be good or bad. Two miles later, Electra saw it was bad.

From a block behind, she watched a pickup truck veer alongside, forcing the Antars to the curb adjacent a strip mall, dim streetlights and light traffic guaranteeing no witnesses. Help would not be forthcoming, so the lightning brain shifted gears. Electra braked, cornered to the right and stopped. The sudden motion grabbed Christi's attention as Electra snapped out instructions.

"We've got a situation. I've got to help Doctor Antar. Drive to the end of the block and wait for me. Call 911 and tell them a mugging's in progress near a strip mall on Jeffers, just past Nagle. Look at the monitor. Do you see where we are?" Christi nodded as she got her bearings.

Electra jumped from the driver's seat, then opened the rear door to find one of her gym bags. *This is no time to get fancy. She wrestled into a dark long-sleeved pullover but couldn't find a face mask. No time to change pants. What I've got on will have to do, as will the running shoes I'm wearing. She was ready in less than a minute.*

"I need to wear the headscarf."

"Let me put it on you. I can wrap it nice and tight." Christi was now in the driver's seat, her eyes wide with excitement. Electra raced through commands one more time, an adrenaline rush washing over her. Though not armed, she would be a dangerous adversary.

Electra streaked to the scene, stopping to view before acting, and what she saw appalled her. The two thugs had shoved Rihanna to the pavement and were pummeling Safwan, one holding from behind while the other punched away. They were heavyset and taller than Electra, but so intent on pummeling they didn't notice her lurking nearby. As Safwan collapsed onto the pavement, the larger thug gloated.

"I think he's had enough. Let's see what we can do to the bitch in the turban. What the—." He was turning around when Electra swooped from behind, grabbing a clump of hair from each head. He landed two solid punches to Electra's nose and mouth, but her grip withstood the blows and she pulled them towards her, collapsing everyone into a heap on the pavement. Electra was pinned underneath but kept banging heads together like cymbals until their bodies were motionless. She struggled to her feet, then began kicking into the inert mass of flesh. Every kick inflamed her desire to kick again.

Get with it, Soldier! Mission accomplished! Go before the sirens get here! Electra's cognitive persona regained control. She looked down; no sign of movement. She looked around; two people walking tentatively to the crime scene. She glanced at the victims; Rihanna on her knees, helping Safwan. A glimmer of recognition sparked in the doctor's eyes, accompanied by a noiseless gasp. Electra raced away, vanishing into the darkness.

Christi was beginning to worry. Nearly ten minutes had gone by, and although she heard sirens approaching, Electra was still missing in action. Suddenly, a creature loomed out of the dark, first at the windshield and then alongside, ripping open the driver's side door.

"Slide over and let me drive. We gotta go. Damn, I'm sweating like a pig." Christi clambered into the passenger seat, saying nothing, simply watching as Electra sped them away. A minute later she swiveled towards the driver, ready to ask what happened but froze momentarily.

"Stop the car! You're not sweating. You're dripping blood." Undetected until this moment, the thug's blows had bloodied Electra's lips and nose. Electra drove until she found a secluded place to park.

"Let me peel off your headscarf so I can see what to do." Christi reached in back for a piece of clothing, then started wiping the blood away. Neither spoke until Christi had the flow under control. "The bleeding from your nose has stopped, and your cut lip isn't badly swollen. Hold my handkerchief in place while I find another piece of cloth."

Electra sniffled, "Check my bag in back." Christi found a bottle of water, using it to moisten a runner's t-shirt, then gently dabbed away the last smudges of blood.

"You're all good. Get us out of here." They drove in silence for ten minutes, the time required for the lightning brain to stand down. Christi watched Electra's transformation and it excited her. Tonight's epiphany had released Christi's genie from her emotional bottle, never to be imprisoned again. Christi craved Electra physically. Electra was incredibly sexy and unaware, which aroused Christi all the more. The scar, the blood, the split lip—all signs of vulnerability, of imperfection, of frailty. It took her breath away. Electra heard the gasp and turned towards her partner.

"Christi, what's wrong?" Christi's lips were trembling. She didn't know what to say or how Electra might respond, but she knew from emotions surging within she had to reveal her feelings or would forever feel broken.

"Please pull over and let me talk." In the dim glow of the street lamps, Electra saw a trickle of tears. She pulled onto the next side street and parked, turning the headlights off and letting the engine idle, then unfastened her seatbelt and took hold of Christi's hands. She could feel Christi trembling and wondered if Christi could feel her trembling too. She would wait for Christi to speak first, but no matter what Christi would say, Electra had to say what she was dying to say for so long.

"Tonight's a tipping point for me, for something that's been building in me. I, uh, I... Dammit, Electra, help me out like you always do."

Suddenly, Electra's emotional dam broke. She knew exactly what Christi was feeling and she knew exactly what she was feeling too. She knew what to say and what to do. She lowered Christi's hands and delicately wiped away the tears.

"Christi, whatever you are about to say, you must hear me first. I have loved you from the first time we played Cinderella years and years ago. And as I've grown, so has my love, but sometimes it hurts. I'm frightened by it. Frightened for you. Frightened for me. I know more about love than I did before, but I need you to help me. I love you sexually, but my love is much more than that...I, uh, I..." Electra could not continue. Her tears washed away unspoken words.

Christi didn't say anything. Her actions did. She leaned toward Electra, pulling her close, kissing her softly on her scarred cheek, then neck, then ever so softly on the lips. Both stopped trembling. The last traces of fear disappeared. They separated briefly, alive in the joy of knowing they were in love, then embraced again, sharing a kiss that suspended them in the timeless presence of being.

Neither could be apart from one another that night. Christi called her parents from Electra's to say she was sleeping over and Electra would drive her to campus tomorrow. It was still early, not yet ten-thirty; they were full of love-engendered energy. Christi showered first while Electra set out a light snack in the kitchen, then it was Electra's turn. They didn't talk, but simply enjoyed closeness. The lightning brain decided tonight was the night just to enjoy being alive. No concerns, no thinking about tomorrow or the day after. Electra took Christi by the hand and led her to the bedroom. Both were fully aware of the joy awaiting.

Electra turned on one light, then slowly removed Christi's robe, and Christi returned the favor. They gazed at one another, Christi the near-starlet quality blonde, Electra the owner of a practically perfect physique and smoky-dark chiseled silhouette. Electra turned off the light after they slid into bed, and then they intertwined under the covers. They talked through the night, interrupted only with occasional tender kisses. They talked about now, about each other, about not worrying what the future might bring. Sleep finally overtook them. Christi's class wasn't until one that afternoon, so they giggled about sleeping in. As she drifted into sleep, Electra recited a verse from Indira:

> "The past is but a memory,
> The future is unknown.
> But the present is a gift we see,
> And meant for us alone."

Both would treasure this night always.

The two lovers were incredibly happy that Monday. It was now four in the afternoon, and Electra was sitting at the lab's workstation trying to finish a report. She was making nada progress because she was thinking about something else. Her brain wanted to delve into issues that must be shared with Christi, so she stood and stretched, sipped her Coke, then meandered into the lab's quiet room to stretch out on a sofa Su often used when working through the night.

Electra knew complexity lies ahead if Christi becomes a longer-term lover.She descended into a self-absorbed reverie until a voice called to her.When she opened her eyes, she saw Indira.

"Why don't you sit up so I can talk to you.Your lightning brain has summoned me to explain last night.But please don't say a word. Just listen." Electra obeyed.

"I'm with you always, your inner voice,ready to discuss whatever you like whenever you like. After last night, your lightning brain decided a more vivid visit would be in your best interests, so it conjured me into your reverie.

"I'm happy for you, for having told Christi you love her. Now I will ask you a rhetorical question, then answer it. What is the comparison between your relationship with Christi and mine with Su? They match, but in opposite ways. Su and I were kindred spirits, so similar in so many ways and loving one another.You and Christi are complementary spirits, so different but so compatible.I died before I could share with Su the intimate joy you shared with Christi last night.You already know how Su feels about me,and she senses my presence in you, for you are an emerging reincarnation, greater in some ways and lesser in others.

"I loved your father also,but in different ways than my love for Su. He never knew how I felt about Su, and she will never tell anyone, nor will she ever be fully committed again, not even to Adom. And that is one of her two major flaws. She clings to what is no more instead of moving on to new possibilities. And it is closely related to her second: she looks to Romantic Love when considering the opposite sex. Do not repeat her mistakes, because you cannot control the path your love for Christi takes. You are both so young, and circumstances or changes in attitude may separate you,and if so,give thanks for what you had and then look to the future.

"You are on the right path, but beware of love's complexities. You want love, and now that you have Christi's you have inherited the outcome of an ancient Chinese proverb: Be careful of what you wish for because it may come true.You are responsible for her and must not overwhelm her. You have much to learn regarding the difference between love and being in love. Perhaps you have a genuine love, but beware of the Romantic Love trap Western cultures set for themselves. And remember what you have learned from Jung: you must own your Shadow. Do not make more of Christi than she is. Make the most for both of you, for you cannot take love, you can only give. Both of you are fond of retro-songs, so I shall leave you with this couplet from the last song the Beatles recorded together.

> 'And in the end the love you take is
> Equal to the love you make...'

"It is time for me to go. Do not worry about what the world might say. No need to tell anyone. No need for anyone to intrude. You and Christi are about to play another hidden game. I shall leave you with this question: What two Chinese proverbs are often quoted with the one I mentioned earlier? Awaken now and stay on your chosen path." Electra blinked, struggling to find words to say, but it was too late. She emerged from her reverie as a glowing image of Indira faded away.

Just then her cell phone chimed. Christi was calling. "Hi, Electra. Can you join my parents and me for dinner tonight?"

"Hello, Luv. I'd love to. And after dinner, I have lots to tell you. We have a new game, and it's for just the two of us. You'll love it. I'm leaving right now."

Electra and Christi didn't need year-end holiday excitement this year because just being together filled their days and nights. They were compatible in all the right ways, balancing intimacy and space so each remained their own person. Electra did not overthink what they shared. She basked in the moment and did not overwhelm her partner. There was none of that awkward, testosterone-induced bluntness or misunderstanding that all too often causes tension in heterosexual affairs. They simply enjoyed one another's company.

And neither of them were man-haters. Christi laughed off the official term—misandrist—because both had experimented with the opposite sex, often having found heterosexual intimacy enjoyable. At one time, Electra was afraid Christi was developing a man-eater's appetite, devouring too many fellows who gave her too many drugs. But the intimacy she found with Electra needed nothing else.

Electra and Christi kept their intimacy private, even bringing to a New Year's Eve party guys they had dated not long ago. At the stroke of midnight, everyone in their group locked arms to celebrate. It was the right time and place to hide a perfect embrace.

"Godspeed Farewell"
(Thread 1 Chapter 4)

JENNIFER CONKLIN'S NUMBER ONE New Year's wish had been fulfilled. Her daughter's promiscuous social life had taken a turn for the better now that she was spending more time with Electra. Christi had been a borderline wild child ever since adolescence, lured by promises of stardom her talents didn't quite match and by an urge for sex with older males. *Electra's always been a calming influence, a voice of reason. I don't know what caused it, but I'm happy Christi's spending more time with her. When she's with Electra, I don't have to worry. It makes the rest of my life that much easier.*

Jennifer's second wish was starting to unfold as she worked her way through certification courses that could launch a post-housewife career her husband Russell encouraged. He would quit his job and help her start a holistic healthcare counseling business when the time is right.

That's her third wish, but there's a major obstacle: the T-Plague. Russell tried to keep Cognicom concerns away from his family, but Jennifer knew he was troubled. Whenever she asked what's wrong, he would smile and say not to worry. It was his job to carry on, and time would make the current muddle better. She gave him all the support she could, maintaining his perfect home and social life. *I hope this year brings the right time.*

So far, the new year had brought nothing better for Cognicom. Su's latest vaccines were only a marginal improvement, and the political pressure continued to build. Electra was working from home alone on a bitterly cold and snowy Thursday evening, dividing time between vaccine and thesis work while expecting a call from Christi. She marveled how Christi's jabbering could give her such happiness and how so many of her suggestions Christi took to heart. She was primed to switch from work to play when her cell phone chimed, but was disappointed because it displayed an inbound call from the lab.

"Hello, this is Electra." She recognized Adom's voice.

"I hope I didn't reach you at a bad time. Su and I are at the lab, and we need you to join us right away."

"I can leave right now, but the snow might snarl traffic. What's going on?"

"Call me from the car and I'll fill in the details, but here's what we're dealing with. Are you sitting down?"

"No, but tell me anyway." "Your father is alive."

Perhaps the snow-slowed roads were all to the good that evening because Electra had an hour to herself while driving. She called Christi first, who sensed Electra had transitioned to a different state. "Thanks for calling so I don't worry. Take care of whatever the problem is. Be careful, and call me when you can."

Then she called Adom, who unloaded a surrealistic story about things she never knew. Jason was barely alive in a suspension chamber, vacillating on the borderline between life and death. He told her about suspension chambers, sometimes called pods, that each team kept in separate pod rooms. She recalled word for word what Adom had said.

"A pod's a life suspension chamber. We put designated T-Plague victims into suspension chambers so we can do testing. They're like a high-tech Petri dish. Bodies are suspended in liquids near freezing; nutrients and drugs are pumped in to keep them alive. If a pod is maintained properly, the body is preserved remarkably well. We can use them as long as the body's basal metabolic rates stay above threshold. But we have to pull the plug when they drop below. When your father blew himself up, Healthguard must have secretly decided he would be kept alive for testing. He's been used for R-Vac testing these past two years. The identities of those in the pods are closely guarded. Su found out because she recently became the tech lead and dug down for the details. But here's the bad news. Your father's basal rates have reached termination level. His body is to be disposed of this evening. We need you to help us figure out what to do."

The idea of suspension pod testing seemed reasonable to Electra's cognitive self, but horrifying to her emotional persona, especially once she stripped away the "veil of ignorance," an ethical concept for making objective judgments. *This is my Father! Is it right to put a near-death body in a suspension chamber so you can do testing? You might say sure, go ahead. But what if it's someone you love? What then? Interesting rhetorical question, but not up for discussion tonight.*

When Jason blew himself up, Electra couldn't do anything because NIH officials said he was dead. But if she had known he were alive, she would have taken all measures, even kill or die, to save him. The thought of killing was no longer abhorrent. She had already killed for vengeance or self-preservation, and she would kill again if her lightning brain issued the command.

Another thought came to mind. *What would Healthguard do to me if they found out I'm a genetic freak? I better steer clear of Healthguard and their partner-in-crime, Securityguard.*

As she drove, her brain raced through combinations and permutations of possibilities, concocting a plan that came in a flash. *We're going to play the shell game. We'll pull Father's body out of the disposal pod and put it in an empty suspension pod Adom controls. Then we'll pull a body out of another disposal pod and put it where Father's had been, covering our tracks in case body counts are matched with pods. Then we'll pump a cocktail of my best vaccines into Father, bringing him back to life. This is as good as it gets. No time to debate, so Su and Adom have to go along or go home.*

When she stormed into the lab, Adom and Su saw an Electra they better not cross. And when she sat them at a conference table, they kept their mouths shut. Electra wasted no time issuing commands.

"Only the three of us can ever know what we're going to do. Not even Mo can ever know. But first, I need some information. What condition is Jason's body in?" Adom looked at Su, who pursed her lips and took a deep breath before replying.

"I haven't actually seen his body, but it could be in surprisingly good shape. It all depends on what it was used for and how it was maintained. There are rumors about suspended bodies waking up." Electra nodded, then pushed further. "Do you think it's worth the risk to revive him?" Su looked at Adom, but he shrugged his shoulders, leaving the call on Su's.

"I honestly don't know what the odds are. You're better than I with numbers. What do you think?" *Dad's irretrievably dead if we do nothing, so the downside risk is nada. And the upside potential's priceless. We're going ahead.*

"It's worth it, so my plan is a go. Now I need answers to these questions. What time is pickup?" Adom knew the answer.

"Four in the morning. The driver rolls out pods one at a time. Depending on the number, it can take up to an hour to load."

"We have five hours until pickup. How many teams and pods are for tonight?"

"When I checked this afternoon, eight teams had ten for disposal. Only one from Cognicom."

"Does the disposal service do an actual body count?"

"I don't know, but if they do, it's done at the disposal site, not here."

"Who monitors the actual pickup from the staging area?" "Healthguard does. The guard checks on his rounds or when the driver gets here."

"Good enough. Here's the plan. As soon as Adom has an empty pod ready, we place it in the staging area. Then we pick the best time when the guard won't check, and we take Jason's body and put it in Adom's pod. Then we take a body from any other pod and shove it where Jason's supposed to be. Then we wheel Jason into Adom's pod room where I treat it with my advanced vaccine cocktail. If it works, we have Jason back from the dead. If not, Adom will dispose of the body in the usual manner. Adom and I are the team to execute this plan. We work together in case we need to change it on the fly. Any questions?"

Adom and Su gaped, unable to fathom how cold and calculating Electra had become. She showed no emotion, only logic and facts. They were dealing with a much different Electra.

Su looked puzzled when she asked, "Where are you going to get the advanced vaccine cocktail?"

"I'll take care of that. If there are no more questions, Adom and I will start now. And I think it would be good for you go home. You need to be fresh for tomorrow." Su was stupefied; Electra was ordering her to leave the lab she manages. Su left without saying a word.

Electra expected Adom's backbone to stiffen for the work ahead. The first task was easy: simply wheel a suspension pod to the staging area, then figure out when to swap bodies. Luck was with them; the guard was just leaving. Adom estimated they would have an hour to make the exchange undetected. That should be plenty of time, but they shouldn't waste a second because swapping two bodies among three pods, then covering tracks would take forty-five minutes if no glitches threw them behind schedule.

They went to work immediately, wheeling an empty pod next to Jason's and using fifteen minutes to make the transfer. Electra told Adom to wheel it back, plug it in, and make preparations for feeding in drugs and nutrients. She would handle the rest by herself: select a pod at random and transfer the body to cover their tracks. Then she would adjust the logs, seal the pods, and hurry back to the lab.

It was surprisingly easy to transfer the body by herself because the suspension fluid provided buoyancy. She used a towel to clean up spilled fluid, then adjusted the logs to make sure the records were in order. She was nearly finished.

After sealing the pod containing the body, she was about to put the cover on the empty one when she heard footsteps approaching. *I can't be caught in the staging area, and I can't run out the door. Where am I gonna hide?* There was only one choice; she climbed into the empty pod, put the cover in place, and waited.

Each pod rested on a separate roller cart, making it tricky to get in but she did. The air supply was limited and she had to immerse all but her head in the cool, oily white fluid, the stench making her gag. All she could hear were indistinct voices. When her pod started rolling, she knew the situation; the pickup truck had arrived early, and she was being rolled out for delivery. The odds of her pod being the first to go were one in ten, but tonight they rolled the other way.

Electra didn't panic. She concentrated on what to do, and while doing so, an odd thought popped into her brain. *Why does the cover have an open-close handle on the inside? Bodies in suspension aren't likely to pop open the lid.* The answer came in a flash. *Of course, it's a government safety regulation, similar to having latches on the inside of refrigerators and freezers. Finally, a government regulation comes in handy.*

She muffled throwing up while rolling to the truck. It seemed like an eternity for the driver to load her pod, but finally she heard a dull thud as the trailer door shut. Electra threw the latch, flung open the cover and climbed out, gasping for air. *I'm a mess, completely soaked and smelling worse than road kill. If I could see myself, I'd look like a ghoul.* It was pitch black, so she groped her way to the trailer door. *Damn! It's locked. Why would the driver lock the door between trips? Maybe there's a black market for these bodies, and he doesn't want to have one snatched on his watch.*

Electra shivered for forty-five minutes in sub-freezing temperatures until the driver was ready to load the last pod. When the door swung open, she timed her lunge perfectly. She slammed the trailer door into his head, toppling him face down, and she pinned him beneath the pod she tipped. Electra flew with the wind at her back across the dark pickup bay to an emergency door that her I.D. badge would open.

When Electra didn't return, Adom retraced his steps only to find the source of the problem: pods being wheeled to the truck. He suppressed his panic, knowing Electra would figure something out, so he returned to the lab and waited. He jerked around to face the door when he heard it click, then rushed to greet Electra, but his eyes and nose stopped him in mid-flight.

"Damn! What happened?" As Electra explained her bizarre escape, her words and appearance brought tears of laughter to both.

"You better use our lab's shower. If you don't have a change of clothes, I'll give you some of mine." Electra did have other clothes, so after a thorough scrubbing she told Adom what's next.

"You're done for tonight, so please go home and get some rest. I'm going to prepare the vaccine cocktail and write up a dosing regimen you and Su can use when you get back. Why don't the two of you come back tomorrow afternoon?"

"Fair enough. I'm beat, so I'm out of here. See you about two." Electra worked as quickly as she could, but by four o'clock she was too tired to think clearly. A catnap would do her brain good, so she stretched out on the quiet room couch, falling asleep instantly. Then a soothing voice broke through.

Electra dear, you've had a hectic night, and there's much more to do. Sit up, please, so I can sit next to you." Indira was about to pay another dream-like visit. Electra bolted upright to behold the glowing aura of her mother. For the third time, the lightning brain had conjured Indira.

"Mother, I need your help. What should I do?" Indira's smile was steady.

"Electra, my precious one, you know what to do, and I am here simply to talk it through. I know you bullied Adom and Su, forcing them to follow you."

"It was the best I could think of to bring Father back. Did I make the right call?"

"It's unfair to judge decisions made in battle from a rearguard position. You had to pull back the veil of ignorance because your father's life rests in your hands. You considered upside potential and downside risks, and you made the decision.

"But did I do the right thing? Indira smiled sadly.

"That is a question only you can answer. And frankly, it's a muddle. You can argue both sides using all your ethical frameworks and paradigms. But don't waste time and energy doing so. Live with your decision. Put it behind and move on."

Indira's words confirmed what Electra knew, but what she wanted to hear. She did not need permission from anyone. She would always accept the lightning brain's decisions.

"We have talked enough. It is time for you to act. My love is with you, and with Jason." Electra blinked, and Indira disappeared in a bright flash. Electra awoke from her dream-like state fifteen minutes later, refreshed and ready to work more.

Adom and Su arrived at two, not knowing what to expect, so Adom offered advice.

"Let's not rush to judge. Let's find out which Electra is here and what she's been doing." Su nodded but said nothing.

Electra was waiting for them in the conference room, ready to provide an edited version of what she had accomplished. She told just enough about the cocktail for Su to understand why it might work, then handed out copies of the dosing regimen.

"We'll know it's working if Father's vital signs climb. And we'll know one way or the other in 48 hours. And then we'll decide what to do next."

"Adom and I will carry on. All of us were stressed last night, so let's put that behind us and do what we can for your father."

"I want to go home and get some rest. Adom, will you be able to take over for Su on the graveyard shift? I'll come back tomorrow morning at eight." Su spoke before Adom could reply.

"I would like to work the graveyard shift. After all, I left too early last night, leaving the two of you to do all the heavy lifting." Adom jumped in to clarify.

"I told her it was heavy lifting to keep my eyelids propped open." Everyone's sense of humor had recovered after last night's ordeal.

"Thank you both, and please call me as soon as you see any change in vital signs."

After Electra left, Adom said, "Well, at least we know the good Electra is back with us, not her evil twin."

"I don't think there's a bad Electra, only a different Electra. And maybe there are others she hasn't shown us yet. Let's not worry about it, because we can't control it." Adom agreed, and they both headed to their workstations.

Electra drove directly home, ready for a hot soaking shower, then some oatmeal and English muffins before resting. Though she was tired, she was too wired to sleep, so she followed advice from her inner voice. *Just lie perfectly still and let your thoughts carry you wherever they want to go. And if you're still awake an hour later, get up and do some chores.* Electra was asleep in five minutes.

Maybe I should call Electra. I'd like to know she's OK. But no, I better not. She'll call me when she transitions back to a different state. I'll be ready to help her then.

Christi was not book smart like Electra but learned quickly when motivated. After Electra piqued her interest in the psychology of love, she surfed the Web to learn the difference between Romantic Love and reality. Until Electra came into her sex life, she never understood she was chasing the wrong kind of love. Romantic Love is a fantasy many cultures unwittingly burden lovers with, forcing their partners to jump through impossible hoops, trying to make them into what they cannot be. Christi was beginning to understand how sex amplifies the better kind of love, the love you give when caring and sharing and letting the other person be what they are. *I'm gonna ask Electra to tell me about the Tristan and Isolde legend. And if she says she doesn't know it, I'll bust her chops for not knowing everything. She'll know I'm kidding.*

When Electra arrived the next morning, she asked Su how her evening had been. "Last night was uneventful. Adom is a master pod technician. He makes it easy to monitor and adjust. Jason's basal levels have been improving slowly, and we are currently twenty-eight hours into treatment. You'll be here during the critical period. Please call when all metabolic levels reach the value Adom told us to look for."

"I will, and before you leave, may I show you my contingency plans." Su stood up and stretched, then replied.

"Let's sit at the conference table so you can sketch them." Not only had Electra already sketched them, but she had extra copies and gave them to Su. "You came up with four? I don't think there's ever been a human being as thorough as you. Please, explain."

"I'll go through them from best case to worst. Best case is Jason comes back with cognitive abilities fully restored, biological systems intact, and muscle atrophy requiring only a couple of weeks' intensive therapy. I'd give that a 10 percent probability. Next, full cognitive abilities with reparable damage to biological systems and muscle atrophy. I'd give that 30 percent. Next, partial cognitive abilities and irreparable damage, 30 percent. Finally, minimal cognitive abilities and irreparable damage, 30 percent. I came up with others, but these four crystallize what we need in order to make the final decision." Electra waited to see if Su would speak, but no, she would wait for Electra to finish, so Electra trekked ahead.

"The decision is whether or not to pull the plug. There, I've said a horrible thing and it's my dilemma."

"I follow what you're saying. You have a better handle on the odds than I do because you know better than I what we've been pumping in. I have more confidence in cognitive improvement. The big unknown is damage to your father's biological systems. Adom and I can do some quick tests if it gets that far. If they're repairable, you might decide to keep him alive, but if the damage is too severe, you must let your father go. And if Jason can talk or signal, we must find out what he wants."

"I look at it the same way. I'll call you and Adom as soon as I see basal rates accelerate upwards. That could happen as early as midnight. I plan to stay the next twenty-four hours, and I hope I call before then."

"I do too. We'll hope for the best, and you've made enough plans to cover all the bases. I'm going home."

Electra kept busy puttering in the lab or surfing the Web, but time grew heavy as it crept forward. Trying not to blink until the North Star moves would be easier than waiting for Jason's basal rates to accelerate. Finally, witching hour came, not at midnight, but at eleven. Jason's vital signs moved upward abruptly; Electra made the call, and Su answered on the third ring.

"Father's vital signs are accelerating upwards. Please get here fast."

Electra dialed up pod temperature and prepared endomorphin-filled syringes in case Jason revives but experiences intolerable pain.

She shuddered to think their collective efforts might do nothing more than increase her father's agony, but there was no turning back. Electra was about to remove the pod cover when her partners arrived; Adom took charge.

"Looks like you've done all the preparations. I'll take it from here. Su, please call out gauge readings when you're ready."

Jason's head was visible now, his body floating just beneath the surface of the translucent suspension fluid. Electra grabbed a towel and gently wiped her father's face. Other than a stubble beard and weight loss, he looked like the father she last saw at breakfast just over two years ago. There was no scarring or discoloration. Electra stood in the background and watched as Adom adjusted the controls.

"I'm dialing up the temperature. How are his vitals?" "Stationary, but let's do quick digital scans of cardio and pulmonary. That's the best we can do to get a handle on bio system damage." Electra studied her father's face, looking for the tiniest trace of movement that would indicate he was coming back. Adom and Su joined the vigil, and Su was the first to detect motion. "Did you see that? I saw eye movement."

Ever so slowly, a flickering motion started beneath closed eyelids. Intermittent at first, then steadier. They fluttered uncertainly, like a butterfly's wings after shedding its cocoon, then faster and faster, and suddenly Jason's eyes flew open. A look of dull surprise, and then a sharper look of a person regaining awareness emerged. Su was the first to speak, and she spoke slowly and clearly.

"Jason, please don't try to talk. Blink if you can understand me." His look changed to that of comprehension, and he blinked one time.

"Jason, I'm Su. Do you remember me, and do you remember being in an explosion? Blink once if you do." He blinked once. "That explosion was two years ago. We were told you were dead, but you were placed in a suspension pod and kept alive. Try swallowing. Blink once if you think you can talk. Tell us if you need water."

They could see him struggling to swallow; it was painful to watch. "I'll get Father the water container." When she had it, Electra carefully placed the flexible straw between Jason's lips. He sucked several times, and a smile came to his lips and eyes. Then his voice faintly rasped,

"Indira, not dead? Am dreaming?" Electra could not to speak; Su answered for her.

"Electra and Adom are with me. Do you remember who they are? Are you able to talk more?" He whispered, "Yes." Adom took over for Su.

"You were reported dead, along with two other researchers. You must have signed some papers long ago that let NIH put you into a pod for research testing. Su just found out, and we brought you out of suspended animation. We need to figure out how to keep you alive. We're doing quick bio scans to see how good your systems are. We want to bring you back if there's any hope at all, but tell us how you feel."

Jason grimaced. "Waves of pain. I hurting." Su used the first syringe.

"We've done digital scans on cardio and respiratory. They're at thirty percent, but they might go up. The glimmer of a sad smile flickered across Jason's lips. He could barely rasp his reply.

"Two years. Too long." Su didn't know what to say, but finally uttered, "Electra, talk to your father."

It took all of her self-control to keep from bursting into tears. She stroked her father's cheek, then said in as strong a voice as she could,

"Hi, Daddy. I love you. I've been working with Aunt Su on T-Plague vaccines." She could say no more, for she had lost her train of thought.

Jason's smile became stronger. "Look like Indy." He winced, then groaned from the pain surging through his body. Su jumped in.

"I'll give you more pain killers, then we'll get you out of the pod and into intensive care. I'll call Med Emergency right now." Jason fought to get the words out.

"Two years. Too long. Let go. Love you."

"Father, no! I'll learn how to restore you. Let me try. Please let me keep you!"

"No. Let go. Love you." A look of finality shone in his eyes. Su took over for the last time.

"Jason, you are right. Godspeed." All three clustered above him, stroking his cheek and his hair, smiling bravely as Adom dialed down the pod systems. Jason's eyes began to flicker once more, but the smile never faded. The flickers became weaker, fading away as he went gently into that good night. It was right for him to go in peace, rather than rage the dying of the light that disappeared from his eyes.

But it was not so for Electra. Emotions overwhelmed her. Confusion rushed in as she gasped to breathe. She gaped at her father, then at Su but could not speak. Instinct took over; she screamed, then ran out of the lab and collapsed into her car.

"Hello Su. It's Christi Conklin. I've been calling Electra's cell, but no answer. Do you know where she is?

"Hello, Christi. Yes, she drove home two hours ago."

"Thanks for letting me know. I'll check to see if she's OK."

Now that she knew, Christi could do something other than worry. It was four in the morning when she parked in Electra's driveway, entering through the kitchen door, using the key Electra had given her. There was nothing stirring; no light or sound. The house seemed to be in a state of suspended animation, waiting for life to return.

Christi spied light coming from Electra's second-floor bedroom and found her face-down on the bed, still wearing her jacket. Christi called out and shook her, but she would not stir. Unbeknownst to Christi, the lightning brain had shifted into its fortress of solitude, not to be disturbed until it was ready to reawaken Electra. Christi's incipient panic turned into action, checking vital signs as her mother had taught. *She checks out OK. I guess she's not ready to wake up. I'll make her comfortable.*

Before rolling Electra onto her back, Christi removed jacket and shoes, and then placed a pillow under Electra's head. She covered her enigmatic lover with a blanket, then pulled a chair closer to the bed, turned on the night light and turned off the lamp on the end table. *It's my turn to watch over Electra. I shall be here all night, and I shall be here when she awakens in the morning. I don't know which Electra will emerge, but whichever one does, I'm glad I can give back for all she's given me.* Christi watched over Electra all night long.

"The Eyes of Texas"

(Thread 1 Chapter 5)

ELECTRA'S INNATE RESILIENCE, COUPLED with Christi's emotional support, brought her back to a normal state of affairs soon after the failed recovery mission. Having pushed to the limit even though the odds had been long, she accepted the irreversible loss of her father and grieved only briefly for what might have been, then buried the experience and moved on to her slate of current activities for which she missed nary a beat.

The mission did bring to life one unintended consequence. The lab's rumor mill stirred with hushed stories about suspension pod mishaps, about bodies being snatched in the middle of the night, about rogue covert operations groups planting moles deep inside Cognicom. A Guardian Party mole heard them all and sent the rumors to his handler, who passed them up the chain of command to a P.R. person who wanted to know more. And that person knew just the person to ask.

Zoe corralled Electra as soon as she arrived one afternoon at P.R. headquarters. Though always busy, she followed orders given by Brandon Sparrows to make time for their prize leaker.

"Good afternoon, Electra. I heard a rumor that Cognicom projects are using a contraption called a suspension pod to put victims in for vaccine testing. Is that true?" *Zoe must know someone who's close to a mole. I can use that person to burrow deeper into Guardian Party P.R. files. If there's a hidden agenda, someone near the top's gotta know. Let's see what I can swap.*

"Hi, Zoe. I heard the same rumor, but I can't confirm it. But I saw a memo that mentioned something I never heard before. Are you aware of a CIA covert operation led by a guy named Elliot Spitzdieck?" Zoe's surprised look answered the question.

"No. Please go on."

"Evidently, it's planting moles in Cognicom, trying to dig up dirt to divert blame from the Administration to someone or somewhere else. And that's not all. There are other rumors about the Administration is sabotaging projects for personal gain." That was enough bait; Electra waited for Zoe to bite.

"We need to let our security team know ASAP. How about we meet with them right now?"

"OK, but I can't stay long today. I have to get to class in about an hour. I just stopped in to make a couple of follow-up volunteer recruiting phone calls."

"Not a problem. They're in this building and I'm sure they'll make time to see us. I'll call."

Brandon picked up immediately when he saw Zoe's caller I.D. He managed several Guardian Party teams that had priority access to Guardian Security and was certain it could use what Electra knew, so he whisked Zoe and her leaker to his private conference room, getting right to the meat of the matter.

"Zoe tells me you have a scoop for us. What's going on at Cognicom?" *This might be the person to hack. I'll give him something to nibble on, and in return I'll dive into his directories.*

"I think the CIA has a covert operations project named Death Shield that is trying to frame someone in Cognicom to take the fall for how the Administration has botched everything it's been doing on T-Plague. If the Guardian Party doesn't blow the whistle on them, who will?" Though his reply was noncommittal, his body language spoke the opposite.

"We at Guardian Party public relations try to keep up with the Admin's excuses for why there are no effective vaccines, so I'll check with our people to see if they've heard your story. Healthguard and Securityguard agencies would want to know."

Electra added, "Most of the Cognicom researchers are worried and feel threatened by the harsh measures Healthguard and Securityguard are putting in place. Do you think that's consistent with the Guardian Party's approach, and if so, don't you think that's going against what the public wants?" Brandon folded his hands and spoke the party line.

"Look, harsh times demand harsh measures. We can't worry about collateral damage. If some bystanders get thrown under the bus, maybe they shouldn't have been standing so close. We have to guard against unusual sorts of people causing unusual situations." The more Brandy talked, the more alarms went off inside the lightning brain.

Father's prophecy is coming true! I can never reveal my secret, especially in these ominous times, especially not to the high-sounding Guardian Party. They'd treat me worse than they treated Father. They'd dissect me if they knew I'm a genetic freak. And I better look out if there's a hidden agenda lurking somewhere near the top. Brandy's Email trail might tell the tale. Electra had just learned all she needed. It was time to go.

"Yes, Mr.Sparrows. I think you're right. I'll jot down all I know about rumors and give it to Zoe. I sure hope this information helps. Zoe, I have to leave for class soon."

Zoe beamed. "Thank you so much. Please do so before you leave. I'll see you next week at our meeting."

Later that afternoon, Electra used the endorphins generated on her ten-mile run to think through what Brandon had divulged, confirming she would need to stay below Guardian Party radar while trespassing into their Cyberspace and picking through places to look for hidden agendas.

Later that evening, the Invisible Man received a call from Headquarters. "What do you know about a covert CIA operation called Death Shield?" He knew nothing, and Headquarters commanded him to dig deeper or risk termination. The order prompted him to call the Invisible Hand, who listened phlegmatically.

"You must find out who or what Death Shield is after. You must get there fast, or else you go home. Do you get my point?"

"Copy that."

"Good. Call back at your scheduled time, and when you do I only want to hear about blue sky, green trees, and ducks swimming." That was not the only covert T-Plague-related inquiry going on. Elliot Spitzdieck was also feeling the heat to get results, and he was grilling one of his lieutenants for more results.

"Look, Elliot, I'm making headway, but you have to cut me some slack. I've delivered more in six months working on this damn project than anyone ever has." Kenton Scraffe—codename Gunner—was trying to convince his team leader not to terminate him. He was a wiry sort of forgettable fellow whose unexceptional career started at a CIA staff position that led him to the field. Now in his early forties, he had a reputation for acting too quickly, hence the nickname for shooting first and interrogating later.

"I've dug up enough on the Cognicom projects to come up with a story we can run with. Hear me out." Elliot didn't say a word, but nodded his head.

"Here's the story line. There's gotta be one big-brain researcher controlling vaccine development, and that mystery person is using stop-and-start progress to their advantage. Maybe the schmuck is selling out to the highest bidder or settling a score with the government. I have my sights set on one person. What I'm about to do is pay a visit, bringing along one of our medical guys to coax out answers. I'm sure this will get us to the next level. Give me a couple of weeks, and I'll get you what you want." Spitzdieck finally spoke. "You have until the 4th of July. Do whatever you need to get cooperation." Gunner had his marching orders and wouldn't let anything get in his way.

Smart as she was, Su couldn't figure out Electra's latest suggestions. She needed a second shift tutoring session where neither professor nor pupil would be interrupted, so she scheduled one for a mid-June Friday evening.

Su had figured out during their failed rescue mission that there were several Electras, each extraordinary though enigmatic. *I'm not as sharp as I was before the T-Plague knocked me down. But I'm smart enough to know Electra can transform her bio-field to become whatever she needs to be. I don't know how she does it, and I can't follow much of her theories when she shifts into one of her high-powered academic states, but I can follow her directions. I miss Indira. I wish she were alive to see Electra in action. Maybe she could understand her daughter better. I'll have to settle for being her reserved and reclusive semi-smart aunt.*

Su had been struggling gamely in her lab's conference room for two hours trying to keep up with Electra. She used a call from the security desk to take another time out.

"This is Doctor Chou."

"This is Security. There's a Kenton Scraffe and an associate here to see you. I checked, and they're from the CIA. Shall I bring them to R-Vac lab?"

"Did he say what they're here for?"

"No, just that his boss, Elliott Spitzdieck, needed some information. Shall I have him clarify?"

"No, just bring him back to my lab." Electra didn't like the expression on Su's face when she disconnected the call.

"What was that all about?"

"Two agency guys want to talk to me. Security desk checked the badges. One of them said Spitzdieck from the CIA sent them." Electra knew immediately this was going to be bad. As the lightning brain shifted to a higher gear, she sprang into action.

"I can't be here. I'm calling my cell number on the speaker phone so I can listen in. Don't let them know it's on or anything about me." Electra dialed, then answered when the call connected. "Say something, so I can test the speaker volume."

"Testing, 1, 2,3. How's that?"

"Good. Stay in this room and get them to sit near the speaker phone. I'll be close." Electra dashed to Adom's lab to gather what he needed. The lightning brain had already figured out what was happening.

While the agents marched to the lab, Electra changed into a Securityguard uniform she kept hidden in her locker and then started eavesdropping as the agents trooped in.

"Doctor Chou, my name is Agent Scraffe. I report to Elliot Spitzdieck. Look, let's not waste each other's time. We think you're near the center of the entire NIH T-Plague conspiracy and want you to tell us all the details. We'd like you to cooperate with us here and now—or at our office if you prefer not to. My associate has the means to make you talk. He's good at needling people we interrogate." Scraffe's cold eyes stared at Su, letting what he said sink in. She sat motionless, frozen like a mouse in a cobra's glare.

"Let me help fill in some of the words. You are holding back on vaccine development. You are selling out to the Chinese. After all, you were born there. You're selling out to the highest bidder. You're working through your volunteer group with Isilabad terrorists because you are a closet Muslim. Take your pick. We can pin anything we like on you and make it stick."

Su blinked and finally stuttered, "Th-this is incredible, just in-incredible." Scraffe was losing patience.

"OK, Doctor Su. Maybe we can loosen your tongue. Tie her to the chair. Start with a normal dose."

Electra had heard enough and had to act before Scraffe overdosed Su. She knew all the nooks on every level in the lab, so she grabbed a flashlight and tools from her locker, then raced to the wing's main circuit breakers. She had practiced before what she was about to do, and as she reached the electrical closet a surge of excitement swept through as her personas merged into one. *This is not a drill!* echoed in her head.

She pried open the electrical box and smashed enough circuit breakers to plunge the entire wing into darkness. Then she flipped on the flashlight, found a fire extinguisher and raced to the conference room, pulling alarms on the way. Flashing emergency lights and blaring horns added to the surreal confusion. Guards and researchers soon would be staggering through the darkness, trying to help or trying to escape. Electra would do both.

Scraffe's partner wasn't getting results fast enough. "Give her another jolt."

"No, let's wait a little longer. It'll have an effect soon." Scraffe was getting more unpleasant.

"Dammit, do it now. If you won't, I will." His associate did his bidding reluctantly. Su's body jerked once, then collapsed, head drooping on her chest.

"She's in cardiac arrest! Her lights are out!" Just then the lab's lights went out.

Electra plunged through the darkness into the lab. As the flashlight beam blinded Su's inquisitors, she yelled, "Fire! Follow me out!" Then she clubbed them senseless with the fire extinguisher and searched frantically for Su, who was dangling deathlike from a chair. Electra's altered state elevated higher. *There must be adrenaline in Scraffe's medical bag for emergencies like this.* She found it, then grabbed syringes and adrenaline bottles, loading two syringes before stabbing one into a protruding vein on Su's forearm. Then she waited for what seemed like an eternity, checking pulse and breathing. Su sputtered back to life when the adrenaline took effect.

Untying Su, Electra propped her up in the chair. Next, she stuffed what she had into the medicine bag, scattered papers on the floor, smashed some of the cabinets, and started a fire. Then she took Scraffe's gun, grabbed the medicine bag, and used a fireman's carry to hoist Su. Electra's adrenaline-charged strength carried the load to the nearest exit, darkness and panic giving all the cover needed. When she reached her car, she belted Su into the passenger seat and escaped unnoticed into the darkness.

By the time Electra reached home, she had scoped out a plan Su could live with. *If Su doesn't disappear, she'll be hunted down and made a scapegoat. I need Christi to do a Su makeover. Su's gotta understand it's the only game in town. My mistake. It's an out-of-town game.*

Midnight had come and gone by the time Christi and Electra had Su back in working order. The shower helped clear her head, and now that she was dressed in Electra's sweats and robe, looked like a carefully wrapped China doll. All three were snacking in the kitchen when Electra began rolling out a plan for Su's future.

"Please tell me again what happened last night. It's still fuzzy."

"We have a problem on our hands. There's a rogue CIA covert operation that's targeted you as the mastermind behind a fantastic plot they've cooked up about a T-Plague vaccine conspiracy. They drugged you to get you to talk. This is all about political power plays and covering for the Administration and its Washington Establishment cronies. They're wrong, but that doesn't matter. One way or another, if they get their hands on you, they'll tie off their fantasy and tie it around your neck, and maybe Adom and Mo's too."

"How is this possible? And what about you?"

"Think about this. All sorts of moles are burrowing into Cognicom. One of them dug up something that put them on to you. Remember a couple of years ago when we were followed to the parking garage after Robin's piano competition? That was an early warning. And don't worry about me. I'm on the fringe and too low in the pecking order. But if they catch you and keep playing charades, I might become a target, so I can't let any of this happen." Su's expression matched her words.

"What do we do now?" Electra took a deep breath and dived into her plan.

"You have to disappear without a trace. The fire will temporarily cover your tracks and sidetrack the CIA, but we have to move you."

"Fire? You mean they started a fire in the lab last night?"

"Yes, but that's not important. Here's the plan. We'll create fake I.D.'s for you. Social security card, driver's license, and passport should do it. Christi will give you a makeover, including new hairstyle, makeup, and clothes. And then I'll make you disappear. We'll get you situated far away in a safe place. But you'll need to keep a low profile."

"What about my name? Will that change too?"

"As long as you're a person of interest, I'm afraid so. Your close friends can call you Su, but everyone else will know you by your new name. Pick something you like and I'll put it on your cards. And starting right now, you can't talk to anyone who can link you to NIH. Not even Adom or Mo can know what's going on."

Electra's partners reacted differently to the news. Christi was beginning to catch on to the game, but Su was thunderstruck. Electra shook her by the shoulders.

"The CIA will not stop until they're satisfied, and they're hard to please, so do what I'm telling you."

"How are you going to get fake I.D.'s for me?"

"Trust me. I'm very good getting what I need in shadow-Cyberspace. I'll get them in the next day or two. Christi, when can you start Su's makeover?"

"How about later today. We'll do hairstyle and makeup. Tomorrow we can shop for clothes."

"Sounds like a plan, and we must keep everything we've talked about a secret; not even Adom, Mo, or Christi's parents can ever know. And we all need to sleep, so let's go to bed. Su, you can sleep in Jason's room. Christi can bunk in my room with me. It'll be like high school days." Christi deadpanned her reply.

"I guess so. Those high school sleep-over days were fun." Electra got in the final words.

"It'll be a good way to end a terrible Friday. Saturday will be much better."

And then she said only to herself,

Especially after a night with you. I'm too wired to sleep.

Electra's cell chimed at nine the next morning, signaling a call from Adom. He was concerned that Su hadn't come home from the lab last night. Electra fibbed by saying she hadn't talked with Su since early yesterday evening, nor did she mention the fire.

"If she calls, let me know. Oops, I have another call coming in. Gotta grab it. Damn, it's not from Su. It's from Mo. Gotta go."

He'll call back as soon as soon as he's finished talking. Electra picked up five minutes later.

"Su's lab caught fire last night. Two people were burned, and she's missing. Mo's already there and I'm leaving now. Please call me if you hear anything, and I'll do likewise." The commotion awakened Christi.

"Hey, bunkmate what's all the excitement?" Electra rolled over and gently wiped Sandman's sand from Christi's eyes.

"Good morning, Luv. Adom's upset about Su not coming home, and Mo called him about the fire. Let's get dressed, get Su, and get some breakfast. We have great games to play today."

Electra started making shadow-Cyberspace purchases right after breakfast. She shopped often in Cyberspace, sometimes paying with bitcoin or similar digital currencies, other times bartering with smart pills she minted while preparing improved vaccines. Drone delivery, perfected before she was born, made the exchange effortless. She would have Su's new I.D.'s by Tuesday.

Her next order of business was to set up—once again online—a series of virtual interlinking corporations whose structures she had planned several years ago, awaiting the right time to create them. They would be needed to insulate all her business activities and partners from prying eyes. Her inner voice reminded how many useful skills she had acquired from sci-fi, action-spy, or Internet videos. A line from one of them popped into her brain. *You have to go to jail to learn to be a crook. Ha. I'm no crook. I'm simply using survival skills and going to Cyberspace to get by in a dangerous world. And crypto-currencies are so much better than credit cards. Bitcoins can't be traced, so I stay invisible. Even in shadow-Cyberspace, I don't leave a trace.*

While Electra surfed away, Christi's magic makeover transformed Su. A new rinse and hairstyle complemented with makeup highlights converted her by dinner into a forty-something who looked ten years younger than the calendar count.

"You look like an older cousin, not my aunt. With the right clothes, friends might not recognize you at a distance."

Christi said, "I'm glad you like my handiwork, but you better fill us in on more of the plan so we can dress Su to fit."

"Yes, please tell. What's to become of me? I'm ready to play an active role, not some helpless survivor." Electra had a path mapped out, starting from Su's grad school days.

"Let me review some background first. Think back to grad school when you Worldstars dreamed about Worldstar Biologicals. Well, you are about to become the first person in the company. I've already set up virtual corporate shells. And Worldstar Biologicals starts by striking a deal with H&H DNA Partners, an Austin-based company created ten years ago by Hudson Haller. Do you remember him?" Su nodded slowly.

"Yes. He was one of Adom's friends. We all liked him. A big guy with a big personality. Adom used to keep in touch. How did you find out about him?"

"By now you should know I know more than you realize. Let me go on." Su flashed a girlish smile; Electra continued.

"I've vetted his company. They're solid, privately held between Hudson, aka Hud, and his father Hollis, aka Holy. According to his social media profile, he likes poker and would bet the ranch to have a bite at developing a T-Plague vaccine that works. We're going to make him an offer he can't refuse." Electra paused to check that her partners were with her, then charged ahead.

"The three of us will fly to Austin on his leased corporate jet just as soon as I confirm an itinerary. Christi is part of this so we look bigger and better, as if we're more than just me and a computer. And here's our cover story for the trip. I have relatives in Texas who invited me and Christi to visit. I'm president of the umbrella company, KC Ventures, Inc. We'll dress Christi up as our Administrative V.P. Su, you're President of Worldstar Biologicals, which is one of the companies under my corporate umbrella. By the way, KC stands for Kittner-Conklin, unless Christi wants to reverse the order to CK."

"No, I'll go with it as long as I get a Beemer company car. I go for designer labels." Electra ignored Christi's humor and continued.

"Let's get to the critical part. We'll put my vaccine formulations into the business and tell Hud they're Su's, but they're not patented. And we won't ever patent them. As part of the deal, Su moves to Austin and works anonymously doing R&D for Hud. And since his company is private, no one needs to know how our businesses are related. Now everyone, take a deep breath. Here comes the deal breaker.

"All this works only if we can trust Hud. He has to know Su is a CIA person of interest, and we have to know he'll keep his mouth shut so Su stays below the radar. And we'll only know his intentions when we meet him in person." Su looked lost but said nothing, so Electra marched ahead.

"I'm almost done. On Monday, Christi will do an image remake for herself and for me. We have to look more mature, more corporate. Also on Monday, I'll take Su so she can pick up stuff at the apartment when Adom's at the lab. Then I'll take her to the bank to close out whatever accounts she has. And on Tuesday, I'll call Hud to set up the trip.So,that's the plan.I know I've thrown a lot at you,but we have to act fast or our head start on Death Shield will shrink. Su, what do you think?" Su had the perfect answer.

"All this is beyond me.You two carry on.I'm going to bake some brownies. At least I know where Electra keeps the mix."

Monday was busy—but not nearly as pleasant—for the other players threading their way through the aftermath of Friday night's bizarre event. Mo insisted Adom join him for an emergency meeting with Bobbi. Unfortunately, neither had anything positive to offer, so she gloomily summarized what Mo had reported.

"So,two agents from the CIA came to our lab Friday evening to talk with Doctor Chou about what? We don't know.About an hour later someone caused a power outage in the wing housing Doctor Chou's lab and started a fire.The agents suffered minor burns and claim someone knocked them out.Doctor Chou is missing.There's no trail to follow,and the CIA is not cooperating.This is dreadful." Mo and Adom sat like stones, so Bobbi continued.

"Let's talk about damage control. When will the lab be open, and what do we do if Doctor Chou doesn't show up?"The dull tone of Mo's voice mirrored his outlook.

"The lab reopens next Monday, but we'll be understaffed. Adom assumes temporary responsibility for Doctor Chou's R-Vac team in addition to his other two,which means Adom is technical leader on all three Cognicom projects.That's too much of a load,so I'll immediately place one senior researcher on I-Vac, and another on S-Vac because those two were at least showing a little progress. Doctor Chou took over R-Vac several months ago, and according to her latest reports, she was working on a vaccine that showed promise. Adom has some familiarity with what she was doing, so in maybe two or three months he might have something to show, but we can't promise."

Bobbi rested her chin on the palm of her hand, then said sardonically, "Aren't we all glad we signed up for T-Plague projects?" She was not looking forward to meeting later that afternoon with her boss.

Elliot Spitzdieck's Monday evening meeting with his section chief went even worse than expected. The hatchet job left him barely standing.

"Jesus H.Christ! You send two agents to burn this Doctor Chou, and they end up getting roasted and Chou missing in action.They claim someone caused a blackout,knocked them out,set a fire,and disappeared like a puff of smoke in a sandstorm. Gimme a break. You think Doctor Chou OD'd on truth serum and is dead.If so,did she get up and walk out before your guys were rescued, or did the person who clubbed them waltz out with her without being seen? If this gets leaked to the press, we'll have trouble containing the fiasco. Can you add anything?" Spitzdieck couldn't.

"OK, here's what's coming. Your buddy Gunner's out. You're immediately demoted into his position. I'll find a new team leader. Until I assign someone, try to pick up the pieces and do something that won't make your Death Shield Team an even bigger joke. If you or anyone on your team shoots themselves in the foot, I'll fire at a different target. Dismissed."

Elliot staggered to his car and sat for several minutes, trying to think of something to do, but his brain fired blanks.

Hudson Haller had been intrigued by a Tuesday Email outlining a business proposal for what had eluded him since starting H&H DNA Partners. When his secretary buzzed him Wednesday morning regarding an incoming call from the person who sent the Email, he took the call immediately.

"Howdy, this is Hudson Haller. How and who are you, Little Lady?" A confident and pleasant-sounding woman's voice answered.

"Mr. Haller, my name is Electra Kittner, president of KC Ventures. Since you took my call, I assume my Email is of interest. I propose you fly two of my senior executives and myself to meet you in person. I know you like poker, so if you're willing to play a high stakes game with us, we can make it a win-win. How do you like the agenda and proposal I included?" Electra knew how to negotiate, knowing when to talk and when to listen. What she heard was just what she wanted. They would fly to Austin Friday morning.

Afterwards, Hud thought carefully about the person he had just spoken with. *So, the Little Lady's last name is Kittner. That says a lot. And I bet she's got the grit of a Texas woman. No matter how tough things get, she's seen tougher. I'm lookin forward to seein for myself."*

Hud liked the proposal as much as what was sitting across from him at the conference table: three attractive, professionally attired women. One of them, a petite Chinese lady looked vaguely familiar, like someone he knew in school, but younger. *If they're half as sharp as good lookin maybe I'll roll the dice for a deal. But don't get the cows runn'in till I check 'em out.*

"Mr. Haller, thank you for meeting with us today. We're here on behalf of Worldstar Biologicals and, if we come to terms, we will contribute to our joint venture what you need to take H&H DNA Partners to the next level. We've vetted several candidates, and you are among the top three. Like you, we know how to compute odds and will decide today if you are the right fit. If we like what you say, we'll be willing to take a gamble." Electra knew Hud would try to maneuver her gambit in his favor, but she would angle him into a corner no matter what he says.

Whether doing business or playing poker, Hud took pride in his ability to put opponents on their heels. This morning's contestant was already wearing an attractive pair, so she would be a pushover. Or so he thought.

"Well now, those are mighty confident words, and if you can deliver the goods maybe we can do business. Are all you East Coast gals as pretty as you three? Three smart and pretty little ladies in one package always looks good to me. We could be partners in many ways." Electra knew Hud's welcoming smile and Texas-accented banter were meant to be harmless icebreakers, but she pounced on them, turning what Hud said to her advantage. She pulled back from the table, feigning insult.

"Mr. Haller, your remarks are a sexist affront to professional women everywhere. We are much more than pretty talking heads having boobs for brains. Please keep your comments on a professional level when addressing us."

Hud squirmed before replying, "Well look here, Little Lady. Don't get your tits in a tangle. Er, I mean, uh, I was just trying to make you feel welcome."

Electra calmly removed from her briefcase a small caliber revolver, placing it next to her on the table.

"Mr. Haller, let's get the facts straight. First, I'm not so little. And second, how do you know I'm a lady?" She picked up the revolver and casually spun the cylinder. Then, while sighting down the barrel, said dryly, "We're here to make you an offer you can't refuse." Later that evening, Su would joke that when Electra pulled the gun, she didn't think it was possible for even Hud's man-sized eyes to open that wide. And Electra's stunt worked to perfection because it brought both sides together, letting them share confidences on which to build trust and a deal both sides wanted. Su has a safe haven and Hud can profit from her vaccines, but he will need to take directions from Electra to avoid being swept up in political intrigue or government strong-arm tactics.

The meeting ended late that afternoon, and afterwards Hud invited his new partners home for a dinner that would extend the conversation, giving his father Holy an opportunity to join in. It was a chance for Hud and Su to blend the old and the new. Hud joked that Su couldn't possibly be the gal from his grad school days; she looked too young. Su replied that this Oriental lady cleverly hides the years, thanks to Christi's magic makeup. She would stay with Hud and his father while settling in.

Memories of the Worldstars came floating back to Hud when Electra explained who she is. He shared stories about Indira and Jason that not even Su had heard. Electra listened, keeping her thoughts to herself. *Too bad Adom can't be part of this, but until Su is out of the crosshairs he can never know her whereabouts. I'll handle all contacts with Austin.* As the jet lifted off Saturday afternoon, so did Electra's worries and responsibilities regarding Su. *I like Hud, his Dad, and Texas even better than I thought I would. Lots of catchy Texas tunes too. I like the peppy one called Deep in the Heart of Texas. Su should be safe down there.*

"Run for Nurse Redux"
(Thread 1 Chapter 6)

ELECTRA CHECKED HER EMAILS Sunday, then called Adom for what to expect at the lab Monday morning. As she had anticipated, Mo would call an all-hands meeting to explain further a major reorganization, but would say little more than he already had regarding the fire's cause or Su's sudden removal from the project. Adom would be temporarily in charge of all projects until Mo found someone to replace her. *Lots of luck. Su's the brightest of the bunch, and just try recruiting on the outside. Who wants to work on a project the researchers have said is dead?*

Mo tried his best to project confidence, but the researchers saw through the masquerade. Cognicom is a corpse if Su is gone, and Electra wouldn't provide clues for Adam because he wouldn't understand the advanced theory. NIH bureaucracy wouldn't trip over the body for months, and it might never know how the ham-fisted Death Shield agents turned Cognicom into a zombie.

Too bad for them but not for me. I don't care a whit about my Cognicom connections. I'm below all the political Sturm and Drang, and can stay invisible just sitting here finishing my thesis. It'll be even easier because I don't have to drop clues. Much as I like Adom and Mo, they'll have to fend for themselves.

Electra did care about using her Guardian Party P.R.connections. An entire week had gone by since the lab fire, and the media had nothing to report because the Administration wanted no one to know. *Well then, I'll innocently leak details to Zoe. She and her P.R. team can create press releases backing the Administration even further into a corner.*

Wednesday afternoon she was sitting in Zoe's office,waiting for a breathless-as-usual Zoe to finish a phone conversation. When finished, she turned to Electra.

"What's up? Got some good stuff for me?" *Great segue,thank you.*

"I was busy with thesis and school last week,but when I got back to the lab I found it buzzing about a fire."Zoe frowned because the Guardian Party mole hadn't reported it.

"I don't think Securityguard knows.What's the scoop?"

"All I know is what the rumor mill churns out, but it sounds serious.The fire was started deliberately.Not only that,but the top T-Plague researcher has gone missing, and the entire Cognicom project is being reorganized."*Enough said. Zoe,please take it from here.*

"Wow.This could be an NIH cover-up for all sorts of bad things. Do you have any hard evidence?"

"No,I'm just a lowly clerk,but I have good eyes and ears.I hope you can use this."

"Say no more."Zoe glanced at the time. "I gotta go, but I'm going to send what you told me up the chain of command.Will you be at your workstation today?"

"No, I have to head back to campus, but I'll be back next week on my normal schedule. Maybe you can let me know if my info was accurate."

"I sure will. And we might have other people who'd like to talk with you.You're a very useful young lady."

The Invisible Man's ears would ring for a while after the telephone tongue lashing he received late Wednesday evening from his Inner Circle handler.

"Why don't you know about the fire in a lab, or about a top T-Plague researcher gone missing? If you and your people can't deliver, you'll be permanently excused."It was time to increase the heat on the Invisible Hand and its moles.

The fourth of July weekend had come and gone, and Robin was aboard a Metra express to Philly after spending the holiday hanging out with her two best friends.Her parents had invited her to join them at the Eastern Shore town of Saint Michaels, but she preferred to be with Electra and Christi.The time had ticked away too quickly, and even though it was only a half hour since they waved her off, Robin missed them.

Robin was staying the summer in her apartment near the Curtis Institute where she would graduate next June, completing her bachelor's in piano performance after only three years. Living away taught more about the people side of her chosen profession as well as herself than if she were living at home. Even though the lessons were painful, it was better to learn now rather than later when choosing another career would be harder.

Robin didn't doubt that her pianistic abilities were as good as many concert pianists. Even her teachers agreed, but she would need to be more assertive. She needed the chutzpah of self-promotion and a self-serving ruthlessness to sell herself, but she didn't have those traits. She was appalled at how sponsors would extract "favors" from artists desperate to succeed, behaviors that violated her moral principles.She balked at the thought of blowing her own horn. She sadly realized she needed to play instruments other than the piano to get ahead,and she refused to learn the five-fingered flute,without which she would never get a rise from those who could promote her.

Decades ago, the performing arts academies officially condemned such practices, ostracizing members who crossed ethical redlines, but the devils in human nature are incredibly persistent. Pockets of arrogant impresarios still remain, trolling the backwaters where incredibly talented but unknown young women fight to break through before economic realities overwhelm them, crushing their dreams and drowning their hopes.

Added to this were lessons Robin had learned from more personal social interactions—particularly with males—in a less sheltered world. To them she was patently pretty, but they tried taking advantage of her innocent and trusting nature. Even some of her instructors tried "hitting on her" in the seclusion of private practice rooms. Robin would have none of this and acquired the nickname the "Ice Queen." How ironic for someone inwardly so romantic, so passionate. Her ambivalence towards males grew; she had learned most were self-centered, blunt, and uncaring, and she had never experienced a satisfying encounter with the opposite sex. Robin mused how different the encounters with the opposite sex had been for her two best friends. Christi's sexual awakening had appeared earliest. She chased after sex and tried mixing it with drugs, which could have led to serious complications had not Electra been there.Christi had better sex control now than a couple of years ago. She still liked to date, but thanks to her friendship with Electra, stayed away from outliers. Electra also dated, but not with the same enthusiasm that used to drive Christi.

Robin mused further about Electra, her stable, enigmatically exciting center. Robin could see what others could not. The relationship between Electra and Christi had become deeper,more private.They shared an understanding, a comfort Robin longed to join, but distance made that impossible. It was probably restricted to just two,and if that were the case she would be happy for them, not jealous.

She compared her career situation to the one Christi had dealt with a couple of years ago. She too had learned she would never make it as a performer, but unlike Robin,Christi exuded confidence and social skills that added to her resilience. She picked another direction that better fit her abilities. She was now a student at the Fashion Design Institute, which could lead to opportunities in clothing, interior decorating, or even cosmetics.

Robin cheered herself up as the train approached her stop, Philly's 30th Street Station. *I'm young, I have talent, and I have two friends who will help me if I ask. And until I graduate, I'll do what Electra told me to do. I'll vanish into my present, into my music.*

Mo tried his best all summer long, but nothing he had done for Cognicom cheered him up. Labor Day was approaching, and Cognicom progress was dead in the water. Even Adom's tireless efforts training the two new tech leaders led nowhere. NIH and Washington bureaucracies sank deeper into the T-Plague morass, and Mo's best network contacts saw no way out. Even his usually upbeat business analyst Nick Rossi seemed depressed. Mo decided the time had come to consider other options. *I'm not gonna wait to be a victim. If the Administration's the wrong horse to ride, I'll find another. What about the Guardian Party? Maybe we need a jockey that's not afraid to use a whip. What about the shadowy Opposition Group? They're trying to get the public to bet on them. It's damn well time for me to place a bet.*

The worst T-Plague outbreak in over a year erupted the last week of September in Philadelphia, followed a week later by a flood of new victims in Atlanta and San Francisco. Overloaded medical facilities had to turn victims away as a panicky public swarmed in, sensing that anyone is vulnerable at any time or any place.

Electra didn't panic for herself or her two best friends. *I have permanent immunity, and I make Christi take my advanced formula smart pills. And I sent Robin another supply of them a month ago. We'll call her tomorrow evening to find out how she's doing.*

Electra yelled from the kitchen for Christi to dial up Robin. Several tries later she got a connection; Robin's roommate Jacqueline answered on the seventh ring.

"Hi Jackie, this is Christi, Robin's friend. We're calling to find out how the two of you are holding up against all the plague stuff going down. Could I please speak with her?"

"She's not here and I don't know where she is now. The T-Plague got her."

"Oh my God, no! Is anyone with her?" Electra came running and waited for Christi to end the call. When it ended, Christi stammered, "Robin's sick." The lightning brain went into overdrive.

"Don't panic. Tell me exactly what Jackie said." Christi shuddered involuntarily, then settled down.

"Thursday morning Robin woke up with a headache and chills, then started vomiting. Jackie took her to the closest place, University of Pennsylvania's emergency room and left her there. The place was swamped. Jackie couldn't get through to Robin's parents. Jackie's leaving for home because the campus is closed." Electra pursed her lips. *I've handled this before, and I'll handle it again. It'll be a variation on the same theme.*

"Let's call Robin's parents. I'll talk first." Christi punched the number, then gave Electra the phone; there was nothing but a voice recording.

"Not home. Here's what we're gonna do. We'll drive to Philly and bring her back. We'll take care of her the way we took care of you when you got sick. You're dressed OK, but I gotta change and collect supplies. It's all stored in Gramp's room. You'll have to drive while I get stuff prepared. Get some towels and cover the back seat with a plastic sheet or blanket. And pack a cooler with food for you and me, and another with as much ice as you can dig out. We'll stop for more if we need it. I'll meet you at my car." Each dashed in opposite directions.

Electra kept a medical supplies war chest always at the ready. She changed into the same nurse's uniform she had worn when rescuing Christi, and looped around her neck an official NIH I.D. badge she had pilfered when Su was in ICU. She selected two surgical masks and lurched downstairs clutching everything she needed. Christi had already loaded the coolers in the car and was waiting for Electra, whose appearance jolted her. "Holy shit, I know you! You were the nurse at Good Shepherd." Electra was all business.

"All in good time, but not now. We gotta make time to Philly."

From Washington, Philadelphia is north one hundred and sixty miles on I-95, taking three hours to drive if traffic is normal, but tonight's post-midnight's travel time would be less. Electra sat in the back seat, preparing massive doses of her advanced formula and loading them into syringes she would inject into Robin. Her instructions to Christi were simple: drive as fast as you can without getting stopped by the cops. Christi had never driven Electra's radar-equipped "little beast" but was a quick study. Soon they were blasting past the few cars or trucks on the Interstate. Forty-five minutes later, the duo swapped places and Electra rattled off more instructions.

"The hospital is going to be operating in chaos mode. When we get there, we'll put on our surgical masks and barge in. Let me do the talking. My role is the NIH nurse assigned to retrieve Robin, who is the daughter of a high-ranking NIH administrator. You're the relative helping find her. I don't think anyone is going to get in our way, but if someone does let me take care of it. Once we find her, I'll carry her and you lead the way out. I'll hook up the IV and then drive us back. And keep your mask on. Robin will be contagious. But don't worry. The smart pills you've been taking are an advanced formulation. We're protected." Christi was afraid, but not for herself.

"What about Robin? Do you think this is going to work?"

"I don't know. She'll be in worse shape than you were because no one's been looking out for her. I'm counting on the IV mega-doses, but we won't know until we use them.

Downtown Philly was deserted as Electra sped off I-95 to the hospital, running all the red lights. She double-parked on the street, figuring the odds of dodging a ticket were in her favor.

"Put on your mask and follow me." Electra was right; even at 3 a.m., the E.R. was a jumble of confusion. They strode right in, past all the people queued for help that might never come. Electra marched up to what looked like a triage station and boomed in a voice that commanded attention.

"We're assigned from DC NIH to extract Robin Setdarova immediately. She was brought in Thursday morning. You need to tell me where she is."

The poor nurse at the staging area looked dead on her feet. Struggling to gather her thoughts, she yelled to another who was carrying a clipboard. "Maria, does Setdarova sound familiar? Do you know where they put her?" Maria glanced at the patient list.

"Setdarova? It's not on my admitting list, but I recall the name. I think she's in the second-floor recovery ward. Electra snapped, "Thanks. What's the quickest way there?" Maria pointed to a stairway down the corridor.

"Take it to the second floor and turn left. It's second door on the right."

"Thanks."The girls dashed to the stairway and raced up to find a room crowded with ten mobile stretchers, then searched madly.

Christi yelled, "I found her! Holy shit!" Electra ran to her side, reading the damage on the digital displays. Several were blaring ominous warnings as Robin lay unconscious under a stained bedsheet. Her pulse registered one hundred, and her temperature pinned the display at one hundred eight.Electra yanked out all the tubes before lifting her off the stretcher, making sure she was still wrapped in a bedsheet.

"Christi, lead the way out!" Christi knew how to handle emergencies; she jostled people aside yelling, "Contagious T-Plague coming through! Clear a path!"It worked; no one got in their way as they charged to the car.

Electra buckled Robin into the back seat. Though she barely fit, cramped quarters kept her from shifting. Electra needed only five minutes to hook up the IV and pump two mega-dose syringes into Robin's comatose body. Then she dumped ice on top of the Ice Queen.

"I'll drive, and I want you to keep as much ice as you can around her.This is all we can do until we get home. Let me know if she goes into convulsions. And hang onto your derriere. I'm going to floor it when we get on I-95."

Electra blasted towards Washington. She could outrun the state troopers, and if they radioed ahead she knew how to handle that contingency. She streaked like a lightning bolt across Delaware and Virginia state lines, doing a hundred and twenty. A state trooper tried to catch her, but she activated the nitro system, and the flashing lights disappeared from the rearview mirror.

Ten miles further she saw the headlights of a hastily assembled road block. *Let's see how Smokey handles this.* "Christi, for shit's sake put your mask back on and let me do the talking."Electra stopped four lengths from squad cars blocking all lanes but not the right shoulder.She turned on the interior lights, then opened the driver's window, and before the burly state trooper could open his mouth, took command of the conversation.

"Officer, I'm a DC-based NIH nurse assigned to retrieve a T-Plague victim. Look at the back seat but don't put your head inside the car. We are contaminated with T-Plague. The victim is the daughter of a senior NIH official. She's in critical condition and we are transporting her to a DC ICU. You're exposing yourself to the virus, so don't stand here any longer. Radio ahead so we aren't stopped. And get tested ASAP. Good luck." That was all Electra needed to say. The trooper sprinted back to his car, getting there before Electra cruised past. Electra pulled into the middle lane and squealed away, saying nothing until Christi unloaded a tension-easing zinger.

"I didn't think bears could run that fast." Electra looked at Christi, and for the first time in twelve hours cracked a smile. "Sometimes you eat the bear, and sometimes the bear eats you."

Robin hadn't regained consciousness, but by the time they reached home she was beginning to stir. Electra carried her to an upstairs bathtub. "We'll check her temperature and pulse, then clean her up. Whether she comes to or not, I'll hook up another IV and load up a couple of syringes that I'll use later." Robin's pulse had dropped to 80, and her temperature to one hundred and one.

Christi said, "She's coming around. I'll make the water lukewarm." Robin's awareness rose, her eyes blinking several times before remaining open. She smiled, then whispered hoarsely.

"You two look so beautiful. I love you." Electra touched Robin lightly on the cheek.

"I love you too. We both do. Don't say another word until we get you some water." Christi returned with it and said, "Just sip while we tell you what's been going on." Christi saw that the strain of the last fourteen hours had taken a physical and emotional toll on Electra.

"Why don't you bring a chair so you can just sit and watch while I scrub Robin and tell her the whole story." Electra sobbed once, then caught herself.

"That sounds like the best damn part of this entire damn plan." Though the fever had broken and she was out of danger, Robin was as weak as a hatchling that had fallen from its nest. Electra lifted her from the tub, then Christi toweled her off and blow-dried her hair. They dressed her in sweat pants and shirt, then tucked her into bed. Robin needed solid food, so Christi spoon-fed a mashed banana with applesauce. Electra joked that next time Robin wanted breakfast in bed, she should do the ordering on the Internet instead of from a hospital bed. Robin said the T-Plague is not what she ordered, then fell asleep as soon as the last swallow went down.

It was now after seven on a clearing Saturday morning, and for the first time in over fifteen hours the girls no longer needed to rush at fever pitch. Christi sighed with relief and asked, "What do we do next?"

"Let's call your parents and tell them what we've been doing. Have them contact Robin's parents. Then all of them should come over here."

Three hours later a collection of anxious parent peered intently at a second sleeping beauty that had been snatched from the T-Plague, discussing what to do next. Russell was first to give an opinion.

"We should do exactly what worked for Christi. Robin should stay here until she's strong enough to go home. She's more delicate than Christi, and she didn't have any care for two days, so it'll take her longer to recover. You shouldn't send her back to school until spring term, but that's up to you."

Jennifer said, "Irena, I know you want to stay with Robin, but she's going to sleep for most of the next day. It'll be better if you let the girls take care of her. They'll call you as soon as she's feeling good enough to talk. In the meantime, keep busy getting things set up for whatever you and Leo decide. And I'll stay with the girls."

Robin's parents agreed; soon all that remained were the former Three Queens and a hover mother, Robin asleep in bed, Electra and Christi dead to the world amidst a swarm of throw pillows, and Jennifer in a chair, pondering what she saw. *How much like days' past, yet how different. How capricious life is, yet how constant the friendship among the three girls, who in so many ways are girls no longer. No matter what life brings, they will always be little girls to me. I can only hope that all their adventures will have happy endings, like the one today.*

CHAPTER 38
November 2116

"Three Queens—Redux"
(Thread 1 Chapter 7)

Autumn's harvest of bad news darkened America's mood. Power and communications outages followed on the heels of September's T-Plague outbreak, and sporadic train derailments made headlines. Add to this Isilabad's arrogant claim that more T-Plague attacks are coming and an ugly picture of America's current landscape emerges.

Only the Guardian Party had a picture worth showing, and that's what Jared Gardner would point to during his election eve prime time broadcast. Pollsters projected the Guardians could win a near majority in the House and add to their Senate plurality. Analysts speculated this could have been the first election sweeping a Guardian Party candidate into the Oval Office, but events the past year had turned so quickly in their favor that the Party miscalculated when Jared should make a run for President. Jared missed a golden opportunity, and one of the media pundits turned a political truism against the Guardians: "When the whistle blows you got to get on the train, for it might not stop again."

What Gardner would say was the question of the day. He could declare himself a write-in candidate, or push for a constitutional amendment to hold a special presidential election. One loud-mouthed pundit even predicted Jared would announce a bloodless coup. Speculation covered all the above, but one thing was certain, the public was fed up with the Washington Establishment. The nation's collective consciousness riveted on Jared's speech.

"My fellow patriotic Americans. Here we are on election eve, plagued with so many dire problems they boggle the minds of even our best and brightest. Not only do conditions boggle the mind, but they have paralyzed the current Administration. Health, security, the economy, and America's rightful place on the world stage are all topsy-turvy, the result of the Administration's mismanagement. Only the Guardian Party has been able to act in our nation's best interests these past few years.

"Thanks to my party's proactive leadership and unflagging patriotism, we have pushed for needed changes. We said right from the start that harsh times demand harsh measures, and that has proven to be the case. Unfortunately, not all the needed changes have been made, and let me take a minute for a civics lesson.

"We are blessed to live in a democracy, but all too often the wheels of democracy, like those of justice, turn slowly. Our great nation normally makes changes gradually from the center. That's what the framers of our Constitution designed. But times today are not normal times, are they?

"I must apologize to the American people for not realizing how quickly conditions spawned by deadly T-Plague and terrorism would propel us to a tipping point. I did not prepare to run for President this election. The party and I planned to solidify a base for 2020. We were wrong. I should be running now. I apologize for missing an opportunity to serve you.

"So, what should you, the American people do? Why not join me in our war to win back our Country's greatness by electing as many Guardian Party candidates as we can. We will guard what makes America great! And then, even though I'm not sitting in the Oval Office, I'm sitting close enough and with enough support to impose your will on Washington.

"There are other choices, but this is the best one for America today. We will know the election results shortly, and we will know soon after the elections if we are on the right path. I pray that we will be, for then we are guarded against harm. But if not, we will be ready to act.

"So in closing, let me urge all of you to vote for your Guardian Party candidate. Let's make right now a turning point, not a tipping point, for guarding what makes America great."

"God bless my fellow patriotic Americans!"

While Electra kept switching among channels to catch the comments made by a host of analysts, Christi's confusion grew. Because she, like most of her friends, didn't follow current events, she couldn't place what Jared had said into a broader context of national politics, so Christi turned to Electra for answers.

"That guy certainly commands attention when he speaks. He's good looking and good with words, but where's he going? What do you think the voters will take from it?"

"People will take from it what best fits their point of view. And I think the analysts are right. The Guardian Party is going to sweep close to a majority. Let's listen to more of them to catch their spin."

Spins were as numerous as the number of talking heads reporting. Those supporting the Establishment downplayed the warnings while those in the Guardian Party's camp hyped an imminent tipping point if harsh measures aren't taken. But they all agreed Jared was deliberately vague on what future actions he and his party might take, implying that next year might tell the tale.

Election results gave the Guardian Party almost everything it wanted. It now had nearly enough seats in both chambers to push through agenda items if some congressmen cross over, but the Guardians could not unilaterally ram whatever they wanted into law. Electra thought this was the best of all possible worlds, and she was not simply parroting Doctor Pangloss from Voltaire's Candide. Time still remained for compromise to head off a Washington collapse. But the gloomiest pundits said there are too few smart people left to make a difference as the T-Plague's insidious to toll continues sapping the nation's strength, dummying down the national I.Q. Electra's inner voice ruefully exclaimed that stupid is as stupid does.

The Opposition Group, the only credible group other than the Guardians to oppose the current Administration, was not stupid. Far from it, for it was comprised of thoughtful statesmen who always put America ahead of personal agendas. They were troubled that the election results were leading to disaster and needed to be ready for whatever lies ahead. Its steering committee chairman assembled an emergency meeting the week before Thanksgiving to cobble ideas into a plan.

"Let's face it. We haven't acted fast enough to keep up with the Guardian Party or the T-Plague crisis. The Guardians have parlayed T-Plague and terrorism into victory, and if we don't get better organized and better equipped, we'll end up victims, not survivors. We have to burrow into what our opponents are thinking and doing, so we have to strengthen our covert operations. Ours is way behind all other surveillance and interdiction organizations. Let's go around the table and lay out options." After two hours of heated debate, the chairman reached closure. "What we've agreed to do makes sense, but we're running out of time. From what Jared said, if we're not ready in less than a year we're history." He pointed to one of his lieutenants. "Please let Mrs. T know the score and the marching orders."

Electra was looking forward to a second Austin trip for two reasons, one weather-related and the other a matter of opportunity. Mirroring the public's trust in its government, Washington's December temperatures had dropped suddenly, while conditions were heading in the right direction for H&H DNA Partners to fill the gaping hole in Cognicom R&D. Su had made enough progress on smart pills and vaccines to get fast-track approvals if her safety and efficacy testing held up. When Electra outlined all the political angles in their favor, Hud joked she better "gallop here yesterday" so they could get started. Electra asked if she could bring two friends with her, Christi and Robin. The more, the merrier was his reply. They would fly this coming Friday on the private Jet Hud charters and return Monday, December twenty-first.

Ever the bold one, Christi, jumped at the chance to join Electra's latest adventure because she always trusted Electra's ability to handle whatever might arise. And though she sensed Electra could be a lightning rod, she knew that Electra's careful planning always insulated her partners from threats.

Electra had one personal dilemma that she could not handle by herself: how to include Robin in the Electra-Christi relationship. Robin's brittle, high-strung personality had caused problems before the T-Plague struck, and though she was recovering physically, emotionally she continued to struggle. She was being treated by a psychiatrist and had to take a break from college to regain her center. She was regaining strength because Electra encouraged her to exercise, and she was reducing stress because a guidance counselor convinced her to suspend coursework. Spring term she would transfer to George Washington University to pursue a double major in music and accounting. He told her musicians are supposed to be good at math, so she could become an accountant and keep music as an avocation. When Electra questioned the career choice, Robin said an artist like herself could tolerate the drudgery of debits and credits because she had already proved she could endure untold hours of piano practice boredom. Electra detected ambivalence but decided not to interfere.

Smart as she is, and in spite of studying all the softer sciences, Electra hadn't deciphered why Robin was causing her such strong emotional pangs. *Why do I have a crush on Robin? I've always liked her, though not in the same way I like Christi. But now I feel a desire for her to be with me so I can take care of her. Until Christi broke through my emotional barrier, I never felt this way for anyone except Dad and Doc. Only Su comes close. But I'm unsure about these feelings. They make me vulnerable, make me scared I won't measure up. How should I deal with Robin? Can I handle a three-way relationship? Can Christi? And what does Robin want? The world is grim, and having another person to worry about limits what I can do. I better talk with Christi.*

A wave of melancholy fatigue convinced her she had thought enough about the quandary, so she went to bed. As she drifted asleep, she recalled a verse from one of her mother's poems:

Or do you want your senses revived?
With quickening pulse you come alive.
Find someone or something to be your new scope,
And vanish within is your last and best hope.

Perfect advice from my peerless mother. I'll never match her empathy. How did she learn so much about life and love while still so young? How did she get so many empathy-mirror neurons? As mother's poem says, opening up to others makes me come alive. I'll sleep on it. I'll be my usual upbeat self in the morning.

Christi hadn't been with Electra for a couple of days and felt the urge to see her now. The Holiday break had just begun, but when Christi asked Electra last Friday to party with her, she begged off, saying she needed time to herself, suggesting instead for Christi to go out with one of her old boyfriends. Doing so would appease Christi's social appetite and maintain their clever charade.

But Christi had detected a hint of worry in Electra's usually confident and upbeat chatter, and that was why she was driving through the bone chilling darkness to surprise her Monday evening. *I'll sneak in quietly and catch her off-guard, but that's hard to do. She seems to have a foolproof internal warning system.*

Electra's house was completely dark, which was odd unless she had gone out, because Electra's high energy level usual powered her late into the evening. Christi climbed the stairs but heard nothing. When she peeked into the bedroom, she was relieved to see what could only be Electra, huddled under the covers for warmth. Christi, shivering from the cold, peeled off her clothes so she could wrap herself in the soothing warmth only Electra could provide. Before joining her, she stroked Electra's hair and whispered her name, rousing her from a troubled sleep.

"Christi! I'm so glad you're here. Come join me."

"I'm counting on you to warm me up." Christi snuck under the covers and wrapped herself around Electra. The two lovers held one other, saying not a word, suspended in time. Finally, Christi was ready to tell why she came this evening.

"Last time we talked, I picked up a feeling that something's bothering you. What is it?" Electra had yearned subconsciously for years to find someone to share her feelings, to understand her. And only with Christi, in the intimate privacy under the covers on a cold winter's night, in the safety of her darkened bedroom would she be shielded from her fears of vulnerability, of failure.

"I don't know what to do about Robin." So, that's it, Christi thought. *I can handle this for her and for me. Christi rubbed Electra's arms.*

"Say no more and let me talk. You've entered my area of expertise, so I'll be the teacher and you be the student. Once upon a time, we were the Three Queens, way back when we were untouched by the complexities of emotions or sex. But all that has changed, and Robin is struggling. She's all mixed up emotionally and hasn't sorted through her feelings towards you."

"How do you know? She never tells me that."

"She talks with me more than with you. It's not that she's afraid, but she's sort of in awe of you. Maybe she's built you into some fantasy. That's for you and Robin to work out. But she does love you. She loves me too, but she's confused. Maybe the shrink will help. Hey, do you like her accounting career change? I don't think it's a good fit, but that's for her to figure out. I'm not gonna interfere, and I don't think you should either."

"I feel the same way. But why do I feel like I need to be with her or take care of her? What am I gonna do about it? And what I do affects you too."

"As I said, you're on my turf because you're asking about love. Love is more than sex. Sex is essentially a physical, self-regarding act, often rather mechanical from the male perspective. Once satisfied, I find it tends to divide rather than unite. And I'm not complaining either, because the physicality of sex is primal and urgent, and I like sex. But love has all that and more by transcending from the physical into the spiritual realm. And I don't mean the religious type of spirituality; I mean the sharing, the caring, the commitment, and the union with another. I don't find that with guys. That's why you and I are lovers. The Greeks coined four words to describe the four kinds of love. Agape for the love of duty and doing what's right,

Phileo for the love of friends, Storge for the love of family, and Eros, my favorite, for erotic sexual love."

"How do you know all this?"

"You're supposed to be the smart one, but I learn fast when something interests me. My psychology instructor covered some of it, and I studied the rest on my own. I guess you feel the love of duty for Robin because she's a friend. And it's affecting you now because she needs help fighting back from the T-Plague."

"What do you think she feels towards me?"

"I don't know. She doesn't tell me and I don't ask. Maybe she wants to hop in the sack with you, but that's between you and Robin."

"Please tell me how you feel about me."

"I do. I tell you often, but maybe not often enough. Our love is special. It combines all four kinds of love. I'm still in love with you, but it's grown beyond that. I love you, and that's even more important than being in love."

"Don't you ever want to analyze it more? I do, so I can understand why it's special and what I need to do to keep you. What will I do if I lose you?" Christi couldn't see in the darkness, but sensed Electra had started to cry. She reached out and felt a wetness on one cheek. She carefully wiped away the tears, then twirled a lock of Electra's hair around one finger before replying.

"I prefer to enjoy our love rather than dissecting it or worrying about it ending. Like drinking a milk shake, I don't think ahead to sucking the air out of a straw when I'm at the bottom. I'm smart enough to know everything eventually ends, and I'll worry then, but not now."

"So, what should we do about Robin?"

"That's easy. Ask her to spend more time with us. Maybe we can offer advice concerning careers or balance what the shrink tells her. And we'll let her do what she wants."

"Won't you be jealous of her cutting into our relationship?"

"If she were a guy, it might be different, but I think an all-female triangle has more chance of success than if you threw a male into the mix. Testosterone would cause problems."

"But what if she finds out we're lovers?"

"Robin's sort of naïve, and I think she's been too preoccupied with her issues to notice. And we've been discreet. But if she does find out, so what? If she doesn't like our sleeping together, it's her problem, not ours."

"I thought I was getting a better handle on emotions and relationships, but you're way ahead of me." Christi saw a segue to lighten up the discussion and went for it.

"Thanks for reminding me. I busted your chops months ago because you didn't know about Tristan and Isolde. You were supposed to explain how the myth feeds into the downside of Romantic love. My instructor said the Psyche-Eros story from Greek mythology could help deal with the downside too. So, I'm busting you again. You're supposed to be the smart one, so you have to tell me both stories. But not tonight. We've talked enough." Christi could feel Electra stiffen.

"Hey, I'm only kidding. You need to lighten up. You have a delightfully whimsical sense of humor when you let it out of the box. Please, try not to be so serious, so philosophical. I think I know what might help."

Christi leaned forward and cupped Electra's head in her hands, kissing her full on the lips. Electra responded in full measure. Both student and teacher would feel better in the morning.

"Please thank Electra for inviting me. And I'll keep all the details a secret, even from my parents. I've never been to Texas, but I've heard it's a big place with lots of wild west history. And please don't tell her you had to explain the men are like springs and women are like wells analogies. I should have been able to figure it out."

"I won't, but I will ask her to explain the Romantic Love myths. They'll help me as much as you. Hey, I gotta go, so sayonara until we pick you up Friday morning."

Robin disconnected the call, feeling better after chatting with Christi because talking with either of her two best friends kept lurking depression at bay.

I'm so glad they're taking me with them. Christi's a dear friend for sharing Electra with me. We're the Three Queens once again. I need Electra's advice to balance what my therapist and guidance counselor are telling me. And I need Christi's advice to understand Electra. I'm lucky they're letting me in, and I'll fit however they want, just as long as they help chase my suicidal thoughts away. And I know they will. I always feel good when I'm with them. Especially when I'm around Electra. When I get stronger, I'll let them know how I feel.

Electra agreed with her travel partners that Hud's chartered jet is the best way to fly because it avoids most airport delays or security searches. While Christi and Robin spent the flight chatting about the landscape below, Electra used her laptop to review what she had prepared for the meeting. That took only an hour, so she planned to use the rest of the time to review enough psychology so she'd be on a more equal footing with Christi.

She knew just where to look for what she wanted: the Capstone Lecture Series for GWU graduating science majors. One of the lectures gave a summary of psychology. *My bad. I skipped the video a couple of years ago, but I'll correct my mistake right now.* Electra went to the Capstone Website and began viewing.

She could tell from the instructor's opening remarks the presentation would help because he emphasized not psychological principles but rather their application. His first slide stated psychology's purpose: to study Human Nature and explain how the brain controls behavior. It also traced how Freud's sex-laden theory grew to be more objective and scientific, thanks to Carl Jung, and today psychology research relies on brain scans and imaging rather than clinical case studies. The instructor paid tribute to Daniel Kahneman's book, *Thinking, Fast and Slow.* Though written a hundred years ago, it is still a good read. But he warned the audience to beware of most self-help books because there are too many amateurs claiming to have all the answers to people's problems.

His presentation provided many helpful insights, one in particular touching Electra's thesis. Free will does exist, but our cognition is aware of a decision only after it has been made. And the instructor said no one is normal. Everyone suffers from mental disorders at one time or another. His next slide listed prevalent mental illnesses, and he stated that psychiatrists call the feelings people are uncomfortable talking about mental disorders. *No wonder the list is so long. Everyone is uncomfortable talking about a lot of things. And according to the slide, I'm a schizophrenic because I see Indira and hear her voice. I never want to see a psychiatrist.*

When it comes to treatment, the instructor mentioned using drugs only when there is a biochemical imbalance in the brain. Otherwise, counseling can help, and a person can get better results for less money talking with friends rather than visiting a psychiatrist, who often misdiagnoses or is deceived by clever patients.

He concluded the presentation by offering practical advice, applying it to a combined topic everyone pays attention to: Love and Sex. He warned not to confuse the two, nor fall victim to Romantic Love.Instead,be "pessimistic."Don't expect too much, nor demand your partner make you happy. People find that happiness comes from within, only when they love themselves first by being totally honest with what they are. And he ended his talk by warning against labeling the so-called love of your life a kindred spirit that cannot be replaced. Humans are resilient and want go forward instead of clinging to the past. He was roundly applauded after closing the talk by wishing everyone good luck, using a variation on a traditional British Royal Navy toast now considered culturally incorrect but witty nonetheless: "Here's to your Significant Others and Lovers. May they be one and the same." *Christi and I are going to watch this together, but not now. We're about to land, and I need to put my game face on so I can control the meeting.*

The H&H conference room was just big enough to hold the brains of Su, the charm of the Three Queens,and the brawn of Hud's Texas-sized personality, a trifecta for which the whole is greater than the sum of its parts. Electra was about to provide a snapshot of the political climate in which Hud could press the advantage.

"Now that's Su's here rather than in Washington, Cognicom is a zombie, still standing but dead on its feet. Adom's left holding the R&D corpse, and he'll soon be reorganized out of a job when a new team of tech and business project leaders are appointed.It'll take NIH about a year to figure they'll never get anywhere, so the best smart pills they'll have are the ones they're selling now. And that means Hud should push his NIH contact for a dual R&D path—

NIH controls one and Hud the other. Let them compare the two smart pills and fill the domestic pipeline with the better one. In the meantime, Hud keeps selling to the Chinese or other countries.Su, when will you have test data to show that your latest pill is better?"

"As soon as I settled in we launched the safety and efficacy clinical trials. I'm writing up the results now. The data show we're better, so we'll file the New Drug Application by the end of January, and it should get fast-track approval by the end of March or April."

"Excellent. Until then, Hud can convert the test data into promo pieces his sales team can use for the domestic distribution network.And keep selling internationally,but let me add a warning. Because of the politically charged climate, you need to be discreet and diplomatic when negotiating. Don't bite off too much of the market too soon. Otherwise, NIH will be even more suspicious or paranoid than they are.Su,what's the likelihood they'll understand why we're better?"

"It all depends on patent filings. If we file and Adom is still there, NIH will have a clue if they ask Adom to interpret. But if he's gone, they won't follow how we're using quantum biology and intra-cellular molecular factories. Are you still recommending we not file for patent protection?"

"Correct. If we do, competitors will get a look at what we're doing. If we don't, they'll never figure us out.No matter how much chemical analysis they do,they'll never reverse-engineer our drugs. How many line extensions do you have ready?"

"I can tweak our formulation for two more, which carries us for two more years. After that, I'll have to come up with new ideas. Perhaps then you'll be able to assist me."

"We'll plan for that. Hud, Su's done her part on the R&D piece, I've done mine regarding NIH and the political angle, so it's up to you to bring in the sales. And remember to keep Su and me and KC Ventures invisible." Hud's rugged features brimmed with confidence.

"Don't you get your, uh,don't you worry Little Lady.Our people know how to grease the skids when dealing with those DC Beltway types,and we know how to reach out to the Chinese.That market's as big as hell and half of Texas. We're all pulling on the same rope, so we've got sales lassoed for a couple of years. I think we've got us all pointed in the same direction, so how about we adjourn so you can freshen up before dinner?"

Dinner at Hud's featured Texas barbeque and two-alarm chili served with lively conversation. When Christi asked how Su liked Texas, she replied it's the friendliest place she ever lived and likes how Texans work hard and play hard. Robin asked if she liked the heat—in the food or weather. Su quipped that even four-alarm chili is mild compared to Hunan cuisine and she would never trade Austin temperatures for East Coast ice and snow.

Electra asked about Hud's family, which consisted of his father and two children. His wife had been killed in a car crash five years ago. He and his father were raising the kids, Seth who was ten and Sadie now six. They were energetic but well-mannered and took an immediate liking to Su, whom they considered exotic. She charmed them with her patience and subtle ways. The conversation continued after dinner in the living room that housed a grand piano; Robin asked who played.

"I want my kids to take piano lessons, and Su's getting them started." Robin blushed when Su mentioned her scholarship-winning recital. Holy picked up right away.

"You might not think an old wildcatter like me knows much about music, but it's a hobby of mine. I go to as many concerts as I can, and Austin, being a university town, has lots. Would you do me the honor of playing?"

"I'd be delighted." She seated herself on the bench, then asked Holy what he would like to hear."

"I'm sorta partial to Beethoven sonatas. Can you play any?" Su provided an instant answer.

"Can she ever! Robin, why don't you play Sonata Number Twenty-Three." Just as she did several years ago, Robin wowed the audience, particularly Holy.

"Young lady, you got the gift. I wish my Austin Seniors Club could hear you play sometime. You're as good as some of the guest performers." Robin blushed again, genuinely flattered by all the attention as Hud wrapped up the evening.

"That settles it. We'll line up a recital for the Piano Lady next time. Robin, you practice some Texas melodies to play when you come back…"

The trio enjoyed a relaxing Holiday Season. They were more mature in appearance and behavior than a couple of years, no longer swayed by peer pressure to race frenetically from party to party. This year, even Christi's social circle hosted fewer parties because people were avoiding crowds, and the public hunkered down at home because frequent power failures and a brutal cold snap made travel this year particularly unpleasant.

The Conklins hosted a New Year's Eve party for the erstwhile Three Queens and Robin's parents. Each grouping had one important gift bestowed that year which made them most thankful: the Conklins for Christi's settling down, the Setdarovas for Robin's recovery, and the Three Queens for being reunited. The party ended just after midnight as everyone toasted a New Year they hoped would be happier everywhere.

That night the girls bunked in Christi's room and talked into the early hours. They sensed once again the magic of friendship and how fragile, how fleeting good fortune can be. Christi bubbled with talk of what she wanted to do and what Robin might like. Electra was happy to listen, keeping her philosophic thoughts to herself. *I made a resolution to lighten up, but I can still do my philosophical musings as long as I keep them to myself. The more I interact with people, the more I sense how the finite extent of each person's days lends urgency to the search for meaning. Perhaps this is mere humanity's transcendental magnificence as well as its ultimate tragedy. Greek mythology told the gods are jealous of Man because he's mortal. This musing is getting too heavy to carry further. I'll switch to something lighter.*

Electra added to Christi's enthusiasm about the coming year, happy to append to their New Years wishes.

"Let's always dream big. We'll follow a quote that comes from Daniel Burnham, one of Chicago's legendary planners. He said, 'Make no small plans. They have no magic to stir men's blood.' We're young, and youth is supposed to be bold.Robin,I hope you're taking in all the words Christi is spewing out."

"I am. And thank you for the quote you gave me from that 19th century French doctor, 'Every day in every way I'm getting better and better.'Thanks to the two of you, I think it's coming true for me."

Sleep finally beckoned, so the trio drifted away. Before falling asleep, Electra recited to herself a poetic reflection from her mother's collection, fittingly titled "The Nerve of Youth."

> Fresh nerve of steel's a treasured gift,
> Bestowed in early years.
> It makes them sure and makes them swift,
> Protects them from their fears.
>
> Alas it does not last too long,
> Time wears it away.
> When energy's no longer strong,
> And caution rules the day.
>
> So propose a toast let Youth run free,
> Have their sights set high.
> Give them strength then let them be,
> May their power never die.

I'm thankful for my inner voice. Mother's presence is only a memory away.

CHAPTER 39
June 2117

"Murder in the House"
(Thread 1 Chapter 8)

Electra's right. I feel better when I think for myself. And thanks to Christi, I know enough about psychology and romantic love to defend myself. I'm glad I fired my shrink. All that talk about dreams and sex and complexes. He was hitting on me. I sure don't envy his penis. I like Christi's advice on sex better than his. Her explanation of modern psychology's combination of Jung and neuroscience makes a lot more sense than my shrink's mumbling about Freud and dreams. And Electra says she'll help me with accounting. No wonder I don't feel so anxious, so uncertain.

Good thoughts like the above helped Robin return to classes when spring term classes began at GWU. Since her scholarship and credits earned at the Curtis Institute had all transferred, she would graduate a year from June if she loaded up on business and accounting courses.

Robin's two-term break from college had helped repair much of the damage sustained last fall. She recovered from the T-Plague, gaining back weight and strength and a healthier attitude. Depression subsided because she knew she could deal with life without becoming a concert pianist, and she was coming to terms with personal issues. For the first time since female hormones intruded, Robin felt good about her sexuality as she transitioned to a better place.

Poor Adom was transitioning too, but unlike Robin, he was rudderless. Though officially still employed at the lab, he was sitting on the bench—a euphemism for languishing in a pool of unassigned researchers—which at his age was the kiss of death for his NIH career. The Cognicom reorganization sent him to a place he had never been before.

I'm fifty-three, and no matter where I land, my career is downward-sloping. But I should be employable for at least ten more years because the T-Plague keeps eating into the talent pool. But a job won't come looking for me. I better start looking. I hear that networking is the way to connect to my next job, but how do I do it?

Adom didn't like this new phase in his career or his life. For the very first time, he was on his own because until now he had always followed the lead of his close friends, who provided social and security safety nets. But time and tragedy had picked them off, one by one. First Indira, then Jason, and most recently Su.

Most associates considered Adom a success, but through the prism of his own conscience he was a disappointment, never quite able to act on his own for what he knew was right. He resolved to use this latest passage to make amends, for he still had time to grow into the person he wanted to be.

Mo's career was also transitioning, but he could build on his demonstrated successes and solid character. His boy scout reputation remained intact, and his resume confirmed competence and commitment to public service, for he had earned high marks on all projects he had managed. Other managerial opportunities awaited, and he'd bring his junior analyst with him. Nick Rossi was smart, diplomatic, and trustworthy.

Mo's quandary was caused by his disgust with the Washington Establishment. For too many years he had done little but observe the slow-motion train wreck. *Washington can't handle the truth about domestic terrorism, and they've dropped the ball on healthcare and domestic security. My folks are gone, and I need to find something to add more meaning to my life. I better start looking.*

Though early June weather was cool and damp, it didn't dampen the spirits of the Three Queens. Christi and Robin had passed all spring term classes, and Electra was making big plans for all of them. She was explaining some details on a mid-June Saturday while the trio waited for Adom to drive them to his apartment.

"Let me sketch the big picture. Depending on career choice, you can work for a company or you can start your own. A lot of people who are losing jobs because of automation start their own businesses, and a lot of recent college grads prefer working for themselves instead of going the corporate route. I can set up a virtual company online if you want to go in business for yourself. According to Mr. Antar, you could start a Middle East women's clothing design business."

"No, I'm not ready to do that. I don't know which career I'll choose, but it will come from fashion design, interior decorating, or cosmetics. I'd like to start by working for a company to get experience, and then think about starting my own company. What about you, Robin?"

"My career choices are down to one. Accounting. It's not as boring as I thought, and thanks to Electra I got through the financial accounting class. And she's gonna help me find a job. Have you done that yet?"

"Sort of. Here's my idea. You can get some experience by working as an accounting trainee for Hud while you're in school. That way, you'll be able to practice what you're learning and decide if you want to pursue an accounting career. I can start you this summer working on the books for Worldstar Biologicals. We can talk about it another time because Adom will be here soon. Christi, do you have the supplies we need?"

"Sure do. I called Adom earlier in the week and he volunteered to get the boxes and tape. I think it's sweet of him to ask us to help pack Su's stuff. He didn't want to do it alone. He says it would be too sad. But he says he needs to do it now. And as a reward, he'll order pizza later." Robin smiled sadly.

"It's too bad we can't let Adom know where she is and that she's OK, but you say it's for his own good. Do you think agents or terrorists would torture him to get to Su?"

"Who knows?" replied Christi. "But you hear stories and see it in the movies, so it's better we keep him in the dark."

Adom arrived at six, hugging the trio and thanking them for helping. He was still the Adom Electra had always known, but now more thoughtful and mature as a result of recent setbacks. He listened to the small talk Christi led, and she asked what he planned to do with Su's belongings.

"I have eight boxes already taped, and I'll put together more if we need them. For such a petite lady, she sure collected a lot of stuff. I'm putting them in storage with some of my things that I've already packed. I might leave DC if the right job turns up. I've started networking, and once I got started, it's been easier than I thought." Adom was indeed fortunate to have the trio's assistance, for having a group of friends help pack provides a party-like atmosphere. While watching as the girls sorted items, he commented on Su's exquisite taste and joked that he could make lots of money selling some of them at online auction sites. The girls played along but knew he would never part with Su's belongings, for his expression said he'd keep her things in hopes that someday she would magically reappear.

Boxes were packed and neatly stacked by ten p.m.Because Adom had just ordered the pizzas,the girls had plenty of time to clean up and prepare the dinner table.Christi and Robin were setting set out plates and silverware in the open area adjoining the living room, placing cans of soda on a sideboard while Electra washed up in the bathroom.The doorbell surprised everyone.

"That's the quickest delivery ever. I'll get it so I can pay they guy." Adom opened the door, coming face-to-face not with the pizza delivery man, but with three thuggish-looking Middle East men who barged through the door, one of them brandishing a gun.

The leader shouted, "Allahu Akbar!"clubbing Adom to the floor; the other two punched Robin and Christi repeatedly,ripping their clothes and gagging them with pieces of torn off clothing. Electra heard the commotion,knowing instantly they were in trouble.The lightning brain shifted gears.

A terrorist cell finally connected the dots from Su to Adom! I bet they want him to get T-Plague virus. I have to act before they find me. Electra didn't panic. Instead, a combination of cool clarity and thrilling excitement surged through every neural fiber as she readied for what could be deadly combat.

She searched the bathroom for weapons,converting the shower curtain rod into a spear. Finding a plunger and wooden-handled scrub brush in the sink cabinet,she pried the heads off both,giving her two wooden clubs,each a foot long.She used a roll of gauze in the medicine cabinet to lash them together,making a nunchuck—a martial arts weapon she practiced with occasionally. *I'll soon find out if the gauze holds.* Electra was armed and ready to attack.

The terrorists didn't spot her spying into the living room. All were thickset and taller than she, so they would be slower afoot. *I can outmaneuver them, but their body mass will overwhelm me if I get cornered.* She could tell from their lizard-like eyelids they were dull, but their relentless determination to kill the Great Satan would make them formidable. One had a gun, another a knife.

None of this fazed the lightning brain; it added to the thrill of deadly competition. *I can't hold back tonight. If I hit hard and fast, maybe I can put them out of commission. But if I can't they can wear me down. I hope I'm in as good a shape as I think.*

Christi and Robin,bound and gagged and bleeding from nose and mouth, were stacked like cordwood against the front door. Adom, pummeled and propped in a chair, was bound arms in front. The thugs clustered about him, ten feet from the entryway that concealed Electra. Suddenly, she felt an electric shock surge through her brain. *This is not a drill, soldier! Get with the plan!* Adrenaline-powered energy rushed through her body, galvanizing her into action.

She hurled her spear, scoring a direct hit on the side of the leader's head, knocking him forward. Then she charged, hitting the second with a horizontal nunchuck spin that broke his nose and threw him backwards,followed by a vertical spin that knocked the knife out of the hand of the third. But the gauze binding the two handles couldn't withstand the force; it tore and she was left holding only a wooden club.She used it to smash him in the mouth, knocking out pairs of teeth.

The gun-toting terrorist was staggered but still standing.Electra needed to get the gun, so she rushed him, using the club to smash down on his hand. The gun dropped to the floor and bounced away, and she used the club to shatter his nose.

As she raced for the gun one of the thugs tripped her, the force of the fall stripping away the club. She scrambled on hands and knees and almost reached the gun when another terrorist grabbed her by the legs, yanking her backwards. Twisting violently, she freed one leg and kicked into his neck, freeing herself to dive again for the gun. She had it in her hands, but as she rolled to the right to fire, the third thug leaped on top, pinning her to the floor, smashing her once in the nose and again in an eye. Her face became a crimson fountain as blood gushed from her nose and an inch-long vertical gash next to her left eye. He punched again, opening a cut on her lower lip. The front of her blouse was a blotter for blood, but she still held the gun.

Just then, Adom leaped into the battle and tore the terrorist off her. She did a backward roll to break clear, then leaped to her feet while still holding the gun. But before she could fire, the biggest of the three leaped at her, pinning her to the wall and grabbing her gun hand. Electra kneed him but didn't have a good angle; he responded with punches that inflicted more damage to her nose and mouth, but she had enough distance to throw a Karate palm strike that broke a third nose. And she still had the gun.

But before she could fire, Adom and the terrorist he was battling rolled into her legs, sprawling her backwards while the gun flipped out of her hand, landing next to a downed thug. She leaped for it, but came up a foot short, the terrorist getting there first. Electra twisted to her left, rolling off the terrorist and onto her makeshift spear. She leaped to her feet, grabbed the spear and stabbed him in the neck, but it was a glancing blow because he jerked his head to the right. He was momentarily stunned, which let her grab his gun hand and twist backward. She could hear the wrist bones and trigger finger snapping, but he wouldn't let go.

The battle was taking a heavy toll on Electra. She was gasping for air and the close-quarters combat had her staggering. Her left eye was swelling shut, and she was bleeding heavily from nose and facial gashes. Adom was still holding his own against one adversary, but the other two were picking themselves up, one still holding the gun.

Electra pounced on the knife nearby. *Never bring a knife to a gun fight!* flashed in the lightning brain, but she didn't have a choice. The gun was still drooping from the broken-wristed hand, so the odds were in her favor. She knew how to handle knives, so she feinted and jabbed to keep the terrorist off balance, but his partner moved in to engage. She feinted once more, than slashed into the gun hand, finally dislodging the weapon. This time it skittered in her direction and she had it in her grasp.

Electra could tell from the leader's eyes he would not give up. He would take a bullet if he could stop her, so she pulled the trigger before he charged, but the gun jammed. Even the lightning brain halted for a micro-second before it directed evasive action. Electra threw the gun at his head, then dashed into the adjoining room, frantically looking for an open space to engage one-on-one.

The terrorists regrouped after pummeling Adom unconscious, and then went after Electra. She started whirling dishes like a discus thrower, and when they were gone she pitched the knives. That didn't stop her adversaries, so she bombarded them with soda cans, scoring direct hits that bounced off their heads, but they kept coming and were smart enough not to rush pell-mell. Instead, the leader snarled instructions in Arabic. When they spread out into the open area, Electra leaped atop the table and then dived into the living room, somersaulting to her feet, facing all three. She searched desperately and found the knife that gave her an advantage, but she needed to act fast before she lost it.

They'll kill me if I stay in the apartment. I can't leap through the window unless I smash the glass first, but there's no time. It's time to exit through the front door.

"Christi! Robin! Roll away from the door! "They did, but not fast enough. The sluggish terrorist brains figured out what she was going to do and rushed her. Electra threw the knife at the leader but her aim was bad. She leaped for the door, opened it, and was almost in the clear, but she was a second too late. A terrorist got there in time to slam the door on her trailing leg, pinning her like a wild

<hr>

creature caught in a trap. His partner grabbed her foot and together they dragged her back into the apartment. She twisted wildly but was unable to kick free. The third terrorist joined the fray, kicking her in the side, knocking the wind out. Then they dragged her to her feet. One held from behind; the second grabbed a lamp and wrapped the cord around her neck. She tried to backflip free and succeeded in toppling everyone backwards, coming out on top but the terrorist pinned beneath would not let go. He found both ends of the cord and pulled with all his might, tightened the noose that cut into tissue. He would choke the life out of Electra if she couldn't break free.

She tried another backflip but didn't have the strength to complete it. She clawed with both hands, trying to find something to pull, but came up short as the strangler arched backwards. She tried putting her fingers underneath the cord but by now it was too tight, cutting deeper into flesh. Her body jerked and twisted uncontrollably, but could not escape from the death grip. Her eyes rolling, her gasping grunts audible, her strength running out as consciousness ebbed. Suddenly, a calmness enveloped as her body relaxed. The last image she saw was that of a bloodied and battered terrorist leering straight into her eyes, dripping blood from his mouth onto her lips. Then her body went limp as all signs of life vanished.

The leader clumsily gaped at the remains of the battle. The terrorist still standing stared mutely while the third, who was pinned underneath Electra's motionless body, released his grip, unwrapped the cord and cast her aside. He stood up and all three numbly stared at the creature they had just killed. They were too stupid to comprehend the picture their violence had just painted on the floor.

Even in death, Electra's repose was that of unvanquished grace, lower body twisted onto its left side, legs arched backwards, slightly separated, as if her feet were trying to regain balance. Her supple upper body lay prone, her head facing to the right, with her right arm and hand fully extended, as if she were reaching for something just beyond her grasp. Her left arm bent beside her with hand palm-up and fingers slightly curled, back slightly arched, as if her arms were about to lift her back into the realm of the living. She couldn't be dead! She was only resting, awaiting her brain to summon her. Only a crimson-colored pool of now stationary blood bore silent testimony to the horror. Electra would sleep for an eternity.

The terrorists had taken a terrible beating. They were bleeding from smashed noses or mouths, cuts or gashes, staring mutely at one another. Their leader finally shook off the mental fog, pointing vaguely and slurring commands.

"Someone must have heard. We must go! I'll take the man. You take the women. You put the body in the trunk." Each collected his hostage, loaded the car, and drove away before distant sirens drew nearer.

Abu's anger grew with every passing minute. He was the handler for DC's reconstructed terrorist cell and demanded performance from his followers, and his kidnapping squad was tardy. It should have been back an hour ago, and he would be late delivering the suspect to the bomb-making lab if they didn't return soon.

Abu had searched long and hard to locate suitable targets, Adom Ola being the prime choice. He needed someone who could handle T-Plague virus and Ola could do that and more. Abu's followers had stolen enough virus to make primitive WMD's but needed a technician to load it into aerosol cans. Ola could be their man, for he worked on Cognicom projects and was linked to Doctor Chou. Abu heard a car in the driveway that could only be his squad returning with Ola.

It was, but Abu got more than he wanted. Along with Ola, his squad dragged in two young women who, though blindfolded, bound, and gagged, were still putting up a fight. And he was stupefied by the condition of his squad; they looked like losers in a street brawl. Abu would call for his cell's healer to patch them up after he drove off with Ola.

"Throw the women on the couch and stay with them. I will take the man into my bedroom for a private talk." Abu pushed Adom towards the bedroom while the three did as told, then sat in stony silence, waiting for additional instructions. Once in the bedroom, Abu shoved Adom onto the bed and removed the tape from his mouth. Adom sat up, and Abu sat down in a chair next to him.

"Doctor Ola, thank you for joining us tonight. We have some work for you to do at our lab. If you want to live, and if you want to keep your women pure, you will do exactly what I say. I will drive you to our lab where you will load virus into aerosol cans. Will you help us?" Adom gasped.

"You've got to be kidding! You want me to make bio-aerosols? I need special equipment to do that!" Abu smiled.

"Good. That means you know how. We will provide all the equipment you need. Come." Nothing else was said as he pulled Adom to his feet and pushed him out of the bedroom.

"Allahu Akbar! You have brought us a man we can use. I am taking him to our lab. Stay here until I get back. I will call our healer to attend to your wounds." The lead thug's brain searched for words.

"What about the body in the trunk?" Abu hadn't expected this complication, but knew how to take care of the problem.

"Bring it into the house and wrap it in a sheet for disposal. And keep your guests quiet until I return. Doctor Ola, please come with me…"

Brumation is the scientific term for reptilian suspended animation. Many species can survive indefinitely by shutting down biological systems until their environment can support life once again. Similar altered human states of shorter duration have been

observed: drowning victims coming back to life, drug-overdose victims emerging from death-like trances.

Electra's lightning brain could do the same. Its lightning bolt of creation had endowed it with extraordinary powers. Until now there had never been a reason for the complete shutdown of life support systems. But tonight, the need was urgent.

Time must have seemed like an eternity before the lightning brain summoned Electra back from the dead. But now it awakened her consciousness, bringing her back among the living. Though enveloped in total darkness, she didn't panic. Her cognitive persona pieced together the current predicament. *Of course! I'm in the trunk of the terrorist car, parked outside a holding area. I'll be ready when they come to get me.*

Let's do damage control. Bleeding's stopped, but I can't open my left eye or swallow. And the cord burn on my neck is raw. Next, she groped for anything to serve as an improvised weapon and found two: a tire iron and a spray can. *All I can do is wait and think about the beating I just took. I thought I was in better shape but I was wrong. I got clobbered. Come on! Concentrate!* Suddenly, Electra began to quiver as her brain shifted to another state, a state that fused all three personas: the physical, the cognitive, and the emotional, powered by a smoldering wrath from which emerged a lusting, revenge-driven monster. The longer in the trunk, the more powerful it became. It had become a killing machine, driven by rage yet fully aware.

The healer, arriving a half hour after Abu departed, patched the three terrorists. Afterwards, they sat like statues staring at the walls, then at the two girls. A flicker of lust crossed into the leader's head.

"Let us initiate the women. We'll start with the gaunt one. "The three dragged Robin into the bedroom. Before closing the door, the leader tossed the car keys to the healer. "Get the body from the trunk and throw it on the couch. Then leave."

The key's turning in the trunk lock sounded to Electra like a starter's pistol. She sprang out and into the healer, knocking him flat on his back. Then she leaned down to clench his head between her hands before rasping, "Where are they?"

"First-floor apartment on the left." She didn't bother to thank him, instead killing quickly and cleanly, twisting his head well past one hundred eighty degrees. She pocketed the car keys, grabbed her weapons and ran into the apartment.

Christi lay on the floor, still bound and gagged. Electra ripped out the gag and croaked,

"Where's Robin? But she answered the question for herself when she heard thrashing behind a closed door. She crashed through, finding Robin stripped naked below the waist, arms pinioned above her head by one of the terrorists. The biggest thug had her pinned to the mattress while the third gawked stupidly. Robin was putting up a tremendous fight, her body violently twisting and heaving, her arms almost wrenching free while she kicked with all her might to free her legs. One leg came free, and she kicked the thug that was on top, nearly knocking him off the bed.

Electra charged into the melee, using the tire iron to club the terrorist who was astride Robin. He tumbled off the bed and onto a night stand, tipping it over and crashing the lamp to the floor. Robin was free and rolled on top of him. Electra discharged the spray can of starter fluid into the face of the gawker. He fell backward screaming in agony, blinded in both eyes. Electra lunged at the thug at the head of the bed and gashed the side of his head with the tire iron. She was about to deal with the last thug moving, but Robin was there first. She had become enraged, swinging the lamp like a baseball bat, catching her opponent on the side of his head, knocking him down again. Then she leaped on top, smashing down twice with the lamp until Electra dragged her away.

The Monster from the Id was not yet satisfied; it wanted more. It leaped on top of each terrorist, striking with the tire iron until all life was driven out. Then Electra stood, completely exhausted, staring at Robin who appeared to be in shock. She shook Robin until Robin's eyes could focus, then rasped out, "We get Christi and get out!"

As they stumbled out of the bedroom, Robin collided with Christi, knocking her down again. They stood her up and Robin untied the rope binding her arms. Only one final act remained. Electra found a roll of paper towels in the kitchen, turning it into a torch, and then set the bedroom curtains and mattress on fire. Then she stuffed the torch into a paper-filled trash can, placing it underneath the living room curtains.

Electra gave the keys to Christi and rasped her last words, "Drive to Gramp's clinic. Say nothing…"

Clarence was happy the graveyard shift had been slow, for it gave him time to finish paperwork left over from a hectic week. Sounds of a car squealing onto the clinic's circular drive, its muffler sounding the final stages of a death rattle, intruded into the calm of the reception area where he was sitting. He joked to himself that his E.R. could be considered a body shop, but one that specializes in organic material rather than sheet metal. He looked up when he heard car doors slam, spotting three young women about to enter.

Even without his glasses, the sight was astonishing: three women in their early twenties, lithe, pretty, and pretty badly battered. The raven-haired one in the middle, blouse caked with blood, had to be propped up by the blonde bookends. The one on the left was buck naked from navel to toes, while the one on the right, though blouse bloodied and nearly ripped off, seemed to be the least damaged. Clarence needed his glasses for a closer look, and when he put them on the entire scene shifted into startling focus. The young women were the Three Queens he had known from Electra Kittner's charmed childhood.

"All of you, into E.R. One. Keep Electra propped between you and set her on the examining table. I'll be with you as soon as I call for assistance." Clarence had nerves that never frayed, and in emergencies he always followed his rule of triage: don't just do something, stand there. A minute later he knew what needed doing.

Robin and Christi would not need stitches, but he needed to clean and use anti-bacterial cream to treat their wounds. Their bloodied lips and noses would heal quickly. Electra's wounds were more serious. Her left eye was swollen shut, and the jagged cut next to it needed stitches. If the punch had landed closer, she might have lost sight in her eye. Nose and lips would heal on their own, but the deep abrasion that completely encircled her neck might be a problem. He would clean and treat with anti-bacterial cream, then have Dr. Antar, the plastic surgeon, take over.

"Here's the deal, ladies. We'll treat Christi first, then Robin because I can patch you good as new. By that time Dr. Antar should be here to look at Electra. How much pain do you get when you swallow or talk."

"Lots."

Clarence carefully explored the outside of her neck. "There's no cartilage damage. The pain should go away in a day or two, and you'll be able to talk normally. All of you be quiet and let me get to work."

Dr. Antar arrived just as Clarence finished with Robin. Because she knew Christi, she greeted her by name and then gave full attention to Electra.

"Your neck abrasion is deep. What caused it?"

"Lamp cord." Dr. Antar didn't expect any more words from Electra, but thought Christi might say more. She didn't, and Dr. Antar knew better than to pry.

"I must take a closer look at your abrasion before I know what's best for you. "Ten minutes later, she spoke again.

"There's nothing to stitch, so there's nothing further I can do. Clarence did a fine job treating it. When you get home, treat it twice a day with the anti-bacterial cream we'll prescribe. You'll be able to wash it in two or three days." Electra nodded.

"It is fortunate the blow that cut close to your eye wasn't further to the center. A little more, and it might have blinded you. Don't worry about the swelling. That will go down in a couple of days. And even though the cut is jagged, my suturing will leave little scarring."

Dr. Antar, assisted by Clarence, completed work thirty minutes later. Neither asked what happened, even though they were concerned the girls might still be in danger. But then they remembered how Electra could deal with almost anything, so they kept away from the subject.

Christi and Robin dressed in hospital gowns before leaving. The sun was just peeking over the horizon when they brought Electra home. They sponge-bathed her, then put her to bed, spoon-feeding mashed bananas and applesauce. Electra fell asleep before the last spoonful. Electra's guardians stripped to shower, Robin first and then Christi. When she came back, she found Robin parked in a chair pulled next to the bed.

"I'll sit here until she wakes up. Funny, but I don't feel tired. I feel energized. Why don't you sleep in her grandfather's bedroom?"

"Wake me up when you need me. I hope she can figure out what we should do next. I don't want to talk about what happened until she can."

Robin nodded then asked, "What about Adom? Should we call the police?"

"No. There's nothing we can do for him until Electra wakes up."

Christi trooped away; there was nothing left to say. Robin would watch over Electra while she sleeps, and she would be there when she awakens. Electra, the girl with the lightning brain who prided herself for never needing help, needed watching over. It was Robin's turn to do just that.

CHAPTER 40
June 2117

"Blown Away"
(Thread 1 Chapter 9)

"PLEASE TELL ME, MY friend, what extra equipment do you need?" Abu had just given Adom a tour of his bomb-making lab—one room of a basement apartment in a ramshackle red brick building located in DC's inner city—immediately followed by an order to stay until he fills all the aerosol cans Abu needs.Smarter than the average homegrown terrorist,Abu used his engineering degree to devise,with help from a Boston terrorist cell,a more sophisticated weapon: a larger container resembling a throwable tear gas canister that would dispense live T-Plague virus. It would be more effective than the typical aerosol can actuated by pressing a release valve because it would explode when thrown,spraying a larger area and allowing the terrorist to flee. The suspension chamber and compression machinery had already arrived, but suitable virus filtration and handling equipment to feed the suspension chamber await selection and purchase.Careful set-up would be needed to prevent a containment breach, as well as to calibrate temperature and pressure settings.

"I see what you have, and I know what you need, and I could hook them all together, but how do I know you'll let me go?"

"We will give you a gun when you start connecting the equipment. You can shoot us if we are lying. Of course, we will shoot back,but none of us want to die,so consider it your mutually assured destruction insurance policy."

"How do I know you'll release the women?"

"We will let you talk with them just before we let you go. You will know they are alive and being treated well."

"Why won't you let me talk to them now?"

"They are still traveling to our safe house. It is better for them not to be in the area." Adom didn't buy the explanations, but he needed to buy time to keep himself alive.

"OK, I'll go along with you. First thing I'll do is give you a list of equipment and supplies I need. Let me logon and check out model numbers."

"How long will it take?"

"I'll ask the supplier when I place the order."

"No.I meant how long will it take for you to make the list? Our people know how to buy equipment, but thank you for offering. Why don't we take you back to your room so you can sit down and write up the list?"

Adom had plenty of time to sit and scribble a list because his room contained only a TV monitor.The longer he sat,the gloomier he became. *The equipment will be here in at most five days,even sooner if Abu's people pick it up.And after witnessing how they killed Electra,I don't foresee a happier ending for myself unless I can think of something between now and delivery day to improve my chances.*

Electra had recovered well enough to venture out late the next night with Christi to dispose of the terrorist car,and the following day the duo reconnoitered Adom's apartment building, spotting yellow crime scene tape plastered across the entrance.When Christi asked what they should do, Electra answered quickly.

"We aren't going to call the police. They've already been here and probably talked with whoever called in the alarm. And there's nothing we can add to the story that would help the police find him. Besides, our injuries would draw suspicion. I'll talk with Mo as soon as I can."

"You better invent a good story. Why don't you tell him you were in an auto accident? And let's hide some of the damage. I'll give you a scarf to wear around your neck. That'll hide the cord burn. And I'll give you a pair of my designer sunglasses. You want mirrored or aviator?"

"Which one will cover more of my swollen eye?"

"Go with the aviators. I think they'll make you look sexy." "That's not my top priority, but I like you're thinking. You're

learning how to stretch the truth to cover up. And Robin's learning some of your favorite swear words. I've noticed she's added the S-word to her vocabulary."

"She can use it to command attention when she's talking. And I'm proud of you too. When you lighten up, your bawdy sense of humor comes out. Robin should add some of your witticisms."

"Maybe so, but I'll keep them to myself when talking with Mo. And until I fabricate an appropriate story, you and Robin must be quiet. Please make sure you tell her that."

Electra met Mo the next day at her new workstation. She had been reorganized onto the one team for which Mo was still the bus-admin leader while helping the new managers come up to speed as he phased out of Cognicom. As soon as he arrived, Electra suggested they talk in the cafeteria because she needed a break; she also needed to keep the talk confidential. Though she couldn't trust him with all she knew about political intrigue, she was certain he'd help find Adom. One look at Electra and Mo knew something was wrong, but he decided not to pry and would let her run the conversation.

"I feel better than I look. My date drove us into an accident last weekend. His car looks worse than I do. But that's not why we need to talk. It's about Adom. I think he's in trouble. Have you heard from him?"

"No. What's the story?"

"I drove over to his place yesterday to pick up some of Su's belongings, but he wasn't there. Crime scene stickers are stuck up all over the place, and we can't get in touch with him. Do you remember a couple of years ago when Su was followed? Maybe Adom was targeted by some bad guys who linked him to Su. He'd be valuable to terrorists because he knows all about handling T-Plague virus. Could you contact the police or your CIA friend to see what they know?" Mo guessed more than his expression showed. *Adom's in deep yogurt, and Electra knows more than she's letting on. I must be her best option.*

"Adom's a great guy and a good friend. If he's in a jam, I'll find out.I'll get Nick to help me.Call me Friday.I'll let you know what I find out."

"Is Nick the right person to work with?"

"Yeah,he's solid and smart,and knows what's going on.We can trust him."

Abu didn't worry that his kidnapping squad had perished in a mysterious fire, or that his healer had died of a broken neck. Instead he would tell his faithful they had died gloriously in a manner befitting the Holy Warriors they had been,and since their lips were permanently silenced there would be no telltale trail to his terrorist cell. Nor did the missing females cause him any concern, for Abu had much better news to give Adom.

"Doctor Ola,the equipment has arrived.My faithful will deliver it this evening so you can set it up and start filling.Please be ready." *Damn! It's only Friday.They must have picked it up themselves.*

"What time will they be here?"

"They will come after dark." Adom cursed again to himself. *Damn, I'm running out of time. Of course, they'll deliver after dark. Harder for neighbors to see what's going on and become suspicious. But in this neighborhood, the neighbors might not be much better than my roommates.*

Though he watched the news, anxiety made it impossible to think about anything other than the evening equipment delivery. *Abu won't let me talk to the girls.It's already six p.m.and I don't see any help on the way. I've got to figure something out.*

Adom felt slightly better when Abu kept his word by giving him a gun, keeping his own at the ready while Adom supervised equipment setup on benches that formed a production line."When do you think you will be ready to start filling?"

"It's eleven now, and it'll take me an hour to get the three components aligned and connected, another hour to complete pressure, temperature and concentration adjustments. After that, maybe another hour to record my notes and get supplies arranged for the first production run. We can start between two and three. How many canisters do you want?"

"Do you have enough virus samples to make nine?"

"No.I have enough for only six,and I'll need to keep enough to culture more. Do you have equipment for doing that?"

"We shall discuss that later. Proceed with assembly. I will have one of my faithful assist you. And let us know when you are ready to start filling." Before going to the living room, Abu handed his gun to one of his followers, ordering him to watch.The other two wanted to observe, but Abu told them to wait.

"No, my faithful, let us have our friend make all preparations. Then we will witness the results of our sacrifices. Allahu Akbar!"

The more Adom worked, the more absorbed he became in building his production line.He was a master at improvisation,able to make adjustments that guaranteed canister filling would work according to his specifications. He was thorough and fast, and by two a.m.told his helper to assemble everyone so they could witness the first run.Adom already had the line primed to start at the press of a button,satisfied from the sound of the compressors and pumps that everything was good to go.

Abu herded everyone around the conveyor belt just before Adom explained what was about to start. "Don't worry about T-Plague virus escaping. The containment and trapping mechanisms are state-of-the-art. Abu, here are all my notes."

Abu couldn't be happier.He had the operating instructions.He had the production line.And soon he would have enough canisters for several attacks. His only concern—and it was a minor one— was the noise of the equipment on the filling line. Perhaps the neighbors would complain, but he would deal with that later. And he would deal once and for all with Adom after the production run ended. He signaled for Adom to proceed.

"We're ready to start. Watch closely how each canister moves off the belt."That was the last thing Abu and his followers would ever see. Adom pushed the start button and dived underneath the benches a second before the pumps exploded,detonating the other equipment and filling the space with deadly shrapnel. Adom had just blown away the terrorist lab and its residents.

Electra was working at home on Saturday when she picked up a call after the third ring. *Mo's calling again. I hope he knows more than he did when he called last night.*

"Hello, Mo. Any word about Adom?" Electra listened briefly, then interrupted to stop his babbling. "Come over to my place right now and tell me the whole story." Ninety minutes later, both were sitting in her kitchen, Mo with arms folded on the table, Electra with arms straight to her sides and sitting on her hands.

"So that's the story. Can you believe it?" Mo had just found out from his CIA contact that a DC terrorist lab blew up while trying to manufacture T-Plague aerosols. Local authorities immediately brought in the FBI, who in turn involved the CIA because the explosion was obviously terrorist-related. The lab was badly damaged but had not burned, so a SWAT team and investigators recovered written notes as well as four bodies. And the notes incriminated a Doctor Adom Ola for being the mastermind behind the lab.

Electra played dumb by asking, "I can't believe Adom did this without being forced. What did the police say about his apartment?"

"I didn't talk to them."

"You know Adom pretty well. Do you still have faith in him?"

"I do. Look, I know you're not telling me everything. Trust me,

I want to get him out of the crosshairs. Please tell me what you know." *I believe him. It's time to tell him more.*

"There was a big fight at Adom's apartment last Saturday. Terrorists kidnapped him so he could make aerosol T-Plague weapons. If he didn't cooperate, they'd kill his friends, and then kill him. He must have figured out they'd kill his friends anyway, so he deliberately blew the place up."

"That must be what happened. His body wasn't found at the scene, so he must have survived. And let me take it further. The media is already reporting the brains behind the blast is on the run, so if Adom goes to the police, the CIA is going to grill him. And they're looking for any sort of scape goat to tie up the mess they've already made. They'll come down hard, much harder than they would if they ever find Su. If I were Adom, I think I'd want to vanish, just like Su. But it's more complicated because he's much more than a P.O.I. If we get some witnesses and a good lawyer, and I do some networking, we might be able to clear him. But first, we have to find Adom. Any ideas?"

"Let me give you all the facts and outline what you need to do next." By the time Electra finished, Mo had his marching orders. First, he would find a good lawyer to handle the legal complexities. Next, he would provide all the facts to the CIA that would exonerate Adom—in fact, make him a hero. Christi and Robin would be his witnesses, saying they escaped when the terrorists first arrived, but didn't come forward until now because they were terrified and had nothing to add. Furthermore, the facts could be spun to make the CIA heroes for rolling up a convoluted terrorist trail intent on making T-Plague WMD's. Neither Adom nor Su would be in the CIA's crosshairs after this.

But for this to work, Adom had to turn himself in, meaning Mo must leak the story to the media, alerting Adom whom to contact for help and priming public support. Mo sat like a schoolboy taking notes as Electra marched through her plan.

"This is all good. I can't think of anything to add. And unless lightning strikes, we should all be in the clear." Electra's inner voice from the shadow spoke. *Lightning played a role long ago, but we don't need it for Adom. There's a less shocking way to transform him.*

The plan worked to perfection thanks to Mo's relentless efforts. After the media broke the story, an uninjured Adom contacted Mo, who coordinated a surrender supervised by a trusted lawyer. Mo became an unsung hero for helping the CIA clear up the local terrorist cell connection to T-Plague weapons, while the Agency became a hero for rolling up the cell, and Adom became a hero in court of public opinion, which was the only court in question because no charges were ever brought.

The entire episode ended in September, which was swift given all complexities that had to be resolved. Adom hosted a dinner on the last day of month at Electra's favorite Italian restaurant, where he and the behind-the-scenes heroines talked quietly about the ordeal they had managed to live through, agreeing never to discuss it again. And they avoided talking about the terrible struggle at Adom's apartment. The image of Electra's deathlike repose was too painful to recall.

The conversation turned to happier topics. Adom's life was returning to normal as he continued searching for a new job.

"I'm dead set, if you'll pardon my pun, against returning to NIH. I'm going to continue networking for a new position." The girls looked at one another, deciding Robin should provide a promising lead.

"Do you like four-alarm chili? If you do, there's a place in Austin that might suit your taste. And we know some Texans you might also like."

CHAPTER 41
November 2117

"The Deadly Mole"
(Thread 1 Chapter 10)

ELLIOT SPITZDIECK TOOK PARTICULAR pleasure listening to the verbal shellacking delivered to his boss by the section chief. And to make matters even worse—or better, depending whose side you were on—the chief dished out the abuse at the Project Death Shield September status meeting. The boss's pain was Elliot's gain because the chief made it perfectly clear whose head was about to roll.

"How is it possible for agents not even remotely engaged in T-Plague to roll up a terrorist cell and lab that was right under your nose? And by doing so they close out not one, but two of your open cases. Don't tell me. I know the answer. You hired them to do your job while you stand around with your thumb in your bum and brain in neutral. Starting immediately, you and Spitzdieck are trading places."

Elliot would have danced a jig if he were standing, because the exchange would halt his career's descent. He might rise again if he could figure a way to repair Project Death Shield's tarnished image. The stunning summer roll-up bought him a little time because it reduced the immediate pressure, which meant he could command the team to focus on his obsession.

Elliot's bulldog determination matched his ruthlessness. Without a shred of evidence, he had convinced himself two years ago of a conspiracy involving researchers on a particular Cognicom project. First, he found suspicious stop-and-go progress. Then, the team leader blew himself up. Next, that brainy Dr. Chou mysteriously disappeared. Then another researcher blew up a terrorist T-Plague lab after he had been promoted and then summarily benched, only to be bailed out by the Senior Cognicom Bus-Admin Manager. All this was too much coincidence to be nothing but association. There must be causation, and Elliot would find it, even if it required dissecting everyone left. He hadn't picked his first suspect yet, but he would make sure his moles keep track of his designated targets. How nice to be in charge again.

Electra had more time to devote to Guardian Party P.R. work since being reassigned a data collection clerk role on a different team, and the terrorist lab explosion details she gave Zoe scooped all others. Zoe was so pleased she promoted her to be assistant speech writer, assigning Jared's upcoming address that would be given prime time Thanksgiving Day. *I know how to spin the words into an explosive message that'll shake the Administration.*

A string of rapid-fire events had erupted in early October. Domestic terrorist cells started using fake T-Plague aerosols if they didn't have deadly virus canisters, the results just as devastating because hapless bystanders couldn't tell the difference and trampled one another just the same. The public's anger grew because its demands for faster and harsher intervention went unmet, many blaming the Administration for failing to implement the latest Healthguard and Securityguard procedures championed by the Guardian Party. Latest economic reports confirmed growing numbers of T-Plague survivors were damaging the economy and clogging the healthcare system, while infrastructure outage or mishap stories became more and more routine, the most recent reporting an airport disaster caused by two air traffic controllers landing planes simultaneously on the same runway. Although their T-Plague positive status had been reported, Transportation Agency bureaucrats had ignored the test results. The guilty bureaucrats and controllers were summarily terminated, but the mistake was irreversible, just like the T-Plague.

Electra remained wary of the Guardian Party. She knew Healthguard would treat her poorly if they ever knew her secret, but the Guardians might do a better job than the current Administration rebuilding the economy and its supporting infrastructures. And she liked Jared's leadership style as well as some of what he said. Her opinion might change if Jared had a hidden agenda, so she continued playing her P.R. game to find it. Email trails hadn't uncovered it yet, but the more she embedded herself in Zoe's department, the deeper she burrowed into hidden directories. *If I find a hidden agenda or something bad for the public, I'll leak the info to the media. That'll derail the Guardians and their chief engineer, or at least slow them down. And if they accuse me of being the leaker, I'll pin it on Zoe.*

Electra's big breakthrough came in late November when she tapped into hidden files and EMails that proved the Guardian Party deliberately fabricated stories that went far beyond the rumors she deliberately fed Zoe. *I'm losing control of the disinformation mill and better do something to regain control.* Electra uploaded files and made hard copies of incriminating evidence she would leak soon after Jared's speech.

Thanksgiving Day's symbolism set the stage for Jared's address. Its galvanizing content would shock as his charismatic delivery would increase support for the Guardians. Electra and the Conklins watched together as Jared spun a message that rocked America.

"Happy Thanksgiving to all patriotic Americans. I spoke to the nation last Election Eve, delivering a message of hope and also of warning. The hope was for Washington to right the ship of state before it reached a tipping point, and the warning told of the dire consequences should it fail. Patriots, the litany of catastrophes since last November's election is appalling and continues to grow. The plane crash victims, the people trampled in T-Plague aerosol attacks, they are but a sad summary for all of us who bear mute testimony to the worst of Washington. Our government has failed to safeguard our great nation. The time has come for all patriots to act while time is still on our side.

"We, the Guardian Party have faith in our people, who, in spite of so many suffering the ravages of T-Plague, carry on. And we want to carry out their wishes. We need every patriot to support us in our efforts to make the current government work for us. Your active,aggressive support will force the Administration to carry out your wishes and will support us as we transform Washington.

"In the weeks ahead,we'll release more proof the Administration is betraying us, and your Guardian Party will take bold steps in the direction you the public declare are in our collective best interests. I cannot promise the path will be without difficulty, but I can promise it will lead us back whence we came: the pinnacle of Western Civilization, poised for an even greater future.

"Let us give thanks to all those brave patriots past,present,or future, who stand with us.Join us in our commitment to guard what makes America great. God bless our great nation and our great Patriots."

Zoe tweaked my words, but the message came out loud and clear as I intended.Watch out for Jared and the Guardians. If we're not careful, they'll seize control of the government, letting the public pick which scenario to unfold, bloodless coup or rioting in the streets. And nothing said closes out options. There's a thinly veiled threat to all parties, no matter their stripe. And no stated deadline keeps everyone guessing.

Tweaked or not, Russell got the message and told all at the table.

"The government has known for years this day was coming. And it just couldn't get its act together. We're in for a rough ride."

"Father, don't get so upset. Electra, what do you think?"

"I'm not sure. Let's listen to what the commentators have to say." A broad spectrum of possible repercussions came to light. Some thought the speech and its ramifications would blow over and Washington would settle back into its normal muddle; others agreed with Russell and said it's time to tighten seat belts. Electra knew the time had come to leak her pirated Emails, and she knew the best person to assist.

"Nick, this is Mo. You and I have to meet with someone later this afternoon. I'll explain in the car. Pick me up at five." As he hung up the phone, Mo glumly admitted he would spend the rest of post-Thanksgiving Saturday working like a political leaker, but he had no alternative.

Part of Mo was energized, ready to act on his convictions. For years he had been part of confidential committees tracking politically charged events, and he was among a handful that had decided a year ago to act on their conviction. He hoped he had picked the right option, and that its leadership could make up for years of fence-sitting.

Mo's career, like his mid-fifties age, was past its prime, as were his physical skills. He had gained weight that settled in his midsection, but his air reserve training forced him to exercise more than most of his peers. Besides, he had been a good athlete, even boxing in college, so his muscle memory retained some conditioning. Mo's energy level and cognitive ability were still good, but he wanted to bring Nick with him to inject vitality into what he'd be doing the next couple of days. Nick performed well in his business analyst role, benefitting from Mo's mentoring and adding to Mo's trust.

Nick phoned ahead, so Mo was waiting outside. Like many upwardly mobile late twenty-something DC males, Nick liked quality, especially in cars and females. His late model Porsche declared his taste, and because women found him physically fit and good looking, the passenger seat was usually occupied. His disarming manner helped pick up Mo's spirits.

"Hi, Mo. What goes?"

"Thanks for jumping in on short notice. How'd you like Jared's Thanksgiving address?"

"That was a political bombshell. I'm not sure what's going to happen." Mo shook his head and continued.

"I think it's time to let the media in on what's behind the Guardian Party curtain. We're going to get some hard evidence that we'll leak to the media. I want you to look at it with me, and then help place it where it will do the most good. We're going to our lab to talk with someone who can give us the goods." Nick's expression reflected a combination of surprise and willingness to help.

"Let's see what we can uncover…"

Electra waited for Mo at her lab workstation. As expected for the Thanksgiving weekend, the facility had only a skeleton crew, and she was the only one working in her lab, keeping busy doing thesis-related work. I have just enough time to run to the cafeteria. I know Mo doesn't like the Establishment, but I still don't know which group he's with. If he's on the Guardian side and grills me, I'll say I thought he'd like to know what's going on and tell him to go after Zoe, not me.

Because Electra had not yet returned when they arrived, Mo headed for a chair at the table in the open area. Mo didn't hear the metallic click when Nick switched the manual door lock, which meant no one could enter. Nor did he see Nick pull a Traser until he was about to sit.

Mo's eyes widened, but he controlled his reaction. "Nick, what gives?" Nick's smirk said it all.

"This Traser gives electric jolts or tranquilizers. And it's about time we jolt some info out of you. You're a two-in-one catch. You've been a source of leaks against us, and you know more about vaccine R&D than you've been letting on. Whoever comes up with vaccines that work wins the political battle." *I'm in deep yogurt. Nick's a Guardian Party mole. I'll bet he's tailed me from the day he hired on. I fell for his cover, but I don't know what tripped me up. Damn, I don't have a weapon. Now's not the time to negotiate, so I'll keep my mouth shut until something turns up.*

Electra hurried back to the lab, carrying a cheese sandwich and a Coke. She was so hungry she had already eaten half the sandwich on the way, but as she glanced through the lab window the view froze her in mid-bite. *Why is that fellow—that's Nick Rossi—pointing a Traser at Mo?* The answer came in a flash. He's somebody's mole. She would be nonchalant until getting closer to the situation, then act. *He locked me out. I'll tap on the window.*

Nick involuntarily turned his head towards the tapping that distracting him momentarily. *What's that simple-minded Kittner doing here?* He regained his focus, but turned back to Mo a second too late. Mo seized the lapse to grab for the Traser by rushing Nick, gripping his wrist and twisting it backwards as he pinned the other arm to Nick's body. The Traser flew out of Nick's hand, crashing against the opposite wall. Nick was able to spring free by smashing Mo on the side of the head with his free hand. They separated, each warily circling the other, saying nothing but fully aware a deadly fight had started.

Electra could do nothing except root for Mo. The safety glass was too strong to smash with the nearby fire extinguisher. She would have to stand at ringside, pulling for the underdog. *Nick's age and condition make him quicker. Mo's height and weight make him stronger. Nick's gonna win if Mo doesn't fight in close.*

Mo charged, but Nick dodged to the left avoiding the rush. When Mo jerked around, Nick slammed a palm fist into Mo's nose, bloodying it and snapping Mo's head backward. Mo's boxing crouch kept him stable enough to swing a haymaker that whistled by Nick's right ear. Nick was quick; Mo had to close the distance, so he forced Nick to the right, backing him into a corner. Mo charged again, this time pinning him and pummeled his gut with a couple of solid lefts. Nick grunted but pulled free by landing a solid left hook that banged into Mo's jaw.

Mo was beginning to tire and soon would be gasping if he couldn't disrupt Nick's footwork. He threw whatever he could find, then shoved the few chairs in the open area at Nick, all to no avail. Nick grinned, sensing the advantage was turning more and more in his favor, but his cockiness caused his first mistake when he leaped for the Traser. He got to it first, but Mo dived just in time to topple Nick forward and Mo sprawled on top. He grabbed for a leg, but Nick was too agile and kicked Mo in the chin, then bounced up and was free again.

Mo rose too slowly and caught a Karate side kick on the side of his head, sending him side-wards and down, but almost on top of the Traser. If the fight continued like this, whoever gets the Traser wins the fight. Nick dived on top of Mo; Mo wrapped his arms around Nick and twisted on top, pinning Nick to the floor and smashing his nose and mouth with a couple of short rights. Blood spurted from Nick's nose; he tried to gouge Mo's eyes, but Mo arched backwards and Nick spun free.

Both opponents struggled to their feet, a sense of urgency energizing them. Nick backed away but fell over an upended chair. Mo saw his chance; he lumbered forward and threw himself on top of Nick. Nick rolled to his left, but Mo grabbed him with his right arm and pulled him close. Then he grabbed Nick's hair with his left hand at the same time Nick grabbed Mo's neck with both hands. The fight had become intense, desperate. Whoever released first would be in the other's death grip.

Mo wrapped his right arm around the back of Nick's neck and using it for leverage twisted with all his weight. Nick started to gasp; one hand slipped from Mo's neck, then the other as Mo twisted relentlessly. Suddenly, Nick's body went limp. Mo had snapped his young adversary's neck. It took ten seconds for Mo's head to clear enough so he could prop himself to his knees. The banging on the window helped rouse him, so he stumbled to the door and turned the manual lock.

Electra rushed in and grabbed Mo's shoulders to steady him, then assessed damages. "You're bloody, but you're standing. We've got to leave."

"What about Nick? We've got to hide the body."

"Help me carry it to the pod room. We'll shove it into one of the suspension pods. Then we'll wipe up any blood and put the place back in order." Mo did the carrying while Electra unlatched the cover from one in the middle of the adjoining room. Mo submerged Nick's clothed body into the suspension fluid while Electra wired it, then sealed the cover. It could take months for anyone to recycle the pod, and by that time any trail would be stone cold dead, just like Nick.

Blotches of blood colored the tiled floor, so Electra hurried to the cleaning supplies closet, then used sprays and towels to clean up the floor after first patching Mo. After that she put the place back in order, picking up a couple of chairs and removing any signs of combat. Time to ask Mo if he's ready to go.

"Did you drive?"

"No, Nick did. Damn! His keys are in his pocket."

"Stay here. I'll get them." Electra rushed to the pod room and back, then collected all her belongings.

"Let's take his car. I'll drive while you take a look at what I brought."

Electra kept her gloves on to keep fingerprints off the interior, and she instructed Mo not to touch anything. They would have to abandon the car in a decoy location because it would become evidence for Nick's mysterious disappearance. As she drove, Mo studied the documents Electra had given him.

"Wow, this will slow Jared down. He'll have to do a lotta damage control. I know just how to leak this."

"I was hoping you knew how to get this to the media. What happened in there?" Electra already had a good idea, but wanted Mo to fill in the gaps. Mo rubbed his eyes before he spoke.

"Nick fooled me. He's been shadowing me ever since working at NIH. He's got to be a mole for the Guardian Party. I must have been careless. Something I said or did tipped him off. But I don't think he had time to call his handler. They might not be on to me. I'll just have to wait and see and be on guard. And if they are, they might feel the same way I do. If Jared approved this, knowing all of it is bogus, he's going too far."

"We have to dump Nick's car somewhere, then you have to drive me back to the lab so I can pick up mine. I'll make a quick pass to see if anyone picked up on what went down. My guess is we're in the clear." A weary Mo said nothing but looked relieved. Electra flashed an inward smile, then drove on in silence.

Two stories dominated post-Thanksgiving news: one blaring Jared's address, the other spouting accusations about trumped-up stories. The result was just what Electra wanted: continued inaction on all sides. She wanted more time to consider other plans. Unknown to her, another group felt the same way.

The Opposition Group's steering committee chairman called an emergency meeting soon after Jared's address, his first sentence getting to the heart of the matter. "The Guardian Party is ready to seize power. If the media hadn't found out about all the lies being spread, we'd be SOL. We are way behind in our contingency planning and resource acquisition. If we aren't ready in no more than three months, we'll be history. Let's go around the table for ideas to map out next steps."

Two exhaustive hours later, the chairman was ready to adjourn the meeting. "We've got our to-do list, so let's get after it. Everyone knows what's expected." He pointed to one of his lieutenants as he concluded the meeting. "Please contact Mrs. T. Let her know the marching orders."

Electra had only one meeting left before Holiday break: a meeting with Zoe to announce her break from the Guardian Party. *I know what they're up to. No sense sticking around. Too bad if my departure catches Zoe by surprise. I like her, but I have to look out for myself. Zoe motioned Electra into her office the moment she spotted her.*

"You can't leave us now. You've just caught on to what works in Jared's speeches, and he likes what you put together. I gave you most of the credit. He's got big plans for you and me next year."

"I'm concerned about the big lies the Party is spreading. They go way beyond my rumors. Don't they bother you?"

"No. The media doesn't have the story straight. I've never seen or heard anything that would even hint at what the news is saying. I can't imagine who gave them such disinformation. I'm sure Jared will explain." *You seem so genuine. Maybe you don't know, but I do.*

"Tell Jared I'm taking a leave of absence because I'm bogged down in thesis work. If other facts come to light, I'll reconsider. But until then, I'm gone." Zoe's disappointment came out in her words and expression.

"I thought we were friends. Friends don't treat friends this way."

"I still consider us friends, but I have to go with my convictions. You and I look at Jared and the Guardian party differently. Maybe reality is somewhere in between. Wherever it is, please watch out for yourself."

Electra walked out before Zoe could say another word. Electra kept a low-key Christmas calendar because she needed time and space to adjust next year's plan due to the recent whirlwind of events. She spent Christmas Eve at the Conklins, and Christmas Day at the Setdarovas, who hosted a party for the Conklins and Electra. Electra came home with enough leftovers to snack on for three days and would be well fed while working at home.

Except for running outdoors, Electra stayed put most of the next week, happily working at her computer workstation. She had just written up additional sections of her thesis, rewarding herself by stepping to the kitchen for a Coke and cookie break. *The hard part of my thesis is done. I've built my neural-mapping brain probe, written the control software, and know how to locate with my new drug all the cognition-related neurons that I can turn on or off with my probe. All I have to do is collect and correlate brain-state cognitive neuron data with emotional and physical responses. And as I proceed, I'll feed enough information to Professor Ravenhill so he won't be stunned when I complete my work. In fact, my diplomacy and empathy are beginning to make him an ally rather than a doubter.*

While in the kitchen, Electra's thoughts turned to the Guardian Party and T-Plague concerns. *I won't see much of Zoe next year, and I hope the info Mo leaked keeps the Guardians at bay. But I will see Adom's face, though in a different place.*

How nice he's in Austin reunited with Su. Her Christmas note sounded upbeat. Adom's becoming the go-to type of person she knew was inside. And I'll give Su enough T-Plague clues so she keeps moving ahead on all vaccines, giving a win-win-win outcome. Hud racks up big sales, NIH looks like they're in control, and the public has protection.

I won't see any familiar faces other than Mo's at the lab. I don't know any of the Cognicom researchers, nor do I care. And it's not for me to help them. Let them struggle to understand rather than be handed what they haven't earned. Only then will they be humbled by technology's transformative power so they won't abuse what they had to work so hard to understand.

Electra returned to her computer, all set to work on a different project when other people came to mind. *I'll see plenty of Christi next year, and Robin too. How different the three of us are, yet how nicely we fit together. I hope Robin can handle accounting without too much coaching from me, and I hope she can handle guys without too much coaching from Christi. She seems to be coming to terms regarding her sexual identity, and when it comes to identities, I've kept my secret hidden through all the twists and turns. Next year's political intrigue should provide even more. I'll need to be careful.*

Electra worked for another hour, then took a second break, reclining on the living room sofa, head nestled in a pillow, and wrapping herself in a blanket as the sun's late afternoon dimming glow cast rays of brightness across the snow-sprinkled lawn and onto the sofa. She was there later, when the streetlight in the distance blinked to life, and she pretended it was summoning the ghosts of loved ones gone but never to be forgotten. A sudden pang told her they could never be replaced, but then an Indira poem came to mind, announcing a future pregnant with possibilities. A ripple of joy spread over her as she recalled the verses:

> "We've reached the Winter Solstice,
> Shortest day of the year.
> Though longest night the stars shine bright,
> Aglow with hope and cheer.
>
> Dwindling days are over,
> Brightness emerging instead.
> Tomorrow's weather getting better,
> Good tidings ring out in my head.
>
> Life too holds many a Solstice,
> Turning points march into view.
> At steadfast pace then turn-about face,
> Take heart joy's waiting for you."

Electra drifted into a dreamless sleep that lasted until the dawn.

CHAPTER 42
February 11, 2118

"Second Strike"
(Thread 1 Chapter 11)

ELECTRA ALWAYS AWOKE on her birthday troubled by emotions lurking just below cognition, force-multiplied this morning by bad weather looming just over the horizon. The weather would be easier to deal with because her friends would postpone this evening's 21st birthday party if travel becomes treacherous. The other would be harder to handle.

Emotions are my Achilles heel, intruding when uninvited, panging in places I prefer not to visit. When they stay too long, my philosophic nature obsesses, making me apathetic and depressed. That's why I make a to-do list every night while falling asleep so next morning I know where to start. My prime directive is survival—to go on living—but for me it only works in a focused, meaningful context. I have to have tangible goals. Otherwise, I lose interest in life and my special talents wither.

Electra checked off the first item by suiting up and getting into her morning run. By the time she completed six miles, endorphins had lifted her spirits, bringing out an irrepressible sense of humor that could be raucously bawdy when joking privately. To satisfy her curiosity, several years ago she had read about swearwords, learning that religious oaths (the Bible is more than PG-13) and biological processes (people have always been obsessed with sex) begat most of them, the Romans then passing them from Latin into other languages that recast the words to suit different cultures and times. Neuroscientists believe they are stored in a more primitive part of the brain—the limbic system—and studies have shown swearing increases a person's tolerance to pain. Electra connected this with what she knew about "owning your Shadow," a concept coming from Jungian psychology that helps explain why bawdy thoughts or behavior may sometimes help a person deal with emotions if the outburst is appropriately self-contained. *Before breakfast, I prefer running to sex. The only quickie I want comes from the oatmeal box, not from some guy humping me in the sack. I won't tell this to anyone, not even to Christi. I'll share it only with my inner voice.* Indira spoke from the Shadow.

"You have the makings of a punster, and today you're twenty-one. Many twists and turns await you, but you'll survive when day is done."

"How do you know that? You told me no one could see the future."

"I'm only teasing. No one knows, but you have survived twenty consecutive birthdays, and I see no reason why you shouldn't keep the string alive."

"Mother, I'll never match your empathy or artistry with words, but I'm getting better dealing with my feelings."

"Yes, you are. And you're starting to apply some of Jung's shadow concept by lightening up. It's good that you are becoming less critical of yourself, and allowing more of your emotions to come out. As you grow by experiencing more relationships, you will realize that doing so gets you closer to the focal point of life. Recall my poem by that name and then get on with your day:

> "It's taken years to understand,
> The focal point of Life.
> But now I see its majesty,
> No more internal strife.
>
> When young we think that all is ours,
> The world revolves round us.

And when our whims aren't fully met,
We make a terrible fuss.

But look beyond your selfish self,
For a selfless path that's right.
Reach out to strive for what makes you thrive,
Your journey comes in sight."

Electra's mood brightened as she completed morning exercises, then dived into breakfast followed by routine chores, although listening to the news was anything but cheery. *Same-old-same-old T-Plague reports and bulletins from Healthguard or Securityguard scaring the public. But at least there's no revolution setting fires in the streets.*

The drive to the lab was uneventful because bad weather remained beyond the horizon, but a thunder-snowstorm might blow in later. *The afternoon commute could become an ordeal. Extraordinary weather may be on the way, but I survived a similar storm long ago.*

That morning she worked in uninterrupted solitude. As she perched in front of her workstation, she mused how pleasantly predictable lab work had become now that she was merely a data retrieval clerk. Most of her time was spent online reading cutting edge articles or attending bioscience workshops whose theories she would apply in the next phase of her academic career. *I have my pick of three postdoc research positions starting next September. I think I'll accept the one at GWU so I can stay put. It'll keep me close to Christi and Robin, and I can live in comfort and safety while taking care of father's house.*

Electra continued making rapid progress on her thesis, impressing even her inner voice. Indira chatted briefly with her during a morning reverie.

"You are truly superior cognitively. It was a stroke of genius to modify your T-Plague vaccine solution path to pave the way for a biotech drug that will bind with cognition-related neurons. It will serve as the foundation for a cellular mapping of the human brain."

"Thank you. And I hope you've notice how diplomatic I am with Professor Ravenhill. I have generously given him credit for assisting me turn what he calls my lucky hunches into a targeted thesis topic."

"Actually, I credit your improved empathy for how well you're handling him. And it will pay off. I imagine he will recruit a thesis review committee that will be smart enough to follow your work. Just remember to dummy it down when presenting to them."

"I will. And I already have a selection of post doc projects that build on my thesis. My brain probe device will be the first. It will take me into robotics and artificial intelligence." Indira added a note of caution.

"You've shared many ideas with me. Just be careful not to expect your associates to understand as fast as you might like. Your Dream Team might always be a dream."

"That's one of the reasons why I'll borrow current technology. My associates should understand that."

"I must say, you're deviously clever building on pirated software. And you don't have to worry about the competition stealing yours, because even if they de-compile your apps, they'll never understand your programming techniques. As you branch into robotics and artificial intelligence, you'll come across corporations that want to steal your inventions, which means you'll need to stay below their radar. But you've already been doing that. It's time for you to return to work. You have a most promising future so I shall wish you a Star Trek farewell: live long and prosper."

As the afternoon ticked by, Electra hiked to the cafeteria for a snack break. *A lot of people have already gone home. I better check the weather. If it's getting worse, I'll leave at four instead of five so I'm on time picking up Christi. And I'll eat just enough to take the edge off my appetite. I think tonight I'll order tiramisu for dessert and an after-dinner liqueur, maybe Amaretto. After all, I'm the guest of honor.*

"Mo, your cover's blown! Two covert operations teams have targeted you. We'll extract you and your handler tonight. Call back at five for extraction coordinates." The impact of the Bad Boy's bad news nearly forced Mo's car into the ditch, but he managed to stop on the shoulder as incipient beads of sweat popped on his forehead. Though struggling to get his bearings, Mo had prepared for this emergency, at least on paper. A year ago, when he committed to fight for a better government, he had outlined a plan. His contact would arrange for escape to a safe location, and he'd be helped from there. But because of recent developments, he now has to retrieve whatever vaccine data he can find, and then pick up his handler. For security reasons, neither Mo nor his handler knew one another's name, rank, or serial number. The Bad Boy would reveal them when Mo calls later. Mo didn't have any data yet, but he knew who might be able to help.

Electra was about to leave when her cell phone chimed. She recognized Mo's number, but had no idea why he was calling. Nowadays she didn't talk with him often because of reassignments and shifts in priority.

"Hello, Mo. How are you?"

"I'm doing OK, but I need to ask a favor. Could you pull together all the background data you have on vaccine R&D? I need it ASAP and can be at your lab in a half hour. I'll explain when I get there." Electra had never heard so much tension in Mo's voice, but she didn't let on.

"Will do. I'll be at my workstation. Be careful driving. The weather's getting worse."

"Yeah, it's beginning to blow in, but travel's not a problem yet. See you soon."

Electra's cloud storage contained a wealth of encrypted T-Plague data grouped into three folders: NIH Cognicom, Worldstars, and My Solution. NIH Cognicom contained everything for the official Cognicom projects. Worldstars held what Su had achieved because of Electra's clues. The My Solution folder covered Electra's work. *Mo can have the NIH Cognicom folder if he tells me what's going on. Something's bothering him. Maybe someone traced the leaks or connected him with Nick's disappearance. That's it! Mo's on the run.*

Electra had prepared long ago for this contingency. No one would ever know she's the mastermind behind effective vaccines. No one would ever know how she defused terrorist strikes or pirated incriminating data that others leaked. The people she works with consider her smart but naïve and simple. *No one—including Mo or whoever's chasing him— will ever connect me with anything I don't want them to.*

Electra liked Mo and would help, but only within limits. She would not risk exposure. *Mo knew what he was getting into and probably has an escape route. I won't pry. I'll give him enough of what he needs, wish him all the best, and watch him exit my life.*

Mo arrived at five and stammered his predicament, matching what she thought, so she made hard copies of what he needed.

"This is all I have. It took me longer than I thought to find it. Hold on, I need to make a call."

"I do too." They sat next to each other while calling. Christi answered on the fifth ring.

"Hi Christi, it's Electra. How are you?"

"I'm OK, but the weather isn't. How's the surf?" Electra's brain snapped to high alert. Christi had never used their coded warning before.

"Surf's fine. How about you?"

"I'm with my folks but the surf's up, so I can't see you tonight. Why don't you call me tomorrow?"

"Will do. Take care." Electra knew that Christi and her parents were in trouble, so the lightning brain began racing through scenarios but it needed to know more. Mo was still on his call; Electra watched and listened.

"OK, I've jotted down times and locations. I'll call you after pickup." Electra glanced at what Mo had written and knew immediately what to do. One of the locations was that of Christi's parents. Russell Conklin was Mo's handler!

"Mo, I know what's going down. Follow me and I'll explain on the way." Just then, the storm knocked out all electrical power.

Christi had arrived home a little before five; getting to the restaurant would be easier from there rather than campus. She could hear thunder rumbling and tumbling in the distance as an extraordinary storm approached. *Maybe we'll have to cancel tonight's party.*

"I'm home," she yelled as she marched into the house, stomping snow off her shoes. Then a stocky fellow she had never seen before startled her; he was leading her by the arm into the living room when her cell phone beeped. Looking at the inbound calling number, she wrestled her other arm free.

"Let me take this call so I can cancel my date."

Electra pointed as she yelled instructions. "You change into that guard's uniform and I'll change into his. Then we'll load them into the back seat. Make sure you cuff them." Mo was still trying to catch up with the train of events Electra was driving. He had witnessed the transformation once before. Electra had become a ruthless commando leader, which meant Mo could do nothing but follow orders.

When the lights had gone out, Electra grabbed a flashlight from a storage drawer and led the way to an exit, windblown sleet adding to the confusion.

"We need something that'll handle bad roads. Let's commandeer the guard vehicle in the main parking lot. I'll distract the guards and you stun them. Here's my Traser."

Electra was now driving an Elite SWAT Cruiser. "When I stop, jump out and roll the guards onto the shoulder of the road. Don't worry. They have enough insulation to keep warm while they walk back." Now Electra was powering the Cruiser through the freak storm towards the pickup site—the Conklin's.

"Here's the situation. Not only is your cover blown, so is your handler's. Do you know who your handler is?"

"No. We're never told names for security reasons. I don't know him and he doesn't know me."

"The address you showed me is Russell Conklin's. He's your handler and whichever group fingered you, CIA or Guardian Party or that shadowy Opposition Group, sent a team to fetch him and you. Who do you think it is?"

"It has to be the Guardian Party. Maybe they tracked me from Russell, or maybe the other way around. Look, I'm not part of any covert operation. I just pass information I think is useful to my handler. But I do know of several groups trying to protect their butts: the CIA, the Guardian Party, and the Opposition Group." It was time for Electra to pin Mo down.

"Whose side are you on?" She didn't need to look at Mo, because he was in no position to do anything but level with her. If he didn't, Electra could dump him in the snow. She had her Traser.

"I've been working with the Opposition Group. I've been passing them information for a couple of years, but last year I decided to act on my convictions." Electra didn't need to hear anything else.

"I hope they're the best choice. Here's the plan for when we get to the Conklin's…"

Three Guardian agents were pleased that Russell Conklin took such good care of everything he owned. The storm was toppling power lines but his backup generator kicked in as advertised, so they were sitting comfortably in the living room, waiting for someone to pick up Russell. Whoever came would be greeted harshly.

The leader stared impassively at what had been, until his team barged in, an ideal family. A successful and distinguished-looking husband with a beautiful younger wife and a pretty daughter. *Too bad he picked the wrong side in the DC political game. Now he's sitting meekly in a chair with his hands tied in front, just like his daughter.* The leader's partners had made an example of what would happen by pistol-whipping his wife if Russell didn't cooperate. He was surprised by the husband's strength and the daughter's feistiness. Both had leaped to protect the first victim. *Well, now he knows what's in store for his daughter if he doesn't cooperate.*

When the leader heard an approaching vehicle, he looked out a window just in time to see an Elite SWAT Cruiser pull into the driveway. Then a person wearing a Securityguard uniform exited the driver's side and was striding to the rear door. *That can't be Conklin's pickup. Why did Covert Operations send another vehicle?* The leader was puzzled, so he pointed to his partners. "You come with me to the side door; orders might have changed. You stay and watch over our host." The two hustled into the kitchen, and as they opened the door a tremendous crash erupted in the living room.

Russell Conklin kept his raging anger under control. He was sitting still, waiting for the right moment to strike back. For his entire life, people misread his pleasant, distinguished demeanor, not expecting him to have second strike capability. But that was wrong, for if anyone crossed his lines, he would respond with surprising force. And his lines were cast in concrete, not sand. These thugs had beaten his wife, threatened his daughter, and were forcing him to turn traitor on the cause he supported. He was sorting through options, all dismal at the moment. Conditions might change when his pickup arrived, but how he didn't know. Suddenly, a human cannonball exploded through the living room window…

"We're a half-block from the Conklin's. I'm getting out. You pull alongside the house. Just drive at a normal speed. There's a good chance they'll confuse you with a backup. Go to the back door. I'll go to the front. Make sure you conceal your Traser, but be ready to shoot at full stun. And knock and speak loudly so I can hear what's happening." Mo nodded, but added nothing.

Electra dodged behind the Cruiser to camouflage her approach. The wind-blown sleet wasn't deep yet, but roads were treacherous. Footing was better on the grass, which worked in her favor. Before she left the Cruiser, she took a thermal blanket from storage—the lightning brain noted how well equipped Elite SWAT Cruisers are—and motioned for Mo to drive on. She crouched low on the front lawn, waiting for some sound to signal that Mo was at the back door. She heard it, so it was time to leap into action. Electra tightened headgear, checked gloves, then wrapped head and torso with the blanket. She took one deep breath and then—like a bolt of lightning—crashed into the living room window, somersaulting across the couch and coffee table, landing prone on the living room floor.

The third-in-command leaped to his feet when Electra crash-landed, and that was all the distraction Russell needed. He leaped to his feet and turned his bound hands into a noose, using his weight advantage for leverage to pull his opponent backwards, tumbling both to the floor, Russell underneath. Christi leaped into action, kicking her adversary. He partially blocked it, which toppled Christi to the side. She bounced onto and off Electra, who had been struggling to her feet. Christi was a dynamo, leaping on top of the pile and smashing a Karate palm strike that broke the nose of the face on top. By now Russell's noose had choked the third man nearly unconscious, but he didn't let go until his opponent stopped moving. He struggled to his feet and picked up Christi, telling her to kick the man senseless if he moved. Then he grabbed the gun lying on the floor and raced into the kitchen. By the time Russell got there, Mo had the situation well in hand. He had Tasered his opponents who were now rigid on the kitchen floor.

Russell helped Mo drag them into the living room. All combatants were now gathered in one place, and the winning side could regroup. Christi had already helped her mother and Electra stand, and as soon as Russell recognized Mo, the cloud of confusion began to lift. Mo summarized why he and Electra were here, and then Russell did likewise. After binding and gagging the three agents, the men started planning another escape.

Jennifer and Christi hurried to put food and beverages on the dining room table while Electra listened. All five ate quickly then remained at the table, listening to Mo and Russell decide what to do. Twenty minutes later, Mo summarized the plan.

"We have two escape plans, not one, because we need to make three more people disappear, all the ladies that are at the table. Russell will take care of Jennifer and Christi. He'll call his contact to get a safe house location where he'll drive Jenn and Christi in the agents' car. We'll load the agents in the car too. I'll drive Electra home because she's in the clear, and then I drive to my extraction site. And we need to leave now, so unless anyone disagrees, let's clean the table, take a bathroom break and go."

Everyone agreed except Electra. She knew she was in the clear and could continue working from the sidelines, but in a flash she came up with a better plan. *If I help the Opposition Group, we can get rid of the T-Plague and terrorists, and we can keep the Guardian Party at bay. Then I can get on with my future.*

"I'm going with Mo. He might need an extra pair of hands to get to where he's going." Christi was the next to talk.

"I want to go with Electra. I'll be safer with her, and we're all on the same side." Jennifer was about to protest, but Russell squeezed her arm.

"Let her go with Electra. It'll all work out." Mo got in the final word.

"I'll call for extraction details. Electra, you drive." Electra decided it was time to lighten everybody up, so she cracked a smile and said, "Roger that. I always wanted to drive an Elite SWAT Cruiser. And now I know it's a blast to drive."

The storm was beginning to blow itself out, making conditions better for Electra to keep a firm grip on the situation. The Cruiser handled as if it were on rails, and though the world outside its headlight beams was black as pitch, she could see where they were and knew where they were going. They were invisible too, because it would take hours to get the power back on.

Electra told Christi to check for weapons and Mo helped. He reported two semi-automatics and four hundred rounds, plus two rocket-propelled grenades. "We can defend ourselves nicely if the element of surprise stays with us." Electra didn't turn her head when she asked Mo who might be tracking them now.

"Possibility air surveillance from a chopper, but only military or CIA."

Electra said, "If they spot us, they could direct vehicles to intercept us. Why don't you show Christi how to use the semi? I'll use an RPG if it comes to that."

Traffic was nada, so they reached the extraction point ten minutes before ETA.

"What kind of chopper do you think they'll send?" Mo scratched his head.

"It all depends how deep the Opposition Group is into the military. If the political infighting escalates, we're going to need good assets to go up against the Administration. Electra spotted headlights approaching, so she cut hers.

"We have a problem..."

Police squads 2101 and 2108 huddled like survivors stranded in a storm. They had been assigned emergency storm patrol in northwest sector grids controlled by the DC Area Command Center, but couldn't do anything until the storm blew through. With the power outage and bad driving conditions, they didn't expect cars to be driving anywhere. They were chatting on their hand radios when a static-charged call crackled through.

"2101 stand by for call patched through from CIA Remote." The driver looked at his partner.

"Can't imagine what this is for."

"This is CIA Remote. We need you to intercept vehicle. Occupants are top priority. Can you radio for back-up, over?"

"That's a 10-4 and with us now, over."

"Roger that, 2101. Here are the coordinates. Radio in when you get there, over."

"Copy that, over." Driver 2101 looked at his partner and shrugged. "Well, let's tell 2108 the good news."

"Mo, there are two cars, not one."

"I see them, and I hear a chopper approaching. I can't gauge direction, but from the pitch it could be an AH-128. They haven't turned their lights on yet. This is gonna get fast and furious."

The chopper pilot could hold his own in any weather against any opponent. He was piloting the most advanced Air Force chopper, the AH-128, which has a top speed of three hundred fifty mph and a range of four hundred miles before using a secondary fuel tank. The pilot hadn't a clue who he was extracting or why; he was just following orders. He had already punched in the delivery coordinates, so as soon as the soft assets were aboard and the chopper airborne, he could set auto pilot on and report in.

The AH-128 was so advanced it was easy to control but needed two to fly: a pilot for maneuvering and a co-pilot for manning the weapons systems. Even an experienced pilot needed a week of simulation training to master all systems.

The pilot spotted one vehicle, then spoke tersely. "I see target. Switching on searchlight." As he swiveled the light, he saw more than expected: three vehicles parked in a triangular standoff, headlights suddenly blazing, doors open, serving as cover for armed personnel crouching behind. Who's who, he couldn't tell. Weapons are useless until he knows the good from the bad, and that he must know before the standoff turns ugly.

"I'm setting down so we can identify human assets. Hold on." Electra peered as the chopper touched down thirty yards behind and to the right.

"They don't know who's who. I'll go tell 'em. Cover me." Electra clutched an RPG, then charged through the darkness towards the chopper, but she was no longer invisible. The headlights silhouetted her against the slush, which thwarted her dodging and weaving. A burst of gunfire brought her down, pitching her forward.

"There! That must be our target!" A bobbing and weaving silhouette had been running for its life towards them. The chopper crew couldn't hear the gunfire over the rotor noise, but they saw the figure plunge forward.

"Let's go get them!" Each grabbed a semi and jumped from the chopper, blades whirring and ready for lift-off. The co-pilot dodged towards the target vehicle while the pilot raced towards the body that was face-down in the slush. A burst of gunfire brought down the pilot, killing him instantly and sprawling him aside Electra. The co-pilot dived for cover next to Mo.

Mo yelled, "We're set for extraction. Three in our party." The co-pilot responded grimly, "Only two. Your runner's down. So's my pilot."

Electra was down but not out of action. She had been grazed in the ankle and was waiting for the right moment to rejoin the fight. As the lightning brain shifted into a higher gear, Electra felt a pang of anguish for the pilot who had sacrificed all for her. While the police shooters focused on the Cruiser, Electra crawled away undetected, still clutching the RPG. As soon as she could, she rose to her knees and fired. KA-BOOM! One of the squad cars exploded, a fireball blasting skyward, illuminating the ground below. Electra used the confusion to rush back to her team, reporting that her would-be rescuer was dead. As the group huddled, no one panicked. The gunfire stopped as both sides regrouped, allowing the co-pilot to take charge.

"Let's get airborne. We'll blast the squad car once we're up if we have to. I need one of you to operate the weapons system. Any volunteers?"

"I'm active in Air Reserve, and I've done simulator training for an AH-128."

"OK. You're my co-pilot. Your people call you Mo, and so will I. What do we call your partners?"

"This one's Electra. That one's Christi. What do we call you?"
"Name's Travis; nickname's Trigger. Either will do. Christi, you shoot like a guy. Here's what's next. No one gets left behind, so Mo and I grab my pilot and load him into the chopper while Electra and Christi give us covering fire. Then Christi runs for the chopper with Electra and Mo covering, and then Electra hightails it with Christi and Mo covering. Once you're in, buckle up. I'll get us airborne. If I get hit, Mo pilots. If Mo gets hit, Electra is weapons control. Destination coordinates already punched in, so the autopilot will take us there. Everyone, lock and load and stay frosty. Nod when ready. We go when I say go." Preparations took less than a minute. Trigger mouthed in a hushed voice only one word, "Go!"

Electra had practiced firing semi's, but Christi surprised everyone. She was learning under fire and matched Electra's marksmanship. She was a natural-born fighter, able to rise to whatever the occasion called for. Their covering fire kept the police shooters off balance, which let Mo and Trigger accomplish the first task. Electra tapped Christi on the shoulder, then pointed to the chopper. "Go!"

Covering fire pinned the police shooters and Christi made it to the chopper, but she fell to the ground trying to climb in. Trigger caught glancing bullets in his right shoulder and ribs when pulling her in.

"Mo! I'm hit! You pilot."

Mo fastened Trigger's harness, then he and Christi put down covering fire for Electra's dash to the chopper, and she dived in unscathed; Mo lifted off before the doors were closed. They were up and away.

The remaining squad car posed no threat, so Electra didn't activate weapons control. Mo switched to autopilot as soon as they climbed to 1500 feet. Autopilot gave a smooth ride, letting the team assess damage. Christi bandaged Trigger's chest wound and put a sling on Trigger's arm after finding the medical supplies, and then she patched Electra's ankle. Everyone could decompress now that the urgency of the firefight was over. Trigger spoke first.

"Let me walk you through the basics. Mo, you first. Take a look at the controls and tell me what you intend to do." Mo studied for two minutes, then replied.

"I can handle everything but pursuit. What do we do then?"

"This bird can outrun anything that chases us from behind. The only problem comes if they vector into our path at less than forty-five degrees. They could intercept us if we don't take evasive action. Can you do barrel rolls or three-sixties?" Mo shook his head no.

"Next best is to dive or weave to get ahead and outrun them. Third option is for Electra to lock weapons and blast away. That could scare them off. Electra, can you make heads or tails of the weapons computer"?

"I've practiced on the Internet flying choppers. I can handle this." Mo cut in before Trigger replied.

"Trigger, if she says she can, she can. Don't worry about her. She's ready. Christi, how's Trigger holding up? Is he belted in tight?"

"Let's ask him. Trigger, how you feeling?"

"Damn, Christi shoots like a soldier and patches like a medic. I'm glad we're on the same side…"

Mo kept busy tracking their flight path on his navigation screen. They would reach destination coordinates in twenty minutes, and by now he was certain there would be no pursuit, so his battle-weary crew could stand down. He couldn't recall much geography, but he did know that flying west by southwest for as long as they had would put them in southwestern Virginia, a part of the state dotted with national parks and forests that could provide landing zones. Even with snow cover, the chopper was too high for Mo to delineate much of the landscape, but he'd do so when flipping on the searchlight during final descent.

As Mrs. T awaited the chopper, wind gusts and distant lightning flashes followed by thunder rumbling and tumbling in the distance worried her. Early today she had learned that cover had been blown on human assets that could get data the Opposition Group needed. Ever since then, she and her Bad Boy had been working feverishly to arrange extraction.

Mrs. T, the linchpin connecting the Opposition Group with British covert operations capability, preferred to be shadowy. No one knew she had written her Cambridge thesis comparing a storied pair of British statespersons, Winston Churchill and Margaret Thatcher, to their American counterparts, Franklin Roosevelt and Ronald Reagan.

Years ago, the British government's top echelon had recognized the United States was heading towards disaster if it couldn't deal with its twin terrors: T-Plague and Isilabad terrorism. So, in typical British fashion, it made plans to protect itself by keeping an eye on the United States. Mrs. T had spent part of her diplomatic career assigned to a covert operation that would spy on America, providing assistance when needed. And the Brits hedged their bet by backing the Opposition Group, while official channels maintained politics-as-usual relations. If the Washington Establishment does collapse, now an almost certainty, British assets would be ready to assist in whatever capacity were needed.

Finally, the sound of a helicopter approaching the delivery zone, an open field in a remote Virginia state park. There could be no better symbolic location, a forest and park named for two founders of the United States, two of its greatest presidents. As Mrs. T stood a hundred yards from the landing zone that was ringed by lights, she could feel the tightness in her chest begin to loosen. The chopper would land before the storm hits, as it was no more than four hundred feet above the ground, making a steady descent in a buffeting crosswind. But her incipient smile froze into a horror-filled grimace when the lightning bolt struck and the chopper plummeted.

Mo was doing his best to keep the descent under control, but gusty crosswinds were difficult to gauge. "Hang on! Buckle in!" he yelled again. His crew looked ready, and the storm looked like it would hold off until he landed. Mo was about to declare victory when the lightning bolt struck with a blinding flash and deafening roar. Electrical systems shorted, motors froze, and the main rotor snapped as the chopper plunged earthward.

The last part of the flight brought Electra welcome relief. After the perils of the last twelve hours, the droning whir of the chopper soothed her senses. It was now almost four in the morning on February twelfth. She had survived a harrowing day. She had survived her birthday.

Christi and Trigger were asleep, Mo was focused bringing the chopper in, and Electra mused about the past and the present. *How odd. Twenty-one years ago, I entered a new world, and yesterday I entered another when choosing sides.* Twenty-one years ago, a lightning bolt had crashed into her world, forever changing what she would be. She kidded to herself that at least this time, her entry was not as shocking. And suddenly, a brilliant flash and thunderous crash engulfed the helicopter. Lightning had struck twice!

Electra was unconscious for only an instant, but in that moment a kaleidoscope of images never seen before flashed through her brain. Images from birth, of her mother and grandmother. There's Indira, radiantly beautiful, surrounded in an aura of pristine white, smiling, arms outstretched to hold her precious infant daughter. It's the Indira from her dream-like visitations. There's her grandmother, smiling proudly, lovingly stroking her perfect granddaughter. The second lightning bolt had brought Electra full circle, completing it, joining forever the past Electra never saw until this moment with the present. They are now with her forever.

Now another image flashes in her brain, that of her father, arms outstretched, pulling her to safety from a raging inferno. But no, it's not her father. It's Mo, frantically loosening her belt, pulling her from the flames. Now it's Electra's turn; she plunges into the chopper and finds Christi, still trapped in her harness. Though Electra screams from the pain of the flames licking at her feet, she will not be denied. She jerks Christi free and they tumble onto the snow-slick grass. Mo drags them to their feet and they run for their lives, away from the inferno.

A second ear-splitting explosion accompanies a mushrooming fireball, splintering the darkness. As a concussive wave of fire sweeps forward, propelling Electra onto the sodden grass and into oblivion, a final question flashes through the lightning brain: WILL I SLEEP FOR AN ETERNITY? And then a final answer: NO! I SHALL NOT!

Glossary

Every book in the Lightning Brain Series introduces abbreviations and terms collected here for convenient reference.

Actual Scientific or Sociopolitical Terms

Atomic Force Microscopy—An atomic force microscope includes a tip mounted on a micromachined cantilever. As the tip scans a surface to be investigated, interatomic forces between the tip and the surface induce displacement of the tip. A laser beam is transmitted to and reflected from the cantilever for measuring the cantilever orientation

CAGE—Conjugative assembly genome engineering (CAGE) is a precise method of genome assembly using conjugation to hierarchically combine distinct genotypes from multiple Escherichia coli strains into a single chimeric genome.It permits large-scale transfer of specified genomic regions between strains without constraints imposed by in vitro manipulations.

Cognition and Self-Awareness—Neuroscientists conjecture that cognition and self-awareness are emergent phenomena coming from billions of neurons forming trillions of interconnected associative patterns in the brain. They draw parallels with force fields (gravitational, electromagnetic, weak and strong nuclear, etc.) that emerge from incomprehensible numbers of interacting atoms.Current research indicates the cognitive part of the brain may be able to self-direct organic development.

Collaborative Consumption—A cultural and economic force that emerged during the "Great Recession" of 2007-2008. People began to share, barter, lend, or swap online for goods and services. The phenomenon launched businesses that transformed the economy by focusing on resource allocation and distribution rather than consumption intersection of supply and demand.

Crowdsourcing—The practice of obtaining information or input into a task or project by enlisting the services of a large number of people, either paid or unpaid, typically via the Internet.

Cryo-electron microscopy(cryo-EM),or electron cryo-microscopy, is a form of transmission electron microscopy (TEM) where the sample is studied at cryogenic temperatures (generally liquid nitrogen temperatures).

Intelligent Design versus Self-Directed Design—Intelligent Design asserts God, a Universal Life Force, hovers just outside man's cognition, controlling man and nature. Most contemporary theologians or philosophers agree the answer to the question Does God exist? is inaccessible. Each person chooses what to believe. Self-Directed Design focuses only on humans, conjecturing a person's cognition affects brain states controlling how the brain and body develop. Buddhist monks' brain scans show how mind control affects brain waves and cognitive states,altering physiological processes like heart rate or blood pressure.Might not prayer or holistic medicine help alter a patient's brain state so the body "heals itself?" Neuroscience research continues to study the phenomena.

Internet of Things—The interconnection via the Internet of computing devices embedded in everyday objects, enabling them to send and receive data.

If one thing can prevent the Internet of things from transforming the way we live and work, it will be a breakdown in security.

MAGE—Multiplex Automated Genome Engineering rapidly introduces changes across a genome.

Microaggression—a statement, action, or incident regarded as an instance of indirect, subtle, or unintentional discrimination against members of a marginalized group such as a racial or ethnic minority.

Terms created by projecting Current Trends

Co-Friendship—Term coined in the 21st century by the LBGT Community that refers to an intimate relationship between two people of either sex. Signifies a serious longer-term relationship.

Co-NFL—Professional football league offshoot created by the National Football League and Cross-fit Training Association. Teams consist of elite male and female athletes. Rules and physical requirements are set to allow exciting, fast-paced competition between offensive and defensive players comprised of both males and females. League formed in late 21st century because women in the United States had achieved parity with men in most careers, and had narrowed the gap in many aspects of physical performance. Though basketball has a similar Co-NBA league, the Co-NFL is the pinnacle combination of athleticism and entertainment.

Cognicom Project—Codename for CDC (Center for Disease Control) project responsible for developing vaccines against the Techno-Plague. It is divided into three sub-projects:

- I-Vac Project: Develops inoculation vaccine that protects

- R-Vac Project: Develops reversal vaccine that cures

- S-Vac Project: Develops symptomatic suppression vaccine that alleviates symptoms and pain

Guardian Party—National political party surging to prominence in the early 22nd century after a string of feckless government administrations and complicit Washington Establishments were unable to protect America from twin pandemics: Worldwide Islamic Terrorism, Global Techno-Plague.

The Guardian Party has its own "Guardian Agency," complete with its own covert operations group, that spies on other agencies, political parties, or governments.

Healthguard—Intrusive national government agency established to guard private citizens against health risks. Championed by the Guardian Party.

Home-Track Schooling—American grade and high school educational systems are more flexible in the 22nd century, allowing customized education for gifted children or those with physical or mental handicaps. Home-Track Schooling allows a child to study at home using computerized learning and tutoring programs. The program is monitored by Healthguard, the agency that tests,accepts,and monitors children in the program.

Isilabad—Rogue Middle East State created midway through the 21st century to reestablish Islamic Caliphate and catapult Islam to its rightful place on the world stage.Capital city named the same.

Mega-Media—Umbrella term describing a worldwide computer network linking all types of communications networks and media. Includes smart cellphones and computer tablets when connected to "Worldwide Internet Grid."

New-Wave—Generic term referring to early 22nd century younger generation tastes and lifestyles.

Opposition Group—An official political organization comprised of concerned Washington politicians and insiders opposed to Guardian Party's harsh policies. It has a clandestine steering committee to which a covert operations group reports.

Project Death Shield—Covert operation run by CIA (Central Intelligence Agency) to monitor how Techno-Plague impacts U.S. government's stability.

Securityguard—Intrusive national government agency established to guard private citizens against domestic or international threats. Championed by the Guardian Party.

Techno-Plague—Also called T-Plague. Disease caused by a mutant manmade virus leading to neural entanglement similar to Alzheimer's, producing rapid cognitive impairment and senility. It spread gradually but inexorably, becoming a global pandemic early in the 22nd century.

Traser—State-of-the-art law enforcement weapon: dual tranquilizer and electric stun gun.

Vow-Cer—The institution of marriage remains in the 22nd century a cornerstone of society, but adjusts to the needs of people. Vow-Cer is a Marriage Vow Contract Certification Ceremony. Two people affirm their commitment to each other, agreeing to honor their written marriage contract. Couples usually become Co-Friends before celebrating a Vow-Cer.

Appendix

The scientific principles and technological applications presented in this book are factual. For readers who might enjoy reading more of the details, this appendix contains charts or diagrams referenced in the book's narrative or dialogue, identified by page number.

Page 46—Jason's diagram placing Electra on Mankind's Evolutionary Tree

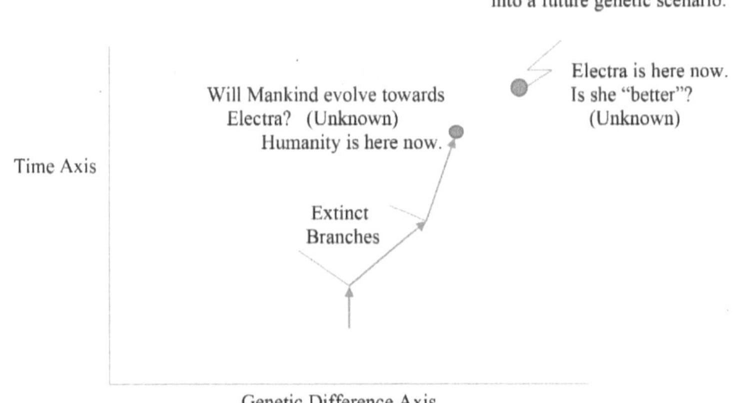

- Solution integrates virology, molecular biology, genetic engineering, and neuroscience using quantum biology concepts

- The mutant virus infects specific bacteria present in humans, causing the virus to spread into the brain.

- Virus targets specific brain control center that produces nano-enzymes.

- Viral infection produces modified nano-enzyme that causes DNA mutation in brain cells.

- Mutation causes neural entanglement leading to Alzheimer's-like cognitive impairment.

- We identify the bacteria/mutant virus combination (Indy)

- We identify brain control center and pain centers potentiated by infection (Su)

- We identify nano-enzyme (Adom)

- We determine the DNA mutation that causes neural entanglement (Jason)

- We use quantum biology concepts—tunneling, coherence, tautomerization, intra-cellular clock, spin tates, entanglement—to reverse engineer so we get:

- Immunization Vaccine (like antibodies or T-cells) Not officially our project

- Suppression/Symptomatic relief Vaccine (modified Immunization vaccine; block pain receptors; stop disease progression) Officially our project

- Reversal Vaccine (dissolve the entanglement; "enzyme inverse") Not officially our project

578

- Outbreaks recur in China and the Middle East New and recurring locations
- New locations—Tehran Boston San Diego Trajectory from urban centers outward Cognitive impairment seldom clears completely
- Fatalities caused by complications, not from T-Plague Growing fear in recurring locations
- China and Israel cooperating with us but report no vaccine progress

Page 125—Mo's Second Bullet Point Summary

- China' Middle Class pressuring Communist government
- China's government maintains control and is more transparent
- Israeli government considered proactive and not threatened
- Iran / Islamic State not cooperating
- No hints yet of terrorist activity
- Europe still observing No political ramifications yet
- Rest of world is watching Developing countries unable to help
- Vaccine research ineffective everywhere except in U.S.
- Guardian Party is using T-Plague hype to grow base
- Current Administration and majority parties will take a big but not fatal hit in next year's elections
- Public sentiment supports new "Healthguard" and "Securityguard" agencies
- Media rampant with conspiracy theories and hyped reporting Main Street still supports government but criticism of current Administration growing

S-Vac Team Drug Development
For NIH—Mo Solstein Bus-Admin Leader

- It's all about Matter and Energy Interaction
- Must understand the Three Levels of Physical World
- Must know "Laws of Nature" for Each

The Three Levels

- Newtonian Large Object World (F = MA Kinetic and Potential Energies, etc.)
- Thermo/Stat Microscopic World (PV = n RT Entropic and Free Energies, etc.)
- Quantum/Sub-Atomic World (Wave Equation Uncertainty Principle Wave/Particle Duality Tunneling Superpositioning)

Lower Levels Often Counter-Intuitive

- Life originates at interface of Second and Third Level
- Nano dimensions measured in billionths of a meter Very Small!
- A New Discipline—Nano Quantum-Biology (built on Classical Biology, Quantum Physics and Nano-Science)
- Utilizes—Virology Molecular Biology Genetic Engineering Neuroscience/Bio-Stats Nano-Technology

Drug Development at the Interface

- Cell is a Factory or Industrial Park containing Molecular Machines

- Large Molecules are the Machines: DNA RNA Enzymes Proteins

- Self-Assembly or Disassembly controlled by "Laws of Nature"

- Self-Directed Design replaces Vital Force or Intelligent Design

- Randomness and Necessity create Order from Disorder

S-Vac Team Development Approach

- Utilize Nano Techniques and Quantum-Biology and apply our training in: Virology Molecular Biology Genetic Engineering Neuroscience/Bio-Stats

- Identify Nano-Enzyme/Molecule utilizing: Atomic Force and Cryo-Electron Microscopy Nano-Chromatography Gene Sequencers 3-D Brain Scanning

- Transcribe into host virus the machinery to reverse/ potentiate new Enzyme or Molecule

- Target specific Brain Centers for Manufacture

Development Pathway

- New Enzyme/Molecule will reverse Neural Entanglement

- Reverse Engineer to "neutralize" T-Plague

- Transcribe Manufacturing Instructions into Host

- Find suitable Brain Center for Manufacture

Easy to State—Hard to Implement!

- Large number of Potential Solution Paths
- Must systematically investigate all pathsMy team played a hunch and "got lucky" with S-Vac (still developing improved formulations)

Going Forward

- Maybe S-Vac Team can assist I-Vac and R-Vac Teams
- No guarantees that we'll again be "lucky"
- Mo is instrumental in our continued success (WorldstarTeam is greater than the sum of its parts Needs Mo Bus/ Admin leadership)

(WHY REASON TRUMPS FAITH)

- The Explosion Principle. Comes from mathematical logic. It's a rule of inference that shows anything can be proved formally if you include among the premises any statement and its negation. (Bible draws conclusions assuming God exists).

- Anthropomorphism. Gods are depicted with human characteristics. (Why should God look like a person, or think like a person?)

- Antiquated Technology. The people who wrote the Bible were just as smart and sophisticated as people today, but they had primitive science and technology that were inadequate to explain the world around them. (Seems unreasonable to believe Bible miracles).

- Original Sin. Humans are born in sin and must be redeemed. (Why were Adam and Eve thrown out of Eden just because they wanted to know? Why should that make me a sinner?)

- Neuroscience and Evolution. Neuroscience connects human thinking with the brain's neural structures. Evolution explains how humans adapt and change. Humans are genetically predisposed to believe in a god, just like humans are predisposed to be afraid of snakes. (There's more of a reason to fear snakes than to believe in God. Sorry, but the facts speak for themselves).

- Bible Predates Science. Ancient theologians did not understand how scientific methods allow humans to draw contingent conclusions. (Although we can never prove God doesn't exist, observations and experiments make Bible beliefs highly unlikely).

(FIRST PERSON REFERSTO ELECTRA!)

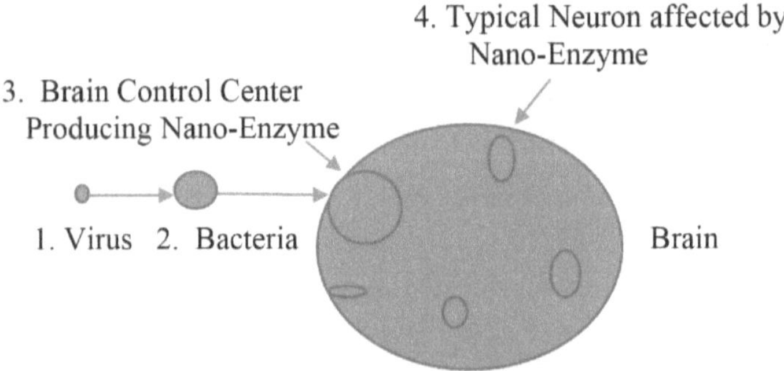

Explanation:

1. T-Plague Virus infects Bacteria.

2. Bacteria targets Control Center producing Nano-Enzyme.

3. Virus takes over Control Center causing it to produce a modified Nano-Enzyme that can cause neural entanglement.

4. Nano-Enzyme spreads to Brain Neurons and damages Neuron DNA so the cell's axons and dendrites become entangled and no longer function properly.

How my Complete Solution Path works:

- I-Vac tags bacteria containing virus so immune system kills them.

- S-Vac gives symptomatic relief at T-Plague pain receptors and turns off Nano-Enzyme production.

- R-Vac uses latest CRISPR/CAS9 techniques to splice into DNA of entangled neurons the modified DNA coding to dissolve entanglements.

Mistakes made by the Worldstars:

1. Indira tagged only bacteria containing remissive viral state. She missed tagging the aggressive viral state. She found only one of the two DNA segments.

2. Su didn't figure out solution paths for both viral states.Hers works only when the virus is in remissive state.

3. Jason edited incompletely the one DNA segment found.He did not edit the second segment.

Other Possible Vaccines (I am the first to think of these. I will develop them on my own when the time is right):

- A-Vac. An accelerator vaccine. Purpose is to accelerate the speed at which the virus causes neural entanglement/ dementia.(Modify internal clock of virus and infected cells).

- Antidote Vaccine. Used to treat massive exposure. (Combination of more powerful S-Vac and R-Vac. Turns off Nano-Enzyme production faster. Dissolves entanglements faster).

(FIRST PERSON REFERS TO ELECTRA!)

- My lightning brain's extraordinary cognition makes most things possible when I concentrate.

- I only have three things: myself, my friends and family, my present moment.

- I can thrive on my own. I must depend only on myself.

- Always keep busy solving problems. People are natural-born resolvers.

- The world is always in motion. Embrace change. If you don't change, you grow old and die.

- Always have a practical, proactive plan for the future, but don't live there. Don't become paralyzed by thinking beyond what you can use right now.

- Don't worry about being the best. Do as well as needed. Don't compare yourself with others.

- Know when to follow orders and when to work around what people tell you to do.

- Emotions are tricky because they're hard to control. They depend on relationships with others. Get more experience. Practice self-control.

- People are tricky. I need more people experience so I learn more about me, about relationships and handling others, about empathy.

- There are more subjects I might like besides science and math. Keep an open mind.

- Perhaps my artistic abilities will grow as my emotional persona grows.And I'll remember to pay attention to other peoples' feelings.

Page 277—Religion/Philosophy Flow Chart

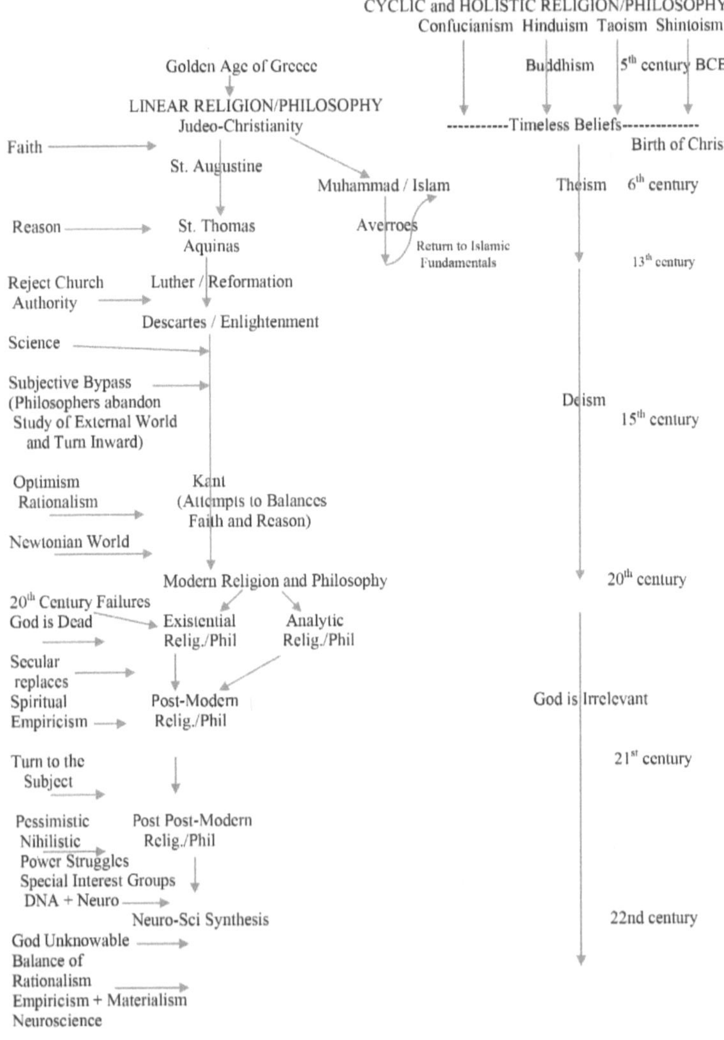

- Mutated virus harder to control
- Latest smart pill doesn't work
- Public patience wearing thin
- U.S. economy/infrastructure might spiral downhill like China's
- Guardian Party linking Cognicom failure to current Administration
- Rumors that Isilabad ready to turn T-Plague into terrorist WMD
- Cognicom researchers may be targets?

- China is unable to contain outbreaks. Western Europe controlled theirs better but suffered from increasing numbers.

- Unconfirmed reports claim international biotech companies use espionage to obtain vaccine formulations so they can supply black market.

- Israeli intelligence reports Isilabad working to weaponize virus.

- Media hyping all the bad news,adding infrastructure issues at home: overloaded hospitals, intermittent metroplex power outages.

- Securityguard and Healthguard agency regulations are becoming more intrusive and restrictive. Former Guardian Party leader David Rushman KO'ed by T-Plague. Slurred speech and fuzzy thinking mark end of his political career.

- Jared Gardner now in charge,replacing anyone not getting results. He's aggressive, hard-charging political animal

- Gardner has charisma: good looking, excellent talker, confident, connects with the public. Washington Establishment worried.

- Guardian Party gaining. Their latest slogan—Harsh Times Demand Harsh Measures—resonates with public sentiment.

- Pressure building to get results now.

(FIRST PERSON REFERS TO ELECTRA!)

PURPOSE: REFINE MY "EARLY teen" understanding. No updates needed for my Oriental Philosophy summaries (Confucianism, Taoism, Shintoism, or Buddhism) because they are holistic, static philosophies. I refined Western Philosophy because it is dynamic, linear and progress-oriented.

Branches of Philosophy:

- Metaphysics: Studies all aspects of Reality.
- Ontology: Considered a major component of Metaphysics and studies the nature of Being

All subsequent categories of philosophy fall under the umbrella of Metaphysics and Ontology

- Esthetics: Deals with Beauty and Pleasure
- Ethics: Deals with the Social and Rational/Rules-Based aspects for what is "The Good"
- Epistemology: Deals with all aspects of Knowledge

(Rational versus Empirical versus Faith-Based orientation impacts approach to philosophy)

Additional categories of Philosophy often classified beneath Epistemology

- Hard Sciences (Physics Chemistry Biology Mathematics Psychology)
- Social Sciences (Economics Sociology Political Science Anthropology)

Chronological Summary of Western Philosophy

- Greek Philosophy: Socrates (Dialogues for exploring the World) Plato (World is composed of Ideas) Aristotle (World is composed of Matter)
- Religious/Medieval Philosophy: St.Augustine (Reconciles Christianity with Greek Philosophy) St. Aquinas (Reconciles St. Augustine with Aristotelian Science)

Philosophy becomes much richer and more complex as Scientific Inquiry emerges

- Renaissance Philosophy: Descartes (Rationalism and Mind-Brain Duality) Hobbes (Social Contract)
- Early Enlightenment Philosophy: Jeremy Bentham and John Stuart Mill (Utilitarianism)
- Later Enlightenment Philosophy: Kant (Reconciles Rationalism and Faith) Adam Smith (Reconciles Utilitarianism with Progress)
- Reaction to Kant:Rousseau (Romanticism:the Noble Savage)
- Extension to Kant: Hegel (Dialectical Idealism: Philosophy's historical trajectory destined to end in Liberty, Freedom, Democracy, Progress)
- Reaction to Hegel: Nietzsche (the Will to Power)
- Note that Hegel is the last philosopher to have a comprehensive Philosophical System

20th Century Philosophers fragment Philosophy to reconcile Enlightenment Philosophy with the New Scientific Findings: Evolution Theory of Relativity Quantum Mechanics

- Existentialism: Kierkegaard, Camus, Sarte (Man is Alienated, Absurd, completely Free)
- Logical Positivism and Pragmatism: Vienna Circle, John Dewey (Apply Rational and Utilitarian discipline to rein in Rationalism)
- Emergence:Whitehead (Higher Order Complexity cannot be explained by analyzing Components: Whole is greater than the sum of its parts)
- Analytic Philosophy:Wittgenstein (Language-Based Logic to avoid misinterpretation by precisely specifying Word Meaning) Uses Logic to analyze Collective Experience

The World War Disasters Confound all Philosophers and lead to Pessimism and Doubt

Leads to Post-Modernism associated with the European Continental Philosophers

Emphasizes Individual's Personal Experience Refutes logical approaches to Philosophy

- Deconstructionism: Derrida ("Kills" Scientific Knowledge by attacking it with its own methods)
- Post-Modern Philosophy brings an end to Philosophy's Enlightenment Trajectory Michael Rorty: There are no Absolutes All Logical Reasoning is Circular

But the "Death of Philosophy" is greatly exaggerated!

Late 20th and 21st Century Philosophers salvage the best by synthesizing the optimistic and pragmatic contents of Post-Modernism branches of Philosophy

- Build on High Energy Physics Limitations and Neuroscience Findings
- Acknowledge the limits of Knowledge
- Realize the Futility of Proving or Disproving the Existence of God (there is room for Faith and Reason)

- Admit that Relativism is ultimately more useful than Absolutism

The End Results:

- Purpose of Philosophy: Contribute to Civilization's Progress by integrating Contingent Knowledge found in Multiple Disciplines
- Purpose of the Universe:To construct increasingly complex aggregates of matter
- Purpose of Life:To survive and to go on living Purpose of Civilization:To extend Rational Progress

I must adjust the name of my philosophy from Neurosci-Extended Deconstructed Kantianism to Neurosci-Extended Deconstructed Emergent Post-Pragmatism.

I am satisfied I have built an adequate knowledge base for dealing with Philosophy, Religion, and Science. In preparation for follow-up academic and career pursuits, I must study Artificial Intelligence and Transhumanism, as well as Sociology, Political Science and Economics.

(FIRST PERSON REFERS TO ELECTRA!)

High Energy Physics a Dead End

- Super-Strings, Multi-Verses and Black Holes exist only in Star Trek Series
- Grand Unified Field Theory unable to control Gravity Waves
- We must obey the well-established laws of Classical Physics, Relativity, and basic Quantum Mechanics
- Atoms and Second Law of Thermodynamics (Entropy) set Scientific Limits on What is Possible

"Merely human" scientists aren't smart enough to make the next breakthrough. Perhaps I can, but I'd rather pursue breakthroughs in Genetic Engineering and Artificial Intelligence

Areas to Pursue

- Nano-Technology, Molecular Machines and Artificial Intelligence will power future R&D
- Plenty of Room for Asymptotic Growth in Genetic Engineering and Artificial Intelligence
- Designer Drugs to improve Quality of Life
- DNA Modification using Molecular Machines found in Bacteria, Viruses and T-Cells leading to "Improved Humans"
- Artificial Intelligence extending Quantum Computing Breakthroughs leading to Transhumanism

- Note: Advanced Computers pave the way for Molecular Machines, Designer Drugs, DNA Modification, Transhumanism

Advanced Computers

- Advanced Computers are extensions of "Neural Networks" that self-learn and self-modify
- They are needed to handle calculations too complex for "Merely Human" Scientists, who are not "smart enough" to utilize today's hardware (Current software not "smart enough")
- "Neural Network Computers"were called "Deep Learning" when first developed and contained layers of neural circuits
- Neural Network Computers today are multi-layers of interconnected microprocessors that self-adapt by adjusting or adding circuitry, accept input signals, process them with feedback loops, and emit output signals.
- "Learning"occurs when the Software self-adapts or brings in additional hardware components

NEURAL NETWORK DIAGRAM

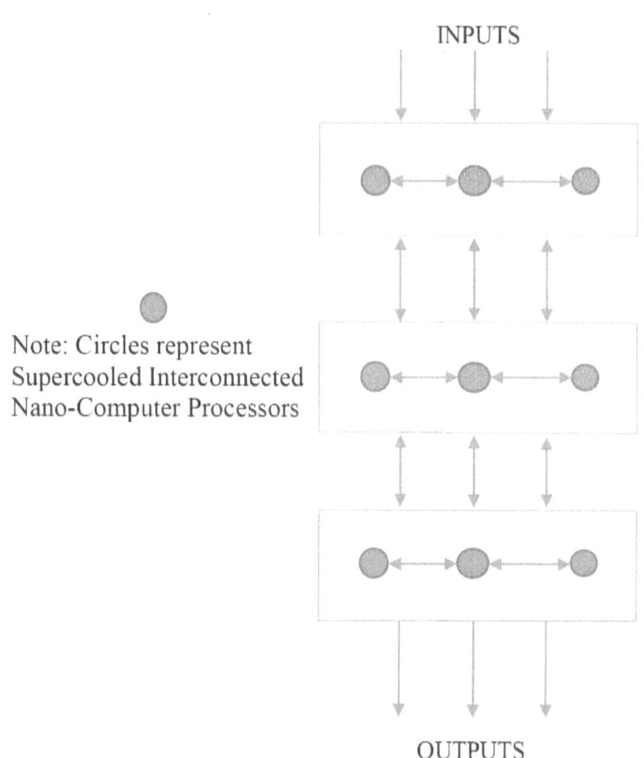

Today's Quantum Computers employ Super-Cooled Neural Networks

- Microchips constructed by "Nano-Machines" (manipulate individual atoms)

- Supercooling needed to stop atomic vibrations and take advantage of Quantum Effects

- Qu-bits store 0's and 1's simultaneously in Atomic Electron Spin values

- Quantum Phenomenon: Superpositioning used to store 0's and 1's simultaneously (highest memory density possible)

- Quantum Phenomenon: Entanglement used for Simultaneous Interaction among electrons Entanglement used for Parallel calculations

- Quantum Phenomenon: Tunneling used to reduce energy requirements in chemical reactions

Why I Can Do What the Others Can't

- Lightning Brain smarter (I can think fast and slow)
- Lightning Brain can apply Extended Real Number System
- to handle "Complexity"
- My self-adaptive, extended object-oriented programming
- language built on massively parallel, autoregressive,
- multithreaded recursive programming exceeds "state-of-
- the-art" algorithmic design.
- I can achieve software breakthroughs using current
- technologies and computer hardware!

What I Shall Do in DNA/Genetic Engineering Short-Term

- Use Organic Molecular Machines and DNA Modification Technology to manipulate Bacteria and Viruses and T-Cells to develop the "ultimate" suite of T-Plague vaccines

- Use a modified T-Plague vaccine solution path to make a drug that will bind with neurons associated with cognition

- Use current Nano-Technology and Quantum Computers
- to map Human Brain's Neural Structure
- Build Brain Probe Device to read/write neural structure

What I shall do in Artificial Intelligence Short-Term

- Develop my own programming language and use it to write
- A.I. operating systems and software apps

- Develop better software for reading/writing/displaying sensory channels
- Develop better software for Computer Network Security
- Develop better software for Immersive 3-D Computer Graphical User Interfaces
- Develop A.I. links between Brain and Computer Hardware

Why I'm Better than Mere Mortals at Mathematics

I know numbers cold. I can build from the Null Set all number systems,from the natural numbers up to and including the Extended Number System and Hyper-Reals. Here's the starting definition:

- Number: a well ordered set such that each member equals the set of strict predecessors.

Even smart science or math types can't reconcile the equivalence of Axiom of Choice, Zorn's Lemma, and the Well Ordering Theorem using this starting definition. And they can't grasp how the equivalence is consistent with the Generalized Continuum Hypothesis.They're swept away by Cantor's torrent of uncountable infinities. They haven't a clue how to construct an isomorphism proving all number systems satisfying basic assumptions are the same if you strip away labels. And why can't they? Because their brains are designed to think fast emotionally, not slow rationally. But my lightning brain is exceptional. Only I can design algorithms running on massively parallel neural-networked chips extending object-oriented relational databases using tightly coded autoregressive and multi-threaded apps. The Star Trek creators knew mere humanity's shortcoming.They got around the problem by creating the Q-Race: an alternate dimension civilization of all-knowing creatures. They also created the Borgs: cybernetic organisms built on silicon chip DNA. Both could outgun man's intellect, but man's emotional persona, man's humanity to man, ultimately wins.I don't always agree.I wish I could build my dream team using Q and the Borgs. Maybe I'll create them…

Possible Organizations

- Guardian Party (covert operations group?)
- CIA (watching the Government's back?)
- NIH/CDC/Cognicom (hiding right in front of us?) Opposition Group (aren't they trying to form a political party?) Terrorist Organization (not smart enough?)
- Rogue biotech companies (possible)
- Foreign governments (possible)

Mole Characteristics

- Low-level job
- Born in United States
- Blends in (male or female)
- Speaks without accent

How to Hunt

- Start with Likely Departments (H.R.Public Relations I.T. Security...)
- Trace People up the Organization Chart
- Hack into: Emails Hidden Directories Department/ Project Files...

Not on the List

- Only Su, Adom, Electra

(FIRST PERSON REFERS TO ELECTRA!)

- I must study biology from the perspective of physics. (Atoms and molecules form cells)

- Consciousness is an emergent phenomenon. (Wave phenomenon analogy—waves emerge from motions of particles and determine "qualia," such as amplitude and frequency, which are the building blocks of waves).

- The brain limits consciousness only to events where it contributes to "survival."

- Consciousness includes Intelligence but is more.It includes Self-Awareness.

- Working Definition:Consciousness is Subjective Experience.

Hierarchy of Consciousness Conundrums

- Easy Problem: How does the brain process information? (Testable)

- Harder Problem: What physical properties distinguish conscious versus unconscious states? (Testable)

- Even Harder Problem: How do physical properties determine "qualia" and what does consciousness feel like? (Partially testable)

- Hardest Problem:Why is anything conscious? (Untestable)

My Thesis Conjecture:Consciousness is an emergent phenomenon coming from billions of neurons and trillions of connections. It includes only the testable problems. My theory is that the brain processes information (external stimuli) by causing a set of neurons to fire, and the physical property that distinguishes consciousness versus unconscious states is the subjective emotional state that I can measure.

How I will test my Conjecture:

- Map the brain's neural structure using a modified T-Plague vaccine to identify neurons associated with cognition.
- "Turn on" a critical number of neural connections to create a conscious state.
- Measure the brain's emotional responses for this conscious state and compare to a reference standard.

Purpose: To provide enough information so you can use Psychology in your Career and Personal Life

What Psychology is: Scientific Study of Human Nature related to the Brain, Behavior, and the Mind

Trajectory of Psychology:

- Freud's Sex-Laden Case Studies

- Jung added Neuroscience and extended Freud using Scientific Methods

- Current Psychology extends Post-Jungian Theory using Brain Imaging

- Kahneman's gold standard Cognitive Psychology book written a hundred years ago, Thinking, Fast and Slow, is still a good read

Psychological Research Methods

- Brain Scans and Imaging to locate/track Neuronal Signaling and associate with Emotional and Physical Measurable Responses

- Case/Clinical Studies to interview patients for tracking Subjective Data

Humans:

- "Think Slow"/Logically Often good for making Decisions

- "Think Fast"/Instinctively Often good for dealing with Feelings and Interpersonal Relationships

Be Careful! Everyone is an Amateur Psychologist

Helpful Takeaways

- Mind and Brain are One-and-the-Same
- Brain filters via Senses What It Experiences and creates Reality
- Free Will exists, but We are aware only after the Decision is made
- No one is Normal

Taxonomy of Mental Disorders (All generally classified under Psychotic Disorders Diagnostic and Statistical Manual—DSM—published by the American Psychiatric Association describes complete classification)

Psychiatrists label Feelings/Emotions people uncomfortable with "Mental Disorders"

Major Disorders:

- Schizophrenia Bipolar Depression Anxiety/Panic Disorder
- Autism Paranoia Obsessive Compulsive

How to Treat:

- Drugs for Physiological Imbalance
- Counseling for Emotions/Feelings

Caution: Psychological Counseling may be Overrated

- Easy to fake Disorders
- Talking with "Objective" Family/Friends often just as good

Practical Guidelines

People today are Stressed Out and Un-Empathetic
Great Success or Disastrous Failure has almost no impact on Long-Term Happiness
Physiological Measurements for Happiness and Love possible (?)

"Think Slow" in Career and in Business Setting

- Don't be "hijacked" by Feelings
- Project Confidence and Leadership
- Command by Power and Influence and Persuasion

"Think Fast"(but carefully!) when dealing with Relationships. Let's apply it to Love

- Separate Love from Sex
- Be "Pessimistic" (don't expect too much)
- Partners can't "Make you Happy"
- Don't expect Partner to "Change" per Your wishes
- Be Open and Honest and Keep "Some of Yourself" to Yourself
- Guard against the Romantic Love Myth
- Kindred Spirits can be replaced
- Before you can love Another, you must love Yourself
- Loving Yourself = Self-Honesty

Good Luck!

www.ingramcontent.com/pod-product-compliance
Lightning Source LLC
Chambersburg PA
CBHW051548100726
47898CB00001B/17